Healer

Slave's Bay
Part III

Healer

Slave's Bay
Part III

Magdalena Kułaga

Table of contents

Acknowledgments

I would like to thank the people who helped me create the book.

Many thanks to Mrs. Izabela for working on the book, great patience for the skittish author and all comments.

Mrs. Maria Cowen, thank you for the English version, making the author's dreams come true.

Thanks to the family, especially my husband, for their support in the final volume. My daughter who listened patiently about the book.

Finally, I would like to thank the people who developed the idea and wrote it down on the pages of the notebook. Damian and Daniel - it's about you.

Katarzyna, whose dark books accompanied me in spirit.

Magdalena, mother of the half-dragon.

Agnieszka, for everything.

And to all of you who have read, read and will read the Healer.

This book is for you.

Magdalena Kulaga

Azram, king of the Slaves Bay, built his kingdom on the suffering and harm of the people he sold into slavery. One day, when he had enough gold to have two kingdoms, he ordered his palace expanded and henceforth be called king. He reigned with a hard, relentless hand, but he still felt he had little. He turned to the demons for help, because he wanted to rule the whole world. Demons have come on call. However, they deceived him. They made him make offerings until he convinced them. So Azram began to sacrifice animals to appease the demons. Then it was time for human sacrifice. The king sacrificed good-hearted virgins, the most tender that were sent to him. Then he started looking for victims among the children, but that didn't help either. Meanwhile, evil was creeping in, growing in strength. Finally, the king got a clue: there are two people in the world whose hearts would satisfy the thirst for the underworld. For evil to help him gain power over the whole world, he must sacrifice the Guardian of People or the Sorcerer of the Heart on the altar.

The king looked for them all over the world, until one day he heard a story about an extraordinary healer...

CHAPTER 1

Vivan was reading the letter.

Lena paused as she walked restlessly around the room to look at her son's face. Her eyes, once marked with despair, pierced with fear. Again, a letter came from this place! From these people! She recognized the seal of the Beckert family, its sophisticated style. There was still a bland scent of perfume. It's the woman! Every letter from that place recently filled her heart with apprehension. There was something ominous about them. As if there was poison in them. All these letters seemed to be hiding something from them. They carried a darkness within them that she could not penetrate. She couldn't bear to see them.

"What is this?" She asked, barely staying calm.

Erlon, her husband, seeing the expression on her face, walked over to the window, trying to hide his nervousness. It wasn't a good sign. She knew about it. He was rarely so upset.

"Is that a letter from them?" She asked to break the unbearable silence. It was more of a statement than a question.

Vivan looked at her. In his eyes she saw the reflection of her own feelings. He, too, sensed trouble.

Since the witch's attack, they both felt everything more than before. Deeper. She didn't know if she had taught them to be careful, or if she had ever had a stronger gift than ever before from her extraordinary son...

"What happened?" She asked, but he didn't answer her. Vivan already knew what her reaction would be to the words she was about to hear. He allowed his father to speak first, though she did not take her eyes off him, with a mute reproach in her gentle eyes.

"My mother is dying," her husband said grimly. "She's asking me to convince my unusual stepson to come. She will provide him with all the comforts. A carriage would come for him. We have time to decide..."

She felt a wave of anger overwhelm her. These people had the nerve to ask for her son?! The ones who abandoned Erlon, swearing never to come to this place?! This horrible woman scolded Vivan in front of everyone on his birthday as if he were an untrained brat! For years they had almost ignored them...

"What words did she use lately?" She asked indignantly, "she said that Vivan was USEFUL! Useful because helpful," she concluded sarcastically.

"I know, darling," Erlon softly broke in on her word, "I'm not trying to persuade you to do anything."

"You gave him that letter!"

"I'm here, mom," Vivan said softly, for the first time since she had come.

She looked at him as if to say, "You know very well why I'm doing this."

"I thought it would be better if he found out," Erlon said, not looking at her.

"Why?! You managed to hide the previous letters from him!"

"Previous?!" reacted Paphian, their younger son, also present at the meeting, "so there were more of them?!"

"Only two. Last week", father replied reluctantly, "I wanted Leno..." he began hesitantly, looking at his wife's face, whose eyes were still on his eldest son.

She waited for his words, verdict in her mind.

"It's his mother," he said softly.

Lena grabbed the train of her long blue gown to find herself face to face in front of it. She couldn't believe the words really came out of his mouth.

"Why are you doing this?!" She asked him with a mixture of anger and regret. "This woman would sell you for a tablespoon of salt if she thought you could be USEFUL for her in this way, Vivan!"

"She asked for me..."

"You are a healer! Who else could she ask for?!"

"Mom..." the son looked gently into her anxious eyes. "You hurt father's feelings..."

She felt as if a bucket of cold water had been poured over her. He was right. She looked at her husband as he said softly:

"She's right, Vivan..."

"This is your mother, Dad," Vivan's voice, who boldly endured his mother's despair and anger, was firm.

"That's why I didn't know what to do," admitted his stepfather in confusion. "I wanted you to know. For you to help me decide... I'm going to refuse her. You're not going!" He said suddenly firmly, "Your mother is right. They treated us poorly all this time. Especially you, and you..."

"No," Vivan interrupted him gently, and sadly, "you."

Erlon looked at his unusual son in a dilemma dictated by despair. He had too good a heart, he knew it. But who in this family didn't have it? Sometimes it seemed to him that they infected the environment around them with their nobility. The world did not repay them the same, and yet they were bound together by an extraordinary bond, the main link of which was his extraordinary adoptive son."

"What should I do?" He asked softly.

"You might not have shown him that," Lena hissed, still unable to contain her agitation.

"Forgive me, Mom," Paphian said finally. "Do you really think you could hide anything from Vivan? One look at father would have made him suspicious. Then he would dig until he found out everything."

"Thanks," muttered the brother in reply.

Paphian smiled at him, though it was a joyless smile.

Vivan stood by the window. He watched the quiet rhythm of the town in silence for a moment. From here you could see the harbor where his friends Valeria galleon was currently moored, as well as several other merchant ships, as well as many smaller fishing boats. New houses and small bridges were built across major mountain streams. More and more streets no longer resembled a beaten track. The trail of these cobblestones started from the gates of the walls and extended further and further with each passing month, supported by the local funds. He knew very well that Barnica owes such dynamic development to him in the recent past to a large extent. He felt a little uncomfortable with that. He never exalted himself because of his extraordinary gift. Knowing that someone was deciding to settle here permanently, to be close to the healer, made him feel a burden of responsibility for the newcomer and everyone else in the town. These people relied on him. They trusted him. And there were more and more of them.

He could only hope they would never be disappointed in him. He will do his best to make it happen.

He didn't like leaving home lately. This trip would surely be no good for him. After all, he was not going to a friendly place. There he could not expect an effusive welcome. This time, it is unlikely to end up healing and sending him home immediately when he is no longer needed. He could feel it.

But it was his stepfather's mother, and he could not refuse him.

"I'm going," he said softly.

His mother sighed loudly. Erlon tried to protest again, but Vivan silenced him with a gesture.

"I'm going with you!" Paphian replied firmly, in a tone that would bear no objection.

"They didn't invite you..."

"I don't care!" snorted his brother. "You will not go there alone!"

Lena gently took the letter from her son's hand.

"They invited anyone but you?" She asked, not looking at her husband.

"No," Erlon replied for his son.

She looked at him sympathetically. He looked down.

"All the more!" Paphian replied fiercely. "You will not go there yourself! They will not throw out their rightful grandson," he uttered the last words with contempt, thereby revealing what he thought about it. "I'm going!"

Due to an important event, the trip was postponed for a few days. The disease Erlon's mother described was serious, but it did not predict a quick death, so the decision was made and no other. Vivan hated delay, but for nothing in the world he would not give up what was to come. Besides, he sensed that there was something behind the disease... He didn't like the bad feelings that haunted him. There was too much darkness in them...

On that day, after a year of discreet waiting in town, one of the couples who were in the healer's close friends' circle was to get married.

On that day, the groom was only twenty years old, but no one doubted that in terms of the experiences and admirable maturity he was beyond the age of others.

Oliver has changed over the past year. He looked less like a delicate youth. He wore short, seemingly carelessly cropped hair that gave him a rebellious appearance, and a distinct stubble that, despite his hopes, even after quite a long time did not turn into a small beard. Unfortunately, that was how it was supposed to remain. He was always springy, and his muscles were well-defined before from incessant climbing. The next year only made it worse.

He was also distinguished by character.

Faithful to Sai, with whom he became engaged in the winter, he still basically avoided people, liking his quiet shop with herbs and spices, for which he would sometimes go with his beloved to distant regions of the kingdom. Then he wrote down what he saw in his travel journals.

Several months elapsed before someone on the crew of the Valeria ship revealed to him that Captain Ross, who was called his brother, although they were not bound by blood, was also writing down his history.

Ross acknowledged this with some hesitation. He was still ashamed of his handwriting and the way he chose words to describe his sea voyages, even though he was doing better and better in both cases. Sel discreetly tried to help him in this and it was only with him that Ross was not hiding. He hadn't read his notes to anyone so far, unlike Oliver, who had been persuaded to do so on some evenings. Back then, people knew that he was not trying to avoid them, but only explored the knowledge in order to be able to present events in an interesting way through gestures or intonation. They knew that this was just a character, perhaps shaped by the past. He was glad to have friends and loved ones now, but from time to time he liked his loneliness.

Everyone wanted him and Sai to succeed. Her past life might have brought dark clouds over the relationship, but the town's sympathy and love for the two, especially Oliver's attitude, who was firmly willing to defend Sai from the echoes of the past, gave hope that all would end well.

Their wedding was today.

Oliver sighed softly as he saw Sai dressed in a magnificent gown, adorned according to the tradition generally accepted in the kingdom. Delicate violet and embroidery, which included elements of local folklore, and a light airy veil combined the symbols of this land, which her heart liked.

He didn't even hesitate for a moment.

He wanted her, not only physically. She combined so many dreams... those about stability, peace, place in life. They both dreamed about it. They will try to make these dreams come true. They both wanted it very much.

Sai spontaneously threw back the veil to give him a kiss as soon as Count Erlon gave them his blessing.

Oliver barely realized there were shouts of joy around...

Many tents were joined together to gather all the townspeople on this special day. The leading position was taken by the newlyweds, next to them the count and his family. Since neither Oliver nor Sai wanted any of their friends to feel left out, a huge, round table was built, which would sometimes take a place of honor in the palace, which was still being rebuilt. In this way, all their dear friends were treated equally, and there was even room for a few new ones to come. Since it was handled by Sel, it was a special and exceptionally impressive work. This table could be reduced as needed or new parts could be added to it. Several of them were still being finalized. Carving his legs in the shape of a tiger - in memory of the brave animals that defended Vivan to death - was a wonderful work of one of the artists who came to the town, who came over the sea after hearing about the healer and offered his services to him. Alvar was delighted to be able to do something for an extraordinary man who had done so much for others and also defeated the demonic witch. Word spread quickly thanks to the sailors. He did not agree to be seated at the table during the wedding, explaining that only friends and family could be there, and he did not belong to any of these categories so far, in his opinion. So, he was honored with a loud toast from the audience. There were already those who made his first orders during the wedding. He asked them for patience, as he had still not fully completed the work aboard the Valeria. There was little left when he led a group of his students. Almost a year after the old Cadelia, only a memory remained, and the new figurehead, or the figure on the front of the ship, depicted Valeria, an old friend and protector of Ross, grasping the wind in her hands. Alvar became so intimate with the crew that he couldn't get used to the thought that he would not be among them one day, since they had spent so much time together. Ross and Sel were already used to Alvar's daily exhortations, looking for his four students each morning. His work and the curling of his black beard as he thought about something. Above all, his pipes, whose mysterious herbs smelled on board every day and which he almost never left. There was also a habit of nervous gesticulating when he was not satisfied with something, and even muttering some words in his native language like an extremely nervous witch. Still, both the students and the crew knew that Alvar's anger, who could argue even with the captain when their visions did not match, were not eternal, and he couldn't really get mad. Avlar cooperated with Sel. He had great respect for his designs, amazed at his developing talent. He was like an older brother, already turning 50. In many situations, his prompts, plus the help of the reliable Silas, who had been in Ross's crew from the beginning, helped the inexperienced captain and his partner in making decisions while sailing. In doing so, they avoided many mistakes and built a reputation for themselves, fueled by the additional, if less welcomed by Ross, tale of his extraordinary talent as a Jewel Sorcerer. In the ports, thanks to the crew, people started talking about the white-haired wizard, the captain of the ship. There were incredible rumors that if he annoyed him, he would send a storm on the insolent. His ship is guided by his power. And when you hurt someone, he will find you and take over your soul with a touch.

Ross was not amused by this part of the overheard stories, but because they aroused due respect, he was simply forced to come to terms with them.

In the center of the table, as requested by everyone, there was a bas-relief mounted separately, and at the same time joining the whole. It showed the jewel that Vivan wore around her neck and the Jewel of Hope...

When Vivan and Ross saw the sculpture for the first time, it caused an unusual stir. Only the two of them wore a ruby held in their hands. For many reasons, it was decided to remain that way.

After all, both jewel owners were unique. The only one in the whole kingdom. And maybe all over the world...

"To the happy couple!" Everyone shouted in unison.

Everyone drank a drink. With so many people around, the impression was truly extraordinary.

Sai hugged Oliver, who is very often smiling, and embraces him tenderly. Her dark, beautiful eyes sparkled.

"Vivan! Ross!" Seme exclaimed when the surroundings went silent. "When is your turn, guys?" then, probably under the influence of emotion, she added without thinking: "When will I have the first children in this group?" She looked at the surprised young couple and the friends, confused by this unexpected remark.

Vivan immediately sensed Ross's tension and Sel's slight nervousness, coupled with indulgence, though he didn't even look at them. For others, it took a little longer to understand the awkwardness of these words. It was the first one who spoke, taking Vashaba's hand.

"Seme," he said gently, "we will not answer these questions for you today."

He glanced at Ross, then at Sel, who caught his eye. He, too, reliably sensed his lover's nervousness.

"Yes," his foster father said, trying to cover up the awkward situation, "Today is an important day..."

"Ross, honey, don't be angry," Seme interrupted him, angry with herself once she realized her mistake. "I said without thinking. I was talking to them about children..." She pointed with her hand at Vivan and the young ones, awkwardly trying to save the situation.

"We can't have children..." Ross replied softly but emphatically, adding to their confusion.

Seme held her breath, now not sure what to say. Perhaps it would be better if she really kept her mouth shut. But now she wanted to get out of it somehow.

"You never know..." she began hesitantly.

A real disaster.

Sel imploringly silenced her with a gesture. He was concerned about Ross's reaction. He felt that he had something to do with it, or rather his ambiguous nature, which he revealed at the House of Pleasure.

He sensed that the neighboring feasters were beginning to listen to this strange conversation.

"We understand, Seme," he smiled at her reassuringly, because he really understood that she had nothing wrong with her mind. These were just jokingly spoken words that could be treated with humor.

Ross surprised everyone with his nervous reaction.

"Sorry, guys," he turned on his and his lover's behalf to the young couple.

Sai smiled warmly at him.

"Brother?" Oliver turned playfully to his new brother, as he was used to doing for a long time. He had no immediate family members anymore. His need to keep at least a part of his former life was related to Ross, who soon became very close to his deceased sister. It evoked memories of Julien, the good ones and the ones full of love. Ross not only understood it perfectly. He was grateful to him for this brotherly bond, and it eased his fear for the future when the two became so closely connected.

He looked at him. He saw a silent plea for forbearance in his eyes.

So, he smiled warmly at Seme.

"I have nothing to be angry with you about," he said. "Nothing like that happened."

It has become. Sel knew this... The poisonous thought had already penetrated their minds. He sighed softly, feeling uneasy. After all, he gave no reason to...

"You know, life can be different..."

It was starting to hurt.

Vivan sensed this poisonous thought, as if in the melody of the world around him he suddenly heard a loud, unpleasant screeching sound. In his heart, it grew into additional anxiety, not least because of his friends. He looked at Vashaba. She clearly wanted to tell him something important. Her gaze betrayed her. Now she squeezed his hand, smiling slightly. If she had wanted to relate to Seme's words in any way, she would have already done so. So, this conversation is not gonna be about the wedding or the kids... No. They agreed on this. They did not want to rush. No words from Seme or his grandparents' glances could make them succumb. They wanted it, but like their friend Oliver, they chose to decide when that time would come. So far, they got to know each other, without rushing. When the quiet time finally came in town life, they spent it on long, secret journeys. They spent it together, immersed in caresses, touch and love. Vivan was sure Vashaba knew all his weaknesses, his nightmares, and the enormity of the emotions he was accumulating. She had seen his good days and days he would cry to keep to himself, but he had no influence on it. He knew that sometimes it wasn't easy with him. Previous painful events had left an indelible mark on him. Vashaba, however, did not leave. Neither his sensitivity nor the tears of yet another nightmare with an echo of the past discouraged her. Unfortunately, he also got to know her well. He knew she would explode with anger sometimes. He knew she sometimes acted under the influence of emotions. When something irritated her, she did not act rationally, and her words cut like a dagger. He belonged to her. Sometimes she expressed it too greedily, as if nothing else mattered apart from the intercourses. Was this what this conversation was supposed to be about? That maybe she could sense his hesitation? He would know. He would have known about it earlier.

Sai rested her head on Oliver's shoulder. She had dreamed about this moment all day long. About the time of the dance, when the market where the wedding tents were set up, slowly lit by lanterns. Candles were placed on the tables, waiting for the night to come with them.

"Do you think about Seme's words?" She asked softly.

She was almost four years older than him. However, especially today, when they finally brought their hands together, he seemed more mature to her than she was.

More composed. It always comforted her. His presence drove away sadness. Today she felt it more than ever.

Oliver hugged her tighter, surprised by the concern in her eyes. He knew the source of this fear. He felt it himself sometimes. Uncertainty. The fear that everything they have rebuilt so far will be taken from them, and anyone who thinks they can do it will try to separate them for their own entertainment.

A trace of Morena. After Ramoz...

He kissed her black, flower-adorned hair, reveling in the familiar scent of jasmine and soap that she liked so much. A fragrance he remembered so well...

"I'm not afraid," he said quietly, but confidently, chasing away his gloomy thoughts, "stop being afraid too. It is behind us."

"I don't want to lose you," she said softly.

"You can't beat yourself up," he told her gently. "I'll be with you, even if you don't see me. We'll get old, we'll get ugly, and all that matters now - will lose it. I will be with you until you are fed up with me and you start throwing objects at me, just to get out, just for a moment," he said with a twinkle in his eye. She laughed softly. "I'll be more and more old and maybe I'll start going bald, and you'll still be beautiful in my eyes. Sai," his voice broke with emotion, "we already have it. Sometimes people spend their entire lives searching, making bad choices that lock their souls behind bars of habits, submission, and resignation. It does not apply to us. You are my part. You are it! You have everything in you that I need to make my heart beat! You will never lose me."

She hugged him tightly, enclosing their little world in her arms.

"Remember you promised me that..." She whispered before she gave him a kiss on her lips.

It was not the end of the momentous events of the day.

At a given sign, Azylas began to summon the inhabitants to his place. Several chairs were hurriedly arranged between the circle of people. Those who had already departed with the advent of the west were feverishly exhorted.

"What's happening?" Asked the intrigued Paphian, but among friends and family no one, except the young couple, knew the answer to this question. They disguised themselves well...

Oliver smiled knowingly at Sai, taking her hand.

"You'll like this," he merely said mysteriously to Vivan.

To the count's amazement, he and his family were invited to chairs hastily prepared.

The blacksmith took the initiative. He cleared his throat a few times to get the right timbre.

"Dear Count," he began solemnly, "Sir Erlon..."

"Azylas, that's enough," Erlon interrupted him with a smile.

Everyone laughed. It was common knowledge in the town that the Earl Erlon never got above himself. Yes, he was firm, if necessary, that's all. Among the gathered were people who remembered when he came here to settle permanently with his family. One of them was the blacksmith Azylas. These people also remembered how much they had accomplished together over the years, especially the dramatic moments when the count had fought side by side with them.

Azylas smiled, looking at him now with emotion. Erlon didn't look much older than when he had come here. In fact, more than twenty years have passed, and many of those who welcomed him then have progressed with age, though not like other people in the kingdom. It was the merit of the healer. It was that moment when, looking at Erlon and his adoptive son, he remembered other moments, those in which both stepfather and son had done so much for everyone.

Especially them, although the rest of the family also helped a lot. The love of these people united the town.

The blacksmith looked around at the audience. He noticed many touched faces. They also thought about it.

"What happened, Azylas?" Vivan asked gently, touched by the kindness that surrounded him on all sides.

He noticed Grandpa and Grandma leaning closer to each other. Vashaba did not let go of his hand from hers, and his stepfather looked at his mother lovingly. He glanced at Paphian, alone in this group. He looked at him.

"Well, since we are all gathered here, with the permission of the young couple," said Azylas, at which many smiled kindly at them, "I would like to solemnly ask all of you here for something."

Vivan got up first, feeling it was going to be something really important. The others quickly followed his example.

The blacksmith grunted nervously.

"That's how I look at you, my lord," he said to Count Erlon, "and I think it's been twenty years since you've been here with us. When I see you still almost as it was then, all those memories of the old days come to my mind." Erlon looked at him with a mixture of sadness and emotion. He was probably looking at the graying hair at his temples now. "Those are good memories, Count. How you got here, how you arranged it all, how you fixed it. And how you had to convince us that you are not like..." he broke off, confused, and Erlon couldn't help but smile, knowing who he meant, "like great lords are," finished the blacksmith diplomatically, to which many nodded their heads. "Look now!" He waved his hand around. "Look how many people are standing here! They know what I'm doing now, they know the wedding is interrupted for now and no one has escaped! See, Erlon? We are here for you..." he concluded with emotion.

Vivan looked at his foster father. Everyone started clapping. Deeply moved, Erlon accepted his wife's tender kiss with tears in his eyes.

"Thank you for all that you have given us so far," said the blacksmith solemnly. "And for our lady countess, our flower that brightens our hearts, good and beloved," now the blacksmith looked at Vivan's mother with tenderness. "We know very well that she is one who supports you, she gathered us together when they took her son to the king. Mrs. Lena, we are glad that you chose our count," he bowed to her, to which she replied with a bow, hugging her husband's shoulder in silence, unable to say the words, "we respect your parents very much and we like how they stand behind you, especially how they replaced our count with his family, when he was denied and left us all to their own fate," here Vivan's grandparents bowed, who smiled warmly.

Grandma touched Erlon's arm tenderly as the words were said.

The blacksmith did not wait for further speech.

"We know that such people could not bring up bad, that's why Paphian..." He stopped, staring playfully at Vivan, thus giving him a sign that he had started talking about his brother on purpose. Moved by such a solemn and cordial treatment of his family, Vivan felt how he began to tremble with emotion, "...he is our pride and glory, as if he were our child."

Paphian smiled, looking down. He waited for words about his brother.

The blacksmith gasped, excited by his role. He called out to the crowd:

"Give me a mug here, or I'll lose my voice!"

Many laughed, including family friends who stood in the crowd next to Oliver and Sai, watching the event.

"Pour him!" Ross exclaimed cheerfully.

Someone quickly complied with the blacksmith's request, who gulped down the contents of the mug, wiped his mustache and threw the mug on the ground. The atmosphere among the people was joyful. For a good while, everyone just laughed. However, Azylas, the master of this modest ceremony, finally made the sign with his hand. There was silence quickly. Everyone was glancing at Vivan now, waiting for more to speak.

Here, however, Azylas decided to tease a little bit.

"Well, that's it, I guess..." he began, pretending to finish.

Then the assembled people began to shout:

"VIVAN! VIVAN! VIVAN!"

Vivan squeezed Vashaba's hand nervously as tears pressed in his eyes. He had never experienced anything like this before. There were many signs of sympathy, that's true. However, he was never honored in this way. He didn't know how to deal with all the kindness he was experiencing. Even the family joined the cheers.

The blacksmith raised his hand again. The audience fell silent.

"I don't know how to say it..." the blacksmith began in agitation. Several women were already wiping tears. "You know very well how much we love you," he said to Vivan in the solemn silence. "You feel it with all your heart, don't you?"

Vivan only managed to nod his head.

"I don't stop thanking fate, Mother Earth and the whole world of all spirits for the fact that we have you here," said the blacksmith warmly. "Thank you, Mrs. Lena, for giving you here, into this world. Thank you, Mr. Erlon, for loving you against all odds and for bringing you here. Finally, I thank you," he wiped a tear nervously from his cheek, which was an unusual sight, that you are with us. And since it is a joyful day, I will not say how much we have hurt, and it hurt us now what has happened to you so far," he added seriously. "I hope that you two will be lucky in life," he pointed to Vashaba with a smile. "You deserve it. We would like you to stay with us forever, at least in our hearts, so we decided it was time to start over. Barnica is associated with everything that is good, but also with what is bad. We would like it to be associated with good from now on. The best that has happened to us. First," he nodded to him, then turned to the rest of the family, "Erlon. And your family. That's why we want to ask you for something. With your consent, we want to change the name of our town..." he waited a moment for the request to fully reach the family standing in the middle. "Our proposal is..." he grunted nervously, seeing surprised looks. "LE - these are the first letters of our sweet lady Lena, your mother, without whom all this would never have started," he bowed towards the touched and astonished Lena, "Count, your father, would probably never look for a home here... Sorry, Erlon, but there is something in it," he added, seeing nervous movement. "If it weren't for them," he pointed to Vivan's family, "you would be stuck with yours, imprisoned in their golden cage. It's for them that you got out of there."

"Yes," said Erlon gravely. "I've never regretted it. And I do not regret it."

"We know," Azylas replied with a twinkle in his eye. "So now I keep talking... VI - from the name of our beloved healer," Vivan bit his lip not to cry. "Finally, because we couldn't forget about you," he nodded to Erlon, "And you need to know that these letters are not only composed of these names. All your names are hidden in it for us," he told the family, especially looking at Paphian so that he would not be offended, "LON - the last, from the name Erlon. So, we stuck it together..." he took a breath, "LEVILON - that's the whole name. We would like to name this town like that. In your honor. All of you," he concluded solemnly.

There was silence.

The family stood speechless in the crowd, not even daring to believe what they had just heard. Victor sat down first, feeling that his legs would not lift him anymore, and after a while his wife joined him, covering her mouth with her hand trembling with emotion. Paphian put a hand on his brother's shoulder. Vivan looked at his foster father and mother, who shook his hand with emotion.

He felt his head spinning.

"Sit down," Vashaba ordered him gently.

He obeyed her, half consciously.

"I think they don't like the idea," said Azylas jokingly.

The crowd laughed softly and quickly fell silent at Vivan's first words.

"I didn't deserve this..." he said in a trembling voice "I didn't do anything special..."

"I think I'm going to pass out," his father added in a similar tone.

"Not the first time..." Exclaimed Seme, amused by these words.

Her sharp wit made a soft laugh as her memories came alive at the same time. This time, however, Seme's exclamation did wonders. Erlon felt the corners of his lips twitch involuntarily. Yes, he remembered...

"Ross," Vivan's mother looked around for their friend. "Help, please..."

She is the only one who has not lost her head, except for Vashaba. They both smiled knowingly at each other.

Ross appeared right next to them, gently touching the healer's shoulder.

Vivan breathed a sigh, feeling impotent departing from him under the soothing effect of the Jewel of Hope. Ross smiled warmly. Then he walked over to the others.

Vivan felt the assembled people waiting for their words. He saw their uncertain glances, their anxious smiles. He gathered himself up. They deserve a vote of thanks.

"We are deeply touched," he told the gathered. "Never..." he broke off, because these words seemed too banal, there was too little emotion hidden in them. "It means a lot to us. I regret that it isn't possible to give the names of everyone gathered here in this name," he pointed with a trembling hand, "but, as our wonderful Azylas said," he let a tear finally run down his cheek, "for us in each of these letters are YOU. Everyone of you. From now on, this name will be associated with this day," he looked at Oliver and Sai, "and this moment. We thank you."

He saw many warm smiles.

"And I will add," said Erlon, his voice swollen with emotion, "that tomorrow at dawn Vivan and I will send a letter to the king and queen, informing them of the new name, asking that all existing privileges, due to the new circumstances, continue to apply, and that the town of Leviron would have full city rights. The town has grown enormously since the last time, so it's time for it to become a fully-fledged port city."

Everyone cried out happily.

"We have to drink to this!" The blacksmith exclaimed, picking up his mug. Someone poured over him quickly. "To our wonderful Beckerts!" he raised a toast. "To the city of Levilon!"

"To the Levilon!" Everyone exclaimed.

Vivan looked at his stepfather. They smiled to each other, raising their mugs to a completely unexpected toast by them.

As the candles burned in the lamps and dusk fell around, Ross watched the lights dance, admiring the subtly introduced atmosphere. He did not have to watch the mood of the guests. He could just enjoy the moment. His white hair stood out in the dark. Bright clothes, sewn in the style of a uniform, as befits a captain, and a hat completed the work. It even overshadowed Oliver himself a bit, some said, but he disagreed. The groom's ceremonial clothes, with accessories in the color of his wife's dress, were simply woven in a different style. Oliver looked great in it.

"What are you thinking about?" Sel asked him.

Ross's calm mood popped up instantly like a soap bubble, but he turned to smile at him.

"About Levilon," he replied softly.

Sel regarded him with concern, sensing the lie. He didn't want the words to hang between them. He would prefer to tear them from his mind. It hurt more than he expected.

CHAPTER 2

The wedding ceremony, now connected with the celebration of the new name of the town, lasted two more days. Meanwhile, Count Elron kept his word by writing a long letter to the king. Vivan, for his part, announced the new fact to the queen. He knew that he could count on her support in this matter, as her two sons.

He felt in a way that they owed him this, but when he wrote to the queen, he made no mention of the past. He didn't want to brood over her.

The last letter was addressed to his foster grandmother. He wrote in it about the planned arrival.

"I can go with you," Vashaba said later, taking his hand.

He shook his head.

"They won't be nice to you. I want to spare you this. I'll heal her and come back."

She kissed him, savoring the taste of his mouth. It was enough for her to feel the need for more. It was as if he possessed her. She couldn't think, do ordinary activities without thinking about him. Sometimes she even gasped at the memory of his touch. He was her personal obsession.

They walked along the bank of the river that ran into the mouth of the port. Even at this hour, voices could be heard from the dock. The taverns were still awake.

Vivan looked at the palace, still only one residential section was completed. The rest was slow to build. At least they could go home now. New home.

"What did you really think when Seme mentioned the wedding?" She asked suddenly.

He smiled.

"I waited for you to talk about it."

"You want it?"

He looked at her warmly, though he felt unease in his heart.

"So?"

"Vashaba," he took her hands gravely, "I'm mortal. I know I can't ask you to. I can't let you watch me grow old and die. I wouldn't do this to you. I know how much you would suffer."

She looked at him in amazement.

"So, you think if we don't get married someday, you'll just let me go?!"

She probably knew him too well.

"I wanted..."

"Vivan..." she interjected softly. He felt his knees buckle at the sound of her voice. There was nothing he could do about it. She was his first love.

"What if I say you'll live with me forever?" She asked softly.

He froze, staring into her beautiful eyes. She took his hand.

"It's not a wedding ring," she said softly when he twitched slightly, feeling the cold touch. With me. Throughout the years...

He looked down at his hand, in which the ring glittered. A simple, silver ring with a small white rose entwined with an intricate crown of leaves - a rare flower that gives long youth and life.

"Adamantis..." he whispered excitedly.

"The rose seed is hidden in the flower," she explained warmly.

He was silent in amazement. He held the dream of many in his hand. A thing so extraordinary and unheard of that it was only ascribed to exist in the stories. Great gift.

Fear seized him. And sadness.

This was not what she expected. She thought she would please him with this gift.

I give you immortality," she pointed out emphatically as the silence dragged on.

Then she saw it. The fear in his eyes. It surprised her and hurt her at the same time.

"You don't want..." she understood, shocked. "Me or the ring?" she felt she had to separate the two matters as if they were separate factors. She had to know that.

What was so important to him? What was he afraid of? Which man would not take immortality?!

She answered that question immediately. She knew people who didn't. They rejected a wonderful gift for the sake of a life they wished to live in peace. Jader, a great friend of her brother Dinn... He has not abandoned his family. Vivan is very attached to his...

"It's because of them..." she whispered shockedly "You don't want to watch them die."

Vivan turned. He looked out over the river in the moonlight. The rushing current was so wide and treacherous that even the trolls did not risk crossing it.

The sound of the waves crashing against the stones conveyed the confusion now reigning in his heart.

"I love you," he said emphatically. "It means a lot to me..."

"For me too!" She replied with a quiet despair "But they are more important... are they so?"

Vivan was silent. He didn't know how to explain it to her. It wasn't about eternity. She wouldn't take his loved ones away. He knew the way.

It was about her.

He sighed in anguish. The thought was like a chain wrapped around him. It tightened more and more, blocking his movements and freedom, taking his life. He stuck links in body and soul. Eternity with Vashaba... One day his relatives will find that they have enough longevity. They will not be able to bear the burden of longing and regret for the past. He would only stay with Vashaba until things slowly changed and faded into the gloom of the past. The whole world will change around many times until there is nothing left of the world that he remembered and loved...

Eternity - it's a very long time...

He loved her, but if he was beginning to fear the future now, what would happen to them later? Month by month, he felt less safe with her. Too sensitive to people, he couldn't bring himself to take the last step. He yielded to her pleas when they were on the verge of parting. His brother wanted to do it for him, but he wouldn't let him. Because of the past. It was her love and devotion that brought him back to life. She had once loved him less preoccupied with passion. In time, lust prevailed, and he participated in it not only because he wanted to. In those moments, she gave him tender words, kisses. Especially at the beginning. And he was ready for a lot to feel it again.

In love, naive idiot. In the rare moments of loneliness, that was what he thought of himself. This time, however, things had gone too far. Eternity would not be a gift to him. It will become an endless torment.

"I can't do that," he replied softly, pain in his heart as he spoke.

"What?!" Her eyes gleamed with mounting anger.

Vivan felt regret. Even now, she couldn't see anything.

"I will not accept this gift," he replied deliberately.

Vashaba looked at him as if he had lost his mind. She has always wanted him. The worst, however, as he slowly realized, she wanted him forever. When they were together at first, he felt euphoric, drowning in passion. Over time, the euphoria turned to anxiety. Frustration. Longing for the old life. He began to suspect, though it still seemed cruel to her, that she was taking his life. Not only by taking him away from family and friends, because she could never get enough. He had never suspected that all desires could be so focused on satisfying the lusts. Couples spent time together, usually inspired by love and devotion. They've been focusing on one thing for a very long time. He did not confide it to anyone, but he was so exhausted by it, as if he had spent this time in extremely arduous physical work. As a healer, he had slightly more endurance than the average person. This trait, however, was based on the continued support of the family. Their concern was his miraculous elixir to restore vitality. For some time, this potion served only to keep his drive up, so that he could please the insatiable elf woman.

It was starting to frighten him.

"You love me?!" She hissed with pain in her voice. "How dare you lie to me like that? Is that your answer? You refuse me and you dare say you love me?!"

So that's how she put it. She had left him no choice from the beginning.

"I cannot accept this gift," he replied, looking courageously into her beautiful eyes, probably for the last time.

She looked at him as if he suddenly became a stranger to her. She did not understand. She didn't even want to understand him for a moment. Feel for a moment what he felt now. That hurts.

"You won't break my heart, Vivan Beckert!" She cried with tears in her eyes. "You let me think that I'm the most important to you. But I'm not! You prefer them over me!"

He sighed heavily, suppressing the rising sobs.

"I want you and them," he replied, his voice trembling with emotion. "Why can't you come to terms with it?!"

"Because I only want to be with you," she said coldly, "I don't want to share you with your whole family!"

"You don't even want to be with me..."

She held her breath for a moment. He didn't wait for her to scream.

"You just want to fuck me," he added, feeling the painful truth pierce through him like an ice blade with every word he uttered. "I return Adamantis to you," he added with a heavy heart, opening his hand. "Let it be used by those who can make such a decision without thinking and it will bring you happiness," he finished, aware that he had just finally buried their relationship.

She stared at the ring gleaming in the moonlight as if she couldn't believe they were parting. It was obvious he had surprised her. Certainly later, when the shock is over, she will attack him with her anger. He preferred them to part with respect, but he knew the emotions would make her angry. He was ready to accept it. He was guilty of it too. He could have finished it sooner. But he didn't want to. Until she threatened him with eternity...

"Keep him," she replied, barely in control of herself. "It's a gift!" She almost threw the words in his face.

She walked away from him with a brisk pace. Without saying goodbye. She didn't even look back, dwelling upon her regret. A cry of despair rose in his throat, but he did not let it break free. So many moments together and now he doesn't even deserve goodbye. Contradictory emotions tugged at him. Anger at her selfish decision. It is a pity that they did not even part in harmony. Solitude. Even relief.

He was left alone.

A sudden movement, a dark hooded figure - that was all he had time to see before the sack was thrown over his head. He felt the impact, then lost consciousness.

The peace that had prevailed for a year had loosened the voluntary guard that was guarding the walls too much. If Alesei were there, he wouldn't be surprised. But the four on the walls were reluctant to watch. The body was carried out through the gate. A black carriage without markings emerged from the darkness of the forest, harnessed by four ebony horses. Lena, the healer's mother, knew about the meeting by the river. As the black coach set out into the darkness of the night, escorted by a large squad, she felt a sudden unease that began to grow with each passing minute. Until there was a pounding on the door.

Ross pulled the entire palace to his feet, guided by his Jewel's insistence and his own fear. He was forcibly prevented from leaving the gate of the walls. The carriage turned at the crossroads, leaving its way to the capital. He hit the road that led to the county, two days' drive away.

He came ahead of time...

The dust cleared by the time the pursuit reached the fork. The darkness engulfed the blackness.

Vivan has been kidnapped.

CHAPTER 3

The black horses were changed once again during the journey.

The carriage arrived at noon, straight to the imposing palace - the Beckert family dwelling, from which the entire county took its name. Foam has already appeared on the animals' mouths. Sweaty sides moved in a nervous rhythm. The heat of the beginning of summer was overwhelming that day. The stuffy air announced a storm.

Countess Sarah Beckert, in all her strength and vitality, but - most importantly - without a trace of any disease, folded her fan irritably.

"Come on!" She cried, "There is still a long way ahead of you!"

"Let's first see if we deliver what we have planned," the count, her husband, leaned toward her. She pursed her lips in disgust as she smelled his sweat. "If we make a mistake, we'll lose our heads sooner than you can beg for forgiveness."

"I never beg for anything," she rebuked him with her eyes like a little boy. "Not even for that you'd be silent forever. But you are right, which is extremely rare. We risk too much not to check it out. Get him out!" She ordered firmly. "Hurry!"

The kidnappers hurriedly obeyed, taking their prisoner out. Vivan groaned in pain, the taste of dust in his mouth and the smell of his own sweat. All the way there were only stops twice. So that he would defecate in abusive conditions, for even then he was kept an eye on and the bonds were not loosened. He hadn't had a drink since dinner last day, and his head throbbed with a dull ache from both the impact that left blood on his temple from a dried cut and the tiresome ride. All he knew was that he was getting away from home with every moment.

The Countess winced in disgust at his appearance.

"Take it off!" She ordered, pointing to the sack. Hastily, she unfolded her fan and began fanning herself frantically, hiding a bit of anxiety in her heart.

The sack was ripped off Vivan's head with a hard tug. He narrowed his eyes under the influence of the light.

When he finally got used to his eyesight, he had to learn another thing as well. The Countess watched with a straight face as the painful amazement and disbelief slowly gave way to regret and a hint of anger.

"I'm here," he began in a hoarse voice, "of your will? Why?"

She narrowed her eyes in irritation, suppressing the nascent guilt as she looked into his gentle, incredulous blue eyes with nervous flaps of a fan.

"As always badly brought up," she said with a hint of carefully mock indignation to mask her true feelings. "It would be nice to say hello, don't you think?"

Vivan's eyes narrowed in anger. She expected this. She heard that his character had changed since the encounter with the demonic witch. It did not surprise her. Such situations in good, brave people can inspire bravery.

Vivan has always been famous for his kindness. His sensitivity was legendary. And how he risked his life just to defeat the witch was admirable even in her eyes.

Pity...

She pushed the thought aside hastily.

"I see no reason to be polite," he replied grimly.

Slowly their shameful deed caused him more and more regret and disappointment.

The Count, her husband, immediately came forward and slapped him in the face. Strong. It was like him. He was always impulsive. However, he was unable to oppose her. She looked at him with disgust. He backed away with obvious reluctance.

Vivan staggered from the pain in his head. Even so, his gaze become hard.

"Do you see it?" the countess asked her husband, assessing the prisoner's behavior. "He is a wild dog, devoid of polite, like his whole family."

She contradicted her thoughts, still hard on her part of the cold bitch.

"Free me!" He ordered them abruptly. "Now! Then perhaps I will forget your behavior!"

The count took another blow against the audacity, but the countess held him back with a blow of her fan.

"Enough!"

"Wolf pup!" Hissed the count, unaware that Vivan had been called that once, "He dare to raise his voice at us in our own house!"

Vivan did not step back.

"I said: enough," said the Countess emphatically, "We have what we wanted. It's him. There is no doubt. We are saved. Our county will get out of debt. His behavior doesn't matter now. He's useful, and that's what counts."

"You...!" Vivan jerked at the words, and several masked people immediately grabbed him. Others were changing horses in a hurry. "That's why you did it?! I was ready to help you! I wanted to come here!"

She was aware of her meanness.

"Yes..." she replied with well-played contempt, "You and a bunch of your sketchy friends: whores and rabble! I didn't want to have all this company that you would probably bring to us! My son defiled the good name of your dirty mother! And that family of hers, a bunch of villagers! It's a pity that our grandson will be wasted in such an environment! And finally, all this Heart Sorcerer, as you call him!" the name almost spat out. "Disgusting, confusing man in a filthy relationship. It's time to put it in order! If they show up here, and I bet they do, we'll put them in order. Once and for all!" She gestured to take him away from her eyes.

Vivan wanted to retort the countess's harsh words at once. Blood rushed to his head with anger. He felt himself losing balance and spots appeared before his eyes. He probably got hit in the head too hard...

He vomited right on her shoes.

A cold fury engulfed the count, who, this time, also did not restrain himself from hitting the prisoner again.

"Take him!" He shouted furiously, turning red with passion.

"Stop!" The countess objected firmly.

She walked over to the aching Vivan who turned pale. Shadows appeared under his eyes. He swayed as if struggling to stay on his feet.

She glared at her husband and her people.

"Which of you hit him so hard?" She asked venomously.

She felt Vivan's gaze on her. She avoided that gaze. Instead, she found one of her people with her eyes.

"It was you, Kraun, wasn't it?" She asked sharply "You've always had a heavy hand!"

"Countess..." the thug began, but he broke off when she came over and hit him with all her strength in the face with her open hand.

Anger, the cause of which she might as well look for in herself, inflamed her senses.

"You fool!" She shouted at him as he lowered his head. "He's a healer! His gift is priceless! How much do you think the King of the Bay will give us if the boy turns into a gibbering country idiot or gets sick and dies? Do you realize what will happen if you deliver him like this?!"

"Sarah..." Vivan said softly.

She froze at the soft tone of his voice. She cannot bend. She cannot show weakness!

It must be so.

She stared at him defiantly but knew now that she hadn't deceived him for a moment. He knew what she really felt.

"You said King of the Bay?" She sensed the suffering in the tone of his voice.

She looked at him carefully and cursed silently. He looked bad. The heat only worsened his condition.

She came over to examine his head. The cut didn't bleed, but it looked nasty. She felt he was on fire under her fingers.

"Why didn't anyone bandage him?" She asked in a cold tone, thus masking her concern. "What about you?! In this condition..."

At that moment, Vivan felt his head light-headed and then feeling sick again. He dropped to his knees. The Countess felt afraid. It was one thing to be reluctant to son's new family and one thing to completely contribute to the disease, or perhaps even the death of the healer.

She did not want to admit the most important thing to herself: she liked this boy for his unprecedented nobility, and only stupid pride made her remain in the attitude of the offended heiress of the old family, whose son had committed a terrible misalliance. She had long followed with admiration, deep inside, his exploits and the abilities of his step-in-law.

But now her future was at stake. If she withdrawn from the treaty, the king would undoubtedly have ordered them all killed. Maybe even Erlon and his family. He made her do it. How naively she had thought at first that she would bring Vivan and the ruler to her palace, where a healer would heal him. There would be no kidnapping, but an innocent trick. The king, however, insisted that Vivan would never agree to help him. The letter was only two days ahead of the request when she changed her plans, realizing that it would also be a very good lesson for her son. She had not forgotten what a blow his betrayal had been to her, and the emissary of the ruler played perfectly on her feelings.

It is a pity that this boy was hurt...

Vivan felt his bonds slashed. He hit the nearest kidnapper. He was captured immediately. He was thrown to the ground and tied again. The count targeted at him again, but the countess stepped in, with a quick flick of her fan, hitting him in the face to bring him to his senses.

It was enough. He pulled himself together as he watched his men pull Vivan to his feet.

"You'll regret it!" Vivan called.

"Really?" she asked coldly, raising her eyebrow a bit, still not leaving the role. "Dress him and go!" She felt remorse saying these words, but she had no choice. There was no turning back now. "To the bay! We lose so much time!" She screamed at her people.

Vivan gave her a murderous glare before he was dragged into the carriage.

"Lady," said another of her thugs, "what if he won't be able to go?"

She looked at him. If it were just some men, she had commissioned him, he wouldn't have been worried about his fate. But it was a healer. He helped many people, defeated the evil witch. This bandit respected him. Well...

She walked over to Vivan once more.

"Don't do it," he said to her. "You can still back out. Don't sell me."

She ignored his request.

"Then you'll stop for a halt. I hope you will be discreet. No witnesses."

He understood that he would not convince her to change her mind. He was seized with anger, which from then on began to accompany him often.

"I won't forget it..." he said with all the contempt he felt for the woman at that moment, compounded by the fact that he knew exactly what she really felt.

"Take him!" she ordered without looking at him.

"Sarah!" He shouted angrily "I won't forget it! I will never forget it! Hear that?! Sarah! I will never forget it!"

She twitched nervously, but quickly regained her composure. He was dragged into a carriage. This time the bag was not put on him. There was no longer any such need.

Her husband watched the whole thing in silence, but with a satisfied smile. She just didn't know whether he felt it towards Vivan or towards herself. Maybe both...

Only when the carriage drove away did she allow herself a moment of regret.

"I was ready to help you"...

She knew there was no turning back now.

"Here's my plan!" Erlon raised his voice, while an agitated Ross protested against his detention in the palace. "SILENCE! By Mother Earth, I'm the Count of these lands! I demand to be heard!"

Ross paused, still agitated. Paphian and Alesei were gone, and they had set out with Dinn in pursuit, with a crowd of hastily assembled volunteers. The assembled family, and perhaps all the rest of Levilon, looked at the count in silence now. Erlon kissed the concerned Lena tenderly.

"Has anyone seen Vashaba?" He asked softly.

Many heads disagreed without saying a word. He sighed heavily, also concerned about her fate, not knowing about the course of the last meeting.

"We must have a second plan!" He began emphatically. "My parents will deny everything! The carriage that they mentioned in their letter will probably arrive at dawn. The carriage that would take Vivan to them. Yes, I know, many of you disapprove of this idea. It doesn't matter anymore..."

"We're wasting time!" Ross said furiously.

Erlon held up his hand for silence.

"You must know something," he continued. "My old family is struggling with debts. They lived beyond their means, enjoying, quite undeservedly, the family connection between the healer and them. They had hosted celebrities overseas, counting on favorable trade deals, but the truth was revealed too quickly when the guests realized that this family was only feeding on Vivan's good name without communing with him or us. You know it yourself. I'm afraid they might have gone far worse. There are, as you already know, people who would not hesitate a moment if they could get my son in their hands. These people know perfectly well that Vivan would never help them willingly. I'm scared, and I'm pretty sure it's something like this this time. Remember my family when they showed up for Vivan's birthday?" Many heads nodded immediately. "There are also those who remember how they looked after Barnica before..." he sighed heavily. "She will not hesitate when it comes to her beloved palace, her own comfort and according to her - the good name of the family. She denied relations with us by prescribing Barnica for me. She disowned me. And Vivan, whom she called a savage. Useful, because helpful," he added bitterly.

There was a silence.

Ross looked down at the ground, unable to find the right words, feeling a pressing regret. He understood how painful the feeling of rejection was. He struggled with it for most of his life...

"I have news," said Erlon in the silence. "Disturbing and terrible. Evil plagues the Slaves Bay. It demands the blood of the innocent, otherwise it will tear down this cursed place..."

"It would be good!" Mikela, the alewife, exclaimed, shaking her fist. "To hell with this place!"

A chorus of voices, mostly from the throats of people who had been kidnapped more than a year ago to be sold in the Bay Area, loudly backed her.

"Yes..." Erlon took Lena's hand in a gesture of consolation. "Azram, king of the Bay, has allegedly made his first sacrifices. Virgins. Children. Often very small..."

"Often?" A woman asked weakly.

"How do you know that, my lord?" Asked the blacksmith Azylas nervously.

Erlon looked pointedly at Ross and his companion, Sel, behind whom were almost the entire crew.

"You were in the Bay?!" The surprised innkeeper asked.

"We know from a credible source," Sel replied, speaking for the first time since his arrival here, "We never go there."

The crowd roared softly.

"Well," said the blacksmith again, "but what does this have to do with our Vivan? And why don't we follow him to the Countess's palace?!"

"They are surely prepared for this," the count explained to him. "You will not catch up with them. Unless you can fly. You can't, can you? So, listen up! To force Azram to act, evil brought him a deadly disease. The ruler of such a filthy world will go to great lengths to save his miserable life. He will bring Vivan to the Bay at any cost. He will force him to heal the disease. And then... I'd rather not say it, but... There is a prophecy," he sighed heavily. "Azram thinks it's about Vivan..."

A wave of angry screams, muffled sobs, and voices of disbelief ran through the crowd.

Ross stood petrified, staring into the eyes of Erlon, who was clutching a shaken Lena's hand frantically.

"I need you," he told him, his voice trembling with tension.

He approached him.

"How can you be sure that all this is related somehow?" he asked incredulously, "it's just guesswork. Your mother, Azram, Vivan. I don't see..."

Without a word, Erlon pulled a packet of sealed letters from his pocket.

"What is this?!" Ross asked, surprised.

"Invitations from the lord of the Bay for a healer," Erlon announced to all the assembled.

The crowd surged with indignation.

"Vivan saw them?"

"He saw and refused every time. They've been coming for two months... Equally every two weeks."

Ross looked briefly at Sel. Suddenly he said:

Ross, that's not all."

"What is going on? Hasn't enough happened already?!"

"Listen!" Sel cried, his eyes communicated with Erlon. "Listen everybody!"

The crowd fell silent.

"That's not all..." Sel began. "When the letters started coming so often, your Count asked for more information about the evil at the Bay and the curse of its lord. We were hoping to find a solution that could be suggested to Azram without the visit of a healer. Vivan realized he couldn't say no endlessly. He is a mighty ruler who will not hesitate to achieve his goal. We just found out about it. Oliver was helping me. And also, his lovely wife Sai," he nodded his head to the couple. "Our expeditions did not only serve commercial interests. We couldn't show up in the Bay. Our crew and our friends did it." He paused for a moment to choose his words.

"Why didn't we know anything about it?" Maya asked, the girl who still wore the black after her fiancé, killed by the dragon sent by the witch two years ago.

"The fewer people knew, the better it was for everyone," he replied, looking into her eyes. "Forgive me."

"What did you find out?" Mikela, the alewife asked impatiently.

Sel looked thoughtfully at Ross, who was frowning.

"What the Count just told you," he continued, not looking at his partner anymore, "and some important facts..."

Then he began to tell a story:

"Azram, king of the Slaves Bay, built his kingdom on the suffering and harm of the people he sold into slavery. One day, when he had enough gold to have two kingdoms, he ordered his palace expanded and henceforth be called king. He reigned with a hard, relentless hand, but he still felt he had little. He turned to the demons for help, because he wanted to rule the whole world. Demons have come on call. However, they deceived him. They made him make offerings until he convinced them. So Azram began to sacrifice animals to appease the demons. Then it was time for human sacrifice. The king sacrificed good-hearted virgins, the most tender that were sent to him. Then he started looking for victims among the children, but that didn't help either. Meanwhile, evil was creeping in, growing in strength. Finally, the king got a clue: there are two people in the world whose hearts would satisfy the thirst for the underworld. For evil to help him gain power over the whole world, he must sacrifice the Guardian of People or the Sorcerer of the Heart on the altar."

"You always told me it was about one man," Ross suddenly interrupted, looking at him reproachfully, "You were talking about one..."

"I was lying," Sel said, "There are two of you. Two of the only ones in the world."

There was a silence as everyone waited tensely. Sel looked at Oliver, who nodded slightly to him. Sai looked at Ross, who was waiting, clenching his fists.

"Tell me," he said softly.

"The Guardian of People," Sel began, "so Azram might think it was Vivan and..." he looked into Ross's eyes with fear in his heart, "Sorcerer of the Heart."

There was a buzz and noise in the crowd. This time, no one doubted it was about Ross.

"You said I couldn't walk on the Bay because I'm too recognizable," Ross said softly.

"I wanted to protect you."

Ross looked at him warmly.

"What now?" Ross asked Erlon among fading voices.

"Go on Valeria," said the other. "Bring Vivan home. I know you won't quit! I will write a letter to the king and queen. They must help us! They owe Vivan their lives!"

"It's true!" Someone from the crowd shouted. "The king must help! It can't be otherwise!"

"The Queen will not leave a healer!"

Our beloved mother!" One of the women broke down, looking at Lena with compassion. "They took him again! What a life this boy has! The king took him, then the witch wanted to destroy him, and now this! Poor boy, oh, poor! And you, poor with him, his mother, because you must suffer too!"

Erlon hugged Lena, shocked at the woman's words. He felt the body of his beloved tremble as she hid her face in his arm. People went on. What hurt them had to break free from their aching hearts...

"And do you remember this dragon? That nearly killed Vivan?"

"And those damned people in the marketplace! Damn them!"

"I hope," exclaimed one of the townspeople, "they slaughtered them all!"

"He barely escaped with his life! Poor boy! After all, if it was someone else, not our Vivan, he would probably lose his mind from it!" Mikela, the alewife called.

"Truth!" Several voices called.

"Ross..." Erlon, with a soft plea, turned to his friend, worrying not only about his missing son, but most of all for his beloved.

Ross touched his arm without hesitation. The jewel glowed with a clearly visible glow the color of blood.

"I'm already working..." he told them softly.

Indeed, Erlon felt consolation slowly envelop his heart. Lena stopped trembling. He kissed her forehead with concern. Ross hugged her for a moment with him.

"It's okay," he whispered in her ear, but in order for Erlon to hear it as well, "He's strong, Lena. Stronger than you might think. He will survive it. You will see."

At the same time, it influenced the mood of the crowd. The alewife's words inspired him to act appropriately...

"Our Vivan has great strength in him," the blacksmith said calmly, supporting Ross's intentions. "They wanted to destroy him so many times, but they failed!"

It was the beginning...

Erlon looked at Ross, frowning, but he showed nothing. He just closed his eyes, still hugging Lena. Out of the corner of his eye the count saw Sel smile sadly. Sel always knew when Jewel and Ross were working together. I think he had a secret bond with them...

"He'll come back to us, you'll see," Ross whispered to the blacksmith.

"He will come back to us," repeated the blacksmith, and as the words spilled out of his mouth, he felt that he was really beginning to believe it, and then his heart was reassured as well. "He will come back!" He repeated forcefully, supporting Ross's hope, "You will see!"

This and that began to smile. The woman whose words so shocked Lena stopped crying and whining. Suddenly, the blacksmith's words worked a miracle. Vivan, their healer, will come home. It has to be. It can not be otherwise.

Ross opened his eyes shining with tears, then moved away from Lena.

The jewel was not shining.

It didn't have to anymore.

People themselves began to believe.

A few of them, suspecting that the sorcerer had helped them a little, looked at him significantly. But their smiles made him understand that they were grateful for this action.

These people were once taken with him on Cadelia's board... and they remained bound with him in bonds of great friendship. He smiled slightly at them; a bit confused.

"Captain!" Said Maya, one of the women who had been kidnapped with him at the time, "You are going on a dangerous voyage. Do you need our help?"

The group he was defending then looked at him with a knowing twinkle in their eyes. He couldn't help smiling.

The rest of the people also looked at him, hoping that he would need them. He looked at Sel and Erlon thoughtfully. Faithful to him from the beginning, Silas stood at his side.

"Orders, Captain?"

Sel met the slightly concerned gaze of Ross, who was still not used to commanding people.

However, Ross did not hesitate for long.

He nodded to Erlon. At the same time, a certain plan began to draw in his head, which, however, required some discussions and preparations.

"I need new people..." he began, and then immediately the innkeeper and his sons moved forward, followed by the others who were accompanying him at that time, "Excellent!" Ross said calmly before gasping for breath. He knew that they would do it. "This time, however, I would also like to ask for help from some of our beautiful ladies," he added, by which he surprised those present. "Sai," he turned to his friend. "Would you like to accompany me on this trip?"

Surprised Sai looked at him, eyes wide open. He did not wait long for her answer. She agreed.

Ross thanked her with a nod. He calmly asked several other beautiful women about the same.

Neither of them refused.

His last choice caused a real stir in the crowd.

"Lena .." he said warmly to Vivan's mother.

Lena looked at him, flushed with tears. Her blue eyes, which the remarkable son inherited from his mother, looked at Ross with steady, determined determination. He recognized that look.

Lena Beckert, although she was the mother of two grown sons, kept her youthful beauty thanks to Vivan. Her age, appearance and complexion, just like her husband's, could have given her twenty-something years. Since her son was seven years old, thanks to his spontaneous decision, Lena Beckert, her husband Erlon and Vivan's maternal grandparents stopped aging.

Lena Beckert has not aged even a day since then...

Before Ross stood a twenty-something-year-old girl with mature eyes, experienced by life. He knew that look. Though he was younger than she was, the mirror sometimes showed him a similar face. In his own eyes.

He knew that Vivan had not inherited his inner strength from a real father. Nor did he take it from his foster father who raised him.

It was she who brought the family between the worlds...

"I know you don't want to stay here," he said seriously.

"Then you must take me with you," she replied as if nothing had happened.

"I have two more men left..." he muttered mysteriously, when almost all of them parted ways. Some of the people appointed by him had to prepare in a hurry for the sea voyage. Vivan's family and their friends still stayed, waiting for a few words of explanation. Erlon spoke first, anxious for his wife.

"I don't agree!" He said firmly.

Ross expected this. He would be surprised if the count did not. Now he embraced his wife like a precious treasure that he was not about to let go of.

Ross's heart twitched. So many years... They stood before him, young in body, almost the same as when they met, but in souls tied together by years of mutual respect and love. They touched his heart.

"I'm swimming with him. For our son," Lena answered him in a tone that could bear no objection, but her eyes showed tenderness towards her husband who cared for her so much.

"With me," he replied, but here Ross and she, both vehemently disagreed.

"No," Ross put a hand on his friend's father's shoulder. "You wait for the reinforcements. Someone has to keep an eye on Levilon. I have a plan..."

"Do you realize that you are taking away what is most precious to me? My son has already been taken," in Erlon's heart, Vivan was never just a stepson, "Lena?! Why she? Why not me?!"

"Trust me," Ross replied calmly.

"Promise you won't leave them!" Erlon said forcefully. "Neither Vivan nor hers!"

Ross looked him in the eye seriously.

"You have my word."

"Ross, why don't you take me?" Suggested Victor, Vivan's grandfather, "I'll help you."

He was prepared for that as well.

"No, Victor," he said with a hint of regret, "Forgive me, but I don't want to endanger anyone else from your family anymore."

Here, however, a surprise awaited him.

"I don't think to listen to you!" Victor replied with a fierce face. Without a word he turned and left, presumably to prepare for his journey.

Ross felt eyes on him. Well, it was likely. He turned to the next person.

"Oliver..." he began, but the latter interrupted him.

"I agreed. Sai will go with you," Oliver smiled with difficulty. "Although it is not easy for me..."

"I want you to come with us."

Oliver looked at him in surprise.

"Why didn't you tell me right away?!"

"Because..." he knew it was going to be one of the hardest things he was going to do today. "I need your permission. Your talents. One talent in particular," he concluded emphatically.

Oliver looked at him suspiciously.

"You want my... skills? The Vermod cat?"

Ross sighed inwardly. Oliver thought about his climbs.

"This too," time urged, he mentally rebuked himself for this lengthiness, "I want a few women to become, of course, make-believe, a gift for the king from a mysterious merchant. I will take care of the entire setting properly..."

"But...!" Erlon began nervously, hugging Lena tighter, but Ross made a gesture to calm down.

"They will be a group of dancers. Not a gift," he assured him. "Remember my skills. In this group I would like to have someone who apparently did a good job during the fights in Vermod, can climb incredibly well, will have the safety of our ladies in mind and above all..." he took a significant break here, "he can perfectly pretend to be a woman..."

Oliver froze. Sai looked at her husband with concern. The rest, including the Victoria crew, did not know where to look.

They didn't have to wait long for the explosion.

"You must be crazy!" Oliver shouted angrily "I said once, never again... Never! Understand?!"

"Oliver, listen..."

"No!" He raised his voice forcefully, "I will not agree to it! And you, just you and Sel," he looked reproachfully at the other friend he had known longer, "you should know why!"

"I didn't know..." Sel looked at Ross, not hiding his surprise.

"Ross, maybe it would be possible..." Vivan's grandmother said gently.

Ross could see how much grief and anger had aroused in Oliver by his words. However, he did not want to yield. Too much could depend on it.

Sai was silent, without even trying to convince her husband of the idea. You couldn't blame her for that. Oliver had a hard time being the false sister of a murdered maid in the royal court.

"I just started a new life," Oliver looked into his eyes, not hiding his bitterness, "I married a wonderful woman," he looked at Sai with determination. "My beauty... My advantage!" He said with anger, "or, as you call it, talent is a curse! It only brought trouble and misfortune upon me... Don't ask me for it, brother..."

He turned his back to those present, avoiding their gaze. Sai touched his shoulder gently.

"Vivan..." Ross began in a low voice, "he's been kidnapped. Someone thinks he has the right to take him as a thing. To have his body and soul as he wishes," he waited for the words to reach everyone and Oliver himself in the silence. "You must know something about that, don't you, Oliver?" He asked softly "Do you know what it's like when someone tries to enslave you? I know that you know."

Oliver was silent.

His decision was awaited.

"Sai," he finally looked at his wife after a while, "is his jewel glowing now?"

Ross would have smiled at that supposition under different circumstances.

Sai looked at him without anger, which he took with relief. She studied the Hope Jewel.

"No," she said softly.

"Because if I look back now and see that that damned jewel is glowing, my word, I will punch you!" Oliver shouted menacingly to Ross as he turned.

Ross didn't even flinch. He stood calmly as his foster brother approached him, watching him closely.

"You've balls for asking me this," Oliver finally told him, pleased with what he saw.

There is one more thing to do.

"The crew!" Ross exclaimed in a slightly hoarse voice. "To the ship! Get ready for the cruise!"

"Ay, Captain!" Silas called before he took the people.

"There's one more left," Ross explained to those who stayed, "I need a man. Unfortunately, I'm sure he won't come with us, unless you," here he turned to Sel, "don't agree to it."

His words surprised Sel again.

"Who is this?! I don't remember knowing anyone here who would need my," he broke off, suddenly realizing everything."

"Talk him," Ross asked, trying to sound firm.

Sel looked him in the eye, thinking of their friend's fate and the words from a few moments ago.

He had to forget about other things. It wasn't easy.

"I can't believe you're asking for this," he replied incredulously.

CHAPTER 4

The rider on the black horse rushed past the group of chasers. Under the hood, no one saw his full face. He was slim though, so it was assumed that he was at least an elf, if not a woman. Dinn smiled.

"Solai," he said warmly to the rapidly departing figure.

"Dinn, stay on watch," Paphian ordered. "Just in case."

He looked at the group he had drawn all the way here, to the former abode of his ancestors, impressively situated among hills and forests. He wondered if he was doing the right thing. Breaking in here will not turn his "grandparents" in a positive light. If, and there was a slight chance of it, they weren't to blame for it, it would be a raid, and so the case would be extremely unpleasant. However, if they are guilty, and that is what his heart told him, they can be prepared for this visit...

As soon as he thought about it, he felt a sudden twinge. He reached to his neck to pull out a thin fishbone, smeared with...

He fell off his horse. Dinn stood on the saddle and swiveled before more hidden arrows were fired. He pulled Alesei away at the last minute.

"Run away!" He shouted, while the brave volunteers fell one by one, attacked by arrows appearing from nowhere.

"Paphian!" The nervous bully pointed to the lying guy.

Dinn wanted to answer that as another arrow hit the target this time. Alesei leaned in the saddle.

So, there was only one thing left for him. He got on his friend's horse behind his back and, holding it, ordered the animal to run into the thicket of the forest. He miraculously avoided the arrows, and Alesei got one or two for him. He ripped them off hastily.

He quickly found himself in the thicket of the still dark forest. Dawn barely brightened the sky.

"All?!" Someone from the woods asked.

"The elf escaped! Along with that bully!"

"Look for him! Take the rest and go to the palace!"

"And our lady's grandson?"

"To the car!"

Dinn looked around quickly, but the chase was close behind him. He cursed silently. He must find another opportunity.

Now was time to save ourselves.

Alesei's horse, guided by the steady hand of a distinguished elven rider, tramped through a thicket of trees.

A few of the less able pursuers soon fell off their mounts or ran into impassable places. Dinn led the horse out onto the track and encouraged him to run faster. There were only two of him here, but still fierce in action. Their arrows apparently ended, so they switched to crossbows and bolts, but they did not perform well in the ride. Dinn was clearly ahead of them.

Suddenly he smiled to himself and stopped his horse.

The riders unexpectedly gave up their pursuits.

He patted the brave animal.

"Alesei," he shook his friend slightly. He touched his neck anxiously and sighed.

It was not a lethal poison.

"We're back," he said to the brave mount, "Maybe they didn't catch my horse."

Suddenly, however, a disturbing thought struck him: why did the riders give up their pursuits?

"If this bitch of yours stayed a while longer," began one of the bandits, called Kraun by the Countess. "I'd hit her in the head to make her die, and then I'd get on with you. I tell you; no woman should give me orders. Do you have that fucking ring of hers?"

Vivan glared at him. The bandit laughed contemptuously, looking him straight in the eye.

"You had the opportunity to tell the Countess about this," Vivan replied quietly. "Before she hit you in the mouth..."

The bandit's contemptuous smile faded immediately.

"He told you well!" Said another with a laugh. "Healer," he turned eagerly to Vivan "I have this ring, calm down. I saw him fall and I found him. I thought that maybe after all..." he extended his hand with a ring that glowed briefly, "you will want it..."

Vivan looked at him. It was he who spoke to the countess out of concern for his health. He respected him, as probably few in his life. But this did not extend to others. In his world, only a small group of people mattered. It was impossible to forget about it.

Adamantis was in his hand...

Vashaba broke up with him in anger...

Her tender words, her touch subtly influencing his senses, pulsed in his blood. Her closeness, warmth, and kisses covered his body more densely than scars, but now it hurt like multiple cuts. Sometimes, in moments of excitement, she whispered his name imploringly, and her lips uttered words that additionally moved him with extraordinary sensitivity. Sometimes he thought his heart would burst with emotion, it was beating so hard when he heard her words.

The gift of compassion.

The breath in him was then torn and quickened. Her body was inflamed with passion like a fever. And she was talking. She said how much he meant to her. How everything in him touches her. The words, the way she spoke them, worked on him like a powerful force. But this state, the state of suspension, when the heart almost stopped, the world hummed with blood, the body burned, and the soul lost itself in an endless feeling of fulfillment, trusting, safe in her hands, outside the world... It wasn't just fire that burned here. Each element pulsed with its energy. All because his emotions, way of feeling and reaction to others were intensified. This was to help him with the help of the suffering. However, when help was not needed, the gift allowed him to experience erotic sensations, which he did not guess until he met Vashaba in his life.

Nobody else felt the world that way...

He felt all emotions deeper. At the same time, tightly. Together with her.

It made him feel barely alive after all. He barely had the strength to get out of bed. He staggered as they returned from their secret places, weak but happy. However, it only strengthened his conviction that he would not convey these feelings to anyone.

Even if it would kill him one day...

He felt a pain as he looked at Adamantis.

He was sharp and poignant. It hurt his soul. And his heart felt as if someone were cutting a hole in it, tearing it apart.

She won't be there anymore...

Suffering pulsed in his temples, making him sick. The blood rushed like a fist in the head wound. Before he lost himself in this feeling, before his eyesight dimmed, he reached for the ring with determination and held it to his heart.

He will probably never feel her body close to his again. He will never hear these words.

He will never see her again...

He would love her anyway. Let the world see that no one will ever get into his heart this way. The very thought that he would never feel such a fusion again caused him a terrible, shocking pain. His heart shattered into millions of pieces.

Deeper...

The ring was placed close to the jewel on the neck. It was the first time that a miracle happened. The gem was originally preserved in a goldsmith's house with love. Hidden in the hand of a statue. It was made in memory of the healer's mother's visit. Lena kissed him and solemnly offered to Vivan when he returned home because Ross had kept the jewel originally offered to her son. Vivan wore it around his neck, sharing his love with his relatives, loving You above all that was dear to him...

It shone like a Jewel of Hope.

He pulled his owner's hand. He made the ring hang around his neck, next to a cross marked with his blood, on a chain that has since ceased to have its beginning and end...

"Oh shit!" Kraun blurted out, and at the sight of it he forgot his anger immediately.

His companion, however, soon became interested in something else. He watched his unusual captive. For Vivan himself barely touched the ring to make sure it was on his neck. After a while, he paled rapidly.

"Healer?" The bandit worried, seeing this sudden deterioration.

The carriage sped fast, shaking on numerous bumps. The other two bandits, seated on either side of Vivan, held him as he leaned forward sharply.

"I feel so bad..." Vivan whispered, feeling he was losing touch with reality.

The bandit did not hesitate any longer. He looked quickly out the window. They passed a small village quickly.

"I know this area!" He exclaimed upset "Right behind the village, there is a lonely hut in the woods. The family of a woodcutter lives there. Let's go there!"

"Are you crazy?!" Kraun was indignant. "And the pursuit?!"

At the same moment Vivan passed out. The furious bandit looked at his impulsive companion. He cringed involuntarily under the gaze.

"We have no choice," he said to Kraun. "If we don't let him rest, he will surely die."

The carriage stopped in front of the hut. The sun was heading west. The woman and her daughter collected clothes from a clothesline. The man was eating at the table outside, clearly weary of the hard work. The ax, his working tool, was propped up against the leg of the table.

Seeing a carriage, black as night, drawn by four dark horses, and a coachman masked on a coach-box, he immediately sensed trouble. He reached for the ax, calling for the wife and daughter who had abandoned their jobs to stand by his side. The kidnappers, however, expected someone to resist them. The bandit who was caring for Vivan quickly reached for his crossbow and aimed the bolt at the father of the family. Two of his buddies revived the unconscious Vivan. Kraun drew a long knife, at the sight of which the mother instinctively covered her child with her body.

"Don't even think about it!" shouted the bandit commanding the operation to the father of the family, "because in front of them I will smash your head!"

"Dad!" The scared girl screamed.

Vivan recovered enough to quickly see what was happening. He felt a familiar chill sweep over him.

"Don't kill them!" He called to his captors. "Don't you dare to move them!"

"Shut up!" Kraun screamed nervously, trying to strike.

Vivan looked into his eyes fearlessly.

"Come on, hit me again!" He said mockingly "The king will thank you!"

Kraun immediately lowered his hand angrily.

"Healer?!" The woman exclaimed incredulously.

"They kidnapped me! I have nothing to do with them!" He explained quickly, and to the kidnappers he turned sharply, "Leave them alone!"

"Do you feel better now?" One of the men asked mockingly.

"Kraun, Befort!" The commander asked them, "take care of them!" He pointed to the family. "To the cottage with them! Quick! And you," he turned to the coachman and the other bandit. "Follow them! Find a bed and put him down!" He pointed at Vivan.

Once they were all inside and obeyed his orders, he sent a coachman to take care of the horses and the carriage. Behind the hut, he noticed some buildings, perhaps a cowshed or stables.

"Now what, Rino?" Kraun asked. "What are we going to do with the family?"

It was clear to everyone that the moment they arrived, they had signed their death sentence. The only question was when?

How?

"You know about treatment?" The one named Rin did not answer him, but turned to the woman to postpone this decision.

"I know this and that," she told him calmly, holding her daughter in her arms.

"Take care of him!" he ordered them shortly, "and you sit quietly," he turned to her husband, who gave him a gloomy look. "Then you will serve us all a meal," he turned to the woman, who had already sat down with her daughter on the edge of the bed, to look at the wounded man.

She didn't answer. Besides, he hadn't expected to do it.

"You must flee," Vivan pleaded to her as soon as the kidnappers started talking, "They will kill you!"

"Shhh..." she ordered him gently, looking carefully at the wound on his head and touching his burning forehead. "Don't say so much. Do not scare. Don't bother your hearts."

She nodded at her daughter. Vivan could see the fear in the girl's eyes. A similar one was hiding in the eyes of her mother and her father's fears. He was stuck in nervous movements of his hands, trembling fingers, furtive glances.

In a low voice, she was giving orders to her daughter, perhaps twelve, who looked at him with a mixture of fear and sympathy. When she tried to ask questions, Rino strictly forbade her to do so. She pretended to humbly obey his commands, but Vivan knew she was thinking about his words all the time, looking for a way out of the situation. Her eyes searched for an escape route that still wasn't there. They were well watched over.

He let them bind his head, worried about his condition, before speaking again.

"Please..." a headache, combined with a strange sense of breakdown and slight disorientation, made it difficult for him to concentrate, "I don't want anything to happen to you..."

He began to tremble despite the warmth in the room. He sensed the bad thoughts of his captors. The growing fear of the prisoners.

It certainly won't end well.

"You need to rest," the woman answered him meanwhile, "to calm down. I'll give you something to ease the pain and let you fall asleep..."

"Not now," he asked, touching her hand frantically. "Do it when they fall asleep."

"But..."

"I'll help you," he assured her softly so that no one else but her would hear.

Rino, as if sensing a desperate plot, looked at them suspiciously. The woman, remaining stoically calm, handed Vivan a cup of water under the watchful eye of the bandit. Finally, he looked away. Then she asked softly:

"How? You're barely stand on your feet."

She appreciated his good intentions, but tried to think logically. Vivan was injured, his condition genuinely uneasy. She was afraid to rely on him because she had seen how bad things were. He wasn't surprised at all. He couldn't look at her without feeling a headache.

"You'll see," he replied with conviction.

He would sooner die than let hurt them.

"You remember me, healer?" The girl asked unexpectedly, as if she had waited long enough with this question.

Once, when he finally fully realized how powerful his gift was and the consequences of having it, he was afraid that if someone asked him a similar question, probably one of the many healed, he would only be able to deny it because he would not be able to remember any faces of his charges. He was afraid of such moments, because he realized how much meeting him meant for these people. Each of them would like to be remembered by Vivan the Healer. Everyone wanted to be someone worth remembering for him, so that they could proudly say: "Oh yes, I met him again. He remembered my name. He remembered how he spent time with me. He asked about what we were talking about then. What a person!".

They remembered. They often kept this memory in their hearts like a treasure, remembering in detail every moment, which unfortunately faded into his memory with time. He knew about it. And he worried about it until the first, second and subsequent times made him realize that his gift... he remembered. A touch was enough to recall the details of events, and even the names. He restored the memory of events as well as helping him determine the cause of pain and suffering...

He took the girl's hand. Almost immediately, the flash of images in memory told him everything he wanted to know...

"You came when the witch attacked the town," he replied softly, moved by the memory. "You were the girl who had a headache, near death," he deliberately did not mention the huge tumor that would have taken her life if it had not been brought to him. He felt the gaze of the little girl's father, full of emotion and tears. When their eyes met, everything else suddenly didn't matter. There was only this moment. The moment when memories came back. The good ones, without the witch's presence, when Vivan took his hands from the girl's head and announced that the disease was over. And maybe, and even for sure, the future was not as colorful as imagined, but thanks to his interference, she had more hope in herself. She had the light in her.

The light now enveloped in darkness...

"Ajane..." Vivan's voice quivered with emotion. "You've grown. You look like a little lady now."

The girl, as he had expected at such moments, smiled happily, pleased that he remembered her. Her eyes lit up. Lush, curly, shoulder-length hair, no longer thin and sparse as he remembered, moved happily as she looked at her mother, sharing the happiness with her.

Then he looked at the leader of the kidnappers.

Rino couldn't bear his gaze. Only a moment, one brief moment, he withstood the silent accusation in the healer's blue eyes. Somewhere deep down, the remnants of his conscience struggled with ruthlessness.

A fight they were about to lose.

Vivan kept his eyes on him, feeling the eyes of a woman on him, the happy memory slowly fading away as she realized a truth that he was unable to accept.

The life of the child he then saved will come to an end.

They will murder her.

They'll kill this whole family.

In his mind's eye, Vivan saw the girl's face contorted with fear, hair that had been beautiful until then, tangled in the clenched fist of a bandit. Blood and scream. He closed his eyes in mounting anger.

He won't let that happen!

Slowly, the bandits began to fall asleep. A hot meal, the only dinner that would be enough for the family for the next day, put them in a good mood. Vivan used this fact to make them sleepy so that they would not discover its effects.

He had never put several people to sleep at once... But he had to. He had to do it. He will not allow the family to be murdered! He would not allow it, although he already knew that he would pay a high price for it... But his future still did not belong to him in these hours. He would not have done otherwise.

So the dream came unexpectedly. Too gentle to them. One by one they fell asleep to the rhythm of the waiting hearts. Rino was the last to fall asleep. He rested his head on the table where he was sitting, almost smashing the empty food bowl.

Vivan closed his eyes for a moment... He was very tired. He felt the wound throb on his head. He must have had a fever.

"Miriam..." he whispered. In memory of his gift, this name glowed with emotions that could light up the gloomiest house.

The girl's mother touched his forehead gently.

"Yes, healer?" She asked gently, making a cool compress for him.

He heard the soft splash of water in the bowl and the calm breathing of the sleeping people.

"Say: Vivan," he asked in a slightly louder, soft tone. "Please..."

It was important to him now.

"Vivan?" She asked him with motherly tenderness, touching her hand gently to his face.

"You must go now," he said to her, accepting the gesture gratefully. "But..."

"Please!" he said the word with emphasis. "You must run away! Immediately!"

He looked at them. Mother and daughter looked at him incredulously for a moment. Ajane broke out first.

"And you, healer? What's with you?"

"Shhh..." her mother ordered her, pointing at the sleepers.

"They won't wake up," he reassured her. "But I can't keep them like this forever..."

The family looked at him now with almost pious admiration.

"It's you...?" Ajane asked incredulously.

It might take too long. Vivan turned his gaze to the girl's father. They agreed without words.

"We'll take their horses!" He jumped up quickly, without further hesitation "Miriam, Ajane, collect the necessary things! We have to move!"

Ajane obediently stood up, but her heart could not believe what she heard.

Like her mother's heart.

"How's that?" She asked in a tearful voice that made Vivan's heart squeeze with emotion. "And the healer?!"

"Honey, he must stay..." Father tried to explain to her.

She looked at him incredulously.

"We're not leaving him!" She screamed.

Miriam glanced hastily at the sleeping bandits, but they, as Vivan had assured, were sleeping well.

"Ajane," Vivan reached out to grasp hers, "I can't go with you..."

"You can!" her tears moved him so much that he felt his eyes fill with them too.

"I can't hold my horse," he admitted truthfully.

These were the first painful words he had to say to convince himself as well.

"We'll take the carriage!" She said frantically, but more quietly, more prudently.

"I don't have the strength for it," knowing that there was a possibility for him to come home, but he couldn't, hurt him the most. He had freedom at his fingertips! However, he had to give it up. That hurts.

"No..." She cried, and then he couldn't hold back his tears.

"Tell..." his voice broke with emotion. "Tell my parents where they are taking me. Take yours away from here. Please... they'll kill you otherwise!"

Parents. The word struck a particular string within her. She gripped his hand tightly. She stroked the seemingly delicate skin of the gloves.

"You can't stay!" She sobbed softly.

"Miriam..." he felt he couldn't take it, and then regret would make him lose control and the bandits would wake up. He needed help.

"Vivan." She didn't need any urging to say his name this time. She did it with love.

She understood how much he was doing for them.

He sacrificed his own chance for freedom, taking away his strength to keep the bandits asleep.

"We have to go, Ajane," she said gently to her distraught daughter, while her husband returned quickly gathering the essentials and coins hidden in the glove compartment.

"Mom, this is Vivan..." The girl stared at them with wide eyes, unable to believe that they were doing something similar, "he must come with us!"

Vivan looked at her fondly. It was he who had to convince her. He knew about it. It should have been done. Only the harsh truth could convince her.

"Ajane," he said softly to the girl, "I'm hurt. I will slow you down. In this state, I will fall off my horse..."

"I'll tell your parents," she whispered, her face wet with tears.

Vivan kissed her forehead tenderly.

Her father squeezed his hand tightly, concealing his agitation.

"I won't forget," he assured him. "Neither that, nor now! Never! You have my hands, my heart and my head! I will help! Always! Remember!"

"I will," Vivan replied confidently.

Miriam was the last to leave.

"Vivan," she took his hand gently. "Please, do one more thing for me..." she looked into his eyes firmly. "Promise you will never give up. Keep telling yourself, "I have to go back to my family." Remember that they are definitely looking for you already. They want you back. They love you. Don't let evil overwhelm you. Don't give them that satisfaction! Show no weakness, because then you will be destroyed. Remember my daughter's tears. Remember it!" She pointed with her finger at the jewel on his neck. "And this..." she added, leaning a bit, lifting his gloved hand. She kissed the inside of that hand, and then the headache finally eased. He sighed softly, feeling tremendous agitation and relief as the suffering finally subsided.

As Miriam passed away and the little world around him filled with the breaths of sleeping bandits, he was still waiting...

He waited until they were far enough away.

Despair was seeping into his heart in the silence.

He first thought about Vashaba...

Yesterday she still loved him. Today he knew she had abandoned him forever, but his heart still couldn't believe it. It's a cruel dream, and if he manages to get home, they'll surely fix it. They were one. Pure passion on a wave of unimaginable elation.

Vashaba will not come back...

He won't see her anymore. He would not feel her warmth in the chill of the night.

He will not hear a whisper bearing his name.

Vashaba will not come back.

Vashaba...

He was close. Very close. Incredibly, almost tangible. He felt the pain building up. This scream rising within him, on the verge of grief, anger and tears, would tear his soul apart.

That scream would probably take him out of his mind.

That scream would surely kill him!

He closed his eyes and took a breath. He let out his breath slowly...

"I have to go back to my family," he repeated Miriam's words softly for the first time.

Time went by. There were no sounds of hope coming from outside. All you could hear was the sound of the wind outside the window.

Help won't come immediately, but that doesn't mean never. He must think about them. He must survive!

He hummed softly to dispel his troubled thoughts. A quiet song that his mother used to sing for him, who came from her secret world.

She did not want him to help Sarah - the mother of her beloved husband. The one he was never allowed to call his grandmother.

She was right.

He was useful to Sarah. Useful because helpful.

Every word in that statement was like a stigma.

Another breath in. Slow exhalation...

With each passing moment, this family went farther and farther...

Secure. Alive.

They were carrying their future and that was the most important thing right now.

He hummed until the weariness caused by recent passages finally overwhelmed him.

Then, before the last tear induced by longing fell down his cheek, he was seized by sleep.

He no longer had the strength...

The bandits woke up only at dawn. Slowly, one by one, they woke up from an unnaturally sound sleep, staring sleepily around the room.

Thanks to Vivan, they got a good night's sleep before the trip, although they did not deserve the rest at all.

Their would-be victims were already far away then.

The hooded rider who had hurt Vivan's heart through and through hid in the shadows. Among the forest paths, three travelers rushed past him. They didn't even hear his horse.

He didn't stop them. He didn't ask for anything.

Walking through the village and forest, Vashaba did not even know where to look for traces of her beloved... She lost her way to him.

Ross was standing on the deck of a ship that cut through the waves in the night. He held the rudder, staring thoughtfully away at the calm waves in the moonlight.

Most of the crew and travelers were already asleep.

He couldn't sleep. Even though it had been a very intense and tiring day for him, he was not yet able to put his head to sleep. There were too many thoughts in it. He was thinking about his crazy strategy, which still had some unknowns. Will he be able to put it into practice? He hoped so. It was a good plan; he could feel it. Quirky, a bit unpredictable, but good. Yes. Good.

Suddenly he had a strange feeling.

For no particular reason, he felt an overwhelming sadness falling on him like a heavy burden.

He did not appear in his heart summoned by thoughts, but literally burst in there with the force of very intense feelings.

They all carried his emotions within them. The one they so desperately wanted to save.

Vivan!

A wave of hope, sadness, and despair swept through Ross's mind. There was more to it, too, but surprised he couldn't make out his feelings. He felt his legs buckle under him. He knelt on the deck. It was too much. He had never experienced such sensations before. It almost hurt.

"Vivan!" He cried softly, touching his jewel instinctively.

It had to be because of him! Like when he heard his friend's voice for the first time when he mentioned his own death. Probably thanks to their jewels. After all, they both had contact with Vivan.

Suddenly everything stopped...

He could no longer sense these sudden, emotional sensations. But he was sure he was right. It was Vivan. Certainly.

"I am here," he said softly, hoping that one word held as strong a power as the strength of his friend's feelings that overwhelmed him. He wanted it to reach him as much as he could. Like a child moving in a fog who doesn't know if he'll find himself in a familiar world. Even though two years had passed and the world had known some of his possibilities, it was still a surprise to him how much he can do now. He was filled with dread at the thought of how great a responsibility was carried by such a power to which even a dangerous witch had once bowed. What he could have done with her help, if he had not been driven by love, was beyond his good heart.

Vivan was silent. Worried about his fate, Ross waited, listening to the echo of the feelings communicated to him. As if trying to grab them to summon him. At least that was how he imagined it. Somewhere out there, among strangers and unfriendly people, was his unusual, sensitive friend. Deprived of loved ones. Kidnapped from a beloved place.

Ross, who, thanks to his unusual Jewel, was able to get into the moods of others like no one else except the healer himself, finally found this binding and sad thought. It was strange and inconceivable because it contained an endless longing for someone dear to Vivan in this world. And yet such longing could only be felt by a man who lost someone forever. Someone who abandoned him...

This feeling dominated the others.

"Vivan..." he began softly.

Suddenly, the Jewel showed him the pictures of the past.

Ring that grants immortality in Vashaba's hand.

Ross instinctively tightened his hand on the Jewel.

He felt a warm drop fall on his hand. Then another one.

He looked at her. In the moonlight he saw dark paths.

Blood.

Too far. Too hard. He shouldn't be doing this! Feeling dizzy, he put a hand to his nose. He felt warm damp.

The jewel glowed.

"Sel..." he spoke weakly.

The darkness suddenly began to thicken. The moon muffled its glow.

"I must know," he whispered to the Jewel determinedly, feeling his grief for Vashaba building up in him. "Where is he?!"

The jewel revealed an image to him...

"Fuck!" A man shouted, tearing at the other's clothes "They all ran away!"

"Not my fault! You were sleeping too!" the other defended himself.

"You were supposed to do it!" yelled the other, you can see very angry, "they should have been killed when the healer fell asleep!"

"And when did he fall asleep?" The other asked him. "Did you see?! Because I don't! We all fell asleep, like at some stupid wedding!

Strange, don't you think? I'm telling you, it's his fault! He did this!" He pointed in the direction of Ross.

I can see through Vivan's eyes! Ross realized quickly.

"Vivan!" He cried, feeling that his time was running out. "Can you hear me?! Please answer! I'm with you, remember! I'm swimming to your rescue. Paphian went to the county! Please give me a sign if you can hear me! I will not leave you!"

"Ross..." Vivan whispered in surprise.

The kidnappers, temporarily focused on themselves and their quarrels, temporarily paid little attention to the healer.

"I'm not leaving you," Ross repeated quietly, while Sel appeared beside him and several other people appeared on board, disturbed by the screams of people. "Do you hear?"

"Ross..." shocked Sel, who saw blood in the slowly awakening light, quickly pulled a handkerchief from his pocket just in case. Just like this. "You gotta stop!"

"Vivan, you are not alone." Ross kept the contact, regardless of everything. "I'm here."

"Thank you," he finally received a soft, thankful reply.

Vivan clenched his hand, unable otherwise to reveal his feelings. His captors drew weapons against each other. Dagger blades flashed.

Even if they were killing each other now, he didn't have the strength to get up...

This was the last image Ross managed to capture.

Vivan was hurt.

The world swirled around and disappeared into a sudden darkness...

Sel, with the help of a few concerned sailors, lured by earlier screams, lifted him carefully from the deck and carried him to the captain's cabin.

Among the volunteers there was also a man who, at Ross's request, was taken on this trip.

Their eyes met.

Sel found real concern in the man's eyes. He hadn't expected it from the ex-killer.

He was even more surprised by the behavior of the other. For before the last man left the captain's cabin, he lightly shook the hand of the unconscious Ross in a gesture of genuine sympathy.

"They're good people," Tenan said. "Both of them."

Sel looked at him. For a moment, to his surprise, he felt a hint of reluctant sympathy for the man. But then he remembered Milera, his wife. This man put a rope around her neck and pushed her out the window... Now he's trying to show him that he respects his partner?!

One look at Ross was enough for Sel to forget a bad memory. The condition of the lover was more important to him now. Above all else...

In a low voice, he asked Oliver to be called.

Meanwhile, the ship rang quickly from voices. Word spread immediately that captain Hope had probably bonded with the healer.

Lena clenched her hands tightly.

The carriage was drawn by only two horses now, but Rino did not spare them. Time was not their ally. The victims fled. The condition of the healer is no longer more important than the fulfillment of the assigned task. They were only an hour away from the port, and they must be there quickly.

He killed Kraun...

Stupid son of a bitch fucked up!

The whistle of the whip quickened the horses' nervous run.

The carriage, swaying on the uneven road, raced as if pursued by death itself.

The healer sat bound and gagged, and Beford held the dagger close to his neck, since the wounded man with unexpected force resisted being dragged into the carriage. Beford was furious. The black eye was already starting to swell after Vivan hit him. Rino barely separated them. The bandit wanted to settle the score with the healer, no matter what. Fortunately, Arst was holding the reins so Rino could focus on keeping an eye on the two.

The carriage rolled through the forest wilderness.

Quite suddenly, wolves appeared out of nowhere.

The horses panicked. They galloped, horrified by the sight of the pack running closer and closer to their hooves.

Arst reached for his crossbow.

"Rino!" He exclaimed, releasing the bolt at the first wolf.

The beast collapsed, screaming, infuriating the pack.

Rino cursed ugly as he peered out the carriage window.

"Watch him!" He ordered his companion, pulling the crossbow from behind his back.

He shot, but he wasn't very good at it. Only one wolf broke away from the cluster. On the other hand, they were quite close.

Their eyes glittered in the light of the lanterns on the carriage. Suddenly one of them looked straight inside the carriage. It took a long time. Very long. It's like communicating with someone inside. Rino looked incredulously at the healer, the only man who could command the pack. This man once held two white tigers. Real beasts. It could be...

Vivan's eyes gleamed with white streaks against the backdrop of blue irises. "No," the bandit corrected himself mentally, "that wasn't it."

They shone.

No ordinary person has had such a gleam in his eyes...

Vivan was staring directly into the eyes of the wolf on the left.

Wolf pup!

That was what the countess called him.

Now Rino understood the full meaning of these words.

A slight nod of the head and the gray wolf leapt courageously close to the horse's legs, snapping his teeth. His job was to scare the horses. They screamed and lunged forward, fueled by fear. The pack was lagging behind. Meanwhile, the carriage hit the road to the port city, which might seem particularly picturesque if traversed at the usual pace, but now raised real fears in the bandits that all this might not end well. Below them, the port of Rened appeared in all its glory. A place where shady business was the norm. A winding road led over a rocky shore that loomed over the countryside, with a chasm and a wide strip of sea to the horizon.

The children of this place did not go deep into the salty waves for several reasons. It was said that the depths of these waters contained creatures that were scattered about in legends. The ships going to the port sometimes gave them a tribute, consisting of things terrible and gloomy but, according to superstitious sailors, necessary. For those who did not offer their sacrifice, for example in the form of a cup of blood, did not enjoy their ship for a long time. The seafarers offered a gift to the secret beings and avoided those who, while known, were no less dangerous.

These included sharks.

Several of them trapped the whale under the rocks on which the carriage was now riding. It was enough for one of the wolves to catch up with the terrified horses and renew the attack...

Loud neigh.

The fading clatter of hooves and wheels.

The carriage left the bumpy road and plunged into the abyss...

At first, there was only a surprise. Then there was pain.

Vivan hit the side of the sinking carriage with the force of falling rock. The cracking glass, under the influence of the impact with water, cut the skin on his arm to the very bone.

He gasped as the interior filled with water. In a feverish haste, he broke the bonds, rubbing the rope against the shards of glass in the carriage window. Blood from his arm stained the small space.

He didn't know what happened to the others until he got out.

Amidst the squeal of horses, desperately trying to stay afloat with the carriage rapidly drawing water, the sound of the waves flooding his face time and time again, he saw two bandits struggling. Rino was winning. However, Beford was not a weak one, and their third companion, Arst, was swimming in that direction, with a crossbow in his hands.

Vivan saw the triangular fin of a swimming predator...

Arst never reached it...

The shark grabbed him, completely surprised by the attack, and pulled him under the water, which was quickly stained with blood.

Horrified, Vivan looked down at his bloody arm...

Looking up again, he noticed a crossbow attached to the roof of the sinking carriage. He grabbed her with the tips of his fingers.

He clenched his hand in a seemingly delicate glove with no fingers on the object.

Both bandits quickly forgot about the dispute, but it was too late. They saw the carcass of a dead whale and two chopping fins above the surface.

Rino dove.

Beford screamed as the first shark attacked the horses struggling for their lives.

Moments later, the jaws of the other shark tightened on the bandit's shoulder.

Vivan didn't wait any longer. The bolt was still in the crossbow.

He fired.

A close-up shot hit the shark in the eye. But he started to yank the bandit without releasing him from his jaws. There was no chance of getting him out of this embrace. Everything was happening too fast.

It was over.

A terrifying act of nature's cruelty.

Vivan looked back one last time. Poor horses died in terrible torments, torn apart by sharks in the depths of the waters. The sinking carriage dragged them into the depths in ripples of blood. The desperate neighs of terrified animals echoed in his head. This finally pulled him into a desperate fight for his own life. He began to flow.

Out of the corner of his eye he saw the triangular shape of a fin approaching him above the waves.

Death.

Fear gave him strength. He had to swim. He didn't know how quickly he did it, but he finally felt the sand with the tips of his fingers. He got to his feet. He was running breathlessly, his heart pounding, but he already knew. He won! He did not drown. He was neither killed nor devoured! He was free. His hand clenched in a leather glove. They won't get it! Not this time! He will come home! He touched with tenderness the gift from his mother - hands encircling the ruby...

"You have lost," a familiar voice suddenly heard.

He felt the cold metal against his neck.

"Healer..." Rino leaned into his ear. "You are mine!"

CHAPTER 5

Paphian woke up on the great bed. The foreign room immediately overwhelmed him with pictures worthy of royal chambers. Daylight fell on his face from the window. There were bars in it. He immediately remembered a similar situation where Vivan had been imprisoned in an identical manner.

So, he became a prisoner...

He felt strangely dull, as if he had drunk too much wine. He slowly pulled himself up from the bed, only to discover that he had no pants. The shoes were nowhere to be found either.

This is another reason to discourage him from escaping.

He walked over to the window.

Once, when he was still a child, he was here with visit. It was an attempt to establish a certain understanding between his father and grandmother. The whole family came here.

He remembered an exquisite dinner. Long family table. Great tapestry on the wall - proof of friendship between the elves and the Beckert family.

His brother, cheerful, overly calm, then twelve years old, did not utter a word during the entire meal. He only nodded his head when needed, which surprised his parents and grandparents.

Paphian remembered the moment when his brother looked up and looked his foster grandmother straight in the eyes. Long. Maybe too long.

She was speechless in mid-word.

Then Vivan said softly but clearly:

"You can't do this to him."

Then he got up without asking anyone's permission, and left the dining room before anyone could stop him.

Father took them home the same day. Paphian remembered that they had returned when it was already deep in the night.

He had met his paternal grandparents again only on Vivan's memorable birthday.

It was he who persuaded his brother to dance on the table. It was just fun. Vivan resisted at first. It was intimidating that so many people looked at him. The whole village was here. In the end, his brother and the wine he had drunk managed to convince him to play.

For the last time.

Vivan is a sensitive man. Paphian knew about it forever. He also knew that his brother was blaming himself for the incident with his foster father's parents, though everyone told him he shouldn't. It was an excuse to finally sever ties with Erlon. Everyone knew about it. At the same time, however, which was not talked about loudly, it was also known that a strange bond had been established between Sarah and Vivan during the last visit to the family headquarters. Probably because Vivan had already seen through Sarah's plan to get rid of his uncomfortable son and his new family - a mother with an illegitimate child and her parents from the countryside and from a foreign world. His words held her back then. Maybe it was some sort of motherly conscience. A few years later, she did not hesitate anymore. She found Vivan just when he was not a remarkable boy awakening her conscience. In her eyes, the boy dancing for fun suddenly became a common rogue, drunk and pampered beyond measure by his stepfather who allowed him such excesses. The healer, who had apparently hit growing fame in the young head, then seemed vain to her, as do many of his age.

Through a short, spontaneous game on the table...

The door began to open slowly. Paphian did not move, although he remembered that he was only in his underwear. Such things did not embarrass him. Sarah, disgusted with his lack of decency, pursed her lips but refrained from commenting. She walked slowly to the bed, holding her inseparable fan in her hands.

"Do you like your room?" She asked, sitting on the edge of the bed with exquisite elegance.

At the same time, her hand quickly unfolded the fan she was holding. The click and gesture were like a warning against a hasty reply, though the voice seemed calm.

Paphian caught one word: your...

"My room? I only know one room that I can call mine..." he replied glumly.

Monkeyshines. For now, they've been exploring the area.

"Where's my brother?" He asked as the silence stretched.

"You mean Vivan?"

"Yes."

"He's not your brother," she said dismissively.

Blood rushed to Paphian's head, surprised by these words.

"Where's my brother? What have you done with him?!" He asked again, however, emphasizing individual words.

"Again," she replied, fanning herself vigorously, "Vivan is not your brother. I'd rather be worried about your friends. They were reprehensible, probably at your urging. Were you planning a robbery?"

"Where are they?!"

"That's better," she praised, tapping her fan lightly, "I was forced to close them. They are potentially dangerous."

"You kidnapped my brother!"

"You don't have a brother who I can treat like that."

It was too much for Pafian.

"Vivan is my brother, like it or not..."

"Grandma," she entered his word, firmly shutting his mouth with a fan. "This is for the beginning. I can't bear it if you start calling me by my name like this stray's son! Out of two bad things, I prefer the traditional form!"

So Vivan was here! Maybe he still is!

"What have you done to my brother, grandmother?" he intentionally maliciously changed the title. It was a bit childish, he knew it, but he wanted to hurt her with a word.

"You are very badly brought up," she remarked coldly. "No wonder if you know what kind of environment you grew up in..."

Paphian ignored the dig. His brother's well-being was more important now.

"Answer me at last," he said coldly.

"You're right," she said, maneuvering her fan. "Enough of these evasions. Time for honesty," she waited a suitable moment for greater effect, to finally confess:

"I sold him."

Paphian was speechless. He opened his mouth, but no sound came from it. Words, so cruel and scary. They slowly began to seep into his brain, then suddenly rolled over him. How is it: she sold him?!

Anger and pain joined him with a sense of terrible injustice. In one terrible moment he realized that he felt the blood-throbbing, anxious aggression again, and only an upbringing instilled in him, far better than his grandmother had suggested, kept him from striking her, after which that face, smeared with the sneaky drink of alcohol, had once been beautiful, showing traces of calculation today, would be flooded with blood. He felt it. Just like when he saw the body of a half-naked witch who wanted to destroy his brother.

Vivan.

His brother. His best friend and confidant. A man whose only drawback was that he seemed too good at times. Too sensitive. He who helped him so many times and put his own life at stake against the witch to save everyone.

He could still hear in his memories how the townspeople chanted his name.

He was so happy.

She sold him. She sold! Just like that. The one he loved as much as brother can truly love his brother. A man whom so many respected and loved for his heart! The one who did not want to lose faith in people so much.

"You're a monster," he finally managed, his voice hoarse with emotion.

"He wasn't even your brother," she ignored his words in a tone devoid of any empathy. "Illegitimate crossbreed. Dirty blood from dirty mother..."

"That's my mother too!" He drawled angrily, but she did not seem to notice him, then continued, "Oh yes, theoretically. Someone had to give birth to you. But for me what matters more is the blood of your father, a descendant of the old Beckert family. No dirty mongrel should live under the same roof with a descendant of a former family..."

"What are you talking about?! What crossbreed?! Vivan is my brother, my mother's son! Me too!"

"He's also the son of his father, dirty like her."

"You don't know anything about that."

"No," here she leaned towards him, "you don't know anything about it. I sent people to a couple of places. I found out here and there. However, I'm not sure of one thing. Does your so-called brother already have all his property in the event of the death of your father and his stepfather?"

Paphian had known the answer to this question for a long time.

"Vivan did not accept the inheritance," he replied with a mocking smile, now proud of his brother's idea. "He only asked to be assigned a small house with land, just in case. If something happened to father, all the property goes to me!"

The old countess stepped back, surprised. He noted with satisfaction how much effect his words had made on her.

Vivan didn't want an inheritance.

"This boy never ceases to amaze me," she thought of the young healer. "It's impossible. People aren't that noble!". But her intuition told her it had to be true, and the memory reminded her of his gentle voice: "Sarah..."

So much waarm... No one has ever said her name so warmly. Her husband, the man she married for his estate, was sometimes helpful to her. He was also the father of her sons, including the one who did not live up to her expectations. But his lips had never said her name with such tenderness before. Not caressingly, not passionately, but just like that. With quiet understanding. A delicacy...

Such people do not exist! It is impossible! Sooner or later, he will reveal his dark face. There must be something in it! Something to calm her conscience...

She sold a good, noble man. The treasure of the kingdom. Always willing to help.

"Well, life is never easy," she replied, trying to be indifferent, although the sudden movements of her fan showed her nervousness. "For no one."

Paphian gave her a hateful look which she noted with pain. She made a mistake. This boy loved his foster brother.

This perfect foundation will have to be tampered with a bit.

"Who did you sell Vivan to?" He asked softly, hiding his fury seething inside him.

"To Azram."

Paphian closed his eyes in anguish. Azram. King of the Slaves Bay.

Vivan never admitted it to his parents, but with him he made no secret of his feelings. He was scared. He said he sensed evil in every invitation that came from King Azram. Though they had always been polite, the mere touch of the paper, his brother explained to him, told him a lot about a man who used fancy words to trap him.

He often saw Vivan shiver with cold as he held the letter in his hands.

"Why?" He asked softly. He felt sorry for him with all his heart. "Why did you do that?!" He raised his voice, suddenly seizing her by the shoulders. "What has my brother done to you that you hate him so much?!"

"He's not your brother," she pointed out again, keeping a cool head.

"He is and always will be!" he exclaimed passionately. "Why do you keep repeating this?!"

"Because this man is the fruit of filthy love. He does not come from any respected family!" She rose angrily to mask her true feelings. "He does not even come from our world! Has this fake brother of yours ever told you about his father? About the real one?"

"It doesn't matter." Paphian replied. "Nothing."

"No?" She asked with malicious satisfaction. "His father from that strange, disgusting world is your mother's brother! Her own brother. Still saying it doesn't matter? Your father married a filthy woman, the mother of a child from a filthy relationship! Isn't that disgusting?"

Paphian looked away. Not because of a disgust he didn't feel. It shocked him. But he knew for sure that this news would shock his brother more than him. Vivan certainly didn't know that. He would tell him. He was sure of that. They had no secrets, especially so serious. He'll probably be devastated. He wondered how that could even happen. Mother has to explain it to them somehow. He remembered a few good times with his foster brother. Playing together, secret trips. Secrets. Vivan's warm, fraternal gestures. The circus tigers he tame for him. Agreement.

Memories cheered him up. Not now. This is not the most important thing now, until she meets her mother again.

Vivan would be disgusting?!

"I wonder," he replied, looking at her, "why did you really tell me about this... did you delude that I would look at my brother differently? Or maybe my mother? I don't know, but I know one thing: Vivan is not disgusting. It was he who taught me to look at people.

There is something behind this story that neither you nor I have a clue today. So, Grandma," he emphasized venomously, tell me finally what this is really about. Know that you will certainly answer for everything to my family. You will be responsible for everything that happens to my brother," he said word "brother" emphatically, "I swear to you, as a member of the crossbred and Becket family! For everything that is dear to me. I don't know how you found it, where you told your people to stick their dirty fingers in the affairs, and also defile themselves at the same time," she shuddered, which he noticed with satisfaction. "You know what I think, grandmother?" He asked, accentuating the last word, this time with contempt. "I think you're trying to slander him in my eyes because you really regret what you did with him. Tell me, am I wrong?"

Sarah looked at him angrily. She lifted her chin slightly, grasping the fan like a stick with which she could hit him.

"Can you imagine that I will be frightened by your words spoken with contempt?" Her face twisted in disgust. "Better than you couldn't scare me. You're just the shit dipped in the slime that you proudly call your family. A proud son of a cuckold and a filthy mother, the brother of a crossbreed who claims to be a god himself. Oh, can't you see how far you have come down?! You are not able to threaten me. I still have the support behind me and the mighty healer, ready to slaughter as a sheep anyone I show them! You and this family of yours mean nothing and you will mean nothing, and your brother, as you insist on calling him, maybe he will finally wipe that gentle gaze off himself, wipe away the tears that deprive him of being called a man, and above all," she leaned towards him, "he will stop growl like a wild animal when he does not like something and he will understand that life is not easy and will not be in his favor forever, because he thinks he is better, someone who should not exist, because he is at the same time repugnant and tempting like the greatest treasures this world. This man is a degeneration! A blemish in nature! In many ways. Understand it, fool! Accept it. He lives because he is useful to all of us! But not for long..."

she smiled with venomous satisfaction, putting her fan to her chest, "and you should forget about his existence as soon as possible and save the remnants of honor that you are so ineptly trying to show to me, as any man who wants to reign over me does and in fact, he's just a squeaky mouse that I can smash with my shoe whenever I want! And no, I don't regret what I did with him! I do not regret and I will not regret it! If I could, I would have done it twice, because it was because of him and his mother that I lost my son. Time to wipe this tribe off our world!"

Paphian came at her with punch in the face...

Only love for his family kept him from doing what could have serious consequences in the future that he only sensed now. Worse than what has already happened. In a quick flash of memory, he realized that his friends were trapped here somewhere, their fate now in his hands. Unfortunately, this monstrous woman, who did not even dodge from him, could somehow influence his fate and Vivan himself.

"Are you afraid of the old woman?" She asked contemptuously at the sight of his hand being lowered.

There was something in her gaze. Something he only caught for a moment, but it reassured him that all that luscious speech was merely a performance. A falsehood that concealed the truth.

He had to stay calm.

What should he do first?

"I want to see my friends," he demanded, trying to control his anger.

She narrowed her eyes at him carefully.

"Put your pants on!" She ordered briefly.

It was a strange and mysterious forest. Full of sounds. A whisper seemed to travel among the treetops. It oozes from dense thickets. Surrounds on all sides. Like sunlight flickering in murmuring streams. Golden strands touching the skin. Darkness fought the golden flame in a small clearing where Dinn laid the body of his unconscious friend on top of the moss. He pulled out poison arrows, six of which were in total. He poured the elven elixir so well known to Sel to his mornings. He was waiting...

He had to do this until evening, before Alesei finally woke up.

During this time, their horses walked around the clearing several times, calmly nibbling on the grass. It was a sign that there was nothing to threaten them around. Until the sun began to set...

Whispers slowly rose. Strange cracks that frightened the disturbed animals.

The forest was dying. In a strange, disturbing way, as if it gave way to disturbing night creatures with dark hearts...

Shortly before sunset, the voices appeared again, a whisper that disturbed the coming night.

"Dinn," Alesei stood up, swaying slightly, but at the same time resting his hand on the unicorn's head - the pommel of the sword he almost never parted with, "what's going on?" He asked without fear.

His skin was covered with sweat. He was still recovering from the heavy dose of poison.

"Ghosts," replied the elf grimly, listening to the sounds surrounding them.

"Ghosts," Alesei repeated like an echo, coming to his senses.

Voices whispered insistently in the darkness of the thicket, but Alesei couldn't understand their language. Leaves rustled as they were struck by someone's violent movement. Twigs crackled in the undergrowth.

Suddenly, the fires glistened in the darkness, giving the scenery a more disturbing mood. Hundreds of sparkling lights. Beautiful, but in the face of strange noises heard around, disturbing. The horses screeched in fear.

"We should leave the forest," said the warrior, stroking his mount soothingly. "I feel that I will not use a sword here."

"I did not expect..." the elf replied softly, "that the forest will change so much..."

"Have you been here before?"

"A long time ago," replied Dinn. "The world was different then. People were more humble..."

Alesei regarded him silently. Probably many at such a moment would ask the elf how long he has been walking in this world. But not him. He felt that Dinn, like many elves, was much older than him, though he retained a youthful curiosity about the world. It was enough for him. He did not play in deeper consideration. For him, the most important thing was what his companion or friend in his heart really was. What kind of woman was the one he wanted at the moment. Ever since he lost his childhood friend in the capital, when he, Ross and a dozen others wanted to save the healer, something broke inside him. When he had to bury Darmon, Ross' beloved babysitter Valeria, and several others, including Sel's murdered parents, somewhere in his mind those images remained forever, distorting his vision of the world. So now he calmly considered some things in his mind. He looked at the dark scenery around. Finally, reconciled to his mental decision, he said softly but firmly:

"Promise me something, Dinn."

The elf looked at him, surprised at these words.

Binding promise.

He didn't discuss whether Alesei should now allay his fears. He made no attempt to dismiss him or ask unnecessary questions. It was clearly feel it in the atmosphere.

Danger.

The final solution.

He knew the aftertaste of this inevitability, like the sound of battle steel. This is how death appeared in the arena. It waited.

"Yes, Alesei?" He asked softly.

"Take care of my Dog," Alesei smiled crookedly at the mention of his pet. "He must be furious at the fact that I left him with Vivan's grandmother."

"You guys never parted," Dinn noticed, smiling as well.

"Funny how it works out in life," said Alesei, not losing sight of the surroundings. "You know that he will be with you for a few, maybe a dozen years. And yet you tie your heart as if it would never happen. This whole end. I had a dog in the house," he noted that Dinn looked at him with a certain sadness. As if he had brought back memories that he had pushed into oblivion. He knew that look. Sometimes he saw them in the mirrors when he wanted to use them. "He died of old age before my father threw me out of the house. I loved him," Dinn's eyes shone. "I thought: never again because it hurts. But I saw the Dog. And it happened. Because no one can live alone. Because I remembered my beloved mongrel. I think you know what it is like. We are such lovely pets for you. Wait…" He raised his hand as Dinn tried to deny it, "you know what I mean, don't you? You used to say to yourself: never again. But that's not possible. You know very well that no. Because then there is a hole in you that cannot be filled with anything else."

Dinn, moved by his speech, was silent for a moment. Alesei took advantage of it. For the first time in a long time, he wanted to say so much. Someone with whom he has been the least likely to be. But deep down, he knew he was talking to the right person.

"That's why I'm giving you my dog, in case I..." he paused calmly, "But I want you to promise me that you will not only take care of him..."

"Alesei," Dinn said finally, "Why?"

"Please don't interrupt," the bully ordered him strangely mildly.

He waited a moment in silence. The one which heralded evil.

"Ross will be devastated," he finally began, pretending nothing was happening, "he'll lose the last person who left the brothel with him. He will lose his best friend. Because you can say what you want, but when you have to talk about things that neither Sel nor Vivan better not know, then we have each other. These are such things, memories, only ours. And a past that we understand best. It's not just about the House of Pleasure. So... if something happened to me," here he felt that he was starting to soften at what Ross would be going through then, "If something happened... promise me that you will try to replace me. You will be his friend. Promise!" He pointed, seeing the surprised look of the elf. "He needs someone like us. No magic, no love and no bedtime. I need someone permanent. Someone to see things from the side. And I know you need it. You will know what to do. Maybe you're not thrilled right now... Maybe you mean what Ross is doing in bed, but..."

"You're wrong!" Dinn interrupted abruptly, not looking in his direction. "It doesn't matter to me."

"Will you try?" He asked him hopefully, without explaining any further.

Dinn looked at him, moved by the unusual conversation.

"Listen," he said firmly, though his voice trembled slightly with emotion, "I'm not going to let you die. Here or anywhere. You are a great friend to everyone, especially this little pet. We elves often value friendship more than love. So, I would like to..."

"Dinn, say what I want to hear," Alesei interrupted him firmly, but with smile. "Yes, or no?"

"If he wants to..."

"You want me to draw a sword at you?"

Dinn knew Alesei was joking, so he didn't take offense for a moment.

"I promise you," he replied solemnly, with all due seriousness.

Alesei nodded his head in agreement. That was what he meant.

"Tell," he added gently, "to our beloved healer..." He paused, choosing his words in his spirit. "Tell him that sometimes it is easier to breathe than to live humanly. Kill instead of saving, but that doesn't mean easier is better. Easier," here he remembered the moment his father had banished him from the house, which he never tried to return to later, "doesn't mean you will do the right thing. Save your heart, Vivan. It won't be easy, but it's right. The most important."

Dinn froze, moved by the unusual words.

"Will you pass on my words to him?" Alesei asked, not looking at him.

Yes..." his companion replied softly.

The wind had risen.

Hundreds of fireflies immediately scattered throughout the forest. Darkness engulfed the clearing, lit only by the firelight. Dark shadows played with fire, shrouding it.

Alesei turned his back to Dinn in a defensive posture.

"This is it," he said shortly.

"You didn't tether the horses?" He asked the elf shortly.

"I never do that," replied Dinn as he grabbed the bow.

"Okay," said the bully. "They have a chance."

"Alesei..." Dinn began solemnly, "if I hadn't survived it..."

"Not on my watch!" The warrior snapped, in his, familiar among friends, phrase.

Suddenly they fell silent when an emaciated girl entered the circle of light...

She looked at them with the blackness of her eyes, silent and calm, as if the forest at night and this place could not scare her with anything. They were not human eyes, but darkness. Her thin body was barely hidden by shreds of clothing. Long black hair covered her shoulders. Long claws sprouted from the fingers. Perhaps she would have been pretty, even in her ghoulish form, were it not for those eyes. Hungry. Wild. Looking lustfully.

The muscular bully caught her attention first, but Dinn quickly changed that with the first arrow.

The girl howled like a wounded child, reaching for the wound.

Hearts stopped beating for a moment.

Alesei was the first to shake off his surprise.

"Okay!" He reached for his sword while the horses ran into the woods, where they were soon to die amid screams and desperate neighs. There was no time for regret. "Let's dance!" He called out to the darkness.

Dinn tightened the string again.

Several more ghouls, similar to a skinny girl, emerged from the woods around.

More followed.

Then another...

CHAPTER 6

Dinn broke free from the last branches of the bushes, gripping his shoulders like hands. His clothes tearing like sharp claws. He broke through the darkness, towards the rising sun, like a drowning man, just pushing forward with the rest of his strength. Blood pulsed in his temples. It stained torn clothes. It flowed from a menacing wound below the ribs. His heart was about to stop beating, but it was his dexterity that saved him. The blow was delivered lower than planned. White hair was sticky here and there with blood where it had been torn out in handfuls when they tried to stop it. Moments earlier, before the branches and the thin hands hidden in them torn his body, attempts were made to drag him into the darkness of the forest forever.

But it was already dawn.

"Save yourself!" Alesei ordered him. "Remember!" He called, before the wraiths jumped into his throat.

He fought. To the very end.

Not for himself, but for him. To give him a chance to escape. There was no chance that they would both leave the forest safe.

The forest has changed.

The forest dragged the lonely ones into its tentacles at night and devoured them.

Those who inadvertently stopped in it.

It was not allowed to stay here. It was possible to pass. It was possible to walk during the day, avoiding particularly shady places. But it was not allowed to stop.

Those who lived nearby knew this and were safe.

Those who did not know this secret disappeared from the world of the living forever...

Dinn pulled himself up on his sore arms.

Skinny hands gripped his legs. They dragged the waist deep into the brush.

The sun had not yet risen, and they refused to give up their prey.

He looked around.

In the shadows he saw pale faces hidden from the light. Dead eyes looked at him.

Their faces were reflected in his green irises.

His breathing quickened with the effort. He wrestled with them all night. He was exhausted. Even the elves' endurance has an end. They need at least a moment of respite that was not given to him. It is unbelievable how far it seems to be from the safe haven that you have seen during the day. Countess's palace. He drove off, pursued by her men, saving his friend. If he had known, he would have preferred not to. Paphian was safe. Alesei was killed. He…

He fought for his life.

He was already so tired...

But they wanted him. He couldn't give up. He hasn't done that so far. There was also a promise. He had put it together, and now it desperately crossed his mind that Alesei, a brave warrior with a big heart, had to foresee that it would be so bad. That's why he made a promise on him. That he wouldn't give up.

He screamed desperately from his shadowy hands, less and less willing to stretch beyond the last bushes in front of the palace wall. It cost him more blood as the claws scratched his flesh. Slowly, very slowly, very painfully he broke out of the darkness. Released from lean hands.

Marking his way with blood, he crawled away from the bushes while the birds greeted the day with their singing. It was so unreal! He fought for his life when the chirping of birds was heard all around. Like a grim joke of fate.

The first rays of sunlight caught him on the road in front of the entrance gate, dirty with mud, leaves, dust and blood, as he fell into the stream while escaping. He lay for a long time resting in that light while his heart slowly slowed down.

He got up like an old man, grabbing at the gate. He slowly pulled himself up with an effort.

He focused his eyes on the forest nearby...

The light of the rising sun played among the trees. A warm breeze moved the leaves gently.

The deadly bushes looked completely ordinary.

Nothing.

Plain view. Another clear day in a picturesque forest.

He felt himself begin to slide to the ground, broken by the image.

No trace. No pale face. No darkness.

If it weren't for the bloody path he had left as he crawled towards the gate, there would be nothing left of the nightmare he had endured.

He began desperately banging on the heavy doorframe, resentful, angry and exhausted to the limit. Someone must have woken up by now! Someone has to find out...

He passed out from the loss of blood before the people came.

The gate swung open cautiously to reveal a few men - servants from the palace.

These were the people among whom Count Erlon grew up. They weren't among the thugs their mistress paid them. They just worked here.

"Oh, mother!" One of them exclaimed, "it must be that elf, friend of the healer!"

"He spent the night in the woods?!" the others did not believe.

"What are we gonna do?"

"What are we supposed to do?" Said the one who spoke first. "When the Countess sees him, she will order him to close like the rest!"

"He is badly injured," remarked another. "He needs to be dressed!"

The first looked knowingly at the others.

"Let's get him! Only silently!"

Erlon sat at a desk in the library, which contained only a small part of the collection from the time when the old palace stood. Many empty shelves gave the interior a feeling of more space and emptiness.

This feeling permeated his heart as well. In the unfinished palace, full of boards and building materials and a lot of dust, there was too much space that there was now nothing to fill. Much of what had previously made up the palace décor was destroyed when the witch Mayene decided to tear it down. Such was the fate of gifts from grateful survivors to a healer, some of them very precious. However, the witch dealt especially vengefully with Vivan's rooms. There was almost nothing left there. The son did not reveal his grief. It only appeared by accident, when he was looking for something. When it turned out that an item had been in his old room earlier, Vivan pressed his lips together and quickly, perhaps a little too quickly, changed the subject, seemingly no longer interested in it. Lena explained to her husband that her son's vengeance hurt more than the lack of these things. Erlon felt sorry for Vivan. There were things that the man appreciated very much. Now his greatest treasure was a gift from his grandfather - an oak tree, carved by him with his own hand, improved for a long time, until it finally pleased the creator with its appearance. So precise that it could delight the masters. Few of the other artist's works could match him.

The memory of the witch faded a bit over time, but never about what she had done.

Therefore, the construction of the new palace began with enthusiasm. It was supposed to help everyone cover the traces of those times. His appearance was completely different from the old one. Vivan's new rooms, already enchanting with their simplicity, were above all bright and spacious.

Everyone knew Vivan didn't like the dark...

Vivan was not in the new palace, full of empty spaces and unfinished interiors.

There was no beloved Lena brightening his days.

Her father, who supported him for years.

Friends, the lack of which he also felt especially. They filled this house with life.

Erlon wrote letter after letter to friends in his spheres, asking them to support him with the king.

His son was brutally kidnapped. Will they be willing to support him to the king to send someone to help?

He didn't know that he didn't even have to ask for it, because very few of them cared only about their own interests in this case. The kidnapping to the royal court during the plague and the terrible event at the marketplace influenced the consciences of the powerful, especially those who were in the palace at that time, that they were no longer indifferent to Vivan's fate. They realized how much happiness was in the kingdom because among them there was a man endowed with such an extraordinary gift that they should care for.

The good of such a great man, or of such a precious treasure of the kingdom (it depended on the approach, as there were also those seeking benefits among them, as always), was therefore on their heart or in their interest. At the time, however, Erlon did not believe it was possible. His heart was filled with the emptiness of his loved ones and a great longing. He spent time trying to escape loneliness and a sense of helplessness. He did everything he could, but it was not enough for him.

He crumpled the letter in his hand...

The library door opened slowly and a Dog suddenly stood in it.

Alesei's dog, a mongrel with black and white fur with ridiculously protruding ears, simply called by him Dog, was taken care of by Vivan's grandmother. "It's a dangerous journey for a dog," the owner told the dog when he told him to stay.

So, the dog stayed.

Erlon has hardly seen him since then, and neither has his grandmother.

The dog stood in the ajar door, staring at him. He waited.

"What's up, boy?" He asked gently, surprised by the visit.

It was enough. The dog stepped inside, approached him slowly, like an old man.

Erlon felt uneasy.

He had never seen a Dog behave this way before.

He stroked it gently.

The dog settled down close to him, touching his leg.

Erlon studied him for a moment. Then, with a strange weight in his heart, he returned to writing the letter and going through the books of receipts.

For the next hour, the animal did not move.

It lay with him in overwhelming silence.

Living among people as sensitive to emotions as his wife and foster son were, Erlon also had a greater than average sensitivity in his heart. Or, more likely, it was stuck in him from the beginning, motivating him to make crazy decisions and great love. After all, he, too, was something extraordinary in the eyes of his own family. So much so that they almost completely cut themselves off from him. For they were so irritated by his sensitivity to the good of others and his great heart.

"Alesei," he whispered in the silence around him.

The dog raised its head. Their eyes met.

Vivan felt the blade of a cold dagger close to his neck.

He felt enormous satisfaction in the bandit's mood, satisfied with the course of events that had allowed him to get rid of his companions for division and not to lose a healer, not to mention his own life. He had great reasons to be happy. He was excited by the thought of a further future with a sizeable purse of gold exclusively for him. He was not going to let Vivan out of his hands.

Therefore, the healer was not afraid of death. Not even for a moment.

He knew perfectly well that the bandit was very anxious to get him alive where he had been assigned. He couldn't kill him.

Miriam's words pierced Vivan's heart like a war cry before battle, as if she had suddenly handed a sword in his hand.

He let the man lead him to the first boats in the harbor. Still, unfortunately, he felt his head start to spin. He paused uncertainly. Rino cursed.

"What the hell?!" He hissed in his ear.

Being among the people, he placed the dagger discreetly against his back. He didn't want to arouse interest. Someone might wish to come to the aid of the healer, which the bandit did not want. Like situations where someone could take a valuable loot from him for his own gain, which was also likely.

However, Vivan suddenly smiled a little, which at that moment seemed to the bandit very suspicious.

"I'm injured."

The gash on his arm, unnoticed at first by Rino, was bleeding badly. The shirt sleeve beneath the coat stuck to the body, and the brown blood stained the coat fabric more and more.

Rino cursed again at this unexpected inconvenience. This wound had to be dealt with. Neither had he thought to do it. He wanted to get the job done and walk away with the reward as soon as possible.

"It's not far to the ship!" He hissed, having had enough of the healer's tricks. "Move! Move! You can do it! They will take care of you there!"

Vivan did not intend to board any ship and be carried away from all who were dear to him.

"You think you have me in your hand?" He asked ominously.

Before the other answered, he simply clenched the fist of his good hand...

It was getting easier than he expected. It was enough to want it very much.

It was dangerously easy to reach for dark desires. Still, he was not driven by the will to do harm. He just wanted to break free. He was far from killing. It was not in his nature.

He has to go home ...

Rino felt a great weight settle in his chest. He was losing his breath with every moment. He understood immediately what was happening, but it was too late. The heart couldn't beat for a moment. Vivan took advantage of his weakness and struck him. The bandit stumbled and fell. The healer did not wait. He wasn't going to kill him, but only to stun him. However, he did not foresee that his wounds would so affect his strength. He stumbled to the first alley he saw. Staggering along the walls of the narrow passage, he strode to another and another, deeper and deeper into the city, while his pursuer recovered from the attack.

Unfortunately, the wounded man left traces of blood on the walls.

Rino reached the first of them. He touched it, smiling contentedly.

The victim will not be able to escape him.

Over his head, the laundry was drying in one of the alleys. He took the scarf quickly hung up and tied the pressure above the bleeding wound with one piece he had won by tearing the fabric with his teeth. With the other he tied up the wound, looking around and moving around in a hurry. He felt Rino following in his footsteps.

The steps heard down the alley confirmed this belief.

He broke out of a dark alley straight into a busy port street, full of stalls, horses, carriages and people. But because of his wound, he found it harder to avoid obstacles than his persecutors. He collided with passers-by, staggering under the weakness of the blood loss. He fell almost under the wheels of the carriage. Meanwhile, Rino tirelessly followed him, shortening the distance. It couldn't have ended like this! Vivan gathered his strength. Strategy. He pushed someone who delayed the bandit's march. He scared the horses from the approaching carriage, whose behavior caused quite a stir and allowed him to disappear from sight. Rino cursed. The healer eluded him. Vivan's next maneuver caused the vegetable stall to overturn. He apologized, but hurried past, dodging among the people. The furious merchant kept people and carts from destroying his goods. The barrels of the wagon became the next target. A quick theft of a knife from a fishmonger, one cut... No one would dare to tackle unbounded barrels! Even Rino.

The red scarf as a makeshift dressing fluttered in a rush as Vivan moved between the people. It itself and he exploits finally caught the attention.

Several men noticed that someone was following him, and despite the refugee's reckless efforts, the distance between them narrowed. They noticed that Vivan was clearly staggering and wounded. Such situations certainly attracted great attention in Rened.

The head of the local gang raised a hand, interrupting the ongoing conversation. He studied the face of the fugitive. Somewhere he had seen a man with an unusual arch of eyebrows and eyes the color of the sky. Is it possible that...?

He furrowed his thick, dark eyebrows in surprise as he watched him escape.

"Healer!" He remarked in amazement. "Follow me!" He called to his companions.

They ran into the alley where Vivan and his tormentor had just disappeared.

"Gentlemen!" The bandit leader called after them.

Vivan paused, panting with the effort. His forehead was covered with sweat. The legs were already failing to obey.

He lost a lot of blood.

Out of the corner of his eye, he noticed that several men quickly began to surround him.

Rino looked after the voice, choking inwardly. No, it can't be...

"Nerden!" He said the name in horror.

Fool! How could he have forgotten who this district belongs to!?

He looked around frantically. Nerden's bandits were already surrounding them. The street has become strangely deserted. The last shutters were closed.

This was the last thing he needed!

"Where are you going, Healer?" Asked the leader of the gang gently, approaching them. "Tell me: is he persecuting you?" He pointed at Rino.

It's over, Rino thought as Vivan slowly turned around.

He didn't wait for an answer. He lunged to the side. He hit one of Nerden's men, clearing his way out. He broke through with difficulty, though he took a few blows. In the end, he was even stabbed with a knife.

"I'll be back for you!" He called after Vivan, before he was out of sight, his hand on the wound, "Remember!"

"You'll die around the corner sooner!" One of Nerden's men teased after him, and to his leader he asked:

"Kill him?"

Nerden silently nodded. Two followed Rino. It was definitely not his best day.

Vivan looked calmly in the eyes of the gang leader.

"You know me," he observed.

"You helped me once, during the plague," replied the other, "In your city. I'm Nerden. I run this part of town. Unofficially, of course," he smirked. "Nothing happens here without my knowledge."

This man will help him. Vivan breathed a sigh of relief. He was safe for the time being.

Nerden held out his hand. As Vivan pulled out his, he whistled in admiration.

"Tut-tut! Real dragon skin!" He stroked briefly the glove on his hand with his thumb. "As strong as armor! A rare sight," he said with sincere admiration. "A gift from a grateful healer?"

"The skin of the dragon that attacked my city," Vivan replied, "a gift from his killer. He saved the lives of the inhabitants."

"The dragon the witch sent?" Nerden inquired. Vivan raised his unusual eyebrows a little. "They tell this story here all the time. The evil witch wanted to get you, sent a dragon, killed people. And you stopped her heart."

"Interesting summary," Vivan remarked with the shadow of a smile. He was starting to feel worse again. He was losing strength. He paled.

Nerden cursed silently. Meeting the healer during the plague was one of the brightest memories in his adventurous life. Now he could see that someone had treated him like an attractive object, and that was, in his mind, unforgivable.

"There's more," he replied gravely, resting him on his shoulder. "We know what you did. Everyone knows it here," he looked at him with concern, "but enough of talking. Come! I invite you to my quarters, healer!" he uttered the last word with pride, glad that he would host such an illustrious personality. He will try to reward him for any bad times. "You will tell me what it's all about."

Vivan gratefully accepted the help offered. He had nothing to fear in hands of the leader of the gang. He knew it.

But he also knew that nothing in this world lasts forever... It wasn't the end of troubles, but just a moment of rest.

It was still a long way home.

Ross's ship sailed out into the open water, headed for Slaves Bay.

The captain knew that there was no ship aboard any of the ships that sailed these waters now. So where was he supposed to look for him?

He slept off the momentary loss of balance, as the state called it, as it stretched further than before. Sel made no comment on the nightly events, reassured by his well-being. However, he looked at him cautiously when it seemed to him that Ross was not looking. Ross thought warmly of this sign of concern, pain still in his heart at Seme's unfortunate words. Will Sel miss real family life? With a wife by his side and children he will love?

What can he offer him to replace it?

The jewel that had always known his thoughts glowed with a warm, blood-red flame; this time speechless.

Love.

Ross closed his eyes sadly, fearing it wouldn't be enough.

It prevented him from seeing Sel's gaze, his eyes sparkling with the quick-buried tears.

"SEL," the Jewel whispered only to him, "HE WILL UNDERSTAND..."

Sel had laid out a blueprint for one of his unfinished designs that he was going to apply to the ship. To the untrained eye, it looked like a set of strange mirrors aboard Valeria. He had not yet said what the idea was, but the fact was that he and Alvaro had already realized some of their ideas on the ship, and they had all been accurate so far.

"Just pretend you are working," he ordered himself, against his feelings.

A rustle of parchment caught the attention of Ross standing in front of the mirror, adjusting the last details of his captain's uniform. His thoughts were distracted when he saw his partner getting ready for work. Despite his apprehension, he smiled at him.

As long as Sel is with him, he will be happy.

Sel did not look up until he was sure that his earlier feelings were no longer visible.

Then he replied with a similar smile.

Then suddenly, as if his lover's smile gave him extraordinary strength, he approached him, surprising him completely with the suddenness of his step and the desperation in his eyes, which reflected his inner will to fight. "Oh no!" Sel thought, "I won't give up that easy!"

"You're confusing me..." he took his face in his hands. "You don't even know what you're doing to me." He bent to his ear as one of his hands moved slowly down his shoulder, descending to the waist where ıt found its way, unbuttoning the buttons on his shirt and parting the cap of his captain's coat. As it touched the warm skin, brushing against his belly and hipline, Ross felt a wave of heat pour over him. Sel, aware of the effect on his companion, had accidentally lost his fingers on his lover's waistband, while his lips pressed against Ross's and his other hand held him possessively by the nape of his neck and white hair. Ross loved his possessiveness, coupled with the gentleness, as if Sel was holding a woman in his arms, but certainly not polite. It was in the twofold nature of Sel. He knew Ross was certainly willing to take more, but caring for him kept him in control. He didn't want to hurt him for anything in the world.

"I almost got dressed..." Ross protested weakly, his voice hoarse with aroused desire.

"Almost..." Sel touched his lips to his neck. Then unexpectedly, a moment after he said the word, he added, surprising himself: "Puss..."

Ross suddenly stiffened, holding his breath.

"What did you say?!" He asked, shocked.

Sel looked at him, slightly confused, wondering why that term had come to his mind.

"I've been thinking about your hair," he said because he had just thought of it. As if something was telling him to say that.

It didn't reassure Ross at all; he could see it. He wondered why at these words Ross gave him a strange look. It had to be a memory. And since his lover smiled warmly a moment later, then winked at him coquettishly, which made Sel want to tear his clothes off immediately, he guessed it was a rather nice idea.

He was pretty sure, judging from Ross's eagerness shortly after, that the memory had nothing to do with the House of Pleasure.

Someone from the netherworld, as Oliver used to say to such strange situations, liked what he saw now.

He gained tacit support in proving Ross wrong...

"Erlon, you won't believe what happened!" Anna was shaking with emotions, finally looking at her age. When twenty-year-old Erlon married her then seventeen-year-old daughter, who was heavily pregnant, her mother was forty-five. Now reaching seventy, though her appearance has not changed since Vivan began to consciously protect his loved ones when he was seven.

Erlon broke away from petting Dog in the library, which he hated to leave since the house had gotten so empty. Outside of this place, emptiness and helplessness seemed to overwhelm him even more.

He was very worried about them...

"What happened?!" He jumped up from his seat.

She grabbed him by the caftan sleeves in a desperate gesture, seeking his support. It was then, for the first time since Lena had left, that he shouldn't cut himself off from the world while waiting for events to unfold. There were still people here who needed him.

Just like her. His foster mother.

"There are people in the living room who met Vivan!" Words began to flow frantically from her lips, "They wanted to murder this poor family, but Vivan saved them! He couldn't save himself..." Tears welled up in her eyes quickly because of the agitation. "Erlon, Vivan is hurt! He is wounded and Vashaba is not with him!"

She started sobbing desperately. He hugged her tenderly, trying to keep his common sense amid the terrible news. He felt anger and pain and grief fight for the main place in his heart, as if a fire had raged there.

He waited a moment, cradling a shaky Anna until the emotions subsided a bit.

"Come on," he said after a moment. "Let's find out more."

It was a very good decision. Amidst feverish words full of righteous anger and concern, they soon knew about the entire course of events. This calmed Anna a little, but still her emotions, which had been searching for an outlet until that moment, were expressed in nervous movements and hands, still touching her lips with anxiety as the family of the woodcutter told their story. Erlon ordered rooms to be prepared for the family in the rebuilt tavern, and paid for their stay for a month from his own resources. The meal was served, which the surprised family ate in the palace, moved by the count's kindness, who assured that the father of the family could start work on the construction of the palace if he so wished.

Ajane hugged him tightly, as hard as a very young girl could. Erlon, quite unexpectedly for himself, returned the embrace, moved by a secret longing for his extraordinary son. Vivan would have appreciated his efforts for the well-being of this family.

Miranda thanked them with calm and gentleness on behalf of all. She was genuinely touched by their behavior, so different from that of Count Erlon's natural mother and her temperamental husband. These people really didn't try to exalt. In the face of misfortune, they became even more open.

"Does that head hurt him?" Anna asked anxiously, thinking of Vivan.

"He felt better when we left," the woman replied truthfully.

"It's because you wished him well," Anna quickly guessed.

"He will come back," she added warmly. "He will come back. I asked him to believe it."

The hosts, however, looked at her with obvious concern.

King Azram ordered the kidnapping. Who knows what else could happen to Vivan...?

"Chrispine, what about him?"

"He sleeps. He needs to rest."

"And that wound on the arm?"

"I sewed it. The scar won't be big. But... did you see those scars? It's monstrous what these people..."

"I know." Nerden sat down in the chair next to the bed, where the wounded healer was now sleeping. "They didn't waste any time, huh?"

"How can you..." the woman rebuked him, after a while she returned to tying the bandage on the wounded's arm.

"Come on," he said warmly. "You know I don't think so."

"But you said it," she still tried to be indignant at him. He loved her for that too.

"I'd rip off the limbs of anyone who tried to hurt him in front of me!" He said decisively, leaning towards her. "You live only thanks to him," touched her blond curls thoughtfully.

She smiled slightly, taking advantage of those rare moments when she didn't have to hide the strength of her feelings for him, or a delicacy none of his companions would suspect her of. She stroked a hand in a leather glove lovingly. She touched the healer's forehead with concern. The leakage of blood had clearly drained him of his strength, but when he fell asleep, she noticed that he looked better than when Nerden had brought him here.

She got up. She grabbed the bowl of cloth which had stained the water with the healer's blood. Nerden spoke softly at the gesture.

"What are you gonna do with it?'

"Pour out," she shrugged. "What else would I do?"

He stood up to gently grasp her hands holding the bowl.

"It's the blood of a healer..."

There was silence. Chrispine stared at him, unable to believe what she had just heard. Finally, a soft, reproachful voice emerged from her mouth, which had so far tried in vain to convey emotions into words:

"It's immoral."

"How many of our actions could you describe like this?" He asked fiercely, "It's the blood of a healer! One day it may be useful to us!"

"Shh," she commanded him with a gesture, "You'll wake him up."

"I won't watch the world die in my arms anymore!" He finished passionately but lowered his voice in accordance with her request. "You are him! This is not the place!" He waved his hand. "Not people, but you! I want a weapon to help me protect you!"

"Or to protect you," she replied.

"You didn't take the blood from him," he remarked. "You don't have to feel guilty! We can use it!"

He knew he was right. She had to accept it. In their world, they needed every help to face their enemies.

"What are you gonna do with him?" She asked, finishing that topic.

"I'll help him get home," he replied confidently. So she figured he'd thought it over before. "You've heard my people. Apparently, this punk that hunts him has already brought friends and they are lurking here somewhere. They wouldn't let him go home in his carriage unless we harnessed the demon horses. I have a plan. We just have to help him get there!"

"Where?"

"On Violet Abigail Meresa ship's board!" he replied proud of his own idea. "He owes me a favor, and besides, he will not refuse the healer himself."

"Fat Violet is in Rened?!" the woman was surprised. "Why didn't you say it before?!"

"We didn't need her before. Her flagship - Bernadette - is docked in the port. It is to set sail at dawn."

"Does she know about it?"

"I've already sent the news."

"There must be Azram's men around!" She exclaimed indignantly.

Vivan told them about what had happened so far and who was behind it. Nerden gave her a smile she knew all too well.

It was attracting trouble.

"Doesn't that sound like fun to you, honey?"

"Lunatic!" She tried to be indignant, but already put the bowl on the table. After a moment a dagger flashed in her hand. "Shall we mug them?" She asked with a cheeky twinkle in her eyes.

Nerden cupped her face in both hands.

"If you want it," he replied humbly, in which one could hear a mixture of seriousness and humor at the same time. "If they try to touch him, we will kill them all!"

CHAPTER 7

"Dinn..." Paphian gently shook the wounded shoulder. "Dinn, wake up!"

Dinn slowly broke free from his delirium. As soon as he began to look conscious, Paphian held a vial with his brother's unusual blood to his mouth. He waited for the wounded man to take a sip, then wiped his mouth gently with a handkerchief.

"How long has he been here?" He asked the cook, who had given him her room, which was an act of courage.

The manservants at the palace did a really great job of hiding the unwanted guest and letting his friend know, who was under vigilant surveillance himself. The people who found Dinn at the gate displayed the cleverness they had developed over the years, carefully selecting those they could trust in this extraordinary mission. The palace itself and its surroundings were no secret to them. The most difficult thing was to bring the wounded from the gate here, but it was also handled brilliantly.

"At dawn, my lord," the cook replied. "I treated him as best I could, but he was badly wounded. Is it the blood of our healer?"

Paphian nodded, bringing a smile to the woman's face with relief and concern for the wounded man.

"Vivan cut her down to size," she said with a smile, calm about the fate of her guest. "He was fastuous and Lord got mad and hit him in the face," she added with a certain pride, glad that someone had acted against the old lord. "And her fan almost breaks, she was so nervous! People saw from afar. Lord, we felt despair when they pulled him into the cart and drove him into the distance, because everyone here knows that the old one..." She hesitated, looking at him uncertainly. After all, he was a close relative, but Paphian nodded his approval. "She sold him to Azram from overseas for debts," she finished surely. "First, she made feasts, asked that important ones, like the healer's grandmother, and then they quickly got to know what grandmother and mother she was, who disavowed to relatives. So, they did not want to do business, and she acquired debts. Oh, here people are angry with her, and they remember the young Mr. Erlon, father, how good a boy he is, because the other one hired thug to his mother and ordered to watch over his property, and he sits in his own land and hardly looks here."

Paphian nodded thoughtfully. They were facts that he already knew, but now he was sure that the people here did not love his grandmother.

"Did he say something?" He asked, pointing at Dinn.

The woman paled and pressed her hands together pleadingly.

"He said..." she began softly. "He talked about the forest. Everyone knows that it is forbidden to be in the forest at night, and they stayed. He and the other," her voice grew to a nervous tone, as if she wanted to say quickly what she knows and not come back to it. "He broke away from them, and they didn't let the other go. They don't let go... Once caught, don't let go. They let him go, but not for long. No. They'll take him. If he stays here, they'll take him. They will not forgive anyone...

Paphian felt shivers down his body.

"Who?" He asked anxiously.

Dinn sat up abruptly, his hand gripping his in a desperate gesture. The woman screamed in fear at the expression on his face. Paphian regarded him fearfully. He had never seen him like this. The gaze of the normally calm green eyes showed madness.

"They..." he said through clenched teeth. "Strange children. Strange children!"

The woman covered her mouth.

"Children," she replied, drawing the attention of both of them, "So it's true what they say..."

Paphian froze in horror. What was happening here was more and more terrifying with each passing moment. He must get them all out of this goddamn place! And if you believe the words of a woman - first, he must ensure the safety of Dinn. He had no doubts that what the cook was saying was true. It was enough for him to meet his friend's eyes. He saw in them what he never expected to see in the eyes of an elf.

Horror.

"What are they saying?" He asked softly.

"Murdered children," she replied in a grave voice. "Outcast children, unwanted children. They say there was once a family. The parents became ill, but asked the uncle of their six children to take care of them after their death. But he ordered the children to be taken deep into the forest and murdered. He did not want them at home. And so it was done. Evil has happened and revenge is happening. They look, listens and does no harm during the day, but catches at night!" She clenched her fist. Dinn cringed in fear. They grab and does not let go, because there was no mercy for them!" She said dramatically. "Children do not know what is good and what is bad but they know when it hurts. It hurts because they hurt. They know it. They hold you and won't let go! Don't let go..." she finished menacingly.

Dinn's hand tightened frantically on Paphian's.

"That wasn't there!" He spat out in a dramatic whisper. "It was a normal forest!"

"When did it start?" Paphian asked matter-of-factly.

"It will be two years," the cook replied quietly.

Dinn paled. He stared at the woman in disbelief. He couldn't understand how evil had poisoned the forest, he knew, so quickly. And that was just the beginning. As time goes on, as more lives die there, the child demons will take over the place.

"There will be no more peace in this forest," he said grimly. "Evil will spread in it and grow in strength. There will be no peaceful day and no fatal night. Everyone will die. I've seen places like this before."

"Can't be helped?!" Asked the woman fearfully. "The road leads to you through the forest. To the capital. You will have to go a long way along an unknown road. It will cut us off from the world!"

"Only good can defeat evil," replied the elf in a trembling voice. "If there is a sorcerer or someone else endowed with good power..."

"You have a sorcerer," she said hopefully, "Sorcerer of the Heart ..."

Dinn looked at her with pain in his heart. Alesei appeared before his eyes. He remembered his last words. Though the wounds were slowly healed by the healer's blood, he could still feel them being inflicted. He felt his small hands dragging him deep into the forest, to death in agony. Hands that were tearing his body apart, causing him unimaginable suffering. Those that fell before his eyes on the body of a brave warrior, whose scream he heard for a long time in the darkness of the night, among the trees. His hands trembled like an old man's. Tears glistened in the long-lived gaze.

"I'll never expose Ross to what happened to us!" He replied firmly. "He has suffered enough."

He saw the surprise in her eyes when he mentioned his past. But she didn't say a word about it. She gently stroked his white hair.

"Dinn," Paphian waited a moment, considering these words, before he hesitantly said, "Where is Alesei? He came back home?"

The elf looked at him with a gaze that took all the last of his illusory hope away from him.

The cook just nodded.

"They don't let go..." she repeated once again in a sepulchral voice.

Paphian felt a burden of responsibility on himself, greater than before. Now he knew how his father must have felt in difficult times when he was burdened with the responsibility of caring for his people. How his brother felt, not only during the plague, when he cared for others, especially those who were dear to him. He felt a foretaste of what they experienced almost every day. Until now, they were responsible for others. He only accompanied them, ready to offer a helping hand.

Now he had to free his own.

It's time to talk to grandmother again.

Violet Abigail Meresa - wife of a diamond mine owner on the border between the kingdom of Tenchryz and the Ice Lands. She herself had four merchant ships with a slightly shady reputation, although officially they were under the flag of the kingdom. She was widely known for her sharp tongue, but it was said that she had a heart in its place, and her charisma could be envied by many men. She kept the crews of her ships in check, even when she was not around. The subjects were as loyal to her as an army. No human could stand her glare for long when she got angry. Her face was able to express anger and sympathy in so many ways that she could successfully play in the best theaters in the world. Despite her rather rounded figure, which no one would dare to call plump in her presence, she moved with as much energy as if she was still twenty years old, the size of her eldest son now.

No one did not get in the way when Violet Meresa set a goal for herself once.

Without hesitating, she destroyed everything in her path.

She was familiar with the hiding places of several gang leaders in the city, so she showed up in person to oversee the transport of a healer. However, most of all, she wanted to make sure that it was indeed a healer. So she entered the room like a queen, though it is possible that if it were not for her dress, she would have kicked the door open.

"Nerden!" She nodded in greeting, seeing a familiar face. "Chrispine!" Her head quickly turned towards the woman who was surprised by the intrusion, but she was already holding a dagger in her hand. "I came for a healer! I swear if now you've tried to cheat me and you don't have him here, won't end up just kicking your ass! Where is he?"

Her voice, low but loud, echoed through the room like chimes.

Nerden stood by his visitor, disgusted with the sudden intrusion.

"Dogs ate my people?! Why the hell do I have them, since you come in here like to yourself?"

"They know me. They didn't resist," she replied shortly.

He decided to discuss the matter with the gang later, though he was rather not surprised that it happened as it did.

"You woke him up," he remarked with a hint of anger. "Healer," he turned to the young man, "please, here is Violet Abigail Meres. You will go home with her. The routes are too dangerous when they hunt you."

Vivan looked silently at the loud woman. Indeed, she emanated a strength to which men of weaker character than his host probably gave way.

He himself, though seemingly too gentle, did not intend to yield to her in anything. He was sure there would be more than one confrontation.

The anger that Vashaba's behavior had aroused in him just waited for an opportunity to grow stronger. He sensed it like a warning sign of an impending storm. He grew beneath the seemingly calm waves in the ocean of his heart.

Violet's silence felt too long for her taste.

"Your visitor lost his tongue?" She asked with a hint of malice. "Is it his nature to lack good manners? What else I heard about him."

Vivan stood up slowly, facing the moment of dizziness and weakness from the loss of blood. He walked over to the woman, feeling a resistance build up in his soul as the distance grew smaller. It will not be easy. From the very beginning she emanated an aversion to him, and thanks to his abilities he understood why. She knew he was the son of a count. She obviously did not like the aristocracy.

"Violet," he said in his well-known healed gentle voice, at the sound of which the woman looked at him with some surprise, "I am Vivan Beckert, the healer."

"The Count's son," she added reproachfully.

"Yes," he replied without elaborating on it.

"The son of a rich man?" She asked teasingly.

All over Violet and her nature. Chrispine looked at her lover, but he only shrugged. He knew Violet's character well.

However, Vivan was not confused. In no way was he going to explain himself to this woman about the privileges he had.

"If you prefer..."

"I'm a great healer, huh?" She asked ironically. "I already know who I will be hosting on board. The next prince."

Vivan chose not to answer that comment.

"So, we have to go to Barnica?" She asked the men. "What will I get for this?"

Apparently Vivan disappointed her with his behavior. She wasn't going to take it easy on him.

"My family will pay you," Vivan replied, interrupting Nerden, "you can be sure you won't feel any loss."

She irritated him with her behavior. He did not like pompous women.

Maybe he would have approached it differently... a few days earlier. Now he felt as if there was a void where his heart was beating. The betrayal of her adoptive grandmother sprinkled salt on that wound. Every human act that caused someone else's suffering increased his bitterness. This slowly changed his view of the world around him. As if he was already crossing certain boundaries.

"Well, I hope so," she growled, lifting her chin. "Are we going? Or will we wait here for them to gather? My people are waiting. We'll go up in a covered carriage." She glanced at Nerden.

"Such a thought crossed my mind," he replied, to which she rebuked him with a truly dragon-like gaze, which he did not care for at all.

"Can you go now?" Chrispine asked with concern, turning to the healer "You have briefly rested..."

"He's ill?" Violet looked at him curiously.

"He's hurt," replied the girl.

Vivan looked directly into Violet's eyes.

"I'm here, Violet," he said with a hint of anger. "You can address me."

"So, what, if you are not willing to talk..."

"Enough!" Nerden was impatient. "Like children! You're gonna be cooing on the ship, lovebirds! It's time for you to happily come home and forget about unpleasant events, healer..."

"Vivan," the healer gently rebuked him. "Only Vivan." He looked at them pointedly, ending with Violet.

"You can do it?" This time her tone softened, no doubt at the sound of his voice.

She liked that tone. It sounded so soothing when there was no anger in it. Like a friend's voice...

Vivan had to think about it. His head was still light-headed. After a moment, however, when he remembered Violet's mention of the carriage, he gestured for Chrispine to hand him the coat.

Chrispine took it, knocking over the bowl of blood-stained contents on the table, and a small amount spilled onto the smoothed wood. The girl's soft exclamation, as she was frightened by the consequences of her own carelessness, caught everyone's attention.

Vivan saw his blood in the bowl. He looked at the startled Chrispine.

There was an uncomfortable silence.

"I don't blame man who protects himself and his loved ones," his eyes fixed on Nerden. "I understand your motivation."

But everyone, including Violet, who understood what had happened, felt very uncomfortable. The healer noticed their deed. But Violet knew she would certainly do the same if she had the opportunity. There was no point in denying it.

Vivan has witnessed such situations more than once. People carefully kept what he used. His blood was priceless. He didn't blame them for that.

This, however, worried him.

At times like this, he felt like a merchandise for sale. So precious that everyone would like a piece for themselves at any cost. He had found out what it really meant when people of the utmost necessity did whatever they could to seize him... He almost died in terrible torment.

He did not let those memories come to him...

If he had allowed himself to do so, he would probably never have left the house again. He would not be able to eat at the same table among the crowd of residents at the wedding of Sai and Oliver. He remembered the times when he had to go out to meet people after Ramsey's smugglers had kidnapped Ross and a dozen others aboard the Cadelia ship. Every moment when his hands trembled and his legs gave way under the influence of turbulent emotions. Until then, even his mother hadn't realized how much it cost him. Overcoming this fear was more difficult than the decision he had made about the witch Mayene. Later it was easier, but the first moments of anxiety turned out to be a real nightmare.

Even trysts with Vashaba would not have been possible if he had not then overcome his fear.

Vashaba did not like walks that gave her nothing. She preferred quick trips to secret places to make love to him. This meeting, which turned out to be the last one so far, would probably have ended like this.

Vivan gripped the sudden bitter thought that burst into his head quite unexpectedly. It hurt.

Somewhere, on the fringes of consciousness, an image of a reality was formed, which the heart did not want to know...

He looked up at those present.

Not now. Not today.

Never.

It was going to hurt too much, and he was definitely not ready for it. Too much has happened recently. Time was not in favor of it. Circumstances as well.

"Help me get home," he said quietly to those present, focusing his attention on them. "Please."

Violet nodded silently.

"I see two," one of Nerden's men said softly to the leader, "I think I see them on purpose. You know what I mean?" He looked meaningfully.

Nerden nodded silently and turned to the people hidden in the shadows.

"They've covered the area, Violet."

"You sent yours?!" She asked sharply.

Nerden's man nodded.

"Ven," the boss said to him, "we're defending Chrispine and Vivan at all costs, you understand?" The question was asked so softly that only the other could hear.

Trusted, and at the same time his right hand in the gang, whose face was marred by a scar on his right cheek, only responded with an eloquent look.

"Can you do it, my lord?" He asked quietly to the healer.

"Yes," replied when asked, his voice confident.

Ven recognized strength and determination in that tone. The healer will not fail. He was sure of that.

"It will be like this," Nerden said, "a carriage will come, we get in and drive away. No delays! Nobody scrambles and stays behind. My people will protect us."

"Ven!" Vivan cried softly. "Thank you. You and the rest."

Ven touched his brimmed hat lightly. He liked it. It reminded him of some matter. He hoped it wouldn't come to that but preferred the healer to know it. From what he heard, the man had no experience with scheming. He was also not acquainted with perfidy. He would have to be sensitized to this.

So as soon as Nerden noticed Chrispine, he said shortly in Vivan's ear:

"Watch out for the blonde!"

Vivan looked quickly at Chrispine and looked away almost immediately. Violet grimaced.

"Now!" Nerden called.

As the carriage arrived, the group quickly obeyed. Several of Nerden's men appeared on horseback, a few clung to the carriage, which immediately moved across the sleeping alley.

Vivan saw Violet's gaze in the glare of one of the defenders' torches. Her hand gripped the dagger tightly. She smiled ominously.

"And back in the carriage!" He muttered.

His defenders did not even give him a regular knife. But he wasn't sure if it was pure distraction.

They had barely reached the road he had run from Rino during the day, and a dozen or so people ran out of the alleys to stop the carriage. Swords glinted in their hands. Two of them carried crossbows. It was only a stroke of luck that none of Nerden's people had died so far. Ven led the escapees. Nerden parried the attacks of the assassins who jumped on the carriage, and Chrispine bravely helped him in this.

Violet put two fingers in her mouth and gave a long whistle.

Her men emerged from the alley in front of them and attacked the mysterious bandits.

Among them, Vivan saw Rino.

He did not hesitate for a moment as soon as he freed himself from his enemies. He raised the crossbow and fired.

Straight into one of the horses pulling a speeding carriage...

The horse lunged in a spasm of pain, tugging at the other. Confusion broke out. The carriage swayed dangerously.

"Out of the wagon!" Nerden shouted.

Vivan grabbed Violet's arm and pulled her with him. The weight of a rather bulky woman and a slap on the back as he hit the pavement almost took his breath away. Violet was on top of it.

"Just don't imagine anything!" She reserved ominously as he opened his mouth.

However, she herself did not avoid foul thoughts. For a moment she had a handsome young man with unusual blue eyes beneath her. The arches of his eyebrows completed the pleasant sight, and the touch, even through his clothes, was alluring. Plus, that thick hair and surprised look... Wait! Doesn't he sense human feelings?!

She jumped up immediately, trying to hide her embarrassment. By all gods! This boy could be her son! And she is not young anymore!

May her firstborn see what her mother does! Well, but still... short, because it was short, but pleasant.

She grabbed his hand to help him get up. She was warm, had long, slender fingers, and was partially hidden by a glove that would kill many. She jerked him a little too hard in the act of helping, true, but he was gathering so strangely.

It wasn't Vivan's fault. He only managed to take a breath when she got off of it. The sensation pierced him like the scorching rays of the sun. He felt strange.

It all took only a few moments but managed to provide both of them with unforgettable impressions.

"What's with you?!" She hissed at him as he stood next to her, rather hesitantly at first.

"I'm taking a breath!" He paused breathlessly, glaring at her anxiously.

She gasped inwardly. Shit, he felt it!

"Not a word to anyone," she reserved sharply, confused by this look, "nothing happened here!"

"No worries!" He replied ironically. "I will not brag about it!"

"Nerden!" They heard a sudden scream.

As they got to their feet, Chrispine and Nerden confronted Rino and his men. A fierce fist fight between the gang leader and the thug was abruptly interrupted by Rino's men who pounced on Nerden. He, however, managed to defeat them. The fight would have ended in victory had it not been for the cross in the hands of the bandit sent by the countess and the bolt aimed straight at the heart of the gang leader.

Ven started running towards Vivan and Violet, but he did so a moment too late.

Chrispine was with them first. Her dagger flashed ominously as she grasped the healer skilfully, placing the blade against his neck.

"Hey!" She screamed furiously.

Rino looked at her. He froze, crossbow in hand.

"Do it," she called to him, "and you'll take the corpse!"

"Chrispine!" Nerden couldn't believe what he was seeing. So is Violet.

Vivan felt the cold blade against his neck, the hot breath of the girl and her fear for her lover.

She was capable of anything to save him...

He glanced at Ven, who silently nodded to him.

"Stand behind me, Nerden!" Chrispine ordered. "You go away, old witch!" She turned to Violet, who, for the sake of Vivan's safety, did not intend to argue. "And you," she turned to the healer. "Stand still!"

"As you wish," he replied with a hint of anger, moved by her action.

"I won't let them kill him!" She explained to him with determination.

"Chrispine, I'm safe!" Nerden said gently as he obeyed her command, "Let go of the healer!" He ordered.

"She won't listen to you…" Vivan remarked softly.

"Indeed," she nodded. "You!" She asked Rino. "Healer for a truce, do you hear? Everyone will go away, only then I'll give him back to you!"

Rino suppressed a smirk that crept on his lips. Nerden was staring at him. He clenched his sword angrily, annoyed by the mistress's strange idea. It couldn't work. How could she not understand this?

"I have a better idea," Violet suddenly said. "Take him off!" She cried suddenly.

Several of her men pulled their crossbows without hesitation.

Rino was dead before any idea occurred to him.

"Chrispine..." Nerden looked significantly at the girl. "Can you finish this nonsense?"

He was angry, undoubtedly. Her emotional behavior damaged his reputation. She also made many resent her.

She raised her head proudly, releasing Vivan from her embrace.

"I did what I had to," she said unrepentantly.

She courageously met Vivan's gaze. He knew he couldn't count on an apology. She said what she thought. Only one thing mattered. Nerden security.

Ven stepped between her and the healer.

It was a sign for Violet. She nodded hers.

"Vivan," she said calmly, "the boat is waiting nearby. Let's go."

But Vivan was still staring at Chrispine, whom Nerden was now approaching. Finally, guilt made her avoid his gaze.

He was waiting for it.

"Come…" he heard Violet's soft but firm voice.

He walked over to her, already surrounded by a handful of his people.

"What did you do?!" Said the gang leader, meanwhile, when the group, observing the actions of others, began to move away. "Chrispine! That was crazy!"

"Nerden!" Vivan heard Ven's voice. "What about the rest of the punks?"

Nerden's voice instantly hardened.

"There are no "others"!"

Vivan stopped walking, but Violet quickly grabbed his hand.

"No!" She said shortly, while Ven carried out the boss's order with his men. "Come on!" She ordered him, looking over her shoulder. "He bought us some time," she explained softly, talking about Ven. "These people only care about themselves! You should try it sometime!"

They got into the boat, followed by the gaze of the gang. Nerden hugged Chrispine against him, clearly trying to hide his confusion.

"That's not how I planned it!" He called to Vivan goodbye.

"Don't take your eyes off them!" Violet muttered to her own people.

"Ay, Captain!" One of them replied softly.

Their crossbows were on standby until Bernadette - an imposing merchant ship - left the harbor...

CHAPTER 8

"This is my Bernadette!" Violet said proudly as he looked around at the underlay. "Come on, prince! We'll find you some corner to sleep and some rum!"

She led him to the captain's cabin, giving orders to her men along the way.

All this time Vivan remained silent, feeling more and more mental weariness caused by the unusual experiences. The weakness was starting to take its toll on him as well.

"You look terrible," Violet noticed, resigning from maliciousness. "Here you have a comfortable bed," she pointed to the four-poster bed. "Yes, I like comfort, that's why I have such in the cabin next door," she explained shortly. "It's not very sophisticated here," she waved her hand, pointing to the cozy cabin dominated by a desk, an armchair and a few chairs, "the wardrobe is in the wall, the mini-bar here," she reached for a globe fixed to the floor, in which bottles and glasses were hidden. She quickly filled two with golden liquid. "Drink!" She ordered, sitting down in the chair. "You look like you need a drink!"

Vivan looked down at the goblet full of rum he hadn't had a chance to taste before. He sat down in a chair with the drink in hand and tasted slowly. After a while he took a long sip. It burned nicely. The alcohol spread to the sore limbs. It lit up in his head.

She watched him with a slight smile.

"You have a flair for it," she noted with a hint of merriment. "It didn't even contort you."

"I have a rather weak head," he replied softly, truthfully.

She became serious.

"Do you feel sorry for those thugs?"

Vivan remembered Rino. The same who wanted to murder an innocent family. He took another sip of rum, seeing the bandit's masked helpers in his mind.

"I'm not sure," he replied after a pause.

Something was slowly poisoning his thoughts. He could feel it. The world showed him more and more of its brutality, and he began to lose the balance between what was good and what was bad in life. So much... He could feel the emotions around him, even the bad ones. He created images in memory, saturated with the colors of these emotions. The colors. Lots of black and red. Dirty red, bloody... blood. Violence... He's been experiencing too much violence around lately. A lot of pain, especially from those who should support him.

Regret saturated his soul, extinguishing the warmth.

Vashaba abandoned him...

Chrispine. He didn't even want to think about her anymore.

"It is past, Vivan," Violet said, watching him thoughtfully. "Now you are with me. We're going home. It's not worth dwelling on the shitty past."

"I know," he replied, feeling his head buzzing with the drink he had drunk. "That's why I'm still alive. If I had thought about it," he looked thoughtfully at the golden drink in the glass, "I would have been crazy for a long time..."

She looked at him silently. She saw a strange gleam in his eyes, a shadow of tears at those disturbing words.

She hadn't heard of such a healer. Too calm and subdued. She felt uneasy.

She looked at him closely. Was he just tired? Why did she hope that was so?

Because the thought that this gentle man, famous for his great heart, was going to fade, filled her with anxiety? Because that would mean that people had succeeded in crushing his strong will, based on his love for the world.

Ihat s what she saw in his eyes. He went out...

Oh, she hoped, she really had, that she was wrong!

She met his gaze. He smiled slightly, but the warmth of that gentle smile did not soothe her at all.

She saw sadness in the blue of his eyes. He could feel it.

"Get some rest!" She commanded him gently. "Then you tell me what's going on here."

His smile widened, sensing the real concern in the tone of her voice.

The eyes, however, were not illuminated by the glow of that smile.

Vashaba, stealing in the shadows, avoided meeting Nerden's men. As he and the woman with him left the pier, full of regret and anger appeared on him.

She's late again!

As if fate had combined all strength to keep her from meeting again.

She wanted to make sure he came home safe. He might have acted foolishly to refuse her offer, but he meant too much to her to suffer again. When she's sure he's home...

Offended pride was deaf to all arguments of reason and heart.

She thought he would give her a hot kiss that would light a fire in her, and then without hesitation he would choose the ring and take her there by the rushing river. He will enter her brutally, but with passion, because they will belong to each other forever. They'll fuck hard until his heart beats dangerously, with the excess of emotion he was falling into, like a whirlpool. Dazed as ever by the sensations she loved to drag him into, watching him feel deeply moved by them, he barely able to get up. She led him home then, observing his weakness so unheard of in other men with a slight amusement. The thought made her feel hot. It could be that good! Maybe when will they meet again?... Maybe she will convince him with caresses. It can't end like this. She must convince him! Must have a chance!

Besides... He must be safe and sound. Safe... Nobody can hurt him anymore. She never wanted that for him. Even when he asked her to leave his room a few months ago...

Vashaba never understood him.

When he returned one day late in the evening, she was so longing that she immediately fell into his arms. Her heart was pounding against him. He had that warmth about him that mistakenly made her lust. She thought their feelings were similar, they had loved so passionately. But Vivan didn't want her caresses and kisses that evening. He wanted to tell her something. She could see that he really wanted to share his feelings with her, the sadness in his blue eyes. She didn't feel like it. He has been gone since last day. Could they not satisfy his longing first and then he could tell stories? Then she would be lazily listening to it with one ear, ready for more after a long pause.

To her surprise, Vivan asked her to leave the room. He leaned against the closed door, ignoring her cries. She heard him fall to the floor. She didn't know what he meant.

Then he avoided her for a week. It would probably have taken longer if she hadn't stopped him, kneeling at his feet, lost and alone. She didn't understand anything.

Sel told her about some girl who was raped. Vivan supposedly nursed her all night. The little one did not want to let him go.

But what's the point of bringing such stories to the bedroom? Agreed, it was terrible. But Vivan helped her after all, and it'll be okay, isn't it? You must go on. The past is irreversible. The child is alive, and this is the most important thing. The rest will come over time.

She had no idea how much compassion had affected her lover's mood.

She hadn't even thought about how the child's suffering would affect him. The girl interested her even less.

Her desires quickly became mostly carnal since she met him. He fascinated her. Soon there was little room for other feelings, apart from an almost childish attachment.

She knew Vivan loved her and was proud of it. Though she cared more at first, the love-affectionate nature quickly overcame that feeling. She had him. The famous healer. She liked him more than the other men. Sometimes she even thought she loved him. At least, she cared about him. This, however, could not take long. Though she was convinced it would last. After all, his love held them together.

She just wanted to keep him with her. Was it so hard to understand?

"He went out to sea," Ross said softly.

Sel got up from the bed to approach him. The face of the beloved was slowly illuminated by the light of the waking day. He was standing in high boots, trousers, and a loose-fitting shirt, fully unbuttoned, which he rarely did. He leaned his head against the window frame, watching the sky thoughtfully. The white shirt slipped temptingly off his shoulder. But something else caught Sel's attention. Scars. Fragments of long stripes.

He felt a pang of regret and anger at the same time.

Poker.

The beating Ramsey gave Ross to beat him to death.

Once again, Sel found himself enjoying the thought that this son of a bitch was finally dead. He hugged Ross silently.

"I asked you..." he began reproachfully after a while.

"...lest I try when I'm so far away," the lover finished for him with a smile. "I just caught it, calmly. And that he's safe now. For now. I'm not trying to talk to him."

"Good," Sel replied softly, thinking of both him and Vivan.

"I need strength today for what I'm going to do..."

"Do you think these preparations will be necessary?"

"Azram won't budge," Ross said calmly. "We must have a plan."

"Isn't it better to plan an armed foray?"

"I don't want to lose people, Sel."

"They risk a lot."

"Tenan will be with them. Oliver too. And I…"

"You can not…!"

"Sel," Ross said gently but firmly, "My power is needed there."

Sel bit his lip.

"I don't like it!" He said sharply after a moment.

"That I risk with others or..."

"How people can perceive you then!" He interrupted him with a hint of anger. "You are not some kind of master of minds! You're a Good Man!"

Ross smiled warmly.

"You know it," he replied, "Victor knows it. Lena. All of you," he sighed softly, this must be enough for me.

Sel looked into his beloved chocolate eyes that evoked so many warm feelings in him. Then his eyes fell on the scars covering his beloved's body again.

Through the open shirt, he saw more of them...

He only had a fleeting hope that he would protect him. So that no new ones appear...

Paphian acted boldly. In the basement, he found faithful companions who went with him to help. With Dinn's help, he obtained the key, then disarmed his brother's mercenaries. A few tried to cut off their escape route, but this time they did not manage to stock up on poison. Time was pressing. Dinn stared at the sky anxiously. With each passing hour, another night came, and his fear grew stronger. He had good cause for concern.

In the darkness of the palace cellar, a hand grasped his hand. The hand belonged to a child with eyes as black as the deepest darkness. She just emerged from the wall… She dug her long nails into his skin.

Were it not for Paphian who yanked him out of that hand into the light coming from the small windows, who knows what further events would have happened. Dinn went numb with obvious horror, while another head began to emerge from the darkness.

A sudden movement and both her hands reached out to grab him! Only a friend's quick reaction prevented the worst. Pale, unnaturally thin hands recoiled from the sun's rays. The creature, born of darkness, hissed angrily. A moment later, the hands emerged from the dark wall...

Released, they paled with fear.

Dinn, still shaken by his earlier nightmarish experience, stared at it as if mesmerized. The sight chilled Paphian's heart. Dinn was brave. Nobody could deny that. Among their companions there were also witnesses of the encounter with the witch herself. Those people, highlanders of flesh and blood, who then took up arms, saw this clash in which even the bravest man had no chance. Dinn didn't hesitate then. But this fear produced a feeling that many already took courageous.

Feeling of helplessness.

Without help, the evil could not be finally removed. Dinn knew it perfectly well. It was not a flesh-and-blood enemy, not a witch who could be struck, but an incomprehensible force that could not be saved from if you did not wield magic.

His fear made Paphian's heart and their companions panic. They were losing combat enthusiasm.

Paphian looked around at the startled people. Both the enemies, locked in the same cellars as his comrades earlier, and the highlanders, showed an increasing fear of the incomprehensible. Some tried to be brave, but what their eyes saw smashed their will to the dust.

He was responsible for his own!

"Dinn!" He called firmly, "Get the hell out of it!" He tugged, maybe a bit too brutally, but it helped. The elf broke out of his trance. "Up to the light!" He shouted to the others "Move! Move!"

At the words: "up to the light", the highlanders took their eyes off the ghastly phenomenon and quickly followed their leader. The imprisoned mercenaries cried out after them, pleading not to leave them.

They deliberately ignored the cries. The wraiths didn't want prisoners. All they wanted was Dinn...

Unfortunately, these attacks wasted too much time. Paphian was sure there would be a nice group to greet them, organized by a zealous granny, before they even went outside.

He was not mistaken. A large crowd was gathered there, and she was in the lead, obviously with the inseparable fan in her hand.

Fortunately, he ordered the mercenaries from the basement to take their weapons...

"Are you going somewhere?" She asked venomously as her men surrounded the fugitives.

"Away from you, Grandma," he replied, deliberately emphasizing the last word.

She stopped the fan angrily.

He acted fast. Before she could say or do anything, he ran to her. The inept mercenaries were overpowered after a brief skirmish with Dinn and the highlanders. The Count - her second husband, standing a step behind his wife's back, whose money she had so generously wasted, only managed to snarl angrily when Paphian tore the fan from his grandmother's hand and threw it to the ground, grabbing her by the throat with his other hand. The count immediately sheathed his sword.

The teachings of the Queen's Guard, which hosted their father's palace during the plague, were not in vain. During those days, Paphian swore to himself that after the stormy events in the capital, he would be a much better protector of his brother and family. He worked hard to keep his word. His speed was appreciated by the guardsmen, and that was no trivial matter. Vivan's kidnappers would certainly have regretted their deed if it had happened in his presence...

"Take it back!" He yanked the woman angrily. "Take back everything you said about my family and brother, old witch!"

"I'm your grandmother...!" She gasped, surprised.

"You are not part of my family! And you never will!"

"You want... everyone to know... about your brother's secret?" She asked slyly.

He released her angrily. She rubbed her sore neck, reaching for her fan with the other hand.

He knew she felt stronger with him. So he stood on the object without hesitation, breaking the delicate structure with a crash.

But he underestimated her. At the sight, she straightened proudly, bringing a mocking smile on her face.

"The son of the Beckerts!" Her voice was rugged but confident. "Loyal and confident! I was right that you are different. That you just wallow in this swamp you call home!"

"Enough!" He ordered her firmly. "I'm leaving this cursed place with my people and no force will stop me from it!"

"Will not stop?" She feigned surprise, still smiling. "Why would I do this? To hold with you this rabble that would have to be finally fed and watered?"

"You trapped them!"

"You really don't understand," her hoarse voice made him anxious. "I was supposed to let you out anyway. I just hoped that I would be able to talk you out of this great love for your ragged stepbrother," she approached him without fear. "The real goal has already been achieved."

She waited a moment, taking in his and his companions watching her people.

Then Paphian noticed a poisonous smile on her husband's face.

He understood before she spoke the words.

"I wanted to slow you down so that my people would take Vivan to where I ordered them. If all went as planned, and I count on it, the healer is on his way to Slaves Bay by ship. And when he gets there, believe me, neither you, nor your traitor father, nor even that shameless friend of yours, you will not snatch him from the hands of the king who is favored by demons..."

He raised the dagger in anger. She ducked slightly, with a mixture of irony and light sympathy as the meaning of the words reached her as well. She sentenced Vivan to a terrible fate...

But now it was too late to scruple.

"Did I mention," she added, choosing her words carefully for a better impression, "that King Azram also asked about your wizard?" As she had expected, this question shocked Paphian. "He was very interested in him. Have you heard the story the travelers tell? What do you think will happen to him in the Bay if he goes there to save his friend? Personally, I hope they will catch him. Demons will be happy to play with him..."

She saw the growing unease in his eyes with satisfaction.

CHAPTER 9

"Gather everyone on board!" Ross ordered. "Ladies forward!"

He waited on the bridge for his men to obey the order.

His captain's suit and triangular hat seemed to be a part of it forever, as did the white hair that the wind brushed now. Sel retreated somewhat, as is usual in such situations, yielding to his authority, which he quickly gained among his faithful crew. After a while, the first officer - Silas, who had served with the captain from the beginning of his sea adventure - entered the bridge. Silas never regretted abandoning his previous ship - the fast Chimera. Living with Ross - the Sorcerer of the Heart, he did not get bored. The predatory hairstyle stuck out like spikes, adding him aggressiveness. The wind couldn't move it. Regardless of the weather.

His presence meant that the order had been obeyed. Ross sighed.

Now he is gonna get hit!

"Ladies!" He began from his seat, noticing a dozen curious glances of sailors for whom the appearance of women, so pleasing to the eye, was a pleasant surprise. They just couldn't take their eyes off them. "You are here because I'm going to implement an idea!"

"I mean, what exactly?" One of the girls, with quite full breasts, asked.

There was no other way, you had to be straightforward.

"I need dancers!" He announced, "groups of great dancers who will add splendor to the feast in honor of King Azram. They will pay tribute to him. Wealthy landowners, smaller aristocracy. They have no other choice. Azram's army has ransacked many villages. They killed many people. There are also many outside the realms who wish to show their support out of fear or common sense. I'm going to pretend to be a wealthy merchant who offers him wealth, and dancing at the feast is to be a kind of addition to the gifts. Of course, I will not give any of you to the king as a gift," he added hurriedly, looking at Lena. "I need your performance to distract from a few of my men who will search the palace for Vivan at the time. We'll take him back! And you will help me with this!" He finished with enthusiasm, which faded slightly at the sight of the faces of the women.

"One moment!" The same big-breasted girl spoke again, while others commented vividly on the revelations they heard. Lena smiled warmly at him, for which he was grateful. She waited for the continuation. "Silence!" Meanwhile the girl roared, to which everyone, even the crew, fell silent.

"You better explain it!" Sel ordered him softly, his voice full of rebuke.

"So, we are supposed to dance and everyone will stare, while someone will go looking for Vivan?!" She asked resolutely.

She hit the nail on the head perfectly. Without long explanations.

"You are...?" He asked with a slight smile.

"Marlene, Captain!" The girl replied, putting her hands on her hips.

"Then yes, Marlen," he replied to the question.

"Okay!" The girl replied briefly, at which a few sailors smiled with amusement. "I have a few questions... First - he will soon find out who you are and what the ship is. He will immediately guess what is going on. He's not blind either!"

At that moment she blinked in surprise. On the bridge now stood Tenan, whom everyone knew from the tragic story he had experienced when the witch Mayene appeared in town. He was in Ross's captain's suit, but his hair was dark. The eyes remained brown, not amber. This particular detail temporarily escaped everyone's attention.

Tenan stepped out in front of the crowd of women, eyeing his double in disbelief. Victor followed closely, watching everything in silence so far.

"You lost your mind?!" He asked in a choked voice.

"I understand you all can see this," Ross said in his own voice.

After a while, the illusion vanished, causing a murmur of voices among those present. Now Ross looked at Sel in mock contrition.

"Forgive me," he said warmly, seeing his embarrassment. "It's for a good cause."

"He?" Sel asked wryly, but his anger was gone.

Ross turned to the others.

"And what?" He asked Marlene.

She looked at Tenan standing next to her, and then at Maya, her friend. Both women nodded appreciatively. Tenan whistled softly. Victor shook his head in disbelief.

"I didn't know he could do that," another girl said softly.

"I don't think anyone knew," said another.

Lena squeezed Tenan's shoulder in a reassuring gesture.

"Admit it intrigued you," she whispered.

He cursed softly, at which she smiled.

"Okay!" Marlene interrupted the discussion with the others, moved by the new discovery. "Will you change the ship too, or what?"

"Maybe," Ross replied, waiting for the continuation.

He liked the girl out of hand for her boldness.

"Another question," at this point, Marlene threw her two braids back in a nervous gesture. "Because… Captain, it's all beautiful and everything for our healer, but… we… this… we don't know how to dance so solemnly. Only our way. Highlander style."

"Ooh, speak for yourself!" One of the black-haired girls suddenly shouted. "We are from there! My sister," here she pointed to her own copy, possibly a twin, "and me! Our family fled the city when Azram ordered the girls to be sacrificed! My family are artists! We all can do that! After all, we also danced like that at the wedding of Mr. Oliver and Sai. What, you don't remember how the boys almost wanted to kill each other, just to stand in the first row?! Then our father told us that there is no point in offering them such attractions, because they will suffer a heart attack one by one! And strange, because we didn't even have costumes..."

"I remember!" One of the sailors broke free, as all eyes turned to him, so he hid quickly behind his friend's back.

"Exactly," said Marlene quickly. "And these outfits?"

"I transport a variety of goods..." Ross began, to which he was quickly interrupted by the buzzing of women's voices.

"Do you have costumes for the dancers?!"

"Hmm..." he replied uncertainly. "Maybe not for dancers, but I think they can be remade. They are colorful, and some have these decorations..."

The women glared at him.

"The captain imagines that we do it all in one day," Marlene noticed, not knowing whether to laugh or cry. "Sew costumes, make hair and still learn to dance like these two, ha!" She laughed like crazy, to which they all replied with a loud laugh.

"You can see it's a man!" The blonde-haired girl next to her called.

Ross felt himself begin to blush. He hadn't really thought too much about it.

"Er... captain?" One of the sailors, who had similar tastes to Sel's, said suddenly. "I can sew..." he began timidly.

"What can you sew?" Marlene interrupted him with amusement. "Sails?"

"See for yourself!" He got up to show his outfit, presenting himself quite professionally at first glance. "The guys will confirm that I sew their clothes like for a great man, when they want to go to brothel. Or go home," he added hurriedly, seeing some of the women dissatisfied.

A few of the sailors nodded cautiously.

"As for the hairstyles..." Ross smiled warmly, pleased with this turn of events. "I think I could help..."

"Oh fuck!" Marlene blurted out. She hastily covered her mouth.

"Whenever you want, honey!" One of the men shouted, while her face flushed red like a peony.

Now the men have joined the group of amused women.

"We actually have about five days," Ross added, "it might work."

"I'll help with everything," Lena assured, to which the women replied with warm glances.

"Lady," Maya said to her, "We'll be upside down and Vivan will come home. You will see!"

"I know," she said, touched. "And I feel he knows it too." She looked at Ross with motherly love. "He knows that his friends will do anything to help him."

He nodded his head in agreement.

"So what first?" One of the girls asked.

Ross looked at Oliver for the first time, standing at Sai's side some distance from the rest. He left the bridge slowly.

"Oren," he said to the sailor, who had revealed his tailoring talent while the women were already arguing with the twins.

"It must be a woman's outfit," he added softly, setting the man by surprise.

"Will there be tits?" The tailor asked quickly.

Ross and Oliver looked at each other.

"I'll strangle you someday!" Oliver announced his stepbrother with a twinkle in his eye.

Ross suppressed a smile.

"Yes," Oliver replied to the young tailor. "They will."

"I propose not too big," Oren pointed out professionally. "Because you are rather small and you have to make them fit in your hand..."

Oliver froze.

"I'll show you," he replied dryly, thinking of the unusual corset he had taken with him.

"So?" Asked one of the dark-haired twins. "Let's not waste time, let's start learning right away!"

The men grinned broadly.

"Hey!" Ross exclaimed, seeing that the crew had already given up their duties, getting ready for the show. "Who gave you the right to hang around?!" He roared immediately in his captain's tone. "Go to work, you lazy lumps! Clean the deck of barrels and ropes! Place to do! Maris, reef the jib! Dinkin! To the kitchen, you slob! Move your butts, goddamn it!"

Still amused, the crew surreptitiously dispersed in a hurry, but not taking the captain's words to heart.

Ross just glanced to make sure his first mate was definitely at the helm. Of course, as always, Silas was reliable.

Tenan met Sel's gaze. Suddenly, sensing that the time was right, he just shrugged.

Sel could not disagree with him. He almost managed to convince him of the lie. Almost. Maya's presence, once at the center of their meaningful exchange, made him feel guilty. But he quickly suppressed the feeling. It is impossible. The man didn't deserve it.

"It's true... he doesn't deserve hatred," whispered his heart.

He hanged Milera in front of his eyes...

Sel eyed him, mentally struggling with the tangle of feelings that sought an outlet for themselves.

Tenan sensed that look.

He hesitated. He sincerely wanted to approach the man and tell him to hope. This plan is insane, so maybe his and Sel's wishes will be fulfilled. Maybe someone will kill him at last... because only that can satisfy them both.

But he didn't. He didn't know exactly why. Was he influenced by the words of his new friend - the innkeeper Wano, who took him in, treating him as a family member? Or was it his own longing for real life, to which he had once been deprived of his right?

He walked over to the sailors who were wrestling with a full barrel.

One day, such a conversation will surely take place...

Now Ross was deciding everything.

Thus began the rehearsals. The highlander women watched the twins' hip movements in amazement, while the men surreptitiously watched their performances with great pleasure. It's amazing how many of them had some minor duties on board then...

Sai pulled out a zither, which she had learned to play in her childhood.

It was one element of her past that few knew about.

Ross remembered her showing up at the House of Pleasure with that zither. After that, he had heard her play more than once, but as far as he knew, she had never told her beloved about the history of the instrument. It was the only trace of her mysterious past.

Her slender fingers seemed to be made to play an instrument that did not really come from the country where her extraordinary beauty came from. How did it happen that the girl of eastern beauty met the zither?

At the age of five, Sai was adopted by distant relatives of her family. They lived in the Kingdom of Tenchryz. That's all Ross found out. What was before and what happened next? This Sai never explained. The zither was the only thing she had brought with her.

Initially, a few girls from simple families protested learning to dance, claiming that they would never do something so indecent. They were ashamed and it was not surprising. The dance from the lands of the Slaves Bay was based on sensual movements of the hips and belly, accompanied by smooth movements of the arms. It was very different from highlanders.

Lena came to their aid. Setting a good example, she dragged Maya with her, and they both started studying.

It quickly turned out that Lena had a real talent for it. Her dance was subtle but sensual, like that of the sisters. A beautiful, apparently young woman danced gracefully, surprising everyone. The sailors couldn't look away. She suddenly seemed to be someone else entirely. Not the mother of two adult sons, not a countess, but... a goddess...

The girls stopped their protests. Somewhat for the sake of a cause, a little out of jealousy, they began their studies with varying degrees of success. Some people were far from sensual, like Marlene, but they gritted their teeth and practiced persistently.

The sad Maya was the second person with hidden talent. Tenan regarded her thoughtfully. Sorrow enveloped the girl like a shroud, actually separating her from the rest of the world. She set out on this journey, probably thinking that she had nothing else to do. To live on, she had to act. Breathe. Look. To dream at nights without hope and colors. To miss but move on. To think, but slowly move away from memories. To love in your memory and blur past moments, old images.

He knew these feelings well...

He met her eyes.

Suddenly, the two broken hearts found a common rhythm. A common longing for taken love. Same pain. They passed each other for so long in the town. Many times, they exchanged a few words with each other. But they had never looked at each other that way before. As if the world had to be reduced to the size of a ship for them to really meet.

Two lonely, broken souls...

Ross was waiting for another dancer to start practicing. Oliver and Oren had been gone for quite a long time. The sun moved in the sky and the twins ordered a first break as Sai disappeared into the cabin. She appeared on deck after a moment, maybe two. She whispered a few words to the first of the sisters who had taken part vividly in the earlier conversation. She nodded in agreement.

"What are they up to?" Victor asked Ross.

Ross knew. So is Sel. He waited anxiously when Oliver decided to leave.

It took great courage.

"Come in..." he whispered softly.

The cabin door opened slowly. Oren was the first to come out.

Sai played a sensual dance melody.

A blonde-haired girl appeared in the doorway of the cabin. Her delicate curls eluded discreetly from the hairpins. They squirmed against the face, covered in a subtle make-up that concealed all signs of masculine appearance and softened the features. Her eyes, underlined with a strong black pencil in the fashion of the Gulf women, looked at everyone with a mixture of uncertainty and embarrassment, which only added to her extraordinary beauty. The blond strands of hair were partially loose and partially held by a delicate tiara. In addition, an outfit revealing a nicely sculpted belly, breasts hidden under a delicate fabric, cleverly concealing the boundaries of a flesh-colored corset. Talia, usually Oliver's nuisance because she had never gotten less feminine, was now a godsend. The whole was complemented by trousers made of sparkling fabric and dance shoes and light fingerless gloves, hemmed with beads here and there, giving slenderness to hands, undoubtedly too busy for a woman of such phenomenal beauty.

Oliver was an extraordinary creature of his kind. As a man, he resembled a slender elf. As a woman, he was gentle, but only on the surface, because his flexibility and agility and character traits were indicative of strength and endurance.

Most of all, at the moment, it was beautiful. A fair-haired girl in an exotic outfit attracted the attention of men, regardless of their orientation. Everyone was amazed at the ability to change. There was a buzz as many began to comment on what they had just seen.

Ross looked at Sai. He could see the fear in her eyes as she looked at Oliver. He knew very well that he had every reason to be afraid for him. He understood fully now, though in those days Oliver wore a dark wig, why Moren had lost his head to him.

He did not envy him.

He approached him slowly. He took his hand to lead him aboard.

The music stopped.

"What you see here," he began, "is not dressing up for fun or sick whims. It's an act of extraordinary courage. We'll have someone who will protect our dear ladies in this way," he bowed towards the girls. "And as one of them he will be perfect for our purposes. The dancers will be able to move around the castle. This might help us find Vivan. I'm only asking you for great discretion. Nobody can know about it. Nobody! Otherwise, we will all be lost!"

After a moment's thought, many began nodding their heads. Women too, still not taking his eyes off the extraordinary girl. The sight worried them. Ross knew he could trust his crew. He had chosen his people properly a long time ago.

"Wait," they heard Victor's voice suddenly. "But what is it? I don't understand."

Lena whispered a few words in his ear, and he looked at Oliver in disguise, so deeply shaken as if he was suddenly told that he was returning to his world.

"Happy?" Oliver asked softly, shaking his hair slightly.

"If you tell me, it doesn't turn you on for a moment - I won't believe it," Ross replied with a smile, knowing his "brother by choice" well.

"Are you crazy?!"

"Hey," Ross winked at him. "Dress-ups, adventure, emotions... Nothing? Really?!"

Oliver couldn't deny it.

"I knew it!"

"Maybe a little…" he replied hesitantly when asked.

"Of course..." Ross suspended his voice significantly.

"Stop, the hell up!"

Now Ross was sure he had done the right thing in choosing Oliver. He smiled slyly. Oliver too.

Since he lost his real sister - twin sister, gaining a miraculously new brother in the form of Ross - the captain of the ship, Oliver's life took a completely different path, full of adventures and dangers. Whether it was because of his unusual brother, nicknamed the Sorcerer of the Jewel or Heart, or his own, it didn't matter. Both were not afraid of the risks that life brought, although they were inextricably linked with each other. Fear wouldn't change anything here. They didn't want to feel no restraint loops around their necks.

"Come on, lovebirds! We keep dancing!" Exclaimed one of the sisters. "Blonde!" She turned to Oliver. "Come here!"

"What?!" Oliver said immediately.

"She's supposed to be dancing with us, isn't she, Captain?"

"Yes," Ross replied, amused.

Oliver flushed.

"Damn it!" He swore softly, "Ross, you will pay me for this, brother! I promise!"

"You need a brotherly kiss to courage?"

Oliver glared at him.

"Don't you dare!" He warned, walking towards the girls with a grim face.

"Hey!" Ross called after him. "Forgive me, but I don't know your name! Or should I call you Blonde?"

Several in the crowd laughed happily.

Oliver pivoted on the spot.

"Call me Fury!" He replied without a hint of his former calmness, though Ross knew perfectly well that all this bad mood was really just for show.

"Or maybe Matilda is better?" He joked boldly and without mercy for his brother's patience. "Hilda? Cunegund?"

"He's going to have smoke coming out of his ears!" Sel leaned close to him. "Have mercy, because he'll tear us all down."

But he laughed at it himself.

Sai, making sure Oliver couldn't see anything, shook her finger at them playfully.

Lena patted Oliver gently on the shoulder. His anger softened. It wasn't entirely real.

"Olivia," Victor said, "if there was Oliver before, let it be Olivia now."

"Olivia..." The blonde-haired beauty said the name as if tasting the sound in her mouth. "Why not?" Noticed ironically. "I'm Olivia," looked at Sai, who stopped the game to come to her. Their eyes full of secrets met each other in silent agreement. Sai brushed Oliver's cheek with slender fingers.

There was no question of cheat between them. There was no camouflage.

However, as they took their seats, Ross noticed something else. Returning to the instrument, Sai instinctively placed her hand on her stomach. It only took a moment. Apart from him, he was sure, no one noticed. Even Sai did not guess that he saw anything.

He hadn't expected this.

He didn't think Oliver knew anything about it. There was no indication of it.

He clenched his fist.

The risk grew even though they hadn't reached it yet. It was the first time he had undertaken such a difficult task. A great deal depended on his new magic.

These people wanted to take a risk. He made a plan of action for them.

"I don't know what else is on your mind," Sel said, "but the beginning seems intriguing."

"I'm afraid for them, Sel..." he replied softly.

"You would be stupid if you were not afraid," he suddenly saw the silhouette of Victor. "The good commander is afraid for his own. Then he works best."

Ross looked at the girls exercising.

"Let's go then..." he muttered thoughtfully.

Aparajita. That was the name of one of the twin sisters, the more outspoken one, Lena had explained to Ross. The other was called Anokhi. As the girls had trouble pronouncing the first name correctly, they quickly began to call the dark-haired beauty Apara. She agreed with an indulgent smile that indicated a certain pride, but fortunately it lacked excessive pride. Anokhi, like Sel at times, was somewhat secretive, seemingly giving way to her sister in reigning over the group. In fact, as a keen observer, she quickly saw mistakes and discreetly guided her sister on the right path and motivated the girls to learn. They quickly agreed that it would be best to combine certain elements of highlander dance with their dance, so that the girls from Leviron could absorb it better, which turned out to be a great idea.

The ship continued. The captain managed the actions of his people to keep them from getting depressed. They must have had a job to give young women a break, otherwise there would have been many incidents. Though now, he had to admit, they were decent behavior. If anything happened, it was rather playful. Marlene won the hearts of the sailors, without a doubt. They often tossed jokes at her, and she did the same. In addition, there were humorous mishaps, such as trampling skirts or bumping into each other in the dance. Oliver was caught consciously by one of the sailors, throwing the slogan: watch out, blonde! which made the boy's face blush, which even a layer of makeup could not hide. He felt an overwhelming urge to free himself from his amused savior.

Meanwhile, Oren was calling the girls one by one to help with the costumes to change without missing much of their lessons. On the sidelines, a few selected for the special mission, including Victor and Tenan, calmly prepared their hidden weapons...

CHAPTER 10

Vashaba visited him suddenly in a dream...

"I finally found you!" She cried, relieved, cupping his hands over his face, "I wanted so badly to finally see you!"

He knew it was a dream. He was painfully aware of this.

"Vivan..." she kissed him tenderly.

In the next moment he felt a wave of growing sensuality overwhelm him. She kissed his neck, knowing how sensitive he was to these sensations. She unbuttoned his shirt, touching the scars with her lips and the delicacy of her hands. He felt the fever build up inside her, her heart beating faster and faster. The heat flared up with every moment his hands began to wander over her body before he was completely unconscious. Her and his sensations permeated his soul. He was lost in it. As always. He was consumed by their shared delight until he was out of breath.

One, two, three. His heartbeat skipped or sped up rapidly, making him tremble alternately with the effort to keep himself from fainting from so many sensations. Their close-ups were always the same: they had a lot of heat and desires, leaving him barely alive after all. Now the beginning also foreshadowed a similar end.

But for the first time he felt the fear of this end.

A sudden twinge in his heart made him slightly awake.

He felt a chill. Like the breath of death on his neck...

"Vashaba..." he whispered pleadingly before he could even think it over.

"Honey," she looked at him with sparkling eyes. "Take it easy..." she put her hand on his heart. "Today it will be completely different. Only you matter. Only you... she whispered in his ear."

He felt chills of pleasure as her lips brushed his skin. Her heart lowered as Vashaba restrained her emotions. The chaos of sensations took on subtle tones.

Suddenly it became really unusual because he finally felt different. He felt fully... She was no longer entering his mind with the wave of her impressions. He could get carried away by it.

But the real Vashaba would never do that for him...

"No!" He shouted softly, as if from the depths of his own consciousness. "No! Stop! I don't want! NEVER TOUCH ME ANY MORE!"

He jumped up abruptly, breathing hard.

"This is not the love I dream about..."

He hid his face in his hands, trembling with emotion. Like any man who discovers a painful truth but does not yet reach a hopeful heart.

No. It is not it. This can't be it! Vashaba wasn't doing anything he didn't want to!

"No?!" A voice whispered to him. "How often did you spend time with your family? When have you seen Dinn for more than a moment? Have you seen what Ross's Valeria looks like now?"

There was no point in making excuses. He knew the answers to these questions...

Time slipped away from him stealthily with her until it was too late or too early.

Then he missed it, in the moments between day and night. He regretted it. He promised himself to change that. Tired to the limit, he promised himself it would be the last time. That he would be more resolute afterwards. He won't let it last that long. He will have time to see the world other than Vashaba.

And he was losing those moments again...

"Vivan?" Suddenly he heard a woman's voice. "What happened?"

A warm hand touching his head with a maternal gesture. Low voice. Real care.

Violet.

He had to shake it off! It is not as bad as he thought. You cannot act rashly.

So why was he still feeling that twinge in his heart that was causing him pain?

"Bad dream," he replied, sighing heavily. "I'm sorry. I didn't mean to scare you."

"A bad dream is no reason to apologize," she replied in a matter-of-fact tone.

He knew why she reacted that way. This was Violet's way of hiding her soft heart. She defended herself against the unknown.

"You're right," he tried to smile.

She touched his forehead. As her cool forehead calmed her down, she quickly found herself at her mini-bar - the globe. She scooped up two glasses, poured the rum, not caring about the amount, then returned to it, this time sitting on the edge of the bed.

"Drink!" She ordered briefly, handing him a glass.

"I don't like alcohol after nightmares..."

"So what were you drinking at home? Warm milk?!" She was surprised. "Just don't tell me that after all the stories I've heard about you, you always sleep like a baby!"

He looked at her, surprised only for a moment. Well, stories travel fast... He reached for a glass to drink the contents without hesitation. She did the same. Rum successfully distracted from dwelling on problems. Or at least it helped him to control himself.

"You slept almost until noon," she told him. "I was afraid you would starve here. I had dinner served before you started throwing yourself in your sleep."

"Did I say something?" He asked uncertainly.

"You were calling her name," she replied, watching him carefully. "But somehow... as if you were begging for your life..."

Vivan looked away. She understood that it was better not to mention this topic now.

"You want another one?" She asked to break the embarrassing silence.

"You want me to get sick?"

"Right!" She slapped her hand on her knee. "You haven't eaten anything today!"

"I've never sailed on the sea."

"Well, be glad that the weather is perfect, because it could be different with you."

"Your sheets are grateful to you..." he noticed with a slight smile. After a while, he smoothed out the extremely fluffy duvet. Under the influence of this movement, the loosely tied shirt began to part...

"Good down sheets!" Violet commented on this maneuver. "Straight from my homeland! Every now and then I have to..." She stopped suddenly, seeing the many formidable scars on his body as the shirt parted too much. "Oh, for all the mothers of this world..." she whispered in shock before she had time to think.

Vivan scooped up his shirt in a hurry, embarrassed by her sympathetic gaze. He avoided showing scars to strangers. Even the family rarely saw them. Vashaba left him the top of his clothes, leaving him to decide what to take off himself. She knew, in those rare moments of understanding, that showing scars made him very uncomfortable. He didn't want to think about it. It was in the past. Just like that. The reminder of this through comments or compassionate glances led his mind and heart to paths he did not want to follow. There was madness in the darkness of these paths as well.

He preferred to live a new, free life. As much as possible.

Violet followed his hands, hidden in flesh-colored dragonskin gloves. For a moment she couldn't utter a word.

She had heard the story of the marketplace and the demonic witch. She did not realize how many wounds he was inflicted at that time. It was still incomprehensible to many people. For a moment her keen eyes caught the distinct mark on her neck from Mayene's bite. Characteristic because it resembles a vampire bite. He wouldn't let her see more, but that was enough for her. As a mother, she was deeply affected by the cruel treatment of a boy close in age to her beloved son. As a tough woman and captain, she had to react with caution, because regret and crying were now useless to Vivan.

"Tell me," she began, however, both curious and suspicious in this aspect, "You are a powerful healer, capable of even stopping people's hearts. But I've heard that you can heal yourself. The concern of others helps you in this..."

"Sincere concern..." he interjected softly.

"Sincere concern," she repeated. "Should I be offended? Do you think I'm not worried enough about your health right now?"

"I'm just telling you the way it is," he replied, slightly concerned by her suspicion, "This person must care a little about me. Otherwise, nothing will happen. You care," he looked boldly into her eyes. "Believe me, I would know if it were otherwise."

"What if I didn't mean well? If I cared because I have an interest in it?" She asked aggressively.

"Violet," he replied in his calm, melodic tone, "I don't believe a wise woman like you doesn't understand what "sincere concern" means."

She blushed.

"I think I'll check your health," he remarked, with a hint of laughter in his voice at the sight of it.

"You better check your head if it is tight on the neck!" She said immediately. "Because I'm going to hit you in a moment!"

This boy has amazingly blue eyes! She rarely saw them. He looked at her now as only a good-hearted man could. In this seemingly calm look, she saw traces of painful experiences and some signs of wisdom in life, acquired through difficult experiences, with an admixture of knowledge of human nature. He already knew a lot for his age.

"You wanted to ask something..." he reminded her as the silence stretched too much.

"Yes..." She shook off her thoughts to follow the one that she had previously thought of. "You can heal yourself," she found the thread, "so, why don't you remove these scars yourself?"

Vivan looked at her silently for a moment.

"I've been hurt…" he began quietly.

"Is that why you want everyone to know about it?"

"I'm not showing them!"

"But everyone knows about them!" She announced to him, like a child who is being told the obvious.

"Should I pretend nothing happened?"

"But that's how you act!" She exclaimed in amazement. "I hear everywhere how brave you are! Because other would break down, maybe go mad..."

"You're not helping..." He cut her off firmly.

She broke off as abruptly as she had started, suddenly understanding. She could read it from his face thanks to her motherly intuition.

"And how..." she began hesitantly. "How to make them disappear? So many people care about you. Family, friends. How, Vivan?"

She felt that the answer would touch her motherly heart.

"Everyone thinks..." he answered softly, "that the scars remain, because I want what was done to me remembered. Meanwhile, I'm not unforgiving," he replied with a flash of tears in his eyes. "And yes... They care about me very much. But apparently something is still missing. However, I have no idea what."

"I'm sure we'll find an answer," she said, embracing one of his hands. "Maybe it's about luck?"

They looked at each other, suddenly dazzled by the thought. Maybe…

"Have I really missed this?" Vivan thought.

He felt like a man who was about to open a locked door with the key, but he almost knows what is behind it and is ready for any good moment related to the unraveling of this mystery.

A sudden knock on the door interrupted the thought.

The chef's assistant brought the longed-for dinner.

"Finally!" Violet exclaimed with a little more enthusiasm than usual, to hide her true feelings once again. The young boy began to put a vase and plates on the table, while he peered curiously at the healer in the sheets and the captain sitting beside him.

"How long can we wait, man!? Many miles ahead of us, do you want me to die of hunger here?"

He did not even comment on her argument. He was used to Violet's screams, as were the rest of them, knowing full well when to really worry about them.

Vivan looked at the plates full of steaming soup. The sight reminded him of hunger. He couldn't remember the last time he ate a meal. He came back from his dreams, dazed and confused. Probably anyone has ever spoken to him that way before. And that was... good. A brief exchange of views brought a lot to his soul.

"Okay, dear," Violet would not be herself, if she had not maneuvered herself out of the awkward situation, which, in her opinion, was too exuberant from a moment before. "Get dressed, in the meantime I will follow him," she indicated the outgoing cook, "to give orders to my people. I will not sit with a man without pants! Just be quick, lunch is getting cold!"

He didn't see Violet's expression as she turned her head.

She allowed the sadness and concern to penetrate her face only for a moment.

Orders were awaited outside.

They ate lunch afterwards, enjoying the peace. They didn't go back to that conversation anymore. Vivan, now fully dressed as Violet had wished, glanced briefly at the seam on the shoulder of his coat. A similar one, the one on his own arm, tugged lightly, Violet treated it with a wound ointment she had not revealed to him.

Another scar...

Probably not the last.

He thought of Violet's words again, linking the thought with his feelings for Vashaba and memories of his own life...

He became acquainted with the members of Bernadette's crew. The sympathy with which he was shown was soothing to his aching senses. Someone still respected him, not treating him as if he were an object. It was refreshing.

These people were devoted to their captain, and the first - Mr. Tipe, as he told himself to speak - knew her habits as if they were his own. Tipe was once a pirate, as he hinted at Vivan with a mischievous smile, impressing with the whiteness of his teeth, his bulky body, his nose and ear rings, clearly shining against the dark face.

He brought some companions with him. Only Violet herself knew how it was possible to keep in check the dark-skinned inhabitants of islands where human flesh was still eaten.

Vivan did not have to fear these people, without any falsehood this time. Healing was a trait valued among Tipe's companions and the sailors themselves. The only, powerful healer - such a figure aroused respect that would be difficult for people like King Azram. Among them, Vivan finally felt at ease.

Unfortunately, he was not allowed to enjoy this state for a long time...

"SHIP ON THE HORIZON!" the deckhand cried from the crow's nest.

Violet looked through the telescope with her critical eye.

"Captain?" Tipe waited silently for her decision. Vivan too.

"Cadelia, now called Valeria by your friend, is a huge but fast vessel in these waters," she finally began.

"Could it be it?" He asked hopefully.

"Unfortunately, not," she replied, disenchanting him. "That's not it. I have a pretty good nose for things like that. Tipe!" She shouted sharply "Get the cannons ready!"

"Ay, Captain!" Tipe replied without hesitation.

After a while he was giving orders to people. Bernadette's six guns were not enough. All weapons were placed at the hand of a well-trained crew. Meanwhile, Violet watched the ship.

"Can't we escape them?" Vivan asked.

"They're too fast for that," she told him matter-of-factly. "We must be ready for this meeting."

"Can you guess who they are?"

Violet looked at the young man with a mixture of anxiety but firmness at the same time.

"These waters are swarming with pirates," she explained to him. "It's a Bandit. A quick, smart ship that has a stupid captain. From time to time, he manages to intimidate a merchant ship whose captain has no experience yet, or a fisherman's boat. For my ships, especially Bernadette, this is a harmless small-timer. Even so, I don't underestimate them. I don't underestimate anyone in these waters. Because a small-timer is sometimes chased by a big fish... A fish big like your friend's sorcerer's Valeria."

The bandit has arrived. The loud and cheerful crew, led by the captain in an unbuttoned shirt and a bottle in his hand, mocked Bernadette and her sailors. It had caused disgust to the old pirates who, like Tipe, winced at the sloppy sight of the brethren's corsair traditions.

The captain spotted Violet right away. His eyes flashed with drunken happiness at the sight of her.

He sensed having a good time at her expense.

"Fat Violet!" He began happily. "Confound it! Are you sailing?! Was your ship built of stone to support a heavy cow like you?"

"If it were built of stone," she mocked him, "it would sink as quickly as your mind in that bottle of rum, Yersey Bean!"

Vivan watched the events attentively. Yersey Bean was beastly drunk, there was no doubt about that. So did his crew.

"What did you rob this time, Bean?!" Violet cried meanwhile, "A few dead hens for which you bought rum?"

The drunk captain laughed hoarsely. Vivan felt a chill sweep over him. The chill this time meant something bad was coming. Someone much stronger, more ruthless.

"Violet, you fat barrel!" Drunken Bean, confident, he waved his dagger towards her. "I'll personally draw your blood off!"

Vivan stopped observing his surroundings for a moment. He didn't listen to Violet's disdainful reply, who had had enough of the whole situation. Anger filled her.

He looked around...

Closer than he expected, another ship appeared on the other side. Bigger than the Bandit, bigger than Bernadette herself. He unhooked the attached scope from Violet's belt to examine this phenomenon.

Who was steering this ship?

A flag with a skull flapped ominously on the mast, surrounded by symbols that, as a land man, he did not know. Galion depicted a half-naked woman holding a saber above her head in her hands. The hand gripping the blade was stained with fresh red paint imitating blood.

Tipe took the scope from him. A short glance was enough for him to understand the situation. The ship was approaching dangerously fast.

For the first time, Vivan saw the unease in the eyes of the seasoned sailor.

"I have a surprise for you, Violet!" Yelled the drunk captain of the Bandit. "You will meet my new friend right away!" He suddenly straightened, losing all semblance of drunken behavior. "We will play with you until you give us everything," he handed the bottle to one of his with sure movement. "Cargo, people," he began to count, while his crew also suddenly sobered up and stood at the ropes. "A even your own fat ass!"

"Captain!" Tipe said without wasting a moment. "Bloody Witch is flowing towards us!"

Violet looked as if she had suddenly seen a ghost. She glanced quickly through the scope, abandoning any further fruitless discussion with Bean.

"He was chasing us for them!" She hissed furiously "They will attack us from both sides!"

"What we do?" He asked quickly.

"Load our guns! Full steam ahead!" She ordered. "We will avoid the clash as long as possible!"

"The bandit is fast..."

"Hell, I know the Bandit is fast!" She replied sharply. "But what else is left for us? We won't win with two pirate ships! I don't want to lose my people, my life and expose our extraordinary guest to the fact that he will fall into their hands!" She pointed at Vivan. "What do you propose then?"

Tipe looked at her thoughtfully. Vivan wanted to know more, but waited until it was time for the questions. Dark shadows accompanied the appearance of the Blood Witch. The sailors were nervous.

"Load cannons!" Tipe shouted, making a decision. "Full speed ahead! Cook the grotto! Quick, move, lazy! You want lords and whips? Or maybe you like skinning?! To work!"

"Violet..." Now was the proper, and perhaps the only moment, when both sides rushed to start their preparations. He glanced at the Bandit. The captain ran a significant gesture along his neck so that Violet could get a good look at the gesture. Then he issued hasty orders to his people. Those eagerly, enjoying the fun, started to act.

Bernadette sailed on, picking up speed quickly. She had a favorable wind.

Unfortunately, there was so much cargo in the hold that even the rats had a problem with it.

Violet had many commercial interests.

"I admit that I would love to see my son again someday," she looked at the young healer with determination. "By the way, pretend to be him for the sake of not recognizing you. His name is Mickael. His father, a great man, comes from the Frozen Lands. I have no other children."

"Tell me something about the Blood Witch," he asked calmly, though there was not even a hint of peace in his heart. It won't end well. Probably everyone on Bernadette's board was aware of this by now.

"You don't know anything about it?!" She was surprised. "It's interesting."

"Why?"

"Who hasn't heard of the Witch yet? About a captain who feared the sailors. People who he captured disappeared without a trace. The corpses he left behind... the Red Captain - that's what they usually call him. Your friend didn't mention him?"

"No," he replied confidently. "I would definitely remember."

"Well, I'm not even surprised," she sighed, looking at the ship sailing towards them. "He and the Red Captain have the same last name. Captain Bernard Hope. The Red Captain, as they sometimes say, serves the demons themselves - that is also part of the stories. They say he and the Sorcerer of the Jewel are two sides of the coin. That they have something in common. Cadelia and Ramsey once defeated the Blood Witch in a match. Once. They struggled out of it and tried no more. But the news got out. Cadelia was the only ship to confront and defeat the Blood Witch. It became a legend. That's why they say in the ports that Valeria will do the same. One day, Cadelia's son will face the Red Captain. They even say that maybe they share a bond. That the Sorcerer is the son of Captain Hope. He really never mentioned it?"

"Not a word," replied Vivan, shocked at the news, though he understood his friend's behavior well.

Violet looked at him thoughtfully.

"I'm not surprised," she said softly.

Unfortunately, the Bandit kept them company despite the increased efforts of the entire crew. The Bloody Witch was approaching inexorably. An instrument of the cruel fate they will face, perhaps for the last time.

"What do you think," Violet began, trying very hard to be brave in the eyes of her frightened crew, "is there any chance that your sorcerer friend is on the way to your aid? I admit that this would give us a chance."

Vivan touched the jewel around his neck before he thought about it. He remembered the unusual contact with Ross, amid dangers and whirling emotions.

But can it be repeated? What if only the Jewel of Hope can do it? It was worth a try though.

"Wait..." he replied thoughtfully, trying to focus in the confusion, "Ross..." he began a little hesitantly, "Ross, can you hear me?"

Violet looked at him as if he were crazy...

"Ross..." the thought, like a snowball, hit his mind suddenly as he bent over the map, holding the compass. "Ross, tell me if you can hear me."

"VIVAN! I hear you," he replied aloud, surprising Sel who was making a journal entry next to him.

"Vivan," he explained silently, to which the lover immediately gave up his occupation.

Sel considered his next move. The jewel allowed him to talk to himself. What if he had allowed him to take part in this conversation as well? He put his fingers to his temple in silent hope, silently asking the question.

"OF COURSE," said the Jewel without hesitation or any objection.

Sel felt impressions and images touching him that he had never had the opportunity to experience before. Stranger impressions, not coming from a lover, but familiar, bringing with it, as it has always been in reality, friendship and warmth.

reatures that were so characteristic of their remarkable friend. Vivan the Healer...

The gesture when he touched his temple was, on the other hand, typical of his lover. Ever since Ross started communicating with the Jewel, he was touching his temples with his finger when he needed special attention. It happened this time as well. It was as natural for him as breathing. The crew quickly got used to the gesture, as did friends and family, no longer imagining how else Ross could display the effect of his gift. Sel placed his hand on the table, watching him closely. He looked for the slightest sign of mental exhaustion that Ross felt on the first such contact. He was ready to intervene, whatever his friend wanted to say. Ross's health was more important to him.

"He's much closer," Ross reassured him, sensing his fears.

However, you can never be too careful.

Even in this case.

"Ask him for the location!" Violet urged him.

Vivan opened his mouth to repeat the question, but suddenly heard his friend's calm voice:

"I heard. Sel?"

He wanted to tell him about so many things, to ask him about so many things. He commanded himself to be composed. Not now. There is no time for this.

Sel, whom Vivan had not heard, had to give the location because Ross had replaced all the numbers and letters that meant nothing to him. Violet repeated them as precisely as she could. Tipe was already waiting with the map.

"Shit!" Violet cursed, clutching the map, "too far!"

"What's happening?" Ross asked worriedly. "I hear your every word."

"We are being followed by pirates," Vivan replied, concerned about Violet and the crew. The captain gave other orders every now and then, but nothing could make the ship faster.

"Tell her not to throw the stuff overboard," Ross advised.

"Tell your friend that I know very well what I'm doing on my own ship!" She gasped nervously. "Goods are our only chance. Let him not teach a mother to give birth!"

"Rough!" Ross said shortly, not harboring a grudge. "Now I'm starting to see with your eyes," he added after a moment, "Vivan, better talk about yourself. How are you doing? Are you hurt? Did they do something to you?"

"Ross, Violet is a good woman," Vivan explained. "She didn't kidnap me. We were swimming home. I'm injured, but it's already much better."

The Bandit was preparing for the first volley.

"Look," Ross said as gently as he could, "Pirates won't sink a merchant ship with the goods until they loot it. If you lose - don't show yourself! It won't help you at all..."

"Ross," Vivan lowered his voice meaningfully. "There's another ship here." He turned so that his friend had a good look at the Blood Witch through his eyes. "Do you see it?"

Ross froze.

"Ross?" Sel looked at him questioningly. "It's the Red Captain, right?"

Ross's glare in response was more than enough for him.

What were they going to tell their friend?

"Change of plans," Ross said firmly. "Come out! It could save a lot of people!"

"You said..." Vivan began, watching the preparations of Bernadette's crew.

"I know what I was saying!" Ross interrupted him. "I'm taking it back! Come out, Vivan!"

"He will give me to Azram," Vivan whispered.

Ross felt regret clench his heart.

"But you will live," he explained calmly. "Do it! I will find you! I promise! You hear Vivan!"

"I hear," he replied despairingly in his heart, "Ross?"

Ross bit his lip, suppressing his emotions.

"I'm here," he replied after a moment.

"Stay with me as long as you can," Vivan said.

"I'll stay," he promised him quietly.

At that moment, the guns boomed. Bandit's Captain thunderous voice sounded a moment later.

"Boarding! Come on, dog sons! Get me that fat bitch!"

The roar of the guns prevented any conversation. This contact required a certain focus for which Vivan no longer had time. Pirates jumped over ropes and planks onto the Bernadette deck. The brave crew of Captain Meres put up fierce resistance. Vivan got the sword to defend himself. He didn't want it, but he knew there was no other way. He was defending access to Violet, who, to his surprise, was doing pretty well. This fight, however, could not bring victory. The Bloody Witch caught up with both ships and threatened Bernadette with fire from her cannons. They had to give up. With heartache, they threw their swords and all other weapons onto the planks of the deck. The pirates were eager to plunder. Trunks with silk, fruit from distant lands, spices, and even precious stones from Violet's hiding place were taken aboard the Bandit to the delight of the pirates. Livestock vehemently protested against this action. Goats and chickens made such a noise that the ears swelled, dragged and carried by sailors. The supplies from the ship were taken with them. Violet's face turned red with anger. Tipe could hardly control the calm of his people and the rest of the crew. The only thing that surprised him was the absence of the Red Captain. He waited at his place, silently watching what was happening now on the merchant ship. Allowing silently for the Bandit to grab all the loot. He just watched with cold calm. Slowly the sight of his seemingly calm figure began to arouse more fear in the sailors than violent action. His face was concealed by the wide brim of his feather hat, casting a shadow over him. The crew looked at him, armed and ready to fight, clearly waiting for the signal.

Yersey Bean ordered the Bernadette's crew to be gathered around their captain. Standing next to Violet, Vivan could see exactly how Captain Bean had set the capture of Bernadette in a good mood.

"Violet, Violet, Violet," he repeated with a smile that flashed a golden front tooth in the sun, "you, my plump dove..."

Violet snorted contemptuously. In Bean's mouth, it wasn't a compliment.

"What else do you want?" She asked. "Are you not enough?"

"Not enough," he approached her, smelling her with the smell of broken teeth. "I'd like you to scrub the deck of my ship with your bare ass..."

"Be careful with your words!" Vivan put in sharply. "Or better, shup up your dirty mouth!"

Yersey pulled out his cutlass. Surprisingly quickly he brought the blade to the captive's neck.

"Leave my son alone!" Violet shouted warningly, grabbing him by the flaps of his dirty coat.

"I guess mom doesn't have to worry about you," Yersey hissed angrily. "He looked down, where the blade of a small dagger significantly stabbed him in the stomach. "Are we looting something on the side, or are we making extra money as an assassin?" He became interested.

"I've been testing your reflexes," Vivan replied, silently thanking the captain of the Queen's Guard for his teachings on survival in the city. Kiernan, seeing that his apprentice was not very eager to fight in hand-to-hand combat, showed him some tricks that might help him out of trouble. In this Vivan showed a certain talent. Of course, when no one suddenly hit him in the head, when he least expected it...

"Someone would have thought," Bean began with a crooked smile, "that if he has blue eyes like the sky, he's such an innocent man. They remind me of my mother's roses..."

A whistle from the Witch's side interrupted his observations. He glanced that way. After a while the cutlass returned to its place.

"Too bad," he grimaced. "I was hoping to have a good time with your mother," he said to Vivan, who sheathed the blade. "He smiled maliciously at the woman. "I take the loot, and he the people. Believe me, you'll wish you had the other way!"

He waved his hand at his people who were carrying the loot in a hurry.

This time Violet did not comment on his words, which was already disturbing in itself.

"What's up?" Vivan asked softly.

"That," Violet replied in the same tone, "that this bastard is right. The Witch trades slaves with merchants from the Bay."

"Ross…" Vivan whispered.

"Bold play, Vivan," he heard his friend's voice, "and I can see you stick to the version with family after all. If so - good. But if the situation requires it, remember what I said."

"And you? How are you doing?"

"Not bad," Ross replied. "I'll stay to see what they do with you."

It sounded a little ominous, but at the moment it made little sense to soften the reality with words. It wouldn't change anything.

Sel looked at Ross searchingly. However, he saw nothing disturbing. Not yet.

The hand was raised to give a long-awaited sign with a slight nod to act.

The Witch's crew quickly found themselves aboard the captured ship. The last stragglers of the Bandit were scorned as they headed for the captives. They circled them, drawing cutlasses, axes, and daggers toward them. Each look had a contempt for human life. Around the captain still standing on the deck of the ship, the rest of the crew dispersed, weapons in hand.

Then suddenly the captives heard groans and muffled sobs.

The captain looked up. His entire silhouette now spoke of his hardly contained anger. The brown eyes, the expression so painfully familiar to Vivan, now looked sidelong at the deck, not glared at any of the sailors. It was enough.

There was an ominous whistle of the whip, time and time again. Several times. From a place where the captives could not see cries and groans. Pleas for mercy. Vivan felt the emotions of the prisoners hit his soul with great force.

Bernadette's crew listened in silence, waiting for the continuation.

Suddenly the captain moved from his seat. He grabbed the rope to quickly move to the captured ship. His high-heeled boots clicked his heels against the deck, loud as thunder in the silence.

Captain Bernard Hope.

Vivan now saw clearly enough the face of a man who had become a terror of these waters.

A face so much like his friend's that any disbelief of the stories he had heard no longer made any sense...

He knew Ross had seen it too.

Ross froze at the sight of the infamous Red Captain. There was no longer any doubt about it. He heard Sel gasp softly, admitted to his gift by the Jewel.

This man had fathered him by rape...

He couldn't call him father. He couldn't and didn't want to. He made Ross's life a nightmare since he was born. He had heard many times from Cadelia's mouth about how Bernard Hope raped her and killed her family. Many times, he paid for it, instead of the filthy man, beaten and humiliated by his mother or her lovers. And only the good of the few who appeared in his life protected his heart from anger and hatred. If it weren't for the wet nurse who breastfed him from birth and her family, he would never have known the taste of a good life. She defended him until her mother sent one of her lovers to her house when Ross was nine, and set him on fire without scruples. Her husband, Naram, and the six children with whom Ross was often associated, miraculously survived the fire. They left for fear of revenge.

Run, Ross!" The good woman told him before they parted. "Run away from her! For yourself! For your heart! Remember, no one can take your right to love and be loved. You have the right to live happily. Whatever people tell you, whatever path you take in life, remember! If you do not hurt others, live to be happy. Live with love so that your heart never dies in the dark. Love and you'll never be alone!".

He started the life of a street urchin, rarely showing up at home. It was enough to catch his mother's eye, when she drank (and she did it often), for him to face severe punishment. Lately, Ramsey has tried to "raise" him. He also said that as the son of a pirate he should not fraternize with men. The son of a pirate and a murderer should be fully male. He beat him with a poker. Ross ran away and never came back. It was then that he met his future friend Valeria. On the street. A year later, at the age of sixteen, he met Nimm... the one Ramsey wanted to torture to death. But with him he would not let him.

Everything sad and painful in his life happened thanks to Captain Bernard Hope, who now stood in front of his best friend. He would have done a lot so that Vivan would never have to meet this man...

CHAPTER 11

In one quick movement, Bernard Hope grabbed Violet by the throat and tightened the grip. He pulled her out of the group, still holding her neck, struggling desperately to breathe, then jerked her violently freeing her grip while forcing her to her knees. Then he kicked her in the stomach. Tipe, who broke free first, deliberately blocking Vivan so that he wouldn't endanger himself, got a hard blow to the jaw.

Vivan, a moment later grasped by the nape of his neck, felt the edge of the dagger against his neck. He froze as he listened for Violet's gasping breath. Hope looked him coldly in the eyes, judging.

"Take them on the Witch!" He hissed after a moment. "I'll watch over this myself!"

Bloody Witch. More than thirty meters long, more than eight meters wide. Draft three meters. Displacement of three hundred tons. Armed with forty guns.

Smaller than Valeria, but that didn't make it any less threatening. The purple sails and the dark color were feared by many sailors. The golden fittings and ornaments showed, at first glance, an unbelievable richness. Inside, gaps were full of treasure, and what could not be contained was hidden on a secret island. The ship's captain could afford to have a ship like the Bandit take the loot as thanks for sparing him the trouble of getting a merchant Bernadette.

There was something in the dark part of the ship that contributed to the Witch's sinister fame. Cages, cells and chains chained to the beams.

Undoubtedly, it can be safely described as a ship that feeds on the suffering of captured people.

A slave ship.

"Full speed ahead to the Bay!" Captain Hope shouted, still holding the dagger to Vivan's neck. He led him to the sternum, gripping tightly on his injured shoulder. Vivan gritted his teeth against the pain. Violet and her crew were dragged from the rear, handling them extremely brutally. Violet didn't dare say a word about it yet.

"Sink the ship!" Hope ordered without thinking.

She couldn't take it anymore.

"You bastard!" She shouted angrily. "It's a solid boat! You might need it!"

"For what?" He asked coldly.

Cannon volleys rang out on command. The sailors pierced Bernadette, which soon began to sink under the fire of the cannons.

"And now the other one," he ordered coldly.

The crew looked at him uncertainly. The first mate of eastern beauty, marked by a history of smallpox and a long black braid, asked incredulously:

"The Bandit, Captain?!"

"Are you deaf, Kim?"

Kim made a short bow and nodded.

The ship began a maneuver to approach the Bandit, completely unaware of what fate was about to happen to it. Orders have been given. By the time the crew and Captain Bean saw the guns aimed at them, it was too late. Vivan caught the look of surprise on Yersey's face before the smoke from the cannons blocked his view for good. They were fired as long as there was something to shoot at...

"What about the crew, Captain?" The first asked, though both he and everyone aboard the Witch were sure of the answer.

The survivors of the pogrom swam, grabbing the remains of the ship.

"Kill them all," commanded the captain, setting his voice in a tone that made Vivan shiver down his spine. "I'm sick of this leech!"

The crew dutifully obeyed the order, firing crossbows and bows.

The screams stopped.

"What do they call you?" He asked Vivan, pressing the dagger to his skin. The blade cut her to the blood immediately.

Vivan looked at Violet's angry expression.

"Mickael," he replied, hiding a tremble in his voice.

Ross groaned softly.

"This is your son?" Hope asked, turning to Violet.

"That's right, you screwed bastard!" She replied rebelliously.

"You don't have eyes like Bay roses, Violet Meresa!" He called to her with a hint of suspicion.

"It's enough that his father has!" She replied without hesitating.

"You look like a porcelain doll!" Hope noticed, looking at Vivan. "A little pugnacious doll, but we'll work on it in a moment. I'll get a really good price for you. Maybe some luxury brothel, where rich women are drawn to, will buy you? Or maybe some aristocrat will buy you and fuck you until you die or break your neck himself? I feel like I'm making a deal of my life on you!"

"I'm not anyone's property!" Vivan was angry.

"You are!" Hope moved closer, embracing him tighter. "From today you are useful to my world, because you can be used for what we like, you hear?" He put his mouth close to his ear. "You are my property!"

"Vivan, please..." he heard Ross's gentle tone in his head, "For the sake of your friends, don't do anything..."

He didn't listen. He could not. His blood ruffled at the words of the captain, so similar to those his foster-grandmother had once told his stepfather.

"Never!" He replied, staring angrily into eyes so similar and so different from the ones he remembered at the same time.

The captain turned him back-to-back again. He felt the dagger at his neck again, but this time Hope embraced him tightly with his arms, deliberately making his movements more lascivious in order to make the victim anxious about his intentions.

"Begin the inspection!" He shouted.

The crew laughed as they looked at Violet, the only woman among the abductees. Kim started first. Without a word, he walked over to her and with a quick dagger cut the fabric at the bodice of her dress. Then he tore the front of the dress with the help of two of his who were holding the leaning woman screaming angrily. Vivan jerked violently. Hope was ready for it. He held him tighter as he moved closer. Vivan felt a wave of heat pour over him. The captain touched him with his thigh, simultaneously bringing his mouth close to his ear. His breath burned his skin like a mark.

The sailors were genuinely going to strip Violet naked. They had already torn shirts on members of the captured crew. Now they were watching them with skill, peering into their teeth and evaluating their muscles, which produced angry grunts. The crew was on the verge of resisting, and they risked spilling their blood. The fate of their captain clearly infuriated them.

Vivan knew that the development of this situation now depended solely on him. This is how Captain Hope set it up, leaving him no choice. He felt tears burning at him, blurring his clear image...

"Ross," Sel said softly. "You have to stop."

Ross bit his lip. He felt a familiar aftertaste on them. Blood. It ran down his nose.

He was running out of time.

"You know he has to give up," Sel whispered. "Leave it. You need to take a rest. You will find him later. We are getting closer..."

Ross felt his head spinning.

"I'm sorry..." he whispered to his imprisoned friend.

"You don't have to..." Vivan replied before contact broke off completely.

Sel grabbed Ross before the man fell and led him to the bed. He wiped his blood away. Exhausted, Ross fell asleep. He only managed to look at him with warm eyes, not having the strength to do anything else. Sel sighed. He has to explain it to others somehow. He hoped Silas would be understanding. This combination complicated many things, but it was necessary. Without him, they wouldn't know what was going on with Vivan, or if the trip still made sense.

But how was he going to tell Lena and Victor about what he had just seen?

"You do not have to..." he replied to his friend, after a moment he cleared his throat and repeated again, to someone else and in a different sense. "You don't have to... be so cruel!" He pointed hard. "Leave her at least a petticoat!"

Captain Hope's crew laughed at these words as if he had spoken a great joke.

"Why should I do this?" Hope asked mockingly. "Why should I care about someone's mother?"

"She isn't my mother," Vivan replied. "I'm a healer!"

The hand holding the dagger trembled.

The crew froze.

"What did you say?!" Hope quickly turned him towards himself.

"I'm a healer!" He repeated stiffly.

"You lie!"

Vivan jerked out of his grip. Hurriedly he slipped off his coat and unbuttoned his shirt, trembling at the thought that he would have to show what few had seen before. He hated it with all his soul.

He slipped his coat and shirt off his shoulders, baring himself to the waist.

The mother's jewel glowed in the sun, along with a cross and a ring from Vashaba. A strong chain slid over the skin around his neck, catching a glint at the bite mark of the witch Mayene, once hungry for his blood.

It was impossible not to notice numerous scars from knife cuts on his body. Monstrous bite marks from human teeth. These were a network of nightmarish memories of traumatic experiences. The long scars, the mementos of Mayene's claws, completed the rest. Vivan's look was: "See what people like you have done to me?"

There was silence.

Even the seamen of the Blood Witch had never experienced anything like this before.

There was a commotion among the crew of the memorable Bernadette. The sight of a man famous for his gift as one who helps those in need seriously shocked them. Even the old cannibals would not have treated a man with the power of a healer like this. The only one like this in the entire world known to them. They would treat him like a god, protecting him with weapons and magic so that no one would touch the toe of his shoe without permission. Those of them who did not come from the lands of Tipe already had tears in their eyes at the sight of the scars. Tough sailors of both ships, drunkards and violent people. However, faced with the sight of everyone's only hope, when death or disease met their eyes, it was they who felt within themselves this once, because of his suffering, something that they had not suspected for a long time. Attachment. Compassion.

It was a healer. Someone inviolable. Untouchable.

Violet felt tears on her emotional face. Clutching what was left of her dress, she looked at the boy who had endured torture in his young life just because someone felt he had the right to hurt and tear as if he were a precious piece of meat, not human. Because he needed it like another thing. Without the right to their own opinion, dignity and respect.

Like a slave.

"I am Vivan Beckert," Vivan began calmly, though he was trembling slightly under the influence of the emotions swirling inside. "The healer," he added, ignoring the facts about his origin and his title. It didn't matter now.

Hope looked at him silently, showing for the first time since the meeting a completely different, more human face. He walked over to him, clearly surprised by the appearance of a living legend on board. Therefore, another gesture made him gain tacit recognition from everyone. He slipped his shirt and coat back over the shoulders of the surprised Vivan. But then he said:

"They won't take you to the brothel with this."

He looked at the silent crew.

"And why are you standing here?!" He suddenly roared at them, making them shudder. "Go to work, lost mugs! Lock them in cages! You!" He pointed Violet with his hand. "You stay! Scrub the deck, clean the ship, and do what the women usually do, but right, you understand?!"

Violet took a deep breath to reproach him properly. But she looked at Vivan and gave up the idea. It was to him that she owed her momentary goodness to the notorious Red Captain. Better to use it.

"This is the last and only thing I do because of you, remember!" the captain reserved Vivan. "This one time."

"What are you going to do?" Vivan met his eyes. He had no doubts that freedom was not meant for him now.

"You will be my personal prisoner," Hope replied coolly. "You probably did not think that I would just free you. I've your hands handcuffed and put a hoop around your neck so that I can always lead you behind me," he waved his hand to the first who, hearing this, gave orders to two sailors, "You are too valuable to just escape from me," the sailors began to do so in a rush.

For the sake of Violet and her crew, Vivan gave up resistance. It wouldn't make much sense either. The ring around his neck, in addition to the chain that had been given to the captain, was the first humiliation he had experienced since he had been kidnapped from his homeland. More than chaining his hand, it clearly testified to the fact that he had just become someone else's property. Even Mayene had failed to enslave him before. Now the fear has become a fact...

CHAPTER 12

"What now?" One of the people asked as they finally left the property of Sarah Beckert and her husband.

Paphian looked up at the sky. The sun was still high in the sky. Dinn, uneasy from recent experiences, found it hard to control himself so as not to rush him. They lost the whole day.

He could swear at anything, but that wouldn't change anything. A group of ten people waited for his decision.

"We're going to the port of Reden!" he ordered. "Hurry! We have to leave this cursed place!"

He set off first, calmly urging his mount. Outside the woods, they had to slow down if they didn't want to overexert the animals.

Now he could reproach himself for being unwise. He let himself be ambushed. He delayed the pursuit of the kidnappers, while who knows what happened to his brother. If he had known about the attempted murder of the lumberjack's family, the clash with the sharks, and the imprisonment of the bloodiest pirate leader aboard, his anger at himself would have increased even more. He did not need any special abilities to sense that his brother was not easy at all now, and surely, as experience has already taught him over the years, he is in trouble again because of his extraordinary gift.

He had failed him.

He was the first to leave, with no plan of action, so focused on catching up with the kidnappers that he forgot other things. Vivan was paying for his stupidity now.

He did not believe his brother was in Reden. This kidnapping was certainly well planned. Maybe he would find out what ship he left and then follow him. She certainly won't leave him.

No grandmother's words could change that.

"I'm glad the Dog pulled you out of the house, Count," said Alvar, seeing Erlon among the construction workers. "Suddenly it was empty here..." he took a pipe in his mouth to hide the agitation in his voice, but Erlon's sensitivity was not so easily fooled.

The presence of Alvar and the Dog had a positive effect on Erlon. He felt needed again, and that suppressed his sense of helplessness.

While Anna coped with it by participating in the preparation of meals for those working on the construction of the palace, he assisted with the manual labor. They both did not care about the count's title. Anna, since she had never been raised royally, did not understand idleness. He, too, has always strayed from his pompous family, preferring to live with people rather than away from them. He was always eager to help, but it was Victor who taught him the skills he thought a man should have, seeing that Erlon was prone to doing things. Without Victor's help, Erlon could not even use a hammer at first. These were times when each pair of hands could help the inhabitants of a forgotten village that Sarah, Erlon's mother, had given her son as a wedding gift. She must have had fun knowing that she was saving to her disobedient son by her name a dilapidated village from which she only collected taxes or food, without taking any interest in her fate. A village with a secret.

Erlon's new family and himself faced a challenge they never expected...

Trolls.

Mountain trolls attacking the village by day or night, depending on their mood. A neglected manor house, which by no means could have been a sufficient shelter for pregnant Lena. Had it not been for Victor's wartime experience, the first days in the village might have ended tragically for them.

Young Erlon made a decision that became the foundation of a new life for everyone. He had to convince the inhabitants to do so for many days, but he did not budge.

A wall had been built at the cost of many sleepless nights. Several clashes were fought with the trolls, including one, previously known as the Battle of Barnica, with the troll leader himself and his great crowd. It was a night to remember. Big as a battle steed, gloomy as darkness, the wild and relentless leader of the trolls bent on Erlon, sensing him as a competitor in the fight for the terrain. Comparing their reasoning to other animals, the female of this man carried the young under her heart. Something about her attracted the troll, which Erlon called the Dark, like the most delicious food. Was it a smell? Did Vivan's presence have had any impact then? Maybe. The darkness wanted to kill the mother and devour the unborn child. When Erlon stood up for them, he became an enemy to life or death. He was looking for an opportunity to get him. Because it was as dark as it was called, it was hard to see in the dark. Erlon's life was at stake. Only a miracle saved him in the final battle.

After that, the trolls never gathered in such numbers, and they were silent for a long time. Until the appearance of the witch Mayene...

Standing in front of a partially completed palace, more like a fortress, Erlon remembered the moment he looked at the village for the first time. Now behind it stood a small but thriving town that has given itself a new name. It had a larger port, and lived off the trade in goods and sheep's wool.

After the clash with Mayene, the trolls became only a memory, and the old house, destroyed by the witch, appeared to the world in a new form.

"Lord Count?" Alvar asked as he saw Erlon drifting away.

"These are only memories, my dear," he brightened up immediately, smiling at him. "They won't hurt anyone anymore. Unlike people..."

Alvar took his pipe thoughtfully.

"Any news?" He asked.

"The Queen will send her escort to us," Erlon replied, pulling a slightly battered letter, bearing a royal seal, out of his soiled trousers.

"We need her now?" Alvar asked with a hint of sarcasm, "Vivan is not here. When he was there, they had been reluctant to send him security."

"You telling me this?" Erlon replied with the shadow of a smile.

Miriam, whose husband worked in a construction site, leaned out of the kitchen, calling for her daughter. She smiled warmly at the sight of Erlon.

The girl's red-haired curls glistened in the sun when she came with the cart, which until recently had two barrels of thin beer. She distributed them to the working people. Now was the time to get the tables ready. The Dog, who had been sitting at Erlon's leg so far, ran in that direction joyfully, sensing that when the girl appeared, he would surely get a treat.

"Traitor!" Erlon called after him, smiling.

The dog wagged its tail uncertainly, stopping.

"Go on, go!" He ordered him gently, seeing the contrite gaze.

There was no need to repeat it a second time. The dog followed the girl into the kitchen.

"They all smile at a pretty one," Alvar smirked, looking at the kitchen door. "And that it's a count, the father of a healer, a grown-up son," he blinked, astonishing Erlon. "But when you look so objectively, neither the father nor the count. A young man who looks like the brother of the healer. Handsome, dark-haired. Women likes such a men.

"Alvar..." Erlon began reprovingly.

"I know, I know," Alvar took smoke from the pipe. "I'm married, and so is she. I love my wife and stuff like that. I understand it perfectly well. But say, for a moment, quite honestly..." He leaned towards him. "Isn't it pleasant when a good young woman gives you such a smile?"

All Erlon's gloomy thoughts vanished in an instant, leaving no shadow. He was confused. Alvar, pleased with the fact that he had managed to distract Erlon for a moment from his dark feelings, laughed softly. He looked at the man with his life experience.

"Don't give up hope," he said after a pause, omitting any titles.

Erlon gave him a grateful look.

Day...

Long hours when anything could happen.

Moments when thoughts wake up slowly, wrapped so far in a warm fabric of pleasure and delight. The blood flows in a different rhythm and the mind follows paths it did not want to go to.

Vashaba has found daredevils ready to seek happiness in the Bay in their illegal plans. Their little ship would not be of interest to pirates like the Red Captain. The elves were not strange to them either. This is not what has been seen in the Bay.

As she traversed the waters of the ocean, she let her thoughts flow freely. They quickly took a course that she did not like. For she remembered her last moments with Vivan. Her anger and regret. So inconsiderate. So childish. Why was she thinking that? Why was she angry with him for loving his family? After all, the family was so important to him. Was she really stupid enough to wish to deprive him of everything? Live with him just for the two of them?

What happened to her? She loved him. His patience, gentleness. His steadfastness in matters of great importance. Sensitivity and strength at the same time. But then other feelings prevailed. Day after day, hour after hour, her attitude towards him began to change, and suddenly nothing else mattered but to relive the delight in his arms. Watching him begin to defend himself against frequent passion, but dream about grasping him even more. Hold it, choke it. To enslave? Oh, was that really what she wanted? Obviously. Lust took away her reason and empathy. She wanted and wanted endlessly. She only thought about how, when and where to use it again. When he pushed her away after the story with the girl, she felt like a drunk without even a drop of liquor. He had to go back to her! He's back. For love, but it was not really important for her.

And then he was kidnapped...

Slowly the veil slid from her thirsty mind, revealing the naked truth as it was gone. He had to disappear from her life for her to finally come to her senses.

The truth terrified her.

Bitter thoughts drifted through her mind now, helping to piece together what she had once truly had with him.

But she knew one thing now.

She would never forgive herself for this.

CHAPTER 13

Evening was approaching. More and more the voices of the prisoners were heard below deck. Vivan listened. Men, women, children... There were many of them. Huddled like animals, probably tired, hungry and thirsty. Violet's crew remained in ominous silence. Not once did he hear Tipe's firm voice. Captain Hope has never come down there since Vivan was aboard. He was dragging him everywhere with him, like a dog on a chain, long enough to move freely. Violet scrubbed the deck, pushed for fun by the sailors, and she did not spare them curses. This amused them even more. Despite her apparent stubbornness, she didn't look very good: her dress was in shreds that could hardly be tied together, her hair barely clinging to the bunched bun. It took several hours for the captured to be close to her. When the opportunity finally came, he did not miss it. He pressed into her hand the dagger used during the argument with Bean, which she quickly hid in the pocket of the tightly bound dress.

"You should keep it!" She admonished him when the captain temporarily ignored them.

He predicted she would say it. He had his answer ready in advance.

"He cares about me," he replied, "about you - no."

They were well aware that everything depended on the captain's whim. This was felt in the behavior of the obedient crew. In their gazes. In the behavior of the first officer, ready to carry out any order, as long as not to incite the leader. These people believed in him, trusted him, and were afraid of him. Not necessarily in that order.

"Vivan," she hissed softly, simulating the polishing of the deck near the healer. "We have a serious problem!"

He looked at her quickly. Violet took the opportunity to check the ship in every corner, practically ignored by everyone after the euphoria of another victory passed. Though she was quickly thrown out of there, Violet looked below deck as well.

"There are over a hundred prisoners on the ship," she reported quickly. There was no way the word "slaves" could pass her throat. These people were captured just like she, Vivan, and the Bernadette's crew. They were kidnapped.

"Go on," he said softly.

Meanwhile, the captain was busy giving orders. The words that reached both of them gave them justifiable anxiety. Violet stood so that he focused his attention on her. He had to understand it right away.

"There are too many of us," she said coldly.

A moment elapsed as they heard the captain's firm commands before Vivan realized what he had hitherto unthinkable.

"Hack the chosen ones!" They suddenly heard the final, ominous order.

The Captain's handsome but cruel face twisted into a grimace that made shivers run down the shocked healer's spine.

He understood...

"Gather the weaker, the old and the sick!" Kim roared to his helpers. "Chain them together! Quick! Don't delay!"

"What are you doing?!" Vivan objected.

He didn't answer, just looking coldly into his eyes. It was a duel of will. Tough ruthlessness collided with a sensitive heart, which was filled with disbelief, regret, and finally anger, when hope finally faded away, overwhelmed by the gloomy reality.

Vivan shivered with a cold that had nothing to do with the coming darkness.

Death among black waves, devoid of sunshine.

Death pulling frightened women, small children and a few elderly people by chains.

What was this man going to do with them? Cut their throats? No. The latter solution, obvious at the sight of the connected chains, was beyond his mind...

The crew chained people struggling desperately. There was the lamentation of the three smallest children, separated from equally despairing mothers and fathers, screaming below the deck. The older men, appointed by Kim, threatened their future torturers and captain. One of the young women, exhausted by a fever that had apparently been consuming her for some time, broke free from being handcuffed, but was quickly caught. The captain faced her. A quick, hard punch to the stomach almost took her breath away. Despite her tears, however, she raised her head to smile at him. Proudly and with contempt. Her eyes, both gentle and powerful, challenged him. Vivan couldn't take his eyes off her. Her courage gave strength to the rest. The captain grabbed her long dark hair, aiming for another blow...

"Stop!" Vivan felt a rush of blood in his temples at the thought of what might happen. "I'll heal them!"

"Him too?" Hope pointed mockingly at the old man. "Will you cure him of old age?" He let go of the woman, pushing sharply away and reached for one of the few-year-old girls.

Vivan had only one glimpse of her.

Their eyes met.

The second girl went with her sister, jerked like a doll in a macabre theater.

"These two are connected to each other!" The captain showed him.

The girls turned out to be Siamese sisters, united by one body, and the dresses cleverly camouflaged this state.

"Can you heal them?"

"I can!" He replied immediately truthfully. As a healer, he had already met twins who were united to each other, also in a physical sense.

"They have one heart!"

"So what?" He replied firmly, though he mentally ached over their suffering and fear.

"It's a waste of time," said the captain coldly. "They're worthless!"

He let go of the child, sore from his embrace and terrified to the point, signaling to the first that he was to take action.

"Throw them all overboard!" His voice was ice cold.

The prisoners were chained to one another. In addition, several shots were tied to the adults to make them sink faster.

Twenty people. Three young children. The old, the sick and the crippled, caught by chance on the death ship...

"Leave them!" Vivan's voice rang out like a thunderbolt amid the screams of terrified people.

He clenched his fists in anger.

A blue glow shone in his eyes, slowly spreading through a web of veins across his face and neck.

It shone in his clenched hands.

His eyes narrowed with the still suppressed anger.

Before he thought deeply about it, desire took possession of him. He could almost see their hearts beating. Each of them. He wanted to crush them until the blood bursts their breasts...

They felt his power working like a blow.

They started to run out of breath...

Violet walked unnoticed towards the stairs that led below deck... Perhaps she was now considering how to free her crew. He saw surprise mixed with fear in her eyes.

"Come on!" The captain croaked, clutching where his heart hid, though some thought there was nothing there. "What the hell are you waiting for !?"

But no one was able to move, torn by the growing pain.

The captain, however, had a surprise in store.

"Kim!" He roared.

The first drew a dagger. He threw himself, with fierceness worthy of the people of his lands, towards the frightened girls. He knocked them over, weakening more and more. But he fell upon their terrified bodies and stabbed the dagger where their only heart was hiding...

"You won't... stop us all," Hope told Vivan.

Inside, below deck, were several crew members Vivan had forgotten.

One of them, with no sign of a heart attack, found himself at Violet's side.

One precise stab of a knife brought her immediately closer to death...

She groaned, looking pleadingly at Vivan, shocked by this act.

"The others... are waiting," the captain reminded him, laying down on the planks.

Below deck, the rest of the prisoners were under threat.

Violet was dying...

Vivan released his fists. The power was gone. He ran to Kim and gave him a kick, which made him roll on the deck, away from the girls. He touched them for a moment, trying to put the strength of his peace into them. He must have left them now.

Violet collapsed on the deck. Her dress was stained with blood.

"Away with you!" He did not care about anything anymore; he did not have time. Her heart was slowing down.

The sailor stepped back with a contemptuous smile.

"Do you remember..." Violet said quietly, while he put his hand on the wound, "I told you that I want to... see my son."

"Not my fault! Too many knives and daggers here!" He replied sarcastically.

The warmth of his hand seeped through Violet's body. The pain is gone. The mind, darkened by the weakness, brightened.

She looked at the captain. He slowly took a breath. He acted cautiously, for the pain in his chest, overwhelming like a heavy anvil, prevented him from making any sudden movements. It was almost indescribable in his adventurous life, to show such a great weakness towards everyone. The expression on his face told her how furious he was about it. One good gesture or two could not change this man's spoiled nature. His head was probably full of revenge plans now, and one was worse than the other.

The wound closed. The blood flowed in the right ways.

"Vivan..." she said warmly to the bent young man, grateful to him for saving her life, although it might have turned out to be futile. "It will not end well..."

He looked at her calmly.

"Sorry, I let you down," he said seriously. "Killing others isn't as easy as I thought."

"I'd be surprised if that were the case."

"You know what to do?" He asked, looking into her eyes.

Strange, but with him she felt confident. No fear. She had never been a fearful woman, and now, looking into his eyes, she felt that whatever happened, with him by her side, she would take it without blinking an eye, like all the other bad things in her life.

She looked back at him firmly.

The captain waved his hand. One of the sailors quickly stood behind Violet. He put the dagger to her throat with firm movement.

Some of the crew on board surrounded the handcuffed people.

"Bring him!" The captain ordered sharply.

Vivan looked at Violet one last time before the sailors dragged him to Captain Hope. Violet reached out quickly with her hand, oblivious to the blade at her neck. Before he could even make a gesture, she lifted his hand and kissed the fingers that were not hidden under the dragon's skin. He felt the warmth of her feelings, like a fire in a fireplace on a winter night. Just for a while.

"When he starts using his power, give him a few lashes!" Hope ordered sharply to one of the sailors.

He looked at him uncertainly, which he probably did not often. He was always ready to obey such orders without reservation.

"Captain, this is a healer..."

The cruel captain's face, so painfully similar for Vivan to his son, twisted angrily.

"You dare to argue?!"

"No... Captain," the sailor stuttered, glancing at the young man with real regret.

"Hit me!" Vivan said sharply, looking at them "I will not stop doing this until we are all free!"

The captain looked at him coldly.

"We'll see. Kim!"

Kim waved his men, who dragged their captives to the railings without hesitation.

In response, Vivan clenched his hands into fists, and his unusual blue eyes shone with a slightly unnatural glow.

His instructions were willingly carried out.

"Do what I say!" Hope, feeling the growing pressure again, did not intend to delay.

The sailor, probably often assigned to this task, pulled a whip from his belt. The strings darkened with the blood of the hapless victims. Meanwhile, torches and lamps were lit to enhance the show.

Feeling a mounting dread as the pain began to take his breath away, the sailor quickly sliced Vivan's shirt open with his knife.

"Scoundrel!" Violet shouted, oblivious to her own threat, "King Azram wants him! He'll skin you when he finds out what you've done!"

The captain looked at her with a slight raised eyebrow.

"Azram takes gold and people from me," he replied disdainfully.

The first lash didn't cut the skin on the back. But it distracted Vivan completely, and it stung more painfully than he had expected.

Not only was he surprised by the pain caused by many braided straps that he had never experienced before in his life.

He did not foresee this...

Ross slept undisturbed by anyone. Sel told Lena and Victor what they had seen so far without making the situation prettier. If things get much worse, it will be better if they start preparing for it. The rest of the time he spent with the girls and crew, supported by a truly devoted Silas who showed friendly support worthy of the best men. Sel had no doubts now that Silas was devoted to Ross with all his heart, almost like a brother. He also respected him unreservedly. Now Sel felt grateful to the captain of the Chimera who had, in his time, apparently guided by intuition, instructed Silas and a few men to take care of the captured Cadelia and her newly appointed captain. These people, because there were several of them apart from Silas, were to come here and they were now the foundation of the crew, holding everything with a firm hand. Thanks to their action, everyone knew their place. There was discipline. It was not the first time that Silas was replacing the captain in everyday activities.

Sel was left to worry about his lover's fate.

The new skills were very helpful. Their power grew the closer they got to Vivan, but Sel thought almost constantly about the impact they would have on Ross's life.

The strain on him to influence people and influence the weather was great enough for Sel's taste, and meanwhile there were visions. He had been able to do it before, yes, but not to that extent. How will it affect him? He had been doing it perfectly so far, as if he and the Jewel were bonded from birth. Will it continue to do so?

He hadn't expected to receive an answer to this question soon.

The sudden thump in his sleep made Ross's heart stop for a moment in surprise. He sprang up abruptly, revealing his back in front of the mirror in a hurry. The pain was burning. Long stripes ran where he could see them from under his shirt. It poured out in sweat, like most people were pulled out of a nightmare dream. A look through the Jewel of Hope gave him the complete picture.

In a moment it will be much worse...

Frightened by this unexpected experience, he looked at the door, hesitating only for a moment. He didn't want to be alone with it. Treacherous tears ran down his face, marked despite his young age with traces of nightmarish experiences. It was happening again...

Vivan's back was marked with human tooth marks and cuts from blunt knives, as were his torso and shoulders. When a sailor tore his shirt, many of those on board were shocked at the sight. The seemingly tough sailors saw the wounds on the body of the greatest amulet, almost sacred, and could not believe it, for just that one thought, the thought of respecting this man, separated them from cruelty beyond human measure. They were glad in spirit that the straps had not cut the skin.

Their joy, like Violet's and those shackled, did not last long...

"Damn it!" Cried the captain, tearing the whip from a sailor's hand. "Why, when something has to be done right, must I do it myself?"

Furious, he put all his strength into it.

The whip lashed Vivan's back, tearing the skin deep to blood with a dozen long stripes. He choked down a scream in agony, gasping for breath.

Ross ran outside just as the captain struck the first time.

The skin on the back cracked under the blow of the whip, quickly staining the white shirt with blood. He cried out in anguish, drawing everyone's attention to himself. He fell to his knees on the deck planks, hands clenched in silent protest.

There was silence.

Surprised, numb at the sight of him, people stared at him, speechless.

Lena's eyes quickly filled with tears...

"Ross!" Sel quickly found himself beside him, staring in horror at the bloody streaks on his back. Blood on his hands. The bitter truth immediately gave him an explanation, without looking into a vision. "How?" He asked, his lips numb as he felt the tears press in.

He had not expected this. Not because of the combination of gems. Crushed, he embraced him gently, trying not to hurt any of the injuries. Powerless. Just like when Milera died...

Ross pressed his face against his shoulder, his hands clenched in despair.

The captain struck again, waiting only for the victim to feel the blows.

Then again. And another one. Time and time again there was a loud lash. In his frenzy, he only wanted the man tortured by him to fill his ears with a longed-for scream. It hurt more and more. His back was severed with straps in pain similar to that when Vivan had been injured by greedy people in the capital's marketplace. A barely muffled scream escaped from his throat, under the influence of new suffering.

The next blows with extraordinary power reached Ross. He screamed, cradling his face in his lover's arms, crying in pain. Helpless in the face of what was happening to both of them.

Sel suffered.

Ross's body was streaked with blows, and there was no way he could stop it. There was nothing he could do!

"Oliver…" Ross whispered.

Sel looked around at the silent crowd. Oliver, pale as linen, stood at the side of Sai and Marlene, who was crying softly.

"Are you OK?" He asked hoarsely, his voice uncontrollable.

Oliver shook his head, watching his stepbrother mute despairingly.

"How is this possible?" Victor whispered, hugging his daughter.

The next blows followed almost continuously, as if the executioner had gone mad.

Ross pulled himself out of Sel's arms, looking for any relief in anguish. He stumbled, trying to get up, but the following times wouldn't let him. So he started walking on all fours, but even that way he couldn't hold on to the blows. Somewhere in his head, his friend's torment heightened his sense of helplessness. He heard him and saw what was happening to him. The images of the old memories of Ramsey and his men tormenting him to death with sticks and a poker were blurred by what he had just been going through, and alternated as he remembered desperately who was whipping them. He must have been crawling towards the captain's cabin, losing his strength. Since they could not help him, he at least wanted to spare everyone the view.

Especially Sel. The blows knocked him down before he could make even a few moves. Several hands stretched out to help him, but Sel, seeing that the wounded man was still shivering from more lashes, stopped them.

Many had tears in their eyes...

Hope fell into a rage, seeing that Vivan was not going to scream out loud. The flogging was obviously not quite painful. Vivan felt himself weakening. Red spots appeared before his eyes. He only stayed on his feet because a thick stake held his handcuffed and chained hands above his head. Blood was dripping from numerous wounds.

"You're gonna kill him!" Violet shouted in despair.

Hope stopped. The crying of women and children barely reached his dazed mind. But he noticed the hostile stares of his people.

They were ready to rebel against him because of the healer.

He moved closer to meet his eyes.

"Blood," he raised his hand holding the whip, celebrating this movement slowly. "More precious than any treasure in this world..." he licked the blood-covered straps.

He licked his lips, slowly tasting the purple, giving the movement a slimy, lascivious grimace. His eyes lit up as the blood began to do its good for him, that he did not deserve.

Vivan mustered the strength to spit in his face.

Ross was lying still on his stomach. The tears flowed slowly, dripping onto the deck of the beloved ship.

It's over...

He closed his eyes in anguish.

He continued like that until his heart slowed down.

Then he stood up slowly, not letting Sel or anyone else help him. Not because he resented them, it was not so. It was better for him to just do it himself. It hurt less.

He couldn't straighten up.

It was rape. Maybe not literal, but it touched him both in body and soul. It entered his mind. He lashed out at him.

Everything was different.

Like when Ramsey tried to beat him to death: Ross knew he didn't deserve it, and neither did his friend. But one thing was important now. A certain line has been crossed. He was in pain again.

He didn't know what to make of it yet. A sense of hurt, shock, disbelief mixed in his head with regret, despair and growing anger.

The jewel was silent.

Suddenly, the crowd around him hummed with stunned whispers. He felt a slight tingling sensation.

The bloody streaks began to fade away.

The pain was slowly subsiding...

Hope wiped his face with his hand with satisfaction.

"Dress him up!" He ordered. "Bring anything stained with his blood to me!"

Vivan looked at him contemptuously, but it wasn't over.

"You!" Hope turned to the sailor holding Violet. "Clip her to the others!"

"Hope!" Violet screamed furious. "You fucking scum!"

The struggling, however, was positioned along with the others. Vivan awoke from the weakness that overwhelmed him.

"Don't do this!" He ordered menacingly.

Hope smiled contemptuously. Kim went back to action.

All the victims, surprised by this turn of events urged by Violet, the victims began to defend themselves fiercely. But their choice was not accidental, except maybe one, which had to be pushed overboard by as many as three people. The others were too weak to resist effectively.

The children started screaming. Vivan struggled in desperate anguish, but then Hope hit him with his whip again without hesitation...

Ross arched violently with another impact. The pain took his voice away this time.

Sel rushed to help. He and Oliver caught him before he fell heavily on the boards.

"To the cabin!" Oliver ordered firmly.

Violet looked at his eyes one last time before she let herself be defeated. Brave to the very end.

He watched helplessly as, one after the other, the chain and the spheres dragged into the endless black abyss of the waters to inevitable death.

Their screams soon ceased as they were all immediately under the water.

He couldn't hold back his tears, shivering with shock and emotion.

"Oh!" Hope looked at him closely. "It must also be worth something."

"Be damned!" He growled angrily at it as the sailors took care of his release with a great care which he disregarded.

"Huh!" Hope waved his hand dismissively. "I've already been. Many times. You just helped me, albeit against my will, to free myself from another curse," he pointed significantly, "and also a few diseases acquired in taverns by the way," he laughed contentedly. "These words mean nothing to me."

Vivan staggered, but the people held him.

"I'll be with you at the time of your death," he announced coldly to his tormentor. "Remember this!"

The smile on the Red Captain's face faded. Like any sailor, he believed such words. They worked too often.

CHAPTER 14

Violet was the first to fall into the water, dragging the others with her. After a while, however, it changed. Heavy shots dragged everyone into the darkness, away from the ship and the light. Darkness swallowed everything.

She found the knife by feeling it with her hand. Opening the shackle lock was more of a problem. All this time, the rest of the desperately struggling people she hadn't even seen dragged her into darkness and death.

Finally, as she began to feel something like dread, the lock released. She was free.

At the last moment, she grabbed the chain before it disappeared into the darkness forever, though that kept her further from the surface. In her youth she dived more than once, so she could withstand longer than others under water. She felt the jerks.

First drowning people...

Young children are unable to breathe in more air. Especially those that never swam. Violet followed the chain until she felt someone's touch. There was no time to wonder who this person was. She found the lock like a blind man and began to scuffle again.

It worked, but the air was inevitably running out. It meant only one thing...

She tugged on the arm of the freed man and began to swim up, while she still knew where she was. When she touched it, she only sensed that the arm was larger, like of an adult, not a children.

She didn't have time to think about it. She didn't want to think about it.

All that mattered now was air. She had to get to the surface.

She had to let go of that chain if she wanted to survive...

She didn't even see them.

It seemed to her that it took ages to finally feel the chill of the wind with her hand, and in a moment her head came out of the sea. She dragged the dwindling figure behind her as she took a deep breath. Fortunately, the rescued soul was conscious and could swim.

"Who are you?" She asked once they could breathe freely.

"Cora," a female voice replied, "I spat in the captain's face."

A sick young woman who showed her bravery on the ship...

"I think it's some new fad," Violet remarked sarcastically.

They smiled in the dark.

"And the others?" Cora asked.

Violet delayed answering. So long that there was no need to explain anything anymore.

"All of them?" Cora's voice trembled.

Confused Violet looked around.

"Darling," she said finally, setting her voice matter-of-factly, "We can't think about it. We have to worry about ourselves now..."

"Why didn't you help them?"

"I ran out of air!" She replied with a mixture of anger and regret. "You understand? End of discussion! They are already over!"

"Catch me," Cora ordered quietly after a moment of silence. "When we get tired, we will swim on our backs. Can you swim on your back?"

"I can."

"I can see the shore," Cora said. "It may be rocks or a small island, but it's not far away. We'll manage!"

"Are you sure it's the shore?"

"Yes."

"Praise the Mother!" Violet called, feeling unspeakably relieved.

The women went ashore, helping each other. As far as she could judge, Violet noticed that it was a rather rocky shore. A short walk showed them that they were just rocks sticking out of the sea.

"We'll wait here until dawn," Cora decided, sitting down on the rocks.

She sat down next to her as close as she could. They huddled together, windswept, wet and tired.

"It's just a few rocks sticking out of the ocean like an ulcer on the ass," Violet explained mercilessly.

"That's good."

"They'll be flooded with water," she said grimly.

"When?"

"Probably tomorrow, knowing our luck. They'll be gone by evening."

They lost themselves in bitter thoughts. Images of people who lost their lives in the depths of the waters nearby did not cease to haunt them.

"I haven't even seen them," Violet said softly. "Dark. So dark. These babies... These people..."

Cora hugged her gently. Violet buried her face in her hands.

"Ah!" She said suddenly, with renewed fervor. "These rocks! The Witch was swimming towards the Bay!"

"I know," Cora replied. "They talked about it."

"Yes!" Violet exclaimed happily, "And that means they're keeping the course! He'll guess that's where they're going! He sure knows it!"

"What are you talking about?!"

"A healer friend, that sorcerer! He must have seen what happened! Earlier he asked me about the course! He knows the Red Captain is a human trafficker!"

"He must have seen?"

"Cora, you don't understand anything!" Violet exclaimed with sparkles of joy in her eyes. "He will swim here! In a few hours, he'll be passing this way, and it will be dawn! He will notice us! You will see! He will save us!"

Ross was lying on their shared bed. The burning and bleeding wounds from the lash disappeared without a trace. But the memory of what happened was alive. Numb after his horrible experiences, he just lay like a log washed ashore. Only his hand tightened on Sel's.

He didn't say a word.

At first, he just let him lie down. Then he cuddled up to Sel, not crying but suffering silently. It took quite a long time.

Through the eyes of the soul, linked by jewels to his friend's soul, he saw the sailors put him on the bed. Vivan stopped talking. He stopped protesting. Weakened by the flow of blood and, like him, by his experienced emotions, he lay there, letting the sailors take care of him. It wasn't that the shocked Ross that worried about it, but the fact that Vivan gave the impression that he didn't care about life anymore. Quietly, calmly, he faded out in the presence of people who were trying to help him.

"It's not good," one of them said finally, shaking his head in worry.

Vivan's soul was permeated with sorrow and regret...

"Vivan," he whispered to him.

He heard no answer. He became concerned.

"Ross?" Oliver asked softly.

"He's going out," he croaked to both of them, slowly breaking out of his dullness. The friend was in danger. Suddenly he decided that this was the only thing that mattered to him now. He must help him. Then he will think about himself. He cannot give in to a moment of weakness!

"Sel," he shook his lover's hand. "We must hurry!"

"What?!"

"We have to hurry!" He repeated, sitting up as quickly as he could, though the sudden movement made his head spin.

"Ross," Sel glanced at Oliver before speaking gently, "You're exhausted. You have a fever…"

Did he not understand how important it was?! He'll be fine, something horrible like this happened to him in the brothel. Although... They didn't actually happened... Does it matter? It will be important after that. Now something completely different is important.

"Full steam ahead! You hear?"

Sel felt a tremor sweep through him, nothing to do with the cold. Ross was burning with fever. His pupils were dilated and his eyesight was distorted, like that of a madman. Crimson circles framed those eyes full of sick liveliness.

Ross was under a strong shock that he was unaware of.

"If you catch up with them, you will fight the Red Captain!" He shouted, trying in vain to summon sense in him.

"Now I won't worry about it!" He only heard.

"BUT I WILL BE!" he couldn't hold out, grabbing his arms. "You won't survive this clash!"

Ross pulled out a small bottle from his chest. He showed it to Sel before taking a careful sip to keep from spilling out the rest of the contents.

"And now?" He asked aggressively.

Sel looked at him helplessly. He glanced at Oliver for help. Oliver put a hand on his shoulder in a reassuring gesture.

"Wait," he leaned in, looking at Ross attentively. "He drank..."

"Vivan doesn't want you to put yourself in danger..." Sel replied quietly, while still wondering when his friend's miraculous blood would take effect.

"He's dying," Ross explained to them. "He's dying of grief. Something terrible has happened... There are people on board who need help..."

"There are women on Valeria's board," Oliver reminded him. "Including Sai and Lena."

"We were planning a risky mission..."

Now it was Oliver who looked eloquently at his friend, who had already considered the decision. He knew that another one could not be taken, and it wasn't because of Ross' stubbornness. That's what they left for. Ross will not accept any other solution. He looked at him again. The circles around the eyes began to fade.

"Full steam ahead!" He finally confirmed seriously.

Ross looked at him with love in his eyes. The jewel glowed with a warm flame.

"Tell him he can never let what happened to you today again," Sel pointed pointedly at the Jewel.

"It wasn't his fault," Ross said hurriedly, "It's Vivan's jewel. He wanted to show what happened at all costs. He's probably learning his power..." He stopped the rest of the words at the sight of his lover's face.

He wasn't too happy about it either. That would mean that he is only a tool under the influence of two powers that test what they can do.

Sel was silent for a moment, jaw clenching to keep in his mind on what he thought about it all. Finally, he raised his hands up in surrender.

"Okay. So let them get along!"

Ross smiled through his tears. Yes, for now they have to stop there.

"Do you know how much I love you now?" He asked softly.

Oliver cleared his throat softly as he tactfully moved away from them to the door. He pretended to be trying to see through the thick colored panes.

Sel leaned in to kiss Ross on the forehead while pulling him toward him with a firm hug purely out of concern.

It did not leave his thoughts even for a moment.

Ross clung to him in a desperate attempt to escape recent events. The thought of it happening again someday terrified him. Also, for Vivan's sake.

They needed a new plan.

Vivan was lying on his stomach in one of the private bunks. Probably this one belonged to Kim himself. This was evidenced by images of dragons, referring to the style of people from his lands. He liked to draw them. He filled every free surface of his little berth with them. His bed had the most comfortable mattress, right next to the captain's, filled with seagrass. And it was not his choice. Vivan heard his angry tone as he scolded one of the sailors for having decided to bring a prisoner here. This one, however, did not care too much. Apparently, he wanted to help the healer, since he failed to save him from the flogging. Now he was entrusted by the crew to dress the young man. There was no intention to harm both him and the captain, although these were completely contradictory decisions.

Through the open door he could hear the crying of women. The mother of drowned girls, whose sailors of the pirate ship did not spare mocking comments, was the loudest who wailed. Her grief permeated the wounded man's soul. She kept saying, "My little daughters... My poor little daughters." She did not heed their words, threats and taunts. Her voice changed from a groan to the desperate howl of a wounded being. The pirates screamed for her to shut up at last. She wasn't listening to anyone. The prisoners were outraged. Their screams and insults for the murderers to shut their mouths at last only enraged the crew.

Vivan was losing his strength.

A helpless would-be executioner who had no idea how to dress the wounds, had pondered too long what to do.

"It's not good," he shook his head worriedly as he watched the captain's victim fade away before his eyes.

The crew finally became nervous.

"Come on, do something!" They urged him. "Don't stand like a dumb lunatic!"

"What's going on?!" They heard the captain's voice from above.

Kim entered his bunk. The anger showed clearly on his face. It was unthinkable for men of his kind to disturb the captain's peace and sluggishness.

"What are you waiting for, Matt?" He reached the frightened sailor, pursing his lips in anger.

I can't dress!" the appointed one explained to him quickly, "I could skin three at once, but I don't know anything about dressing!"

"Here and here is skin and meat," Kim told him, clearly not understanding what the problem would be. "Clean the wounds, dress, pour rum. Do something, whatever!"

"The captain killed Oman for putting stitches on his wound. I don't want to end up like him, goddamn it! Give me someone who knows more than me, Kim!" said the sailor angrily, "because if I kill him because of my ignorance, this time we both will answer for it!"

Kim glared at him silently.

"Anyone here know how to treat the wounded?" he called deeper into the rooms, "answer me!"

In the silence, only the loud wailing of the unfortunate woman was heard.

Kim's face twisted at the cruel thought.

"Stop!" Vivan croaked, knowing what was next.

But it was too late...

Kim approached a mother who had lost her children. Vivan clenched his hand in helpless anger.

The woman looked at the man who had caused her despair, stopping loudly crying over her fate for the first time in a long time. It was then that Vivan realized that she had been waiting for what was about to happen from the beginning. Without a hint of fear. That was her goal. Her eyes rested on the wounded man for a moment. She smiled warmly, as if to say to him: "I don't blame you. I know you tried to save them". A wave of sincere, heartfelt feelings washed over his aching heart. But it did not ease his guilt. It only made him feel a little better. The pain eased.

The woman courageously grabbed Kim by the legs. Maybe wanting to knock him over, or maybe she just didn't want to give up without a fight. She dug her teeth into his calf like a wild, desperate animal, holding him tightly. Kim screamed, struggling to pry the woman apart. He kicked her angrily. Then he grabbed her hair so she could see his face before she died. Tipe jumped to his feet, revealing his presence at last. The chain prevented him from getting close to the fighters, the chain prevented him from getting closer to the fighters, jerking backwards like a beast in a captive. Meanwhile, the guards pulled their cutlasses, threatening the other prisoners.

"Bitch!" Kim hissed contemptuously, cutting her throat with his dagger.

He waited until she died before shoving her contemptuously to the floor.

"Throw that carcass overboard!" He ordered his men. Then he turned to the prisoners: "I'm asking one last time! Who knows about dressing wounds?"

"Me!" Said a male voice from deep inside the deck.

"Excellent! Take him to a healer! And this one," he pointed at Tipe, "give him five lashes! Just don't cut the skin, he's too valuable!"

Vivan's eyesight turned blurry. So he didn't see Tipe's contemptuous look when he heard about the punishment. He was falling asleep. Or maybe it wasn't a dream, maybe it was something else... He held out his hand, trying to summon someone, to ask for help. He felt himself moving away, and yet he was not going to. The hand was looking for some support, but found nothing.

Until finally a strong foreign hand gripped her, carefully clenching her fingers.

"Relax," he heard a gentle male voice, "I'm here. I'll not let you go."

"Vivan," he heard a little later, "It will hurt now. Then you will fall asleep and rest. I have to prevent infection. I will not act like that fool who once had a leg's wound burned when a dragon attacked you! Yes, I know this from stories. People talk a lot about you. You are their favorite hero. Me and Cora..." The man's voice broke suddenly and stopped.

The man crouched down so that the wounded man could see him. He was older than him. Several gray hairs adorned his temples. He could be his stepfather's age. If Erlon had aged like the others, he probably would have looked the same.

"Cora was my daughter," he explained to him with tears in his eyes. "It would be enough for her to get the right potions. We know... I know them. But they decided to drown her!" He hissed angrily. "My beautiful, talented daughter!"

"Shut up!" Matt threatened, watching everything from the side, out of Vivan's line of sight.

"You're a medic," the healer said quietly. "I've always admired your skill."

"It's an honor to hear such words from the mouth of the most powerful of us," replied the man with a sad smile. "I'm very impressed with your gift! This is great power. And great responsibility. We should carry you in our arms and worship you like a deity..."

"No, you shouldn't," Vivan interrupted quietly, "All I want is to live in peace and help you. People. Everyone. This is my sense of existence. My heartbeat and my every breath. That's all I've always wanted."

Matt approached them, looking at Vivan with a mixture of amazement and admiration.

The silence after these words indicated that none of the men assigned to him had been able to find the right words for a long time.

"You're right," finally the medic agreed with him. "Sorry, I went too far. What I meant was that we all owe you respect and gratitude."

"Exactly!" Even Matt lowered his voice, making him softer. Even so, in the falling silence of the night, many heard their conversation.

Vivan smiled painfully in his heart.

"You owe me nothing but peace."

His words were delivered in a whisper.

Tipe looked up, listening.

"Here," the man told him, handing the bundle. "It's Cora's shawl. It belonged to her mother before. Clench your hands on it or place it over your mouth if you want to suppress a scream. My dear beings would not mind if you would."

"It belonged to them..."

"Vivan, I want the scarf be with you. At least I'll know what's left of them is in good hands."

Vivan's hands tightened around the scarf.

"Hold him!" The medic ordered Matt sharply. "Now it will hurt," he warned his patient one last time. "Then you will rest," he reached for the bowl, in which the white contents glistened in the light of the torch for a moment.

The next moments turned into a nightmare. Pain pierced the bloody stripes on his back. The medic tried to comfort him in a calm, matter-of-fact voice. He spoke gently, intermittently. He did not get angry. He did not scold him. He patted his head once or twice. Vivan's hands tightened on the scarf. It muffled a scream. He hid his tears in it...

It was finally over.

"This is the end," he heard from the mouth of the man. "Give this clean cloth," he ordered his involuntary assistant, who obeyed all his orders all the time. "Cover him now. Gently. That's right... Did he have no other clothes but a shirt?"

"Got his coat here," Matt reached for his coat hanging from a hook.

"Cover him with it. These blankets are rough."

Vivan was given tea to drink, the composition of which the medic ordered from the ship's cook.

They did not have to wait long for its operation.

He was falling asleep.

Before that, however, he had to explain something. Something very important.

"Tell me," he asked, before the medic was taken, "what's your name?"

"Eric," the medic revealed. "Rest now."

He wanted to take this advice, but something was bothering him.

"Haven't we met before?" He asked, "Your eyes seem familiar to me."

"No, healer," he replied, "I have never left my land before. Only after what happened to my daughter..." He broke off, unable to finish because of the sob that suddenly welled up in his chest.

As long as he could care for the wounded, he put his grief aside.

Vivan, oblivious to the pain he felt especially during the movement, grabbed his hand. He thought about his home. About the stepfather who was probably worried now.

"What...?" Eric began. After a while his gaze softened. The breathing calmed down.

He looked at Vivan with the warmth only eyes full of tears and love can show.

"Thank you," he whispered.

Kim, who had come to look after everything personally, took him personally, looking only at the healer. However, his attitude towards the medic changed. Eric's personality seemed a little more important to him. It was not known, however, whether he meant value in the Bay of Slaves or as a human being. Still, there was a subtle difference.

Vivan looked at the place where the mother of the unfortunate girls had been kept until recently.

The empty chains lying among the other imprisoned women were the last image before he closed his eyes and fell asleep...

Ross lay with his eyes open in the darkness of his cabin. Sel was asleep, pressed against his back. Oliver decided to take the matter of faster travel with Silas's help. He forbade him to leave the bed. Sel ordered to watch over him. This time Ross had no intention of protesting. Despite Vivan's gift and best intentions, he was too weak to stand.

Mentally, he wasn't feeling well either. He needed strength when the next events came. What they were supposed to be and how they could end for him - that he preferred not to think about now.

The most important thing was that the wind was favorable to them.

His thoughts circled around Vivan. Luckily for him, the jewels might have taken Sel's warning or, more likely, learned a bitter lesson.

Thus, the dressing of the wounds took place without his participation.

Ross touched his lover's hand on his side.

His gift was getting difficult. He devoured too much. He was not as sure as he had been two years ago that he would be able to deal with him. If it gets really dangerous, will Sel stick with it? Will he endure the peculiarities that surround him? If so, Ross can handle it. He will control it just as he will control the influence on others.

What if not? What if Sel starts to fear him?

"I think too much," he muttered softly. "Right?"

"TRUE," said Jewel, "HE DIDN'T GIVE YOU THIS REASONS."

"Thanks," Ross smiled.

Vivan got help. Ross knew about everything, but it didn't really occupy his mind anymore. It allowed him to breathe. The jewel simply told him what had just happened without imposing images that would burden his psyche. This made it easier for him to recover from previous events. It allowed him to focus. He will definitely appreciate it later when he will be less tired.

At least he knew that he had gained the distance he needed.

However, that didn't mean that he was less worried about his friend's fate...

She will try to establish a bond with him. Tomorrow...

Before he could count the time, the dream distracted his thoughts, indulging him in peaceful dreams.

CHAPTER 15

Dawn rose slowly along with gusts of strong wind. Most of the people on board were still asleep. Until late at night, the tragic incident on board the ship was discussed. Now it was silent.

Victor nodded to the sailor at the helm. Once used to getting up in the morning, he usually woke up at dawn. His favorite drink was also cereal coffee with milk, which he usually took with him. He often used to say that here they cannot appreciate the taste of good coffee. Here, or in this world, he has found few who have appreciated its taste. He accepted the goat's milk with a sigh. Even in the palace he did not lack milk straight from the cow in the morning. Unfortunately, Ross did not take with him any good gnome whose sight evoked warm memories in the older man. The smell of coffee pleasantly filled his nostrils. He leaned against the railing on the bridge next to the helmsman.

"Good wind," he began a casual chat.

"Aye," he remarked calmly.

Suddenly the wind stopped humming around their ears for a moment.

And then they heard a scream.

"What's that?!" He asked the steersman as they looked at each other in surprise.

Then, over his broad shoulder, he saw something...

He grabbed the telescope with a quick movement.

The two women were standing on what, a few hours ago, might have been above the choppy waves. Now they hugged each other and their knee-length legs were immersed in the water. One by one they called out to the passing ship, waving their hands desperately.

"Man overboard!" The helmsman called to the other two on board as he took over the telescope. "Tell the captain! Man overboard!"

Victor looked gloomy. He was sure that the women had left the pirate ship they were chasing. As sure as the stars in the sky.

"I almost drowned!" Violet irritated in her style. "You took your time! And I thought you cared about Vivan!"

The news of saving the two women spread quickly among the crew and the traveling girls. They all came aboard, surrounding Ross and the two perpetrators of the uproar.

"Hello Violet," Ross bowed slightly, fully dressed in his captain's outfit. He could dress really quickly when needed. It had to do with his childhood when he was left all alone. Naram had to leave, and he was left to his mother's moods. Having anticipated this, the wet nurse had taught him about many things she knew as the mistress of the house. She taught him to wash his own things. Take care of cleanliness. She showed what herbal decoction drives out lice, and what fleas or bedbugs. Thanks to her, he was able to darning. Sew on patches. Fix shirt fasteners. Tie any knots decently. Never beg, with work to earn what he needed at the moment. Never steal. Make a fire and put it out.

Life taught him the rest...

White hair was held in place by the triangular hat as always. He was the captain. Naram could be proud of him now.

Someone made sure to give the women blankets. The young woman at Violet's side has yet to speak. Her eyes caught Ross's attention. They had a certain gentleness and, at the same time, extraordinary strength that life forced her to do. Ross was sure he knew that look already. It bothered him.

Her long auburn hair, blown in the wind, reached almost halfway down her back.

"And you, madam, you are...?" He asked, genuinely curious about the answer. He hoped she would give him some clue.

Here, however, he was disappointed.

"I'm Cora Freizer," the young woman replied, lifting her chin. "Is that what they say about you: the Sorcerer of the Heart? The White Jewel Sorcerer? Troublemaker of Thoughts?" Listing the last ones, she tilted her head with a shadow of a smile. "You look younger than I expected."

She had a low, sensual voice.

"Troublemaker..." he began hesitantly, surprised by the unpleasant term he heard.

Violet made a firm mental note that it was time to interrupt.

"Have you seen enough?!" She asked aggressively from the crowd, cutting him off half a word. "Captain, I demand dry things, warmth, food and drink immediately. We're both going to freeze here! This woman is sick! Has a fever! Then we'll talk as much as you like! I trust you still follow the Witch?"

"She demands, can you hear her?" Silas mocked softly, leaning toward Sel and the crew.

"Wait!" Sel raised a finger pointedly, smiling slightly.

"Only if you ask me, Violet Meresa," Ross replied firmly, "you will get what you need."

The tone of voice he gave his words smothered Violet's belligerent mood. Marlene huffed with amusement. If that bag thought that the captain would be at her command like some snot - then she was wrong. Their captain will not let him get push around.

The crew sent Violet malicious smiles. Many have heard of Violet Meres. But on that deck, there was only one captain of Valeria.

Cora stepped forward.

"Captain Hope," she said to Ross like an officer, giving her voice a basic tone, "Please help us and give us shelter."

The ship girls smiled with amusement at the sight of their captain's face.

Ross straightened up. He tried not to show his confusion. He was still surprised when someone treated him with such respect.

Then he suddenly understood why Cora's gaze seemed familiar to him.

The jewel glowed a faint red.

"Request accepted, lady," he replied, thinking of the absentee.

He desperately missed him, wishing he would be safe now, and returned home with them.

Cora reminded him of Vivan...

The women changed in Lena's cabin and then ate the prepared breakfast. Ross took care of the sick Cora first, before they began to tell their story, without hesitating forcing her to drink a drop of Vivan's blood. He was surprised by her reaction. At first, she claimed she could handle it, but was dissuaded by the idea. In the present situation, he couldn't let her get sick and possibly infected someone else. She accepted the gift, looking at the vial sadly. So poignant that he felt moved. Cora barely recognized him, yet she was already thinking of him as if she had known him for a long time. It was noticeable. The attachment was different from Violet's motherly concern, more intimate. She couldn't hide it from him. Sel looked at her with obvious sympathy, and Ross knew exactly what his partner was thinking. He liked Cora more than Vashaba, though they knew her only for such a short time. It took just a few moments for him to like her, and that didn't happen very often.

They spent the next hour surrounded by a few trusted people, listening to women's stories about what happened on the Witch. Lena was holding Sai's hand tightly, which embraced her in a gesture of consolation. Ross struggled to control himself when they started talking about flogging. However, those experiences were too painful and fresh for him to be distant. He struggled with difficulty until their story reached a dramatic point: nineteen men, women, and children, appointed by the first mate and his men, died. This unimaginable drama finally distracted him. Violet described the way she freed herself from the shackles and helped Cora, unfortunately, the only one. Saying this, she shed the mask of a tough woman, sobbing at the memory of the drowning children, the darkness of the dark depths, and most of all her own helplessness.

Ross took her hand gently. At first, she wanted to move away, she was not used to such tenderness. However, she gave up on this idea, it seemed so nice to her. She needs so much now. His hands were warm, a little rough inside. Just like her own. She gave up completely when he poured her rum. Even Cora didn't refuse when he offered it to her.

"You're a good man, Captain Hope," Violet said, patting him bluntly on the back. "Completely different than expected," she poured herself another serving without asking. "Even your threatening expressions won't change that," she smiled. She tipped the contents down her throat. "I see it in people, you know?" the drink was starting to work. "In their eyes," she explained, leaning forward confidentially. "You have a good heart. Big as the whole ship," she showed carelessly and drank it all up again. "Vivan has a child's heart," she continued. "She," she pointed at Cora. "She is tough and vulnerable. He," now Violet showed them Sel, "he loves you more than life," Ross looked warmly at his lover. "And this one," she waved at Oliver, "could be cut for you!"

She took another cup before adding:

"I've seen a lot of good people here, Ross. But no one as bad as your father." Her voice changed tone, revealing a hidden fear. Ross's smile faded. "This man is dark," she said softly. "And your good compassionate friend fell into his dirty hands..."

Ross clenched his hand in anger.

"He's not my father, Violet!" He got angry.

"Yes," they heard Victor's voice. "That bastard is not his father. I'm it and that's it!"

A hand trembling with emotion touched Oliver.

"Don't be angry, son. I know about my uncle."

Oliver looked at Ross with emotion as he heard the words Ross must have dreamed of.

"I'm his father!" Victor repeated solemnly.

His hand rested uncertainly on the shoulder of the seated man, as if he was afraid that he would be indignant, maybe even laugh at the words. She stayed there. He bravely waited for a decision. Ross was speechless. As Victor revealed how much he cared about him, which was rarely the case, Ross's heart was bursting with quiet happiness. He was afraid to speak back then, so as not to spoil the moment in any way.

Violet, already quite drunk, freed him from his trouble.

"It's good for me!" She announced, tapping the goblet on the table to strengthen the effect of her words.

"I'd like to try something, Vivan," Ross thought silently as all but the women he found had left his captain's cabin.

Violet, drunk with rum, was now sleeping on his bed next to a tired Cora. There were no other places, at least for now. Sel went with Oliver to announce a change of plans. Everyone had to be ready to fight. Oliver was to see that Tenan and Victor were in the preparations. He assumed that this option would surprise the girls a lot, but he didn't feel up to talking to them personally.

Sometimes they glanced at him, trying to hide the grief and sympathy on their faces after yesterday's events. The men watched surreptitiously with a similar look.

Now he wished he had run out of the cabin and showed what had happened to him. Maybe those looks and sadness wouldn't be there if he had hidden it behind the door… He was looking for help. But they couldn't help him. Even Sel, and he couldn't look at his suffering and helplessness.

"Please tell me if you can hear my thoughts," he asked quietly in his mind.

Silence answered him.

"Vivan?" He asked softly, still in his head, losing hope.

"Yes," replied his friend, "I hear you."

He also said it in his mind.

Ross breathed a sigh of relief.

"What are you doing?" He asked.

"You just woke me up," Vivan replied warmly.

"Sorry," Ross felt guilty.

"Don't apologize," his friend commanded mildly. "I'm pretending I'm still asleep."

"Clever!"

"Are you following us?"

"Of course," he replied hastily, "I'll meet you soon."

"Do you think I'll see you again?"

Ross became concerned.

"Where do these words come from?" He asked, "I'm close. I'm sailing for you."

"Miriam told me..." Vivan began sadly, "Promise you will never give up. Keep telling yourself: I have to go back to my family. That's what I did... But I feel that this time will not end well."

"Who is this, Miriam?" Ross asked. "She's a smart woman. You better listen to her," he remarked with a hint of amusement.

"I helped her family escape," explained the friend shortly. Suddenly, unexpectedly, he blurted out, "Ross, what happened? You are different."

Ross bit his lips to keep from cursing. Vivan was sensitive to emotions. What had he revealed to him?

"I'm worried about you…"

"No," Vivan immediately objected. "That's not it."

Ross stared at the waves outside the cabin window.

"Not now, Vivanie," he asked, clenching his hands together.

Vivan fell silent. Ross didn't know if he had offended him by the request or made him more upset. His gift was slightly different.

"I don't want you to fight him," he said finally.

Ross sighed.

"Do you have any influence on it?"

"If I can just prevent it - I'll do it!"

Ross has stopped seeing the waves. He closed his eyes, plunging into a darkness similar to that of a friend. In the dark beyond everything.

"Vivan, I have to tell you something," he began, wanting to distract not only his attention from the near future as quickly as possible. "We saved Violet..."

He told about the whole incident, about the story Violet told him. It was better that way.

"There is a young woman with her," he added, opening his eyes to look at the sleeping woman. "Her name is Cora..."

"Cora..." Vivan interrupted him. It doesn't matter that he had no idea what the rescued looked like. "Her father is here with me, the medic."

Why, when he spoke her name, he saw the face of that sick, brave, young woman who spat in the face of the captain himself? The image was still vivid in his mind. Vivan thought about it endlessly. This one and others. Brave Violet. Rebellious old people, three crying children... He remembered each of their faces.

He remembered her face again. Those eyes.

"That's good news," Ross thought silently. "At least she's still alive."

"Cora..." Vivan thought, forgetting that Ross could hear all his thoughts.

Ross caught a new thought in that word, an emotion that his friend quickly hid, even from himself. Sorrow and regret replaced it.

"Turn back," he heard unexpectedly from his friend, "I don't want anything to happen to you. You are all I have. All I have left. I don't want to lose you! None of you!"

"Vivan," the tone with which he addressed him surprised Ross. The words also made him uneasy. He sensed a bottom line in them, not only concern for the safety of friends and relatives.

"She made me choose," the tension in Vivan's voice vibrated in Ross's mind. "You or immortality. She or you, Ross. Understand?"

Now it was despair.

Ross understood immediately.

Vashaba... he thought in disbelief that quickly turned to anger as he realized the fullness of his friend's suffering.

"Leave me, Ross," Vivan's voice was apparently calm, but full of sadness. "You'll be safe. I love you…"

Ross became concerned. Vivan's voice faded.

"Vivan!" He exclaimed in his mind, "Don't say goodbye to me, do you hear? Don't get me away!"

Silence answered him. But he felt that his friend was still with him. He still hears him.

He couldn't let that happen!

"I'm not leaving you; can you hear?" He called to him.

What was he going to do now?

He quickly approached the sleepers. He shook Cora's shoulder gently. He didn't know why he had thought of it, but he felt he wanted her to know it. So, she would know what was happening to Vivan now.

"Cora," he said softly, his voice trembling with excitement, "Please, bring Vivan's mother..."

Cora, though she knew him so briefly, stood up without hesitation.

"If I go..." he tried to explain himself, feeling how his eyes were starting to sting him with rising tears. "And they will see me like that," he pointed to his face with a wave of his hand. "It will be a drama, and I don't want it..." He broke off when she touched his face with a reassuring gesture.

"Fine," she said warmly.

She hugged him gently.

Suddenly he felt the familiar feeling again. Something that quickly got him back on his feet. He knew it, but hadn't felt it in a long time. Since there was no Valeria...

He calmed down immediately.

Cora, seeing the positive change, kissed him lightly on the cheek.

It surprised him in a very pleasant way.

"I'll find her!" She assured hastily.

And she was gone.

"At last!" Lena said simply, appearing in the cabin with Cora. "Finally, you decided that it was time to ask for help? You both try to be so independent, so brave! So stubborn!" She sighed. "Ross, come to me," she hugged him tenderly. "Pass him for me," she commanded gently, stroking his back. "Pass on what I'm trying to give you," her touch confused him. He couldn't define the feelings he was feeling now. They reminded him of those he had bestowed upon his mother, and later on Valeria. These feelings, in his opinion, could not get carried away. After all, the warmth of motherly love was not meant for him...

"Ross," Lena said, still hugging him. "You've helped us so many times. Do you really think now that I'm doing this with only my son in mind? You are as dear to me as he is. He will always be dear to me, just as, better never reveal, even Paphian is not. It doesn't mean I don't love my other son, oh no. It's just that I and Vivan have what cannot be shared with others. The bond of blood and tears. Tell me, does he feel what I want to give to him?"

Ross closed his eyes, no longer hearing anything around him. Even Violet's snoring on the bed.

The heart beat faster. The rush of blood drowned out all other sounds.

And suddenly he felt. Bond.

There was so much in that one word.

Touch. Heat. Love. Sadness. Joy. Strength. Memory...

If they could be grasped... Mentally naming them made a pause between them that just wasn't there. They all appeared at once, like waves slapping against a rocky shore.

Vivan felt his mother's love. Like the waves of a warm sea, it washed him of worry and pain. Her strength and sincerity started the healing process in him. The whip wounds began to heal. Soon, only narrow lines of scars became the only evidence of committed cruelty.

Hope and the will to fight returned.

Vivan's thoughts flashed to his mother.

"He." The Jewel of Hope glowed purple, and Ross felt that he was barely able to speak under the influence of all those powers that were still challenging him. "He thanks you," he said softly.

That was not all, but that was the only way Ross, who was just learning to name in many ways feelings and sensations by reading books and associating with Sel, was now able to express it.

"You feel?" She asked softly, surprising him. He thought it was over.

"But what?" He asked helplessly. It wasn't for him, it shouldn't have... It was like stepping into someone else's room.

Cora had never found herself in such a situation. She had never known anyone who expressed her feelings like this. Her love for her father was strong and full of strength, and it was mutual. But they had never shown her so much. So intense.

But as soon as Lena looked at her, any considerations about it no longer mattered. Words became redundant.

"What are you doing?" Ross asked meanwhile, feeling his heart leap out of his chest, it was beating so fast and hard.

Lena kissed his cheek with the sweetest mother's kiss.

"What do you think?" She asked with a soft smile.

He looked at her. Then to Cora.

"Lena, I... can't tell it to Vivan," Ross explained in confusion. "I don't know how."

"It was just for you," she replied softly.

He hugged himself with arms in a nervous gesture. Before him he could see a young woman accompanied by another. His mind lost its way to reason.

"I don't know what that means," he said softly. "I don't know what it was," they saw how hard he tried to put into words what was unusual for him. "Once..." he broke off, remembering two women dear to his heart from the past. "Don't do that," he asked, his voice trembling as his movements became nervous, "I don't know what to do! I don't know what I'm allowed to do!"

Lena clenched her hand. Cora touched her arm lightly. She understood before he spoke again:

"You are Vivan's mother," he said, close to panic.

Hurriedly she hugged him again.

"Ross," she said calmly, though she felt both resentment and anger inside her toward a woman who had never given him what she should have given him as a mother. "I just wanted to convey how much I care about you. Cora…"

He didn't let her finish.

"You cannot!" He stepped back abruptly. "I'll never do that!"

Both women looked at each other fearfully.

"Lena loves you like Vivan," Cora explained as simply as she could. "Like a son."

He looked at her, completely confused.

After a moment, he took a deep breath to calm himself down. It was just as he had thought at first, before his mind wandered off.

"I'm not sure I know what that means," he replied sincerely to the shocked women. "I'm sorry. I got it all mixed up..."

It was enough. They both hugged him again, touched by his repentance. This time he answered them with a similar hug.

Even Violet's snoring did not interrupt this moment of respite.

Vivan stood up slowly, waiting for the pain that hadn't happened anymore. With some relief, in front of the surprised fellow prisoners, he put on his coat casually. Kim was already standing in front of the bunk, refastening the chains. He stared at him, not trying to hide his amazement.

Tipe leaned out of the shadows, dragging the chains behind him.

"Healer..."

Vivan walked over to him quickly. He put a hand on his shoulder. It was enough. He sensed the times given to him. Kim didn't make empty promises.

No need," Tipe was about to move away. He did not make it anymore. So did Kim trying to pull him off. He was probably still asleep after yesterday's nap in someone else's hammock. The power of Vivan's gift spread over Tipe's body with soothing warmth. The red stripes disappeared without a trace. He was relieved. He nodded in silent thanks.

"Eric," Vivan looked for the medic. "Are you here?"

"Here, my lord!" The man from far down the deck called.

Vivan cheered silently. But the good news had to wait.

"Come!" Kim grabbed his arm. "The captain will be glad you are good so quickly.

Vivan looked at him coldly.

They had only taken a few steps towards the stairs when the trapped women began to shout:

"Don't go there, healer! Do not go!"

There was both despair and terror in those words. As if something terrible was happening upstairs. Some of them were reaching out to him with desperate eyes.

They tried to stop him. Kim was furious at their behavior. He reached for the whip. Vivan grabbed his hand raised above one of the victims:

"No!" He banned briefly, but in a tone that did not bear any objection.

Kim hesitated. Vivan sensed a certain respect in him for his gift, for the desperate courage he had shown last night. It was probably only because he had put the whip back first with a smile that Vivan did not like very much.

As soon as they were outside, he understood why.

Vivan felt the hair standing on end on the back of his neck. The mind was defending itself against what it just saw.

There was a woman on board.

The door to the captain's cabin was wide open. Many sailors were happy to see the show. Hope raped the woman on the table with strong, violent pushes, pulling her hair at the same time.

Vivan was out of breath.

The woman cried, groaning in pain under her rapist while others waited their turn. Kim led Vivan ruthlessly to the table itself as the captain finished with a loud cry of satisfaction.

The sailors now waited in silence for the healer's reaction.

"Here is our hero!" The captain sneered, putting on his pants.

The crew laughed maliciously. Even Matt, who was in this group and like the others, was waiting for his turn. The unfortunate woman tried to slide off the table, but Hope leaned against her carelessly, holding her in a humiliating position.

"That bitch cried all night for her bastard who we drowned yesterday," explained the captain to Vivan. She had no balls like the mother of those freaks of nature," he waved his hand disparagingly. "I have nothing to do with her. At least she will keep us entertained since she gives birth to crippled children."

Vivan felt a chill.

For a moment he allowed himself to think about his mother and Ross, and about Miriam's words telling him to fight to get home.

He was beginning to think that he would not keep that promise.

"Well?" Hope stood in front of him with a malicious smile. "You won't say anything today? You will not do anything?"

"I will," Vivan replied coolly.

He couldn't use his power again to stop their hearts. His body couldn't stand it. There were more of them here than then. The captain must have guessed this from his penetrating gaze.

"Captain," Kim said in a warning tone, "He seems to have healed himself."

"Really?" Hope asked ominously.

Both he and Vivan knew what had to come next. There was one option: kill the captain himself...

Vivan clenched his hands into fists. He knew perfectly well how little chance he had to do anything. But he had to try.

His eyes glowed blue.

At the cue, Kim hit him on the head. Not too much, just to daze him. He succeeded fully. Hope immediately grabbed Vivan by the neck. He pushed the screaming woman off the table. Vivan was in her place, in the same position. Hands shackled briefly with handcuffs did not allow for effective defense. The captain tugged the chain around his neck, standing behind him as he had been behind the raped woman before. The trapped felt a flush of panic and heat as he realized where he was. He had not expected such a turn of events at all. Everyone will be looking at it... When he thought that nothing worse, what he had experienced, could not happen anymore, fate showed him just how wrong he was.

"We'll start the fun, will you obey?" The captain asked, lying down on him eloquently.

A curved dagger appeared before Vivan's eyes, with which Hope made an ominous move. He will cut his pants in a moment...

Vivan made the captain meet only the hard gaze of his glowing eyes. His only defense in this situation, though inside he struggled with an overwhelming panic.

Hope felt a warning pain in his chest. He smiled as only a madman could, without bothering himself with it. He would scare him pretty well; he was sure of that.

Only the dagger at the neck made him realize that there had been an ominous silence around for a long time...

"Hope," said one of the sailors sharply, covered in thick tattoos, even on his face, "I advise you to get up, right now!"

"Vincent!" Hope hissed angrily, not feeling any fear for a moment, but angry that his fun was interrupted. "You mean, treacherous viper!"

"If you want to teach him a lesson, have him flogged again!" The pirate ordered him menacingly. "But don't touch his ass, do you understand?"

"If I don't fuck him, we'll be scared for our lives until the end of the cruise! Do you understand, you blunt noodle?"

"If you fuck him, he won't be good for anything!"

"He still has flesh and blood. Hair, tears, and semen if you need to! I don't need his soul!"

Vivan sprang up abruptly, taking advantage of captain's distraction. With a strong right hook, as his grandfather had taught him, he hit Hope in the jaw before anyone could stop him. Hope stumbled from the blow, more from surprise than from pain. But he couldn't hit him, because the crew hastily stopped them. Angry that he had to yield, he looked at him grimly.

"You'll pay me for this!" Vivan shouted meanwhile, struggling in the hands of the sailors. "I'm not your property, Hope!"

"Yes, you are," Hope replied coldly, filling his eyes with his impotent anger, "You are here to serve us. By all possible means."

"In your sick dreams!"

"Shut him up, or I'll do it," the captain ordered, making a careless gesture with his hand as if he were pushing away an intrusive fly.

In response, most of the crew pulled their cutlasses toward him. He raised his eyebrows in disappointment. These fools had a little filthy respect for the healer. It would not be too prudent to play with him. He realized that he had to respect their will if he still wanted to be captain of the Witch.

He straightened, pulling his victim by the chain to the hoop around his neck like a disobedient dog. Vivan looked at the crying woman sitting on the floor, surrounded by sailors. He grabbed the chain. He jerked violently to help her up. Then he placed her in front of him, shielding her body from the others.

"Touching..." Hope mocked at the sight.

He looked closely at the people around him, ending up with the sailor who first threatened him.

"I'm listening, goddamn it!" He shouted impatiently. "What conditions are you setting?!"

Give him only five lashes and send him back to the deck," Vincent ordered. "I know your greed, Hope. You think I don't know what you are storing in the chest?" He pointed to the chest by the wall. "There are blood and torn shirt of the healer!" Vivan looked at the captain with contempt. "You count on huge profits because you know that what you have now is worth more than many pirate treasures!" the sailors began to murmur among themselves. "And you are still not enough! You want more, that's why you bully him! I'm telling you - five lashes and that's it!"

Hope measured the sailor with a mocking glance mixed with irony and anger. Then he looked at Vivan and the young woman hugging him.

"That's all?" He asked with a crooked smile. "What about the girl?"

"Give her back to us!" Several voices rose before Vincent opened his mouth.

"Agreed!" He replied coldly.

Several volunteers immediately grabbed the woman by the shoulders, trying to yank Vivan out of her grip. She started scream. Vivan didn't mince words. His eyes glowed with a dangerous glow again. Chaos reigned. Hope lasted only a moment, losing patience with the whole situation.

"What the hell are you waiting for?!" He shouted to his men. "Take him away from her!"

It was easier said than done. Neither of them let themselves be separated, despite the fact that many people tried to do so.

"Damn it!" Vincent shouted finally, looking at the desperate struggle between both of them.

He pulled a dagger from his belt and without hesitation plunged it into the woman's heart...

"No!" Vivan shouted, but the mortally wounded let go of him, weakening immediately.

They no longer let him come near her.

She died during the crew's curses, disappointed in Vincent's deed, who responded to the healer's accusing gaze with a calm nod. Vivan understood, but at the same time was unable to accept the fact. What was this place? What kind of people were deciding the fate of others now? But worst of all was the feeling that nothing could be prevented. It cannot change this reality or help. This time he was left with only resistance, which meant little. It didn't change anything.

He was quickly dragged to the mast to be punished.

"What you doing?!" Yelled the captain, seeing that they wanted to cut the coat. "You don't appreciate a decent job! This is the work of a master tailors," he smoothed the fabric. "Take it off!"

Torn by Matt and the people, Vivan saw the tattooed sailor pick up the woman's body and walk across the deck, then toss her overboard. He couldn't thank him for the shortening of her suffering, though he felt he should.

He offered her a better death. But it was death, after all.

"Five times, Captain!" Vincent remarked as he approached them.

Matt handed the captain his whip, again not wanting to hurt the healer. He watched captain with an angry look as he snatched it away from him, remembering the faces of the first rebels well. Especially one of them.

"I wanted to take the dog out today..." he pulled the chain by the rim. "But you must have spoiled my mood again!" he shouted to Vivan. "You're rebelling my crew against me!" His face twisted angrily. "Do you think I'll give you back to Azram?! Let the demons rise up if that happens now! You belong to me! And you'll bleed on this ship for the rest of your life!"

He swung with all his might.

Vivan closed his eyes...

When Sel had to leave the cabin, he couldn't find a place for himself. Ross ordered them to get ready to fight the Blood Witch as soon as they had breakfast. So, the sailors hung around the guns and checked their weapons. This and that also took care of the girls. For now, the bolder ones, like Marlene and the sisters of the dancers, hung around them in search of a suitable weapon. Valeria had a lot of it. After she fell into their hands, then called Cadelia, Sel, Alvaro and the blacksmith Azylas started to work with her. First, the ship was heavy. Despite the removal of many unnecessary ornaments and sculptures, showing too much admiration for the wealth of the previous owners, the replacement of many materials for lighter ones, and the use of Sel's new inventions, Valeria was still and was to remain the Fat Lady. That was the name Alvaro used when Ross didn't hear. The Fat Lady, 65 meters long and 1,500 tons heavy, reached a maximum speed of 8 knots after numerous combinations, unless magic intervened. Then even 22 knots. It was therefore the fastest ship in these waters. With a very durable hull.

It had a beautiful staircase leading to the captain's bridge, an impressive bell, many berths and a lot of hiding places in which treasures, documents and weapons were kept. Few people knew about their exact number on the ship.

Oliver joined Sai, already giving instructions to Lena. Victor was checking his crossbow. There was a strange triangular box at the waist, though that might not be the proper name. A dark object that seemed to shine protruded from this strange triangle.

"What is this?" Sel asked, intrigued by the shape of the object.

Victor looked at him thoughtfully.

"You are smart in such matters," he said slowly, busy with the crossbow. "You enjoy various news from our world, I know. Would you like to know about them..."

"Dad," Lena gently admonished him, "Sel is a great inventor and you know it."

"But he doesn't know that," Victor replied with a sly smirk.

"I told you why. They don't know many things here yet."

They. Lena rarely used this phrase. Just when it came to technology. Sometimes about medicine or religion.

Victor smirked in response. Sel wondered if he should be offended. While Vivan's grandfather finally took Ross into his heart, thus proving to everyone that a lot can be changed when it comes to upbringing and tolerance, his attitude towards Sel was, however, much cooler. Sel knew the cause. In Victor's eyes, Ross was what he was. But Sel had had a wife once, led a normal life. Now he was living with a man, and that was even more difficult for Victor, older than him, than Ross's behavior. It was almost a betrayal.

For this reason, Victor held a grudge against Sel, which he hid from Ross.

"You're not going to show me this?" Sel asked, remaining calm solely for the sake of his partner, who liked the man a lot. "You don't have to!" He remarked, intending to leave immediately, before the quarrel started.

It was then that he bumped into Cora, the gentle-eyed woman whose gaze reminded him of Vivan. He immediately apologized to her, and she replied with a polite smile that was meant to keep men at distance. She didn't have to do that with him, he thought. He sensed that there had been a change in her from the moment she tasted Vivan's blood. He knew her symptoms. Thunder struck softly but hard and decisively the moment he saw Ross for the first time... Then, like the girl now, he hadn't realized it. Circumstances were also not favorable. And yet... He watched as Cora asked Lena to come with her to the captain's cabin. He might have been interested if it weren't for Victor, who grabbed his arm. He unexpectedly pressed the object into his other hand, which intrigued him immensely.

"This is a gun," he explained matter-of-factly. "From the war in our world, Sel. You are just getting to know gunpowder here, which is why Lena asked me not to use it. Unfortunately, we live in such and not other times. You may have to use it. Then I won't look back at anything."

As an inventor, Sel immediately focused on it, while Lena and Cora flew away.

"It's working," Victor explained, "I care about it."

"How it works?" He asked, looking at the item curiously.

"I can show you; you are good in this!" Victor said matter-of-factly. Sel almost smiled. He just heard a compliment from his lips, which is rare. While Vivan's grandfather undoubtedly valued his skill, he tried to show admiration so that Sel was unlikely to notice. All interested parties in the immediate circle of both of them, who were somewhat amused by the old man's behavior, kindly informed Sel of any kind words about his inventions. Sometimes he himself had the opportunity to observe the quiet appreciation of Victor, who was puzzling like Sel, clueless about the technique of his world, had this or that idea. Vivan once laughed in a conversation with Victor, when they both thought they were alone, that the shed by their palace would explode from these experiments. On Valeria, Ross's pearl, no potentially dangerous thing was allowed to be investigated or any daredevil who dared to do so would be flogged with nettles, as the captain himself pointed out.

As the thought unexpectedly turned to his friend, Sel felt regret. A fucking fate that brought such misfortune on Vivan!

"Stand here!" Victor ordered him, while several people watched the whole scene with curiosity.

Tenan approached slowly, as did Sel, curious about the object's operation.

Meanwhile, Victor was giving Sel a short lesson...

"Stand like this," he commanded, "shoulder like this! Find your target... Oh, yes," he said, pleased. "And now everyone will be watching, because I don't use bullets for fun." He loaded the gun, handed it to Sel. "There," he pointed to the training target, away from people. He touched his thumb on the trigger. "Pull the trigger. Now!"

Sel obeyed.

The bang scared almost everyone. There were shouts here and there. Surprised by the operation of the gun, Sel lowered his pistol. He stared in disbelief now, as did everyone else, at the hole through which the sky could be seen.

Right in the middle of the shield.

"Nice shot," Victor commented, taking the pistol from a surprised Sel. "Now you know what I have. And you have a good eye. You are born to be a warrior. You will deal with everything," he leaned towards him, so that others would not hear his words and, convinced that this was the end, they departed for their activities. "But why are you so strange?"

He left as soon as Sel could think of an answer. He met Tenan's gaze...

He was standing by Maya, examining the sword that had just been chosen for her.

For a moment it looked as if the man was about to say something, perhaps a compliment to his accuracy. But after a moment he changed his mind and pursed his lips. It suddenly occurred to Sel that he might like it. He would like to hear something friendly from this man's lips. Everyone treated him so friendly and respectful. Maya stood by him, letting him teach her how to wield the sword, if only to a basic degree. Completely at ease.

She didn't see what he saw...

He turned his back to him before the warm thought could sprout in action.

Ross was already sitting on the bench in front of the cabin, absent again in spirit. He paled like linen in front of his eyes. It made Sel forget about all other matters immediately. He was beside him, silently sitting down. He slowly realized what had happened. He felt his eyes welling up with tears, more with anger than with regret.

The jewel showed him.

In the midst of people busy with conversation, exercise and daily routine... Amid carefree laughter and friendly jokes... Somewhere in the ocean in front of them. At the same time as breakfast was being started... The captain was flogging their friend again... Vivan was suffering again.

Ross tightened his hand on the hilt of his sword until his fingers turned white.

Sel looked at him with a mixture of relief and concern at the same time. At least this time his lover did not suffer with Vivan. It does not change the fact that something happened again, which strongly influenced not only their friend. He was afraid for Ross. For his health. His life…

The jewel glowed faintly to the beat of the heart.

"I will murder him, Sel!" Ross said finally, his voice full of suppressed rage.

Sel closed his eyes for a moment, pondering silently.

"Do you know why he does this to him?" He asked softly.

Ross looked at him, nodding silently.

Sel, who had previously tried to convince him to give up the fight with the Red Captain by handing it over to him, was now sure Ross would not listen to him. He won't listen to anyone anymore. He was not as vindictive as he put it in words. But the pain and grief were as great as the heart can feel, sensitive to the harm of loved ones.

They sat in silence as long as the flogging lasted.

Ross got up. Many people had been watching him stealthily for a long time, fearing future visions. He realized that he looks and feels worse and worse. The recent events had an impact on his psyche, barely giving him time to rest.

He had to make some important decisions.

"Sel," he looked at his partner. "I need to talk to Tenan. It is very important."

He didn't really ask him. He knew he needed to have this conversation, but he didn't want Sel to feel removed in any way. Though Sel had no degree on board, he was more of an advisor, builder, and cartographer, Ross was always careful to show him how important he was to him. They made many decisions together, supporting each other in overcoming difficulties. Some things Ross was on his instincts, and then Sel pulled away, knowing that if he could take his gut feeling, they would come out of it unscathed. It always worked.

"I see," Sel replied, trying to hide his anxiety as usual in such cases.

Ross walked over to him. Though the steps to the bridge on either side were equidistant from the bench they had sat on earlier, Ross passed his lover only to brush his hand over his.

When the fingers touched, they met their eyes for one moment.

They showed affection among people discreetly. Not because they were afraid of the opinions of others. They didn't care about that. They were only trying to maintain the intimacy, the apparent randomness in a secret caress that inflamed the senses.

Ross needed this now, and a lot more, but he couldn't even dream about it right now. He had discovered long ago that love was his power.

"Hang on, damn it!" Sel said suddenly, taking his hand before walking away.

He looked at him again with a gaze of unfettered tenderness. Everything he would like to express in words is included here. In silence. In the reflection of his eyes. Suddenly he was afraid that something might take him away due to inconceivable forces. He didn't know where he had come to think of it. The thought made him uneasy.

He couldn't lose it.

Ross smiled shyly, making him feel more tender. He loved that smile the most about him. He was so innocent, meant only for him.

"Sel," he said softly, feeling the eyes of those present, thankfully too far away to hear them, "I must go now..."

"Do you remember?" The words broke suddenly. Darkness was slowly enveloping their lives, Vivan was hurt again, and Ross was suffering with him just hours before. So he had to talk about it now. To break free, even for a moment, from this insane trap by taking him with him. Only now he had the opportunity, he could feel it. Before the world takes their freedom, it forces them to rush to a gloomy future, where one event after another could turn into a nightmare.

"Lots of things," Ross said gently.

He pulled his arm into the shadow of the stairs so that they would no longer be viewed with such curiosity.

"We are running out of time..." the beloved began, and then Sel asked softly:

"Do you remember our first night?"

Ross opened his mouth, but the words dared not come out.

"At the House of Pleasure..." Sel reminded him, although he did not need to be reminded, "I told you that never before..."

"I remember," he gasped, hearing the rush of blood in his ears.

How could he forget? It was then that he began to feel again. As if his heart awoke from a deep sleep under a blanket of snow. Against everything he decided to do.

"I wasn't scared for a moment. I told you," Sel blurted out the words, not wanting to lose his mind of what he really wanted to say to him now. Finally, remove from their memories the words of Seme that entered their souls. "I said I wanted it. I want to be with you!"

"Yes..." Ross whispered.

He also remembered that after that night he was afraid that there would be no tomorrow. Sel would not come to him anymore. The next day he asked mother to let him rest. He couldn't pull himself together. It lasted for several days. That's when she told him, "Ross... You know you don't have to do this. Violet and I snatched you from death. I never wanted you to sell yourself. You thought you would chase away your own demons this way."

Sel was returning. Until he decided to marry Milera to save her from ruin.

With this decision, he almost broke his heart.

"I trusted you," said Sel meanwhile. "And so, it is today. Now I'm asking you - you, trust me. Don't create obstacles that are not there. Will you do it finally?"

"Sel," he whispered, touched.

Sel embraced him tightly, torn by emotion and anxiety.

"I love you," he confessed softly. "Remember that..."

Lena was sitting inside the captain's cabin.

Cora sat down next to her, taking her warm hand. She stroked it slowly, comfortingly. It was becoming easier and easier for her to understand from the observations of people close to him that something bad had happened to Vivan again.

She remembered his gaze. That look of despair as it cannot help them.

He tried...

She heard about how he killed people in the marketplace and a witch in his land. He stopped their hearts. This moment when you are sure that there is no other way is painful for many good people. She heard these stories. His power helped people. She could only imagine how difficult it must have been especially for him.

The killing was certainly a terrible experience. Whatever the reasons. Therefore, he only killed these people in the marketplace when they forced him to do so.

The witch, on the other hand, perished, almost dragging him into the embrace of death.

He didn't want to kill anyone.

"Why are you sitting like at a funeral?" she heard Violet's voice suddenly, "Cora?"

"My son is suffering again," Lena replied softly, "and we are still too far away to help him..."

She wasn't looking at them, lost in her own painful thoughts, maybe even in visions of what the other women couldn't see.

"Are you Vivan's mother?" Violet asked softly, surprised.

Lena looked at her through tears. Now Violet had found it easy for mother to resemble her son. Eye color, though less blue than Vivan's. Their expressions, facial features. Hair color. Thick, dark eyebrows.

This was not the time for admiration, so Violet refrained from making any comments. But she mentally admired again the effect of Vivan's gift. The young woman in front of her could be her daughter.

Incredible, but it was possible for him. She put aside those empty delights. She knew well what it meant to be a mother, though her son had never experienced even a part of such love as Vivan.

"Spinner," she said gently. "Do you know what is happening with him now?"

"I know one thing," Lena replied in a low voice. "Someone made my son suffer. Whoever it is, I want him to pay for it!"

Violet nodded solemnly.

"Me too!" She replied firmly.

The body of an innocent woman floated on the water.

No wave could wash away the stain of blood on the dress where the stopped heart was hidden underneath.

Her hair rose around her face like a dark crown.

Her eyes were half open, as if she was squinting them against the glare.

Nothing could move her anymore. Even when the scaly ridge appeared next to her...

The blow of the snaky tail shattered the waves.

The creature swam around the abandoned body as if wondering.

Then it grabbed it instantly.

A ship appeared on the horizon. By the time it swam, there was nothing left on the surface of the water.

Valeria swam over where the monster had previously appeared.

She was approaching the Blood Witch.

She had company.

CHAPTER 16

He was below deck again. This time Matt knew what to do. He brought Eric in immediately. Meanwhile, Kim ordered that food be served. As if nothing happened.

The captain used all the anger he had at that moment to inflict pain on him. The sailors immediately regretted their approval. Especially since it wouldn't have ended up five times if they hadn't stopped him. Vincent helped bring him back. He probably felt guilty about the situation, but... he didn't stop him from lashing.

The healer's blood was tremendously precious.

The pain penetrated deeper than Vivan remembered from the previous time.

He felt as if in some places an attempt was being made to cut him in half. This time it was stronger. Eric looked at them angrily. Maybe it would be better to put on the seams? Applying the previous method would also cause Vivan more suffering.

The blood was still dripping.

Of one thing he was sure: even if he had told the healer to stop standing at every turn, Vivan would not have obeyed him. This was not a man who silently watches the suffering of others. Eric was convinced that if Vivan remained in the hands of Witch's Captain, he would die one day, he would probably be whipped to death. Such nobility in people spoiled by evil only causes aggression. This boy did not realize yet that his days were already numbered.

No matter what the crew do, the captain will get it.

He sat down next to the wounded man, wanting to collect his thoughts for a moment before he started.

Eric, Vivan whispered.

He felt a chill engulfing him. It made him tremble in pain, adding torment to him.

The medic approached him.

Vivan just glanced to see if Matt was around. The latter got into a conversation with the sentries, eating his portion. The prisoners were given nothing to eat.

"Free Tipe," Vivan ordered the medic, his voice breaking, "He's the one who got the whips right after me."

"Are you crazy?!"

"You have to help us!" Vivan's hand tightened on his. "Free him! I can't beat them alone!"

"Beat?! What are you talking about?"

"If you free him, no one will ever raise a hand against us," Vivan assured him, tears of pain streaming down his face. Memories also played their part. "Help us all, please!"

"I'm a medic, not a suicide..." Eric began hesitantly.

Vivan looked at him meaningfully. Eric felt stupid. This man was not afraid to risk his life for the benefit of others, and he lacked courage? What would Cora have thought of him?

"I will help you," Vivan assured him as calmly as he could, "but first you must help us!"

He closed his eyes.

Eric looked at him hesitantly.

Upstairs, the crew ate their meals, and downstairs as well. Seemingly nothing disturbing happened. After a while he heard the first yawn.

Matt and one of the sentries sat down, leaning against the stairs. They ate their bread slower and slower. Until they stopped eating and started to snore. They fell asleep with bites of bread in their mouths.

The second guard sat down at the bunk entrance. He set the cup down.

He also fell asleep.

Vivan's breathing slowed.

"Mother Earth..." Eric whispered, suddenly understanding everything.

Now. He can't hesitate!

"Hang on! I'll be back to you soon!" He promised the wounded man who gave him time to act.

He took the keys of the shackles from the sleeper by the bunk. He reassured the prisoners with a thumbs-up gesture. They understood.

He walked over to the dark-skinned man indicated by Vivan. Tipe straightened proudly, waiting to be released. Only once did he look with concern at the wounded healer, already focused on the ideas he intended to implement. He knew that they might not have such an opportunity anymore, so he was going to take full advantage of it. He did not want to disappoint the hope placed in him.

"Quick!" Eric ordered him nervously.

"Vivan!" Ross shouted in his mind, standing on the captain's bridge, "It will be soon."

"I forbade you to sail here."

"I will not let you die!" He clenched his hand into a fist, throwing him reproachfully in his mind.

After a moment that seemed to go on forever, Vivan replied:

"And I won't let you die there."

"Captain?" Silas, at the helm, looked at him questioningly.

Ross straightened up immediately.

"Do you already know what to do?" he made sure.

"Captain, I don't even want to hear about it..."

"You have to!" He ordered him firmly, "Silas, you are my best man on this ship. He has no idea about it."

"I understand, Captain, but that doesn't mean I accept it," his first mate replied gravely. "You are and will remain my captain. Captain of Valeria."

"Thank you," he looked into his eyes, seeing only friendship there. "Summon Tenan."

"Aye!" Silas nodded. "The captain calls to the bridge, Keeper of Secrets!" He exclaimed, pointing to Tenan, surprised by the title.

"Keeper of Secrets?" Ross asked, raising his eyebrows quietly as the summoned walked up the stairs.

"I found the title appropriate, Captain," explained the first, somewhat confused, "Besides, I don't know his name."

Ross smiled slightly.

"Captain Hope," Tenan bowed slightly. "You summoned me?"

"Yes," Ross replied. "Our plans have changed. I have to be prepared for anything. Let me explain something to you..." He approached him to make the conversation more confidential. Fortunately, they all took care of other things as if on cue. "I'm making you a Keeper, as Silas mentioned. The keeper and protector of our ship people."

"I suspected that I should watch the safety of women..."

"You will make sure everyone reaches Leviron safely, Tenan. I appoint you the expedition commander, keeper, guide and whatever you want. The most important thing is that you drive people home. Use any means to do so."

There was silence.

"Ross..." Tenan began, skipping the title. "You are Valeria's Captain. I cannot..."

"I gave the order!"

"But I'm not a crew member! Explain it to me, or I'll bring Sel over here immediately, who'll put you over his knee and belt your ass for this ridiculous idea!"

"Shh..." Ross ordered him, glancing at Sel, who regarded them suspiciously from below.

"Tell me what's going on!" Tenan hissed softly.

"The Red Captain will expect me to fight him," Ross began, trying to shut down his fear as he said the words. "As you mentioned, I'm the captain..."

"This is crazy!" Tenan replied immediately, his voice still low, seeing Ross' gesture to keep calm, "You can't beat him!"

"Thank you for believing in me so much..." Ross made an ironic tone. "I feel more confident right away."

"You know that so far you have had more luck than skills..."

Ross looked at him meaningfully. Tenan paused, hardly waiting for the continuation.

"Someone has to take care of the crew and the people in case I'm gone," he explained seriously.

Tenan didn't speak anymore, looking at him in a way that was enough for any words. Out of the corner of his eye he saw only Silas, who turned around with obvious concern.

"I thought..." Ross sighed, feeling the weight of fear and concern in his heart at the same time, "that I must take care of it. Someone has to take care of them all, even if not everyone wants them." He looked meaningfully at Sel downstairs, occupied by a crate by the side, the ropes of which departed towards the sails, towards the mirrors mounted by the sailors. He had no idea what he and Alvaro had put together this time, but they obviously had a reason. "You're the most appropriate person in this time of chaos."

"Ross..." the right words did not come to mind.

"I've had many roles in my life..." Ross began again, this time looking into his eyes. "I was a bastard. The streeter. A helper. A lover. The victim," Tenan looked at him understandingly. "Also, a male whore. A lover for life and death. Friend. Part of a big family. Finally - the Jewel Sorcerer. But now I'm, first and foremost, the captain of this ship!" He stressed. "As a captain, I have to be responsible for the people on board! I'm responsible for their protection and safety. That is why I entrust their fate to the hands of a man whom I know will surely guide them, that he can keep a cool head when others get lost in their emotions. You are such a man, Tenan!"

"I am not, I am a shadow of whoever you knew anything about!" He interrupted abruptly.

"We both know that's not true," Ross said calmly. "So, I ask... Will you do it for me? Will you take care of them if I'm gone?"

"With an emphasis on it," Tenan pointed out.

Ross waited silently for an answer. Tenan considered, dragging out a decision he had already made.

"I promise you," he said gravely.

Ross replied with a firm handshake.

"Thank you," he replied. "I will write the relevant documents in a moment."

"Lady," began one of the deckhands, "It's too much of a risk."

"You said yourselves that this ship..." Vashaba pointed in front of them. "That it must be Valeria."

"Yes, my lady," confirmed another seaman. "But it is dangerous to go in a boat here."

"It's always dangerous here," said the deckhand, who was the first to persuade her, hurriedly, "These are the waters of the Bay. Various strange creatures swim here..."

Chills ran down her spine as she heard the tone of his voice.

"Well," she said proudly, "you don't want to catch up with Valeria, so I'm taking the boat. I paid for it!"

"Aye!" Agreed the captain of the smuggling schooner who had taken her, marking this statement with a spit aside in disgust. "But it seems to me that even the elves cannot cope with what is sitting in these waters."

"It's none of your business anymore," she replied somewhat rude, glancing nervously at the ship.

"We don't want to meet the Sorcerer, even if it's the only good thing about this place," the captain explained, while Vashaba waited for her boat to drop. "The Troublemaker is cunning. He can deceive the monsters into eating us instead of him..."

"Who told you such nonsense about Ross?!" she got upset. "You don't want to - ok. I will go alone!"

"Good luck, lady elf! It will certainly come in handy…" The captain bowed with a malicious smile.

She drifted away, muttering curses under her breath. Brazen fools! Eventually, she will catch up Ross, and then...

A boom and a deafening crack interrupted her thoughts suddenly, making her scared. She looked back again.

The schooner split in two under the blow of mighty tail. The crew raised a desperate cry as a great reptilian head peeked out of the ocean. What came out of his throat was a loud hiss. The mighty sea serpent tightened its tail in a loop on the unfortunate schooner until the boards flew out. Sharp teeth gleamed in the sun as he began his hunt. The first to die was the captain, crushed in the grip of his jaws. The blood of the next beast gushed from the mouth of the beast, furiously attacking its victims. The waters of the ocean ruffled at her sudden movements as she hunted the still living eagerly.

Vashaba squeezed the oars tighter, trembling with fear. She had to swim without looking back.

It was impossible to help them...

"Ship! Ship, Captain!" A brief torn from the crow's nest a moment earlier. "It's a Bloody Witch!"

Ross froze. His heart leapt into his throat. When he could plan in peace, trying to anticipate everything, it was much easier.

The time has come.

He swallowed nervously.

"Hope you're all set!" He shouted aloud to Silas to show the others that he wasn't scared, which was obviously one big lie.

He always had the Jewel...

"Yes, Captain!" Silas replied, as did he, trying to sound confident for the sake of the passengers "Ship ready to be boarded!"

Ross smiled knowingly at Sel.

"When was the last time we did this, Sel?"

Sel pretended to be calm as if it were one of their many adventures that had not been missing over the past year, with Valeria already officially sailing the waters.

"Last year, before winter. The Invincible said goodbye to his name when we got him and then took the imprisoned."

"A few rich men among them generously showered us with gold for this feat," Ross added, smiling mysteriously.

"Because of you," commented Sel with the shadow of a smile.

"I just offered them that they should be grateful for their help. Valeria needed new sails..."

"You and your Valeria!" Sel shook his head, looking at him with emotion.

Then he said silently, looking him straight in the eye:

"I LOVE YOU."

Ross was about to answer him when a sudden bang, and a moment later the scream of a crow's nest deckhand interrupted their conversation.

"Captain, sea serpent! Big as a mountain!" he pointed in the opposite direction.

Ross looked quickly through the spyglass while almost everyone was watching the sea tragedy. He felt a mounting unease. He had so many people close to him on board. A faithful crew. He wasn't going to lose them!

Sel took over the scope.

"There is a boat," he remarked. "It's flowing towards us!"

Ross looked ahead. They were approaching the Witch.

"They wouldn't be safe with us anyway," he muttered.

"Captain?" Silas looked questioningly.

"Full power ahead!" ordered him. "Our plans do not change! We're sailing for the Bloody Witch!" he emphasized emphatically.

"Aye, Captain!" The first replied without hesitation.

Ross took a deep breath.

Now!

"Everyone in position!" He commanded. "Cannons on the right side!"

The crew frantically began maneuvers. The Witch was getting closer. In a moment they will be able to see them at a distance of a crossbow shot.

"Max!" He called up. "What about that snake?!"

"He's following us, Captain!" The boy replied with obvious fear.

"Just what we need," Ross muttered to Sel and Silas, standing next to him. "Lower the boats on the left!" He ordered firmly. The order was handed over quickly and the implementation began. "Quickly, gentlemen, this is not some fest! Oren!"

"Yes, Captain?" Said a sailor with a talent for tailoring.

"Flag!"

"Aye, Captain!"

"Nils!" He called to another. "Ring the bell!"

"Aye!" Shouted the broad-shouldered sailor, rushing to the bell. The rest were work like billyo, summoned by the lower ranks."

"Aren't you worried about boats?" Sel asked, looking back.

Ross did the same and immediately regretted it. The waves raged behind the sea serpent, in a rush almost sliding over their surface.

"I'm more worried about people," he replied anxiously.

The snake dove into the depths, almost right behind them.

"Tenan!" Ross did not dare order Victor, even in such a situation. "There are too many people aboard!"

"Yes, Captain Hope!" This time Tenan did not discuss the matter. "Go back below deck!"

"Are you kidding?!" exclaimed exuberant Marlene immediately. "I'm not going anywhere! We're going to meet the Witch soon!"

"Meet the saved life, woman!" A skinny sailor cried nearby.

"Captain?!" she yelled towards the sternum with reproach. "Girls! They want to bury us here like some luggage! Are we giving up?!"

"Shit!" Sel swore, hiding a smile as Ross gave more orders, "Here comes Violet..."

"Of course not!" Violet yelled at it, standing so that Ross could see her, "Captain, there is my crew and a healer on the Witch! I will not hide below deck like a rat!"

"There is Vivan!" Sai, to Oliver's amazement, stood beside her, proudly raising her head.

Oliver joined her, silently admitting they were both right with a shrug.

"For the pirates!" Violet called, holding her fist up.

"For the pirates!" The dark-haired Apara called.

"FOR THE PIRATES!" Everyone on board shouted.

The crowd looked at the captain.

"Oh," Ross replied softly, reflecting.

Everyone waited for his words. He held them in this uncertainty for a moment, savoring it before the captain's loud, firm voice exclaimed:

"All right then! From now on, you are all crew members of this ship! You are to obey my orders! Understand?!" He did not wait for an answer, because time was pressing. "To the positions! Weapons on standby! Get ready to board! FOR THE PIRATES!" He finished in a loud voice.

The old and new parts of the crew shouted joyfully.

"Aye, Captain Hope!" Violet cried, gripping the ax tighter in her hands.

"Do I really have something else to say here?" Ross muttered ironically to his companions, seeing how everyone tried to obey orders. The new ones surrendered to the three-hundred-person crew that had commanded so far. The commands were interrupted by the last moments of peace.

"Always, Captain," Silas replied. "Unless you hand over the ship to her," he added with apparent carelessness.

The captain glared at him, which Silas didn't care too much about.

Ross looked away from what was happening on the ship. They were approaching the Witch. He rubbed his temple with his index finger.

"I need to focus..." he said seriously, pushing aside any other thoughts.

"Where are you?" He asked mentally.

As Eric retired to the bunk currently occupied by Vivan, Tipe released two of his men.

All prisoners were soon free.

"Let women and children keep quiet!" He ordered sharply.

As he had ordered, silence fell among the crowd. Several people tied up and gagged the sentries.

Eric prepared everything that he might need. This time, he had both salt and enough rum. He even considered breaking his promise and burning the wounds, although he decided to spare his patient the stapling. He had no helper. He would have to deal with that as well. He reached for the rum and took a sip.

"You'd better have a drink too," he said gently.

But Vivan didn't want to get up.

"Stop! A woman's voice said suddenly in a soft, firm tone. "Don't do it!"

A woman from such warm islands as Tipe, with skin as dark as he, approached them quickly.

"It's enough of this suffering!" she pointed out firmly.

"He's gonna bleed out..."

"Nena," she introduced herself. "Do you love someone?"

"What? What does this have now...?!"

"Answer, please."

"I loved," he replied impatiently, "they're dead now!"

Tipe gathered a group of the best armed, ordering them to stand behind him. The rest lined up behind. Women and children stayed where they were. He looked determinedly up the stairs.

"Ask yourself," he said softly to those present. "Do you want to rot in the Bay or live as free people?"

"Or die," one of the men said sarcastically.

"Die then! I will die when I want it myself!" He hissed angrily. "Now I'm going to fight and win! Who else thinks like that? Who is going with me?!"

Most of them immediately raised their hands in a gesture of determination.

Tipe looked at the injured one last time. Vivan clenched his hand into a fist, showing his support. Tipe nodded at him with the respect due to the faith practiced on the islands in his part. One by one they looked at the wounded man, remembering previous events.

Bernadette's crew. Women and men who decided to fight for common freedom.

He was a hero to them.

His determination and suffering fueled their anger. Vivan knew there might be many among them whom he would never again see alive. He would never know them better. He tried to remember their faces watching him for that one moment. Keep this amazing image in his memory.

"So, I will ask otherwise," he heard Nena's voice suddenly. "Do you care about him? Do you want him to heal?"

"Of course..." replied Eric.

"Then make it happen!" she ordered him. "Because only the warmth of our hearts can cure love... That's how it works. He helps us and we help him. People forget it, as do you, because all too often they only care about themselves."

Tipe smiled at Vivan with brotherly tenderness.

"Get well, healer," he said warmly. As if he wasn't going to fight in a moment. Violence had not yet overshadowed his good thoughts. The memory of home and instilled respect.

The others also smiled at Vivan before climbing the stairs to seal their fate. A sincere, not contaminated by anger feeling. Each of them said goodbye to him with a cheering smile.

They left.

After a while there were screams and sounds of fighting.

"Look!" Nena whispered softly to Eric.

The wounds on Vivan's back began to heal. Close.

They turned into narrow scars.

And unlike many other wounds... they disappeared without a trace.

The smile of those going to fight was filled with happiness.

"It's good that you are with us."

The enslaved had only one option to gain the upper hand. They just needed to get weapons as soon as possible. Disarm battle-hardened pirates. Few had any chance.

And yet... Initially, they gained the upper hand. They were helped by the attack of the sea snake on the unfortunate schooner, which distracted the crew and captain, delighted with the vision of fighting the greatest enemy in these waters, flowing the magnificent Valeria. They followed her as she prepared the ship for boarding. They considered the appearance of the sea monster a good omen, but the creature dived into the depths and had not yet appeared.

"Captain!" Tipe called after he snatched the machete from one of the pirates' hands.

Hope looked at him with a certain impatience. He was waiting for another match and it was a pity to waste time on that darkey. He stared at him coldly. This man won't be able to change his plans... He must die quickly.

Vivan got up. Nena handed him her coat with a friendly smile. Eric was glad that he did not have to cause him suffering.

They both agreed that they would be of better use here in treating the wounded, which should be soon.

In fact, this resolution became their only defense against fear. They did not know who would win this fight and what would happen to their fate. If Tipe had been defeated, the fate of Nena, as well as the fate of other women, both of the four mothers of the children aged ten, twelve and those above, would be doomed. As for Eric, his skill might have saved him, but that too would depend on the humor of the winning crew and the captain himself.

Mothers and children touched the healer in a gesture of welcome. He barely responded to their smiles with the same gesture. They couldn't sense the same as he... And he had to do it. He did not want to lead to an even bigger massacre. Chances were good they'd get the ship before Ross arrived. Fewer people will die. Tipe will defeat the captain...

Suddenly he sat up abruptly, feeling dizzy.

What was he imagining?!

Everyone will kill themselves there! It will be carnage!

Eric ordered the women and children to hide in the bunk.

Vivan closed his eyes. He recognized emotions.

Tipe fought the Red Captain. Two men besieged Kim and stabbed him in his chest, taking revenge for murdered wives and children. Three women pounced on a certain pirate. One of them picked up the ball and wanted to drop it on his head.

Why did he feel worse and worse?

He already knew the answer.

His gift hated violence, anger and soreness.

The entire ship exuded a lust for fight and revenge. Defeated women were cruelly murdered. Men had their throats slashed, their limbs cut off, and they rejoiced at their suffering. There was no dignity in the fight. It covered the deck with blood. This is how Ross and those who come with him were going to fight?! Was this madness to embrace them as well? Who was swimming with him? He sensed that Lena was there.

Mom... Every heartbeat brought back images of childhood and mother's care.

She would kill?

There is no nobility of any kind in killing...

He wanted to get up and leave, against the protests of Eric, who had been trying to reach him for a long time, but to no avail. He took the first step towards the stairs, determined not to allow a massive battle, even if he himself was to fight Captain Hope...

Neither side of the warring party touched him. Meanwhile, Eric locked himself with the women in Kim's bunk, ready to defend them with a cutlass taken from the bound guard. The last bastion of the enslaved. Each of them had something to defend themselves with. Then suddenly he felt it.

"Where are you?" Asked a friend, "We see you."

They are already here...

Suddenly there was this familiar feeling.

He always knew when she went to him.

Quickly, like a red flame blown by the wind, her hair flickered in the sunlight that fell on the stairs. She carried that scent with her, drenched a little with sea salt and sweat. So dear to him, and so painful at the same time.

She fell into his arms, oblivious to the fighting around her, taking no danger at all.

"Vashaba…" he whispered with an involuntary shrug, surrounded by the warmth of her shoulders.

Surrounded by the touch of her lips, he was unable to say more.

"Come!" She ordered him, stepping back quickly. "I have a boat here!"

"What?!" he realized immediately.

All his fears returned.

"I'll take you to Ross…"

They went upstairs, where there were major fights. He let himself be led, surprised by her presence, happy… Wait, is that for sure? No, it wasn't luck. It was supposed to be, but it turned into something completely different. He felt an old fear. After all, it will never be like it used to be.

First, he saw the massive Valeria overboard. Then he looked at the deck.

Captain cut Tipe from the crutch to the up. Blood-stained clothes. The wounded man instinctively grasped under the influence of pain, boldly looking into the eyes of his murderer.

"Tipe..." Vivan broke free from her embrace, guided by his gift. "I have to help him!"

"Vivan!" She exclaimed impatiently.

"There are women and children in a locked cabin below the deck!" He said quickly, "Take them to the boat!"

She looked at him carefully, composed as when they first faced the witch Mayene two years ago. Suddenly his heart skipped a beat. With hope? Oh, how he wished she would come back! Just like it was then. His Guardian, she used to say. His lovely girlfriend.

He was on the verge of believing that this would be the case. He missed it so much.

"You know I won't leave you..." she began to say.

He remembered that moment. A beautiful, redheaded warrior. In clothes of masking colors, with a sword at his side, a bow in his hand. With a twinkle in his eyes.

He felt so much relief...

Before he knew it, a great wave flooded them from above. A massive tail hit the hull, meandering between the Witch and Valeria.

The sea monster has returned.

"What more, for fuck's sake?!" The Red Captain cried, furious, as chaos reigned on the deck. Almost everyone was frightened by a huge beast capable of crushing both ships like nutshells. Only this saved Tipe from another blow that would end his life.

Vivan froze for a moment as he saw the beast's head above his head.

But not for long. His instinct was deep within him, ignoring the danger.

"Tipe!" He shouted towards Vashaba, running to the wounded man.

Vashaba followed him, drawing an arrow from the quiver on her back. The captain looked at them sullenly.

Before the monster reappeared, Ross looked nervously through the spyglass again.

"What the hell is going on there?" Sel muttered.

"Rebellion," Ross replied.

"Are you sure?"

"Yes."

"What now?"

Ross looked at Silas a little helplessly.

"Cannons..." Silas began quietly, accustomed to the fact that an inexperienced captain must sometimes be assisted in making a decision.

"We can't shoot or we'll kill everyone..." Ross didn't understand.

Silas cocked his head significantly.

Ross nodded his thanks at him shortly before shouting,

"Don't shoot without orders!"

"Aye, Captain!" A few voices in reply.

"Prepare!"

He was wet with sweat under his sailor coat. On the other ship, he saw the Red Captain himself among the combatants.

He will kill him.

He wasn't allowed to think that. He has looked after the people and the ship! Vivan is counting on him.

No matter what he told him. It didn't matter now. By the demons, he was the captain of Valeria! Only that was important now.

He must give another sign!

"Vashaba?!" Sel snatched the spyglass from his hand. "Where did that leech come from?"

Ross involuntarily looked at him in surprise, distracted from his gloomy thoughts.

"Leech?!"

"Don't tell me you don't think that," Sel replied irritated. "She sucked on him like a greedy bi..."

"Sel!" He cut him off abruptly, glancing down at the deck.

Sel paused, realizing he had gone too far in his comment. He decided to express his opinion anyway.

"Sometimes I think she's worse than Mayene. And all because he trusts her..." he added very softly.

Perhaps Ross should have denied it now, but he couldn't.

"I know you agree with me," Sel looked at him, but he didn't answer. Not now. Not here. Not when Vivan could hear it...

"It's Vivan!" Oliver suddenly called. "Look, Vivan's over there!"

Ross looked hurriedly through the spyglass, grateful for the change of subject.

Vivan was discussing something with Vashaba. This time he had no shackles. Well, he was flogged again. Despite all these experiences, he moved very smoothly, without a frown on his face caused by the pain. And that could only mean one thing: something happened.

Ross smiled in relief. It was good news.

The ship, thanks to Silas and his commands, has just positioned sideways to the Witch. Ross thought he should think about the sides, not the sides... He forgot about it all the time.

The waves around him suddenly piled up as the sea serpent unfolded its tail between the two ships. Ross looked around. He looked fearfully at the further scrolls of the great monster. A mighty head rose from the depths to rise above them, obscuring the sun.

Ross looked down to the deck. There was only one thing in the faces of those present: fear.

CHAPTER 17

"Everyone in position! Cannons on both sides! Boats to the sides! Come on, move on!" The captain threw a series of orders to free them from this fear. "Crossbows ready! Don't shoot without orders!"

The crew tried to obey orders as quickly as possible, despite the strong rocking of the ship.

"Captain!" Violet yelled. "The snake entwines us!"

"I can see Violet!" He replied with apparent composure.

"Maybe we should shoot below the draft line after all?"

"How about giving him a snack?" He asked with a hint of anger. "What do you say, Violet? Do you prefer to be on a tray or jump off a board?"

The old crew laughed loudly. This relaxed the tense atmosphere a bit.

Violet blushed but didn't say a word more. She wasn't going to apologize, and Ross wasn't expecting that of her. She had learned a lesson.

"Silas!" He asked his faithful first mate. "Take care of the helm!"

"Captain, the snake is..."

"It's my worry, do you understand?" He looked at him significantly.

"Aye!"

"I'd sooner break his head than let him destroy Valeria!" Ross muttered angrily.

Vivan kept his hand over Tipe's cut wound. At first, the blood was draining out quickly, and if it weren't for the hands, perhaps the insides would have flooded out onto the deck. Tipe was holding the wound with a trembling hand, feeling it tighten under his fingers into a single whole. He followed the healer's blue eyes with his great astonishment, refusing to look down for fear he would lose all courage. He could feel the soothing warmth spreading through his body in waves. He felt neither cold nor pain. He glanced once or twice at the elven woman accompanying Vivan, about whom the recent stories in the ports had told. She watched the captain, who took advantage of the common fear of the opponents and ordered everyone, without exception, to defend the ship from the sea monster. Like no one, he was able to force obedience with the tone of his voice, therefore, due to the impending danger, the fight for a common cause was abandoned. It was obvious, however, that no one could be trusted in such a group.

"Come on, you damn bastards!" He yelled at everyone. "Crossbows ready! Shoot without order! Load guns!"

The caves piercing the flesh lit the beast, and it tightened its tail around both ships, apparently wanting to crush them.

"Take Valeria, you stupid overgrown reptile!" He screamed. "Away from my Witch!"

Tipe felt the healer's hand grip on his shoulder.

"Can you get up?"

"Yes."

With his help, he managed to do it, happy to be still alive.

"Get down!" Vashaba shouted.

A huge head dove for its victims, breaking one of the masts. It took the lives of three random people, whom they never even had a chance to get a good look at.

Vashaba looked at Vivan. Anyone could die in a moment.

Out of the corner of her eye, she noticed the man rescued by her lover move away discreetly, seeing her gaze. It's nice that he thought about it.

Vivan was staring at her.

She knew he meant that conversation. Adamantis hung around his neck, next to the jewel and the cross. So, he had no idea...

They had neither time nor favorable circumstances. She had to hurry. They clung to the ropes of the ship swaying by the waves, lashed by the salt water and gusts of wind.

"No matter how you wear it!" She explained, pointing to the ring, "as long as you have it, you are immortal!"

"I don't want it!" He replied immediately.

"Too late, it's yours!"

Vivan looked at her in horror.

"You are immortal, Vivan!" and then explained to him what needed to be explained from the beginning. Perhaps everything would have been different if she had understood then and had not allowed her emotions to get a little out of hand, as usual. "As long as you are, they too are immortal. All those you protect. You will never lose them, as long as no one kills them."

Vivan looked at her seriously.

"I know," he replied finally, surprising her with this. "I don't want such a fate for us," he added after a moment of silence.

"It depends only on you," she feigned indifference, though deep in her heart she felt regret. "Don't worry. Perhaps we will die in a moment anyway."

"Vivan!" Tipe yelled suddenly, falling on the deck.

Vashaba pushed Vivan onto the boards without hesitation. Instantly she reached for the arrow, turned towards the growing noise, and sent it from her bow straight into the eye of the great snake. The latter tossed his head furiously, cowering in pain. Everyone froze when the Witch began to crackle.

She turned back. Vivan hadn't had time to get up yet. Meanwhile, the healthy eye of the snake was looking for its wrongdoer. Just as she sensed...

She looked into Vivan's eyes, wanting to remember this image last.

"I'm sorry," she said softly, sending a mental memory to him as he returned from the battered girl. The memory of how he cried softly behind closed doors, devastated by those experiences while she was then unable to understand him.

If she had enough time...

The snake grabbed her with its teeth. She saw darkness. She felt a sudden pain.

Then she felt nothing anymore...

Valeria creaked under the pressure of the mighty weave.

"Hey!" Ross yelled at the snake.

He went downstairs, passing Sel. He snatched the crossbow from someone's hands without looking back. He took aim, cared more for attention than for accuracy.

The bolt lodged in the beast's neck. It hardly noticed it.

"What's he doing?" The women asked the crew, "Are you mad? He draws attention to us!"

This monster just killed Vashaba...

"Don't think about it," Ross told himself. "Don't get too deep into it. You need to focus. Otherwise, we will all die."

However, it did not help. He could feel the despair of his friend on the other ship seeping into his heart. As if he was standing in two worlds now. Before him he could see the enormous muzzle of a monstrous snake. The teeth of the creature, which was closer to dragons than the grass snake in the woods, had gnawed through Vashaba's body moments earlier.

The cold penetrated Vivan, numb with despair and terror. He needed help. Someone to let him feel sorry now.

There were over three hundred people on the ship. Now, however, no one could move from here, despite their great intentions. Their lives depended on Ross...

If he survives it somehow without going insane, he'll probably get drunk.

Poor Vashsba... He couldn't like her. But that didn't mean he didn't feel sorry for her.

He held out his hand and someone immediately handed him a second bolt. He shoot again. With no result. So, he reached for a bow from one of the old crew members.

"How about that?" He asked teasingly.

The arrow hit the one Vashaba had shot. Dangerously close to the eye.

The snake immediately turned its head towards him.

"At last!" He whispered as he waited in the center of the deck.

The reptile glided towards him. The crowd moved aside in a hurry, ordering him to flee, apparently thinking he was mad. He didn't listen to anyone. A big head was against him.

Ross was pretty sure what the reptile was thinking. Is the man in front of him so brave or so stupid? Or was it his imagination? Snakes don't think that way. They are hunting. They are waiting for a move, even a small mistake. Meanwhile, he was wondering if he would get wet in his pants in a moment from fear.

"Hey, sweetheart!" He asked, making up for himself with a confident face. "Get the tail off my ship!"

The snake lifted its head quickly, intending to devour it. Ross saw a row of bloody sharp fangs right in front of his face.

"No!" He shouted abruptly.

The snake froze, surprised by the imperious cry that echoed in his head.

His will struggled with that of the sorcerer, trying to free his body under the magic of the Gem. The ruby red glowed, emphasizing Ross's focused gaze. The enormous head hung over the ship, held in place. Meanwhile, the creature trembled nervously, moving Valeria as it did so. People grabbed what they could.

It was so great! But this time it wasn't size that was overwhelming Ross, it was stubbornness. The snake wanted to tear the strange man to pieces and crush his ship in anger, then devour everything that moves.

Still, it couldn't do it! It was beyond its understanding. How's that?! It0 always did what it wanted to do. Why now is some mysterious force preventing it from doing so? Maybe then it would try to cheat, avoid. Deception. It was an ordinary snake, perhaps a bit like a dragon, but a snake nonetheless.

In fact, Ross wasn't prepared for this. The reptile saw only one form of solving the problem and blindly pursued it. He wanted her with all his might. Eat it and destroy it. Easy. Too much. One pure desire. A steadfast will.

Ross felt it press against his own will. The sight of the sharp teeth and the enormity of the beast did not help him to resist. Just below the surface of his consciousness, he felt that something was wrong with Vivan. He wanted to look at the ship beside him, but at that moment the snake would kill him. He would kill the others soon after.

He fell into a trap.

The only option was to force the monster to leave them alone, but the plan could prove impossible. The serpent was not going to give way at all. His will pressed against Ross's mind so much that he felt his skull burst open in pain.

The hum among the crew made him realize that something new was happening.

"Look!" Someone shouted, "The witch wants to run away!"

"Shhh..." a few voices calmed him down quickly. "Don't distract the captain, we'll all die!"

The snake stared at Ross with its reptilian eyes, devoid of any gentle features. Cool as ice. Unfriendly.

Vivan was lying, unable to move at first. It took a moment or two for him to realize what had really happened. Then he trembled with suppressed despair, unable to even get up. With each passing moment his heart was beating faster and faster, and his breathing quickened. He wanted to scream. At the same time, he couldn't make his voice heard.

Vashaba...

Dead. She is dead! This time he couldn't hope. He couldn't count on a miracle. She saved him. Then she died.

The accompanying shock began to slowly, very slowly fade away, releasing the body paralyzed by the sudden shock and outburst of emotions. Then he felt his throat tighten.

Captain Hope's face appeared before him. He felt a pain in his neck and realized that the man was forcing him to move, wrapping the whip around like a collar before. He was choking him! He cut off access to air.

"Get up!" He hissed angrily.

Vivan saw only the quick movement as Tipe lunged at the captain's back, knocking them both over on the boards. The two men engaged in battle. He quickly found himself with them. He tugged the captain by the collar of his shirt and coat, then delivered a blow without thinking.

"Thanks!" Tipe threw to him.

One of the pirates turned to send him an arrow from his bow. Vivan warned him with a shake of his head. In the line of fire, the archer killed one of his companions.

"Here's the boat!" Vivan shouted. "Gather the people and run!"

"I would have listened to him!" Hope appeared next to them, putting a dagger to the healer's throat.

"You're not gonna kill him!" Tipe replied, furious with this turn of events.

Hope quickly cut the skin on the hostage's neck. Vivan groaned.

"Check me!" replied coldly. "Do you prefer a ship and a dead healer or freedom?"

"Tipe!" Vivan shouted urgently.

Tipe regarded the captain with a cold stare.

"Please…" Vivan began.

"To the boat!" Tipe shouted to his people, "Don't straggle!"

The tied boat was quickly found. Tipe felt bitterness. He knew perfectly well that Vivan had not begged for his life. He asked him to save the crew and the imprisoned. At that moment, he mentally cursed him for this nobility, which nevertheless matched the behavior of the gods he knew from his native islands. But he was different from them because he was a flesh and blood man. Now Tipe felt confused. He couldn't leave this man. To leave him to the Red Captain meant to hand him over to Lady Death herself, the dark guardian of the people, as she was called in his hometown. He was not going to do this. The God of Life would never forgive him. He couldn't forgive himself. Therefore, he ordered the crew to help only the imprisoned to regain their freedom, deliberately delaying so that only they would leave the ship. He didn't have to explain their reasons. Some of these people were not from the islands, and yet they thought the same. If they are to leave the Witch, it will be all together. If they can't - they must get it!

The snake was still immobilized by the wizard's will. It was trembling with tension, unable to even wag his tail. You could almost feel the tension between its will and the young man's determination. It fought Ross's will for its desires.

The ship moved slowly forward, away from the snake and Valeria. The long tail was carefully avoided, heading out into the open waters, taking advantage of the fact that the reptile was too busy.

"Slowly, boys!" Hope ordered quietly. "We don't want to distract it."

Pirates tried to stop people from sneaking out. They were afraid, however, that the snake would finally attract their attention more than losing their prey. So this time they gave up the fight and rapes. Now their focus was on avoiding death. They were saving their ship.

Stealthily, the crews of both ships exchanged malevolent glances. Ross's crew glared at the Witch angrily, with an overwhelming sense of helplessness. Everyone was afraid of the snake that literally hung-over Valeria. Beneath the pirate ship, a dozen or so men fought damage to the hull after its massive tail tightened its knots. Valeria, pampered by Alvaro, seemingly made it unscathed, though the original purpose of placing the hull reinforcements was to withstand violent waves and extreme speed.

"You see, your sorcerer friend bought us some time," Hope explained briefly, loosening his grip a bit, "in this state you cannot focus..."

Vivan mentally agreed with him, albeit reluctantly. However, he did not miss the action of Tipe, who was just taking Nena and mothers with children under the escort of his people. Eric, walking next to him, in a low voice, showing his nervousness, was explaining something to him, or rather convincing him. After the women got into the boat, Tipe looked at him.

Eric did not leave the ship. Vivan saw understanding and determination on his face as on Tipe's face. After a while he was convinced that the pirate crew had guessed their intentions.

So, his pleas had been of no avail... He felt disappointment but mixed up with a bit of gratitude and concern. These people were either so brave or so crazy!

"Ross!" Violet hissed, oblivious to Cora's and the girls' warning jabs. "They're murdering my people there! The ship is leaving!"

"Violet!" Apara looked fearfully at the captain. "Shut your mouth!"

Ross felt a tear roll down his cheek. He was already very tired. His head was splitting. He could barely stand on his feet.

Everyone saw that he was barely holding on, he knew it. He had to do something...

Sel bit his lip as people began to whisper anxiously. Blood appeared under Ross's nose. It began to flow out of the ears. After all, he could die trying to stop this beast!

He looked helplessly at the departing Witch.

"Hey!" Violet felt an unease that quickly turned to fear in her heart as she noticed the young captain's condition. "People! We have to do something!"

"Violet!" Marlene hissed softly. "You will kill us! The captain protects us from the snake!"

"It's killing him! Can't you see it?!"

"What are we supposed to do?" One of the crew called.

"What? For the fuck sake!" She yelled at him, revealing her explosive nature. "Shoot the snake, damn it!" She took the crossbow from the hands of one of the girls, aimed it at the body and released the bolt.

"Violet..." Ross groaned desperately as the snake pressed his will furiously against his will, under sudden pain.

Sel approached him.

"Hold him, love," he whispered in his ear. "And we'll kill him."

Ross wanted desperately fell into his arms at that moment. Get away from it all. But he knew he couldn't do it.

"Stay with me..." he asked with difficulty, feeling such a pain in his head that he almost lost consciousness.

"Always," Sel replied, his voice trembling as he stayed by his side. He touched the fingers of his lowered hand.

The jewel glowed. The pain was much less. Ross took a deep breath, like a man surfacing. He saw clearly again.

The great serpent's head hung in front of him again, obscuring the rest of his surroundings.

Ross suddenly became certain that only a being of the female kind could turn out to be such vindictive stubbornness. In this way, his memories helped to recognize feelings, while imposing a view that had its source in the past.

There was only one way he could vent the feelings he had accumulated over the years. He took advantage of it.

"You bitch!" He hissed, picking up the crossbow and applying the bolt. "Die finally!"

He shot the beast right in the eye. The snake shuddered desperately, but under the influence of his will, supported by Sel's love and concern for people, he could not move. So he shot it in the other eye. The snake stuck out its tongue. He almost touched their faces, but neither of them stepped back.

"What are you waiting for, Christmas?!" Sel shouted in frustration before using his crossbow.

Violet also fired the crossbow. The others finally woke up. Although only those with crossbows managed to injure the snake, it was evident that it was at its end. Then it moved.

Violet looked at the departing Witch and the boat on a circular route. She did not see her people on it.

She understood what was happening.

They'll be too far to stop them in a moment.

"Take care, brave boy!" She shouted to Ross. "You have a wonderful captain!" She called to the people around her, "I'm going for my people! And my new goddamn ship!" She climbed onto the balustrade.

"Violet!" Cora shouted after her, grabbing her hand. "This is madness!"

"For all the waters of this world!" Violet frowned. "Who is not crazy here?!"

She jumped into the depths of the water. Cora leaned out behind her, anxious for her fate as the dying snake retreated, churning the waves. Violet, however, was doing very well, quickly catching up with the pirate ship, which, slowed down by the serious damage to the hull, was slowly moving away. Soon she grasped the dangling ropes and protruding ornaments with her hands. She was out of sight.

Cora looked up at the deck of the pirate ship, feeling Valeria tremble as the snake twitched in convulsions.

The captain kept the healer as his captive. There was a possible fight on the ship.

She was worried about Vivan's fate. She was thinking of nothing else. She had no suspicions about the essence of these feelings. Her thoughts slowly returned to Violet. She looked for her. It was at that moment that she felt the tremendous jolt of the entire ship.

The snake wasn't going to give up easily.

CHAPTER 18

Valeria's deck shook with the mighty beast's movements and the waves lapping against the sides.

The snake hit its head, breaking the middle mast. Ross stood more firmly on his legs apart. The jewel glowed purple. The young sorcerer raised his hand as if summoning something. He needed this gesture to help his imagination. For Ross did not know any magic tricks. He was self-taught. The summoning, which looked like an introduction to the arcane art, was just a gesture that made him think that this was probably the way it should be, if he wanted to achieve his goal.

All his magic was based on this: intuition and sensing. He's been doing well at it so far. Magic for peasant reason, he used to say. Sailing from Leviron, however, he knew that the next days would make him face obstacles he had never faced before. He wasn't ready for it, he sensed it. And yet, seeing how much everyone counted on him, he faced a challenge, ready to do his best.

He was afraid to think about the consequences, but he sensed that he would certainly pay dearly for it. Maybe even with life...

He wasn't going to drop out.

After a while, a powerful gust of wind rocked the ship and flapped its sails. A wind charged with purple magic struck the snake in the neck, kicking its drooping head, then pushed it away, away from the ship a boat's length. Ross ordered the Jewel to make sure everyone was safe.

A boat with fugitives from the Witch was floating on the waves. Some of the people jumped straight into the water, hoping that they would swim to nearby Valeria.

Ross made up a whirlwind in which he placed the head of a dying snake. He slowly pulled it back so it wouldn't fall on the fugitives. He was losing strength. He decided to just let go of the snake. He relieved him of the vortex with relief, and the reptile's head fell heavily, splashing the deck. He sighed, already tired.

Then the snake's head rose again. It quickly tightened the strands on Valeria, so that many people fell to the deck. Its head was searching its tormentor, hissing menacingly, though it was already weakening. Ross held his crossbow towards it, determined, above all else, to fight to the end. At the same time, he made another attempt to control the snake's mind, but here a headache prevented him, striking the wave with such force that he almost lost his balance.

Blood flowed from the ears and nose again. He felt dizzy.

A loud bang sounded several times on board. A hole was formed in the snake's head from which a narrow line of blood flowed. Many hands rose to grasp the head in a vain attempt to keep it from falling to the deck. Ross lowered his crossbow and struggled to lift his hand, pushing his head safely away from the ship again, while Victor calmly holed the pistol and walked over to it briskly.

Sel was ready. When the snake finally disappeared under the water with splash, they both caught the falling Ross. The crossbow clacked hard against the boards as Ross released it from his weakening hand.

The hat rolled at Cora's feet.

She picked it up as the men began to carry the sorcerer to his chamber. She walked over to them. Despite captain's outfit and white hair, he now seemed even more delicate and younger than ever.

At that moment, it seemed ridiculous to her the dismal fame of the Troublemaker of Thoughts that she had heard about recently. The White Sorcerer. The White Captain - the alter ego of the cruel Red Captain, his fate, as it was eagerly told. Yes, it was more appropriate. But when he thanked her for returning his hat with the hint of a smile on his weary face, he was neither the Troublemaker nor the Captain. Behind all these titles was a young boy whose eyes had already seen a lot. She recognized the gaze of street children that she had seen more than once in her hometown, bringing help. Probably, like them, he had to grow up faster, but (and she had seen it more than once in the street urchins) he did not lose the most precious treasure hidden in his heart. Something that no one in him could kill, although it was probably tried.

This was why he was a welcome victim to Azram's demons.

She shivered as she remembered the prophecy. He saw it.

"Don't worry," he said weakly as she accompanied them to the door, like many others, "They say a bad thing never dies."

How did he know what she was thinking?

The jewel pulsed and dimmed.

Ross closed his eyes before they carried him inside.

"Bad - no," she said softly, though he couldn't hear it anymore. "But good?"

She met Lena's anxious gaze.

They both thought of the same thing.

Among them were two jewels, more precious to demons than any treasures and souls in these lands. It wasn't about rubies in hands.

"Tell me what you think," Lena asked seriously.

Cora looked at her. They had known each other so briefly, yet she felt as if she had been here a long time.

That was why the things she had seen so far did not surprise her.

"Why are the demons so anxious to get them? Not because to free the Bay," she said calmly, "They want to get them..."

"Because both of them are people's only defense against them..." Lena finished quietly. "The Bay and Azram are just an excuse."

"You're an ass, not a companion!" Sel heard as soon as they laid Ross on the bed.

The angry words escaped from Victor's mouth, and now he couldn't find a place for himself. He felt helpless seeing Ross like this.

Sel opened his mouth to respond appropriately to the remark but paused as he saw Oliver leaning on Tenan's shoulder.

Sai accompanied her husband.

"I feel weird," Ross whispered softly through chapped lips.

Sel immediately focused his attention on his lover. First, he gave him water to wet his lips. The blood from his nose was still flowing, so he reached for the handkerchief from his pocket, holding it there thanks to a habit he had acquired from home. His father did that too. A sure sign of remembering him was repeating this practice, which brought back many memories.

The blood from his ears worried him. Oliver, meanwhile, sat down on the floor, propping his back against the bed with a soft sigh. It was more comfortable here. Due to his sudden weakness, he could not hold his chair.

He was used to such situations from birth. However, his bond with Ross was usually only about their life force being combined. It did not interfere with feelings, did not browse through thoughts. It didn't even send pictures of what was happening now. The fact that he was losing his strength meant that Ross had put his entire self into saving everyone, endangering their lives.

It was not the first such situation in the history of their fusion.

Both were not living a quiet life, coming to the conclusion at the beginning that it would not make much sense. After all, life always has some surprises. Sitting at home would imprison their souls, hungry for freedom and impressions.

"Can you, do it?" Tenan asked softly.

"Go," he ordered him, keeping his composure despite sensing Ross's condition. He preferred not to see certain things, otherwise he would have succumbed to a hidden fear. That would upset Sai even more, and he didn't want to, "People need you now."

Tenan squeezed his shoulder in a comforting gesture. Oliver smiled weakly at him for encouragement. He failed. The smile was too short, and his breathing felt heavy as if it had been made of great effort. He faded in his eyes.

Tenan hesitated. Sel won't want to see him here. But he always cared for those who showed their friendship to him. Oliver was one of these people, as was Sai. And Vivan, even in spite of the dread he felt at first at the sight of him. Vivan could not, or rather did not want, to hold grudges indefinitely.

Some of his friends might learn from others at times.

"I gave Ross Vivan's blood, so he'll be better in a moment. Then Oliver will also get better," Sel said sharply at him. "You are not needed here at all!"

Tenan looked at him, jaw clenching to suppress angry words. As always, Sel was reliable when it came to malicious taunts about him. He was slowly getting fed up with it.

"Why are you treating him like a lousy dog?!" Victor suddenly shouted in the embarrassing silence. "Maybe you would have a better look at what you are doing yourself?!"

"Why don't you tell me what you mean?!" Sel said aggressively, glancing at Ross, who closed his eyes, too tired to speak. That should already have worried him, as Ross would certainly have prevented the argument from happening. Concern for him, coupled with Victor's harsh words upon entering the cabin, made him lose his temper and lose his mind.

"Don't do this..." Oliver asked, hugging Sai against him. She handed him a cup of water, which he accepted gratefully. She had to help him.

"Perhaps you will go to your cabin after all," Tenan remarked softly.

"I prefer to be here," he replied weakly. "Brother!" He exclaimed with difficulty, "Ross?!"

"I'm sorry..." the sorcerer gasped, frightened by his own condition, also for his sake.

He wanted to say more but was now unable to. Vivan's blood was unexpectedly insufficient. His condition was improving, yet he was still surprisingly weak. He felt as if he was slowly sliding down into darkness and gloominess. He fought it with all his might. It also exhausted him. It was bad. Very bad.

Oliver...

The fear of a friend in his life did not help. For the first time in a long time, Ross was really concerned because it wasn't just about him anymore...

"I'll tell you what's going on in a minute, you bastard!" Meanwhile Victor was nervous. It was a shocking sight for everyone present. It took a lot of effort to throw him off balance. "Why the hell are you doing nothing?!"

"What do you mean?" Sel asked with a trembling anger in his voice, though he was already beginning to guess the reason for this argument.

"Sel, it's very bad..." Tenan chimed in, looking at Ross anxiously. "Look..."

He wanted to point out to him that the blood wasn't helping, but Sel wasn't going to listen to him about anything right now. Sai got up. The very first look at the man made her feel more anxious than ever before.

"Shut up!" Snapped Sel meanwhile, "I'm talking to Victor, not you!"

"Tenan..." Ross made an almost superhuman effort. "Promise..."

The ship was left to itself. Except for Silas's actions, probably wondering what he should do. The captain was not fit to fight. His successor did not appear.

"Damn it!" Tenan, ready for a verbal skirmish with Sel, immediately let go of the words. "I promised I would take them to Levilon! Ross!"

"Follow Vivan... Follow him..." Ross whispered before he passed out.

Sai was with him. Her eyes followed alternately his condition and her husband's behavior. She considered action frantically.

Tenan struggled alone with the decision. Oliver could barely breathe. Ross was barely alive. And these fools were blinded by their own quarrel!

"Go!" Sai ordered him gently, even though her voice was trembling "I'll handle it!"

"Don't let them die…" he asked her, giving Sel an unfavorable look.

Meanwhile, confident in the action of the healer's blood, he decided to winkle out from Victor the true cause of his anger.

"What do you mean?" He growled.

"Why are you allowing all this?" Victor shouted angrily, "Why don't you stop him? Can't you see what's going on? Do you only care about your own lust? You tricked him because you imagined something in that sick head of yours and that's all you care about! He'll kill himself in the end, and all you rely on is lovemaking!"

Sai held her breath for a moment.

There was silence.

Sel fought with himself not to say words that could change everything...

"So you think I seduced him?" He asked regretfully.

He tried to control the tone of his voice. Feelings of injustice demanded escape in anger.

"Sel..." Sai spoke gently, moved by his pain.

She knew Victor's words had nothing to do with the truth. Victor knew it too, she saw it. He couldn't take them back anymore. Now he clearly feared the consequences.

"Sel, listen! Ross needs to eat a meal. Blood alone won't help him! Do you have red wine or rum? Answer!" She tried to distract him, sensing in it a rescue from a powerful brawl that could destroy too much.

Sel looked at Ross fearfully. Silently he pointed to the shelf where they kept their drinks. She touched his face in a reassuring gesture before moving from her seat. She wanted him to be reasonable.

Oliver silently watched his friend as he slowly walked over to Victor, trying to calm down at the same time. Like it used to be, when he controlled his emotions, when he was still terminally ill with his heart. He still remembered how to do this, for there were nights when his old fear choked him in his sleep.

"You know..." Sel began quietly, looking into the eyes of his interlocutor. "What I do when you think I'm doing nothing... It's the most difficult thing in the world. I had to accept it, although it is not easy. You can't even imagine how much. I love him," he used the words for the first time in Victor's presence, but this time he didn't even hesitate. "I have to grit my teeth when I can't help him. I must be strong when I want to howl in despair. Sometimes I listen to his heartbeat and wonder if this is the last time, I hear it. What can I do? At important moments, such as that fight, I'm completely helpless. I have no magic to support him!" He felt a treacherous tear running down his cheek. "Do you know this feeling? Surely. That's why you're basking on me now. You are angry that you could not help either your grandson or even him..."

Sai listened, whispering soothing words to Ross. She gave him red wine slowly. Ross's eyes glistened with tears. He was silent.

"I shot..." Victor tried to defend himself, "and you couldn't kill him..."

Sel sighed.

"If I were you, I would have used it earlier," he bit back, but without a hint of anger.

"He was doing quite good..." Victor felt awkward too, even more than after his earlier words. "I don't have many of those bullets anymore. After the Battle of Barnica..."

He fell silent, no longer finding excuses for himself.

Sel pondered what he might say now. He might, for example, wander into it, reminding Victor (feeling hurt) for being too slow, even though he supposedly cares so much about Ross. He would also try to humiliate him by telling how they actually met with Ross at the House of Pleasure.

He didn't do any of these things.

Though the words of the deceit still hurt him, he locked them at the bottom of his heart.

Ross respects this man. Victor loves him like a son. He wouldn't stand between them, even if it hurt. Not now. They need each other. This is an important piece of the puzzle that strengthens the power of the Jewel. Their bond.

He will leave it. For now.

They both found out how much the power of the Jewel was supported by their feelings during careful observation. The bulk of this power, formed by the accumulation of love, from Vivan himself to Tenan, the last one to give the Jewel to Oliver's sister out of love, remained strong and unchanged. But what else he could do depended on...

"Sometimes I really don't know what to do," he said quietly to Victor, "I'm actually alone with this. He has you. He has Vivan who shares his experiences. I stray in the dark... I don't have anyone anymore and I've never had anyone..." he hesitated a moment after these words, remembering his friend, who later turned out to be a cruel and murderer. "Ross is my closest person. And Oliver," he smiled at his friend, who clearly felt better now, sipping his red wine slowly from his mug, "Oliver has a life of his own. Ross has a lot on his mind. And every day I look for the golden mean in all of this. Alone. That's how I learned. I'm not sorry because I prefer to look for new solutions. I don't expect this from you," he raised his hands before Victor began to speak. "So, let's not go back to the past."

He withdrew calmly. He helped Oliver to stand on his feet and led him to the bed, urging him to lie down next to Ross. Then he sat down on the edge of the bed. He shook his lover's hand with concern, who looked at him warmly, in complete silence. Sai kissed her husband and went out to take meal for both, also without saying a word. The strength of her calmness and small gestures were enough to lift the spirits of everyone present.

Victor approached them. He studied Ross for a moment, pleased to see that his condition was improving, but only slightly.

Then he looked at Sel, who was seemingly focused on his friends, as if he had discovered something about him that he had not noticed before.

"You're wrong," he softened a bit, "You've mentioned now that you don't have any magic to help him. But you do. The strongest magic in the world... Learn to use it better."

He turned around.

"Learn to use it better."

Just before the sea snake died, the touch of two hands changed everything...

Sel held his breath for a moment.

He hadn't yet believed that it was so critical to Ross's magic. Throughout his life, up to the events in the capital that brought them together, he gave himself secondary importance because of his past. In the family home, the mother showed no higher feelings, despondent at the loss of other children. The son, terminally ill with heart disease, was only a shadow. Fortunately, not for everyone, but this sense of invisibility, because it was not about low value, but the illusion of existence, it was still there.

Until now, he considered himself a witness, a devoted audience in the wizarding arts of Ross's emerging talent...

Ross, sensing his thoughts, smiled. Barely, but still. He felt a dark force that had been unknown before him, the effect of a powerful mental effort. He managed to overcome the collapse, also because of the wine he drank, forced by Sai. If it weren't for this... But it still felt like he was on deck.

He needed his help.

"Sel. Help me..."

"What should I do?" He asked immediately.

"I've never experienced anything like this before," the words flowed out of his mouth quickly, filled with fear. "So strong, so..." in panic he was looking for the right word, taken from the books, "intensely..." he whispered, feeling how fear is beginning to choke him. "I still think that she is there!"

"She's still alive?!" Oliver asked, bewildered.

But Sel already figured out what Ross was struggling with.

"No," he replied softly.

He pulled Ross towards him, hugging him tightly.

"I'm going crazy…" Ross whispered in fear.

For the first time since the Jewel had allowed him to do so, Sel knew perfectly well how close he was to meet the threat.

"He's an ordinary boy," worried Victor sat down next to him. "It's a bit too much for his..."

Sel silenced him with a gesture. He had to think about it.

"Give him some vodka!" ordered after a moment, guided by a sudden intuition. "Do you have your canteen?"

"Surely, I have!" Victor replied quickly, already reaching for it.

"I don't want to drink, I'll get lost…" Ross protested weakly, but Sel wasn't listening to him.

"Trust me!" He asked firmly, and nervously to Victor, "Don't skim!"

"Drink Ross as they say," Victor said, eyeing Sel suspiciously, "I've got a little more of this on board..."

Then he added the word Sel was waiting for. He predicted that this time it would not be without an anecdote about life in Victor's world. He was not disappointed. The old man in spirit added mysteriously after a while:

"A gift from Vivan's father. The real one. Patrick. A good boy, when he sends those parcels of books, gives the old man such a gift. A kind of souvenir. This is my son," he added with quiet pride.

"Please, go on!" Sel asked mentally, seeing that it was paying off. Ross's attention shifted to the words spoken.

He himself was surprised by them.

"Son?" Ross asked, not believing what he heard, "Vivan's father?! But Lena..."

"Yes, Patrick is my son. And Lena is my daughter," Victor began to say, seeing that he aroused the interest of those present. "Just don't tell anyone!"

Ross took another sip of vodka in his rush. Then another. It was important. At all costs, he preferred to concentrate on explaining the mystery now rather than hearing the Snake's still relentless thoughts. The burning liquid did a great job at this.

Sel was a genius!

"I guess it's starting to work..." he confessed to those present. After the second sip, he felt the turns of his head, which effectively suppressed the echoes of the snake's willpower. "I guess even too much..."

Victor handed him the canteen again, insistently encouraging him to continue drinking. He couldn't say no without being rude at the same time.

"I don't feel good with this..." he tried to protest weakly.

"I don't believe it," replied Victor deliberately. He preferred to drink him rather than watch him curl up in anguish under the influence of something he didn't quite comprehend, but he knew it would certainly do damage to his mind. Vodka will at most cause a hangover.

"Anything left?" Oliver asked.

"I don't give to adolescent!" Victor reserved.

"Adolescent?" Oliver protested animatedly. "And who is Ross? He's in my age! Plus, I'm married!" He concluded proudly, with a hint of rebellion in his voice.

"Take a sip!" With a sigh, he handed him the drink, while observing with interest the effects of its action. Unaccustomed to such specifics, of course, Oliver immediately choked, but he made up for it bravely.

Tell me... Ross asked, struggling desperately to stay focused after drinking too quickly.

"We'll probably catch up with those soon!" Victor protested weakly, but then Sel kicked him in the ankle.

Victor, understanding his intentions, sat down in a free chair and began to speak. In frustration, he chose the way his hometown was spoken:

"There's not much to talk about here. There was a war, I once said. Those were terrible times, you know. At the beginning, we were stationed in such a city. And I met one nurse, Wanda. The kind that cares for the sick and the wounded. And as we were young so we... hooked up," he was confused, unused to talking about such matters.

"What?" Oliver was surprised.

"You know, and so do you and Sai," Ross explained disarmingly sincerely, stunned by the drink.

Victor gave up staring at him, continuing the story:

"Then we had to go on and we didn't see each other anymore, as it used to be," he said calmly. "We didn't even write to each other. She is there, and I'm at the other end of this, as you say, land. It's like the whole world back then. A few bloody years passed and the war was over. I returned home, and new ones came there, to my village. They occupied empty houses. And there was Anna. Anna. My love. My quiet happiness to a soldier. We got married. Lena appeared, then grew. She went on such; you call it an expedition. She looked after the children there. Well, Patrick also got there..."

"They got hooked?" Oliver asked.

"What did you think?" Ross remarked a little gibberish.

Sel smiled at the words.

Good that works.

"Well, you know, they were young. And then they decided to get married. They wanted the families to get to know each other."

"A great tragedy has happened..." He hung his head, silent for a moment. He took a sip from the flask Sel gave him. "From word to word," he began with apparent calm, "we got along with Wanda. She said that she persuaded everyone that Patrick's father had died during the war, she arranged the papers. Oh, such an adventure for life. My son. There was crying and lamentation, because the young people did not want to part with each other, and Lena was already pregnant. But it couldn't be like that. I promised Patrick," he sighed heavily, "because he was not guilty or she, if they didn't know anything? I promised him that I would allow these packages. Sometimes I will write to him about Lena and the baby. I promised. It's my son. Innocent of anything. I made him this promise..."

"Vivan knows?" Sel asked softly.

"I told him not to ask," Victor announced. "This topic is over and that's it! He has life here, not there! What if he ever wanted to meet his son? Can you imagine? No, you have no idea. He with this gift of his... There they would grab him and do research until he died! It would happen to you too!" He pointed at Ross, who shuddered at his scream. "He has Erlon, and he's a good boy, the best! Only my grandson knows a lot. He touches you and he knows already. He doesn't have to ask much. Maybe he already knows the truth, but he didn't tell me. He didn't tell anyone about it, I asked. Erlon also knows the truth, because he was angry with Patrick, so he had to know. Should know. And Vivan doesn't tell us everything that goes on in his heart. Just like now with yours... He was afraid..."

The sudden entrance of Tenan and Sai cut him short.

Sel made way for the young woman to sit down with a tray of food. She quickly explained that the rest were waiting for them on the cook's table.

"Ross," Tenan approached with a firm step. "Valeria has a leak and a broken mast, they'll finish fixing it, and we keep going. The Witch is not far away, it's at anchor, and it's even worse than Valeria. We watch them through the telescope. They will not escape us! The second ship is perhaps the worst problem. Silas says there may be trouble."

"What kind of ship is this?" Ross asked not very smoothly, and Sai winced as she smelled the alcohol. She gave Victor a meaningful look, who pretended not to know what she meant.

Ross's mind was already finding balance, though truly under unusual circumstances. The distraction helped him a lot.

"Silas says it's the Avenger," Tenan replied. "It has a pirate flag."

"It's going to attack the Witch..." Ross said.

He paused. He was overcome with such unexpected powerlessness that he ran out of breath. He gave his all. As soon as he stopped seeing behind the fog, he saw faces marked with fear all around him.

"Enough of this!" Tenan said firmly. "You said when you were gone, I was to take charge, right? The captain isn't able to command the ship, you are witnesses..."

"Before you say something stupid...!" Ross gathered the strength to counter his arguments, but Tenan wouldn't let him speak.

"As the commander of Valeria, while the captain isn't on board, I will order the necessary stop to repair the damage..."

"You said...!" Ross interrupted him indignantly.

"...and to improve the health of a captain who is unable to fight either the Red Captain or anyone else, unless I have to replace him in that as well, which I will be glad to do!"

"We... will not leave... Vivan to his fate!" Ross fought himself to beat another wave of nausea.

"Captain, there are children on board!" Tenan protested sharply "Not to mention the women!"

"Children?" Sel asked, surprised.

"Yes," said Sai. "People kidnapped by the Red Captain escaped with the help of Captain Violet. They're on our ship now."

"Hide them under deck..." Ross ordered nervously.

"Ross," Sel said. "This is crazy. You need to take a rest!"

"Sel, since when have you been in charge of Valeria?"

"I'm in charge of it," Tenan interjected to him. "And I make all the decisions. It's a courtesy to be here now."

"WE ARE SO CLOSE!" Ross shouted in frustration.

"There are two ships..." Sai whispered.

"Apologize to him for me," Tenan asked calmly. "As soon as you get better and we help these people..."

"Ross," a familiar voice suddenly heard in his head, "Give it up...".

There was silence.

Ross was not a mindless madman. Hearing about the troubled fugitives from the Witch, he already knew that his stubbornness could lose them all. Two pirate ships, a sick captain, a commander with no experience, women and children. He could have led it anyway. Could. With the help of his extraordinary magic.

But he was unable to stay on his feet. He could barely collect his thoughts. He closed his eyes. He nodded his head in agreement, trying to hold back the pressing tears of helplessness. They were so close!

Tenan bowed slightly. He left, discreetly pretending not to notice anything.

"He knows we won't come to his aid," Ross revealed to those present.

Victor hung his head.

"He told you to yield," Sel reminded him softly, "I heard."

"Really?" Oliver asked, lowering his voice as well.

Ross nodded silently. Oliver sighed and rested his head on his shoulder.

"Eat..." Sai insisted, but he fell asleep before she finished speaking. She looked questioningly at Ross.

The jewel glowed purple.

Ross nervously squeezed Sel's hand.

"Rest at last," his beloved ordered him gently. "Please..."

Though he would have preferred to act now, he had to grant him his request. He had no more strength for anything. He closed his eyes. He fell asleep immediately, weary to the limit, without even moving his meal.

The miraculous power of the healer's blood took effect when he finally allowed himself to rest.

CHAPTER 19

Violet climbed aboard as the first shots from Victor's gun were fired. She made the most of it. Ignoring the shortness of breath, she took out her cutlass and placed it against Hope's neck, intrigued by the unusual noise.

"Hello, lover!" She hissed furiously. "Let him out now, or I'll make you a new rum hole, you furiously red face!"

Bernadette's crew smiled happily at the sight of her. All their weapons immediately turned towards Captain Hope. He smirked at them.

"You think my crew care a lot about me?" He asked ironically.

Apparently, it was so, despite earlier disagreements, as his men had halted all activities, now following the course of events. Though actually… Did he not hold a healer in his hands?

"Unfaithful dogs!" He hissed at their address.

Reluctantly he released him.

Vivan took a deep breath. His first thought was to get rid of the sinister whip, so he snatched it from Hope's hand and then threw it overboard. Hope only said it with a crooked smile.

"And what now?" He asked mockingly.

Vivan faced him. His eyes, to the surprise of those present, shone bright.

"I said I would witness your death..." he said ominously.

Violet froze, watching him in surprise. Like Tipe.

Vivan clenched his hands into fists in angry silence. The desire for revenge for the wrongs filled his mind.

The captain paled, clutching at his heart. He fell to the boards.

Vivan felt nauseous and dizzy almost at the same time. However, he extended a warning hand towards the Hope's crew, forbidding them access.

"You are not a killer," Vincent pointed out calmly, "You are a healer."

"Shut up!" Someone from the Tipe crew shouted.

Vivan met Vincent's eyes, panic rising. Something was wrong! Hope was already dying, and yet he felt that with every weakening breath of the captain he was losing his strength. And the growing pain of the whole body...

He trembled, suffering more and more.

"Vivan…" Violet said softly.

At that moment, Vivan's body burned with increased pain, taking his breath away. The gift of healing denied him his power, sensing his anger and vengeance. He understood it moments before he fell beside the captain, half losing his consciousness. He should never have done this.

Violet got scared. Vivan began to shake violently, and foam rolled out of his mouth.

"Stand back!" Eric ordered quickly, pushing everyone away.

He hastily removed the belt from his pants to place some between the patient's teeth. Vivan's ominous blue glow faded. Shaken by his convulsions, he banged his head against the deck.

"Get something under his head, quick!" Eric shouted.

Vincent quickly pulled off his shirt and it was immediately beneath Vivan's head.

"What now?" Violet asked.

"We have to wait for the attack to pass," replied Eric matter-of-factly, holding the sick man's head, "He cannot kill on your behalf!"

Everyone looked at the captain lying next to him. Eric hurriedly checked his pulse as he saw the healer's twitching stop.

"He's alive," he said shortly.

"Wait... And didn't the healer kill before?" One of the Witch's crew asked.

"Only in defense," Tipe explained shortly, remembering the stories he had heard. "Captain, orders?"

"She isn't the captain, if there is no ship..." another Witch's sailor laughed mockingly. The others followed his example.

"I have two more, you...!"

"Hey!" suddenly came the voice of a skinny sailor from the crow's nest. "The Avenger is coming to us!"

"Vincent, stop the ship!" Another sailor ran up to the man, red in the face. He quickly realized that he was the only one capable of making decisions. "The Witch is quick to take water! If we continue to sail - we will go down!"

Vincent glanced after Valeria. She was lagging behind. It meant it was in trouble too. The Avenger was still a long way off. The captain will probably recover soon.

"Only misfortune with them," said Matt suddenly, "since we have them, we have been chased by a sea snake, we have lost a precious cargo of slaves, the ship has pierced like a harlot's panties, a wizard is chasing us... And now the Avenger is coming! The healer brought us bad luck; I tell you. And that fat hen too!" He pointed accusingly at Violet.

"Pay attention to your words, you rotten bastard!" Violet yelled at him.

The mighty, tattooed Vincent thought for a moment. He looked at the assembled crew. Several of those present silently nodded. Matt was almost begging him with a look.

They might not have had a better opportunity.

"Here's my suggestion!" He said. "We need agreement on board to face Valeria if she catches up with us. It's not far to the port. We will give the Avenger something that will effectively stop its aspirations. Don't worry, we have something to make up for." He waved his hand towards the captain's cabin, where there was a chest with Vivan's blood.

"What will it be?" The same seaman who spoke second on behalf of the others asked.

Vincent smirked at Violet.

"It seems that a bit too little of you," he said with a twinkle in his eye. "And you have a bad omen among your people!"

The Witch's crew pulled their cutlasses towards them.

Violet raised her head proudly.

"Boys!" She turned to her people with deadly solemnity. "We are taking over the ship!"

"Are you sure about this, Violet Meresa?!" Vincent asked ironically.

At his nod, two men pointed crossbows at the semiconscious healer.

"You're not gonna kill him." She remained calm.

"The situation has changed," he replied.

"It's a bad omen!" Matt exclaimed anxiously.

Several of the other sailors nodded affirmatively.

"Damn pirates!" She hissed angrily.

"A gift from Vivan's father... Patrick... My son... I knew, Grandpa..." he thought without a trace of anger. "There was a war... I met one nurse, Wanda. And as we were young so we... hooked up... Anna, my dear... We got married. Lena showed up..., ...they were young... A great tragedy has happened...

There was crying and lamentation... Lena was already pregnant. But it couldn't be like that...

I told him not to ask... This topic over and that's it!"

Vivan caught an escaping thought:

"My father's name is Patrick..." he remarked emotionally.

He felt that they were carrying him somewhere. He didn't have the slightest influence on what happened to him. Rather, they won't kill him.

"Silas says it's the Avenger," Vivan heard Tenan's voice say, "He has a pirate flag."

"He will attack the Witch..." it was Ross.

"We... will not leave... Vivan to his fate!"

"Best friend..." he thought warmly.

"Captain, there are children on board!" Tenan protested sharply. "Not to mention the women!"

"WE ARE SO CLOSE!" exclaimed irritated Ross, "SAIL AFTER THE WITCH!"

"Poor Ross is barely alive..."

"Apologize to him for me," Tenan asked calmly. "As soon as you get better and help these people...

"Ross" sent his friend a thoughtful thought for all of them: "Give it up."

He fell into a dreamless sleep...

He woke up inside a strange cabin. He was lying on the bed, still clothed. There was a carafe of water and a mug on the next table. He reached for it slowly, like an old man, now hearing raised voices and sounds that were probably signs of unloading or loading. A foreign, dominant voice gave orders to the sailors.

Violet, Eric, or any of Bernadette's crew were not with him.

Under the cover he saw a piece of roast meat, some cheese, and bread. He ate some cheese and bread, feeling sick at the sight of the meat. He felt better. A bit.

Everything swirled around. He sat down on the bed, and then he saw a fragment of the port. He felt a cold chill.

Slave Bay.

So, they did arrive...

The cabin door opened slowly. A still quite young captain, with a blindfold and a large-brimmed hat, entered. His clothing was typical of the people of his profession, from high boots to coat and belt, beyond the shadow of a doubt. A flesh and blood pirate.

"Welcome aboard the Avenger," in his voice Vivan recognized the one who had given the commands before, "Although it will be a rather short visit. I'm Captain Yosaya Marten. A squad will soon be picking you up to take you straight to the King of the Bay. He promised to shower me with gold for it."

"Where are my friends?" He asked softly.

"You mean Violet and her people? Oh, I'll be glad to sell them at the market as soon as I have a deal. I admit, I was a bit surprised by the Witch's offer, but when they confessed to me that I would get a healer..." he smiled with satisfaction. "You understand, don't you?"

"You locked them up," Vivan said bitterly.

"What do you think?" The captain replied nonchalantly, "They could try to free you. They had so many good intentions," he grimaced. "Sit and rest while you have the opportunity."

Vivan got up.

The captain produced his cutlass dangerously close to his neck.

"No!" He said stiffly, without a trace of prior humor.

"I know," Vivan replied. "Profit and fame count, right, Captain?"

"Exactly," he was still holding the cutlass.

Vivan feigned discouragement as he sat down again. He felt so tired... But if he didn't... He wouldn't make that mistake again. He just hoped what he was about to do wouldn't kill him now.

"Easy," he said in his exceptionally gentle tone, which worked on the needy. "I don't have the strength for this."

He used his gift slowly, carefully checking to see if he could still do so.

The captain lowered his cutlass.

"Lie down and rest," he ordered.

After a moment, maybe two, he sat down on the edge of the bed. Vivan, pretending to be a sleeper, eyed him intently. He didn't notice anything.

The confusion outside began to subside.

"I have to see personally that you get to them," explained the captain with deadly solemnity, "otherwise he'll send demons to me."

Vivan's blue eyes glowed with a warm glow.

Interesting color, Marten remarked, like roses from my mother's garden...

The warm thought made him more docile. He bowed his head as he fell asleep.

Vivan focused on the crew. He began to hum a song from his homeland.

One after the other...

He was falling asleep when the cabin door swung open. He didn't even know how much time might have passed.

Violet waved her hand to Tipe and two others.

"Quick!" She pointed the healer, "Take him away! We're leaving the deck!"

"Violet..." he whispered when they hid in some alley. The rest of the crew hid nearby while King Azram's troops stepped aboard the dormant Avenger.

"Not now, son," she ordered him frantically, sending Tipe on scouting.

"If I die, burn me," he ordered her.

She looked at him as if he had suddenly lost his mind.

"Are you crazy, Vivan?! You will not die!" She replied sharply. "You need to rest, and I know where it could be done! Relax! Violet's gonna take care of it, okay?"

"Captain!" Tipe appeared quietly.

"Talk!"

"Yehudis in port. Barus finished doing business with her this morning."

"He'll take us?"

"He's afraid they'll find out how he does business with your ships. He arranged for a carriage. We'll be leaving town in a moment."

"And the rest of the crew?"

"They'll scatter. We'll meet outside the city. I sent one to Judith. She will be waiting in the cove."

"I hope it works!" she summed up shortly.

The carriage did arrive quickly. The royal soldiers did not manage to leave the deck. It had gone on for a while.

"Violet," he said, suddenly noticing it. "Where's Eric? The medic... He helped me..."

"Yes," she replied thoughtfully, "The one with the tattoo kept him on the ship."

He felt uneasy about his fate.

They were about to move when they suddenly heard commotion.

"Boys, come on!" He heard the captain's voice.

A fight broke out on board.

"We drive!" Violet signaled the coachman.

Suddenly there was a loud wail in the air. The people, still wandering around the harbor stalls in the glare of the slowly setting sun, scattered with screams of fear immediately, abandoning everything. A moan and noise scared the horses as they pulled the carriage in fear, cradling their ears.

The sun was quickly blocked by a dark mist.

"Demons..." Violet explained to Vivan.

The king's soldiers left the deck in a hurry.

Winged ghostly figures hovered over the pirate ship in the cluster, only to fall on it quickly like arrows. There were screams of those torn apart and pleading for mercy. The carriage grew farther and farther away from them, amidst other fast-moving and fleeing people.

The street around the unfortunate Avenger quickly emptied. In houses, the shutters were closed with a crash and the first candles were put out. Confusion and the crackle of shutters accompanied them until they left the city gate.

Vivan trembled all over in the chaos as he listened to the fading screams of the pirate ship's crew.

It was he who prepared this fate for them...

"I murdered them," he whispered.

"Either them or us," she replied sternly. "A miserable life of the pirate, Vivan."

She looked at him firmly.

"He sold you. He would sell us as well. Think what the fate would be for all of us. I'm sure Azram is preparing a special death for you for the joy of the demons. Very slow and intense. Here's what Captain Marten was going to give you!"

"I'll always be sorry for them..." he replied, his eyes shining with tears.

"I know," she replied. "Because you are who you are. I know those who would curse your sensitivity now. I don't. I don't have to agree with it, but I respect it. It makes you a healer."

He was silent, so after a while she added softly:

"Don't lose it. Never."

Tipe silently nodded, agreeing with her words.

Vivan closed his eyes.

He saw no glow of the fire. The death of the Avenger came right after the brave demon-fighting captain was murdered, until two others jumped down his throat and torn his insides.

It was said afterwards, though it was not known where these stories came from, that Captain Yosaya himself had killed a dozen of the monsters that wanted to murder his crew. His cutlass dipped in their blood as black as night until they caught him. Among the harbor taverns there were legends about a survivor among the waves who once told the story to escape the demons. It was passed on eagerly. Due to the demons, not even the wreckage remained, as if they had never been. Only the story remains.

The demons smelled the scent...

Before the fire consumed everything, they burst into the cabin looking for victims. The captain's bed smelled of something so incredibly tempting, so tasty, they wanted to devour it all to feel it deeper. They torn the bedspread to pieces, beating themselves for a moment as it it was the most precious prize, until they discovered the plate and the cup.

They sniffed the chewed bread and cheese greedily. One licked carefully. He chuckled approvingly. He was here. He was for sure. He gripped the bread greedily with his long fingers. He rose into the air amid the blazing fire.

He will carry it. He will be delighted!

Another sniffed a piece of the taken quilt. That smell...

Here! In this dark alley! Good meat was here! And then...

He rose into the air, grimacing angrily.

He escaped! The scent mingled with others, especially those with four hooves and paws, as if this man were part of their nature.

But he will find it! He won't miss it!

He took a nap in the carriage before they met the crew of Judith. The carriage was hidden among the rocks, ready to go in the event of an emergency, and Tipe and the coachman watched the area carefully, not only on the ground but also in the sky.

The demon appeared soon, almost silently. A few more are behind him.

"Not a word," the coachman whispered.

Vivan was fast asleep. He didn't see the silent landing of the demons as they approached the horses, sniffing around as if searching for something. Violet raised her eyebrows. Their behavior was strange. They didn't touch the horses, as if they were a little afraid of them. Instead, they approached the carriage.

A door was opened on each side. They stuck their long mouths in, sniffing everyone.

Violet froze in horror at the sight of the teeth in those maws, still bearing traces of human blood. She was afraid not only for herself, but also for Vivan, completely unaware of the danger. But the coachman gestured for her to remain calm, making no unnecessary movement as they sniffed his clothes and Tipe standing outside.

One of the demons prodded Vivan harder, waking him.

The healer opened his eyes.

Opposite him he saw two eyes completely devoid of human features, a long muzzle and pointed ears. The creature stared at him motionlessly, as if waiting.

Though a sight might be terrifying, he remained calm. He was responsible for the lives of these people. His eyes took on a glow, like the eyes of a wolf, suddenly found in the darkness.

"You are not looking for me," he passed in thought, keeping a cool head.

This gift never let him down. Vivan usually seemed delicate to people. Meanwhile, for several years he had been hiding a wildness, contrary to his usual nature. The animals felt a respect for him that few had ever seen.

Looking straight into the demon's eyes, he challenged him. And although he was usually more emotional, at a moment like this he was completely indifferent.

He tilted his head slightly. The creature moved. Violet suppressed a groan.

Other demons gathered around. They sat at carriage. They surrounded them, disturbing the horses. Vivan knew, however, that he had a leader ahead of him, for they had not jumped into anyone's throat.

He calmed his breathing.

The demon finally turned its head and body, staring at him greedily. He sniffed again. The smell did not match him, and neither did his eyes. It was like this one, but different. There was no fear in him. It couldn't be him. He wasn't looking for him.

He groaned in disappointment as he backed away.

Behind him, the whole crowd flew away.

"What the hell was that?!" The coachman wondered. "We know that they are usually not to attack without orders, but this... It was unbelievable! Who are you?!"

"Nobody!" Violet cast before anyone else spoke.

They didn't reveal much, except that they were in trouble.

"You are not that white-haired sorcerer," the coachman did not give up. "But did I not see on the neck...?"

Vivan looked at him silently. His eyes still shone. Right now, he was the least of the legendary one. He was like the demons of this world. The coachman broke off in the middle of a sentence.

"I'll check on the boat..." he said fearfully, backing away.

"You are full of surprises," Violet remarked, smiling crookedly at Vivan. "Keep it up!"

Judith.

The second of Violet's ships. Actually, a schooner. A perfectly selected crew, loyal to the owner of the ship. She inherited it from her father, just like Augusta - the last one. Bernadette was her pride, but Judith was just a little different from it. The only difference was that Bernadette was sponsored by get gold or earned for the rest.

Under the cover of the coming night, a boat was sent for them to take them aboard. The moon appeared in the sky, no longer obscured by any ominous fog. The lights of the Bay could be seen in the distance.

"Violet!" Shouted the man with a little stubble, undoubtedly the captain, "On Mother Earth's chest! What are you doing here?! What about Bernadette?!"

"Nathan, you old devil!" Violet exclaimed happily, which was far from true, as the man could be at most thirty. "I can see that you have completed the task! Please meet," she turned to Vivan, because Tipe already knew the people of Judith, "this is the curviest smuggler in my group, Nathan Nils!"

Vivan barely managed a slight smile. At that moment he felt himself losing his balance, and not because of the rocking of the ship. He felt fatigue.

"Oooyo," said Nathan seriously, grabbing him and Tipe under his arms, "Your companion is very tired, Violet..."

"I'm not surprised," she replied. "Nathan..." she made a significant pause. "Meet Vivan Beckert. The Healer."

Nathan opened his mouth in mute amazement. The apparent shakiness of his unusual visitor quickly made him abandons all social chatter.

"It's a real honor for me," he only said to the young man, not hiding his concern. "Come, I'll take you to the cabin, where you will rest. Luckily you won't be sleeping there with Violet. Believe me, you have nothing to regret," he leaned in confidentiality, leading them to the cabin. "She is snoring terribly!"

"I heard it!" Violet tossed menacingly, following them.

"But you have company there," said Nathan, ignoring her words. "I met them in the port of Reden. I didn't want to place these two below decks, but I had to ask their companions for it. I don't think you will mind..." he finished with a mysterious smile, opening the cabin door for the guests.

Vivan looked up with difficulty.

"Vivan!" incredulously he heard a familiar voice. "Oh, Mother Earth!"

Paphian immediately approached him, locking the healer in a firm, brotherly embrace. Dinn was right behind him."

"Paphian!" Vivan forgot his weariness immediately, feeling the surge of unrestrained joy.

He missed him so much! Him and his family. Their love. He was saved as long as he had someone close to him. It was as if he had been kept in a dark dungeon until now, and now he has finally come out into the sun. All warm feelings surged within him.

He hugged him tightly, holding him with all his might, as if he was afraid that he would disappear and see him again.

Paphian became concerned.

Vivan was upset. It wasn't normal behavior, even for him. Violet noticed the fear in his eyes.

"He's been through a lot," she explained quietly.

He carefully moved his brother aside to study him. He felt a surge of anger immediately.

"What is this scar?" He touched the head, where was the scar from the blow. "These bastards did this to you?!"

Vivan was unable to speak for a moment. He embraced him again, and then, quite unexpectedly, the words that heralded that he was under a really strong shock came out of his mouth on his own, assisted by the memory:

"The city should contain your name," he said, agitated. "You must be there. You are my brother. You have to be there!"

Paphian froze in surprise.

"What?!"

After a while, a wave of tender brotherly love flooded his heart. No words from an old, stupid grandmother could change what he had always felt. And now Vivan, who had been kidnapped in terrible things, judging by his condition, in his first words proved to him that he never forgets about him.

"Vivan, you crazy!" He hugged him again, not hiding his emotion. "Did you think about it all the time?"

Vivan trembled as he tried to hold back a sob. Time and time again he felt that he really felt him, as if he did not believe his own senses.

His behavior really shocked Paphian. Just like the appearance. Only a few days have passed...

"I'll bring him clean clothes," Violet said, hiding her emotion with difficulty. "Take care of him well!"

"And you are...?"

"Violet Meresa, the owner of this boat," he introduced herself. "And you must be Pafhian," she noticed, looking at Vivan with concern. "There is one of the last elves in our lands - Dinn, right?"

Dinn nodded silently.

"Give him a break," she added, before retreating with her men from the cabin.

They were left alone.

Vivan held him for a long time, unable to move with excitement. Paphian waited patiently for his brother to calm down. They didn't say a word. Vivan neither complained nor asked for anything. He just enjoyed his closeness, gathering strength. He trembled as if he were about to fall apart. Thoughts flashed back to the most painful memories.

Finally, Paphian felt he couldn't take it anymore.

"Yell if you want," he suggested. "I can take it."

Vivan hid in his arms as if he was just waiting for it.

Paphian endured his torment.

That night he did not leave the cabin. As he once sat at his brother's bed, keeping watch. He held his hand, dressed in an unusual dragonskin glove, dreaming gloomy ideas about what he would gladly do to his grandmother for what happened to his brother, or to the thugs who kidnapped him. He thought about the distant future, and how long Judith would sail to their hometown. About what was here and now.

Most of all, he remembered his piercing scream muffled in his brotherly arms.

CHAPTER 20

Vivan opened his eyes.

The first person he saw was Paphian. He slept next to him, still touching his hand lightly. He was immensely grateful to him for this gesture. It helped him more than a warm meal, a bath or a change of clothes. If it weren't for his support, he wouldn't have done so many of these things around him. He was so tired then...

However, it worked and now he was restored, although it was sore after the ordeal. He felt that he lacked inner balance. Everything was wrong... All that anger, violence, cruelty... His not-so-glorious feat of trying to kill Captain Hope. Strange, so far somehow, he has not regretted it. He should, but he couldn't. He reached the inner limit where his goodness ended and his anger for wrongs began. Too soon for him lately. He fell into some inner anger that deprived him of his ability to feel different, warmer. Everyone had moments like this from time to time, at least the ones he knew about, but in his case, such emotions weren't good. As a healer, he had had a lot of patience so far, not to mention tolerance, mercy, or other such feelings. Anger or violence isn't the best for him at all. Thanks to them, he fell into a debilitating disease, just like when he was imprisoned in the royal palace. The environment was then so saturated with perfidy, sadistic motives, and finally with a lack of conscience that he could not sleep even one night without nightmares and internal, devastating cold mixed with regret. He has changed since then, but his attitude towards the world has still not made him immune to its horrors.

It was never going to change.

He had realized long ago that being in the midst of bad emotions, as he ironically put it, was simply exhausting him. He has learned to control himself. He went through a wave of rebellion against this state of affairs when he was a teenager. He was furious with his over-indulgence, tendency to cry, or sensitivity, which some even gave reason to gossip about his orientation. He usually did it alone, until Lena found him in a hideout by the river. Then she gently explained one thing to him. Being good and feeling hurt is not a bad thing. People have learned to see it as a weakness, and it really does take a lot of willpower sometimes to keep it inside when the world tells you to be tough. Hence, many give in and succumb to pressure. It's easier that way.

"You cannot give up," she added gently. "The gift is your strength, not a curse. I know it's hard, but nothing good in life will come easy…"

He sighed, holding back the pressing tears.

He's already lost so much… Especially her…

He pursed his lips, fighting the wave of feelings, only some of which were warm and tender, among those marked by regret, sadness, and even… fear, to finally go to those hidden from everyone in the depths of his heart. It was first and foremost… a relief.

He hid his face in his hands, ashamed of the thought, but she refused to let him hide it in the dark. She was too real for that.

He did not tell them, much less to her, about his hidden fears. Feeling that their relationship was starting to destroy him, not only physically but emotionally, distancing him from his loved ones, making him penetrate their emotions with all his vitality, to experience them twice, Vivan understood that all this brought him closer to his own death…

It started with a memorable tragic event with a raped girl, maybe even earlier. Just before the last meeting, he was sure this relationship would kill him. When she gave him Adamantis, he realized that she would never let him share his time with his family and friends too. She just wanted him for herself. One day they would have stayed, maybe just the two of them... If not for time, not for the coincidence of events, then his constant absence and destruction would distance him from everyone. Their paths would diverge forever.

He stifled a groan. Was he selfish? He loved her. He loved them. Why is this irreconcilable? Why did she not want to share family life with him? He lost her, making her feel every shade of pleasure.

He froze as the thought penetrated him...

So it was his fault! He was afraid of her, but he had made it all happen himself!

He felt his heart prickle like a touch of ice.

He can never let anyone get so close to him again.

It influences the people around it too much.

He felt hot tears on his face as he tried to swallow the bitter thought.

He must be alone...

It hurt more than anything he had ever experienced. It was tearing him from the inside.

But was there no truth in it? It was enough to look around at the immediate surroundings.

He messed up their minds! Everything they did was revolving around him. All you had to do was look at Ross. Over time, their bond grew so strong that it even dimmed Ross and Oliver. A friend came to his aid, ready to sail the world to help him! As if his own life didn't matter anymore!

It was similar with Alesei.

The family had long been ready to get killed for him.

Vashaba? She wanted him to the limit of life and death!

Wasn't that crazy? What did he do to the minds of these people? Why did they want to forget everything that their stepfather had done to give the town a new name?

Yes, he was helping them. To each of them. But did this give him the right to confuse people's minds, making him almost worship him?

His existence began to threaten their lives. Why had he not noticed it yet? He wreaked havoc wherever he went...

He was destroying them with his devotion. He did not allow them to live as they should, enjoying their own happiness, sharing their own troubles and worries.

He tied them too tightly together.

And he dared to dream about having them always with him! Vashaba knew. She wanted him for herself, pushing others away, but was it just a selfish act? Did she not want to protect them from his influence?

So much bad happened because of him...

The sudden touch of a warm hand pulled him out of the tangle of false assumptions and conclusions that filled his heart with bitterness and sadness.

Dinn.

He sat down with him on the edge of the bed. Out of the corner of his eye, Vivan saw the makeshift bedding on the floor. He couldn't even remember when they fell asleep. Yesterday he was not himself.

"Why are you crying?" The elf asked softly, leaning towards him. "If it's because of Vashaba, know one thing: I already know about her death."

Vivan wiped away his tears. His bleak vision of the future and depressing thoughts did not allow him to calm down.

"You mourn her?" Dinn asked sadly.

"Yes," he replied, because it was true. Despite everything, or rather because of what he thought he had learned about himself, he missed her. If he had guessed earlier, maybe he wouldn't have let...

"My sister wrapped you up," Dinn said firmly, his voice serious as if he had been thinking about it for a long time. "I know that you should talk bad about the deceased. But I know you. I'm sure you now blame yourself and your gift for all the misfortunes in your relationship."

"It's because of me," Vivan replied firmly.

"No," said Dinn, "I forbid you to think like that!"

"You can not! You're not in my head!"

"Do you remember how she was hanging out with men?" Dinn asked. "You treated her like a partner. You resisted her the longest and that attracted her to you. She finally grabbed you!"

"Don't say that!"

"I knew her better than you do," Dinn continued imperturbably, trying to make his tone softer, "She'd been doing it for years. You haven't had any experience. I'm sorry, but it was true. She wrapped you around. My sister knew how to do it."

At the end he added softly, sadly:

"Everyone knew it, Vivan. She was a leech. The truth was, she ate you alive, and you put up with it because you loved her. Don't make yourself guilty. Don't come up with a new theory to make sure it's your fault. I live in this world for the third generation of people. I know, it's not much for an elf, but for a human it's years of experience. I find that you are inclined to take any guilt for yourself, even though the evidence shows otherwise. Especially those with a great heart and sense of justice, like you. One word of advice: don't think so much. Maybe there was a little bit of your fault in it, I don't deny it, but this time listen to the older brother of the one who used to love games. I know what I'm talking about, Vivan. Vashaba liked you very much, I'm almost sure she loved you, but she was a big Cuddles, if you know what I'm talking about," he forced a smile on his face. "I loved her too, and she loved me, but... I know that in my heart you also know the truth..."

Vivan was silent for a moment, still sure of his pathetic new truth.

"I wrapped her around," he said softly. "Like everyone else. That's the truth, Dinn. They all live what happens to me. I'm getting them in trouble. And Vashaba? Okay, she liked it. If I didn't like it, I wouldn't have surrendered to her will. But it was me who made her want me so much! I'm the one with the gift that wraps around people like poison ivy. It penetrates their minds. Makes they want my good..."

"They hit you in the head too hard," Dinn said firmly, interrupting his word, "It's not true! Do you know what is it? We all just love you very much. And yes, it is remarkable what the bond is between all of us in this violent world. But it is because of this, now listen to me carefully that we have a man among us who cares for others like no one else. It makes our hearts full of good feelings. We have more patience and tolerance, but also courage and dignity. We have a passion and don't give in to the imposed rules. You make us want to live and our thoughts shine. You are changing us, and we are changing the whole world around us. And if," now he smiled sincerely, "you start talking about yourself again, or worse, thinking such nonsense, I'll personally kick your ass!"

Vivan, however, did not easily dismiss his theory. One thought still haunted him.

"I could help others," he revealed regretfully, "And I couldn't."

Dinn looked at him calmly.

"Go on..." he asked.

Vivan briefly told him about the events on the Witch.

Dinn was shocked by the actions of the captain and crew. Such a precious gift as life was destroyed in such a ruthless way... Human cruelty constantly surprised him.

"I wanted to use this... power of mine," Vivan explained in a bitter tone. "And I couldn't. I didn't help them. I could kill everyone and then I would have saved these people. I didn't do that. Now I'll always remember them. About how they died before my eyes..."

Dinn sighed.

"I'm not surprised you weren't able to kill those people. No matter how bad they were, you aren't like that. What distinguishes you from many good people is that you were born to help, and your whole self fulfills this mission. This force... This murderous, crushing power, as you call it, helps you."

"But I couldn't use it to protect them!"

"You wanted to defend them?" Dinn tilted his head, making his slightly disheveled long hair peek out from behind him. "Did you want to murder those people who hurt them?"

Vivan wondered, overwhelmed by memories.

"Murder is always murder," Dinn added quietly. "A brutal act taking life ruthlessly. Do you feel capable of it? I don't think so. Therefore, even using this gift in righteous anger, and especially in an act of revenge, destroys you."

Vivan felt the familiar feeling chase away all bad theories, leaving behind reflections like shadows on his soul. His gift. His strength. His motivation...

"I should be more responsible," he said softly but firmly.

Dinn was surprised.

"What?" He asked, moved by his words.

"I'm a healer," Vivan clenched his hand into a fist, as he once faced the witch Mayene in desperation. "I should protect you as best I can..."

"You mistake your calling for a guard..." Dinn interfered with him, but he was beginning to understand why his friend was saying that.

"You rely on me," Vivan added, lost in his own thoughts, "I should have tried better."

"You can't fix the world..."

"No," he agreed calmly with him. "I heal..."

Dinn would have given a lot to know Vivan's thoughts now.

At least his mood changed for the better. He reminded himself of himself from before the kidnapping. Despite how much he has lost and gone through.

Suddenly, he felt calm. The fear of demons is gone. He was safe again. They couldn't get him anymore, finding him in the darkness. His thoughts about You changed. Feeling sorry for what she had done to Vivan flew away. His love and longing were soothed. Mourning has been replaced by sadness. Unpleasant memories gave way to good ones, from childhood to the last conversations.

Such was the gift of his friend.

The healer.

"Vivan..." he whispered deeply touched, feeling the calm flowing over his thoughts.

Vivan looked at him, surprised by his reaction. As if even for a moment the thought that he was doing something extraordinary had not crossed his mind. It was as obvious to him as the fact that he was breathing. It was part of it. And ever since Dinn met him, his friend always wondered how people responded to his gift. As if he kept asking, "Did I do something unusual?"

He didn't even know how amazing it was. Or maybe he knew, but did not pay attention to it? He was born as a healer.

"Dinn," Vivan smiled with a smile they had rarely seen him lately. The one who made the hearts beat faster with emotion. "How good I have you," he said warmly.

Dinn thought the same. He felt that emotion was pressing on him in full swing, so he politely apologized to his companion and left in a hurry. Vivan was a truly remarkable man. He was proud to know him.

"What happened here?" Paphian spoke unexpectedly.

Vivan wiped away his tears hurriedly, managing a hesitant smile.

"Have you been here long?"

Paphian stretched slowly.

"I guess I missed your conversation with Dinn, if that's what you ask," he replied easily.

Vivan sighed silently in relief. He wanted to keep this moment in his heart without his brother's comments.

"How are you?" Asked Paphian with concern.

"Much better," he replied.

He sensed a change in his mood. Now when he was feeling better, they can have a more daring conversation. He knew what was coming. There was a storm coming. Thunderbolts are about to fall on his head. He deserved it.

Paphian waited, watching silently. Vivan was agitated. The conversation must have been interesting. He wished he had missed it.

He won't ask about it. The brother obviously doesn't want that. But you don't have to be a genius to figure out what it was about. It had to be about Vashaba.

Does not matter. He will not skip this conversation. He is his brother.

"You got kicked again?" He asked brutally.

Vivan remembered the flogging. Brother was shocked when he saw the scars, but he did not have the strength to tell him about his fate yesterday. Now, looking at it all aside, he admitted bitterly that he wouldn't have put it otherwise... Too much indecision. Fear of the consequences.

"It seems so," he replied, waiting for the harsh words of the reprimand.

"You really must like pain..." Paphian began ironically, but Vivan had no intention of listening to the insults with humility.

"You have no idea...!"

"About what?!" Paphian shouted angrily, entering his word. "Why did you let it?! AGAIN! Haven't I ever reminded you how to act? Why didn't you handle this just like the people in the marketplace? You got abducted like a child!"

"I had no choice..." Vivan lowered his tone. He didn't want to talk about his fate, although that would explain a lot.

Right now, it all felt like a cheap excuse.

He did not deserve any consideration.

"You know very well how the people in the marketplace died. It was an accident. Mayene... It was the only way," he waited a moment before speaking again, "I fear what might happen. Own power. Defense is not the same as deliberately killing someone," he remembered the elf's words about murder. "I feel that then something dark is trying to take control of me. Absorb me and everything around me. I'm not sure how it might end so I hesitate. Believe me: I know very well that I screwed up!"

Paphian looked at him closely.

"Will you finally tell me what happened?"

The latter, however, remained silent.

Pafian understood that he would not get anything out of him now. It was almost unbelievable in the behavior of his brother. So, he tried another way. He decided to provoke him.

"You didn't use that killer gift? Not once?!"

"NO!" so it was the bull's-eye. "This degenerate should rot in the depths of the ocean! I couldn't kill him! Neither him nor that damned crew that drowned innocent people! Even Ross couldn't help but fight the snake, even though I felt his suffering! That's why Vashaba died! It's all because of me!" He finished, in the blink of an eye kindling a blue flame within him that burned in his eyes and flowed through the veins to the palm of his hand.

Even beneath the dragon's skin, the glow could be seen.

Paphian acted instinctively, taught by the experience he had acquired over the years alongside an extraordinary brother. He placed his hand where the aching heart hid, and at the same time pressed Vivan to his brother's chest.

The healer felt he was losing strength again. Immediately dark circles appeared under his eyes. Fury was burning him like destructive poison. His breathing was shortening.

Suddenly he felt relieved. Hot brotherly love took its beginning from the hands on his chest, then it wrapped around him like arms. The destructive blue flame was extinguished, choked by the green color of spring grass, a symbol of reborn life. He felt a warmth inside him and a power surging through him... The only one he had always cared about. The gift of healing. He breathed a sigh of relief.

"I think I already know why you didn't," said Paphian, excited.

The boy looked in amazement at his hands, shining with a web of green glow.

He recovered again. But more important was what they just found out.

"You're welcome," added his brother with a smile. "Since when do you change colors like fireworks?"

Vivan looked at him, both surprised and scared.

It was something completely new.

When Paphian heard of the Red Captain's deeds, he was at first silent.

Finally, in a low voice, he apologized for his earlier violent behavior. Vivan didn't want the apology. He did not think he deserved them. He told him about it. Then he saw the expression on the other's face.

Paphian looked at him with eyes full of genuine sympathy. The feeling pierced deep into his heart, disturbed his breathing. It brought tears. He could barely control himself, though at the same time he was overwhelmed with tenderness for his stepbrother. Plus, after all, Paphian was gentle with him, as if suddenly Vivan had turned into a glass statue. Considering how much Vivan has been through so far, it was a bit annoying.

As for Ross and his abilities, he was full of undisguised admiration for his dynamically developing talent. Apart from warm words about his devotion.

"It's really surprising how much they both developed their skills," he told him. They looked like two sides of a coin, magic and a gift. Was it for sure a coincidence that the Jewel was given to the dying Ross? Paphian did not know where this certainty came from, but he was convinced that the Jewel was due to their friend. Maybe because only he loved someone then? Or maybe it was because fate gave a gift to an abused street kid, a male whore, thus giving a chance to someone who deserved a better life?

He wondered if he too, now aimlessly, would soon be marked by life? Or maybe he himself will finally discover his path that will lead him to a dignified future?

From the bottom of his heart, Vivan wished him not to discover any unique gift within himself. Only after a while Paphian thanked him for this, understanding that his brother would like to save him from a fate like his fate.

Violet was still asleep, as were Tipe and his men, now below deck when Vivan decided to leave the cabin.

He reached into the pocket of his new pants. The scarf was still there. He did not allow it to be taken for washing or thrown away. It carried so much soothing energy. The warmth of the feelings of those who had her before. It cheered him up.

Eric stayed on that damn ship. May fate protect him...

He was glad that they found Judith.

He greeted the captain and his men. Each of those currently on deck watch wanted to shake the healer's hand personally. It was soothing. Paphian forbade him to blame himself, but Vivan knew his. He left guilt to his conscience.

Ross, from what he sensed, was still asleep. Then he had to ask Sel for help... He was already bustling about the deck with his grandfather. They watched the Witch.

The Avenger sailed away, which was a surprise to them. He knew perfectly well why. Without Ross, they didn't know what happened. Now that was the most important thing. They had to know.

"Have you come to get some air?" Dinn asked when he saw him.

"Kind of," he replied, studying the waves.

"I haven't told you yet..." Dinn sighed heavily, but before adding anything else, Vivan, on his peculiar gut, announced:

"Alesei is dead."

"So, you know…"

"I figured out by the facts..."

"Pretty good," Dinn said with soft admiration.

"Tell me better: how did it happen?" He asked.

They both set out to help him. Alesei would never stand at the door of his room again, a voice as strong as his trained body awakening him to his morning training. He will not give a friendly pat on the shoulder, encouraging him when words are of no use.

Ross will take it badly. When the two decided to help Oliver and then the healer, they finally left the House of Pleasure, which had been their home for several years. They dragged a few people with them. Most were already dead.

Ross was grieving over the deaths of each of them. He had better memories from The House of Pleasure, though a brothel, than from time living with his mother. He had the opposite of Alesei, which seemed like a chuckle of fate. They had been true friends since they broke down the final barriers of prejudice when they were at Sel's house. They could talk about anything, including things that they did not want to tell their loved ones about.

Alesei reasoned everything in a simple way, without a combination. In his spare time, he enjoyed cooking, which sometimes made the cooks angry because he made a terrible mess around him. He wasn't put off by it at all, and they couldn't be angry with him for too long, charmed by his simple-heartedness and innate charm.

Vivan felt a growing sadness in his soul.

It all happened because of him...

He touched Dinn's hand. It only took a moment for him to learn the details of this gruesome story. He saw it with his eyes. He felt how severely the elf had been mutilated, and he was close to death. He also knew what saved his life.

Dinn realized his intentions too late. Getting to know it didn't take more than a moment. He had always been impressed with this ability in Vivan, though it was a bit scary.

"Stop risking your life for me," Vivan said softly, struck by the enormity of the tragedies associated with him.

He looked at Dinn, begging him to grant his request, but Dinn refused, shaking his head firmly. He was not going to listen to him.

He felt an enormous weight in his heart. Why are they doing this? Why can't they understand that everyone can die because of him? Coming to his aid may result in even more casualties. He was starting to hate himself for it.

He turned to leave, resentful. Then Dinn asked:

"You know why we do this, right?" When he did not receive an answer, he added, "We do it because you are important to us. You help everyone without hesitation. We do it because we love you..."

"Then stop it!" He looked into his eyes. "I don't need dead friends who loved me! Stop loving me! Stop helping me! I'd rather you live than die because of me! I prefer you to sit safely in your homes without worrying about me, than to count how many of you are left!"

Dinn narrowed his eyes without a trace of anger.

"You don't want our help?"

"I don't want you dead!"

"They'll find us, whether you want it or not," Dinn observed. "They'll do anything to get you, and then they'll hit wherever it hurts to make you do their own thing. You do not understand this? We're not going to be safe at home. And I would never forgive myself warming my ass by the fireplace when a friend who is ready to give his life for us needs help. You can't stop me."

Vivan felt the grief leave him. He was right.

"You'd better say thank you," Dinn smiled slightly at his confusion.

"Thank you," Vivan replied agitated, unable to find other words. "Only... You know that I love you too. That's why all this..."

"Oh, don't whine anymore!" Dinn patted him on the back. "I know you don't normally nag like that!"

He left him alone and returned to the cabin. Vivan looked after him for a long time, thinking about the conversation. About the people who helped him. He was worried about them.

He will miss a strong, good friend who looks like he can crush stones in his hands. The world around him again impoverished for another kind soul.

He now had to take care of Ross and the others so that they wouldn't make hasty decisions.

"Sel," he tried direct contact through the Jewels. "Can you hear me?"

Will a friend near him, now away from Ross?

Sel stopped suddenly.

"Vivan?" He asked aloud, ignoring the stares of those present.

"I'm safe. We are sailing on the Judith, Violet's ship. That's not all..." the words came out of his mouth in a nervous rush.

"So, this is what it looks like in full..." muttered Sel, not hiding his joy mixed with the instinct of the researcher, "but how did it happen?!"

Vivan briefly told him their fortune. He made it through the Avenger's demise with difficulty. Sel made no comment, but Vivan, who knew feelings like no one else, sensed that his views on the subject coincided with Violet's.

"What are you doing?!" Victor, who had been watching Sel for some time, finally got impatient. "You look like madman!"

Sel looked at him, barely concealing a child's joy and pride at his relationship with Vivan. Vivan was touched by his sincere sympathy. He had known long ago that he was very lucky to have such friends around. Thanks to them, he felt like living.

"Vivan is safe now," Sel explained meanwhile. "I'm just talking to him."

Victor sat down on the nearest barrel, moved by the news.

"And Ross? How is he feeling?" He asked after a moment in a trembling voice.

Sel simply nodded. Vivan smiled involuntarily, watching his grandfather through his eyes. Well, he impressed the dear old man!

"And what is he telling you?" Victor asked, barely concealing his disappointment that even Sel could talk to his own grandson and he couldn't.

Unless?...

"Grandpa..." he tried carefully, "I'm safe."

Victor looked at Sel with fearful eyes.

"Oh, it didn't seem like a good idea," Sel said quietly.

"Did you do something?" Victor lashed out at him. "What are you playing at?"

Sel decided it was better not to explain anything. They confused him enough, even though their intentions were good.

"I should have known this would throw him off balance..." Vivan worried.

"I'll take care of it!" Sel said briefly to him, and he turned to Victor calmly, "I'm sorry, I wanted to check..."

"Come on!" Victor said angrily. "Don't talk to me in my head!"

"Forgive me, Victor," his friend replied, without going into details. These words were so rare in their relationship that they took effect immediately.

Victor looked at him, suppressing his anger with a glare that made it clear that he shouldn't do it again.

"No such tricks!" Still angry, walking away.

"Sorry," Vivan said, "I didn't think it through..."

"He'll be fine," Sel remarked nonchalantly. Vivan sensed a hint of merriment in it. The whole incident amused his friend rather than upset.

"I'm glad you're safe," he added after a moment, in line with the emotions he felt. "I'll tell Lena about it in a moment."

Vivan leaned back against the ship's railing, looking out over the sea. Cook, glad to find him, brought him hot chocolate. He smiled happily as he accepted the mug. The boy felt proud of his own idea. Vivan toast him to please him. The boy's eyes shone with joy as he walked away.

He did not know his name yet. He must ask about it. You must remember this.

"Sel," he told his friend silently, "Try not to answer aloud," he remarked with mild amusement.

"Well, that's right," Sel smiled happily. "I must look like a madman!"

"Nothing new!" The nearest sailor said cheerfully.

"It's normal on this ship!" Another one immediately noticed.

"Mr. Adios!" Cried another from above, "Greet the healer from us!"

I hear, Vivan smiled emotionally. "Thank you."

They still like him...

"He thanks you!" Sel called to everyone.

Nearby sailors shouted joyfully. Then they passed the heard news to others.

The healer was safe.

Soon the message reached Tenan. Straight to the captain's bridge.

"There is something else..." Vivan added.

Sel decided it was time to try some good advice.

"You already brightened up my day," he remarked cheerfully, this time in his mind, "could be better?"

"Paphian and Dinn are with me. And the townspeople they took."

Sel pondered the news, feeling a sudden unease that quickly shattered his gaiety.

"And Alesei?"

Vivan frowned. The joy at talking with friend faded away quickly, muffled by the recurring mourning.

"Alesei won't come home anymore," he began sadly.

Sel felt a pang in his heart.

"Tell me everything," he asked softly, glancing toward the captain's cabin.

He cut himself off from Sel as soon as Tenan gave his orders. He without hesitation ordered to return home, enjoying his freedom. He hoped Ross would also be pleased with the decision.

Joy at the last moments faded as soon as he was alone.

Vivan hid himself from the eyes of others. He could feel Ross' grief, to whom Sel had passed the dark news. Thoughts so similar to his...

The waves reminded him of the drowned.

Every death he did not prevent...

He had done more harm than good to everyone. How did it happen that instead of helping, he destroys everything around him?

It can't be a blessing from heaven, as his grandmother used to say. It is not a gift! It brings only misfortunes!

The world does not want to leave him alone, and his relatives and friends only suffer from it.

"I hear crap you think about yourself," suddenly he heard a familiar voice, much stronger than a few hours ago.

He smiled with difficulty. Ross didn't cut himself off from him.

"It's good that you are finally free," added his friend warmly, "You will probably tell me later how it happened. Now tell me better - why do you feel so bad of yourself?"

"I think maybe I should have died a long time ago, on my birthday," he told him straight from the shoulder. "Then the world would stop hating me."

"The world doesn't hate you, Vivan," Ross remarked thoughtfully. "You know why, let's put it in general, bad people usually want to suck you up, gutted you, or tear you apart?"

"Bad people?" He asked uncertainly.

"Vashaba..."

"Vashaba was not bad! She was lost in the action of my gift."

"Let's say you got all the secrets out of her..." Ross remarked in the tone of a former professional in his trade.

"Ross!"

Ross sighed.

"They want something they lack. Something that will make their lives better, fuller," he said, "A good person has to endure many bad things in life that lurk at almost every corner. Why? Because he has something that the world secretly envies him. Strength. Because good is not a weakness, but a strength. It takes courage to be a good person."

He fell silent, sinking into his own memories.

"Beautiful words," Vivan whispered.

"They're not mine," Ross smiled at his thoughts. "One time, when I was lying unable to move for pain, the woman I loved told me as if she were my mother. Because she was. She will always be her for me."

"More courage, Vivan." He added after a moment, "You can die as an old man or during a fight. We need you in this world. Of course, we won't all bite you," he remarked ironically. "I personally don't like raw human flesh. I'd rather be careful with your new companion, Tipe. His people come from the Namala Islands and thus they treat brave people. But I and the rest of the ordinary meat-eaters we know well miss you. And believe me, if you were missing, the whole world would miss you. Because you bring with you the good that gives us strength."

Vivan pondered his words. Once again, someone told him how much he meant to others. However, at that moment he did not feel it at all.

CHAPTER 21

"As if this escort is a bit too big," Alvar observed sarcastically when the arrival of the royal force was finally announced.

Erlon watched the oncoming closely.

"The royal carriage," he observed with a hint of amazement.

"The king himself came to us?" Anna asked surprised.

"We'll see," he muttered, reluctant to such a visit. "Dog, calm down!" He ordered the animal just in case, although there was clearly no such need.

The dog knew how to behave. Alesei had taught him that.

A small group of two maids and cooks employed in the palace kitchen to give dinners to the builders, accompanied him outside the unfinished building in silent waiting. There was also Alvar with a group of his men as working representatives. Workers stopped work while waiting for the arrival of guests. Like Erlon, they saw the carriage.

The royal coat of arms, depicting a woman in a crown, holding a green branch in one hand and a sword in the other, was a symbol of the blessing of Mother Earth herself - a deity recognized as common in most lands, by mutual acceptance centuries ago. The mother wore a crown - a symbol of royal power. Her sword pointed at the castle - so she gave the king the right to rule over her land. The branch was a sign that harmony would be kept, so nature was not allowed to be undeservedly destroyed throughout the kingdom. Cutting down trees was allowed as long as new trees were planted and only in fixed amounts. The shortages were filled through imports from other countries.

Erlon still remembered the teachings of a private tutor from his childhood.

Also, a legend about how the kingdom was created.

A beautiful, always with child Mother, outraged by the tribal fights in this land, appointed a woman queen one day, endowing her with the power that helped her to unite the warring tribes.

Calteymaya. That was the name of the young girl. A purple rose, pierced by yellow streaks, was then named after her.

When the carriage door was opened, the first thought in his mind about the visitor was the last mention of that legend.

Calteymaya was said to have had the same fiery red hair color. The Queen, even though she was older than her legendary predecessor now, still exuded beauty, just as, according to ancient tales, she did.

She showed clear surprise and confusion as soon as she looked at him. The faces of the women accompanying her looked similar.

"Oh!" She barely suppressed the cry. "You look even better than I remembered you..."

He could feel himself starting to blush.

"Still young, as all these..." she bit her tongue in time.

Alvar looked at him pointedly. Erlon felt the situation getting a little out of control. Everyone around them was watching them. Including Anna and Dog.

"Your Majesty," despite the compliment, he has barely made the necessary courtesy, for a very specific reason from the past. "To what do I owe this unexpected visit?"

The women in the carriage stared at him raptly. Behind him, he heard some soft, amused comments from the workers.

"I was expecting a similar compliment, as it usually is in a good tone," the queen remarked, already in control of herself. "But I am not surprised by your coldness, Lord Count. After all, our relations have not been the best lately," she noted, trying to smile cheerfully, even though his appearance and posture clearly upset her. "I'm here to help!" She concluded firmly.

There was silence.

Erlon knew perfectly well that he should thank her now for her favor. Not to mention the visit he was honored with. But he couldn't do it. Not after what they did.

Fortunately, the queen was not like her sometimes impetuous husband. Otherwise, the whole situation could have been fatal for the reckless Erlon.

"Queen," he said at last, when the prolonged silence had already begun to be commented on in a whisper, "Welcome to my humble home," he stretched out his hand to lead her, "And everyone with you." He smiled compulsively at the women in the carriage and then at the others, finally recognizing among them some welcome people who tried to keep a straight face as they watched the meeting.

The queen pretended not to be offended by his behavior. She had to admit that the handsome count was bold indeed. He needs to be tempered a bit. Alvar waited until all the guests had passed.

"Oh, how cute he is!" He heard one of the women say.

"Did you see how nervous he got when saw her?" The other asked with excitement, even though she was a little older than she was.

"His anger suits him," the young woman sighed dreamily.

Alvar smiled as this little parade passed.

"It will be fun!" He said, then turned to his men, "Gentlemen, help the Count, as we agreed! Come on, take care of the horses and the rest! We don't want to bring embarrassment on our count because he doesn't have all the help yet!"

The only ready room capable of accommodating all guests was the library with rows of empty shelves and only a dozen or so surviving volumes on an oak desk. Here stood a round table with a relief of a hand with a Jewel. It wasn't big enough for everyone to sit down at. First, it was intended for family members and their friends. So Erlon ordered it to be dismantled and moved, expecting a royal force. He asked to be lent him tables, so many brought what they had. The missing seats for the distinguished guests were hurriedly replaced.

The inhabitants did not disappoint the quiet expectations of the impoverished count, who, after the palace was destroyed by the witch Mayene, really lost almost everything. So they brought tableware, tablecloths, chairs and benches, and even flowers in vases. When he fully saw the effect of these actions, which had been prepared until the last moment before the entry of Queen Constance, he felt a wave of emotion tightening his throat. He looked with admiration and gratitude at the people around them who pretended to be his ministry that day.

Many of them did not accept any payment. Those who chose to do so were in too difficult situation to refuse. They were mainly new residents who had little possessions with them. They were simple people. Usually, they lacked good manners. They made up for it with diligence and enthusiasm. They smiled at the count surreptitiously, seeing his emotion. They tried really hard.

Constance watched it all with amazement. This man had the backing of a ruler of a small kingdom. People obviously loved him. Many could envy him such support. A few would feel threatened, even knowing that the Count Beckert and his family never pursued power. Unfortunately, she knew those who would destroy this city only because of what they would see today. And this discipline! She spotted looters, ready to go to the unfinished upstairs rooms in search of loot, though from what she had just seen, she wouldn't have expected too much in their place. The keen eyes of a few of the guys, apparently led by this red-bearded, tobacco-smelly man, caught them quickly. They were led out the threshold. Like those who wanted to steal something from a silverware that some kind soul had brought.

She looked at Erlon with a faint concern. It wasn't just his extraordinary son. All these people were like one big family.

If they only wanted to... This thought was not appropriate to the situation, yet she felt the unease that more than one ruler would probably feel.

She pushed it away from her.

Marcela and Klara, two brave maids, were hastily instructing Miriam and her daughter, as well as several other women who had come to help, how to serve the gala dinner as it was the time to start the ceremony. There were a few stumbles and a few small mishaps, after which the women, frightened by the unusual guests, almost ran out, but as for the less royal sophistication, everything went very well.

Erlon led the queen and her two companions to the hastily prepared spots, feeling prouder of his people than he could express.

Constance cast a glance at her ladies, who were simply enchanted by him. Handsome, sensitive and daring. No wonder they make a hit with him. She smiled thoughtfully.

She was far from similar thoughts, though she was undoubtedly impressed.

Everyone waited anxiously for the end of the meal in these unusual conditions. It was feared that the queen would get angry at the inexperienced staff. But Constance had not even thought to be angry about anything like that. She knew perfectly well that everything here was still under construction and preparation. She was not like other mannered rulers for whom material goods are the most important.

On the contrary, she was captivated by this place and the people.

Erlon noticed her soft delight and a kind smile for her subjects as the desserts were served, perhaps less exquisite than those served outside, but extremely appetizing.

For a moment he thought more warmly about his distinguished guest, seeing her posture and hearing the soft tone of her voice as she addressed the intimidated women. She was talking to Anna. She even thanked Ajana, Miriam's daughter! Seeing the pride and happiness of the girl, he smiled slightly.

"You look good with a smile, my lord count," the queen remarked, wanting to soften his demeanor.

Unfortunately, she only made that smile fade instantly. This time, however, he had to make some effort to do so.

"I'm just stunned by what's going on," he replied, looking at his surroundings. "It's just wonderful."

Constance smiled at the emotion in his voice. He couldn't even imagine how many there would be at her court who would use it against him and destroy this little world. He did not have the slightest idea about everything, which made it difficult to move freely for rulers. It was great to finally breathe among normal people.

"I know what you are thinking, Lady," he suddenly became serious, "This man would not be able to cope with the royal court. Fortunately, I'm only a lesser count."

He surprised her, that's true. A sharp mind.

"You are also the father of the healer," she replied. "That's why you must be careful."

He looked at her quizzically.

"Probably," he said after a moment, though she would have sworn he was initially about to say something different.

It was time to get down to business.

"May I speak with you privately, my lord?" She asked.

He nodded his head in agreement, waiting for this conversation from the beginning. He motioned for the Dog.

Like the palace, on which work was started after lunch, the garden was also in the preparation phase. It has already gained its unique atmosphere, being full of shrubs and trees in the middle of summer, creating alleys full of almost fairy-tale nooks and crannies. This, too, was different from the royal gardens, smoothed and translucent to a fault after the plague had passed.

The trees and bushes were young, but you could hide among them with a dagger.

It is terrible that such a thought crossed her mind! Unfortunately, as she knew perfectly well, her world was just like that.

She quickly focused her attention on the black and white shepherd dog, the Count's companion, running freely along the alleys. Another peculiarity.

The exception was the labyrinth, low but neatly trimmed. It will definitely be an attraction with the now closed fountain in the middle. It wasn't big, but it was going to be a lot of fun in the future.

"You have a real treasure here," she said, giving up title for the first time. Her two ladies walked nearby, marveling at the beauty of the roses and the emerging multicolored butterflies.

She will never regret coming to this place. It was almost dreamlike. And it grew stronger.

"I know," he replied, walking beside her. "That's why I have to ask for something. My son said you treated him well, Lady. I trust you have such a good heart as they say."

"What is this request?" She asked, looking him in the eyes.

She had a beautiful look. He only succumbed for a moment.

"Please don't tell anyone what you saw here today, lady," he urged, "on behalf of my people."

She looked at him, savoring the sight.

"What are you willing to offer me for this?" She asked with a gleam of merriment in her eyes.

She wanted to tease him. Indeed, he immediately felt tense at the question. She laughed at the sight of his expression, perhaps for the first time in a long time, with a real sincere laugh.

"Oh please, Erlon!" She cried, "It's just a joke! Don't be so scared!"

It was impossible not to like her.

"Lady..." he began hesitantly.

"Of course," she said solemnly, being more seriously, "I promise you. I will not tell anyone." He really surprised her.

"Thank you," he said simply.

She noticed the sadness appearing in his eyes. She knew its reason perfectly well.

"Can we talk privately?" she asked, getting to the point. "Let's skip all titles."

"As you wish," he replied.

Nervously, she adjusted the sunshade that protected her from the sun. It didn't save her skin from freckles because she had never applied to it. The husband loved those unruly freckles, treating them as a highlight rather than a blemish on flawless skin. She didn't have to hide them under a layer of powder.

"Why did you come here?" He asked directly.

"Why the library?" she interrupted him. "Why did you accept us in the library?"

Music sounds came from the palace. A few people came to keep the guests entertained.

The townspeople did not cease to amaze him today.

"I asked it to be finished first, because in the event of rain, many workers could take shelter there."

"And not because of the books?" She asked.

"I don't have many at the moment," he replied, increasingly convinced she was trying to flirt with him.

She only smiled, easing his fears.

"As I mentioned, I came to help," she began to say. "First of all, the king and I will take care of this construction. We will cover its costs, we will hire more workers. The palace will be built faster, it will resemble a fortress. Additionally, there will be walls around..."

"Stop!" He shouted suddenly, cutting her off. "No fortress! No walls!"

"The healer must be protected so that no similar incidents happen in the future!" She replied firmly.

"A little late for that..." he began, but she cut him off.

"I trust we will all do our best to get him home safely."

"First of all: by bringing people here - you will break the promise you made to me!" he remarked. "Secondly: my son is and will remain a free man. By creating walls and a fortress here, you will make him choke as if in a cold cage, just like us! Third," he raised a hand not to interrupt him. "We will not separate ourselves from people! Never!"

"Look what happened when you used these methods of yours!" she could not stand it.

He looked at her carefully.

"You mean the brutal kidnapping of Vivan by your general, hitting my wife, hurting my other son, and threatening to kill the entire village? Or maybe just the last kidnapping?"

She snapped up.

"Oh, by Mother Earth!" She shouted resentfully. "You don't know much about diplomacy!"

"I'm even proud of it!" He replied ironically.

"This is stupid!" she looked into his eyes. "If you were talking to my husband like that, he would order you to be killed for insolence!"

"This audacity helped me break out of my family home," he replied. "And besides, I'm talking to you," he added teasingly.

She saw the gleam in his eyes. Oh, he probably wished he could say it! She was sure of it!

She couldn't blame him for that.

"It's not up to you!" She said, trying to assume a firm tone, as befits a queen.

"Oh yeah, what about the treaty of independence you gave to my son and our family on his way home?!"

Oh, she forgot about it! Of course, he had to mention it!

She fell silent. Erlon, feeling anger mixed for some reason with amusement and a hint of satisfaction, watched her inner struggles. Apparently, he had upset her. Probably, she really liked him.

"I am to understand that kings change their minds when they want, like little children?" He added, even though he knew how brazen it would sound.

She looked up at him with sparkling eyes. He wondered if she would attack him with her fists.

"Still, I've had a better opinion of you lately," he added in a calmer tone to ease the situation.

He surprised her again.

"Ah, she replied mockingly, still angry with him. "So, we have gained your favor after all? In the name of the king and my, we thank you for this, great count, ruler of this land!"

"After the plague you helped your subjects," he began to calculate calmly, not being provoked. "You lowered the taxes. You gave the lands to the poor. You have opened the royal granary. You have opened a home for the sick and the lame. Orphanage for orphaned children. Elementary schools in several cities. You helped the people of Adelaide to lift the city from its fall. In the port of Verdun, you gave people a job building ships for the future army, thanks to which the city revived very quickly. These are good decisions. Better late than never."

She calmed down at the soft appreciation in his voice.

She thought about the next words that could change a lot.

"Sorry," she said suddenly, lifting her chin like a queen.

At least she was trying to look proud enough.

"What for?" He asked.

He felt it, she was sure. Just like his son, whose father did not appear to be. He knew what she was thinking before she spoke the next words. Therefore, the tone of his voice became more benevolent. Is everyone in this family so special?

"For the harm that happened to all of you," she replied sincerely.

He stared at her, still distrustful. He was right about that. Kings rarely admitted their mistakes.

"We had no idea how bad the general would treat you," she continued, looking him in the eye, "or that it could have ended so tragically if not for the help of your friends. Please accept the apology on my behalf and on behalf of my husband. This one time. Before you answer anything, consider the words carefully."

Erlon knew that this situation hardly ever happened. It was a royal gesture. So this time he followed her advice.

He never expected to hear it ever again.

"Apologies accepted," he replied, his voice slightly trembling with emotion.

She smiled with a little of the superiority befitting a queen.

"Let me help you," she said gently, contradicting her attitude.

"Don't build a fortress," he replied in the same tone.

"So what do you want?"

"A home that will give him relief when he comes back. Bright and full sun."

"And the walls?"

"Will I get these funds?" he made sure.

He saw her smile again.

"Yes," she replied shortly.

"So, I'm gonna move the city walls inland. It's getting a bit tight."

"Really?" She asked teasingly, thinking about what she had observed today.

"I will think about the walls around the palace," he added after a moment's thought, "but I'll hire my own people to carry out the project."

She managed to push something through.

She was sure these walls would be built.

She nodded silently to him.

However, the conversation was not over yet. She needed a break.

"Erlon, I also came here to announce to you the royal decision," after spending an hour in his enchanted garden, she picked up the subject.

Time was pressing. Decisions have already been made.

"As you well know, we appreciate Vivan's gift very much," she began matter-of-factly. "We believe that he is the greatest treasure of this kingdom..."

"He is first and foremost a living man!" he pointed out firmly.

"He is!" She admitted imperiously, to nip this discussion in the bud, "I predicted you would say that. So, I will start from a different side. Because of what happened to him and the harm he suffered in the past, she emphasized, "we will do everything to get him back home. We found gold and jewels, once stolen from us by the viceroy. That is why we tried to help our subjects," she explained. "You mentioned ships for the future army. This army is no longer the future. My eldest son will soon take the throne. The husband will be his adviser. Rather, he is resigned to it. This is what tradition dictates. The son will marry Princess Teresa, daughter of the neighboring kingdom of Vakadelmaria. It's his choice. Thanks to this, we gained support in the form of troops heading for the capital. These troops and the soldiers we recruit will be our army. We counted on the help of the Kingdom of Ice Lands, with which we also live peacefully, but apparently a civil war will break out there in a moment. The king was murdered, and the usurper sat on the throne. However, the Seal Keeper appeared, according to their local legend, so maybe in the future..."

"Wait!" He interrupted her anxiously. "Why are you telling me this? Why are you gathering an army? What does this have to do with my son?"

"You know the prophecy of King Azram?"

"I know," he replied shortly.

"He can't just take our land's most precious inhabitant!" She announced firmly. "Our spies have already sailed to Slave Bay. If we find out that Vivan is his prisoner, the army will sail towards the Bay, support him in the fight against Azram, or take him from his hands so that he will not be murdered. This prophecy is one big lie! His death would not only be a tragedy for you and all those who mourn him. Demons will take over the Bay and will soon take over the world! Including Tenckryz. We cannot let that happen!"

Erlon felt a shiver run down his spine.

"Are you saying you'll send an army to the Bay to save Vivan?!"

"The ships you mentioned," she explained to him. "They're ready. Six ships and the recruited ships of those who can fight. Do you know where your friend the Jewel Sorcerer is at the moment? His ship and himself would be of great help to us in this fight..."

"Ross went to rescue Vivan..." he replied, increasingly nervous.

"Excellent! He will be there if..."

"Azram has demons to serve him. Thanks to them, he wields power. He makes sacrifices to them..."

"I know these stories!" She interrupted him.

"They're real!" He assured her. "You will send soldiers to death in agony!"

"Put more hope in us. We can defeat the demons. I have heard that without the support of the Dark Circle, they are mortal. Until the Blood Gate is opened..."

"Many people will die!"

"Even more will die as the Dark Circle takes over the world!" She admonished him angrily. "Do you want more witches, like the one that attacked your present Levilon, to show up here? They can be even stronger than her. Not to mention any other creatures that might pass into our world if Vivan dies! She nearly decimated the city. They will murder everyone! There will be nothing left of this fairy-tale corner of the land! Nothing! And nobody!"

He closed his eyes for a moment.

The middle of summer.

The place around them was teeming with life. He heard bees flying around the flowers. The happy barking of a Dog that was entertaining the court ladies nearby. Workers' voices. The thunderous voices of the queen's guards, flirting with the young women helping them today. The clatter of dishes and free conversation of the cooks through the open kitchen windows. Musicians' music. The sounds of nearby farms. Sheep bleating. The horses neigh in the pastures.

"All this will cease to exist if your son dies," said Constance, thinking of the same thing.

He swallowed hard, mouth dry.

"I understand," he replied hollowly.

After a moment he added firmly:

"Constance," he looked into her eyes, "You forgot something."

She was surprised. Not only because he said her name.

"About what?"

"You mentioned Azram's prophecy. It says about two people. One of them is Vivan. You have to protect the other, too, if you don't want it to prove to be true."

She wondered.

"Keeper of the People..." she remembered aloud.

"And the second?"

She looked at him fearfully.

"Sorcerer! Sorcerer of the Heart! His power is just developing, I thought of him as support all the time! I forgot..."

"You must protect Ross, too," he told her gravely, dreaded by the upcoming events, "I couldn't stop him."

"Lord Count," Kirian greeted him kindly.

"Nice to see you again..." Erlon hesitated, noting the other's uniform.

"I am now the commander of this unit," explained Kirian, seeing that look. "Captain Teron took command of one of the ships in Verdun Harbor. By the queen's order, we will stay here to protect you in these uncertain times."

Erlon looked at him closely.

"You know the king's plans?"

"Yes, sir," replied the commander solemnly, "the Queen sent us here, hoping to inspire your trust."

"You did excellent last time," Erlon admitted. "Actually, I'm grateful to the queen for this favor. I'm glad you're here again."

"Glad to hear it, sir," smiled Kirian. "May I ask, how is the situation now? There is new news about Vivan?"

"I'll tell you," Erlon revealed. "What I know and guess."

"They all came to help him?" Kirian asked thoughtfully.

"I couldn't stop them."

"Lord Count..." Kirian leaned closer to his interlocutor, feeling a bit awkward. "By the king's order, the soldiers are to capture Countess

Beckert and her husband and lock them in the royal dungeons for treason. Their property will be confiscated."

Erlon looked at him, feeling a mixture of surprise, satisfaction, and unease at the same time. It was his mother, as well as Paphian's grandmother. She never wanted a connection with his new family, so he had no thoughts of linking her with Vivan or Lena, especially after a memorable incident where she was indignant at Vivan's completely innocent behavior on his own birthday. It was just fun! Could a young boy not dance to the music on the table? Paphian persuaded him to do so, and he also danced on the table. And yet the mother decided Vivan was a bad influence on her grandson, and he was a vain, crude bully. As if she were just waiting for an opportunity to humiliate him!

Poor Vivan was so taken over by this that he never got involved in such games again. He blamed himself for severing family ties.

However, there was really nothing to break up. They have never been closely related to each other.

"Haven't the queen told you about it, my lord?" The young commander asked anxiously, seeing his confusion.

"No," he replied, trying to chase away unpleasant memories, "It's truly amazing how much envy people have..."

"Lord...?" The interlocutor looked at him questioningly.

"I didn't believe it," Erlon said thoughtfully. "Meanwhile, my son was right to fear that it would cause some misfortune in the future," he looked at Kirian with sadness in his heart. "One moment of carelessness can trigger a war."

He spent the hours of the night bitter meditating in Vivan's room. The dog accompanied him, sensitive to his every movement, lying on the bed next to his side. The Queen and her maids took their bedroom and Paphian's, suitably prepared by the amazing townspeople and maids.

After supper, he gathered everyone when the queen had already gone upstairs. Not hiding his emotions, he thanked them for the enormous amount of work they had done today.

They liked it immensely.

Tomorrow will bring anxiety into this small, peaceful world.

He let Lena on this risky journey, knowing that Ross could become a target.

One of his sons is in danger again, and he still has no news of the other.

Anna vainly concealed from him her fear for her beloved husband.

He sent people on an uncertain fate. There were already the first victims. This hunch could not confuse him! How many of them will not return to their homeland?

Why did Vivan deserve for this fate? And Ross? The great sorcerer... A boy quite plagued by life, as is his foster son. Can they really not be at peace? Live and build their future?

A knock on the door interrupted his thoughts in the middle of the night.

He reassured the Dog with a gesture as he sprang up abruptly.

Cautiously he opened the door.

Queen.

At first, he felt the blood rush to his head. Why has she come? What reasons did he give her to believe that he was prone to such a tryst? He would never cheat on Lena. He was going to make it as emphatic as possible. Even if he was a bit rude. There is no way he would agree to it! His reputation could already be at stake if someone saw her outside the room now.

"Erlon," she smiled brightly, as if not noticing his barely concealed indignation, "can't you sleep either?"

She noticed he was still dressed. Just like her. This surprised him.

"It's inappropriate..." he began, but she hushed his words by placing her hand over his mouth.

"It's so hot," she said, "Let's go outside. I noticed you have a large balcony here."

"Not finished yet, lady," he explained. "There is no support."

"You can sit there though?"

He hesitated.

"Do not be afraid," she smiled warmly. "I do not want to seduce you. My ladies would probably like it, but fortunately they are asleep. Let's talk. We both need it. You have your worries, I have mine. We both have sons whose fate we constantly think about. Before I return to this world, full of intrigue and hypocrisy, I would like to be able to talk to a man who appreciates honesty at least once. Will you agree to it?"

There was something in her voice. Some secret longing that was also in his heart.

She was telling the truth. She risked their reputation to show up here. If he had refused now, he would have offended her feelings, and perhaps would have endangered her. Young ladies could listen in on the entire conversation.

He surprised himself by discovering that he didn't want to say no, not necessarily for these reasons.

He needed this conversation as much as she did. He felt he could trust her. She won't reveal its details.

Finally, he nodded, agreeing to the idea.

Like two old friends, they spent a hot, muggy night with a little wine, with the Dog as their only companion. Talking about the things that were on their mind.

Although it was the Queen who revealed much of her life to the count reluctant to reveal family secrets, neither of them regretted this conversation even once.

When she left, he thought about his mother being taken to the dungeons of the royal palace... He thought about the words of Constance, who finally told him about it, full of understanding and determination.

Then he gathered all the inhabitants.

He told them that a war might soon break out...

CHAPTER 22

They chose the course for the home port. Sel waited for Ross to take a bath and eat breakfast. He already knew Vivan was safe, and that made him feel good. There was no point in contacting the Witch. Tenan decided so. It was more important to take the survivors to a safe place. The women from the town were a bit disappointed that the show didn't come. On the contrary, Oliver did not regret it. He could sit quietly on the deck, listening to Sai's lyre play as long as he wanted. Free from intrigue and embarrassing disguises. Sai focused on the instrument. That's when, according to him, she looked most beautiful. Her black hair was lightly brushed by the wind. The slightly slanting eyes reflected a state of spirituality, a wandering mind somewhere beyond the worlds.

The smile she was sending him made him wonderfully tender.

Apart from the duties of the sailors, the atmosphere was calm. People clearly relaxed.

In addition to the rescued Nena, the dark-skinned girl who helped Vivan, there were sixty-four people. Lena met each of them, from a man to a child. She listened with her father, sitting below the deck with them. They told her and the crew about how they ended up aboard the Blood Witch. Forcibly taken from ships carrying goods and travelers to different parts of the world known to them. Merchants, noble births, poor people looking for work - they were all here. Too late, she noticed the young man who had been sitting among the survivors for some time. She had seen him too briefly to remember the face. Touched by a hunch, she followed him as he left. She saw him among many people standing at the railing. Then, as if nothing had happened, he leapt into the waves.

He drowned.

Silas and Tenan searched in vain for him. Nobody has found a man who so easily gave up fighting for his life.

"Did anyone know him?" She asked the rescued, shocked by the deed.

"His daughters were swallowed up by the sea," explained Nena. "And his wife had her throat cut in front of our eyes. He connected with them."

"There was one more," added the woman, the mother of the girl maybe nine years old. "He lost his son and wife. He defended us until he had to. Once in the boat, he allowed himself to be killed by one of the pirates. I saw it as well as I can see you now."

"I remember!" Exclaimed one of the men from the group. "They were swimming to the healer. The son had some weakness. I think he had a bad hand."

"His wife had a nice voice," said another. "She hummed her son lullabies at night."

"The girls were so happy!" One of the women sighed, touched by a sad memory.

"They are gone," Nena finished her tragic tale.

Lena lowered her head. Long brown hair covered her face.

The rescued fell silent, engrossed in silent mourning.

"Ross," the sun was at its zenith before Sel decided it was time. "How are you now?"

Ross smiled slightly, again the same as he had started on the journey, and Sel silently thanked Mother Earth for the existence of their extraordinary friend, a healer.

Only his eyes showed that the captain, fully clothed and ready to return to the bridge, had been through a difficult passage. He regained his health and strength.

"Good," he replied in a nostalgic tone that also had a more sensual note.

Spontaneously, in a slightly feminine gesture, he tilted his triangular hat back.

"I wish..." he leaned forward suddenly, following his desire. Longing pulsed to the beat of his heart. It changed his senses, sharpening them under the influence of hidden fantasies. He wanted him so much that he began to feel pain when he couldn't touch him.

He needed him.

He woke up stronger. Broken down and full of life at the same time. Full of longing for his presence...

They could finally be alone. Probably not for long.

His kiss was passionate. He dispersed all thoughts. He awakened a desire that could only be quenched in one way. So Sel embraced him, his hands running beneath his cloak, until he pulled out his shirt, carefully hidden under his pants, and placed his hands on his lover's warm skin. Ross groaned softly, sensitive to his touch. Sel forgot what he wanted to say to him immediately. Now he couldn't do it. As his fingers ran over Ross's body under his pants, reaching below his waist, he knew he wasn't going to stop there. He ran his hand over the throbbing penis. He felt Ross tremble as he succumbed to him, biting his lip so as not to be heard outside.

"I just wanted a kiss..." he whispered in his ear with a seemingly innocent smile.

Spoiled boy. A kind of innocent.

He remembered the moment he saw him for the first time. Sitting casually in an armchair. With his shirt unbuttoned, his pants slightly pulled down, showing a fragment of a firm buttock. Seductive lines of a slender body. Brown hair disheveled from sudden jerks. Knee-high boots. A goblet of red wine in a hand. Rose in the second.

The face of a gentle boy. No "porcelain" makeup.

That's what he drew him then. Later, after the first night together, he turned the page to include both of his lover's faces in one sheet...

Without hesitating, he added a new torture to him. He covered his neck with his hot breath. A kiss that touched a pulsating vein.

"We're not alone..." Ross tried weakly to defend himself, shivering at his caresses. "I can't stand it. I'm gonna scream and make... Sel!" He moaned, feeling the sensual massage of the most sensitive place on his body. "No... please!" He suppressed the last words, cradling his face in his arms.

"Ask!" Croaked Sel. "I love it when you do that..."

Ross looked him in the eye. He was lost.

A sudden knock on the door made them motionless.

"Captain!" They heard the voice of one of the sailors. "Captain! Talk to me!"

Ross felt his heart beating hard. He can hardly take a breath. He turned to the door, frantically collecting thoughts that did not want to pile up at all. His body was burning like a fever.

"And what did you do?" He asked with affectionate reproach.

"We'll just finish…" Sel consoled him, still touching.

Ross focused. With difficulty.

"What happened?!" He shouted, trying to sound confident.

"The Witch is following us, Captain!" was the answer. "It looks like they want to catch up with us! The Guardian is waiting for your decision!"

Ross pulled out of Sel's embrace, feeling the chill seize him. Sel didn't protest. Not in this situation.

Darkness fell on Ross's soul.

"He's after me..." he whispered.

Sel was immediately filled with fear. For his life.

"I'll be there shortly!" Ross shouted, returning to the role of captain for a moment.

He allowed himself a kiss. The blood rumbled so hard in his ears again that he didn't even hear the answer.

"Let the world collapse…!" He whispered with determination straight into his lover's ear.

He tore the shirt on his chest to give him a desperate caress of his lips and hands, reaching lower and lower. Sel did not resist it.

He gave up without a fight.

"If you remember the location well, Healer," Captain Nils said, "We'll be meeting your sorcerer friend soon."

Vivan smiled faintly, silently thanking Sel for patiently sharing the news.

"Good," he replied thoughtfully.

"You'll be home soon," the man consoled him, nudging his shoulder. "Do you have any good inns there?"

"I have a palace," Vivan sensed his sincere sympathy, and this had a soothing effect on him.

The captain laughed sincerely.

"Not for me palaces, healer! Have a few glasses of rum with me, with good music, among simple people like me, and I'll be happy!"

"Agreed," Vivan looked at him with a twinkle in his eye. "Unfortunately, I am a weak companion. One and you will have to take me home, or you will just leave somewhere in the ditch..."

Nils grinned at him.

"Yes, for real? So, I have to teach you to drink!" He announced cheerfully. "And then we will dance on the table until the splinters fly!"

Vivan's smile faded instantly, as did the cheerful mood.

Nils noticed it immediately.

"What is going on?" Asked a little anxiously. "Can't you dance?" He added playfully, in a futile attempt to summon good humor.

"I don't dance," Vivan replied calmly, as he had learned to answer similar questions over the years.

A distant boom distracted the captain before he asked another question.

They turned to where the sound was coming from.

"It's gonna be a big storm, Captain!" the deckhand ripped from the crow's nest.

Vivan looked at the billowing clouds with concern.

He was not afraid of the storm. Rather what it preached.

"Oh!" Ross blurted as he finally left the cabin.

Probably everyone was on board. Well, maybe almost everyone. A few of the watchmen and Silas were missing. After all, everyone must rest sometime. The voices slowly died down. Sel left shortly after him buttoning the last button on his shirt. Seeing so many people waiting for them, he was a little scared, probably thinking, like Ross, how long they had been here. The nearest Tenan has kept his famous calm. The smile of Marlene and a few other girls, aside from the knowing glances among the crew, had betrayed him a lot.

Especially when Oliver laughed at his expression.

At that moment, he wished for a moment that the floor would suddenly collapse beneath him, hiding him from the eyes of those present. Judging by Sel's expression, Sel must have dreamed the same.

He breathed slowly, trying to stay calm.

Unexpectedly, Cora's warm gaze helped him a lot. He nodded at her gratefully for the little gesture.

There was something far more important to him than the sensation they both had caused.

"Captain," Marlene could not bear it. "Let's sail with all our might! What do we care about this carcass?!"

"We cannot!" Apara replied firmly before he could speak. "If the captain goes away now, he will be disgraced in all the seas and oceans!"

"Exactly..." he interjected but was interrupted again.

"Why so?" One of the blonde-haired girls asked resolutely. "Why should we waste time on him?"

"He must fight the Red Captain!" The bearded sailor explained to her patiently from the crowd. "If he floats away, it's as if he has escaped. Everywhere they will spread the news that he did not want to fight him out of fear! He's gonna be a coward!"

"What if the Witch follows him to Levilon?" said another. "What then? They can attack the town!"

"It's a matter of honor!" added another, waving his hand at the same time. "Captain has to fight with Hope."

"He must fight his father!" Another shouted from above.

There was silence.

They didn't take their eyes off him.

Calmly, with some carelessness, he reached into the inside pocket of his coat. At the sight of what he had pulled out of there, Sel made a face of disgust. Well, he couldn't quite get over it. Especially when he tried to hide the tension.

He lit a cigar.

Everyone knew how rare this happened.

He sucked the smoke into his lungs, celebrating the moment thoughtfully. Then he let it go slowly.

"Well," he said quietly. "Looks like I have work to do." The cigar glowed again. "I think you too. That's why…" He paused considerably, "I may know why my people aren't ready yet?" He raised his voice, giving it his captain's tone. "Why aren't we ready to board, land rats?!" the crew twitched nervously, some people began to rush away to their duties. "I should do everything for you?!"

He waited for the preparations to begin.

The women were still standing. Some of the men accompanying them also.

"There will be a storm, Captain," Tenan announced.

As if on command, they heard a nearby thunderclap.

"Ship, Captain!" yelled the sailor from above. "Ship on the horizon!"

"Vivan's ship, I suppose," Sel said, reaching for the spyglass hopefully.

Ross was still calm as he considered his next move. Or at least he thought he was doing it. His hands were trembling slightly.

"I won't let he fall into his hands again…" he muttered.

"They can help us," Tenan observed matter-of-factly.

Ross looked at him seriously.

"We won't drag them into this," he said firmly.

"Two ships are better than one..." he tried to protest.

Sel grimaced at the words. Serious mistake. The captain's decision is not questioned in the presence of the crew.

"Are you questioning my opinion?" Ross's voice grew cold.

"No, Captain," Tenan replied solemnly, noticing Sel's sneering glance at the same time.

"Nobody's going to whip him anymore..." Ross demanded discipline. His people were not to blame for the fact that he was all in nerves now. "Relax, Tenan, we can do it," he added with a slight smile, well aware of the mood of his lover, who purposely stood behind him so that he would not notice his behavior.

The conflict lasted too long.

"Gentlemen!" He shouted to the crew. "What about that ship on the horizon?"

"It could be Violet Meres' ship, Captain!" Cried the sailor from the crow's nest.

"Vivan? Do you see us?" He asked mentally.

"I see you and the Witch," replied his friend immediately, "Ross, please wait..."

"No!" He abruptly cut in on his word, "I will send women and children to you. Notify the captain!"

"Ross..." Vivan began, who, thanks to his sensitivity, already knew what it was about.

"Hush, Vivan!" He ordered him a little too sharply in his mind. And he said aloud:

"Crew, drop the boats on the right! Get women and children out of here!"

"I knew!" Marlene threw at it, glancing at the other companions.

To his amazement, all the women stood in front of him. Though they feared Ross's reaction when they uttered their first words, their expressions were firm.

"Captain," Marlene began, as the bravest. Apara and her silent sister stood next to her, as did Lena and Cora with Maya and Sai. Oliver took a fighting stance, this time giving way to his wife, and Tenan, on reflection, stood beside him, supporting his friend. Sel raised his eyebrows in disagreement.

He admired the courage of women. The one who ordered them to revolt against the ship's captain's orders.

The effect of the first was very interesting now.

"Listen, Marlene," Ross figured what they would want, but was adamant about it.

At least he thought so.

"You can have us locked in an orlop, but only some of us will go to Violet's ship!" she began with a strong voice. "Mothers with children will sail. And those who can't fight," she hid the usual fact that some women were afraid of pirates. "The rest of us... stay!"

"I gave the order..." he began firmly, while the sailors were already letting the boats out.

"With all due respect, Captain," she said nervously. "You didn't say which women to take..."

"Marlene!"

Was she trying to make an idiot out of him?

The women separated. Some of them solidly concentrated in their group and embraced them in unison, thus letting them know that they would not be able to move.

The crew stopped their activities, observing the event with curiosity.

"We're not leaving you!" Apara announced firmly.

Ross looked at Lena.

"We're in this together, Ross," she replied to his silent question. "I'm not going to abandon you because Vivan is safe now. You wouldn't do that!"

"Are you doing this for me?" He asked, surprised and agitated at the same time.

"Not only for you, Captain!" Apara asked.

It was probably the first time he heard her twin sister Anokhi's voice:

"We are not like a flock of chickens in the yard, which can be chased from place to place so that they do not harm. We are part of the crew. You said it yourself, Captain. So... If we have to fight - we will fight!"

He looked at her, for the first time he had the opportunity to do so. So much had happened... The ship was full of the people. He knew each of the faces of the women who came out with him. But he didn't get too many opportunities to get to know them better. Maybe it's time to change that.

Anokhi was not as beautiful as her sister. She had the beauty traits of the people of the Wanderers she came from. But there was something about her... a certain gentleness.

He froze.

Suddenly he heard a laugh. That girl had a temper. It remained a part of his soul since he was reunited with her brother. Julien.

She figured it out... Ghosts know a lot.

"Oh, stop it!" He asked mentally, confused.

He could do it. One more, one last time...

Anokhi smiled shyly at Ross' confused. She knew this incident was a chance for them to hear them out. The most important thing for her was that the captain noticed her unexpectedly.

Yes, women liked them both. But they knew they didn't stand a chance.

She hadn't thought of herself as a competition to Sel. She knew deep in her heart that it was impossible. They were tightly bound together.

Ross looked away, frightened by their startled glances, not quite understanding how it actually happened.

Quick as a flash, a memory flashed through his mind.

Julien's kiss...

"It wasn't that bad," he once told Alesei when he asked about it.

No, it wasn't. He refused to admit it to himself, sure he had known what he wanted for a long time.

He looked up, looking beyond the assembled group. He desperately looked for something that would break him out of this strange state and, most of all, stop hurting Sel. He didn't have to search for too long.

The Witch was getting closer.

It's time to face reality.

"Do you know..." he asked the girl seriously. "What can you threaten if we lose?"

Anokhi looked at him boldly, still touched by his earlier reaction.

"We aren't going to lose, Captain!" She replied firmly.

Her audacity almost made the fear disappear. Almost.

He nodded her head in agreement. He looked at the women around him with appreciation but, what was less common, with apprehension for their fate.

Even those who knew him less were touched by this concern. Highlander women loved him for it, and the men looked at him with a mixture of jealousy and amusement at the same time. Hard here, soft there. The captain was such a mixture of emotions they had never encountered before. But that's what they liked him for.

"Well then," he said, "Let's do it, ladies," he said to mothers with children and the rest of them. "I'm sure Violet Meresa will take care of your safety. Time is running out. May the waves be kind to you."

Several of them came to thank him personally. Some of them had children in their arms who had barely outgrown infancy.

With the help of the sailors, they left the deck.

All but one, about sixteen years old. She stood astride, scowling and close to tears, measuring the captain with a look full of rebellion and pleading at the same time.

"I'm staying!" She said proudly.

All eyes turned to her. Ross looked at her. He quickly concluded that the young lady must be taken seriously, especially since the others tended to disregard her. He will do otherwise.

"What's your name?" He asked.

"Daryenne," she replied, bent on defending her position vehemently.

He leaned in a bit because she reached his shoulder.

"Daryenne," he began calmly, "You are brave. I can see it and really appreciate it."

He looked around quickly, but no one was waiting for her. Apparently, she was alone.

"Don't send me away!" She half asked and demanded with tears in her eyes.

"You don't have anybody?" He asked softly.

"No," she replied with a trembling voice. "They killed the babysitter because she was too old."

So, he didn't have to explain to her how cruel pirates can be. She saw it.

So, he started on a different side:

"Please do something for me."

She looked at him suspiciously, brushing back the unruly dark fringe that obscured one eye.

"Have you seen the healer?" He asked.

"Of course," she replied quickly, "He was wounded in the cabin of this who helped the captain to rule. He ended up there twice."

"He's my friend," he explained.

"Everyone knows that, Captain..."

"Promise me that you will take care of him," he cut in on her word. "Tell him I told you to. Help him."

"Captain, but I...!" she tried to protest. He silenced her with a gesture.

"I have such a feeling," he confessed. "I think you should be with him. Promise me, please!"

She looked at him closely.

"Well..." she replied, letting go of her anger. "But you have to defeat the captain. Promise me."

Several people smiled at the words spoken with girlish solemnity.

Faced with destiny, Ross managed a slight smile.

He looked thoughtfully at his brother by choice. Oliver smiled at him with a warm, friendly smile that was filled with emotion. After all, he was responsible for his life.

Sai waited for his words. Involuntarily, for a moment, his gaze fell on her belly. He surprised her, knowing her secret.

Then he looked at Sel, his eyes expressing all his love for him. Sel, moved, nodded at him. Anokhi gave him a warm look. Cora and Lena too. Victor hid his concern, which was similar to him. The crew waited. He was responsible for the fate of all of them...

"I promise you," he replied with complete certainty that he would do anything, and even more, to make it happen.

Daryenne hugged him goodbye before disembarking.

He waited a moment, looking at the Bloody Witch thoughtfully.

"Gentlemen and ladies!" He finally shouted in a captain's tone. "All hands-on deck! Flag on the mast!"

"Ay, Captain!" The people shouted, "Flag on the mast!"

Ships caught up with each other, side to side. The crew of the pirate ship shouted derogatory words, mainly aimed at women, although there were also some fighting shouts and bloody promises to the other members of the Valeria crew.

Ross eyed the Red Captain, now watching him through the telescope with a contemptuous expression on his face.

He felt nothing at all.

He almost convinced himself that seeing this man did not evoke any emotions in him. Several years in a brothel taught him to surround himself with a wall of indifference when necessary. Especially the time he started working there, after he had been put together.

Oh yeah... He could suppress emotions.

He has not lost this skill so far.

It was in him, wrapped in vigilance, ready to act when the world around him began to trample on his dignity. He didn't need it. For a very long time. He listened to the captain's thoughts, slipping through them like a snake...

Curiosity. This is the first thing he senses. He was like a cat trying to surround a mouse. He wants to destroy him. That's for sure. No youngster can beat Captain Hope! Even a wizard! Son? Bastard, not a son! There are plenty of such in the ports. This one stood out from the group of other worthless rubbish. He intrigues him.

"Were you hoping for something else?" He asked himself ironically.

He caught that one thought.

"...he stood out from this (...) rubbish..."

Had he sensed a note of admiration in his words?

"Take a look at me," he ordered with gentle emphasis. "Who do I remind you?"

"Similar to me," Hope remarked in his mind, "I wonder if he has character, or if he only makes up for it with magic, because he is a tearful fagot?"

"I'm not afraid of you," he sent his thought straight into his mind, though it was not entirely true.

The captain looked at him coldly, as if he were nothing more to him than the worm he wanted to trample.

Ross looked at him thoughtfully. Such people are not afraid of the unknown. Even magic seeping into his head. It showed a certain strength of character.

"Fire!" He ordered, keeping his emotions under control with the Jewel's help.

"Fire!" Silas yelled.

Several of the other sailors echoed the cry eagerly.

The guns boomed.

A moment later the other side replied the same.

The volleys of both ships brought people aboard Judith. The approaching storm answered them from behind their backs. The waves got higher and higher. The wind whipped the onlookers.

Meanwhile, the boats from Valeria were not far away, fighting the rising tides of the impending storm.

"Are you sure that's what he wants?" The captain asked.

"Unfortunately," Vivan sighed resignedly.

"Ross can rule his own backside, not me and MY SHIP!" Violet said firmly, showing her nervousness once more since he had presented her friend's plan of action. "Neither I nor Nathan are agreeing with this, damn it! Violet Abigail Meresa may not be the captain of the greatest ship in these waters but let the firebolt hit me if I have nothing to say here!" She said firmly.

"Violet..." he began with apparent calm, feeling a growing concern for his friend.

"He will die!" She exclaimed in his face. "A cruel, painful death! What else do you need to believe? You've already met the Red Captain!"

"It's a matter of honor..."

"This man has no honor!" She pouted. "Your friend is a gifted sorcerer, but something tells me that he is a rather bad warrior! And this bad apple owes me a ship!"

Even he was not convinced of the rightness of Ross's decision. Violet was right. Too few people from Valeria had boarded Judith. His mother was not among them.

He nodded. It was enough for her.

"When the passengers have boarded, go to Valeria!" She ordered the captain. "We will not leave him without help!" she added.

Anger permeated her face for a moment. Vivan looked at her. It was becoming the rule that one knew exactly what the other was thinking.

Ross waited for a moment of silence before giving orders.

"Captain!" He raised his voice until the people closest to him huddled painfully. "Battle or duel? Do you prefer to send your dogs, or do you dare to fight with me here and now? Choose!"

Sel looked at him as if he had lost his mind. So did the crew.

Ross ignored it. He couldn't imagine Lena fighting these murderers. She, Maya, Anokhi… His crew. He wasn't going to lose anyone.

He snapped his fingers.

Under the influence of his magic, lightning struck from the sky straight into the waves between the ships. The wind whipped them until the men had to hold their hats.

The second and third lightning strikes in the water rang in their ears. The jewel glowed purple.

"Enough!" He heard on the other side, "Enough of these tricks, you fucking bastard!"

The Red Captain and some of his companions left the ship with the help of ropes.

Lightning struck around Judith as if receded under his gaze. Everyone around watched the famous corsair like a sinister phenomenon. He ignored them.

He approached Ross confidently, as if he was here at home. He even looked around with interest that clearly showed appreciation for the value of the potential loot. He scanned the assembled women with a quick glance. He concentrated on Cora for a moment, trying to remember how he knew her face. The memory put him in a better mood. Oh yes… he remembered.

"You'll be mine!" The words lapped the air like a command.

Cora narrowed her eyes in anger. He just disregarded it. He didn't care about her feelings. His cold, indifferent eyes fell on the young white-haired captain, and his mouth twitched in mockery.

"Well?" He asked sarcastically "Shall we finally start?"

"If I win, the Witch is mine," Ross said, taking a firm stance.

"You will not win," said Hope shortly, not honoring him with a longer statement, as if it were completely obvious.

Ross kept his composure.

"Promise for your pirate honor!" He demanded firmly, even though he himself did not believe it.

"Ok, ok!" The Red Captain replied dismissively, making a gesture with his hand as if he were warding off a troublesome fly. "And what do I get in return? I will wait for your reply, though it is a waste of time..."

Ross did not get upset. Such situations had happened to him before. Due to his young age, he was met with a similar mockery from the beginning of his career as a captain. Until fame began to overtake him.

"Nothing!" He entered his word sharply.

Hope looked at him as if he was talking to someone extremely light-headed.

"So, how am I supposed to agree to that?" He asked mockingly, casting a knowing look at his surroundings.

"They say you're not losing," Ross remarked sarcastically.

"I'll tell you what it's gonna be, you little bitch!" Hope quickly approached him at a distance of a hand. Sel immediately drew his sword towards him, as did many around him, but the Red Captain ignored his move. "When you lose, I'll rip your guts off, starting with cutting your pathetic dick off of the used porcelain, then when you finally die and stop navigating these waters, if you mean anything, I'll fuck your lover before I have him impaled." He pointed at Sel without hesitation. "We'll kill all the crew. We'll fuck all the women you surround yourself with like a woman. And then we'll take them and sell them to the worst harbor brothels, if they're still fit. I will rob your little ship of valuables and everything of value and sell it where they make outhouses and toilets for the rich, so that each of them will shit on its shitty size and power!" He grimaced sarcastically. "What ass do you have to be to make such an offer to your opponent, huh? I guess I didn't fuck your mother enough if she gave birth to such a misfit!"

Ross's eyes flashed with anger. The crew hummed.

"You're not getting anything!" He hissed furiously. "This is my offer! The final one!"

Hope stepped back a bit thoughtfully.

"That's better!" said matter-of-factly. "Although it still sounds poor, but with a confident voice and without unnecessary explaining. That's all?"

"It's really happening," Ross thought, feeling a mixture of desperate courage and despair within him.

"You ruined her life..." he remarked.

"The stupid bitch did not want to give, so I took her by force. Then she ruined your life when you were a kid, until you ended up in a brothel where you drank, smoked herbs and gave yourself a fuck to anyone who wanted it," Hope explained disparagingly. "What, he didn't talk about it?" He asked Sel, looking provocatively in the eye.

"Don't let him talk…" Sel warned quickly, but it was too late.

"Actually..." Hope pretended to think. "I was visiting this brothel then. The best in the capital. I took both this and that. No difference…"

"Shut up!" Sel warned him, sensing where this was going.

"I didn't know you could be Cadelia's bastard," the Red Captain finished mercilessly, ignoring him. "And you gave yourself to everyone," Ross paled. "What do you think? Have I been with you?"

Ross drew his sword, shivering with emotion.

"Jewel..." he asked, controlling himself with the last of his strength.

"YES..." Jewel replied shortly, stifling the visions his imagination was already suggesting.

Ross stood confidently in front of his opponent, who bared his sword with satisfaction, forgoing the cutlass in favor of unicorn-headed steel.

Ross attacked first.

The swords clashed together with a ghastly scrape of steel. The strength of the elderly, seasoned man pressed on the desperate youth of his opponent. The captain flashed Ross a contemptuous smile. But this one was not going to succumb to him.

"What's this?" the Red Captain sneered. "The mouse is attacking the cat?"

Ross deftly dodged several attacks, wondering briefly himself how he had done it. The answer was to react to a swift charge aimed at his head. The blade cut the skin on his right cheek as he reacted too slowly.

In his field of vision, Oliver put his hand to his face in the same place.

A red streak cut through his skin.

Ross shuddered in awe.

He did not deliberately look at his brother. Oliver, fearing that what was happening to him might distract him, retreated hastily to the captain's cabin. Sai followed him.

Ross hit his opponent in the face with a heavy blow. But he couldn't beat as well as he did. Perhaps he did not want this. At the next opportunity, Hope firmly and hard hit him with a few blows to the stomach and head. Moments later, Ross was barely able to defend himself from the blade. He tasted blood from a split lip.

"Tired?" asked the Red Captain mockingly. "Or maybe you will use your magical power now? Come on, beat me with spells, clumsy asshole!"

Ross ignored the words. From the beginning, he decided to fight him on an equal footing. No one can say that he defeated him with magic. It's a matter of honor. He will pay him back for his fate...

He did not pay attention to his surroundings. He couldn't be distracted now. Nothing was that important. Here and now mattered. And this man.

His shoulders ached. Hope didn't have to make an effort. It seemed impossible to tire him. He watched with obvious pleasure as Ross, wet with sweat, was torn over and over again. Ross used the sword less often than he used magic. Now such a practice took revenge on him mercilessly.

He got hit badly. Jewel tried to suppress distracting thoughts, such as the one about Oliver, so that he could concentrate on the fight. Ross's mind, so far open to his surroundings, eager for new experiences and learning, was choked in these limitations as if in a cage. He quickly realized that the Jewel's good intentions only bothered him.

Too bad, he will have to be intuitive.

"Enough" he ordered an extraordinary existence who faithfully accompanied him, who was still learning the rules of maneuvering in this extraordinary world.

The jewel carefully withdrew from any intervention.

Ross felt as if the hoop was too tight from his head.

Much better!

This time his surprise blow had a positive effect. The Red Captain's smile finally faded from his damn mouth!

Ross didn't wait any longer. He did not have many chances in this fight, so he did not intend to lose the one he got. A few quick counters, a sharp turn of the enemy, and now he was with the sword at his neck, turned by an extraordinary coincidence towards the deck of the neighboring ship.

Out of the corner of his eye, in the raging rain and wind, with the blast of lightning, he saw his friend closely watching this fight. Vivan was staring at the defeated captain now. Hope, as if attracted by his gaze, turned his gaze in this direction. Their eyes met.

"I will witness your death," he recalled those words.

Clearly Vivan was thinking the same thing. The captain's face twisted into a mocking smile. Young has what he wanted, doesn't he? His son is about to cut his throat. Well, he deserved it. Without a doubt.

"The fate of a pirate!" He said ironically.

Ross hesitated. Images from the past flashed before his eyes: rape and murder of innocents. The suffering of a friend. His own painful life...

"Shit son of a shit father!" his mother shouted to him more than once. "You rotten apple! Punk! You fucking rat! You even have a face like him!"

"What's up?" Hope asked impatiently, when the failure lasted too long. "Don't squeal now, for fuck's sake! I was beginning to have a better opinion of you!"

"I'm not like you!" Ross replied angrily.

"And I'll never be like you!" He screamed. "Kill me or I'll come back for him!" He hit a weak spot, pointing to Vivan. "You'll regret it when you find out what I'm going to do with him now!"

"You have to try harder..."

Hope jerked, but at that moment Ross finally saw the most important things in his mind. What he had heard from his mother many times. The moment that changed everything. Rape in front of murdered parents. Immediately after that, a memory made him think of an image. The same man who is now standing with his sword at his neck wanted to enslave his friend and destroy his life...

"That's for Vivan!" He hissed angrily in the ear of his opponent, mentally distant from the calm self he was presenting to his friends.

The only way this man will not hurt anyone anymore is to die... He slit his throat with a quick movement. Then he waited for the Red Captain to choke. Before death would take him, he added:

"And this is for my life!"

He took a swing just as another bolt of lightning struck the water. Cutting a bloodied unicorn stripped the cruel captain's head.

Blood splattered his face.

Ross lifted his severed head to meet his opponent's eyes one last time.

The last moments of his life were still smoldering in it. The jewel told him about it.

This has always been the law of war...

"And this," he added at the end. "For the murdered!"

He threw his head into the depths of the waters to merge with the bodies of the innocent.

Perhaps it was just his imagination, but he was sure that he saw a slight smile on Bloody Captain Hope's face. It must be an illusion, but there was pride in his fading eyes as well...

He looked up.

Vivan looked at him in that peculiar way of his that was filled with unlimited compassion and understanding. With the eyesight that clearly defined him as a healer... The one who spoke so much.

Silence was enough for them.

Ross lowered the bloodied sword. He let the wind and rain beat it. He felt no guilt within himself. Perhaps it should have been so. Maybe he should feel it, but it was different. He was slowly filled with a sense of satisfaction and relief at the same time. Most importantly, it's over.

Never again will the Red Captain raise a hand against anyone.

He saved himself. Oliver. Vivan... Everyone he could hurt, including Sel... It's the end of this nightmare.

Only moments later, as the wave of relief faded, did a fully understandable feeling arise.

He won!

He screamed, venting his emotions.

He turned, noticing to his surprise how many people were still aboard in spite of the terrible weather. All these people were staring at him intently, in silent expectation. Unsure of his reaction.

He looked at the headless body.

Sorrow penetrated his thoughts.

Sel came over. Out of the corner of his eye he saw Victor, who also started toward him.

He hugged Ross firmly until he groaned in pain. He did not defend himself, but quickly replied the same. Suddenly and greedily, because that was what he had been waiting for.

Sel felt a surge of emotions conveyed through the Jewel. Shaky, held only by a strong rope of self-control, exercised since they took over Valeria. He stepped back a little, assessing his condition with concern. Cut lip. Black eye. Sore spots hidden under the coat, cracked or even broken ribs. The old son of a bitch had a lot of strength. Judging from what he saw in the images of the Jewel, the stronger Vivan was struck down like a boy. Ross would have broken like a match if he hadn't dodged.

Not to mention what he did to his psyche.

As they became friends with Vivan and his family, amidst many new experiences and a time of relative peace, Sel got into the sumptuous Beckert library.

So many books... They gave him a insight into an unknown world. Before Lena hid from him (he had a good memory of pictures) part of the collection, after he started asking uncomfortable questions about inventions in her world, he looked at human anatomy, he learned important things about survival. He also found in the literature a few tips he needed, which helped him to deal with the complicated moods of his partner and lover. The heroes of the books had problems similar to his problems and dramas from the past. Their survival was sometimes encouraging him as he began to struggle to cope with himself.

He and Ross were both severely shattered by fate. The more he admired Oliver's fortitude, who dealt with it perfectly, precisely thanks to love.

"Give him to some others!" Victor released Ross from his partner's arms. "You did it!" The man called, hugging Ross, who immediately focused his attention on him. "Are you good?"

It's strange, he was too pleased, even for the situation. He was just as happy as a little child. He squeezed Ross's hand, speaking fatherly to him, while Sel stood aside, having the overwhelming feeling that they were just pushing him aside, this time not because of their relationship, but something else.

He felt emotion tighten in his throat.

Victor was talking. Ross listened with all his might, staring into his eyes as if there was no one else around. He struggled with the weakness that overwhelmed him, resulting from simple exhaustion, both emotionally and physically. Victor knew about it. He led him calmly to the captain's cabin, all the while talking about, as Vivan had noticed on the other ship, about Cora, who saw her father on the Witch, about the captured bloody captain's companions, who were already waiting in their orlop, unable to shake off the shock. About everything but the duel itself.

Sel asked for everyone to go to the staterooms and designated areas. He was surprised to see that the storm was clearly beginning to calm down.

Did Ross influence the weather?

Ross calmed down enough to start thinking about other things. He paused in front of his own cabin. There is something else to do.

After all, he is the captain.

"Mr. Silas!" He shouted a bit hoarsely.

"Aye, Captain?" Cried the faithful First Officer, staying close as always.

"In a moment I want the pirates who came from the Witch in my cabin!" He ordered, struggling to do what barely resembled a captain's knack. "My other ship needs a new captain!" He exclaimed firmly, almost as before.

Sel met the anxious gaze of Anokhi as she descended below deck.

They both knew Ross' attitude was appearances.

"A little more," Sel whispered straight into his ear as he managed to get closer, "It'll be over soon..."

"You don't even know..." Ross whispered to him dramatically, glancing at Victor.

"Yes, I do," Sel replied warmly, breaking his word.

Ross managed a weak smile, exclusively for him, before stepping inside the cabin.

"You're Vincent," he said coldly.

The tattooed man who apparently commanded the group looked at him suspiciously.

"Aye, Captain Hope," he confirmed carefully.

Ross assessed their behavior. It was clear that captured pirates feared more him than Victor, Sel, and the few other armed men who surrounded them inside. You must use it somehow.

"Vivan, is Violet with you?" He asked his friend mentally, deliberately prolonging his observation.

"She is here," was the immediate reply, "We'll wait a moment longer and get into the boat right now."

Ross raised his eyebrows. Several of Vincent's companions shifted nervously.

"What she will say about a new ship?" He asked mysteriously.

He looked at the frustrated captain with his eyes. Violet's bad mood faded in the blink of an eye as Vivan conveyed his words to her.

"I'll say: Aye, by all the demons, White Captain!" She replied with a twinkle in her eye.

He smiled. This disturbed the pirates in front of him even more. This was what he was counting on.

"Listen to me carefully," he began to say to the man with the tattoos, evidently the leader of this lousy gang, "Violet Meresa will be your captain, but you all report to me first and foremost."

"Over my dead body..." one of them blurted out nervously.

The next words stuck in his throat.

Ross, pretending to be impatient, rubbed his forefinger at his temple. He didn't know what he looked like now. The effect he achieved was better than intended. They feared him. He knew perfectly well that stories about him circulated among the sailors, sometimes exaggerated. Shivering horror. Whether he wanted it or not, this built his reputation as the Troublemaker of Thought. This time he was grateful to the stories. At the same time, the Jewel glowed a shade of purple, not very strongly, but it was impossible to ignore.

"Better not to tease him," he ingeniously suggested directly into the mind of a superstitious sailor.

"You think your tricks will work on me?" Vincent asked angrily. "I won't listen to any woman!"

"As you like," Ross replied to him with apparent, still echoing old life carelessness, with a feminine gesture emphasizing the words. "You can refuse," he said to everyone. "But remember... There will be no place on land, air and water where you can hide in front of me. I took over the Blood Witch. If you oppose my will, you will oppose the will of the captain and the sorcerer. I will find you everywhere! You will never know peace! Unless you obey me or, if you prefer, respect my will."

Vincent raised his head proudly.

"I won't be your minion."

"No, you won't," Ross assured him firmly, surprising him, "You'll be following Violet's orders, but I have the last word. If you don't want to serve her, leave. Likewise, the rest of your companions. If you stay - you fulfill my conditions."

Vincent looked at him thoughtfully.

"Your power doesn't go that far," he said incredulously.

Ross stood fearlessly in front of him, looking him straight in the eye. Even though he was younger and shorter than he was, he had a certain pride that was respected even in this tall man. And yet Vincent would not be himself if he not find it to his's cost in front of his people. He was not intimidated. The "sorcerer" didn't look too threatening. A young boy with a soft look. His white hair suited him even, though he had nothing to do with the elf, except for a slender figure. He was certainly not too heavy. He grabbed him by the lapels of his coat and lifted him up. Without any special effort.

Ross immediately stopped his companions with a gesture from intervening.

"What are you gonna do so I don't break your neck now?" Vincent asked menacingly.

"I'll convince you," Ross croaked, gasping for air. He kept his eyes on him.

"You really have nothing against me," he told him silently, "You hated Hope. Or what he was doing with Vivan. You're curious what it's like to be under the command of a sorcerer."

Vincent gripped his cloak tighter against his neck.

"Stop it right now!" He roared until everyone shivered. "Stop talking in my head!"

"Then let me go!" Ross commanded him with difficulty, feeling that it was getting harder and harder to breathe.

Vincent dropped him violently as if burned.

Ross took a deep breath and calmly straightened his clothes, waiting for his decision.

They both knew he was right.

Vincent looked at him thoughtfully. Ross saw disbelief mixed with anxiety in his eyes. It was impossible...

People very often reacted that way when he started using power. He wasn't surprised by this. Usually, it took a while to get used to it.

He didn't quite know why, but he didn't want to lose the man. Maybe it was something in his eyes, or maybe it was his behavior on the ship. He had a feeling it would be better not to kill him.

And it would be best not to kill anyone else. If only it were possible...

"How can you know anything about me, huh?" the pirate did not give up easily, in the end their conversation was watched by his people. "You are using some fucking power to read people's minds?! What do you know about what happened on the ship?"

His companions watched them anxiously. Vincent could sense a superstitious dread of the young captain, as if he had suddenly become the embodiment of the demon in the story. However, he had to admit that the young man skillfully used his gift. He did not try to influence his will, to subdue him like a slave. He preferred to convince him without depriving him of his dignity, respectfully, but lined with a certain hidden threat that now seemed very likely. Seemingly so innocent, and there was something dark about him. He probably didn't think he wanted to see what was hiding at the bottom.

He was starting to like it. He'll be a great captain and sorcerer. It felt like a expensive perfume. An attractive mixture, subtly attracting. He was beginning to understand why there were so many people on board around him.

"Sorcerer…" he muttered ironically.

Ross heard it. His gaze seemed to harden. He didn't like the nickname.

Vincent almost smiled. Young has a good character. It is worth checking what life would be like under his flag. The old man under the rule of a young man with magic - that could be intriguing…

"Troublemaker of the Thought…" Matt whispered. His voice trembled slightly.

Ross honestly hated the nickname.

But he had to admit that it was quite accurate. What else was he doing now, he did confuse his thoughts with his "talent"?

"Let's say," he began calmly, "that I have my own ways of knowing it. Is this answer enough for you?"

Vincent looked at him for a moment, pretending to be indecisive. Finally, he quickly reached out his hand, making the final decision.

"Okay," he replied firmly.

Ross shook the offered hand, pleased with the turn of events.

"One more thing," he added seriously, "There will be no torture or murder. Robbing as well," he saw disappointment on the faces of some of them. Vincent himself was not surprised by this. "Captain Hope's treasure, which you hide so in your trunk," the sailors shifted nervously. "Yes, this is about it," Ross added with vengeful satisfaction, "is going to be used to restore the ship. No chains. It's all over!"

Vincent smirked.

"Maybe this power of yours is not as powerful as you think. What will you do when we cut Violet's throat and take over the ship?"

"Do it and you will die," Ross replied coldly, not losing his confidence for a moment.

Something about his attitude, especially his eyes, made Vincent believe that he was telling the truth. It was enough for him.

Unfortunately, not everyone shared his opinion.

"I don't think so!" One of Vincent's companions shouted. "It's all a lie! You will see! Pure rumors! Nobody in the world has that power!"

Ross didn't even move. He was tired, battered, possibly wounded, and yet he stood with such unwavering confidence that can give chills. The sorcerer was not to be tested. His appearance and age were deceptive. Old Red bastard has found out about it already.

Meanwhile, the reckless seaman stepped back toward the door, confident.

"Get on your knees!" Sharply, like a lash, the order was given.

Without a moment's thought, even the slightest resistance, the pirate obeyed the order. It was as if he had no will of his own.

There was silence.

"How...?" Asked the sailor, his lips trembling with fear.

Ross looked at him. There was no emotion in his hazel eyes.

These were appearances, but only relatives could find out about it.

He did what he had to do.

"Do you want to die?" He asked. His tone changed. Stranger. Almost inhuman. It was an illusion he had planned, forced by the situation.

The sailor looked down at his lap, not understanding how he might have done so.

"No, Captain," he replied with pious fear, giving up his rebellion entirely.

Ross looked pointedly at Vincent. The man nodded silently.

When the pirates left the ship, he stopped pretending. He just froze motionless.

Like a puppet from a theater with its strings cut.

His eyes lost their brilliance. It was as if he was about to collapse. Only the breath revealed that he was still alive.

Everything he did from the first moments of the duel to this point was a desperate attempt to survive the hardest. He fought, and he killed. He slit his throat with vindictive satisfaction! He was steering someone, depriving him of almost free will.

And going deeper into it... He met darkness. And blackness, deeper than many seas in this world.

"I have to be alone," he told everyone dully.

They hesitated. They all knew him in some way, from the sailors to Victor and Sel. They knew he was in rather bad shape, nothing like that firm attitude from a moment ago. They understood that he had done to the rebel what he had to do, only to prevent a fight.

They saw that his endurance was running out. He had reached the line which it was better not to cross.

Sel signaled the others, appreciating their concern. Everyone, except for Victor, left, looking back at the hunched figure of the captain, which had almost no life.

"Son..." Victor began, not even waiting for a moment. Showing his affection in public still frustrated him, so he was relieved to indulge when the only three of them were left. With Sel in love with him, which still raised mixed feelings in the older veteran, he could afford to be exuberant.

"Raise your head!" he ordered firmly and gently at the same time. "Come on! You have to hold on!"

"I have to...?" Ross asked weakly.

"Hey..." Victor frowned. "There is no point in giving up. It's over now. You handled."

"Victor..." Ross's voice trembled.

Sel barely made his way toward them, ready to help. But his gut told him that Victor's help would be more useful here than tenderness.

Victor noticed the inner struggle of the young inventor. It was truly amazing for him to see two men so in love with each other. Amazingly, they looked so… innocent.

In fact, their feeling didn't bother him anymore. With these two, everything seemed so normal, as if it were natural for a same-sex relationship. He hadn't dealt with this type of relationship very often, and yet he was getting used to it.

Sometimes they were afraid of what would happen if he will see others…

"It can be Victor," the old gentleman agreed good-naturedly in spirit. "I don't want to leave you alone like this. Sel doesn't want that either. If you are to cry, cry with us. Always nicer in company. And if you get mad, go ahead. You can too. You just have to stay sober mind, you understand?" He forced Ross to look him in the eye, finding his gaze. "You can't! Not because you will break my heart. And not because you will break his heart," he nodded to Sel. "But because now you can hold your head high. You didn't get killed! You saved not only yourself. I repeat myself, but it's true. You saved everyone! It's over, Ross! You are alive, and this is the most important thing!"

"Did you see what I did with that pirate?" Ross asked grimly, though he wanted to feel joy at his earlier words, "I'm a Troublemaker…"

Victor looked at him seriously, completely calm.

"You are a hero to me."

Sel smiled warmly.

"You hurt him?" Victor asked. "You didn't deprive him of his free will forever. You gave him a chance. Few have the opportunity to afford it. You know very well that sometimes there is no other way. Life is full of difficult choices. It's important what kind of people they make us."

Ross's gaze was clear. There was the warmth of all shades of feeling in his heart. Their sign was the purple light of the Jewel, not very strong but visible. But there was something else in that glow…

"I meant nothing to them..." came the soft words.

Compassion made Victor's eyes glow dangerously with tears. Only then did Sel carefully step in.

"It's important that you mean a lot to us," he embraced Ross gently. "You are everything to me."

Paphian appeared on the Valeria's board only moments later.

His dark, long hair was disheveled, and his eyes were pure despair.

"Ross!" Vivan was washed off the deck by a wave as she rescued Violet!" He shouted upset.

Ross staggered. He really needed a rest. Sel grabbed him immediately.

"Have you been drinking?!" Paphian indignant, looking at him in disbelief. "Now isn't the time to celebrate! Vivan has disappeared and we can't find him!"

"You lost him?!" Ross asked, not very conscious, but that didn't mean he deserved the words he heard in a moment.

"You have no right to reproach me!" The other shouted. "You are not a family member to remind me of this! It's enough that I have to hear it from my mother!"

Ross froze, hurt by his words.

Sel would gladly slap Paphian's face for it now.

His heart ached at the sight of Ross's expression. His resignation...

Half the crew was already crowding at the cabin door.

"This isn't the time to celebrate!" Cried Paphian reproachfully, not noticing anything, not only thanks to tears, "You have no idea! You all don't know anything! You don't know what he was like when he came to us!"

Oliver pushed his way through the crowd. Shocked, Lena stood closest, listening to this conversation, assisted by her young friends.

"You're forgetting yourself!" He spoke sharply to Paphian.

He wasn't the only one who was concerned about Ross's condition. This one was now pale as a sheet. Oliver felt dizzy.

He called him out softly. Ross just hid his head in his arms. It was terrifying. The brave, formidable sorcerer was gone. Ross was a mess.

"And you have no idea how he feels..." Sel replied in a low voice, pointing at his beloved with a dramatic gesture. "You just told the man the degenerate father was trying to kill, and his mother had tried before that, that he isn't a member of your family!" he looked for Victor. "But you always told him that he is! So what's it like? In case of trouble, do you kick him out like an old dog?!"

"What the hell are you doing!?" Victor joined indignantly. "Maybe start thinking before you say something!"

Paphian was speechless. He realized that he had gone too far.

There was silence.

"He's alive," Ross said suddenly, softly but clearly. Those who heard him whispered his words to the rest.

Paphian immediately joined them. Sel gestured for him to keep his hands with him.

"Do you know anything more?" He asked Ross hopefully.

Ross looked at him grimly. Paphian felt remorse. Even his grandfather glared at him.

"He's alive," replied his friend calmly, "He's unconscious, but alive."

"Is he in the water or on land?" Paphian asked frantically.

Everyone waited for this answer.

"On land," he confessed after Ross listened to his feelings.

"And Violet, Captain?" Asked one of the sailors from the crowd. "It washed them away together! And two sailors!"

"I don't know," said Ross truthfully. "As long as he's unconscious, I don't know anything else."

"Ross," Paphian gently, gaze begging him for forgiveness, put his hands on his shoulders. "You know those waters. Where could it have taken him?"

"Here are the Cursed Islands, sir," explained another sailor from the crowd.

"There are about twenty smaller and larger islands," Ross added explaining, "Hunters come from all over the world. They look at people who are captured like cattle. Healthy, strong, pretty, needed they are taken to Kartaman..."

"Artaman, I guess...!" Some sailor remarked from the crowd.

"You're wrong... We and the captain rioted on the island, and now there's nothing there. Everything is destroyed, the market does not exist," Silas explained proudly.

Victor looked at Ross appreciatively.

"You didn't say anything…"

"I didn't mean to brag," Ross explained evasively, but at the recollection of those moments he smiled slightly, as did many of his sailors.

Well, the use of power was justified there.

"Life is full of difficult choices."

"The old, the sick, the crippled... They kill those," he continued in a weak voice. "After I rioted and freed the kidnapped, they transferred everything to Kartaman. There is a market there now. The heart of the main profits of the Bay of Slaves. King Azram's own beating source of wealth."

Paphian turned pale.

"He must have been here somewhere, close to..." he said softly. "Ross..." he began pleadingly.

"I'm not a family member," Ross replied without a trace of anger, while the Jewel glowed a warm red, "but I'll always be a friend, Paphian..."

"I'm a mindless fool!" Paphian snapped, angry with himself, but Ross cut him off calmly, as if he didn't want to come back to that case anymore.

"I'm not a family member," Ross replied without a trace of anger, while the Jewel glowed a warm red, "but I'll always be a friend, Paphian..."

"He could have ended up here on one of the islands. But if we don't find him, we'll only have the Kartaman market."

CHAPTER 23

Nimm never wanted to seduce him. He once found him in the street, sick and without strength, when he was returning from the House of Pleasures. He made him go home with him. The aunt with whom he was staying recognized the boy, who willingly did various jobs in the city for a small fee or simply for food. Without hesitating, she accepted him under her roof. Ross had a good reputation on the streets of Vermod. He has never stolen. He tried to take care of his belongings, though he spent more than one night in darning. Usually, people would give him new things and shoes, in addition to the payment. Sometimes he stayed with them. Everyone saw who he was, but he never wanted to accept their help for free. He did not ask for alms. He had to run away from home that night, even though he was very sick. Another lover of his mother wanted to "raise" him. He burned him with a poker for fetching wood from the shed too slowly. Nimm and his aunt took great care of him. He didn't even have the strength to protest. He spent the next three days in bed with a high fever. The burn did not heal.

It happened a year before the tragedy that changed his fate.

He thanked them when he recovered. He helped out in the stable for a time while Nimm practiced archery before joining the royal army. One day, after the first archery lessons that Nimm had given him, Ross discovered the truth about his orientation. He noticed this when he spied on him while visiting the House of Pleasure.

At first he was shocked, unaware of the truth about himself. Is it possible that a beloved friend...? It didn't matter that Nimm had never touched a sensitive fifteen-year-old in an intimate way. He was very responsible for his nineteen years. He told him that the enrollment in the royal army was supposed to be a trial that his father had persuaded him to do.

He wanted to see how he would handle it. He was not afraid of challenges. Of course, the father never found out what the secret was kept by his son.

Nimm was very concerned when he realized that Ross had learned the truth. He had promised him he would never touch him.

Then, unexpectedly for Ross, the roles began to reverse.

Ross found his friend occupied almost all his thoughts. Not a day went by without his face appearing in flashbacks, and what he saw then in the House of Pleasure, although he did not wait until the end, really influenced his imagination.

There were occasions for meetings almost every day. Nimm's family, both his own and his widowed aunt, were famous for breeding horses. Business was great and help was needed often. Although Ross had never ridden a horse, he had learned to take care of it.

In his spare time, he learned to shoot a bow and crossbow, under the watchful eye of Nimm.

One day he found the courage. He kissed him.

It was a shy kiss but caused a great storm.

Nimm firmly asked that he never come to his aunt's house again for his own good. He can't do this! He himself does not know what he is doing, and it could end in a great tragedy!

Ross was devastated. After all, he felt that he had just found his place in life! Why then?...

His mother sent her lover to him when he returned home, nailed after many days of happy absence. He was not ready to defend himself, then his heart was confused.

The brawling petty thug eagerly took to the little boy to show himself in the eyes of the still beautiful woman Cadelia was.

Beaten Ross had nowhere to go. He wandered the alley leading to the House of Pleasure, full of despair and desperate hope that he would meet Nimm there and then confess his feelings to him. In front of the brothel, however, his courage left him. Sore and unhappy, he hid in the shadow of the House.

There, again by a coincidence that happily gave him good people in his life, or maybe they were some good powers, Valeria found him...

Ross has recovered with her. Later, still bearing traces of beatings, Nimm found him.

He apologised. Ross insistently urged him to make a special apology...

They lived in this idyll for several months. The aunt, who had guessed everything from the beginning, did not reprimand them. At his parents' house, Nimm would not have had such freedom. Ross worked wherever he went. Nimm joined the army. They saw each other in their free time, which was not very often, but intensely. Cadelia then met her Ramsey, a smuggler. Her life has changed for the better. She planned a future together with him. Ramsey out of love gave his ship her name. She seemed softer, especially since the son did not live with her, but with Nimm's aunt, or visiting his new friend Valeria, who cared for him as a mother should.

One day his mother was walking with Ramsey through the marketplace that would in the future nearly become Vivan's death place. There she noticed Ross with Nimm. They both hid their feelings daily, yet Cadelia had that sense, that nasty instinct she always used to touch her son painfully.

Ramsey did some research. He soon discovered the truth.

The attack was planned. He and a few confidantes waited until Nimm had a day off. Then they attacked them as they walked through the city. Nimm quickly realized they were chasing them into a trap, but his concern for Ross clouded his judgment. He was young, full of good intentions, but insufficiently experienced. They had no weapons. It was forbidden outside the city walls.

They surrounded them.

They wanted to ensure Nimm's death in torment. They had a poker in their hands, torches and who knows what else. That Ross never found out. Nimm deserved because he was older, he was supposed to be in the ranks of the army. While there were many like-minded men among the soldiers, it didn't matter to Ramsey. He was appearing, so he was supposed to pay for it.

Nimm wouldn't let them do that.

He knew what they were up to for him. Therefore, when he gave up hope, he secured himself a dignified death. He snatched a dagger from one of the smugglers during a fight and stabbed himself right in the heart...

"Don't give up, pussycat," he said softly, before dying among the furious torturers.

Pussycat... That's what he used to call him. A wild pussycat from the street, walking its own paths. That's how he once described it.

Angry that one of his victims had eluded him, Ramsey punished Ross. One that only thanks to Valeria's persistence the boy was able to walk again...

He managed to survive. Thanks love.

Love that has become the heart of a powerful awakening power.

He needed to rest.

While in Lena's cabin, Paphian told his family about his meeting with his brother, aware that the walls had ears, apart from intimate details, Sel took care of him with care, as did Nimm. Ross gave in with a weariness that was more dominated by sadness.

"Maybe I should call him?" He asked quietly while Sel unbuttoned his shirt.

Once he was helping him, still in the House of Pleasure, when Sel had run out of strength after what happened. Ross remembered those times. Completely different, and they were different too...

"No," replied Sel calmly, but definitely, "he probably needs rest, too. Taking Violet Meres with himself requires a certain amount of strength…" he cast a seemingly indifferent tone, hoping mentally for a reaction.

It worked. Ross smiled weakly.

"You're incorrect," he said with a hint of merriment. But he became serious immediately. "You think she's with him?"

"Yes," Sel replied, "Violet isn't a woman to be killed by any storm. I feel they are together. They will help each other."

Ross looked at him fondly, which the busy Sel did not see. For what he saw when he unbuttoned his shirt worried him. He touched the ribs lightly. Ross shivered with pain. It was enough for him. Without hesitating, he reached for his small bottle of liquid.

"Don't be against!" He ordered firmly.

He looked at his lover as he took a small sip. He was starting to change colors. Swollen, split lip. Impact mark under eye, possibly some broken ribs. Traces of blood. Ross looked like he had been fighting wrestlers in an illegal arena.

He waited for the gift to be beneficial.

"He slipped out of our hands again," whispered Ross. "By the Great Mother! I saw him! He was so close…"

"It happened," Sel put a calming hand on his. "Now we just have to keep looking for him." He was relieved to see the first signs of his healing power.

Ross slowly reached for his hand. He put his hand around it thoughtfully.

"Sel…" he began hesitantly, "I don't forget about you…"

Sel looked at him in surprise.

"You know," fatigue made it difficult for him to concentrate, but he felt that he had to throw it out, as if his life depended on it. "I've so much…" these words seemed stupid to him. "You still help me," he began again. "I'm still the one, which everyone is interested in…"

"It's not your fault you're at the center of these events…" Sel interjected, but Ross did not let him continue. "You probably think no one cares what's happening to you," he added. "But it isn't. I care. Always…"

Sel looked at him fondly.

"I know," he replied warmly.

He kissed him lightly on the cheek.

"Shut up and let me take care of you," he added after a moment, more animatedly.

In every touch of him, Ross sensed the beneficial effects of the most powerful magic…

Somewhere on the verge of dream and waking, between what might have appeared and what existed, he saw a female figure. He must have dreamed, but his dreams were not very peaceful. They did not bring him comfort. He worried too much. He still remembered. He had seen people dragged into the abyss by Vivan's memories.

"Do you miss?" She asked gently, somewhere beyond his vision.

The silhouette leaned forward. She was at his bedside. He heard a soft splash.

But it wasn't she who was talking.

"You know…" he whispered.

"I think she'll be a good friend," Julien said warmly. "Although I envy her. She is with you. She is close to you. And him…

Tenan."

Cup. It was a cup! The figure poured something on it, and now it was leaning towards him.

Julien was leaving. He felt it. She was like smoke that he tried in vain to catch.

"Don't go too far," he whispered.

"Ross," she said, ever more softly, "I'm always with you…"

The female figure sharpened. He recognized her now.

Anokhi.

Ross felt uncomfortable with his condition. Probably sweating like a pig. He felt restless. Terribly shattered, as if his soul had also been bruised. Despite all of Victor's warm words or Sel's soothing touch, as he helped him wash and change, and even wrapped him up like a baby, which already smacked of exaggeration, somewhere out there, seemingly elusive, supposedly suppressed by Julien's appearance, there were painful and shaky memories.

The man who caused him pain... His unnecessary, too late recognition in his fading eyes.

"...you will cease to navigate these waters as if you meant anything..." Words of Paphian...

"Ross?" He heard Anokhi's calm voice.

Oh no, no, no! It's falling apart...

"Anokhi," he said to her, completely awake from his restless visions, feeling that he was in greater danger than ever. From the side where his weakest point has always been... "If I break now," he heard his voice tremble, "you'd better kill me!" he ordered sharply. "Do you hear? I don't want anyone to see that I have finally lost! I've fought all my life not to give up. I don't want to become a mumbling, insane wreck!"

"You're not going to," she assured him, showing no fear for a moment. "It's just too many thoughts. Unpleasant memories," the tone of her voice was soothing to him, just like Vivan's voice. "Drink this, please," she showed him the cup. "And when you wake up, you will gain strength again and chase away sorrows where they will only be in the past."

"No tea has that power," he smelled the herbs. He knew it a little because Oliver was passionate about examining them. He began to suspect that it was his brother who accidentally made this nasty for Anokhi.

"Tea - no," she replied with a smile. "They both knew you'd say that. Sel and Oliver. That's why they sent me," she added mysteriously. "I'll give this tea a boost."

A moment ago, he was barely in control of himself, shaken by tiring dreams. Now he felt that bitterness and anger began to dominate that feeling.

"If you think that I..." he began, resentful of the actions of his beloved and brother, as well as the girl who agreed to such an arrangement.

Anokhi leaned over calmly. Then she kissed him on the cheek.

Somewhere behind his head he heard a fading laugh from Julien.

"And what is there to be afraid of?" The girl asked with a spark of mirth in her eyes.

He smiled, embarrassed by his behavior.

Suddenly he felt his good mood returning to him.

"Vivan is awake," he whispered.

CHAPTER 24

Vivan woke up on the sandy shores of an unknown land. The wave swept him off the deck of the Judith as forcefully as if a battering ram had hit him. He gripped the ropes too weakly, holding Violet with his other hand. He had not traveled by ship during a storm before. He did not expect it at all.

He stood heavily, feeling dizzy.

He looked around with desperate hope. No sign of the Judith or the Valeria.

So, he is away from his again...

At first, a wave of disappointment and anger made his eyes streak with tears. However, he quickly took control of it. This time he took it better. As if this outburst, expressed in a scream in Paphian's arms, allowed him to tame his emotions, at least for the moment. Now he felt better prepared. After all, he knew what was happening to him all the time. Nobody hit him on the head this time. On this shore, he found himself exhausted from struggling with the waves, helping Violet.

This is not the time to be weak. Where is she?

He saw her quickly. She was lying nearby. He immediately started running. There was a large bleeding gash on the unconscious woman's temple. She is alive! He touched her head, simultaneously assessing the state of the rest of her body with his inner sense. All right. Only one wound. No fractures. His power began to work quietly, gluing together the torn tissue from the impact on the rock.

All scratches and bruises disappeared with her wound.

"Healer..." he heard the call.

On the other hand, two sailors appeared.

"It's great that you are all right!" One of them rejoiced, the one with the short-cut hair.

"Nachim," Vivan squeezed his hand while examining the condition. It will be fine. The scratches will be gone soon.

The other sailor did not need to remind him.

"Something weird happens, we can't part with each other," Tipe smiled, grinning white teeth on the dark face and at the same time shaking his hand. "Like a marriage!"

Vivan smiled at the remark, welcoming him happily. Slit on the back... Coastal rocks again.

"Hey..." Tipe felt the warmth spreading around the wound. "Do you use your tricks?"

"You were injured," Vivan explained.

Violet just woke up cursing under her breath. All said and done, but the lady's behavior was definitely far from her. The men looked at each other knowingly before helping her to stand up.

"It's good that at least I changed into men's rags!" She muttered. "If I had a dress, probably its fucking weight would pull us down!"

"Captain with us again!" Tipe noticed with a smile, hearing this remark.

Vivan tactfully hid a smile.

"Hey," heard the familiar voice in his head, again full of old enthusiasm, "Are you okay?"

"Ross..." he muttered to the others explaining, stepping away a bit. It must look weird.

"We're good," he replied to his friend.

"Where are you?" a quick question was asked. "Paphian freaks out of despair."

Vivan caught something else in those words. Something Ross didn't want to reveal. He found regret among his feelings. And a hint of anger. They quarreled. Harsh words were spoken.

"Do you know where we are?" He asked his companions hopefully.

Only now did they look around at the place where they were.

"Ross can see through his eyes," Violet explained, "Vivan mentioned something."

"Look over there, healer!" Nachim pointed to the place along the shore. "The lighthouse!"

Vivan looked in the direction indicated.

Unfortunately, it was not a good sign. He saw no joy in the eyes of the survivors. Rather a lot of concern.

"We have to hide!" Violet ordered firmly.

"Why? What is this place?" He asked surprised. There must be people here. Maybe thanks to them they will get help.

"Else!" Ross recognized immediately, "Get out of there now!"

"He says it's Else," Vivan explained aloud. "He said we must run."

"Your friend speaks well, Vivan!" Violet started tugging at his arm. "This is the slave traders' reloading point! The lighthouse attracts ships unfamiliar with these islands! They crash against underwater rocks! Let's get out of here! It's a miracle they haven't spotted us yet!"

"Healer?" Suddenly they heard a young voice.

A young girl with tousled hair appeared from behind the rocks by the shore.

"I'm Daryenne. I was on the Judith."

"Was the wave washed you away?"

"No," she said confidently, "I jumped myself. I was drifting on broken boards."

They looked at her in surprise.

"It's not my fault Judith's deck is a mess," muttered Violet with disgust, but a little appreciation.

"Daryenne," Ross recognized her, as surprised as they were by her courage. Or rather, madness.

"The captain ordered to watch over you..." she began to explain, while Vivan was already beside her, assessing the condition. All the bruises and wounds healed immediately. She felt a warmth spread through her body, soothing her senses. So this is his gift...

He looked like a kind man up close, and warmth radiated from the bluest eyes she had ever seen. His touch was nice too.

A friend of the people.

"Oh, by Mother Earth!" Ross groaned in Vivan's head, hearing her words, "I didn't make her jump into the sea in a storm!"

"You're really brave," Vivan remarked warmly as they started walking, ignoring his comment.

"I guess rather stupid..." Violet muttered under her breath. "We don't need some snot..." she added sarcastically.

"Any help will come in handy," Vivan said firmly, looking around anxiously.

"Ross will be looking for us?" The woman asked.

They glanced at him.

"You can be sure of that," Ross replied.

"Yes," Vivan replied on his behalf.

"LET'S GO!" Ross shouted as soon as he stood on the bridge. "Open up the caverns! In this wind, we will set all the sails!" He ordered. "Full speed ahead! Come on, you lazy idlers!"

The crew smiled furtively as they heard the next commands spoken in a familiar tone.

They hastened to obey orders. Among those on board, one could hear another command of the boatswain, a firm and energetic graying man with wiry hands, accelerating the entire maneuver. Ross looked pointedly at Silas, who was at the helm as usual. Despite his position, he did not resign from this function, although it was quite early.

"Mr. Silas!" he said firmly. "Please go to sleep! That's an order!"

"Captain..." he tried to protest.

"Mr. Ernst!" Ross called a burly, gray-haired sailor from the deck. "You will replace him!"

Ernst was the second confidant at the helm that Silas himself had instructed Ross. At the sight of him, the resistance of the interesting events, but the clearly lame deputy, disappeared.

"Aye!" The other steersman exclaimed vigorously.

The order was immediately carried out.

"Silas, goddamn it!" Ross quietly said to his faithful friend. "You've been up for hours, haven't you?"

"But…"

"I'll need you later!" Ross pointed out firmly. "Tenan doesn't know sailing, not to mention me. Please!"

Silas did not protest any longer. He understood the situation perfectly.

"An order, Captain!" He replied respectfully. "Nice to see you on board again!" He added with a smile as he left, coming off the bridge.

Ross nodded to him kindly.

He felt Sel's scrutinizing gaze. He smiled warmly. There was no cause for concern. It will never be.

The sudden appearance of the casually dressed Paphian interrupted any further considerations. A worried Lena appeared right behind him. Everyone else was apparently still discussing or taking a nap. Only his sailors were running on the deck, following orders. There were no women.

Tiring night.

"You know something!" Cried Paphian immediately, running up to him anxiously. "Tell me!"

Ross looked at him firmly. Nobody will order him on board the Valeria. Even for a good cause!

Not to mention other circumstances...

"We're going to Else!" He replied firmly.

"Is Vivan there?"

Ross looked at him irritably. Somewhere in his mind there were still harsh words that were hard to forgive. Forget? No. It was no longer possible.

Hidden in him, the neglected, wounded boy was sometimes stubborn in similar cases...

"It must be obvious," he replied, softening his voice at the last moment.

Paphian sensed his resentment.

"He's alive and well," Ross turned to Lena. "I hope we find him."

She nodded, watching him with concern. A faint smile appeared on her lips.

Ross looked much better.

She didn't want to ask him anything. Perhaps they should wait for quieter moments? She also left the whole situation with Paphian. It's just a matter between them.

"I was worried about you," she said gently.

Ross looked at her with her old friendliness well known to her. I don't think he would ever be able to take offense at the Beckert family. She was sure even the resentment he felt for Paphian would melt away quickly. Especially when they want to communicate.

Sel meanwhile moved closer to Paphian.

"You thought it would go easy?" He tossed sarcastically into his ear.

Paphian pursed his lips in frustration with the whole situation.

Anokhi appeared at the bottom. Ross nodded to her, then looked up.

The Judith started a similar maneuver, but the Bloody Witch did not.

Smarties...

He sighed. Yet this!

"Are you going to disobey me?" He asked bluntly, using the power of the Jewel that glowed violet for a moment.

The first response was the obvious panic of the sailor. Apparently, despite the rumors, he didn't believe his abilities.

"The captain did not show up on board," was finally the sly reply.

"Who are you reporting to?"

Vincent knew the answer perfectly well.

He saw Paphian's worried look. He probably wondered what he was doing now. He touched a finger to his temple. The sign was familiar. He preferred to use it, or else everyone would wonder why he seemed suddenly absent.

"I order the Witch to follow me!" He announced loudly for the benefit of those listening to him. "Support may be necessary! Vincent, you're in charge until I say otherwise!"

Vincent did not dare to disagree. Especially when it turned out that everyone heard the last words in their heads.

Now they began to fear him.

He took it calmly. Too bad. There is no other way.

After a while, they began the maneuver.

"Oh, crap! By all the old kings!" Ernst called at the sight on behalf of the others.

The crew watched this event with genuine admiration.

The Witch followed Valeria...

In the port of the kingdom of Vakadelmaria, the last ships were ready for the first voyage.

It still remained to complete the crew and the army.

Much gold was delivered to County Beckert in a well-guarded chest. It was possible to start building the walls.

Erlon's hand tightened on one of the coins, thinking with concern for his adoptive son. About all those close to his heart. As always at such times, the liveliest heartbeat accompanied thoughts of Lena.

CHAPTER 25

The trouble started moments after they approached the first trees near the coastal rocks.

A long whistling whip wrapped around Violet's neck, dragging her to the sand.

A group of dressed according to the custom of the Bay people appeared as if out of nowhere.

Vivan felt the blade against his neck. Opposite, he saw Nachim in a similar position. Tipe showed greater reflexes, which is why a few jumped at him. He gave up after a few blows, albeit more out of reason than fear. Violet gathered up, freed from the whip whose owner was now watching her with signs of contempt.

She took a breath.

A few nervous shouts immediately distracted him. There was quite a stir. One of the hunters, for Vivan was sure that it was them, certainly the leader, as he was distinguished even by a blue and navy-blue outfit, ended with a peculiarly arranged sash around his head, gave firm orders.

"Nobody can get away!" He shouted to his own. "Capture her! I said: Catch that little viper!"

Daryenne ran away. One of the hunters ran after her, holding a bleeding hand that (Vivan could have sworn because he knew the marks very well) showed tooth marks. Excellent!

"Ross, can you see this?" He asked his friend in his mind.

"I can't believe my eyes," was the reply. "Stay calm. If they wanted you to be dead, you would already be."

"Poor consolation."

"We got caught like children!" Nachim hissed angrily.

"I'm not denying it," Ross replied with a hint of sarcasm.

Vivan silently agreed with them.

"And what?" The leader yelled, meanwhile, when he saw his people returning from different directions.

"She's gone," the bitten ventured to answer.

The boss without hesitation struck him a blow in the jaw, against which the other did not even defend himself.

"What do we have here?" He asked, looking at the captured man.

"Bravo, Daryenne!" Ross said proudly.

Vivan agreed silently.

"Fat woman and three nice pieces," the leader of the hunters said shortly, staring at them shrewdly. His eyes were framed by a dark rim, his eyebrows and hair were dark as the wings of a raven. All his people were of the same type of beauty, except for a skin darker than Vivan.

"These two are fit for work," he said, pointing at Tipe and Nachim. "And this..." he looked Vivan straight in the eyes. "What a color..." he looked. "Where can you meet people with eye color like yours, huh?" He asked mockingly. "Just like the color of the roses from my mother's garden!" He called to his friends, who were also watching Vivan with interest, "We'll sell him to the brothel!" He decided, grabbing his chin.

Vivan gritted his teeth, tearing at him angrily. The scornful smile on the thug's face fueled his power. He felt him begin to burst...

It had nothing to do with benevolent healing.

"Get your hands off you freak!" Violet yelled meanwhile, struggling in the hands of the other hunters.

The leader immediately fell to her. He aimed a hard cheek until she gasped loudly in pain. Vivan clenched his fist...

"Shut your mouth, bitch!" The bandit ordered menacingly, clenching his hand on her throat.

And then, with his free hand, he gave the order.

"To Kartaman!" He ordered.

Everyone who was holding the hostages hit them on the head.

Losing consciousness, Vivan noticed that the leader had struck Violet personally...

"VIVAN!" He heard his friend's voice as if from a distance.

He was hit on the head again. The anger began to rise within him as soon as consciousness returned. He was getting fed up with this abuse. Why can't he be with loved ones? Why do people still do wrong?

He woke fully, thrown unceremoniously to the ground.

"Get up!" Someone yanked him sharply, bringing him to his feet.

First, he looked around for the rest of the captured. They were still alive, but as battered as he was.

Violet's nose was trickling with blood.

"Come on!" He was ordered, pushing brutally.

"Where am I?" He looked around as he approached Violet at the same time.

They were standing on the edge of some abyss. Next to the wagon with the horses they were probably brought here with.

"You must be more alive," explained the leader of the gang contemptuously, seeing his surprise. "You have to be moved!" He pushed him.

"Don't touch me!" He ordered him abruptly, his anger rising.

"Heh, this threatening face is to scare me?" There was a dismissive answer. "Not such things I saw."

"You surely haven't seen ones like these..." Vivan replied silently.

Just before he was about to clench his fists again, he felt Violet's touch.

His power eased immediately, and his anger faded. This time he remained calm.

She was hurt. He had to help her.

He touched her hand as he walked. She looked at him gratefully, feeling the pain recede.

"Look!" She ordered him, looking straight ahead.

In front of them, the taboos of people gathered. Hunters similar to those who captured them rebuked the poor unfortunates with whips and screams. Behind them was a city with an exotic tower towering over its surroundings.

"The governor's palace," Ross explained quietly, "Scumbag probably screwed up to Kartaman after we destroyed the market. I haven't seen his dead body."

But it was not the governor's palace that attracted his attention. Right in front of his eyes, closer and closer, the tragedy of civilization was unfolding...

People captured in captivity acted on his sensitive senses. Some cried, unsure of their fate. Others welcomed him, numb with despair. The rebels were punished with a whip. Despaired by their terrible condition, they fell from sudden blows. Many of these people were born free. Their peace and intimacy were brutally violated. No wonder they reacted with a whole range of actions that testified to their rebellion against the reality in which they found themselves. They did not give up in spite of the pain or gave in in sobs and hysteria. They panicked. Anger seized them.

Chaos reigned. Only a few knew what slavery meant. They aroused Vivan pity, unaware that with their humility they let their torturers think that they were nothing.

The hunters screamed at their victims. They hit them with a stick. They jerked and threatened using fear and confusion. They were accompanied by dogs resembling emaciated wolves, reacting aggressively to children and screaming in fear of people. The hunters were clearly having a good time letting the animals bite. They listened to the shouts of pain and terror with evident pleasure, though they were only trying to intimidate. After all, they did not want to lose a valuable commodity, but to obey it.

"Violet," Vivan felt all that pain, anger and crying cut his heart in half. He swayed under the weight of these sensations. "What is this world where people destroy others for their own sick pleasures?"

The child's cry, full of boundless despair, prevented her from answering for a long time. An ominous whistle of a whip from the group on the opposite side and moans of pain broke into the scream, making the sensitive healer shiver noticeably. She could easily imagine how he felt at the moment.

"Real," she said firmly, trying to stay calm.

For what they saw as soon as they were in the middle of the rallying point before entering the city was beyond their comprehension.

The child who screamed so horribly was maybe a year or two. One of the hunters dressed in navy blue was holding them. Before their eyes, he threw the child to the ground with all his strength, then he reached for his sword and before they could react - he chopped off the baby's head...

"They choose the goods." Vivan heard Tipe's voice in the hum of pulsating blood.

One of the hunters pulled an old woman out of the crowd, led her to the abyss right next to them, and then pushed...

Everything was happening too fast around here.

The fat man resisted the two hunters.

On the other side, a young woman was crying terribly, whose torturer was tearing off her clothes to evaluate the goods.

Clothes...

They stripped everyone...

By depriving them of their clothes, they wanted to weaken the resistance of the unfortunate enough to make them feel more vulnerable. Only a few could afford to maintain a sense of dignity in this situation. Many succumbed to the constant intimidation, screams, aggressive behavior of animals and the general mood of boundless despair.

Vivan felt his breath run out. Violet snuggled against his shoulder. He saw the cold gaze of the leader of the group who had taken them, piercing them right through. He wanted to enjoy their fear before starting the selection himself.

He had already chosen the first victim with his eyesight...

In the blink of an eye, Vivan recovered from the choking flood of sensations, struck by a terrible premonition.

He will kill Violet!

He won't let him do that, oh no!

"Remember what I told you about my son?" She asked, pressing her hand too tightly on his shoulder. "Pass it on to my husband, too, if you see him."

Everything happened very quickly. Hunters appointed by the leader began to strip Tipe and Nachim. He himself grabbed Violet's arm. She looked at Vivan for the last time she thought. She had no chance against so many people from this gang. She knew it perfectly well. Not that she wanted to leave without a fight.

Two hunters tried to overwhelm Vivan, intending to take off his shirt.

Violet with all her strength delivered a blow to the bearded jaw of the leader!

Vivan hated to expose his scars. He hated it when someone tormented another human being.

He hated such violence with all his soul!

This time the fire did not start slowly. Blue flashed through his veins, liquid like volcanic lava. He groaned, feeling the pain pressing as his whole existence protested against the use of such power. The surprised hunters loosened their hold. He glared at them angrily, clenching his fists.

Violet was frightened by the sight.

Under the influence of a liberated, aggressive force directed in the power of vengeance on all those around who had caused the suffering of many, shadows appeared under Vivan's eyes, dark as the darkness that burned him away. His face, usually soft, as if sunken, sharpening his features. The arch of his brow that characterized him suddenly made him look predatory. His eyes, like the glow in the web of veins, blazed with a cold blue glow.

It was destroying him...

But the bandits had no idea about it.

The head of the hunters fell in amazement, clutching at his heart. His men and all the hunters in sight behaved similarly...

Confused slaves looked around, surprised by this turn of events.

"Vivan, stop it!" Ross's voice broke through the raging storm in his senses.

"Don't kill them! You are not a murderer! You'll kill yourself!"

"Stop!" Violet tried to speak to him. "Stop it!"

The sight of this man, so kind and sensitive, who killed others, destroying not only his life but also his innocence, was to break her heart. Here's what the humans eventually got to do!

Vivan sat down next to the weakening leader, grabbing his clothes. His power deliberately carried the pain slowly because, contrary to what he had guessed, he didn't want to kill everyone. He just wanted to teach the torturers a decent lesson, hoping that they would be able to remember each other, thereby compensating for their earlier slow action.

He shows them what they deserve!

Though that was also wrong...

"See those dogs?!" He asked angrily, pointing to the hunter's animals "I will call them now and they will listen to me! Without hesitation! Do you know why? I will tell you..."

"Stop!" Tipe, shocked by the sight, tried to stop him, but Vivan stopped him with one sharp gesture.

"You think he'll stop because you tell him to?!" Violet shouted in anger, "It's us, we all brought it to this!"

"When I was about fifteen..." Vivan began, weakening the force a little in order to be heard by the shocked victim, now not very violent, "...a dragon attacked me. He ate my horse and tore his leg with his teeth. His dragon venom infiltrated my blood. And you know what?" his eyes shone not only with a glow, as if he had finally revealed the dark shadows of his soul, caused by the tangle of nightmarish events in his life. "Something else happened!" He shouted like a madman, pointing with one hand at the nearest dogs. "Before I could convince every animal to myself, but it took a moment or two," the dogs whined, thus summoning the others.

Soon they were all waiting for his command. Vivan's eyes became a silver gleam. The head of the gang froze with terror. The three closest ones moved slowly towards them.

Violet looked anxiously at her people. How would they stop the healer? He must have gone mad with despair and anger. But whatever came to her mind to stop it, she wasn't going to rush it too much for now, at least.

"Now," finished Vivan coldly, summoning the dogs with his gaze, "Each of these animals is at my command. You know why?" The scared hunter tried to shake his head. "I have a dragon in my blood!" Vivan shouted in his face. "No one will survive the venom of the dragon but me, you worm! I have survived its operation and the burning of wounds ordered by a certain medic. Now, I'm the most powerful predator of these lands!"

"Please…!" the chief's voice lost all traces of the imperious behavior from moments ago, when he saw the dogs getting ready to attack. "You are a healer! You are not killing! I would never have laid my hand on you if I had known! Nor against your friends!" He assured him eagerly. "Don't make them do this, please!"

Time dragged on mercilessly as Vivan stared at his victim thoughtfully. No one would have guessed from his face whether he was sated on her fear or just looking for the familiar signs of humanity.

"Stop!" He finally ordered the animals who immediately obeyed the order.

Tipe frowned. Was Vivan really giving in to these pleas? What would happen now?

Vivan lifted the weakened man with remarkable force.

"Think about it," he heard Ross say in his head. It echoed through recent experiences. "It won't fix anything."

Vivan gripped the leader tighter, who was just wondering if he had anything to thank him for, or if he should start screaming.

The world has stopped.

The bandit hangs over the precipice. The healer's firm grip was now all that saved his miserable life.

Vivan held him, fighting the fury bursting him. This man personified everything that made him rebel and anger. He probably hurt a lot of people.

Yet he did not want to kill him. He could not.

It was not in his nature...

He knew exactly what he was looking for in his eyes. It wasn't about something as obvious as traces of good or guilt.

In the dark wells of his eyes, he wanted to see understanding at last...

He found it. At the last moment, between life and wisdom buried in cold calculation and death...

He attracted him to a life of thought.

Tipe and Nachim immediately captured the bandit, without waiting for an order. He didn't resist, staring now at the healer with a sparkling gaze of silent respect.

The healer...

Vivan's companions, surprised at this sight, were speechless.

Dark, transformed, and shining with a cold blue light, the man was not the one they had met before. But his angry color changed, glistening for a moment with green, gold, and finally vanished without a trace, ending the glow with the glow of the purple jewel glistening on his neck.

The healer...

The dogs still listened to him, snarling at the hunters, but the hunters felt better now, slowly getting up from the ground. It took a moment or two for the liberated to understand what this meant.

Vivan was starting to lose strength. That dark power had severely damaged his strength...

Violet shook her shock first. They had to act!

"LISTEN!" She called to the crowd amidst the prevailing chaos, "The Healer will not free you by himself! Do you want this man who helps others to kill on your behalf? You must fight! Defend your freedom! Nobody has the right to take it away from us! You have to defend yourself!" She clenched her fists, just like Vivan, from now on giving the gesture a symbolic meaning. "Defend yourself!" She repeated sternly, "Or you will never be free again!"

"For freedom!" Tipe clenched his fists, shouting to the crowd.

"For freedom!" Those who resisted the oppressors immediately repeated.

A young woman in a torn dress tore the sword from the reclining hunter. A fat man on the brink of the precipice threw one of his would-be executioners into the boiling abyss.

This started a fight.

The would-be slaves pounced on the conscious hunters. The dogs jumped on their owners.

Blood flowed. There were screams and indescribable clamor. The clash of weapons pierced the air as the rebels seized their weapons.

The surprised hunters could not beat their pack of dogs and the desperate crowd. Death pursued its own plan. So brave defenders of the oppressed and would-be traders died. The unscrupulous owners killed obedient to Vivan's dogs, also standing up for those they were supposed to bite before. Frightened children were hurriedly flocked or taken from the battlefield. The mothers, having obtained weapons, went head-to-head, killing the hunters surprised by this turn of events.

The victims finally resisted their oppressors...

"Vivan..." Ross tried all this time to reach his friend's heart. "Please calm down..."

"Vivan..." Violet gently embraced him without fear. "It's all right... Stop it. Please stop..." she felt tears in her eyes.

Something bad happened.

Vivan stopped clenching his fists. He felt tears of pain and growing despair at what he had just done. His legs buckled under him in silent anguish.

"I wanted to defend you..." he whispered, his voice weakening.

Ross knew all too well what was going on in his heart. He had only experienced it a few hours earlier...

Violet hugged Vivan tenderly, like a mother. She felt hot tears streaming down her face as the fighting around was almost over.

More and more people from the crowd of the freed gathered around them with pride and victory in their eyes. Few of the hunters tied up were brought to the edge of the abyss. Everyone assumed that Violet and Vivan were the people who would decide their fate. Especially a healer who has shown a will to fight like you've heard of in stories. Ready to do anything to defend them...

Slowly, as they gathered around them, many learned about what had just happened...

Seeing the tears in his eyes, many felt regret. What had the world forced this man to do? What did it induce them to do?

They felt confused. They won. But at what cost? Why did they have to defend themselves against such injustice by violence? Why in the hearts of others such a lack of respect for other people? What resulted from this belief that you can enslave another creature like yourself to your own dark ends?

"Talk to them," Ross ordered gently. "You must, Vivan. They are waiting for your words. They should be proud of themselves. They defended themselves and their loved ones. They won freedom! Tell them that!"

He stood on the balcony, away from prying eyes. Too much would have to be explained, and now is not the time to do so.

Only Sel, busy practicing before a possible fight, knew the truth. He hid what he had just learned by applying more to them.

But little could be hidden from Oliver's intuition. Sometimes he knew or saw more than Ross could have suspected. Maybe because the

Jewel used the same power to save his soul. Or perhaps because the gift of the twins permeated that gift as time passed more and more intensely.

He didn't tell Sai about everything. Especially now that she was taking the sea voyage so badly. The next day she vomited until he made her, with gentle persuasion, taste Vivan's blood, genuinely worried about her.

Possessing a gift that often revealed its effects suddenly, Ross was not entirely in control of his emotions. He tried, but sometimes it was almost impossible. Therefore, when he could afford it, he went to his cabin or balcony to gain more freedom.

However, his crew always knew when he used these abilities. They already know him well.

The news spread instantly: something happened with the healer again...

Vivan kissed Violet slowly on the forehead.

Did he really deserve so much devotion from everyone with whom he surrounds?

Yet he felt that he did not entirely regret his actions. No matter how much it costs him. He hated times when people hurt each other.

He will protect them, even if he eventually finds himself burned alive by his own power.

"Don't let hatred win," he heard Ross say, "It's a strong feeling. It gives you strength, but it will never give you love. It will not fill the void."

Only love will give him a sense of fulfillment. Maybe for others it is just a banal cliche, but for him it is the essence of existence.

Free people stood around. They were safe. And that mattered. That was the most important thing now.

"You're free!" He called out to the crowd, his voice still trembling with emotion. "And I am proud of you! You know sometimes there are no good choices! We all found out about it today! Let's remember what happened today! Remember that we did it to be free people! To defend those, we love! Those we care about! We made it! We won!"

"What about Kartaman?!" Someone from the crowd called, "Are we really going to let them go?"

"Today we, and tomorrow someone else will be here!" Cried the fat man who had miraculously escaped death.

Tipe stepped forward.

"The city has weapons and guards," he reminded them. "Are you ready for this fight?"

They got mixed up. Among them were women, children and the elderly.

"They must know what happened here," Violet remarked sharply. "They will gather the army and come after us!"

"I have two ships under my command" Ross's voice was firm. "And the Judith is sailing with us. Wait in hiding!"

Vivan felt a chill.

Open War!

"It's time to deal with this habitat of snakes, Vivan!"

"Azram will find out about us..." he involuntarily spoke the words aloud, making everyone shiver with fear.

"And good!" Ross said shortly, recently reassured by his relatives.

"Vivan, what's Ross saying?" Violet asked hopefully.

"Ross - the sorcerer" it was said immediately to the clamor of voices, "White Captain!"

They both heard soft comments reaching them, overheard rumors. Vivan was looked at, thinking of his friend, whose magic grew stronger.

Were these two communicating with each other now? If this is true, what does the sorcerer say about it?

Vivan lingered, full of conflicting feelings. War. These people did not realize what they could unleash here in a moment. There will be no turning back. Everything's going to change.

He started it all...

The frenzy of feelings put not only his future on the knife's edge. Kartaman will become a flashpoint in the fight for freedom! Many will die...

"Vivan, you've already started this..." Ross remarked calmly.

He did not understand the most important thing. Vivan had known this was going to happen ever since the idea of the attack on Kartaman was born.

However, he will not come home...

"No, it's still possible to quit! We'll hide and wait for you, and you'll pick us up and that's it!"

Before he finished speaking, he knew he had no choice. There are more important things than one life. He already knew it.

"If only it were that simple..." whispered Ross. "Look at the sea, Vivan! It's time!"

Three ships were approaching the island.

Some of those released also noticed them.

"Time to choose, Vivan! Will you hide from Azram's soldiers for the rest of your life, or will you stop it once and for all? Neither you nor they will stop suffering when you run away! Think about it! This is how the words of the prophecy come true..."

"I am a healer..." he whispered to both him and the crowd around him.

He was trapped.

There was no other way.

He quickly realized that he had a new worry.

He won't be able to command these people! The violence will kill him!

There is only one thing left for him...

"Don't get me wrong," he began firmly and calmly, "I will defend you, but I cannot be your leader! I am a healer!" He reminded everyone with the power to make them aware of the essence of his gift. "I protect and help! I am not a fighter! Killer! I was created to defend life as long as it lasts! Fight! I will support you! As long as my heart beats in my chest!" the faces of many fell. "I'm not asking you to understand this," he assured, trying to smile, which was supposed to cheer them up. "Don't worry about me," he straightened up in pain. "Burn Kartaman! Burn the marketplace! Let Azram feel that the times when people are treated like things are over!"

Ross froze, reproaching himself for not having thought about it sooner. He never thought about it. Vivan was always willing to sacrifice anything to protect others. For this he almost died when the witch wanted to take over him, the village, and maybe even the entire kingdom. And he never thought that he might really die then.

Vivan is first and foremost a healer.

Violet understood more than that. Her heart recognized all that he had not said. He really wanted to help but was limited by his gift. She had seen the power that stories told about him destroying him. Did she nearly kill him the first time, at the marketplace in Vermoda, when he was dying of those who wanted to hurt him? And when the witch Mayene wanted to enslave him, he killed her by stopping her heart, he did it even though his own was barely beating? Yes. He defended his friend from cruel death, and his relatives from its cruelty. The dark side of his gift also served to protect the people, but by using it, he destroyed himself. Even so, he continued to do so. Even if the rebellion kills him, it will not stop them. He will die helping. It was just like that. He helped.

"I will lead you!" she shouted to the crowd. "Who encouraged you to fight?! Me, right?!"

A few voices she exclaimed briskly, giving her support, including her two sailors.

"I'm Violet Abigail Meresa, the captain of the Judith and the Constance! I'm the captain of the Blood Witch!" She announced triumphantly to everyone. "I have a crew of mean pirates with me, who will gladly skin anyone who wants to enslave you!" she saw clear support in the eyes of the crowd. These people were eager to believe it, although not all shared the growing enthusiasm. Mentally, she asked

Mother Earth not to let the last words turn out to be an empty fairy tale. She had no idea what her new crew would do. "They'll be right here! They and the White Sorcerer himself! You cannot lose with us!" She cast a keen glance at their faces, "The Healer gave his all!" She looked at Vivan appreciatively. "We know he is ready to die for us! Let us not fail him!" people looked at Vivan warmly, finally fully understanding the essence of his gift and determination. "I'm ready to fight for my freedom, his freedom and any other human that Azram wants to enslave! Who is with me?"

A mighty chorus of voices answered her. Violet breathed a sigh of relief, though she was also filled with unease. She wasn't sure how the whole thing would end.

"Great!" She cried with the verve that moved her entire full figure. "Wait for the White Sorcerer!" He ordered firmly, sealing everyone's fate. "I'm not going to attack these bastards without him!" She pointed at the city.

"Let's find a hiding place!" Tipe ordered. "We will go to the city soon!"

"Thanks for thinking of me at all," Ross said humorously, "I already thought she was going to run there alone! Amazing woman! I gave my orders while she spoke. She can talk!"

"I went out to be a coward," Vivan remarked, with a hint of sadness mixed with a sense of injustice. He was what he was. He wished they knew it now. He wished he could have done more, but he was different. It was true.

Tipe gave directions to people as if he were back on the ship.

Violet looked at the young man with a motherly gaze that made his heart warm.

"The hero cannot be a coward at the same time," she explained warmly. "You have become our symbol."

"Thanks to you," he remarked with a hint of irony, and at the same time proud of his friend.

"You didn't need my support," she pointed out confidently.

He smiled slightly, not entirely convinced.

"Tell me," she approached him with concern. "Is it all true? Can all this chaos kill you?"

He looked at her gently. She felt chills even before he could speak.
So, after all...

"Don't think about it," he commanded calmly, in that wonderful voice of his that took a special tone when he cared for someone.

"How the hell am I not supposed to think about it?!" She yelled in her own way, drawing a few concerned glances. "You're going to die here, and I'm just not supposed to think about it?! Are you crazy?"

"Captain, they open the city gates," Nachim stood at a safe distance, not wanting to get hit by the agitated woman. "I advise you to wait in hiding!"

"If we hide you out of town... Will you survive?" She ignored the words she heard, grabbing Vivan by the flaps of his coat. "You must know that! You know what you can and cannot!"

"I will not hide when you go to fight!" He shouted in response, irritated by this, in his opinion, an absurd idea.

"Move your butts, goddamn it!" Tipe got angry, meanwhile watching the traffic at the city gate.

"So, it's true!" She shouted triumphantly, ignoring the exhortations again "It will help!"

"You can't make me...!"

"You're an idiot!"

"Violet!" Tipe couldn't stand it. "Soldiers!"

"In a second!" She screamed at him. "Even if I had to tie you...!" She shouted at Vivan, tugging at his cloak. "Do you hear?!"

"Don't do this!" He half demanded, half asked, seeing where she was going.

"Tipe..." she began.

At that moment she noticed mysterious pendants hanging on a chain. They flashed through the open shirt. She would swear that...

"Why haven't I seen them a moment ago?" She asked nervously, "You wear them all the time, and sometimes I see them and sometimes I don't. How is this possible?"

"I think the ring hides them," Vivan explained quietly. "They're often invisible."

"That's why the whole leader of the people who captured us didn't even talk about it!" She shouted understandingly. "And not only him!"

"Can you discuss it another time?!" Nachim was getting nervous. They weren't visible here in the shadows, but that might change soon.

"They protect you?"

"No," he replied, wondering where she was going. "You see..."

She pulled him to where Tipe was leading them, glad that they could finally move.

"The ring is the work of the elves. I've heard of adamantis. The gift of immortality."

Vivan thought painfully about Vashaba.

"It doesn't affect my gift," he explained quietly, seeing Tipe's gesture.

She looked at him, touched by a hunch.

The soldiers reached the place of the fight. Apart from a few overturned objects and trampled ground, they found nothing here. The bodies of the dead were hidden or thrown into the abyss.

"Look here, folks," Vivan heard a familiar, teasing voice in his head.

Suddenly the entire squad gave up the thought of searching the area. The ships from which the boats had already been lowered were shown to each other nervously.

He should thank Ross for that...

Moments later, after a short deliberation, the soldiers decided to return to the city, which they did in the greatest haste.

Tipe smirked at their retreat.

"Courage is a valuable commodity," he remarked sarcastically.

Violet removed the scarf from around her neck. She unceremoniously tucked it behind Vivan's shirt before he could protest, then pinned it down at heart-height where she had hidden it. She looked at him expectantly.

"What are you doing?!" He asked in amazement.

"And how? Do you feel the difference?" She asked, examining him with her eyes.

He looked at her suspiciously.

"It's not quite that…" she muttered to herself.

Now even Tipe and Nachim watched her actions with interest.

"You feel better when you help others. I noticed that," she muttered mysteriously. "What else is triggering this power?"

He felt the soothing warmth on his chest, where she hid the handkerchief. Her kindness was sincere. She really cared. Emotion squeezed his throat. Sometimes she reminded him of his mother. He hoped Ross wouldn't let his brave friend fight. May he do it for him…

"I think it works, Captain," Nachim remarked, noticing his movement in the meantime.

"I'm sensitive!" upset Vivan noticed, embarrassed by the fact that his emotions are now the subject of their strange experiment. "This is not news, is it?"

They stared at him thoughtfully, as if they were waiting for something.

"What are you doing this for?" He asked, trying to control himself. "It's not fair…"

He broke off as Violet gave him a juicy kiss on the cheek.

"Oh! Our healer turned red!" Tipe noticed with a soft cackle.

"I think I found a way!" Violet hurriedly explained to the confused boy. "Vivan, we need you!" Tipe nudged significantly, who quickly added, with a somewhat excessive, but disarmingly honest, effusiveness on his swarthy face:

"We love you!"

Vivan looked at them as if they were crazy. Surprisingly, the pain and fatigue passed quickly. He straightened up involuntarily.

Violet's wet kiss burned his flushed cheek.

Nachim just offered him a firm hug that made him breathless for a moment.

"You won't die with us," he added kindly.

The shadows under the eyes have disappeared.

A satisfied smile spread across Violet's face. It might have looked a little like a smug toad, but her eyes shone with emotion.

"Bloody hell!" She exclaimed. "I haven't butter someone up like that for a long time! Just everybody's mouth shut, or you'll regret it! It's a secret!" She ordered everyone firmly.

It remained to nod.

"You have two options, Vivan," she looked at the boy firmly. "Either we tie you up and hide you outside the city, or..." She pointed with her finger at the place where she hid her handkerchief. "Hold on to this and all the thoughts that give you strength. Wear this handkerchief over your heart. Even if you lose her, we'll be here," she pointed out his heart.

Memories returned. It seemed so long ago... The moment Oliver first appeared in his life, then in a woman's disguise. With all the kindness he could do at the time, despite his own problems, Vivan embraced him warmly, eager to help him.

He remembered that feeling. He was depressed, frustrated. He felt tainted, and the falsehood and intrigue deepened his gloomy mood and desperate longing for his loved ones.

Then Oliver showed up.

His concern lifted him more than his words.

He was silent for a moment, searching for the right words. However, none of them seemed to be that way.

"Thank you," he said finally, holding out his hands to them.

They embraced it with emotion. They had never experienced anything like this before.

"I'm sorry," Ross said. Immediately afterwards, however, he quickly corrected with a female gesture. "Wait, no! I'm not sorry!"

"ROSS!" Lena shouted angrily, tugging at the bars. "Let us out now!"

Among the women who were caught by surprise, there weren't those who had shown a certain bravery so far. Cora, Marlene and both dancers - twins, to the despair of Ross and Maya, who were worried about a new friend, did not allow themselves to be imprisoned. Like half of the "dancers", they successfully fight for the right to decide about their future. On Sai, who had not yet revealed a secret to her husband, a way was quickly found. Ross ordered Oliver to be kept under guard, much to his anger. Sai lost her strong argument, but his adoptive brother did not hide his indignation.

"Ross, that's not fair!" He shouted at him, holding out his hands angrily. "We might as well die because of you!"

Sai looked at Ross searchingly. She wanted to read on his face if he knew it and what it actually meant.

He hasn't even found the time to talk to her...

Suddenly he realized how much he had neglected his friends.

"I'm a bad friend," he said, half regretful, half sarcasm, "I promise I will look after my ass."

"I'd watch too!" Oliver muttered dissatisfied. "You would find out!"

"Ross..." Lena began, pushing her long hair away from her face. "There is my son!"

"He doesn't want you to fight," he replied calmly, revealing his friend's thoughts.

She looked at him with concern.

"This bond does not tire you? You are connected to each other almost all the time..."

"Not all of it," he replied calmly, "Some things that the Jewel says I'm supposed to see, I see later."

"You and the healer share every thought, Captain?" One of the girls, imprisoned because of too slow escape, as she thought, asked curiously. This question was her retaliation for unfair treatment. He could read it clearly in her face.

"This is a very inappropriate question..." He suspended his voice significantly, wagging his finger at the same time.

"Alina!" She raised her head proudly. "We have to stay, because what? We can't fight? With these hands," she raised it angrily, shaking her blond hair. "I grabbed the troll and stuck my pitchfork into it until it died! And more than one! And now you're locking me up? So I don't break my fingernails?!"

Several other girls supported her eagerly.

"I've already made up my mind," he replied firmly, walking towards the exit.

He appreciated their bravery, but he really didn't want them to fall into the hands of the governor's soldiers. They obviously couldn't understand that he was doing it just out of concern for their fate.

"You know the orders!" He looked at his people, who nodded in response.

"What orders?!" Lena cried. "Don't let them go until it's too late?!"

"Release them when you need to defend yourself!" Replied her father, who had been accompanying Ross so far in silence. "May you not have to fight, dear!" he added, saluting goodbye, in accordance with the laws of the army from their now so distant land. "Kiss your mother for me!"

She froze.

He said goodbye. There was only one last look left for her, threaded with helplessness and anxiety.

It was that time...

Suddenly, the dispute was no longer relevant.

She could only hope to see each other again.

Her older, unusual son... somewhere among the enemies. He is sensitive and does not tolerate violence. The younger one, probably also getting ready to fight, though she had seen Ross order him to stay on the ship. Even so, he probably sifted through his combat equipment, selecting his weapons.

Father...

He almost looked like when they crossed the border of the worlds. With the stigma of military experience hiding in the eyes. Another fight, maybe a war ahead of him. And he was walking alongside their young, devoted friend, to support him with military fortitude and experience, although not long ago he said that he would not like to take part in the war ever again.

What would she tell her mother if something bad happened that she didn't even want to think about? She wasn't afraid for herself. But the fate of those close to her made her dread.

Vivan must feel the same, knowing that they are risking their lives for him.

Erlon has no idea about this...

Maybe good. Otherwise, he would probably have joined them himself.

Ross... Trying as hard as he could to command so many people, not to mention the ship and the Jewel's magic growing within it, the bond with the healer, and the constant lack of time for a proper rest.

"If only you saw them, dear..." she thought warmly, thinking of her husband, at the same time proud of all of them: relatives and friends, so brave in the hour of trial.

Maybe she should say goodbye to them instead of arguing? No. They shouldn't be saying goodbye. They will definitely see each other again. It cannot be otherwise...

She looked at her companions. She put her hand on the shoulder of the unhappy Alina with a comforting gesture.

"Put our weapons against the wall!" She said firmly to the sailors guarding them. "Better to be ready for the worst!"

She didn't have to tell them that twice.

CHAPTER 26

With the help of his men, Ross assembled the crews of all three ships.

The seamen of the Valeria and the Judith looked at the Blood Witch pirates with reasonable suspicion. Their hands rested on their swords as a warning whenever they did not like the looks of the Red Captain's former sea robbers, as was often the case. Captain Nils reassured his people in a determined tone, not losing sight of the temporary pirate commander, whose appearance could disturb many seafaring souls. He was also curious about the immensely Valeria's young Captain, whom he thought favorably about given his recent exploits. Indeed, the attention of everyone gathered on the beach was in a rush focused on him. Now, however, Ross, supported by the sympathy of many and his relatives, has got used to the almost unusual situation. The term "almost" was key here. He was supported in this by echoes of the past, when he found himself in a brothel before the eyes of a wide clientele.

However, it was still something new. Though he had a crazy thought that somehow, he wasn't afraid.

Of considerable importance was the fact that Sel was at his side, and so was Victor, not counting the women and a few seasoned sailors, such as the boatswain and the second helmsman, because Ross not allowed Silas, like Tenan to participate in this extraordinary undertaking.

"We're supposed to defend the slaves now?" Vincent laughed. "You've lost your mind!"

"Pirate honor?" Ross asked lightly, not at all concerned, "What if I say that in return, I will let everyone plunder the governor's palace and the rich who have grown gold on human blood? Everyone!" He remarked, looking around. "Not only the old pirates!"

"What if we don't want to share?" Vincent asked ominously, clearly implying that no lion would suddenly become a docile lamb unless he proved his advantage again.

And what was the advantage of the young captain, freshly commanding a crew of cruel pirates? Vincent wanted Ross to prove his worth to his people. Not everyone has been convinced by his demonstration of power yet. It took more than magic for that. Preferably in front of everyone.

Ross understood his intentions perfectly.

Everyone was looking at him now.

He raised his head proudly. What will work on them the most? The promise of loot was a good idea.

"Can you fight?" He asked with his special, intended for moments when he was going to use persuasion, tone. "Or is it just talking? So far, we haven't had a chance to know how much you are worth. Maybe you can't do anything? Perhaps the only thing you know is to attack defenseless women, children and the elderly?" he sneered, to which several dozen cutlasses and swords belonging to the sailors of the Valeria and the Judith issued a warning screeching. "Maybe it was not worth keeping you alive?" He asked, looking into his eyes fearlessly.

"Very good," thought Vincent, suspecting that the captain knew his thoughts.

"Or maybe we will not listen to any fucking woman?!" one of the pirates could not stand it, on which Vincent was counting silently. "Do you think you will scare us because you asked something in our head?" He smiled with a smile presenting missing teeth. "Do you have us for a bunch of fools? You defeated our captain by luck! You have no balls! No well-groomed doll is going to push us around!" He pulled his cutlass towards him. "Not with such…!"

Ross felt a touch from the past...

"Sleek, like a princely!" The mother shouted. "What are you imagining? Who do you think you are?!"

He was standing in front of her, wearing the best things Nanny had found. He wore shoes from one of her boys, and a trimmed coat. The white shirt gleamed like new. The neatly combed hair was a bit ruffled by the wind, but it was clean and trimmed.

"You told me yesterday I could go to school," he tried to remind her.

"What?!" She shouted incredulously.

"You said I could learn," he persisted.

She did say! Yesterday. In a rare rush of motherly care. He didn't make it up! He will not allow himself to be told that he was dreaming about it. Nanny heard it too.

"What are you talking about?!" She shouted as usual after drinking.

"All children my age can read and write," he argued, keeping his composure, even though he could see what was going to happen. And the nanny wasn't there yet. "You said I could go..."

She stood in front of him in a see-through nightgown, her hair disheveled. She looked at him with familiar eyes as if he were merely a worm, or even something much more meaningless. Not even something, but nothing.

He knew that look all too well, even though he was only nine years old.

"Listen to me, you little shit!" She came up to him surprisingly quickly. "You will not study, did you hear? You are too stupid to learn!" She grabbed his clothes; it was carefully prepared for this festive day. The best he ever had. "Not a single letter will get into your empty head! I'll make sure of it! That bastard's son will never know anything, you understand?! You are nothing! And you're supposed to be nothing for the rest of your life!"

He felt tears under his eyelids, but then he raised his head proudly.

"I'm nothing! I'm the son of a pirate! I'm Ross Hope! My future belongs to me and only to me! Naram told me..."

He felt a hard slap in his face that made him dizzy.

"That bitch will regret it!" His mother shouted in his face. "So are you!"

The jerking out of her grip ended for him not only tearing his beautiful shirt and patched coat. Not only the pain in the face, hands and arms after the blows that left their mark for a long time.

The night he ran away to the nanny, Cadelia sent her lover and his buddies to set fire to Naram's house..."

"...We fought with stronger people than you! You are ordinary punk!" The pirate shouted, savoring his own words.

Ross looked at him coldly.

Nobody will call him that with impunity!

Perhaps the belligerent pirate was expecting another magic show. But Ross didn't want to shield himself with it. He would spend half his life on the street, coping without it, and though the Jewel now shone purple and ready to support him, he, as he has always had it since he owned it, was on his own instincts.

The blow came quickly and suddenly. The knuckles of his hands should burn him as they hit his face, but he felt nothing. Another blow, harder than ever, filled with rage. The pirate shielded himself too late, but when he finally did, blocked it quite effectively. Then Victor interrupted the fight, wrapping his arm around the thug's neck.

"Enough!" He ordered.

"Only that appeals to you!" Ross yelled at the pirate. "You got what you wanted, now go back to yours and shut your mouth!" He strengthened his last words with the effect of the Jewel.

Victor let go of the pirate as he tried unsuccessfully to express himself, but no sound escaped from his throat.

Ross straightened up.

"I know it might be too hard for you," he said, calming his emotions thanks to the effect of the Gem. "But you won't say a word until you sincerely help someone. You can be sure of it."

The pirate looked at him, wiping the blood from his nose. It was no longer a mocking look, but a respectful one. Not because Ross used magic, but because of how he used it. He moved his jaw, judging by his expression that the blows were pretty good. Then he nodded to him.

"We're wasting time!" Ross exclaimed to those present. "We must take on board the people who opposed their oppressors! I don't think Else Governor will look at this calmly! Perhaps we will get the city! Free the other enslaved! Me and the Valeria crew are ready for it! Among these brave people is the healer and owner of the Judith, as well as the captain of the Witch! What's your decision? Are you with me?"

"You have my word, Captain!" The Judith's captain firmly extended his hand to embrace. "We are with you!"

The crew backed him eagerly. Ross looked at Vincent.

Vincent raised his fist up. A chorus of thunderous voices filled the space.

Eric was not sure if he would ever see his daughter again. Only child. The meaning of existence. His joy and support. Only she was left for him.

And although he almost stopped believing it, he regained her.

As they all started marching off, he held her tightly, alternately crying and laughing. He urged her to return to the ship and at the same time was glad to have her by his side again. Brave again. Adventuresome. They failed to break her...

Ross saw Cora and the man who was probably her father.

He froze for a moment, watching the sight that touched the silent longing of his heart.

He should go, yes... It was as unusual for him as it was for others to discover a precious treasure.

So, this is what it looks like? A parent's love for a child? Yes, he did feel a similar warmth when Naram was with him. Then Valeria. And then the Beckert family, the Semeralda's family, and the elderly couple who only left the house in the mountain. It was similar. But whatever it was, it would never be the same. He will not be given it...

Sel stood beside him, discreetly silent.

For a short while more, before they moved on, they stared at this unusual sight, enjoying their happiness.

The crowd waited where the fighting began.

Notified by the scouts, men, women and children gathered in a large crowd, armed with weapons of hunters, whose several volunteers guarded nearby, circling them.

At the head of this enormous group was Violet, her head proudly held high. Tipe stood on one side of her, while Nachim watched over the man many had been looking for for so long.

The Healer.

Vivan stood with his throat tight with emotion. It was them. His grandfather, brother, Sel and many inhabitants of the former Barnica. They came here for him!

He had brought so much harm on them by his existence, and yet they were here now.

Among them was the only person in this world who knew him almost like a mother.

Dearest friend.

He didn't know whether to run or wait for them. He felt his legs buckle beneath him and he was unlikely to get far, as tears began to blur his image.

Ross stopped. He glanced at Victor. Vivan was convinced that his friend was giving way to his family, not wanting to disturb these moments. He secretly regretted, because now the most important thing in the world he wanted to say was to say hello to him. Not because he didn't care about them. He wanted it because of their relationship with each other, the understanding of two souls who understood each other best. So he was a bit distracted when he greeted Paphian again.

He concentrated more when his grandfather greeted him. He deserved his full attention. Like Sel, whose kindness warmed the heart. He hoped that he had shown them with all his strength how much he was enjoying this meeting. He saw understanding in Sel's eyes. Sel knew perfectly well the longing with which they both had been waiting for this.

The moment had finally come. They stood facing each other for a moment longer. Too long for Vivan's taste, most prone to exuberance of all. That's why he couldn't stand it. He felt the need to embrace him immediately, otherwise he would burst into tears that he sometimes shed too much anyway.

So much time until all thoughts on this moment finally come down to a few simple words, filled with the sincerest dedication.

"Without you, I wouldn't be able to do it!" His voice failed him, turning hoarse with muffled sobs. He gave Ross a firm, warm embrace.

Ross reciprocated, feeling the warmth of his friend's feelings, driving his gloomy thoughts away and his heart filling with happiness.

At last! He found him! Almost as if they were already home.

He had the overwhelming feeling that Vivan's warmth, which had become almost legendary, was as intense as ever. It carried so much relief, a sense of security, and even care that he had never experienced from him. The friend seemed to radiate an outer aura. He could almost see the glow. It wasn't just luck with the meeting. Certainly, it had a meaning here, but the power, or he couldn't have called it otherwise, was beyond that. There was no demonstrative brilliance. Just a strong, indescribable feeling. Even so, Ross stared at Vivan as if mesmerized. He had never experienced such strength of spirit from him before... As if someone had lit torches in every dark corner of his mind, heart and soul. The burden he felt after fighting the man who fathered him almost vanished. The past ceased to sit on his neck like a nightmare, allowing for distance. It finally became only a memory.

Bitter but not bothersome. The world suddenly took on color, the heart pounded with a strong rhythm.

People surrounded them. They also wanted to say hi to the healer.

Ross was quick to find in many similar signs of calmness and even spontaneous joy.

Vivan, once surrounded by a bloodthirsty crowd, did not need to fear them. He certainly sensed it. That's why he didn't even think about it.

At first, he was surrounded by people from the Valeria and the Judith. However, when they began to be enthusiastic about this meeting, not hiding even for them unexpected emotion and tears of joy, the pirates joined them hesitantly.

Ross watched in amazement as the tall, tattooed Vincent squeezed Vivan's hand with some embarrassment, not knowing if he could. Everyone waited for the healer to react. Even he himself was curious about what was going to happen.

Vivan looked straight into Vincent's eyes.

At a time when he was still able to help normally, he moved among many people. He saw many faces; he knew many characters. All of this only helped him in part to know their hearts. The gift was helpful in this. Now, shaking Vincent's hand, he sensed a change in him that gave him hope that this heart would change.

The fate of this man was in his hands. If he tells others that they will never get to know the better side of him, they will surely kill him.

Fortunately, to be completely honest, he didn't have to say similar words. He felt a warmth in him that did not go out. It was hidden.

"Stay with us," he said, returning the hug tightly. He knew it would make the right impression on a pirate who was accustomed to strength.

Vincent looked at him. He felt the exceptional solemnity of the moment.

Vivan looked different now. He had some features of all the deities he had heard about in the stories. It appealed to him. Surely there would be people like their former captain, for example, who would care nothing for the importance of such a meeting. After all, he had seen how he treated the healer when he appeared. But it mattered to him. Before, he just thought he was a healer. He helps others, he cannot be tormented, because he will still lose his gift. Now he thought he deserved a respect they had not shown him before. They should never torment a person born to help others in such a selfless way. On the contrary, they should protect him from greed and ravenousness, so that his gift is never broken in him.

"You may not be any deity," he began with a slight smile. "You bleed like us and shit like us. But there's something about you that makes me want to cry. I'm starting to think about my mother, my house and my own boat, somewhere where I was born. You change people's hearts if we only give you the chance to show us this heart." He put his hand on his shoulder. "You are a special man, Vivan Beckert, the Healer of Tenckryz." He smiled at him. "May you never run out of that damn stubbornness to do good."

Vivan smiled. His gift, devoid of bad colors that consumed his strength, worked on people, making people smile, and that was what he loved the most.

The last time he felt like this after a fight with a witch, he appeared in a reconstructed village. Then the warm welcome of the inhabitants and the joy of Vashaba in love (or her strong infatuation) increased his gift.

"So, this is what it looks like," Violet muttered to Ross, watching Vivan allow the pirates to greet him, approaching it carefully and deliberately.

Ross, who had never seen a friend say hello to the townspeople because he was busy rebuilding his ship with Alvar at the time, watched with interest.

"What's next?" She asked, shaking off her pleasant satisfaction. "What's our plan? We still have some, right? We have not given up on it because we have what we came for?" She pointed at Vivan. "He is radiant because people showed gratitude and cordiality," she began to explain. "This is where his strength lies. He helped the wounded and the sick. People love him now. They will follow him everywhere! If we give a sign, Vivan will encourage volunteers to fight. If we take him and other people..."

"Violet," he interrupted her speech with nonchalant calm, "Do you think I brought everyone in to give you a great escort to the ships and take you home?" He looked at her with irony.

Several commanders moved closer to them, waiting. Vivan looked at them for the sign.

Violet greeted her captain from the Judith and a group of sailors from both of her ships. Quite a large group. And well armed, she noticed. She also welcomed the women and sailors of the Valeria.

At last, the pirates faced her - her new crew.

She raised her head proudly, though she was shorter than the stalwart Vincent.

"Give me a hand, right now!" She cried in her captain's tone. "I won't kiss you!" She held out her hand. "You are Vincent, I'm Violet, the new captain of the Witch!" She patted him luscious on the back. "Enough?"

"It won't be better!" He grimaced.

She considered that smile.

"Captain!" She shouted at Ross loudly. "Time is pressing! The market in Else is been going on! What do you say?"

"It always falls on me," Ross thought ironically, lifting his head in his triangular hat. "I guess I should get used to it."

"We're going to Else!" He shouted.

"But..." one of the liberated paused. "How will we get behind the city walls?"

Vivan looked knowingly at Ross. He already knew.

"Some of you will escort women, children and old men to the ships!" Ross ordered. "Everyone else - follow me! We'll do..."

Else prepared to attack.

The residents had enough time for this. They even prepared kettles with boiling water and tar. The archers took their positions. The mounted unit was ready outside the gate. The soldiers fully armed themselves waiting for a signal to begin their defense.

Many rich people paid with gold to mobilize as many people as possible to fight. They protected their lives, property and interests. News came about the deeds of the Troublemaker who were heading for their beloved good. They did not like such a visit. Some people even panicked when they heard about his appearance in these parts. The few fugitives, those from the skirmish near the city, also spoke of the new, extraordinary power of the healer, glistening with blue steel. A few were even willing to swear that Vivan had burnt those who did not return with them.

Therefore, struck by this news, the governor ordered a pigeon to be sent to the castle of King Azram himself.

Ross, on a premonition, watched the birds fly, and a winged messenger hid between them, starting a series of events that seemed to end loudly.

Azram will find out soon. Certainly, he will not leave these matters alone. If they procrastinate, perhaps they would get his sullen assistants, the winged demons that were rumored in the harbors of the royal capital.

He wasn't going to wait for them.

He adjusted his triangular hat and coat nervously.

"Okay!" He exclaimed eagerly to cheer the people accompanying him. "It's time to start having fun!"

Vivan narrowed his eyes as he watched him make his way to the city gates. What friend was going to do now, probably anyone has seen before.

Out of the corner of his eye, he saw grandfather put his hand on the gun, watching the walls.

"Hey, you there!" Ross called meanwhile to the soldiers on the walls and in the turrets with narrow windows, "Open the gates!"

Silence answered him. This was what he expected.

He touched his temple with a calm gesture. Vivan saw Sel clench one of his hands. He wanted to soothe him with a gesture, but refrained from doing so.

"What are you waiting for?!" Said a nervous voice from above. "Shoot him, goddamn it!"

The archers tightened their strings. They tracked the target with their arrowheads.

"He's not immortal!" The same voice shouted again. "Come on!"

Ross tilted his head in careless curiosity. His mind found the screamer among the soldiers. Long robes, expensive pants. Belly a bit too round. Self-confidence for show, tinged with a hint of fear.

Commanders raised their hands.

Sel held his breath.

"Don't move," Ross ordered calmly, hoping to save time.

All the soldiers stopped in their current positions.

He felt a growing fear, mixed with irritation, from the archers. They were still in position ready to fire. Some people's hands started to tremble slightly.

"YOU FLEW LAST TIME!" He increased his voice so that those standing closest huddled a bit. "Castello, open the gate!"

The puffy little man felt he could move again. However, he resisted his demands in a blunt manner.

"Get the fuck off!" He shouted, losing the last remnants of his grandeur.

The awkward position was taking its toll on the archers more and more.

Ross waited patiently. The drunk, lazy mind of the governor of the island was no match for any of his opponents so far. Sharing his fists and waving his fists at him, Castello made his way inevitably towards the guards opening the gate.

"I sent a pigeon!" He shouted between curses, "The king will send demons here! You're over, you pirate bastard! You're dead! Wait, wait a moment and you'll see!"

Ross calmly followed his actions.

"Throw out your bows," he said quietly, aloud, so that his companions could follow the course of events.

The archers lowered their bows with relief, removed their arrows from their strings.

"Not everyone listened," Victor remarked, looking at the whole situation.

At Ross's signal, sailors with bows and crossbows reached for them.

Most of the archers on the walls obeyed.

"Why not all of them?" One of the pirates asked.

"Some are more courageous," muttered Paphian.

"When Castello opens the gates, the fight will begin," Ross said to everyone, "Don't count on avoiding it."

In fact, he was already trembling slightly with the effort. It took a great deal of concentration to concentrate on all the soldiers and their behavior.

"Okay, okay," he heard the governor's voice through the Jewel, "Open this gate!"

The gate creaked ominously, then flung open...

"Now!" Ross yelled, relieved to free the will of his opponents.

The accompanying archers fired the first arrows, killing the reluctant.

The pirates let out battle screams, being the first to burst into the city.

The others followed.

Vivan's heart beat violently with anxiety...

The clash of steel and the screams of combatants merged into the chaos of battle. Ross was undermining the morale of the soldiers by constantly influencing his decisions, shielded along with Vivan by the squad with his relatives and family. It was not entirely fair, but the residents were also not famous for their honesty. The lighthouse deceived the shipwreckers in its vicinity without expecting a trap. And then the soldiers from Else dealt with these unfortunates, more than once murdering, robbing and raping. Castello was hiding behind them, trying to distance himself from the white-haired sorcerer, who allowed him to have the illusory hope that he would finally slip away to safety. Time was pressing because the demons sent by Azram might not be there long. The city had to be taken at all costs.

Pirates were ruthless when finally allowed to do what they wanted. Cutting their throats and cutting their limbs was their element, and Ross, busy weakening his opponents, this time let them off the leash, but making sure that they were keeping their oath of allegiance with a part of his attention. How his mind was working at that moment was known only to Vivan, Sel and, to some extent, Oliver, already freed, watching the city anxiously from the deck of the ship.

Fighting the snake was something completely different, although the excessive effort of the will then paid off. Ross felt emphatically that it was not enough just to want to be able.

He figured he would be in control of everything, but keeping that control turned out to be quite an effort.

Battle frenzy is not easy to handle. Teaching cruelty, Castell's soldiers would have smashed less experienced volunteers unimaginably cruel if he had not stopped their efforts.

At the same time, his people, ranging from pirates to liberated people who were driven by revenge, also wanted to show some ingenuity in killing. He had straightened their ideas not only for their own good, but for a friend who was ready to fight, if necessary, but his pale skin tone and faster breathing indicated that this element was a huge burden for him. Vivan found himself in the middle of the fighting - a place where it was harder to find mercy or warm feelings, and violence dominated. Everything the combatants were guided by attacked him directly in the gift, mind and heart. It was unimaginably hard to bear for a person who was helping others, with his whole being focused on giving it.

However, he did not want to leave his friends.

Finally, Ross got bored of playing cat and mouse with the governor, who tried to lock himself in his stronghold.

He grabbed him by the neck, holding a dagger to it.

"This time you will not be well!" He hissed in the face of him. "Did you really think I would forget about you? Even after you gave the order to kill all the slaves in the marketplace?"

"Besharam. One of the meanings is "unscrupulous"..." grunted Castello, trying to make a mocking smile. "Besharam will find you! And his too!" He pointed at Vivan.

Ross looked deep into his eyes.

There was only darkness there.

"He already sees you..." the captured rejoiced with a joy that marks madness.

"POSSESSED," the Jewel of Hope warned.

Ross pushed him away, and Sel swung his sword and severed the head, which fell to the ground, making a loud noise. As if a huge drum had been hit...

Vivan staggered.

There were still fighting going on around.

He realized that it had to be that way. It wasn't his world. His friends, his family, they were all in a fight that they all agreed to. Including himself.

He was trying. With all strength. However, the violence around him wreaked more and more havoc in him. It was taking away his strength.

"I need..." he whispered in his mind, thinking of the house.

It can't end like this! He cannot fall!

Violet's handkerchief did little when he saw her killing opponents. The handkerchief Eric had given did not have this power while he himself fought and killed.

A girl was helping him. That brave girl from the Red Captain ship. Daughter...

His daughter.

So, they met.

The thought was reassuring until, in front of him, one of his opponents hurt her badly on the shoulder.

Suddenly he was shocked to see this.

"Wake up Vivan!" He ordered himself indignantly, "You are a healer! Protect them!"

He grabbed her arm. His eyes gleamed briefly as the gift worked. The deep cut began to heal quickly, faster than before. The torn tissues fused together. The blood has returned to its paths. Eventually even the scar disappeared without a trace.

He met her eyes, and healed the effects of bruises during the fight.

"Thank you..." she said softly, surprised by his action.

And suddenly it happened...

He always knew!

Always.

How... What... For what cruel reason... Like ropes, the ghastly ties between the victims he healed and their tormentors tied it all together. The order of events. Spoken words. It all took a moment, maybe two, and for him it was almost forever. Picture by picture. Sentence by sentence, blow after blow... Thrust after thrust... As a compassionate witness, he classified a rape as one of the cruelest acts that can be committed.

He became more sensitive to him when he almost became a victim of the Red Captain...

These feelings almost merged into one. And in its history, they supplemented with missing impressions...

He staggered, turning pale. He lost track of time and place.

It was a perfectly planned trap.

Cora was supposed to go to the allegedly in labor. Her father was stopped by another case. One of the thugs previously disliked her words about treating women with respect after he had beaten up a street maid who was assisted by Eric. He decided that she would pay him for her audacity...

Three of them. The empty house they dragged her into. No chance of winning against strong, seasoned men. The red-haired, bearded tormentor of that girl tugged hard on her neatly combed bun, rushing to act. Vivan felt a pain as if his hair had been torn off his head, almost immediately coinciding with the pain of the punches and kicks of the thug and his colleagues.

"Vivan!" he heard her voice vaguely. "What's going on?! Help!"

"No," he wanted to say "don't yell. This is not really happening. It will pass. They're actually memories. This is not happening..."

Thoughts fled in terror as the thug opened her legs...

"But I just...," he thought desperately, but it was to no avail.

He was there. He was her. He felt what she felt then.

The bearded man was the most brutal. And he was her first, which he noticed with malicious satisfaction.

It took a long, long time. Paralyzing pain.

He couldn't feel anything else anymore. He saw nothing else. Like then, with the poor girl, mutilated by her uncle, the bastard who tore her to the anus...

Rape was a brutal act that he was never ready for...

Three had her one by one...

Only then did the paralyzing vision disappear.

A moment or two passed.

For her, for the people around him.

Paphian called to him, terrified that Vivan had fallen shortly after Cora's thanks.

Cora was shaking him, demanding a reaction.

One moment...

Few hours...

The baby in her womb.

Third month.

"Please say something," her voice finally reached him. "You passed out. The blood is running from your nose. Lie down, do you hear? Can you talk? Understand me? Tell me what your name is!"

He looked at her, unable to stop the tears from pouring out of the strong shock.

"Viv... an" he blurted out, still bewildered by the crowd of images and impressions.

And she smiled! She smiled despite what they did to her. He wasn't sure right now if he would ever smile again. Although it was not the first, and probably not the last time. He always wondered how he managed it. How he can live knowing so many faces of cruelty. And he always found an answer... But now it wasn't enough.

"He must be exhausted," she said to Paphian, looking for clues in his behavior. After all, he knew him better. He knew what his options were.

Paphian knew his other secrets as well. So he looked at her only briefly, fearing that he would betray something. Instead, he gently helped him to sit up, to her surprise, embracing him in a firm, brotherly hug. He understood.

"A little food, a sip of wine and he'll be good," he decided for the benefit of the girl and those present.

"Let's take him and the wounded to the Valeria," she asked, while several armed men, escorted by Ross, protected them from the few opponents.

Paphian shook his head to try to hold him back, but Vivan was too upset to listen to his brother.

"It's not to blame for anything," he began in a trembling voice. "Please think about it..."

Cora paled, as did Paphian, who instantly understood his words, though he did not know the full story. However, his brother's behavior revealed a lot to him about it...

Cora stared at Vivan. The disbelief in her eyes quickly turned into the belief that he was telling the truth. Until then, she had been hoping that everything would be fine, that it was the end. Wasn't she suffering enough? Will she remember this for the rest of her life?

"I'm pregnant?" She asked hesitantly, her confused future before her eyes.

He was scared. It often happened that aggrieved women or their family members who found out about it focused all their anger for the harm they encountered on it, powerless against the absent perpetrator. It ended in various ways... Now he knew perfectly well what was going to happen, but he didn't feel up to it.

He would like to get as far away from here as possible. But the phantom, excruciatingly real pain in the groin did not do much to him. His face was burning with the blows. His body was sore. But there, where her femininity had been wounded, it hurt the most, making him want to howl.

Unfortunately, he had to answer her. She deserved it.

"Yes," he replied, shaking with emotion. "In the third month."

As he had predicted, she came to him almost immediately, punching his chest with her fists as if she wanted to make him silence.

"And you know about it?!" She moaned desperately.

Vivan tried helplessly to shield himself. He wished she would stop. It was causing him double pain. Paphian restrained her from further anger.

"Maybe I call Eric?" he was concerned.

Vivan bit his lip. He'd let him do it only to get a chance to have an intimate conversation with Cora.

"I have a special gift..." he whispered as the other walked away.

He also predicted it.

She slapped him in the face. Strongly. Crouching, he groaned softly.

"What else do you know?!" She screamed painfully. "What else do you know about me?!"

He wanted her to know. Maybe then she will stop beating him...

"Everything," he looked at her boldly, struggling for a little sympathy, though his condition barely allowed him to speak.

She froze, struck by the news, as if nothing worse could happen to her. She hid so much with her fear...

"You can't know that..." she blurted out regretfully. "You can't! I didn't tell anyone! I can't be pregnant! I can't be... I can't..." She hid her face in her hands. "Say it's a lie!"

"I can not…"

"How am I supposed to live now?!" She asked, looking at his face with eyes full of tears. "So? Every day look in the mirror and see what happened to me?"

"It could be you..." he whispered, seeing a cruel face in the images of his memory.

He contradicted his own thoughts.

"Or one of them!" She screamed regretfully. "Or maybe you still know which of them is the father? Do you know?! Talk!"

A single tear ran down his face before he could speak.

"I know."

She looked at him, resigned.

This man was the only one who...

"He had a beard," he said, feeling his heart poundingly in his chest. "He had red hair..."

He felt sweat beating on him. They did it! They broke into his intimacy! Her intimacy. He didn't know anymore. From despair, he felt that he was already losing his mind.

"Vivan!" he heard Eric's voice suddenly behind his back. "Cora? What happened?!"

Apparently, he didn't see much.

Everything went blank. Apparently, Ross made sure of that.

Few of the troops were still slipping towards the center of Else, eager to muster their strength there for their final defense. The townspeople looked shyly through the small windows. They won this clash.

All the winners now looked around with a smile of satisfaction.

Only he wanted to disappear.

Eric just looked at his face. He understood everything faster than his daughter, without further explanation. He touched his shoulder reassuringly and walked away to summon Paphian. They talked in low voices.

"What's going on with you?" Cora finally worried about his condition. "You have a fever..." She touched his forehead with concern.

The medic's sense immediately replaced the jittery one as anxiety won.

"You told me this because..." she began slowly, "do you have the gift of clairvoyance?"

"The gift of compassion," he croaked with difficulty.

It took a moment for her to fully understand the meaning of his words. Her eyes widened in disbelief.

"Did you feel...?" She asked quietly, closing the world to their two and a secret she had so far managed to protect.

He no longer felt her anger, only a growing compassion.

He nodded.

"Oh, gods..." she whispered in horror. "It's not a gift. It's cruel."

He closed his eyes.

"It's the essence of my existence. I live to help you," he whispered.

She watched him anxiously. He preferred not to see it. He wanted to go out of here now, away from her. From everybody.

"Hey..." Ross finally showed up. "I have to go on, to the market. Paphian is here. They'll take you to the ship. I'm so sorry... I say that to you too, Cora. You will rest, Vivan. You know..." He broke off, feeling all the hidden suffering of his lying friend inside him.

Oh, he's seen it before! At Sai. Same look. The same apparent bravery that made Vivan stand up with his head held high.

"I have to help the wounded," the healer croaked.

"You should..." Paphian began softly, but Vivan cut him off abruptly.

I should help! Let me do it!"

Cora watched his movements. Impossible for him to play that well! And since he wasn't acting, that slow, effortless step by step was as real as hers when she came back at night from a dark alley where her torturers had abandoned her.

"I didn't know..." she whispered, "that so..."

He could barely walk. Just like her then.

She would never wish that to anyone! Meanwhile, he...

Vivan staggered, falling into his brother's hands. No wonder the three brutal strongmen didn't let Cora go right away. They played until late at night...

"Leave me some men and go," Vivan croaked, feeling everything swell inside, demanding a scream.

Ross finally decided to stop it.

"Listen," he began gently, "Eric will go to the wounded and..." He looked at Cora, who, shocked by the healer's appearance, managed only to nod her head, "Cora will help him. I also see that there are several of ours who know how to help the wounded," he looked at the liberated one.

He called one of the sailors. He ordered him to fetch Oliver and a few of his crew's women who were already hanging around with the people.

"You don't understand..." Vivan waited a moment, trying to control himself. "When I help them..."

"Not this time!" Ross remarked sharply, depriving him of all his illusions.

"It's the same as with the little one, Vivan," added Paphian. "Do you remember how difficult it was for you to recover then?"

Cora watched them, unable to move. She had herself in front of her eyes... From those moments when she had surreptitiously, overwhelmed with pain, returned home. Before her eyes, an unacceptable thing is happening. She both laughed hysterically at the news she heard from him and despair at what she had inadvertently done to him.

She knew very well how much he was suffering at that moment.

She had no doubts that he was telling the truth. Every gesture he made testified to it. So, when she was finally able to move, she just went to him.

"You should listen to your loved ones," she said.

She held out her hand to give him a comforting gesture. But she hesitated. What if it worsens his condition? Enough bad has already happened.

She turned to leave.

Then she heard his soft voice:

"It isn't your fault."

"I know," she said, before she left.

She didn't look back anymore. She did not dare to meet his eyes again.

Ross was unable to accompany Vivan. They still had a lot to do. He said goodbye to him with a tender embrace, promising to come as soon as he could. He whispered a few soothing words for which his friend thanked him with a handshake. A makeshift stretcher was made on which several people carried him outside the city. Vivan covered himself with the blanket he had brought, hiding his face. He couldn't bear the stares of the people he passed. Regret was tearing him apart. He was failing them at the most important moment. But Ross was right. He was unable to help them. He was the victim of a brutal rape. His mind refused to acknowledge that it was just an impression. It was not. Only moments after the incident, the signs of beating appeared on his face and body, he preferred not to think about the intimate area. He had lost the wall protecting him from such visions. Probably due to being in the middle of the fighting. Now all he could think about was when he would finally be alone in his cabin. He focused on persevering until this point.

Meanwhile, Ross went to the marketplace. He couldn't have done otherwise. After all, he had promised these people, even though his heart was eager to see his friend. He tried to help him mentally, but Vivan kept him away now. So he focused on the next target.

There were many people at the marketplace. Mostly merchants, their escorts and the soldiers of the slain governor. Ross lifted his head from under the triangular hat, standing just in front of the entrance.

Wooden stairs led to the landing, where the salesman praised the goods on display: a group of people of almost every age group in which they could still serve their future masters. It didn't matter in what capacity these people were sold. Was it a housekeeper who works great in the kitchen, a sturdy man, suitable for hard work, or a few years old girl with blonde hair and big blue eyes.

All these people were naked.

Stripped of clothes, they huddled in front of a large audience, concealing their intimacy and trying to save the last remnants of their dignity in such a dramatic situation. The terrified little girl stared at the trader with eyes full of tears and fear as he praised her qualities to the merchants who loudly appraised her white skin, breast buds, and young womb. They were probably merchants with brothels in the Bay or outside the capital, interested in buying merchandise for discerning customers, for whom there was never a place in the House of Pleasure where Ross worked. Mother never sold children, even though such shameful offers were made.

Another one who had just sold a strong man was standing next to him, and now praised the culinary skills of an undressed, no longer young woman, quietly shedding tears.

"There are more of them there," he heard Paphian's soft voice, indicating a large group near the landing, guarded by armed guards.

Those who had freed themselves slightly stepped out to watch with horror this extraordinary spectacle in which they almost took part.

Pirates and...

Ross looked at Vincent and the man with him who had helped injured Vivan on the ship. They and their evil companions looked at it, judging. Some of them assessed the value of the goods sold - old habits. Others looked as if they were seeing it for the first time. On the other hand, Vincent, whose character Vivan understood well, and his companion Matt and a few of their companions - these had a strange twinkle in their eyes.

He would have sworn they were tears.

The women were deeply moved. Apara and Anokhi, who sought support in his arms, clenched their hands with eyes full of tears, looking at the suffering of the girl and the old woman. Violet cursed to herself. The women of the liberated men nervously wiggled their weapons, ready to leap out at the traders and merchants with screams of anger.

The hype among his people grew, while the market continued to bustle with life, as if nothing notable had happened. Had it not been for the soldiers of the city who had signaled the nobles to prepare for battle, the trade would have continued, as if the nearly eight hundred men next to the marketplace had not been cared for.

These rich men were so confident that they thought it could be settled easily - with gold or with a system favorable to them. They were business people.

Possibly their numerous escorts will overcome this jumble easily. They were deeply convinced of it.

Ross felt himself on the edge.

He could not allow these people to be simply murdered, no matter how heartless they were. They were not soldiers, but civilians. Well prepared, but still...

What was his decision to make?

He had never found himself in such a situation before...

"Ross," Sel leaned toward him anxiously, "They don't run away like in Artaman..."

"Yes…" he whispered.

In Artaman they had captured, terrified merchants fled in panic, fearing for their precious life. And yet Artaman was the center of the slave trade, the second in the Bay, outside the capital - the filthy Dolorporta (Latin dolor est in porta - pain is the gate).

Else was just a minor port.

Apparently, after he carried out the revolution, the merchants broke their spheres of influence into several smaller ones, so as not to lose too much this time.

Or be better prepared.

All the gentlemen, traders, hunters, and guards turned slowly towards them. Many chained their personal slaves and purchased "merchandise", surrounded by their own small force. Either they did not trust each other or they were cautious after the events in Artaman. The sellers' voices ceased. Voices of other merchants praising vegetables, fruits, fish and other goods nearby as well.

Everyone was looking at them.

On him.

So were his people.

"Captain?" Asked Nils significantly, commanding the crew of the Judith.

Ross calmly took a cigar from his coat pocket. Celebrating the moment with excessive carelessness, he lit it. He puffed on, aware that everyone was watching this maneuver with a certain disbelief.

Meanwhile, between one puff and the other, he managed to penetrate the minds of each of the potential opponents. In the remaining, very short time, he judged that most of the townspeople had no intention of taking part in the fighting. They barricaded themselves in their homes with their families.

"BELIEVE ME," he increased his voice. "You don't want to do this!"

The answer was mocking smiles and a slow engagement.

"Captain!" Vincent shouted impatiently. "Maybe enough of this show? Let's kick their asses!"

He blew smoke at the merchants and guards.

It grew rapidly larger, enveloping everyone, biting the eyes and blinding them.

"Are you waiting for something?" A moment later he asked mockingly the pirate as the smoke attacked. Only enemies, avoiding chained slaves.

Vincent smirked as his opponents began to cough and rub their eyes.

"Forward!" He exclaimed, rushing out first.

This time Ross did not follow him, allowing the others to do so. He and the people who were his closest escort were in the back.

He had to control the course of this battle.

Pirates captured and tied their opponents, this time killing only the most stubborn. Ship crews and freedmen did likewise, quickly gaining ground where they were for sale. It wasn't long before he saw Anokhi and her sister, accompanied by Marlene and Maya, rush to the podium, tending to the terrified girl and the woman accompanying her, while a mob of freedmen snatched the newly sold man from the hands of his would-be master.

Everything was perfect. Some of the merchants escaped, the rest were imprisoned. Less combat guards disarmed. This time, far fewer enemies were killed.

Else was taken. The first shouts of victory were raised, and a satisfied Violet let proud Vincent embrace herself.

The battlefield was beginning to fade away.

And that's when they appeared.

Demons.

CHAPTER 27

Long, membranous wings, the color of mud mixed with white. Dark as night itself, slanting eyes and a long muzzle with a tongue that is too long, twisting.

The demons in Azram's service were the size of a goose, but their size did not detract from their effectiveness. Both Ross and Vivan knew they were attacking in packs looking for signs of rebellion. Both of the overheard stories, which, as it turned out, were in line with reality.

Vivan heard them first. They were almost on the beach.

In the blink of an eye, he thought of his companions carrying his stretcher. His gift always put the fate of others first. Especially at times like this.

"Hide yourself!" He tore up the blanket in panic.

They left him immediately. They hurriedly looked around for the hiding place. But they were already on the beach, too far from the ship to hide.

The demons will kill them.

One thing remained for him: to distract the creatures of the underworld.

"They mean me," he looked at the brave men who boldly drew their swords. "Stand back!" He ordered them firmly. "Immediately!"

"Healer..." one groaned in disbelief at the words.

But Vivan knew it was their only chance to survive.

"Azram needs me alive," he added, struggling to keep calm while the demons were already descending, "he will kill you. Stand back!"

They hesitated, but seeing his steadfast gaze and a cloud of beasts diving towards them, they were forced to make a quick decision.

"We'll tell the sorcerer," said Vivan who spoke first.

They backed away in despair and anger. Vivan nodded his thanks before his claws lifted him into the air...

They jerked him up and began flying towards the sea, undoubtedly wanting to take him to the king himself.

Vivan felt claws cut through the skin of his arms and hands as they gripped his coat tightly. The grip ripped through the thick fabric and thin shirt.

He felt a piercing pain, but he knew he couldn't give up, otherwise he would be taken away.

He reached for the dagger. However, he could not move his hands freely.

He had to stop them.

The blue power barely faded in his hands, glowed in the whites of his eyes.

Quickly, definitely stopped their hearts.

Too late he realized that he was already far from the shore. Far from Else. Now he could see some unfamiliar shore, like a vast desert, cut here and there by tufts of grass and stunted trees. Nearby, the killed demons released him from their clutches. They were only minions, created to be undisturbed in the human world. Therefore, they were subject to the laws of all living creatures.

He fell into the sea with them.

For a moment he thought he was sinking as the water flooded him. He was below the surface, falling like a stone. He did not give in to fear. He had been through this once before, when he was going down with the carriage. He had to fight for himself! He surfaced, though he thought he was going to do so endlessly. He took a deep breath, looking for the land he could see. He was far from his people again, completely on his own.

At least the cold water eased the pain of the unreal rape.

Finally, he started to flow.

He found himself on the shore, relieved at first. Then the pain returned, compounded by the pain of his injured arms.

He groaned, finally venting to the terror and enormity of suffering that pierced his soul. He started screaming in anguish, struck by the enormity of the cruelty that befell both Cora and him. And now this too! As if the world was about to hurt him! He was overcome with rage at the torturers, at the powerlessness he felt. He felt despair at Cora's suffering that day. And his own suffering. He felt as if he was a victim himself...

He screamed while he had enough strength.

He remembered other victims of bestiality. The little girl who spent the night in his arms, struck by what had been done to her.

What was done to him as well.

"Why do you hate so much?" He asked quietly of the people who lived in violence.

He couldn't do anything else anymore. He could die now. Lonely. Injured. Sore.

Overwhelmed with sadness for the people for whom he was ready to help.

He closed his eyes in anguish, surrounded by the bodies of demons whose cruelty was due to nature. People who hurt others developed a taste for violence, although they might as well follow a loving heart. They loved being demons in human skin.

Therefore, for others, Vivan was a hero. Among the demons, you had to have the courage to continue to be good. Despite what happened.

The demons that attacked the people under Ross' leadership were unable to overcome the strength of his mind. They quickly gave up their bloodthirsty intentions. However, immediately afterwards grimaced maliciously, gathering high above.

They were given a clear order.

The goal is the one who imposes his will on them.

There were almost a hundred of them.

Many were killed by the swords of the white captain's defenders. Some of them flew away, discouraged by this turn of events. Others continued their attack, continuing to catch him, even at the cost of his death. They rained like hail on his escort, knocking everyone over with their weight.

But as they pecked Viktor in the head and dragged Anokhi along the ground, fear permeated. Awhile. It was enough.

Sel took the pistol from Victor's still motionless hand and fired. The bang scared the mean beasts. Unfortunately for a short time.

So, he stood with his back to his partner, ready to fight the demons.

To no avail - they were not interested...

They jumped at Ross in a whole crowd, quickly scooping him up into the air. So, he used every bullet... He fired all the precious rounds Victor had saved for the most extreme necessity. As if using this kind of weapon was something completely natural for him. He remembered well the lesson Victor had given him on the Valeria's board.

He shot accurately as if he had been born with the gift.

Even so, there were still enough to take Ross so high to his despair that he almost lost sight of them.

And flew off towards the Bay...

Chaos reigned among the victorious troops. The town and palace were conquered, but the people were not given the opportunity to rejoice at the victory. There was no leader. The white captain who made everyone fight.

Another loss was soon found out. The sailors who were helping Vivan returned to share the grim news. Their regret was touching the heart.

Vincent lost control of his people, who in retaliation began to murder prisoners, plunder the palace and surrounding houses. Violet threatened and cursed them in vain. Without the presence of a sorcerer who might already be dead, the pirates felt immediately completely unchastised. They even threatened their existing allies in the fight, especially women.

Momentarily, their willfulness was becoming more and more common.

Until finally, a triple bang in the dusk interrupted their actions...

Victor appeared on the landing where slaves had previously been sold. Stoically, he loaded the next and last rounds to the pistol, hidden in a pocket that Sel had not checked in the confusion. Next to him, Paphian and Sel aimed at pirates with crossbows, made for multiple shots - a special weapon designed by Sel. They were surprisingly light, despite the six-bolt drum, smaller than before, but just as deadly.

There were few of them in the Valeria, but they certainly wouldn't be in any kingdom. These were only part of the armament of the mighty ship.

Victor spotted one of the slimy pirates trying to grope Marlene.

He shot him without hesitating. Sel glanced at the old soldier, remembering the memories Victor had shared with them in the living room of the former Beckert Palace.

He had to behave like that in the war...

His unwavering confidence motivated Sel to keep himself in check. It wasn't easy. He still saw Ross kidnapped by bloodthirsty demons. But the world around them did not stop. It was impossible to forget about it.

The corpse slumped slowly to the ground.

There was silence.

Violet joined the three, holding the cutlass toward her rebellious crew.

"Vincent!" Violet called to her first. "Who started first?"

Vincent glanced slowly at his companion, still holding the loot in his hands. There was no friendship in the world of these pirates.

Victor fired again.

The roar of the gunshot, the immediate execution and the death of the pirate immediately calmed the rebels' aspirations.

"Everyone," Violet said loudly, when the roar of the shot faded away, "who will behave like you, a similar fate awaits. Is it clear?"

The silence was the only confirmation, though the rebellion in their eyes clearly contradicted it.

"Captain Nils, please order a return to the ship. Vincent - the same! We're sailing in the direction they disappeared. To the Bay!"

She waited for them to begin following orders.

"Sel," she turned calmly to the young man, who, despite his best efforts, still looked deeply agitated. "Do you have a bond with Ross? Similar to the one that connects the two?"

"Only when I'm close to Ross," he replied, his voice a little shaky truthfully.

"Are they alive?" Victor asked immediately, despite these words, not losing hope that he would find out something. "Come on!"

Sel focused on the sensations. They were definitely weaker, but still palpable.

"Ross is alive..." he replied after a moment in a low voice. "I only know that."

The old soldier tried not to show his disappointment. After all, in this crazy world you can't have everything. They'll find Ross, and they'll find out about his grandson. That's good, too. That must be enough for him for now.

"Be strong!" He firmly looked into the eyes of the depressed young man. He is alive, and that's the most important thing! He patted him on the shoulder, which had hardly ever happened, but this time Sel was in no mood to judge the old veteran's behavior. "You have to act!"

"Who's in charge of the Valeria when Ross is away?" Violet asked them on the way back.

"Tenan," Sel admitted reluctantly, "along with Silas, the First."

His voice cracked visibly. He fell silent.

"Notify if you find out anything," Violet asked, thinking mostly of Vivan.

He just nodded.

He needed to see Oliver.

"I'm burning," Oliver announced, when they were all on board again. "It hurts and irritates me terribly," he explained to worriedly Sai, touching one arm and the other alternately.

"Come on, I'll see it!" She asked as one of the sailors announced that the crews were returning from Else.

He sat down on the barrel, letting her slide his shirt off her shoulders. Lena was watching them from her seat, full of bad foreboding.

She was not wrong.

The skin on the arms, also around the neck, and even on the back, was covered with thin stripes and strange red patches. Their number was startling.

Sai groaned softly.

"That bad?" Oliver worried, hearing her reaction. He looked down at his shoulders at the strange, disturbing marks, then frowned at his fear.

"You have no traces..." Sai noticed quietly. "You have something like a shield. You said yourself when Ross was injured on the ship..."

"I know..." he hurriedly put on his shirt, then took her hand. "Maybe it's a... a jewel? Maybe it wants to tell me something, I don't know..."

Sai embraced him anxiously, hugging his back as gently as she could.

"Don't worry," he tried to reassure her, although the manifestation worried him, too, "It will disappear in a moment. Nothing special..."

"These are claw and clutches marks!" Sel, who came first on board, interrupted him.

Oliver looked around immediately for his brother by chance, but did not find him at Sel's side, as was usually the case.

"Oliver..." Sel began as calmly as he could. Lena approached them quickly.

"Where's Ross?" Oliver asked worriedly, instinctively clenching his hand on his wife's. However, this was mainly the concern for her future fate, because he was used to the thought that accompanied him, at least all his life, that his existence was connected with someone else. A bond that could drag him to the grave, no matter what he wanted, for he had less control over it than a mere mortal.

Sel froze for a moment, with a painful awareness that he used to push away from how much Oliver's life was related to Ross's. Yes, Ross's life was also tied with this bond the other way around, but it was Ross who drew trouble to himself much more often. Even so, Oliver never complained.

"I'm sorry," he didn't answer his question. "Because of how vulnerable you are. Really. It's like a curse of fate. Like Vivan's gift, which over and over again does him more harm than good. And all the Jewel magic that Ross has..."

Oliver looked at him with the serious gaze that marked a life maturity of more than a century.

"I live every moment of this existence precisely because it is like this," he replied. "Every moment can be the last. Thanks to Ross, I can love and be by the side of Sai," he looked into the eyes of his beloved. "Believe me, there comes a moment in life when only what is most important count. Love and friendship is just that for me. If I were to die now, I would be happy to have known these feelings. And you," he looked into his eyes, "will definitely save him."

"It's impossible," Sel said, but Oliver smirked.

"I'm proof that the impossible does not exist, Sel," he replied with a twinkle in his eye. "Now, please tell me everything..."

"...I don't know where they took him," Sel finished his brief account after a few moments, "I was hoping that maybe I would learn something from you."

Oliver ruffled the little stubble thoughtfully.

At that time, the ships were already filled with people. Violet gathered the surviving part of the former Bernadette's crew and took control of the Blood Witch, giving loud commands to her suspicious pirate crew. Tenan, assisted by Silas, led Valeria out into the high seas. His actions at the moment cared nothing for Sel, who, apart from Oliver's good health, was only consoled by the thought (which surprised himself) that Victor was here, busy talking to a shaky Lena and a strangely silent Cora, accompanied by her father - a medic.

Sorrow welled up in him as he glanced at Lena from time to time. Once again, her son was in danger from which she could not protect him. There was an almost human malice in it, an extreme meanness. As if he had taken on Vivan, trying to annihilate him. Just for what reason? Human greed, of course. His life, since the king ordered him to be taken to the palace during the plague, has become a streak of evil adventures. People wanted to enslave him, appropriate him, as if he were not a human being, but a valuable thing. It's terrifying.

Paphian and Dinn, as he heard from Victor, decided to stay on the Judith.

"Gentlemen," he heard Tenan's voice above him. "Do you have any news for me?"

"One," he replied irritably, as the latter interrupted his gloomy thoughts, "We don't want you here!"

"I remind you that I'm the captain of this ship for the moment..." Tenan began calmly, which irritated him even more. How dare he even say anything? He will never be entitled to that ship!

Sel, despite Oliver's attempts to stop him, immediately jumped up to face him and interrupt him in a gruff tone:

"You'll never be the captain of the Valeria, you fucking murderer!"

There was silence.

The crew of the Valeria and the people of Leviron had long expected that a similar situation would occur. Especially now that Sel was mad with anxiety about Ross.

Maya stood in Sel's field of view, but Sel tried not to pay attention to her presence.

"I got clear instructions from Ross..." Tenan began again calmly, but more firmly. "If I had known anything about his position, I would have ignored them, but if you don't tell me right away, I'll do what he told me to do. If the Valeria loses the White Captain, I'm to set course for Leviron. Even if…"

"Are you going to leave him?!" Sel said indignantly.

"Sel..." Oliver tried to cut in. "Listen carefully. You are blinded by hatred..."

"Can you imagine that I will let you do that?" Sel ignored his words as he faced Tenan. "It's like you've already killed him! How you killed Mira and Alen, servants who were better to me than my family. And almost the same as you killed Milera! Wanna kill ALL I LOVE?!"

Tenan had expected this for a long time.

"MISTER," Oliver heard suddenly in his head.

The surprised boy felt dizzy.

Sai held him down, seeing him turn pale.

"You are restless, and I understand it." Meanwhile, Tenan made a final attempt at agreement, more and more sensing how his new reputation was shrouded in the darkness of his audience. "But we won't talk like that..."

Victor stopped Lena, who tried to intervene.

"We're going in search of Ross," Sel remarked emphatically, looking him in the eye angrily, "And you have shit to talk about..."

It was necessary to give up trying to reach an agreement. It couldn't go on. Tenan hit with a strong right hook. Several women screamed softly in surprise.

"I HAVE TO DO IT QUICKLY," Oliver heard that calm, gentle tone of voice, "YOU DON'T HAVE THE SAME RELATION THAT BINDS ME TO VIVAN. THIS COULD HARM YOU."

"But what?" Oliver was surprised, whom Sai wanted to take away from the quarrel. Lena looked after them.

"WE NEED YOUR HELP," said Jewel, for it must have been him, judging from what Ross sometimes said, "I WILL SHOW YOU THE PLACE WHERE WE ARE. HURRY UP!"

Sel returned the blow almost immediately, with sheer satisfaction. He had been waiting for this opportunity for a long time.

This time he was not a sickened, emaciated boy on the verge of death.

Tenan calmly prepared himself for the fight among the crowd.

"Come on!" He turned to his opponent.

Sel didn't wait long for himself.

Oliver closed his eyes.

The town... On the seashore. Facing the houses, he could see the royal capital in the distance on the great mountain of the Bay of Slaves. To the right.

Demons... Other than the long-mouthed ones. More like humans, though not in behavior. Smoke. Fire. Screams.

The end.

Everything went silent.

The jewel was gone from his mind.

He opened his eyes...

Sel and Tenan pummeled each other in dark silence.

There is no time for settle an old score!

"Valeria's crew!" He shouted, taking Sai's hand and entering the circle for the fighters. "I need your help!"

The two fighters immediately stopped hitting each other with their fists. You can already clearly see puffiness under Sel's eye.

"We are listening, lord!" A voice called from the crowd.

Oliver explained to them how the Jewel had bonded with him. Then he began to describe the images he saw.

The sailors inquired about details. How far was the capital city from here? Was it really a town, not a village with thatched huts? Has it had a port? Did it have a view of the open sea or were there any mountains? Oliver didn't know all the answers. But he knew one thing for sure.

"It will be easy to find this place," he said, turning to the gathered. "There is smoke, fire... and death there!"

CHAPTER 28

"Hey... Healer, can you hear me? Speak!... Vivan, I can't do it alone, you have to help me... Finally! I thought they would really take you, but you killed them! I stole a horse and followed you! He told me to watch over you! Captain, your friend... A little more, oh yes... Here is my horse... I'll hold you, just ride it... A little more... Don't fall asleep, Vivan! We will go a bit... Driving here I saw rocks, a small grotto... There it is!... We're already there... Vivan..."

He dozed off, sliding slowly off the horse's back. He only felt that he was held by some hands... The girlish voice kept talking to him, but he didn't have the strength to listen to it anymore...

"My name is Daryenne," the young girl said, "I was a prisoner on the Blood Witch when you got there. Captain Ross asked me to watch over you. Well, I keep an eye on you. When the demons took you, I was there on the horse. I went right behind you, but they were so fast. I heard you scream..." She broke off in confusion. "You fell as if dead. We got here somehow. I found water while you were sleeping..." she handed him a small water bag. "Luckily it was in the bag by the saddle... Drink slowly," she ordered with excessive seriousness. "Oh, that's right..."

Nothing else mattered at first. Just those few sips. But then his thoughts made sense.

"How long...?" He asked hoarsely. "How long have I been asleep?"

He remembered her now. She escaped the hunters on the beach near the lighthouse.

She hesitated.

"Long enough," she said hesitantly, after a while, "that the ships with help have already passed through..."

He felt a twinge of fear and deep disappointment.

"I stood hidden among the rocks and watched them float away without us," she said sadly in her voice. "It was a terrible feeling. Like when pirates killed my nanny because she was too saucy in their opinion. And she was just defending me. She loved me..." She broke off, shaking her head. "I had to do that. The dead bodies of the creatures that kidnapped you are lying around. They got the attention of all kinds of dark types, people who trafficked other people. They were here. They would take us sooner than any of your friends' ships could land or send boats! Or maybe even..." Her voice broke a little. "Maybe they would kill you. They don't know who you are. They might not believe me! You can barely keep on your feet and, on top of that, those terrible scars... For them, as a human, you are worthless..."

He wasn't going to be angry with her. She acted prudently.

"Come here," he asked gently, his voice soothing the sad hearts of others.

He held out his hand.

She saw the cruelty. Her gaze, distrustful at first at these words, made him understand that a similar, supposedly friendly gesture on the part of the man was a deception intended to lure her into a trap. And the hesitant step towards him strengthened his conviction.

With sadness mixed with a hint of anger, he thought of the changes in the world since he had been kidnapped into the king's palace to serve him. No matter the price his family would pay for it.

Daryrenne approached, though not immediately. She took his hand with obvious hesitation. But when she touched him, the distrust vanished. Thanks to the soothing touch, she was in his arms.

He felt a surge of strength under the influence of her trust and concern.

"Don't worry," he said softly, "We'll find them."

The consolation was that the pain after the alleged rape had finally disappeared.

"Thank you for following me," he added in a whisper. "You helped me a lot."

"Find the ships," he asked rushing. "Don't save me!"

Before she tried to stop him, he fell off his horse, rolling on the sandy ground.

The last time he looked farewell to the silhouette of the girl and the horse. Daryenne's face, surprised by his action, quickly obscured the mouth of one of the hunters.

"Chase her!" The leader of the detachment ordered.

Vivan managed a dismissive smile. They had no chance of it. A single rider horse, aided by his benevolent action before, was now racing like a whirlwind.

"What are you laughing at, blue-eyed devil?!" One of the hunters roared, intending to punch him in the face.

"DO NOT TOUCH ME!" Vivan's scream, sharp and not very profound, was heightened by a hint of blue vengeful magic that pulsed in several veins in his face. "I am the Healer, Vivan Beckert of Tenchrys! King Azram will probably pay a lot for me if you take me to him! Do not destroy valuable goods!"

The hunter froze, hand raised, surprised both by the magic and by the words themselves.

"The healer doesn't wield magic!" The leader said sharply.

In response, Vivan grabbed the jewel and the remaining symbols around his neck, revealing their presence.

"And this?!" He raised them slightly. "What does it look like to you?"

The hunter quickly recognized the Jewel and the mysterious symbol of a strange religion he had heard about in the stories.

He smiled slyly. He felt that fate was on his side.

"So, my lord," he scoffed. "Come in our humble thresholds!"

The hunters returned quickly, cursing the demon horse that had carried the girl away from them as if it had been carried by the wind. Vivan only managed to glance once at the trapped, crowded on the ground, and bound like animals. They were mostly men. Several women huddled together in despair.

He was trapped in a tent surrounded by guards and tied to the main stake. After a few moments the same commander appeared with food and water. He assessed his appearance with an expert eye.

"There will be a bath tomorrow," he informed sternly. "We will go to the village. There is not enough water here!"

He had enough freedom to eat his meal. He also got a bedding. However, he did not feel well knowing what conditions the other companions of misery were condemned to.

Nevertheless, sleep overwhelmed him after an hour.

There was an attack at dawn.

They were the men of a rival clan of hunters who set out to grab easy loot. Vivan's brief conversation with one of the men quickly gave Vivan a sense of the situation. The loot was tied and ready to be picked up. So it was worth the risk, since you did not catch anything yourself. The enemy clan's hunters were ruthless. They slaughtered their opponents brutally. After a short but dramatic fight, the camp was conquered, and the winners decided to celebrate the event with defenseless women. During this time, the men were quickly separated. Vivan was dragged out of the tent amidst screams and rapes. When he tried to stop the bestiality, he was rendered unconscious with a quick blow...

The penultimate thought, relieved before he resisted, was the thought of Daryenne.

Fortunately, she did not fall into their hands...

"…son of a rich man, not from this side. See that coat of his? It was a decent thing until something tore it apart."

"That's why they kept him apart. They were probably counting on a ransom."

"And the handles with gloves of strange leather? A body full of scars? Some quite fresh."

"You see he is traveling a lot like that," remarked a sharp voice mockingly.

"Or he's been on the run for quite a long time," added his interlocutor.

"What are we doing with him? We will ask and count on a ransom?"

"We won't be fools like our predecessors!" the voice commanded sharply. "Those who counted on it either bite the sand or they escaped! I take what they give me! Yahys will buy what we bring and pay us generously. He's still short of laborers!"

"He has paws like a priest except for the scars," remarked the other with a cackle.

"He has a young body! Just right to work! Just watch him! Let him feel what work means!"

Vivan didn't open his eyes.

Yahys turned out to be the chief supervisor of the mine where Vivan ended up the day after. He clucked and clicked loudly, pretending to be dissatisfied with the quality of the merchandise on offer. However, in the end he bought a whole unfortunate crowd of men, apparently paying a very good price, for the hunters departed satisfied with the profit, sparing Vivan a sneering glance, which attracted the buyer's attention. Vivan looked back at the caravan that had brought him here. Of the few women captured by the hunters then, only two young girls were still alive. He wanted to help them. He really wanted it. He was not even given the opportunity to come near them. Perhaps he would have relieved their battered bodies. The last image he saw were women hugging silently, looking with fading hope at the supervisor and the entrance to the mine.

The sight left its mark on his heart. He found a place next to the raped girl, whose fate had not touched Vashaba in its time. And a few others that could not be forgotten.

"You!" Yahys said sharply when the caravan started to move away "What are these gloves?"

He looked at them critically. Dragonskin gloves, the color of his body, still too pale in the hot sun of the local climate, did not look too attractive. Their main activity was protection. They masked themselves, changed color, cooled when needed or heated. They let the air through. They were very durable. And incredibly valuable.

Here, however, only rumors of dragons in other lands were heard. Yahys had no idea that the film on a captive's hands was of great value. With one glance, he judged that this invention would soon go to shreds when the enslaved set to work. They were worthless to him.

For Vivan, they were a lifesaver. His hand, badly scratched and wounded as he defended the cross given to him by his grandparents during a desperate and maddened crowd attack that had tried to tear him to shreds a few years ago, would have been fit for any work had it not been for these gloves.

They helped soothe the pain of damaged muscles. Vivan had never improved her condition since the court physician took care of him. Only love could help him. At first, he was sure his condition would improve after Vashaba entered his life. The pains that haunted him in bad weather would pass, and perhaps even the scars would disappear... He was sure that it would be possible if he only found someone who, apart from his family, was very concerned about him. But as the next months passed, their sensual intimacy flourished, but their condition did not improve. After the first warning pang of his heart, following particularly intense close-ups, he understood that it would never happen...

If the hand were without the glove, he too would soon be of no value to Yahys then... unless he would reveal his identity again.

"Delicate hands, huh?" The overseer sneered. "I'll keep an eye on you, Prince," he casually parodied the bow, giving him a nickname that would cling to him from then on. "Come on, get them to work! Today they can work for a few more hours before sunset!" He roared loudly to his helpers.

Diamond mine.

Work in the rings, in an open space that is not allowed to be looked at. In dust and toil. In the glare of the hot sun, soaking my feet in muddy water more than once. Endlessly sifting stones and sand in search of precious metal, in an oval funnel that is enlarged every day, with the power of strong hands, hammers and pickaxes.

They were not treated decently workers. Paid, with the right to meal breaks. They were slaves, dependent on overseers, fed carelessly, and used beyond their strength.

Many died of exhaustion, disease, and hunger.

Vivan took one careful look to judge the tragedy of his position.

The inexorable blue power flared up inside him like fire. The glow that lit his gaze for a moment aroused suspicion in one of the overseers. He stifled it. It was hard for him, but he knew he had to do it. The force with which he would attack the oppressors could kill even all of them around... But then there would be no help for him.

If he had not died soon after, the power would have confused his head and driven him insane. Already, by the tragic events in their lives and in the lives of his charges, they seriously disturbed his psyche. The last thing he needed was to vent his rage.

It was not in his nature, but in the nature of the dragon that had once attacked him. Over the years since that event, Vivan had dealt effortlessly with the beast within him, though more than once he was morally tempted to bring justice to the wrongs he had seen. There, in a darkness of frustration and anger, the dragon disturbed. Or maybe it was just fueling what was always in him? He did not go into it. But now he knew one thing for sure...

If he doesn't make an attempt to escape now, while his strength will permit him, he will never attempt it again!

He would die like the others before him, too weak to withstand the conditions here.

The world closed behind him for the next few days, as if he ceased to exist. Limited only to what was in front of him, he fought back the rising panic. His whole life ran through the open expanses of the mountain valley in which he was born. Hills and peaks along a wide river flowing out to the open sea. Travel to places more or less distant from home, under a changing sky. The only place where he was kept for some time, and which seemed to him an age, was a royal palace. For a moment, a moment's hesitation, he considered revealing his identity this time as well. It was a godsend from his fears. But somewhere in heart a different fear, a more primal one, was waking up. He felt it like the dread of the fire that could burn him.

He was too close.

He could feel it with every nerve. An unnamed, evil force lay in wait for him. She could almost touch him now! It was one thing to be lost among the hunter tribes vying for loot, and it was another thing to be here in the mine where the ruling tyrant's army was overseeing the jewel mining. He saw them around. They surrounded him, guarding the working slaves. He could have attacked them, that's true. But the price he would pay for it might be too high. Therefore, when he was given a pickaxe, he undertook the hard work, pressing his lips together in impotent anger. He thought frantically about a way to escape. His hands, until recently helping the wounded, were holding a pickaxe, so unusual for them. Yes, sometimes he helped rebuild their home. Grandfather did not allow the grandchildren to just watch the work, as he called it. Even his stepfather never shirked his job, despite the title. But the arm that had once been broken out of the pond by the witch Mayene, healed with difficulty by his gift, did not allow him to work hard for too long. Vivan felt pain in his heart to admit to himself that his endurance was no longer the same, despite his young age. Each attack left an indelible mark. Unlike the ones he healed, Vivan felt the effects of the wrongs he had done. Maybe his disturbed psyche helped him, as he could withstand subsequent misfortunes with great difficulty? Seemingly strong, more than when his adoptive mother's sharp commentary made him quit dancing forever. In fact, however, battered inside as much as outside. And when it seemed to him that he was getting straight, he was faced with other adventures, tragic in their consequences. Nevertheless, more than his own suffering, he was hurt by the suffering of his relatives and friends because he was the cause of it. Therefore, his thoughts became bitter more and more, tending to the conclusion that perhaps it would be better in this world without him...

The thought brought back a different memory to him. His friend's uplifting words. And that, in turn, reminded him of him. During this time and everything that happened around him, he did not even think about it. But... What struck him as strange: Ross didn't say anything either. Not once.

Sudden fear made all my other thoughts run away, scattered and squeezed into the darkness...

CHAPTER 29

The pain was acute. Demon claws pierced the layer of his captain's cloak, reaching his body. At first, he only thought of it. But the closer he saw the capital, the faster his consciousness returned to him.

He will not allow as the wounded and the weak to drag him to Azram.

Besheram...

The name rang in his head like an alarm bell. Black eyes stared at him without a hint of human affection.

Whoever he is, they shouldn't take him lightly. He and Vivan. May Vivan not allow himself to be dragged there...

"Let me out, you hideous beasts!" He hissed, putting all his anger into these words, but above all the power of persuasion. "Lower me down and die!"

The last time he used all his willpower in the fight against the sea snake. Now he was just as desperate!

It didn't take long for the demons to slowly lower the flight and land him on the ground. Right in front of the village, beyond which you could already see the damned capital itself in the distance.

He clenched his fists, thus boosting his willpower. The ghastly creatures, this time helpless in the face of such a powerful magic, not disturbed by surprise and fear, with a groan of disappointment and anger, died around him, scattering like distorted flowers in a frightening circle, as a sign of submission and devotion.

After a while, there was only silence...

He staggered under the pain and weakness. He glanced at his shoulders. The cloak was soaked with blood. There were open wounds between the torn material.

He won't get far that way. He reached for his own vial around his neck, filled with the healer's blood. Sel devotedly offered him the contents of his own bottle, not wanting to waste valuable time. He thought of it, taking a long sip. May what's left be enough for the next meeting.

He had to wait for the blood to heal him...

He sat down groaning in the sand, staring absentmindedly at the village. It was his only escape from the pain that slowly faded away.

Therefore, it was only when the pain disappeared that he noticed that something disturbing was happening here...

"We gave you everything!" Someone shouted in fear. "Everything!"

"You hid gold supplies!" An inhuman sounding voice answered him.

"It's money for food and our vital necessities," the male voice belonged to the man who clearly had power in this village. Now he crouched in fear, frantically trying to convince the creature to be one of the huts hidden from Ross's gaze.

"And children? You were supposed to give us back the children!" The creature added firmly.

Ross felt a chill in his heart.

The man saw him suddenly, abandoned by the dead demons on the beach. His gaze showed a fading desperation. This man has killed the demons! Whoever he is, he has suddenly become a hope for the people of his unfortunate village! He looked again at whoever he was talking to, raising his head like a man who knows there is no rescue for him. His fear was gone, fueled by a new thought.

"Which mother will give her children to the demons?!" He asked with a hint of undisguised anger. "You will not get anything from us!"

Ross saw a silhouette twinkle in the rush. The mayor was staring at him, not assuming that it would be the last painting he would be able to see in his lifetime. The nightmarish, fearful creature snapped his head off with one powerful tug, pouring blood on the sand.

Ross took the Jewel in his hand.

He was driven by an impulse known to him from the old days, when he fought to survive in the streets of the city, supported by the belief in the possession of magic, the advantages of which he had yet to discover.

He wouldn't have had time to hide.

He needed a miracle.

And a miracle happened.

When the ghoulish thing looked his way, all she could see was dead demons.

Then he realized that this was just the beginning...

Children. They ran like frightened mice, looking for new hiding places. They appeared in Ross's eyes for a moment, then disappeared like shadows in nooks and crannies as the demons entered. They watched fearful as demons leaped onto the panicked adults and tore them to pieces amid shouts of agony. Of course, those who were lucky and managed to hide cleverly. Others have been torn from the hands of loving mothers and their eyes gouged out.

Beating hearts were torn out.

The shrill screams of suffering mothers and fathers were quickly replaced by the death whinnying. The demons, other than the ones he had killed, strode among terrified people, mercenary and cold. Though their silhouettes resembled humans, he could not find any warm feelings in their eyes. They were fast. Terrifyingly fast. Before he shook off the initial shock of their ruthless cruelty, they had killed at least twenty people around him, surrounded by an aura of invisibility! He had no time to waste if he did not want to disappoint the murdered village chief. Though he himself was steeped in fear of them, fear of pain and brutal death, he took action. His heart pounded in his chest as he jerked violently from the demon's claws the child it was holding, and then disappeared with him behind a veil of invisibility. Ross took in his hands the ward miraculously torn from the demon. The girl clung to him without a word, while the surprised creature angrily searched for its victim. Ross didn't wait. With the girl in his arms, he was impulse to approach future victims. Sometimes he would take them abruptly like a baby, and sometimes he would just pull them out of hiding places that weren't at all safe, and then hide them behind his back in the magic of invisibility. The demons quickly realized something strange was happening. They searched in anger, searching everything around. They carried the walls of houses. They started fires. Ross has not had time to save someone. He wanted to hand the baby over to some of the surviving adults to have more freedom of action. But the girl, five or six years old, apparently, was not going to let him go. She clung to her savior with all her strength. With the power of a childlike courage that is still unaware of the consequences and disarming innocence, she even tried to help him! She extended her hand to the rescued adults. She pushed demons away fearlessly with a small hand. Ross couldn't help admiring her, though he was all sweat with the effort. She could see that he was tired already. Once, with a brief respite, she stroked his hair with a serious expression.

As she did so, his heart twitched.

He felt a feeling inside him that he had never suspected before. It was nothing like the previous ones. There was something tender about it. Something he has never felt before. It was a bit like feeling for Valeria, maybe even for Lena, when he discovered how foolish he was, suspecting her of malicious intent. It was…

Was…

He felt a great responsibility for the life of this little one. As great as a paternal love he was born of, which he would never have suspected.

For the first time he thought he would like to be a father...

And he will do anything to prevent any harm to her or any other children he has saved. Their parents and the rest of the village close to him, realizing quickly how necessary it was to survive, developed an additional tenderness in him.

"Listen," he said to the adults, some of whom hugged their children, "It's not enough to save you. If you want your children to survive, we must defeat the demons! We have to kill them!" He called, summoning the power of the Jewel, but the Jewel whispered to him that there was no need to.

There was no determination stronger than the desire to protect whoever is dearer to you than yourself. The power of the Jewel has increased. Mothers and fathers silently agreed to his words.

Hidden behind a veil, they attacked the ghastly creatures with pitchfork and axes. They chopped off their heads and stuck them in the ground. The gem pulsed. Only a few demons attacked the village. No resistance was expected. They retreated before the Jewel, and it glowed incessantly with a warm light, red as blood. It pulsed to the beat of his heart. They were afraid of it. The strength in it. But not all of them. One of them looked defiantly at him, as if it had seen him. Ross knew it was rather impossible, though the demon moved quickly towards them...

Ross held his breath. That demon saw him! Or, more likely, it knew how to find him. All he had time to think about was not to let him capture him, because then the veil of invisibility would cease to exist. Even one demon could have extinguished this entire village, and a large crowd had already gathered behind him. An attempt to go further into the village for one or two inhabitants ended in exposure and a quick, brutal death.

Everyone could be killed in an instant.

"NO!!!" He shouted, instinctively stretching his hand out in front of him, and the other clutching the girl harder.

The demon could not hear his scream. The barrier was tight. He passed through it, suddenly among the crowd of survivors. They moved away from him as if they were burned. He walked between them, traversing the area several times. Each time they moved away, making a way for him. Two other demons passed through the people once or twice, suddenly appearing, but still, they did not even sense them.

The people followed their journey in silence, ceasing all combat activities, as if they knew that now their activity could harm the white sorcerer's focus.

Their instincts were telling them well. Ross felt the narrow trickle of blood begin to trickle down his nose again. He focused with all his strength to make people and himself as transparent as air. Undetectable. He could feel the girl's serious gaze and his body trembling with the effort. Finally, he looked at the first man with a pitchfork in his hands. The latter nodded slowly to him.

They were waiting for a good moment.

Finally, one has arrived.

The inquisitive demon stood right in the middle of the crowd. His two helpers were right next to...

All armed villagers raised their makeshift weapons.

The first blows softened the effects of the aura of invisibility. The blows had to be effective. But if it was supposed to be so, there were other, more serious consequences...

The attack of the demons was terrifyingly quick. Whoever was within reach immediately joined the wounded or murdered with cruel ruthlessness. Whether it was a child or an adult defending it, it didn't matter. Human life was of no value to demons. They came here to exterminate, and were just fulfilling their mission with terrifying precision. But they met with resistance. A determination bordering on madness that can only be achieved by those who defend the lives of loved ones. The sorcerer's presence magnified their actions. Ross was attacked by the demon leader with fierce fury during the fighting. Strengthened by his friend's wonderful blood, still flowing in his veins, dirty, sweaty, mentally and physically aching, he rose from the trampled ground, shielding and defending the life of not only the accompanying child, still fighting like a wild animal, but also brave people fighting for life. That was all that mattered now. Therefore, despite their incredible dexterity, strength and speed, two of the demons were finally killed.

In the final act of final destruction, their hideous bodies were chopped up until they were just pieces of bone and flesh...

Before that happened, a few more brave people had lost their lives. Two mothers died in defense of their children, torn apart before their eyes so quickly that the murderers' actions were barely noticeable, only to see the bloody effects of their brutal actions. The man who had communicated with Ross at the beginning was killed almost immediately as he drove the pitchfork into the demon. But the others, encouraged by their victory over the two, pressed ranks together, attacking from all sides simultaneously, biting with axes, pitchforks, knives, and anything suitable for weapons in the haste. Ross's role was to defend them. Two died when the demon caught him a couple of times, nearly killing him. Once, when he attacked a girl. He could be and was so terrifyingly fast as to attack several at once, especially the white-haired leader.

However, he underestimated the child.

Another attack, as the demon grabbed the skirts of the captain's cloak, intending with the other evil-clawed hand to tear out his throat, collided their bodies. The girl, showing unprecedented heroism, which only people who do not know fear or those in desperation can do, without hesitating, stuck her fingers in the demon's eye...

It howled, surprised by the unexpected attack. This moment, one short and quick as a heartbeat, was used by the villagers. They stabbed him from the sides, pulling him away from Ross. And before he could free himself, as he had done so many times, two alternately hit the demon's neck with their axes. Dark brown blood spattered all around. There was something beastly and primal about human action, at this last, decisive moment as they chopped the flesh to pieces, massacring it with the zeal of murderers, holding their axes. Ross grabbed the little one, stepping back from the slaughter. The fingers of her right hand were covered with blood. He almost forcibly turned her head away from the bloody spectacle he couldn't stop looking at himself. His heart beating rapidly, he watched the bloody slaughterhouse, as did the other villagers, making sure the monster wouldn't attack anyone else. Finally the hitting stopped. Someone quickly brought a torch, someone else brought a bundle of hay. What was left was set on fire.

All the bodies of inhuman torturers...

The stench of burning meat mingled with the stench of burning houses.

People stared at the fire for a long time in sudden silence.

Dead bodies lay among the survivors. The fire consumed the carcasses.

Flames have recently devoured vibrant homes.

CHAPTER 30

"Why are you staring at?!" One of the overseers shouted, pushing him brutally. "Look at him! He has gloves on his handles, like a prince!"

It was the second day of his work in the mine. Vivan wanted to groan as his once-broken arm crashed into the wall.

"Because it's a Prince!" Cried another. "Look at that tattered coat! He was probably worth a lot. And this doll's face..." he added ironically. "Well, if he's a Prince, he must have gloves, because his hands are so delicate," he grimaced at the end, his hands spread theatrically.

"Prince?!" the brutal supervisor grabbed Vivan by the shirt-skirts. "Is he better than us?! Or maybe he wants to get hit by this beautiful face right away, huh?"

"Zarin, fuck it and get them to work!" His interlocutor glanced at the exit, fearing that the higher ranking will soon punish them for their tardiness. "You'll have fun later!"

Zarin's face, marked by cruelty and, his dominant trait, a fondness for alcoholic beverages, froze in contemptuous anger as he appraised his victim with his gaze. It was not difficult to understand that Vivan had made an enemy of him from day one, though his stay here had not yet begun in earnest. Unfortunately, it was too smooth, as the overseer judged him mentally. In addition, he looked into his eyes with courage, which Zarin did not like very much, but very much. Before him, all slaves were to stand fearful, staring at the ground, as if apologizing for the very fact of existence. Because he is their master here. And this one is referring to it as some rich man's son. A real prince! Zarin never had enough money, at least in his opinion, although he did some extra money in dark business. That's why he hated the rich who thought they were better than him.

"Prince!" it sounded insulting. "We'll see if you know what it means to work in a mine!"

Vivan met his eyes defiantly, though his heart felt cold like the touch of an icicle. Zarin's behavior was a sign of great trouble. Unjustified acts of cruelty. Snags for a reason. He has already met people like him.

He had no illusions about it.

The first day of hard work was the best proof of that. Zarin made sure Vivan did the hardest work. Before the end of the day, he was loading the stones into the carriages. He carried them for hours until the end of the day, until they were finally given a meal and ordered to sleep where they were today. Vivan was strong. He ignored the overseer's open taunts, which the unfortunates caught with him greeted with some relief, but still filled with compassion (they had been here too briefly to be indifferent), because the malice distracted Zarin from themselves. He also knew that it would be a day or two before the arm, once broken off by the witch, healed with considerable difficulty, would react with such excruciating pain that he would not be able to move it. He probably won't even be able to get up. The sight of the miserable soup and a piece of stale pie had stripped him of all his illusions. The worst part was that they were not allowed to leave this place with the coming of night. And they had tunnels, which they had carved without going outside. In this dust, among dirt and stones, they were to work until their strength ran out. The dark part of his soul burned with an inner anger, saturating his thoughts, awakening a blue glow that he smothered with difficulty.

Oh yeah... He wanted to get carried away with this anger! Inflame! Destroy Zarin and all the oppressors in fire! Because of them, people now lay down, suffering from pain that gave them no chance to rest! Through them, the quiet cry of the terrified enslaved person expressed the fear of tomorrow, which would probably end his life with a cruel death from flogging or beatings. There were so many sick and suffering around him that his inner instinct to help wreaked havoc in his heart and soul. The dark side fought his true gift without giving him a break. Boiling below the surface like a waking volcano, anger was as strong as the gift of helping. Vivan already knew that he would not fall asleep that night, too, with conflicting emotions. He wanted to help and end the whole situation at the same time. Perhaps the blue will win a moment later, extinguishing the whispers of the mind and the heart.

When they were finally allowed to sleep, he tried to calm the inner demons in the darkness.

He was a healer.

The word was a balm, but he needed more than just repeating it to himself ad nauseam. He needed support. People who loved him.

He had two options.

He could search with the help of the now hidden Jewel of a friend. His presence would certainly cheer him up.

He quickly understood why Ross was not making contact with him.

Until recently, he struggled to survive facing demons. After that, he helped people hide, keeping an eye out for the Valeria and other ships from the beach. His determination and courage had not ceased to amaze Vivan lately. His inner peace has been disturbed. He lived in constant tension. The Valeria, with Sel's help, finally found a handful of unfortunates whom Ross was helping with all his might. Vivan didn't want to bother him now. Ross was the one who needed the support more of the two. He had done so many surprising things since he set out to help him... Too bad, with him, a healer marked by dragon's anger - there will be what has to be. Ross needed his help. And he would rather lose himself than leave a friend in need.

He really worried about him genuinely.

Ross aroused genuine respect among his people, even love. However, his endurance had come to an end. Probably even Sel was not fully aware of the seriousness of the situation.

Caring for him helped Vivan to suppress his bad emotions.

The anger burned inside him, though he still had control over him. He barely managed to tame him when he helped the captured. However, a destructive force remained in him. He had suppressed it for years, in spite of the cruelty he recognized, burying it inside. But the pain inflicted on him in the marketplace by the crowd revealed that power for the first time. The necessity to stop the witch's heart awakened him anew. Even so, he was still coping. Thanks to the love of Vashaba. Now his disappointed feelings, a sense of loss, the perfidy of his grandmother selling him like a thing, stoked the flames in him until he almost lost himself. And they did not want to go out.

Three days earlier, according to Oliver's words, the village had been found guided by smoke and fire. The Valeria, shining majestically in the rays of the setting sun, waited for the survivors to be brought on board. The other two ships were cruising nearby.

The sky was burning red and red that day. Many of the elderly sailors nodded in glum silence at the phenomenon. They told the others that this is how the gods of all peoples wanted to convey the news of their atrocities.

Arriving ashore, they saw a surprising group of people. Most of them were children. Several men were just finishing filling in the mass grave of the murdered, interrupting their activity only for a moment, only to return to it with an expression of determination on their solemn faces.

The women, on the other hand, hugged each other, sitting in silence. Those whose children were among the few survivors kept them as close as possible. Some of them hugged orphaned children with their free hand.

They were all sitting around one figure holding a sleeping child, so ragged and dirty that it was impossible to recognize the gender at first glance.

Like it, it was a sight that made the arrivals pangs of heart.

Under the layer of blood of the slain demon, dirt and rag, which until recently had been the captain's cloak, he looked like a specter of doom.

Only the eyes glistened like the gleam of the first symptoms of madness.

The group merely raised their heads in silence at the sight of the boat. Even the children stopped crying. The women closest to Ross touched him immediately in silent plea for protection.

Sel looked briefly at Oliver, feeling tears welling up. Ross didn't come out to meet them. He did not greet them with joy. He didn't move, still cradling the baby in his arms. His eyes only revealed that he recognized them.

"He's exhausted..." Oliver explained quietly.

Sel nodded slightly. He didn't have to tell him that. Though he was not as connected to him as his brother, his heart had a different bond.

He knew him. He knew as himself.

Ross was acting solely for the sake of the baby and the people who sought his support. Something happened (again, which was more terrifying) that forced him to use everything he had learned so far. And much more.

What he probably felt now, and what the Jewel showed, shining a faint purple glow would be hard to explain to Sel's accompanying crew. It was associated with suffering, incredible determination and great attachment. The child he so desperately held slept confidently in his arms, exhausted by his experiences.

It was only after a while that Ross gestured for the women to let Sel go over to him.

"You're alive," Sel began softly with a hint of relief, afraid, not knowing what. Whether that he would wake the little one (he could finally see more up close) or that he would violate the fragile peace of his partner or a group of survivors. Maybe it was both?

"She only has me..." Ross spoke in a voice unexpectedly strong, though hoarse with exhaustion. His tone sounded both a request and a decision to keep the little girl.

Sel, with some irony, remembered the incident at Oliver and Sai's wedding that seemed to take place many years ago.

"...because we cannot have children...".

He remembered Seme's answer as well.

She was right: life can be different, although this was probably not the solution, she had in mind at the time...

"She'll have us now, kitty," he replied softly, feeling as if in the back of his head that a ghost from the past was trying to tell him these words. This time, however, he did not have to intervene. Sel knew from the start that was what his words would be.

Child. His hidden dream. His secret hope.

Only... will the little one accept this state of affairs?

Now was not the time, but it was to be expected that their question would be answered soon.

Ross looked at him, surprised again at the caressing word. It broke something about him. The wall he set up to resist.

"Come on," Sel said, calm but firmly, keeping his emotions in check as he used to do. He motioned to Oliver, who was willing to help him pick up Ross and the baby. They both knew without words that Ross was not going to give the little one them, so they didn't even offer it. Oliver quickly stroked his foster brother's head, speaking gently to him. He said anything, trying to control his fear. Ross, always ready to stick his nose in the cookie jar, as Victor once said. Ross so dedicated to the cause. With a mocking smirk admitting the insults of enemies. Bold. Full of ideas for magic he didn't even know well, and he only knew that he had to help. A sorcerer driven by heart. White Captain...

He didn't look like his old self.

Now he was like a victim of the war, taken from Victor's descriptions of his former life. At the sight of him, usually tough Victor, who was waiting with Lena on board, broke his soldier attitude. Tears glistened in his eyes as he patted Ross gently on the shoulder, as if afraid of damaging him. Lena followed them to the captain's cabin amid the silence on the deck. The crew greeted the survivors with silence. Children cried as the door closed behind Ross. Ross then broke free from his numbness. He looked at her pleadingly.

She understood.

"Let them in," she pleaded with the men accompanying her.

After some time, Marlene and the volunteers accompanying her helped the women rescued from the slaughter wash the babies and feed those who managed to eat something. There were twenty children, including Ross's girl. Several babies. Eleven kids up to the age of nine and five teenagers.

Only six of them had mothers.

Father's only one.

For a time, commotion reigned in and around the cabin. Survivors stayed close to Ross, like candlelight in the dark. He had no choice but to help them. As he sat in the armchair with the baby in his arms, calmly explaining and reassuringly, though Sel and the entire crew with him saw that he was barely able to speak, he evoked a certain unprecedented tenderness in them all. It wasn't that he was a captain, a friend, or even a... lover. They sensed that they were witnessing something much greater. The birth of a legend. And only once in their life so far have they had the opportunity to feel something similar. Just when the Healer appeared among them. They experienced feelings at the sight of Vivan, and whatever he did, admiration for him, tenderness, and even concern to protect someone so extraordinary, accompanied them from the very first moment. Looking at Ross, everyone thought of Vivan, who was still not safe. These two needed protection. They were an amazing spark of this world. As long as they existed, the hope for a better life did not fade away.

When Ross, with his gift of persuasion, managed to calm the children and adults down enough to be accommodated somewhere in the staterooms, he finally took care of himself and the baby. The girl hadn't said a word yet since their arrival. Sel quickly figured he couldn't count on even a little privacy today. Maybe it was some form of silence after all, because all the babies who had been left without their mothers and aunts stayed with Ross. All the sheets and blankets and bedspreads were left on the floor. There, Ross hugged the little girl and fell asleep almost immediately. At first, Lena and Sel wanted to look after the other children, but they did not let them. The five little ones clung to Ross.

Only then did they fall asleep.

Sel had only serious concerns that the children would be able to sleep peacefully in such a large group of people. However, it soon turned out that there was an unprecedented harmony between the sleeping people, probably again thanks to Ross. Nobody was in danger of overheating. It wasn't the only strange situation about the group Ross had brought with him. Cora drew friends to the peculiar behavior of the survivors. These people went through a nightmare. The children lost their parents under terrible circumstances. Mothers lost part of their family. The men of those they loved and knew. Eveybody on the Valeria should hear the lamentation of the despairing. The incessant crying of frightened and lonely children. Meanwhile, the survivors were silent. Too quiet. As if someone had put a shroud on them. It was just as if they had had an exceptionally hard day of work behind them, and they went to sleep. The exception was nursing mothers, who without problems fed both their own and other people's children, setting the feeding times among themselves beforehand, so that all children would satisfy their hunger and they could rest. This unusual harmony had so far escaped the attention of the crew members who were on watch in succession. But Cora, who had gone through terrible experiences, quickly noticed it.

These people acted as if in some trance...

This was the only explanation for their composure and their ability to help each other.

The gift that allows others to be manipulated according to the wizard's needs had something dark about it. And as noble as the goal was, the thought of what he would have done with them if he had wanted to, was tainted with a hint of horror.

Oliver and Lena took turns watching, getting up to meet the toddlers when it was time to change, drink or even hug one of the toddlers. Sai was playing the lyre while Ross was calming his charges. Now, amidst the quiet conversations and breaths, a certain harmony was lacking without the music. The uniqueness of this stillness was like a false note, still floating in the air.

Anokhi cared for everyone, with special care surrounding her new friends.

Ross himself was asleep, seemingly oblivious to everything that was happening around him. He wouldn't be able to do anything more except at the cost of his own life. He surprised everyone again with the scale of his gift.

Confidence that Ross was still protecting survivors was given to everyone by Oliver. In the middle of the night, he collapsed from exhaustion, quite violently. The increasing emphasis on the barrier Vivan had once placed for the two connected to lead a normal life was cause for concern. Something was happening that Vivan had not foreseen. Surely his help would be badly needed now. It didn't bode well. Sel remembered Ross's story about the encounter with the witch Mayene. He wrote down her words at one time in his journals, left at home on the hill. But he didn't need them now to remember the beginning of a sentence she had said. Was she really aware of the possibilities inherent in the gift of his partner?

Was he really capable of, in accordance with her words: be more powerful than the foundations of the earth?

Sel knew few people who could imagine what the words meant. And even he himself was not able to see with his imagination the power of such a gift...

The little one, with whom Ross hardly parted, slept, unlike other children, without even waking up for a moment. Sai, who came to replace Oliver, finally expressed concern that the girl's life was related to Ross's. Sel was sure that his beloved was driven solely by concern, so he plunged her into a dream that was supposed to help her simply rest.

The jewel pulsed with violet light continuously.

Throughout the night, Sel bent close many times to listen for his lover's silent breathing...

There was a certain tenderness in this watch. Like a touch saturated with love.

The one who had never known enough closeness was willing to give everything to the man who finally gave him it. So, he trembled when he thought he couldn't hear his breathing...

Again and again, he made sure by touching his face that this one was still there. Safe. And this time evil has no access to it. Until finally he leaned against the wall next to the makeshift bedding. Rocked by the calm rocking of the ship, he fell asleep, with his beloved's head within reach.

Ross was dreaming, stuck between dream and reality. Part of his consciousness remembered he was aboard the Valeria, surrounded by children on makeshift bedding. But that other part, made up of memories, has now blurred the lines between what was and what is. He thought he was asleep, surrounded by his nanny's children. Next to him, Tayen was sleeping, the girl who drank mother's milk with him, who was a month older than him. She was a family to him. So are her five siblings and their father. These people were his home, his mainstay. These children played with him, ate and slept. Stealthily, they taught him to write his name. And Cadelia threatened to burn them all alive if they tried to take him with them...

Now it felt like when they sometimes fell asleep together after having finished playing and having dinner in a hurry. While he slept among them, safe and loved. Until he opened his eyes, he could still dream that Tayen was asleep next to him. Manni, her brother a year older, is asleep with his back as usual, and the rest of the siblings next to them or on the other side of the bed. That is why they often joked about who's feet stink the most today. The family was not rich, but strong ties were shared between its members. Children, when they were small, often fell asleep together on a huge bed, made of all quilts and pillows, right on the floor. Their mother loved these moments.

"Tayen..." he whispered; with a silent hope it wasn't a dream after all.

Only soft breaths answered him. Tayen would not be silent.

He felt sadness overwhelm him.

"Nanny..." he half whispered, feeling the grief, longing and loss coming.

He never found them... As if they had fallen underground.

It really hurt. They loved him, even asked Cadelia to let them take him away. And then nothing.

Not even one letter. No attempt to meet him.

After all, they knew that he sometimes ran away from home. They knew his hiding places...

They just abandoned him. But could he blame them? Cadelia was his mother, what more could they do?

At first, he dreamed that one day they would come back for him. Then years passed, and finally his hope died...

Suddenly, as his heart seemed to clench with pain, the relentless and now hungry for warmth, he felt a hand on his forehead. The soft, familiar voice answered tenderly, in a tone he had heard extremely rarely among women:

"Yes darling? What you need?"

It wasn't Anhoki. He was sure of that.

I m scared..." he whispered to the voice, slowly realizing where he was and who he was talking to.

He felt a hand on his head. It stroked him as if he were a child. Just like the nanny used to do.

He trusted her.

"Lena..." he said after a few moments, during which he let the quiet happiness fill him, as she still gently stroked his head, "Please stay until I fall asleep."

He remembered the blissful state of falling asleep in Nanny's arms. Sometimes she cried softly and tried to hide it. It was definitely about him. However, in those moments all that mattered to him was that he felt calm and safe in her arms, because Cadelia and her lovers, having fun and drinking then, never thought to come for him at night.

"Okay, honey," Lena replied warmly, making his heart feel the tenderness of his childhood.

Long after he fell asleep, Lena was still watching over him, touching his head. Her thoughts circled around the mysterious nanny, who fell in love with the unwanted child, but failed to take him with her. She thought about how much she had given Ross. She kept her sensitivity and a good heart in him, despite his bad fate.

One time, after he and Sel had checked all the leads, and there weren't many of them after the plague had passed, they heard a man who fled the capital in fear a few words that they could never confirm. It was a rumor of a terrible murder many years ago. The family, quite numerous, was attacked on the road by thugs. They murdered everyone without exception, and the bodies were abandoned in the forest, where they were accidentally found and buried. There was a time when it was loud in Adelaine, because it was in this village that they were attacked. It was a strange murder and a very mysterious one, because yes, there was no cart and horses nearby, but some coins were found with father, so the robbery was not a case. More about scores. Or revenge.

Since they had learned nothing for certain, Sel decided not to tell Ross anything. He sent letters to all the villages in the vicinity, describing the family as accurately as he could, including the time to leave the city. All messages about them were to be passed on to a trusted administrator in his former house in Vermoda, who was to send him a predetermined sign, if it was something important. The mark hadn't appeared before Vivan's dramatic kidnapping, but Sel was hopeful. In the end, he managed to find his family, so there was little hope that this story would also have a good ending. Milera's family met with him. A symbolic funeral of the deceased was organized, and at the end they parted in agreement. There was nothing to add. Nothing connected them anymore. Both sides agreed.

But family of Ross's nanny...

Sel instinctively sensed that the tragedy he and Lena had learned was about them. He couldn't understand how you could be so cruel...

How much vindictive satisfaction and a carefully nurtured sense of injustice was there in Cadelia, capable of poisoning the life of a child - the innocent victim of her revenge.

He did not want such a truth for Ross, who often remembers his childhood years and the only bright moments associated with this family.

It was to them that he owed the good he had known from him. Not only he... He was sure of it.

It was overwhelming to think how many loved ones Ross had lost to bad fortune, starting with Nimm, his first love. Then there was Valeria, his good friend. Home friends. Julien, Oliver's sister. And finally... Alesei.

When Ross found out about his friend's death, he was speechless for a long time. He didn't leave the cabin for long, giving the impression that his mind and will had vanished somewhere, turning him into a living figure. Then circumstances forced him to take action, but when he thought no one was seeing it, his face twisted for a moment with stifled crying.

Sel knew well how pain could tear apart from the inside, breaking a soul into a million pieces. He recognized these symptoms. If the rumors about the fate of the nanny and her family turned out to be cruel truth, he might not recover from it.

Ross was on the border, but he was revealing it to no one, assuming the pose of a brave wizard and captain in front of the admiring crowd.

He was starting to fear that she wouldn't get him out of this.

He revealed his fears to Lena.

She looked at the sleeping Ross, mentally admitting he was right.

Fate favored Ross only seemingly. In fact, he was stealthily taking those he cared about the most.

It worried her. For it was no secret that, apart from Sel, who was the axis of his existence, Ross cared about one more human being the most.

It was her older son.

CHAPTER 31

At dawn on the third day, a loud wail interrupted the sleep of another watch. Below deck, in the women's section (such a division was made when some of the survivors from Kartamanu had to be taken care of), a woman who lost her entire family moaned. The despair over the murdered children was as inconsolable as a loving mother's heart could be. Then another one joined in, with only one child left, without three siblings and their father. Another mourned her parents. Another was recovering from traumatic events. It was like a wave washing over the deck. Bringing pain in its depths. Orphaned children cried out to cry because of fear and longing for their mother or father. Their despair was breaking hearts. One of the men decided to throw himself into the depths of the water, but, though with difficulty, he was stopped from doing so. Sleep did not soothe their thoughts, it locked them in the jar of Ross' extraordinary gift where they were within reach, but they did not hurt until the sorcerer lost control of them. Ross was only twenty-one years old, had too many hardships behind him, and his skills continued to expand. Controlling the thoughts of a whole group of people, ignoring previous achievements, was for him as great a challenge as the mental fight with the will of the sea serpent. No experienced mage helped him. For if there was such a person, he would have to deal with the layers of emotions flowing from the whispers of the heart and intuition. Ross' magic was based on the heart, as was also given to him. Her power was limitless. And unpredictable.

Now, however, ordinary human endurance has failed. Even magicians sometimes needed rest. Ross has known little of it recently.

This made the unfortunate villagers wake up from the calm imposed on them...

A great deal of commotion broke out on and below the deck. Tenan jumped up from his hammock below deck to get the situation under control, but soon found there was little he could do. The desperate families of the murdered apparently woke up from lethargy or Ross lost his vigilance, exhausted by his experiences. No arguments, kind words or hugging attempts reached the hearts of the suffering. There was no way to comfort them somehow. The thoughts of what the survivors might have experienced and what the desperate eyes of the children saw in the minds of the witnesses filled with fear and compassion.

"Captain..." Tenan did not relinquish Ross's rightful title, although technically it was his right now. However, the entire crew knew Captain Hope was aboard, and as long as he was, it was up to him to command the Valeria. This matter was not up for discussion.

Ross was sitting at the table next to the rescued girl. With his back to the door, as if to cut himself off from everyone.

There was something disturbing about the pose he assumed. The slight movements he made only deepened the grim image, making Tenan suddenly wish the captain would not turn around. As if he was going to see something that he never wanted to see. Something no one was prepared for.

He was right.

Ross's face, though apparently calm, expressed the deepest pain. He began to lean steadily back and forth, back and forth, back and forth, ceaselessly, locked in his own world that, in the darkest moments of his life, helped him to disconnect himself from the brutal reality.

"I know what you came for..." Ross began, his voice breaking, which in itself had a murmur of uneasiness in the crowd. Lena put her free hand on Sel's shoulder. The child cuddled against her only stared at Ross, as calm as children living in constant fear can be. Too quiet for children.

Ross also stopped swaying for a moment in a disturbing way. Tenan saw now that the girl was clinging to him, frightened by his condition, but bravely trying to support him. What an extraordinary child it was!

"I can't help them," Ross continued in a sullen tone that was ominously different, as if there were too many conflicting emotions in his head that could not be matched. "Because what would I tell them?!" He suddenly shouted, until they all shuddered. "What words would I find?! You can't imagine what I saw. These images are still in my head!" He indicated with a nervous movement. "I let them rest, calm their thoughts, even for a moment. I myself calmed down for them!" with a female gesture, which happened to him only in exceptional situations, he pointed to the girl and children accompanied by their caregivers. "I asked Jewel to extinguish their thoughts. But…" He paused dramatically, during which his face twisted into a sarcastic, half-demented smile, "…I can't do this anymore," he shrugged as if it were a trifle. At the same moment, blood from his nose rushed out in a larger trickle than usual. "I know and remember! I feel, although I poured cold water over these feelings, you understand?! I can't stop!" He laughed hysterically, starting the morbid back and forth motion that was his momentary escape from reality.

"I see," he replied calmly, deciding that the best he could do right now would be to let him talk.

"You know the words that will soothe their hearts?" Ross asked quietly, suddenly returning to normal for a moment, as if caring for others was his last stronghold before the madness to come.

Tenan brought up memories of his murdered brother. A child with a hole in his chest where his heart was ripped out… Nailed to the door.

"Maybe teach me the control you exercise over yourself," Ross asked mockingly, not quite logically thinking. "Maybe if I could, like you…"

"Ross…" Tenan began calmly.

"I have to do something! I have to do something with myself…" Ross began repeating the mantra, meanwhile Tenan saw the suffering face of Sel out of the corner of his eye. "Because what will happen, what will happen… If something happens to me?" Ross ran his hand nervously over his face. "Who's gonna help them? Who will help Vivan? What will Sel do if I lose my mind?!" He looked despairingly at his partner.

"Ross…" Sel said softly, "maybe you should rest longer…"

"I was resting, weren't I?!" Ross raised his voice nervously. "I've been resting all night. And what did this rest give me?!"

"We both know you were awake…"

"Yes, we know that. This is the only thing we know… Because I still don't know anything!"

"Wait!" Tenan silenced the rumor by taking his hand. His voice was as controlled as his thoughts. Someone must have kept a cool head here, "Try not to say anything. Awhile."

Ross paused, letting only the tears flow, without any hope.

Everyone tried not to make a sound to give Tenan time to think, even children who had an intuitive sense that something was wrong. Tenan was sure Ross was aware of that as well.

"I can't teach you something that was forced on me," he explained calmly. "I would like to learn from you feelings that I was not allowed to…" he looked into his eyes. "Why don't you call him for help?" He asked.

Ross blinked confused. After a while he replied softly:

"He's in captivity. Locked in the mine. Guarded by guards."

"Did the presence of the guards prevent him from starting a rebellion? Wake up the blue flame?"

Sel looked at him, perhaps for the first time in appreciation.

"You don't need a blue flame here," Ross remarked confidently and to the point.

Tenan looked at him thoughtfully. Ross calmed down as soon as he was given something to think about instead of descending into despair. He was strong-willed. All he needed was support.

"Vivan," he turned suddenly to the most extraordinary and, at the same time, the only man who could remedy the situation. He must have done it for the first time in several years, "Ross needs help," he looked into Ross's eyes. "I know you can see and hear with his eyes with this," he pointed to the Jewel on Ross's neck. "So please: do something!" He ordered forcefully, still touching the jewel that glittered red under his fingers. "Do what you do best! Now you can take care of everything. We need you."

Ross stopped. After a moment, that mocking, deranged smile appeared on his face again, as if he did not believe that Tenan had just done what he had done.

"Why are you talking to him like I'm not here?" He asked suddenly, with tone chilling the blood in the veins.

Out of the corner of his eye, Tenan saw that Sel turned pale.

"I'm here, Tenan!" Ross pointed out emphatically, in a voice that had so far echoed the hidden echoes of the past, when her own mother in a fit of humor ignored his existence, then changed her mind, only to torment him.

Sel touched his shoulder, recalling all the care and love. He knew perfectly well what dark demon of memories was now permeating his lover's emotions.

"I exist, Tenan!" Ross pointed out, losing some obsessive strength after Sel's intervention to prove his worth. "Don't talk about me like I'm not here!" He shouted with pain hidden years ago, now dragged to the surface under the influence of nightmarish events that could not be ameliorated.

Sel pulled a handkerchief from his pants pocket, trying to remain calm.

"You're bleeding..." he said softly, putting the handkerchief to his partner's nose with a concerned gesture.

Ross involuntarily held down the handkerchief, deeply moved by his behavior. He suddenly remembered that it was completely different now. Someone cared about him, someone loved him, and he misunderstands the situation. Remnants of sober emotions tried to defeat him with his shaky mind. And they were about to lose this battle...

"May he hear...," Tenan told him.

Ross looked helplessly at Sel, who immediately stood up and hugged him tightly. Then the girl hugged him. Sel caressed the little one on the head with his free hand.

Feeling the touch of both of them, Ross thought, apprehensive about their future.

Things were certainly not going well.

Tenan's words came to him as he loaded the stones again, pain rising in his shoulder.

He looked through the Jewel...

Suddenly, the dragon's anger ceased to matter to him. In the face of a friend's suffering, the flame had no right to overwhelm him. According to what he feared, Ross needed help. That was all that mattered. The muted gift of healing and the trampled desire to help awoke in his body without any effort. They have always been there. They were stronger than the blue flame because of their love for people. After all. The flame could not win against this. Not now. Not today.

There was only one obstacle to taking action... A very serious obstacle.

"Hey, Prince!" Zarin called, seeing that Vivan was not working. "Did you fall asleep?! Do you need whipping for encouragement?!" He walked up to him with a quick step, glad that he could punish him again. "Get to work!" He raised his hand to hit him with a whip.

Vivan, with a swift movement, struck him with the shovel in his hand without thinking.

Zarin fell to the ground with a groan. Vivan's intention was not to kill him, but merely to stun him. He still hated killing.

"Shut up!" He ordered him shortly.

Ross desperately needed help. Vivan suddenly looked around. The world seemed to freeze, surprised by this act of rebellion. At the same time, he also saw himself from a completely different angle. The act of violence woke him from his long sleep. He thought about his past. He let himself be beaten and pushed. He lacked decisiveness, because the sight of the cruelty around him felt emotional, shocked and deafened by the actions of evil people. But if he acted like this again, he would lose his friend this time.

He wasn't going to let that happen.

"Maybe it's enough of this whipping?" He asked Zarin, thinking not only about him.

The tone of his voice, the language he used, touched those present. Vivan began humming... Along with the soft melody came memories of the beginning of the journey that had brought him all the way here. A girl with beautiful hair. Her parents. Were they able to find a safe place? How far has he already grown from that self? Where will all this lead him?

When the overseer fell asleep a moment later, the companions in captivity exchanged bewildered whispers among one another. Meanwhile, two more overseers, who noticed the movement, lay down on the rock bedding. He knew that more would come. One moment more. Maybe two.

"Do you want to be mistreated endlessly?" He asked his closest companions of misery, impatient with their hesitation. "I'm not going to die here!" He said firmly. He began humming again as he saw more overseers. More and more people saw it in action. As successive overseers fell asleep, the Jewel on the Neck appeared. The murmur of voices was heard again, but not yet recognized.

A voice after a while made the situation change at last.

"Why are you standing like sheep?!" A young man with dark skin asked everyone firmly, "They can use bows in a moment!"

Without waiting for their reaction, he approached Vivan with a quick, firm step. His gaze scanned his silhouette, finally stopping him on the Jewel and the other symbols.

"I'm Azim, my lord," he bowed slightly, but with evident respect. "There are two Jewels in the world, as they say, and you don't have white hair," he observed with a twinkle in his eye. "It's a Healer! He called out to everyone with an energy that was both pride and joy."

The slave crowd passed the information on. It quickly ran around all the sidewalks in circles.

Azim stood firmly at his side. Vivan already knew that he was pleased with this turn of events and would be willing to face his opponents.

"Speak," the new companion ordered firmly. "What do you need?"

"Time," Vivan replied shortly, sensing the warmth of friendly feelings in him.

Azim looked straight into the blue of his eyes that first caught his attention.

"You got it!" He replied shortly, tighter grasping the pickaxe in his hands.

Vivan's comrades captured by the hunters were among the first to fight. There were quite a few of them, about thirty men of all ages, from boy to old ones. For the warden, it was the number that mattered, not the people. They were to work until the very end, just like their predecessors. Weakened, ailing slaves also joined the rebellion, wanting at least a moment of freedom, or because they had no other choice in the face of the rebels' advantage. Vivan helped sometimes by putting some of the guards to sleep. Azim stopped him very quickly from this action. The slaves, hungry for revenge, murdered their oppressors in a dream, and this he was not going to support. Vivan agreed fully with him. As long as they were going with a group of volunteers to the chief overseer and his dozen of his people, he tried to sense how badly Ross was and how much longer he could wait.

He had little time.

Waiting for his help, which still wasn't coming, Ross asked Tenan for a painful favor. Thoughts and images swirled inside his soul, demanding an escape with brutal violence.

Vivan was angry about his own helplessness in the face of events. Everything else ceased to matter in the face of the suffering of a friend who more than once risked his life to help him.

Much depended on how the rebellion turned out.

Yahys had the best of them with him.

"I can end this!" Vivan said firmly to his companion. "With one song..." he looked straight into the eyes of the fearless overseer, licking his lips with satisfaction at the sight of him.

"You will take away people's chance for a worthy victory!" Growled Azim. "Leave it to us! He will not get away from death!"

Yahys was sure of his. No slave can cope with his men, armed with swords and daggers. In full strength. He forgot in his pride that he had only received a fresh "delivery" yesterday, determined and ready to resist him. These people drew the able to fight with them, and Azim, whom they all chose without hesitation as their leader, probably due to his bulky stature and, above all, the presence of the famous Healer, dragged the people with him. The fight grew fierce. Yahys hid behind his backs as long as possible, quickly losing confidence when it turned out that the enslaved would not give up despite their losses.

Finally, there was an unexpected end.

A girlish figure with a whip in her hand galloped among the fighters on a horse.

The horse rammed the guards, giving the dark-haired girl a chance to show off, who lashed with a whip, hitting the warden hard. He cringed in pain, screaming almost girlishly. Daryenne, because she was the said girl, slashed the guards with an untrained hand, sometimes hurting herself. Azim waited for Yahys to reach for his own sword. The fight seemed a doomed, and in fact it was so. A few strokes could no longer delay the sentence.

Blood was shed on the warden's neck in one fell swoop. He ensured a slow death in front of the freedmen, making him a symbol of overcoming oppression.

The battle cry that escaped from the victors' throats announced their freedom.

Vivan staggered.

The inner struggle of the two forces in his soul became devastating.

Azim saw disturbing changes in his companion. He managed the people, finding his closest associates in the captured. He ordered them to distribute the diamonds they found between the winners and the supplies. He left a few with him, taking them inside the imposing warden's house. Daryenne escorted them.

Vivan was in mortal danger.

This time he was an enemy of himself.

"Talk to me!" he ordered him. "What's going on?!"

"A girl..." Vivan replied uneasily, not seeing his brave new friend.

Azim wanted to scream. He was leading the healer to the bedroom. Frightened slaves ran away from the chambers in panic. The overseer's fat wife and her two sons tried to flee the palace. The liberators captured women and children. They robbed rooms.

A battle cry and the thud of hooves told them that Daryenne had burst into the hall on her horse, stopping him at the imposing staircase leading to the private rooms.

"Hands off the women!" She shouted loudly, and the echo of the hall carried her voice. "What about you?! They are also victims!"

"Nonsense!" One of the freedmen remarked consciously, holding the overseer's wife with his companion. The little boys clung to her dress.

Vivan looked pointedly at Azim.

"Women are to be safe!" he ordered with a flash of blue heat in his eyes. "Children too! Otherwise, everyone will know my anger!"

There was silence.

Azim nodded slightly.

"Lock up the overseer wife and her children in her bedroom! You two," he appointed two people he knew. "Watch over them! Let the women go free! I'm ashamed for you! Are you liking our lords?! Are we not sharing the same fate?!"

The liberators mingled.

"A few will stay with me and Vivan!" He ordered the rest of the group. "We have to bring order here!"

"Those who handed out the supplies are back!" One of the swarthy companions told him.

"Okay!" Azim nodded approvingly, while Daryenne dismounted the horse and tied him, "Let they help you! And one more thing!" He added as they left, while Daryenne was already with them. "That girl and her horse are untouchable, okay?"

"Little heroine!" remarked one of the companions with a smile. "I would not come close when she is holding a whip in her hand!"

The others laughed kindly.

Daryenne threw herself into Vivan's arms, a little embarrassed by their interest. The group quickly agreed on their responsibilities and departed as planned.

"You were supposed to run..." Vivan remarked with a smile, hugging the girl.

"Me and the horse got along quickly," she replied with a spark of cheerfulness. "I'm going to take him to the ship."

"It was her idea," said Azim. "We didn't get on your ships after the sorcerer had conquered the city. We decided to look for you on the road. We were counting on the demons to release you quickly. In the end..." he smiled crookedly, leading everyone to an empty bedroom. "They didn't kidnap ordinary man!"

"They walked past us while you were sleeping in the cave," Daryenne added.

Vivan looked gloomy. So many things could not have happened...

"Glad we've met now," Azim remarked.

"You say we," Vivan said, lowering his voice.

"A handful of insurgents against Azram's rule," Azim explained. "There were more of us, but the king's fucking adviser quickly sensed us and sent his demons out before we collected our weapons. There were maybe twenty of us left. Me and a few got caught to see if you were here. We are together now. The others have already joined."

"The king's advisor rules over demons?" Vivan asked seriously as his thoughts returned to Ross.

"Besharam is evil incarnate," said Azim shortly. "Better for you not to meet him."

Vivan felt a chill as the name faded into the air.

Unexpectedly, a cold gust of wind blew through the windows, sending shivers down the spine.

"Maybe it's better not to say his name," whispered Daryenne.

Vivan shook his head.

"I won't hide from him," he replied softly, with a strange note in his voice.

"It's not your witch..." Azim remarked. "It's not enough to find a heart here. Maybe he doesn't have one at all."

"He lives in our world," said Vivan wryly. "He must be subject to certain laws of this world."

Azim looked at him half mocking, half admiring.

"You're crazy if you think about it!"

Vivan replied with a similar smile, guessing his feelings:

"I'm not the only one."

CHAPTER 32

Azim took Daryenne to the kitchen, leaving Vivan in the care of two trusted companions. The palace was silent. Here and there quiet conversations could be heard. The released women got acquainted with the liberators. Those who remained were mostly Azim's companions, or too weak or too sick to leave. The others took their share of the loot in the form of small diamonds and provisions and quickly dispersed. They gained freedom. They preferred not to risk the wrath of the king and his gloomy adviser.

Vivan knew, as did Azim, that they couldn't stay in this place too long.

They probably won't even stay the night. Time was pressing. So he was relieved to see the moment when he was finally alone to bond with Ross.

"I'm sorry…" he whispered.

Several hours had passed since Tenan summoned him to help. Ross was sitting in the corner with his chin on his lap during this time. After several attempts to reach him, Sel took care of the hapless girl who was only interested in her rescuer, ignoring her own needs. With great caution, he managed to pass her a few spoons of soup. She looked like a wild animal. It was terrifyingly sad. Sel was tormented by nightmarish thoughts at the sight of her marked dependence on her partner's mood, which was also becoming increasingly lost. He felt he was losing both of them. The awareness broke his heart.

Both responded only to him, but relatively rarely. They seemed to be a ghost in a completely different world. So, when Vivan finally spoke, Sel almost burst into tears with relief. He himself did not realize how much tension he had been living in the last few hours. Lena took care of him, gently surrounding him with motherly concern. She did it with some apprehension. Sel knew even less about maternal tenderness than Ross did. His mother treated him coolly. She waited for death to take him away from a serious heart defect that had been cured by Vivan's gift. She did not live to see this moment, which Lena sometimes regretted. She would have a lot to say to this woman.

Cora watched as the closest to Vivan clung to each other for solace. Once again, she caught herself thinking if it was because of this strange man, whose image did not disappear from her memory, but remained alive, even though he had hurt her with his meddles, as she liked to call his compassionate ability. Everyone was so emotional...

She hadn't known them before, so she didn't know that Vivan's presence had triggered feelings in them that they had been forced to suppress before. She didn't even know how much what was about to happen would surprise her.

"Ross..." Vivan called his friend softly, in a tone long unheard of.

If he didn't act his gift in any way every day, he felt empty.

Only now, reaching into Ross's mind, was he beginning to realize that voidness was a feeling he had never defined before, but which was what defined his gift. He felt her if he had not helped someone for a long time. He could not live without it, although the gift did not always bring him happiness...

He grabbed an ornate pillow from the great bed on which it settled. He felt that something he had never tried before was about to happen. He was not yet sure of the nature of the event, but the very thought quickened his heartbeat.

He peered into his friend's mind. To the feelings. The good and the bad...

At first, Ross felt a warmth in his chest. The jewel glowed with a soft purple glow, responding to the call of its former owner.

Then he felt as if he had drunk something that warmed his body up to the tips of his fingers and toes. He gasped as a mysterious warmth enveloped his head. His mind filled his nanny, her husband, who treated him like his son. Their children, whom he grew up with. All those good moments, even those forgotten like the warmth of a nanny's milk; her soothing presence and scent suddenly returned. They filled him with tenderness, a wave of emotions. But most of all, they inspired him with joy that chased the gloomy images into shadow and gloom.

"Ross, remember..." this wonderful woman once told him, "You have to take care of yourself! I didn't bring you up so that you would grow up to be a bad person!" She shook her finger warning him. "Be who you are! Not the son of your father and mother! Be a good man!" She concluded firmly.

Memories burned sometimes. Like when he watched their cart until it disappeared around a bend in the road. The cry of the man who should be his father. He shouted that he would find him. That he would come back.

He hadn't come back yet, leaving a childish longing in his heart.

The thought went away, suggesting other moments. Bitter. Painful when he returned to the times of the uprising on his body cigar scars... After the poker...

Vivan gave new meaning to these pictures, although it was not easy for him.

Valeria.

She had appeared in Ross's life by accident, one rainy night, when he had to run again and he didn't know Nimm yet. She gave him a place to sleep and food, in the middle of the groans and sighs of the House of Pleasure. But it was better than fear of his mother. Better than cold and wet clothes in a dirty alley. Valeria recognized the boy who was helping the merchants for a bowl of food at the marketplace. Quiet, slim as a stick, but moving with a dignity that was sympathetic. Old clothes, mended with a not very skilled hand, were always clean, and so were the shoes. She had promised him that he could always come here, and it happened to him more than once after that... until he met Nimm.

And then that terrible night when the beaten dragged himself up to the brothel...

Ross recalled the days she had taken care of him with a mixture of love and guilt. And then those when he repaid her concern like a moron, motivated by suffering after losing a loved one. The days and nights of darkness when all that mattered was wine and herbs and fucking, as the Red Captain described it.

Fortunately, love won once again. This time to a wonderful babysitter, caring and warm under a layer of life roughness. He came to his senses to make plans with her about the future. After all, Sel, who awakened his senses and heart, was to remain a beautiful memory forever...

Ross's face changed as elation woke him from the dark night of his thoughts. And as his heart skipped a beat at the memories of the first moments with his lover, Ross felt he couldn't take it anymore. Love and joy lit his soul with an inner fire. He felt that he was going to burn if he didn't do something...

And Vivan, the soul healer, knew exactly what he needed now.

"Yes, Ross..." he smiled, feeling his friend's well-being penetrate and him, like the sun's rays after many days of rain, "Laugh!"

Ross laughed heartily, surprising everyone, and then the chain of fear, insecurity, and dread broke in his heart, then disappeared for good.

He felt hot tears on his face.

Vivan, on the other hand, felt as if the soothing balm of his happiness enveloped his lost heart.

At times like this, he preferred to be alone. Others would find him too sensitive for a man. Perhaps they would mock his sincere, passionate feelings. He knew from experience that men were restrained by too much exuberance, perhaps out of jealousy that it was not seeming for them. Or maybe because they find it funny? Devoid of masculine character? Long ago, it was his mother who had told him emphatically that his imposed habits did not apply. He is the essence of feelings. He is a healer. He must be sensitive. Otherwise, he will be just another medic without an vocation...

He was himself. Nothing less, nothing more.

"Do what I ask you to do," he said to his friend, feeling a special emotion. "I will help you."

Ross replied from the bottom of his heart that he would agree to everything, knowing now that something completely extraordinary was about to happen that he had never experienced before.

"Touch and hold for a moment those closest to you," Vivan ordered him gently. "And then do it for the others. Everyone you saved..." He paused, feeling his heart beating rapidly, fueled by his uncertainty. "And then everyone else," he concluded with determination.

Ross froze, not believing what he heard. But before a question was asked, Vivan calmly repeated:

" Yes. Touch everyone."

Vivan cringed, clutching the pillow in his hands. An unusual golden-green aura shone on his skin like a torch. As more and more people were soothed, an extraordinary, the only power in the world penetrated his veins, piercing his heart and soul. The sinister force of blue anger was forced to yield, muffling the flame to just one spark etched in his heart forever. Vivan sensed Sel's happiness, who was relieved to see Ross's overall mood feel better. Peace and quiet joy of the rescued girl who hugged her sorcerer with gratitude that only an innocent child can express.

Then it was Lena's turn...

Vivan poured into his mother's heart the enormity of his longing and love. He encountered the same feelings that filled him, losing him somewhere in the worlds with such a blissful sense of comfort that he took his breath away. Feelings full of memories, warm, evoking a sense or security filled his mind and heart with the peace that was close to him...

Mother... In that word, in the pictures, soul and memories, there was a lot of emotions building his personality and gift. She was his beginning. His motivation.

His thoughts about her penetrated Ross's soul, awakening a bond he had once buried.

In this one, the most important one, he never managed to wake up warm feelings...

But she let others love him, as if a little bit of decency won the fight in her heart for a moment. She had sustained her for years as nanny and her family raised Ross as their own children. She did not interfere with their devotion until they asked her to give him back to them forever.

Their request smothered any remnants of warm feelings in her. She aroused a lust for blood. They wanted to take away her right to revenge...

Suddenly, the stream of the gift was disturbed as Vivan found one important message in Ross's mind. Ross learned of a brutal family robbery outside the city walls. A murder done with perfidious precision, without justification. This family had no enemies, it was said. Modest family, quiet people. Someone recognized them. Ross found out from the people at the marketplace who had been murdered...

His heart did not acknowledge it. He pushed the news out of his mind, feeding his thoughts with a false hope in which he had finally believed. It was because of it that he thought that they were alive somewhere, only that they were afraid to come for him. It couldn't be about them! She wouldn't be so mean...

This thought, sealed in the heart, opened to Vivan's mind. He almost reminded him of the truth when he found it.

He left it as it was.

Other, equally serious challenges awaited him. The families of the murdered. And although he was grieving over the fate of his friend, who had suffered many misfortunes in his life, he cleansed his mind of painful emotions with the skill he had had for many years.

He started with the children.

He didn't instill in them that nothing had happened. He wasn't going to cheat them. It might have had an impact on their future lives. He has already met people who are hiding the truth after the great tragedy. Thinking stories supposed to help ease the pain of a loss. Sometimes it did help. Usually, however, these were exceptions, and revealing the truth caused more suffering. These children saw what really happened. Perhaps it seemed to others that since they were small, they would not remember. Vivan already knew that such forgetfulness did not exist. He reveals himself in the fears he has chased away. The nightmares he had to deal with. Spiritual and mental development, even under the influence of great trauma. He knew and healed the effects of many dramatic events. So, through Ross, he touched the heads of these children and soothed their pain. Protecting his friend from the visions in their heads, so that he would not relive the events in the village again, he numb with horror. At the same time, he felt deeply sorry for them, seeing how their mothers, who tried to save them, and the fathers who were defending their families, died. Hot tears, filled with golden light, fell on the pillow clutched in her hands.

He had to stick to it.

The parents are gone. He blurred drastic scenes, recalling memories full of warmth, tenderness and love so that in the future they would know that they died protecting them because they loved them so much...

He had some influence on how they would handle it in the future. He gave them distance to events to help them survive, but he also kept their memories alive by defending their hearts with peaceful memories.

He quietly hoped it would be enough.

He knew that he lacked years of experience that would perhaps have better prepared him for such help. He made up for in intuition and still a good heart.

His actions were already bearing fruit. As he likewise helped the women in the room, and then Ross went to the other survivors, Vivan's shoulder no longer ached. His tired complexion glowed. All pain is gone.

In treating others, Vivan always helped himself as well. Now he did it on an unprecedented scale. He had never done this before.

Perhaps the urge to undertake it came from the need to return to himself, without the blue anger that wasn't so much in his nature that it was slowly killing him?

But he forgot about one thing while helping aching people. By silencing the lamentation and comforting with the hands of a friend whose extraordinary action more and more made him a god on the ship.

Ross was helping, excited about his task, touched by the fact that for the first time he really felt how Vivan's gift was working. He was almost one himself, acting on his behalf.

Vivan saved him from penetrating too deeply into the images and emotions of the people being treated.

But he forgot to protect him from his own emotions.

So, Ross knew what he felt and how much he felt when he met everyone, they were helping at the moment...

And as he walked from one person to the next, he thought about how much he loved this extraordinary man. A love greater than lust, views, blood ties. He alone was able to see so much. He wanted to embrace Vivan and thank him, not with the adoration that a priest of a nascent religion might feel, but with a commitment to pure friendship and care.

He had never come across such an absolute, devoid of profit-making good.

He understood now why in the town where Vivan was born, they worshiped him so much.

Why do people throw themselves into his arms for help.

And finally... Why each of the fear-obsessed people in the marketplace wanted to have at least a fraction of it...

Vivan will never be safe...

Because the gift he had was what they wanted forever.

The glow on Vivan's skin finally faded after three hours. He felt completely exhausted as they finally touched the last member of the crew. He knew Ross had crawled to his cabin in silent admiration. He fell back on the makeshift bedding and fell asleep immediately. Daryenne and their new companion, shocked to see him returning with their meal, flatly refused when he ordered them to leave the palace without him. He was so weak he could barely speak. But he had never felt happier before.

He was filled with a wave of warmth and gratitude from the ship. He fell asleep calmly, although he knew that this state would change when he woke up. Finally, it did what it was made to do. He felt really good about it.

CHAPTER 33

The only thing that occurred to Azim was to be impudent in the palace and pray to all the gods he knew that the king would not send demons to them.

It was clear that Vivan would not survive any journey if he was moved from the warden's bed.

Azim explained to his people what happened. They agreed that they did not want to hurt the healer for anything in the world. So they decided to arm themselves and send someone to find the Valeria. The warden's widow and her children decided to let free when they left the palace. Reluctantly, they were given some food, still under guard.

The attack did not take place.

The demons would attack anyone without exception, even the warden's family. Azim could tell the woman was aware of this. However, she hid her fears from her sons, keeping watch during their sleep until dawn.

Daryenne fell asleep beside Vivan. With him, she felt most confident. Even while sleeping, he had a soothing effect on her.

Azim wanted to do what the girl did. He felt that he was close to it. However, he told himself that he did not want to disturb. This desire struck him as strange, as if inappropriate, though there was nothing wrong with it. This was how the gift of the healer acted on him.

So, he was surprised when he woke up next to Vivan in the morning. Not because he was attracted to him, oh no. He would be the first to mock this ridiculous thought. Rather, it was about missing someone dear to him. It was soothed by the proximity of the healer. It's all strange, but so fascinating.

In addition, he felt fantastic. No pain, as if he spent yesterday morning meeting his family. These were the associations that came to him as he tried to comprehend it all. He regarded the healer with a mixture of admiration and concern. Yesterday he saw that guy shine! He had little chance of anyone in the house believing him...

Vivan looked good. And even very well, as if he did not have a hard time behind him. Even the scar from hitting the head was gone. Azim cheered in spirit. They will leave today for sure. He would escort him to the White Captain's ship. Then you will see...

He went to his own to begin preparations.

Vivan opened his eyes.

Full of tears welling up before his eyelids, he could see almost nothing but the colors. Nearby he could hear the calm breathing of a sleeping young girl.

He knew who she was, as well as that the tangle of colors above him was the canopy of a bed in a palace.

His mind quickly stopped worrying about it. Thoughts flashed towards the images seen without ceasing, stubbornly circling around the experiences of the people whom he had helped. Ross's memories of survivors in particular attacked his heart, awakening a stream of tears running down his face, while his body went numb from too much of an experience. He was paralyzed by the fear of witnesses to brutal murders. Horror, causing his heart to pound faster and faster, was awakened by the sight of torn hearts and innocent hearts. So loved, hugged, now helpless and helpless against monsters. What he saw with their eyes could not fit in his heart or mind.

His quick breathing woke Daryenne, and the fear in his eyes made him realize immediately that it was very, very bad...

There were too many stimuli. Every despair after losing in such a brutal way a person close to his heart pierced his heart like a thorn. Shock, disbelief, shocking truth, inconsolable grief... Vivan drowned in the abyss of others' suffering.

Daryenne was intuitive, far more mature than her actual age. She did not call for help. No one could help him now with their fear of seeing him like this. She simply stroked his cheek with a compassionate heart, remaining calm.

He looked at her.

Slowly, he sat up like an old man, taking her hand in silent thanks.

Then he hid his face in his hands.

She hugged him silently.

"You look like shit," Azim remarked sarcastically as they left two hours later.

"You look blooming too," Vivan replied sarcastically, smiling slightly at the remark.

Two hours of Daryenne's soothing concern helped him soothe his emotions. Faster than after meeting Cora. He hoped his ability to distance himself from what others felt might be returning again.

"Can you finally explain to me what happened to you after the capture of the palace?!" Azim blurted out suddenly, not without irritation. Vivan had yet to explain himself about the incident, and it was not something normal.

Vivan glanced at Daryenne with a knowing smile.

"I helped my friend," he replied calmly, "It's a bit complicated..."

"You shone like a fucking lantern!" Azim couldn't hold back, hearing the evasive answer. "Can you tell me how the hell is it possible?!"

Vivan thought for a moment.

"I've never had anything like it before..." he admitted, "and so blue anger..."

Azim looked at him closely.

"You mean you don't know where the light comes from?" He asked with a hint of disappointment.

"I know," Vivan replied. "It's a sign that my power, gift, or whatever - is growing. Someday I will burn in this fire. Maybe when I save others. Or maybe because I'm consumed with anger for the harm people do to each other? And maybe then it will all end... Maybe the world will forgive my relatives and friends and stop persecuting them because of me..." he finished gloomily.

Azim looked at him with an irony marked by experience.

"If you want peace for yourself, your relatives and friends, you have to fight for it," he remarked. "There is no other way here. Not for you. You always have time to die. Sooner or later, Mother Earth or some other god will wave its hand and give up the ghost. I prefer to fight. For a decent life, a safe life, yes... It's worth fighting for! To live with your own people - that's the real goal! Only it matters!"

"I'm not looking for death..." Vivan protested, but Azim silenced him with a wave of his hand because he hadn't finished speaking yet.

"If you are to die, defend them! To die when you murder others is a mean death, the death of people who cannot afford good. Those who don't know how to be good. I despise such people! A warrior is a warrior. The real one has heart and courage. Skunk only thinks about hurting others. It is not worth remembering. If you have to die, die according to your heart. Not in anger. But take your time. For your relatives and friends, you will be more precious if you are alive. Without you, their world will lose a lot. Die when nothing else can be done! Only then!" he pointed out.

"You thought so..."

"Yes," he immediately broke into his word. "I thought that a man who is a living legend is going to give a bad account of himself..." he concluded shortly.

Only their march broke the silence now, sometimes the snorting of a few horses. They gave two of them to the chief's wife and her sons, releasing them on the way. She knew well that she could not return to her palace. The king, furious that her husband had not suppressed the slave revolt, would have ordered her killed. This man was not famous for his mercy.

"Are you over?" Azim asked after a moment, not hiding his irony.

Vivan looked at him with a twinkle in her eyes, while Daryenne watched them from her mount, wondering if they were insane.

"It's over," he said simply.

"Praise all gods!" Exclaimed Azim with mock relief, causing laughter among his companions, "We have two days ahead of us to the sea. I'm not going to listen to the moaning. Let's find the White Captain and finally put it in order! No one can claim you as if you were a thing! Nobody! And forgive me, but you're getting down to it badly. You don't have the sense to fight, but it's your nature you can see. You don't like to hurt anyone. It won't work, Vivan! See what it got you to. More determination! Just like your friend does, the captain! They won't leave you alone until you catch them by the murder and tell them to stop!"

Vivan looked at him silently. Violence in his case meant trouble. But he did not want to provoke another outrage from his companion.

He, however, guessed his thoughts.

"I know what you want to say," he looked into his eyes. "I remember blue anger... But you have to be firm at last! You gotta get angry sometimes! Otherwise, they will kill your family and friends to do it for you! Understand?"

Vivan felt anger mixed with embarrassment and guilt.

"How many of yours still have to die for you to understand?!" Azim asked.

"Nobody's gonna die anymore." He replied firmly.

"Why didn't he attack us?" Azim wondered once again.

They stopped for the night in the hills, far from the Hunter's tracks. Azim has appointed a few men to be on guard duty. They made a fire to roast the birds on the way. Daryenne firmly refused to pluck the feathers, so the men had to take care of it themselves. There were no other women. They decided to try their luck and find their way back to their family homes. So, the group consisted of about twenty people and a few horses.

Vivan remembered the last demons attack that had taken him from the battlefield by force.

Then the demons from the village where Ross ended up...

"Maybe he's waiting for us to meet the captain?" Daryenne remarked.

"No," he replied. "That's not it."

"He had the perfect opportunity to send demons after you again," said Azim. "After all, we are few... Why didn't he?" He asked thoughtfully, thinking about it once more.

Unexpectedly, Vivan felt a shiver run through him, as if someone had stepped behind him. He already knew the answer.

"He's planning something completely different," he explained to his companions. "A trick."

"A trick?!" Azim repeated with surprise. "How do you know about this?"

A gust of wind came suddenly, strong and cold despite the warm night.

Though Vivan knew there was no one behind him, he couldn't help feeling that he was wrong.

"We're close to the Bay. I feel his presence..."

"The king?" Azim asked.

"His adviser," explained Vivan. "Bes..."

"Enough!" Daryenne interrupted him. "Don't call him up!"

"Besheram," he ignored her warrant without a trace of fear, "He's waiting for us to come closer. He doesn't like to bother too much. Ever since Ross attacked the Hunters, we've got his attention. The demon plan has failed, so he will do something else..."

"And how do you know that?"

"Ross has a talent for sensing others. Once he knew perfectly well where the witch that persecuted us was. Besheram made contact with him in Kartamana. His Jewel connects mine. I will know more when I'm next to this villain," he explained patiently. "These are such powers. Mind powers."

"So..." Azim wondered for a moment. "Do you sense him?"

Straight to the goal.

"Yes. The closer, the more."

"It doesn't bother him?"

"We don't know much."

Daryenne shifted nervously.

"How far is the captain?"

Vivan looked at her and then at the others. They waited intently, taking the fact of the unusual bond for granted.

"At this pace, we should meet in the morning."

"He's going this way?"

He nodded his head in agreement.

"How many capable to fight people are there?" One of Azim's companions snapped.

"He won't fight us, you heard," Azim reminded him. "He is preparing the trick. Only what?"

"Extremely treacherous..." Vivan replied grimly.

CHAPTER 34

Sel sipped his coffee slowly, watching Ross do what he was doing. If he looked down, perhaps he would have seen the last strips of smoke dark as a deep water, slipping into the black liquid in the vapor. He would probably have also drawn attention to the fact that someone handed it to him with a strange absent gaze, previously succumbing to hypnotic whispers carried by the wind. But it was not a stranger, so he simply thanked him, too absorbed in his partner's observation, while the latter returned to his seat, standing faithfully at his side again.

This is what turned out to be fatal.

It was late evening and Ross was still scheduling for the next day. On Tenan's advice, he persuaded Violet and the Judith's Captain to regroup their forces. There were too many civilians on the Valeria. Women, children, the weak and the old. The ship's supplies were plummeting. Certainly, these people were not safe on the ship where the man was that king's mysterious adviser and King Azram interested in. Ross introduced his friends to everything, telling them at lunch what Vivan had mentioned. The Judith took the unfit to fight on the deck and set off regretfully for Leviron.

They said goodbye to one another with great kindness, due to the many miracles done by Vivan through Ross, who among all now enjoyed genuine admiration and respect, without a chaotic rebellion. The healer's spectacular feat impressed even the pirates who finally realized the power of his gift and the possibilities of both him and Ross.

Sel didn't think they would go to sleep in the next hours. Ross was just arguing with Violet and Vincent, with faithful Silas and his substitute by his side. They were standing only a few steps away from him, so he didn't lose any of their conversation.

The plan was to seize Vivan as soon as possible and set off on their way back, not to think about the fate of the Bay and its prophecy.

Violet did not think this plan would work. Fate will probably get them anyway, so maybe it would be better to face it now? Ross considered the possibility.

When he mentioned what a precious gift Vivan was to everyone, Sel froze as if struck by a cold spike.

"LOOK HOW IT'S GETTING UP FOR A MEETING WITH VIVAN..."

Sel shook his head, dismissing the thought. So what? After all, that was the purpose of this trip...

"HE CARES A LOT ABOUT IT..."

Ross has always cared about Vivan's well-being. This is nothing new. He was his friend; they shared the same bond. Such a thought would never occur to anyone. After all, Vashaba was...

"WHICH ROSS DIDN'T LIKE...".

It's fact.

Sel tapped his cup against the saucer, feeling deeply uneasy. Something was wrong. He had no such thoughts! Never. Vivan had never, judiciously, displayed such an inclination. He caught Ross's gaze, so he managed a slight smile that lulled his alertness.

"WE WILL SEE HOW TOMORROW HE WILL WELCOME WITH HIM. THEY ARE RELATED TO THEMSELVES..."

Oh no! It was way too much! These thoughts came suddenly, out of nowhere. He felt a confusion in his head. He was not himself. Probably, he really needs to leave, maybe he will talk to someone? Maybe even with Victor?

No, he never thought that... Ross loved him. He knew about it. They've gone through so much to be together! What are these ideas...

The seed has been sown. The crop was to be harvested soon...

A few riders saw the ships on time. It was almost noon. Vivan's heart beat rapidly in his chest, urged by impatience. He hated these breakups. Each time he was afraid that he would see someone close to him for the last time. Or that he would never see them again.

The bay was perfect for both ships to drop anchors here. The depths of the clear waters seemed endless. It was easy to get to the shore. The beach was separated by a strip of shallow water, several meters long, right in front of the underwater abyss.

The two boats traveled quickly. Apart from Vivan and his companions, only one horse was taken at the request of Daryenne, who had attached herself to her horse.

The ships broke with cheers as soon as Vivan put his foot on the deck. Vivan froze, surprised by such an enthusiastic welcome. The joy on the faces of the people was great and undeniably sincere, and this stage of the journey finally seemed to be reaching the longed-for end. The healer was finally among them...

There were so many shades to this feeling...

Vivan remembered with emotion all the times he had been greeted and thanked with genuine joy. Giving a new name to their rapidly growing town. Rescued... Blacksmith Azylas, who regained his severed hand... He remembered the circumstances of these emotions. People gathered in their house, admiring the miracle with delight, even though they were threatened by trolls. The witch wanted to kill anyone who stood in the way of her plans. He remembered how he and his family had lost the family home soon after. The same one who was ruined and empty, as Erlon once told him, had received the once-disgraced son of the countess and his newly wed wife in advanced pregnancy. There was nothing there... When Vivan was born, the midwife mercifully made the bed available to the mother in labor...

Vashaba stood beside him as he folded the hand of the agitated blacksmith. He remembered her breathing. Her scent. The taste of her skin and lips.

Then she loved him...

Nobody loves him now. Not the way he wanted to.

And as people greeted him, shaking hands enthusiastically and patting him on the back in a friendly manner, a bitter thought crossed his mind: why is there no one close to him here? He saw the crowd happy with his arrival, true, but less familiar to him. They surrounded him on all sides so closely that for a moment he felt his old panic attack.

It was then that he felt warm, so familiar arms encircling him. He was finally safe...

"Mum..." he said the word softly, softly, as if fearing that she would lose that lovely touch.

His confidant. A friend. Support.

She released him from her arms as she felt he was ready for it. Victor's strong hands embraced him, then Paphian, who examined him carefully, only shaking his head at the turmoil of fate. Violet hugged him and kissed him like her own son. Dinn appeared, silent as at the beginning of their relationship. He wanted to leave quickly, giving way to the others, but Vivan would not let him.

Dinn wasn't guilty of anything.

He whispered in his ear that he knew very well what was going on. He was deliberately stuck in this relationship, though it was destroying him. It wasn't just Vashaba that was to blame.

Only now, during the greeting, did he let the memories he had effectively dismissed come to the fore.

He greeted Oliver with relief, finally feeling that the welcome, though pleasant, was coming to an end.

After so many sufferings, Tenan's handshake, as well as the sight of him, ceased to evoke unpleasant associations in him. He could see the gratitude in his eyes that they could go further in this relationship. At Tenan's side he saw a girl from Leviron. The sight warmed his heart. Tenan seemed dead inside, but Vivan knew it was mourning his many misdeeds. Now he was finally allowing himself to live.

At last.

Then suddenly he saw her...

The sight of Cora suddenly touched him. He felt his heart twitch as she approached him. And he never wanted to allow himself to do that again...

"It's good that you came back," she said. "And in one piece."

"Our last conversation..." he began hesitantly, but Cora touched his hand.

Vivan closed his eyes for a moment, listening to her heartbeat. In the beating of a tiny heart in her womb...

A kind of tenderness overwhelmed him as he caught the tone of the unfolding tiny life that he so desperately wanted to exist.

It was safe.

"Dreamer," she said suddenly, without a trace of anger, "Come back to earth!"

He looked at her. She smiled slightly.

"Sorry," he whispered in confusion.

He was losing his head with her.

She stopped him with a gentle gesture.

"It was terrible..." she noticed softly, thinking about his suffering.

He looked at her, surprised by the unexpected concern. She shrugged slightly.

"What happened to me, in some way also happened to you..."

"It's not quite like that..."

"Yes, I know," she interrupted, "but even if you know the memories are not yours... That fear..."

He froze. She saw it. She stroked his shoulder lightly with a reassuring gesture.

"You have the same fear in your eyes that I see in my reflection every morning," she noted.

Vashaba died in his defense. He cannot have desires...

It will be best for everyone when he will be alone.

She walked away; her eyes bid him farewell.

He shouldn't be thinking about her! Imagine their world together, full of conversations, walks, kisses... He can't dream about it!

Hurriedly, his eyes searched for friends who had not yet welcomed him.

They weren't on the bridge. And even among people, some of whom patted his shoulder and clasped his hand smiling.

He found them only in the captain's cabin.

Sel stood in front of Ross with an angry look. Behind the young captain's back was a little girl, covered with an arm by him. Probably Ross acted instinctively, because the anger on the partner's face was not aimed at the child. They both seemed surprised by his behavior.

Vivan soon shared his feelings fully.

"Oh, here you go!" Exclaimed Sel triumphantly. "You have him at last! He came here himself! Run to him! You have to give him a big hug!"

Vivan slowly closed the cabin door, thereby cutting off prying eyes. Something was definitely wrong. As if there was some evil aura in the air, like dark smoke enveloping the room.

"Sel..." Ross began calmly, and then something completely unexpected happened.

It wasn't a warning. With all the force of a strange, unbridled rage, Sel punched Ross in the face. With his open hand, he aimed a cheek so hard that Ross almost lost his balance.

The girl squealed in surprise, and Vivan felt all his resolutions to extinct the blue fire will not happen. In an instant, the blood boiled. He won't let him beat him, never again!

He was near them immediately. He grabbed Sel by the laps of his clothes, feeling a hot wave of fierce fire flow through his veins. His eyes flashed blue. Meanwhile, Sel laughed mockingly at the incident.

"Oh yes!" He cried. "Baby's jealous, Ross! You have to pet him now!"

"You hit him!" Vivan croaked, ignoring Ross's startled and terrified look.

"So what?" He asked mockingly, completely unremitting himself. "I was supposed to thank him? Since yesterday, he's been ready like a whore to greet you. Prepared clothes and cabin! And then this saying: Vivan this, Vivan that! He might at least not do such a show in front of everyone! He humiliates me, and I love him so much..." He stopped suddenly after these words, as if overwhelmed by what he had just done.

"I'll be fine, Vivan," they heard Ross's voice tremble slightly. "Let him go! Please..."

Vivan released Sel, giving him a look of disbelief and disgust. Then he quickly turned to Ross, assessing the damage.

The friend's face turned red from the blow. It must have hurt.

He looked again at Sel, who was just waiting, unable to react.

Suddenly he understood everything.

Puppet.

"Having fun?" He asked directly.

Sel looked at him. His eyes were filled with the blackness that got inside thanks to coffee...

"JUST STARTING," he replied in a strangely altered voice, at the sound of which Ross hugged the girl accompanying him.

Vivan quickly picked up the relevant information in the thicket of emotions. Sel was possessive of him during the night. Abruptly and regardless of his surroundings, he demanded sex in a rather unusual way. Ross pushed his brutal advances away in front of the baby, but to prevent things that would be hard to forget, he stayed awake all night.

During the day, he faced a wave of insults. He was also hit during a joint meal with the contents of Sel's cup.

"Victor said Sel came to him, stood up like a stake, and then left. He never acted like that. Never..." Ross whispered.

"It's not him," Vivan replied.

Sel suddenly laughed in obvious sneer, making them shiver.

"It's not me," he grinned, which made Ross feel another wave of disbelief and regret. "So, who am I?"

"Having fun?" Vivan asked again with icy calm.

"Great, so far," Sel replied easily, "And I'm going to have even more fun," he started for the exit.

Vivan looked over his shoulder at him, feeling the chill seize him.

"You must be forgetting who I am," he said aggressively.

Sel paused with some hesitation, dictated more by the curiosity of the one who possessed his body.

"A molly who bothers everything and constantly sheds tears?" He asked mockingly. This time, however, his eyes did not participate in the malice. They turned cold.

Vivan stared at him, thinking of his imprisoned friend.

"A healer."

The blue anger gave way to golden-green light as smoothly as if it had always been doing these things. He thought of two things. About the fact that he has to suppress this glow for the energy to focus mainly inside. Then about it, although it happened almost at the same time, that it is time to make a proper presentation.

He grabbed the puppet body by the arm and pulled it toward himself.

"Introduce yourself!" He ordered firmly.

"I'm Besheram," Sel replied in a strange voice, staring at him with the blackness of his eyes.

"Excellent!" At last, you found your courage, you vile coward!" Vivan hissed in his face, without a trace of fear, "Don't ever try that again!" He ordered angrily.

And suddenly - in a fit of a spontaneous decision - he kissed him.

The girl squealed. Ross froze, surprised by this turn of events. Vivan felt his surprise as much as the taste of Sel's mouth, who somewhere, pushed into the depths of consciousness, was regaining free will again.

He might wonder why he chose this method. After all, he had never kissed a man before. But he felt that this was how he would get the most, and indeed the surprise factor was of great help here. King

Azram's dark adviser had not expected this at all. Like the incredibly strong power of his gift. He was displaced before he was able to counteract it in any way.

The healer was also famous for breaking all spells.

He underestimated him.

He missed an opportunity.

It had been a long time since Besheram had been so helpless. This made him enormously angry. After all, he was watched! What a disgraceful fiasco!

There was nothing he could do to stop it. Not even for a moment. It was so obvious it was almost absurd. It aroused genuine rage in him. He will regret it already! He will bitterly regret it...

Echo of these feelings reached Vivan before he removed it from Sel's mind for good. Strange, he didn't seem to care much about it. Since he helped everyone on Ross' ship, his attitude towards the hostile world began to change. As if he had finally made a crucial decision. Azim's words only reassured him that it was time to finally take up the challenge and face adversity with his head held high. True, he hadn't been a coward before, but he was too deeply affected by emotions. If he wants his action to benefit everyone more than using the gift aboard the Valeria, he must silence it. Just enough not to let them go, because they were his fire in his veins, but to let him act logically. Otherwise everything will collapse. It will allow you to destroy the lives of people close to him, and finally his own...

Enough of this impunity!

This time the chill engulfed him for completely different reasons, to give way to a soothing warmth, as Sel, devastated by the encroachment into his soul, nestled into his arms. He was trembling hard, under the influence of the buzzing emotions and muffled sobs.

"Cry..." he gently commanded him, with that one word releasing tears from his friend's clenched eyelids.

"Glad you came back..." Sel whispered from the bottom of his heart.

All other thoughts vanished into darkness where they came from. There was never a place for them here.

Then he felt a different touch. Ross hugged them both first. However, quickly driven by a passionate feeling, he pulled Sel from his shoulders, then hugged Sel tightly until he groaned. He didn't say anything. His eyes full of tears, his gestures full of emotions did it for him. Vivan could sense his friend's quiet despair of concern. By drawing the attention of King Azram's gloomy adviser to himself, he made the latter not hesitate to harm Sel by making him a puppet in his hands. It burst into his soul again. At that moment, Ross began to wonder how much longer they would be able to endure rough handling. Which of them will eventually find that he cannot take anymore?

What will happen to the baby then?

The girl became close to him, through the dark beginning of their acquaintance, until now. Always ready to side with him. She reciprocated her devotion to him from a sincere heart in which falsehood and hypocrisy could never really warm up the room. The child's fate made him uneasy, the only feeling that could influence his decision. It was this decision that tied the lives of all three, maybe even four, if it was possible to mention the girl whose kiss was disturbing her senses.

Ross's eyes met his.

Vivan now understood that a decision could be made.

He wasn't sure if he would ever be able to take it.

"Sel," he looked into his friend's eyes, in the falling darkness of the coming night, "Tell me."

"He handed me my coffee," Sel began anxiously. "He just handed me the fucking coffee!"

"Who?" Ross tried to stay calm. He was hugging a very quiet little girl.

Sel felt sad about it. The child has been through a lot. He was making contact with her slowly, and now they were back to square one.

The little one may never pull herself together. Even with the help of a healer.

She didn't trust him anymore...

"It was..." he began.

A scream interrupted them at the same moment.

They rushed out of the cabin immediately with a premonition that what they were about to see was certainly related to Sel's possession.

They were not wrong.

On deck, surrounded by a group of sailors and women, was Silas. His hand was on his favorite knife, now at his throat. Until now, this small, inconspicuous knife had been an object he loved to play with from time to time. Now he was an instrument of death.

Silas's eyes were wide. Shifting like madman's eyes. It was as if he did not believe what had just happened to him.

Another puppet...

"At last!" He exclaimed with obvious satisfaction at the sight of all four, then quickly slit his throat.

CHAPTER 35

One of the women screamed in fear. Confusion broke out immediately. The chorus of voices caused a noise filled with emotions. People started to panic. The sailors began to look for their amulets or mumble prayers in the tongues of their ancestors to ward off evil spirits. Vivan walked between the people before they tightened the circle around the wounded man. Someone had tried in vain to stop the blood from the throbbing wound with a dirty bandana. Vivan touched the worried sailor, ready to help his colleague. He gently directed him to lay the wounded man down on the planks of the deck. At this point, all the noise stopped...

The whole scene was watched in silence, observing every movement of the healer who, accustomed to such attention, focused on the necessary activities. For Vivan, everything else didn't matter at the moment. He knew perfectly well that this was not the time to panic. There was no time for any other unnecessary words and gestures. Only quick action could save the fatally wounded victim of King Azram's evil adviser.

He cupped his hand around the wounded man's neck, in the place of the ever-weaker throbbing cut. Ignoring the blood, he spoke gently to him, forcing him to be calm and patient, as if it were only a temporary ailment.

The blood stopped flowing after a while. Then the wound began to close, and a chill enveloped the damaged muscles, relieving the pain at the same time. The wounded man calmed down as his eyes widened as they gazed at the healer now. This continued until Vivan joined all the tissues together, leaving a barely visible scar on his neck.

"Vivan!" Croaked Silas, excitedly, clutching the healer so tightly that he for a moment lost his ability to breathe.

He seized him with tears in his eyes, terrified and at the same time so relieved that he could not pronounce any more words without nervous sobbing.

Vivan returned the hug as he heard the crowd cheering around him. He couldn't celebrate at that moment. It was not a victory. It was merely a skirmish won. Although it meant much, much more to Silas. For him as a healer too, but he knew that was only the beginning. A terrifying beginning. And as the crowd rejoiced at the miracle they witnessed, he was already thinking of the victims he might no longer help, in the name of fighting the power of darkness... Did these people realize what was going to happen?

He sincerely doubted it.

"I didn't even know what was going on..." Silas was sobbing, which itself was a shock to many. He wasn't the type of man to lose his temper. "She made coffee; I gave it to Sel... I didn't know it was inside me! Captain!" He turned desperately to the pale Ross "I'm sorry! I didn't know! I didn't know anything!"

Ross was standing between two of his dearest friends in the world. Silas's words reminded him, however, that someone in this group was missing...

"Who…?" He asked hoarsely, his voice full of tension. "Who made the coffee, Silas?"

There was a silence, filled with a tension that made the blood pulsate in the temples.

Vivan, overcome with a bad feeling, buried his face in the arm of the man he had saved.

Silas swallowed nervously.

"Anokhi, Captain," he replied hollowly.

Suddenly they heard a shrill scream.

"Anokhi!" Her sister's voice echoed in the silence like a thunderclap. "No! Please don't do this!"

Anokhi stood on the railing.

Naked.

Wounds adorned her body, and the wind whipped her hair. She begged for help with her eyes.

The noose tied to the railing left no illusions.

Vivan sprang up abruptly before she let out a sigh of muffled sobbing. In a hurry he made his way towards her, among the surprised people.

When she jumped, he was no longer alone.

Two sailors and the woman who had screamed before seized the rope and the falling body.

Then it happened...

Black smoke filled her eyes. She screamed inhumanly, hitting blindly, like a puppet pulled by strings. Her strength was so great that she pushed her saviors away. The beautiful Apara will never dance again. She broke her spine and smashed her skull.

Two devoted to Ross sailors who was helping her, shared her fate. One broke his neck, hitting the railing ahead before he fell overboard. The other, Anokhi broke his ribs and crushed the heart with one blow.

She fell overboard moments later. The smoke vanished like a memory of a nightmare.

Vivan grabbed the rope. He knew the pull was strong, so the odds were weak. Several willing hands helped him.

Together, they put the body up aboard.

He put a hand under her neck, focused only on helping her.

But it was too late.

Death took her away immediately, with a sharp tug on the rope.

Anokhi was already dead when they dragged her in.

And he couldn't bring anyone back.

Heal, yes, but not resurrect...

"Do something!" Ross shouted, shaking him in the silence. "Why are you doing nothing?! Save her!"

Vivan was silent, letting his grief and despair mixed with anger focus on him. Ross pushed him angrily, eyes full of tears, hating him now for his stubbornness in refusing to help.

"She didn't do anything!" He shouted furiously at him. "She was under his influence!"

Vivan was still silent without looking at him. He hated that moment forever. It happened, not very often, but still that he did not have time to help. He then let his loved ones pour out their anger on him, because he believed that he was rightly entitled to him. He should have helped, and he didn't make it.

He deserved this rage.

He let them scream over him. They cried.

They made words for which they apologized more than once, although he did not count on it.

He should be able to resurrect.

For why was he a healer who couldn't do it?

"Maybe you don't know yet that you can?" Ross suddenly asked. "Have you ever tried? Whenever?"

"Ross…" Vivan heard his mother's warning voice.

He had tried before… He remembered it well.

"At least try..." Ross began pleadingly, taking the girl in his arms. "Please..."

He looked at him apprehensive. He had reason to be afraid.

"No!" Mother cried, "Vivan, I forbid you!"

Mother certainly wasn't as scared as she is now in a long time. He could feel her fear. Everyone around heard it. The order sounded hard, but it lacked a sense of authority. She knew the final decision was up to him. Always been like that.

He could try...

There was a shadow of a chance it wouldn't be this time. After all, he only tried once...

It was within a few minutes of Ross's pleading plea. But Vivan knew that time was of the essence. He placed a hand on Anokhi's shoulder, causing great agitation among the people accompanying them. Ross looked for the girl standing by Lena's side. The little girl did not trust Sel. It was perfectly understandable, though evidently Sel hated it.

Vivan would rather be somewhere else now. In the palace. At his house on the edge of town. Not here, not now at least. But Ross was waiting for his help so much! He hated to say no. He almost never did.

He felt the body lying in front of him. It was completely lifeless. To bring them to life, it wasn't enough just to make the heart beat. He had to do several things at once, and it took a lot of effort. He heard a soft murmur as the crowd saw the green glow of his gift spread slowly from his head to his entire body.

Mind...

He did all the activities. He stopped the cells from dying. He woke up the heart. He warmed the blood a little, giving it its former fluidity. He moved stiffening muscles and joints. He sent the wave to the nerves (thanks to the books sent by his father, he knew the names of many elements of the human body, and he knew anatomy better than any doctor in the kingdom of Tenchryz and probably beyond). Like a lightning strike, he shook them, ordering them to take up their recent work. He repaired the damaged spine with a loud bang that made Ross and many others jump nervously. At last, he reached the head... the vapors of dying thoughts, the last impressions. The link between what was still here and what was already THERE...

The last images still played back, depicting life and the choices made.

But when he tried to grab them like thread...

In one moment, he realized that he had made a serious mistake. Anokhi is gone. These were merely memories. Her soul was no longer here, and he was trying to revive the corpse...

He turned pale as the dead body began to suck energy from him, hoping to prevent his annihilation. The abrupt end of life interrupted the processes it wanted to continue. The fear of death was preserved not only in the dying mind, but also permeated the memory of the whole body.

He felt the pain.

Growing pain, greater than with the attack of the witch who once wanted to suck his blood. This body wanted to suck the life out of him in order to survive on its own!

Within a moment, he began to scream in anguish, breaking contact immediately. But he did it a moment too late... The body moved like the torso of a hen whose head had suddenly been severed. It shuddered violently. The eyes widened. A rattling sounded from the mouth.

Ross hid the baby's head in his arms, staring in horror at the macabre spectacle. Lena ran to her son, who fell on the deck in a spasm of pain.

"Cora!" she said quickly. "Give me some gag! He's about to get an attack!"

Vivan felt foam in his mouth, making it difficult to breathe. He felt the gag given by Cora with a firm hand.

"Hold on!" She commanded at the same time and asked, studying his face with concern.

He looked into her beautiful eyes, framed by thick lashes. He wanted to grant her request, but all he could do was hold back from further screams, which tired him faster.

He knew something was going on, something wrong, because he caught a glimpse of the frightened glances of Ross and those around them. His mother asked them to leave, and they immediately agreed to allow him access to air. Cora released her hand from his grip, too tight, he could feel it. He almost crushed her hand. The world began to tremble. Lightning bolts pierced his eyes. The voices came chaotically and as if from a distance. Only her gaze, her voice was his salvation. He clung to it as tightly as she and her mother held him down during the attack.

Until finally the world calmed down.

He felt himself weakening. He still felt the pain, but he couldn't scream. He was exhausted. He felt drowsy, as if he was floating somewhere deep.

"Vivan!" He heard her voice. "Not yet, don't fall asleep! Look at me!"

He forced himself to obey with a great effort.

"Drink it!" She gave him, patiently waiting for him to drink, though he thought it would take forever. "Does it still hurt?"

"Yes..." It was even hard for him to open his mouth.

She smiled slightly at him, perhaps for the first time. Each of her smile was the first and unique for him. This one was sincere, full of genuine compassion, caring, with only a hint of great responsibility when she wanted to remember who she was handling.

It was more important to her that he survived. And he didn't suffer anymore.

"Cora..." he pronounced her name, feeling the benevolent warmth of self-healing suddenly spread over him.

They both wanted the best for him. At that moment, however, her kindness was more important to him.

"Oh, Vivan, just don't start," she muttered, glancing at Lena. She set a tone of mock resentment in her voice, not feeling it at all. "Rest! We're in Ross's cabin!"

So, he was transferred in the meantime… He didn't even know it.

"Don't let me go... I want to see you again..." he whispered, closing his eyes to doze off.

He saw her surprise before he lost consciousness.

CHAPTER 36

He opened his eyes slowly.

First, he saw his mother. She was holding his hand as she sat in a chair that wasn't too comfortable. Her head tilted slightly during her nap. He felt tears welling up. Poor woman, she must have been with him for quite a long time. It was definitely uncomfortable for her. Her back was already feeling the effects of sitting in a chair without any comfortable support. He decided to get up and gently persuade her to rest next to him.

As it used to be, then when he was recovering from terrible ordeals in the marketplace, when attempts were made to tear him alive.

He felt a great need for someone to hug him.

He was unable to make any move.

He felt dizzy. As if a pillow had been put on his head. Very exhausted. He held his eyelids open with difficulty.

"Hey," he saw Cora again, just like he had dreamed of.

But now he could barely look at her.

She held the candle close to him, carefully examining the pupils. She touched his forehead. She grabbed his wrist, counting softly. Finally, she cursed under her breath, frowning in obvious concern.

"I have to listen!" She said quickly.

Unexpectedly, with quick movements, she unbuttoned a few buttons on his shirt, in great haste. He wanted to protest, but could not. The last thing he wanted was to show himself scarred as if an animal had torn him apart.

As it happened to him more than once, she, too, froze upon seeing them. She looked at him quickly, eyes full of warmth. It completely baffled him. She had treated him so far as an intruder, stepping into her intimacy with boots. Suddenly, the sight of such a scarred body made her concerned. Her eyes softened for good, as if those moments when they argued over an unborn child had never happened.

She laid her head against his chest, listening to his heart beat rapidly under the influence of emotion. Her hair looked soft.

They smelled with a delicate hint of herbs, which reminded him of a meadow before the evening in his home region.

Its warmth soothed the pain.

"Try to breathe normally," she ordered him, setting her voice in the tone of a medic, but the trembling revealed that she was feeling some emotions as well.

Cora felt the almost legendary warmth of a healer. But her thoughts weren't just about the nature of his gift. Vivan's rapidly beating heart certainly wasn't desperately trying to keep his exhausted body alive. However, this will happen if he allows to continue succumbing to emotions that are dangerous for him.

He tried. For two reasons it was now more difficult than it seemed.

"Don't be childish!" She growled. "Are you fifteen? Be warned that if I feel, if only by accident, something in the area of your pants, you will be screwed!"

"I feel pain everywhere..." he remarked softly. "I wouldn't count on it," he added with a hint of sarcasm.

She hurt his feelings. She cursed silently.

"Your heart is strong," she noticed getting up. "You'll stand on your feet. In a moment I will put my ointment on you in several places, give you a potion that I developed with my father. It will definitely help you. It's never failed before," she said quickly, trying to hide the nervousness under his gaze.

His touch was so soothing...

"Focus!" She ordered herself firmly, "He needs your help!"

A treacherous tear ran down Vivan's gaunt cheek as he tried his best to hold on. All he wanted the pain to go away was her loving touch. But he knew the reasons for her reluctance perfectly well.

They would be remembered forever.

"One moment..." she asked, taking what she was talking about from her bag. "I had to do everything all over again. Fortunately, I remember the recipes," she said with a slight smile of pride. "These are the things I use the most! There is a lot of pain in the world..." she added thoughtfully. "Where does it hurt the most?" She shook herself hurriedly, waiting for his reply.

"Here," hand of Lena, who had awakened from her nap a moment earlier, wandered towards her son's beating heart without hesitation. "You should start with this." And when Cora looked at her uncertainly, she added, "Yes. That's it. That's where you should start. From concern. Compassion... A little warmth, not professionalism..."

"Mom..." he asked softly, but Lena kept talking.

"My son is very sensitive..."

"Please stop!" He tried to say it louder, though it was not easy.

She fell silent as he wished, looking at him warmly.

"But..." Cora didn't really understand. Was she supposed to handle with him like a child?! He's a grown man! Yes, he is very broken, but...

Lena sat down on the edge of the bed. She kissed her son on the forehead with concern.

Vivan closed his eyes, feeling the soothing effect of a mother's concern. The pain is gone. The relief was almost overwhelming. And perfectly visible to both women.

"It's impossible..." Cora whispered, watching his condition improve.

Lena smiled understandingly. Vivan wanted to collapse into the ground. He has always felt uncomfortable when people discover what works best for him.

Fortunately, he was saved from his embarrassing situation by a vigorous knocking on the door.

"Open it!" He heard Ross's emphatic voice from behind them, "I won't be dismissed this time!"

"Oh, Mother Earth!" Cora sighed heavily, looking at Lena with irritation, "He comes here for the tenth time!"

"Let him in at last!" Lena smiled. "He certainly feels that Vivan is awake already."

"I told you," Cora began, opening the door, "that Vivan needs peace! Take care of the girl..."

"She's with the women!" He interrupted her firmly, "They'll come tell me if she needs me!"

"So, take care of Sel!"

"I gave you the entire captain's cabin!" he noted. "It is rather difficult to find intimacy below the deck!" He smiled slightly, reaching with satisfaction for words that had their sources in his past.

"No, it..."

"Cora..." he interrupted, significantly lowering his tone. "Don't make me act like a captain on my own ship!"

"I'm not your subordinate!" she interrupted him sharply. "And in matters of the sick and the wounded, I decide what and when can be!"

They looked at each other angrily. Vivan finally decided to stop this discussion. He didn't want their quarrel.

Cora could be firm, he had to admit it. Who knows how long she had been chasing Ross from his own cabin.

"Let him in," he said softly.

She reluctantly relented, glancing askance at Ross, who only smiled smugly as he passed her quickly.

Before Vivan could greet him, Ross lifted him a little and hugged him tightly, putting all his concern, almost brotherly affection, his fear for him and tremendous guilt all in one.

"I'm sorry..." he whispered in his ear, trembling with emotion.

Vivan could smell his sweat, which he didn't mind at all now. Ross had not washed and changed from the events on board, too worried about what had happened, as well as his duties to his relatives and crew. It was unusual for him, but so understandable at the moment. He always put the welfare of others above his own.

"I wish I had succeeded," he replied, suppressing his tears, "You did so much for me, and I couldn't help you..."

"You could have died trying, silly," Ross smiled fondly, pushing him away a little. "Don't let me ask you to do this again. Never."

Vivan looked at his tired face, the shadows under his eyes glistening as if in fever. Ross was barely standing again. Even so, he came to give all the love of his best friend, knowing full well that this was what would do the best.

He was right. Vivan was now able to move and sit up on his own. He knew he would slowly come out of it.

"How long did I sleep?" He asked.

"All day," Lena replied. "And all night. It's just dawn."

Ross did not lie down during this time for even a moment. Vivan had felt the path of his emotions over the last few hours. Funeral of the murdered. Despair for Anokhi and sorrow for her sister. Moving words about two devoted sailors who died bravely trying to save the endangered woman. Tender care for a girl who needed him like the father he was becoming for her. A love for Sel, devoid of prejudices, which he soothed his needlessly remorseful lover. Friendly care for the rescued Silas. Instructions for the crew. Conversation with women. A constant fear for him lying in his cabin, pale and exhausted. Excruciating guilt and despair when Cora wouldn't let him in. Nevertheless, he had control of himself. He wasn't alone here, and everyone needed him. Precautions taken. Conversations with Violet and Paphian who came to the ship after seeing the funeral. Fear of the unknown...

He needed it. Only together can they stand against this disgusting advisor to the king, who turned out to be more formidable than he himself.

Vivan placed a hand on his friend's face, surprising him with the gesture.

"You can rest," he said, smiling slightly. "I'm here."

There was no trace of a priestly tone, no divine superiority in his gentle voice.

Ross tried to protest but was unable to. By the power of his gift, Vivan made him feel overwhelmed almost immediately. He only guessed that it was because of his friend, who wishes him the best. He felt relieved to lay down next to him, no longer thinking about anything. He saw nothing inappropriate about it, or even had time to think whether he should think so. He was safe here. Just that, as well as the memory of his touch as he touched his face as if he were a child, was important to him now. He trusted him immensely.

Cora felt emotion tighten in the throat. She had never expected to witness similar events one day.

Or that she will know the effect of the healer's gift...

She was beginning to understand why Ross and so many people around him, including her father, had a genuine, almost reverent respect for Vivan.

To limit this to the description that these people were willing to give their lives for him because he was willing to give his without hesitation would be a great understatement.

These people and Vivan had an unbreakable bond. Without them, he wouldn't have recovered so quickly, and they knew they could always rely on him.

Was she also under the spell of this bond? Her dislike of the unborn child paled visibly. Ever since Ross was found, and then like a priest, giving everyone the blessing that Vivan stood for (otherwise his actions could not be called), she caught herself thinking about the baby as her baby, just as Vivan said. About what it will be like.

Rape had already been thought of as a terrible experience in the distant past that would not break her. She will not allow it to affect her further fate! She pushed them into a corner, ready for a new tomorrow. It makes her stronger, tougher, but not devoid of feelings.

So, when Vivan looked at her while her mother covered Ross with a blanket, she remembered that he almost felt it as if he were there. In her place. But did she feel sorry for him, or did she still reprimand him angrily for invading her secrets, even if he was against himself?

He actually paid a cruel price for it...

"I'll tell the cook to prepare you broth. He should be awake by now," she remarked hastily, trying to sound like a medic at all costs.

How was it possible that this man had upset her so much?! Her mind analyzed all their meetings, reaching unbelievable conclusions. It was impossible. There are no people like him and all these people here are trying to portray him. You can't be like...

He looked at her with the blue of his eyes, which they had seen a lot. As if his gaze penetrated through.

"What is it about?" She asked, stopping yet. "You wanted to see me again. Have you not seen enough?"

He did not answer. So she approached him, gazing defiantly into the blue depths.

"Thank you," he said softly.

He knew what she was thinking thanks to his gift of compassion and observation. She wondered if the nightmarish incident belonged to him or if she should sympathize with him.

He sensed a hesitation between resentment and sympathy.

Sometimes he would like to know less.

Why has this changed?

"I was sure you would handle it," she suddenly confessed, surprised by her own sincerity, "She looked as if she was starting to wake up."

"She has already been too far..." he whispered, trembling at the mere memory.

She sat down beside him. Lena sat quietly on the other side, waiting for the question she probably wanted to ask him herself.

"Did you know that? And yet you tried to revive her?!"

He considered the answer.

"If it was about your father..." he began softly, as if afraid of returning to those experiences. "Wouldn't you try?"

She mentally agreed with him, looking at it from the point of view of both daughter and the medic. She wouldn't hesitate for a moment.

"You'll kill yourself someday," she warned him, softening the words with the warmth in her voice. "You can't take that risk. Apparently," she looked at Lena and Ross asleep, "a lot of people care about you. Don't make them look at your suffering."

She touched his shoulder lightly in a gesture of understanding.

As she closed the door, she thought maybe she was wrong after all.

Maybe this man is as she has heard of him.

That would mean he really is unique. There was only one other man apart from him who displayed a similar sensitivity, though he did not have his gift in him.

It was Vivan, if the rumors were to be believed, who by chance had put his life in a completely different course when the Jewel of Hope came into his possession.

The healer's influence made huge circles.

Larger than even he had expected.

Maybe, with the emphasis on this word, she should look at him differently?

She hadn't realized she had been doing this for a long time.

CHAPTER 37

In the afternoon, while Vivan was still recovering slowly, many people passed through the captain's cabin. Cora let them in after dinner (she didn't even give in to Sel, who absolutely wanted to see how Ross was doing), one by one, as if everyone interested had to wait for an audience. First came a girl who did not want to reveal her name to anyone. She stayed. So was Sel. Victor stayed until evening, talking to his grandson for a long time, and when Ross woke up, the discussion turned to possible future action plans. Meanwhile, Silas appeared to thank the healer for saving his life. And Daryenne, who just burst in to see a healer.

Sel pointed out to everyone that the action of the king's advisor had fortunately resulted in only a few casualties. Dark smoke passed from one person to the next as if it were looking for a host. Fortunately, something was holding him back, because from Anokhi's behavior it could be seen that the dark smoke endowed its victims with superhuman strength.

"It was a show," said Victor bluntly. "I've such power, I can trick you. You don't know the day or time when he'll attack."

Vivan mentally agreed with him.

"He's going to hit again," said Violet, who appeared for the debate, "The only question is: do we want to wait passively?"

"What do you suggest?" Asked Paphian with nervous impatience. "Attack the Bay?"

"This is crazy!" Lena asked, looking for support in the eyes of her father.

An argument ensued, and Ross perched imperceptibly on the edge of the bed.

Vivan looked him up and down.

He sensed Ross was guessing as well. They were to face the king and his adviser. All they had to do was find a way to do it on their own terms. It was madness to go to a place full of demons and troops. Attack this place even with the help of the crews of two ships - murdering people devoted to them.

No good solution was found that day. It was hard to blame anyone for this. Rather, there was no good plan that did not require sacrifice.

In the evening, Cora kindly asked everyone to leave, except for Ross's loved ones. Vivan was too tired to argue that night. Though he hadn't complained a word all day, she could see it in his movements and eyes.

Ross was looking much better, but he also needed some rest. He put the girl to sleep on a makeshift bedding, asking Cora to accompany her. At first, she wanted to say no. She wanted to stay awake, but the previously sleepless night made itself felt and finally she was overwhelmed by sleep.

Lena returned to her cabin, calm about the fate of her extraordinary son.

Sel fell asleep in one of the armchairs Ross and he had kept here, seeing that the two friends wanted to be left alone.

At last, there was a silence, broken only by the breaths of the sleepers, occasionally making themselves heard from the conversations of the guard that Tenan had arranged between the seamen. Whenever Ross was unable to carry out his captaincy duties, Tenan undertook them without hesitation, with a natural ease that showed a strong sense of duty.

The ship could not be left unattended. After all, there were now two of the most precious to the wicked king on board.

Tenan, unfortunately, did not know well enough to sail with Ross.

Each of them had a trait that could bring misfortune under favorable circumstances for the enemy...

"What are we really doing?" Ross asked softly.

He was going to ask this question hours ago. But they both knew that the people with them might not like the answer.

Vivan looked at him warmly.

"We have to be ready for anything," he replied grimly certain.

"Yes…" whispered Ross. "We have to."

There was silence. They remembered all the bad things that had happened to them so far. These were not comforting memories. They carried the fear of the unknown.

"Cora caught your eye?" He asked after a moment without a trace of a smile.

Vivan was silent. He sensed Cora was awake. She listened for his answers now. Considering the increasingly painful memories of Vashaba, he preferred not to answer this question. He also knew what the friend was up to.

"If she finds out you love someone..." Ross began warningly.

"Yes. I know!" He cut him off sharply, wanting to end this conversation.

Ross pondered his and Sel's fate for a moment. Their uncertain, dangerous future.

"I should have told him to take the little one and go back to Leviron," he said quietly, glancing at them both with concern.

"He won't listen to you..."

Ross suppressed a sigh.

"Cora is pregnant..." he pointed out. "Do you have any idea what they can do to her to hurt you?"

"I wouldn't worry about that," Vivan replied, trying to smile a little. "She hates me. With one touch, I discovered her most painful secret and burned all chances. You don't have to worry."

It was not entirely true. He sensed agitation in Cora's mood. For a moment she hesitated to correct his remarks, but gave it up. Vivan met

Ross's eyes, knowing his friend didn't quite know his thoughts. Being close, they rarely linked their minds. Then he would discover that he had deceived him a bit. Cora thought that the healer didn't always read moods perfectly. He preferred her to see it that way. As she talked to him, she kept trying to judge what he really could do. It was frustrating. But he wasn't surprised she wanted to find out. He had come across such a reaction often.

"I'm afraid of what we might find there," Ross looked away, "He murdered innocent people. I mean the king," he reminded him, "And that one? We do not know his possibilities..."

"Mayene told you," Vivan lowered his voice, "that you are powerful. I believe her."

Ross flinched at the name of the witch who had nearly killed them.

"I have no idea what that means," he replied uncertainly.

"We'll see."

"And your blue power?"

"It'll destroy me when I use it," Vivan explained firmly. "I'd rather do it as a last resort. You may need me."

Ross looked at him in a particular way that disturbed him when he saw him exchanging that look with Sel.

Ready for anything.

"Don't think about how to die," he told him. "Think about what you can do. Die - this is the easiest thing to do. We all face such a fate sooner or later."

Ross smiled slightly.

"I think I know how to start," he replied.

Ross looked at the polished dials that were to act as mirrors according Sel. It was basically their joint idea, based on books found in the Beckert library. Sel insisted on having them mounted on a ship, saying they would be used.

He was right.

Ross decided to use them, using his power to do so.

"We have to protect our own," he explained to the Jewel, "let's make use of them."

He touched the ropes and the lever of the steering mechanism that helped to angle them to catch the light. Several of the sentries on board and the steersman looked at it curiously.

"Let the glow illuminate the dark when all the lights fail," he ordered softly.

The jewel glowed with a warm red glow, helping him in doing so. It was about the protection the sorcerer cared for. This desire was from the bottom of his heart.

"I wish they would be safe on board, at least. Aside from him as well…" Ross explained softly to him as the red glow flowed down the ropes to the attached shields. It spread slowly over their surface, gradually revealing a bright glow flowing from within by magic.

Everyone was watching the extraordinary spectacle begin.

It turned out to be fatal.

Vivan was right. Besheram continued with ideas, avoiding those that didn't work for him. Demons not only had wings; they could also hide in the depths of the water…

A dark, unnamed force sent them from the fortress on the top of the city straight into the depths, terrifying the sea monsters and the gentle people of the sea.

Hiding from the eyes of people, both from the pirate ship and Valeria, they waited for the right moment…

The first attack was only meant to cause fear. Inside the bottle was the power of a grim adviser. The dark creature seized the opportunity. She crept in the shadows of the coming night to pour a grim will into the ear of the thoughtful girl, which told her to take the coffee prepared by the cook. She handed one to Silas, asking him to take the other to Sel, and as he looked into her eyes with curiosity, the dark smoke from her fingers mixed with the dark drink, hiding inside him. It muddled the minds of its victims. He penetrated the body and soul of the girl, enjoying her fear. He gave her no chance.

Now the beings had a new task.

They barely resembled humans because they had no faces. No eyes, mouth, nose or even ears. No sign of human emotion. Black as night, they blended with her, almost invisible to the human eye.

There were quite a few of them, submerged by the hull of the ship. One was on its mission again, but this time the others waited for a sign to launch an attack.

When Ross activated his magic, they realized they had to hurry. There will be no more opportunities later. The glow was shocking to them. They backed away in fear, waiting for this one, hiding in the fading darkness around the ship as the glow of their shields grew.

This time, the creature opened a vial right behind one of the sentries. She opened her mouth, blowing the smoke straight into the back of his head, and as it disappeared inside her, she backed away hurriedly.

The glow caused a faint stir among those who had not yet slept.

Oliver stroked the sleeping wife. Day by day she seemed to him more and more beautiful, as if it was illuminated by an inner glow. Since talking to Lena, her well-being has improved. She stopped suffering from this terrible nausea.

He loved her.

Every day he was grateful to fate for finally giving him a chance. Thanks to Vivan, he could finally have a world of his own. Thanks to Ross, his life began anew.

His only regret was that his sister was not so lucky.

He still missed her, but told no one about it.

Suddenly he felt he couldn't just go on deck to see what his brother was doing there by accident. As if he had a feeling that he had to do something this time. He could not leave Sai without saying a word.

He accepted this state of affairs.

"Sai," he said softly, "thank you for each day. I love you."

As he left the cabin, he wondered why he had used these words.

But he felt they were right, so he quickly dispelled his gloomy thoughts when he saw Ross's handiwork.

"You can not sleep?" He asked playfully.

Ross turned to face him. His white hair gleamed like the whitest snow in the rising glare of his shields. The jewel, in turn, shone with a glow of soft red.

He wanted to ask him what the idea was with the shields. What is it for? It was then, right behind him, that he saw a dark figure fled from the glare into the dying shadows of the deck.

The mere sight of it made the hairs on the back of his neck rise, and an unnamed fear seized his heart, almost taking his breath away and extinguishing a smile on his face.

Then the creature swung to throw. Oliver saw the harpoon gleam in the glare of the shields. In the blink of an eye, he realized that Ross was the target.

Without hesitating, he ran towards him...

Vivan was resting. Ross had warned him of his actions, so the rising glare did not bother him. On the contrary. Thanks to him, and thanks to his friend's soothing gift, the night promised to be peaceful. When he falls asleep, he will not be haunted by nightmares from the past. Eventually Ross was able to calm him down. Vivan blessed the work of the Jewel, which, among other things, went in this direction.

Troublemaker of Thoughts? Possible... But not only.

The warm glow of the shields illuminated the faces of the sleepers. A little girl with no name was sleeping cuddled up to Cora. Sel was snoring softly in his chair, covering his eyes with his usual neck scarf, which was changed every morning.

He stood up slowly, frustrated by the thought of the toddler and pregnant woman sleeping on the floor while he lounging in bed. He wasn't going to listen to Cora's instructions. This behavior was against his nature.

He approached the girl carefully. In a gentle tone, he explained what he was doing to keep her from getting scared. The little girl confidently cuddled up to him. He felt joy fluttering like a scared butterfly in his heart. So familiar and close when he helped children. No blue was his gift. It was always this one. The essence of his existence...

He put her on the bed, gently covered her with the duvet. Then he went back for Cora to lie down as well. Yes, he used his gift to make her sleepier, but he was afraid she would try to protest.

Cora allowed herself to be picked up. He had planned it differently at first, but she was really tired. He had to try.

He carefully picked her up.

He felt his heart begin to beat hard, and it wasn't because he was making more effort. Frightened that she would scold him for this maneuver or maybe even slap him in the face again, he carried her slowly, which made him feel it would take forever.

But it was okay.

Her head was resting on him. He could feel the warmth of her body through the layers of clothes. The smell of her hair and the scent of the soap she used was intoxicating. He had never felt so safe, as good as now, when he held her in his arms. She opened her eyes, feeling someone touch her. Her first instinct was to defend herself.

"What are you doing?!" She asked fiercely, fighting the weariness at the same time.

If he answered honestly, it would not sound very good.

"Quiet!" He ordered, but in a voice so saturated with tenderness he had not expected of himself.

He saw a flash of surprise in her eyes as he laid her down on the bed next to the sleeping child. He covered her with the duvet, feeling his cheeks begin to burn under her gaze. He looked up...

Their eyes met for a moment. Between one breath and the next...

He endured it. He bowed slightly to say goodbye. There was only one thing left for him. But it was better not to think about it...

He encouraged Sel, who was still sleeping, to take some of the available bed, then finally lay down nearby.

He couldn't calm his heart.

It all took perhaps a few moments as the warm glow of the shields grew. Even when he heard voices outside the door, he was still torn by emotions.

He closed his eyes slowly, calming the storm in his heart...

Someone burst into the cabin shouting his name. One of the sailors on watch that night. Ramon, it was probably his name. It wasn't important, but his words. Oliver hurt. Something's going on with the captain.

He jumped up from the bed. Sel ran right after him, he knew that.

The next moment Ramon grabbed his shoulders. He squeezed it until it hurt, then pushed it against the railing. Surprised by this incident, he looked into his eyes, wanting to ask what he was doing.

The sailor's eyes turned black, dark and gloomy, like magic that changed them...

The next moment the man grabbed him and threw him overboard.

He felt hands grab him.

Lots of black hands and eyesless figures.

The immense fear he had held so far, the one that had settled in him after attempts were made to tear him alive in the capital's marketplace, now awoke, taking his breath away.

He was drawn into the depths of the waters...

CHAPTER 38

Ross saw Oliver's expression changing. Instantly he changed from delight to fear. There wasn't enough time. Oliver found himself beside him, taking a harpoon blow.

It's a miracle he didn't kill them both at once.

He pierced him right through. Ross only managed to catch him when he felt he was going to pass out. The world began to spin. He sat down heavily with him, numb as he saw the blood pouring out of his mouth.

"I'm sorry..." Oliver croaked with difficulty. "I didn't think... Poor Vivan..."

Strange, he, too, thought at first about Vivan, who would be left alone with it all...

Maybe because he and Sel had been thinking about a similar situation for a long time? They talked about it during the long nights, when they captured and destroyed the city that fed on the suffering of the enslaved. He hadn't thought of Sel first. But that didn't mean he didn't care.

He felt his arms around him. A feverish whisper against his ear as the pain grew and senses went mad with the sensations. Something about everything going to be okay soon.

He forced himself to look at him.

The strange, ghastly faceless creature stopped his gaze. In a panic, it avoided the glare of the mirror, which, thanks to it, searched for the source of the darkness with the power of magic, to which it had tuned it. The being fled, dragging one of its sailors, Ramon, with it.

Overboard he heard his painful scream. Ross imagined a sea of formidable creatures tearing the unfortunate man to shreds.

He saw it for a moment. The picture was as frightening as if he was looking at it with someone else's gaze, though it was impossible. Vivan was...

Sel tugged at the chain, pulling off the little vial of blood, then pouring the contents into Oliver's mouth. Ross would like to stop him. After all, Vivan was on board, he'll help them soon! But Sel was trembling as if he had suddenly taken a fever. Ross felt a dread engulf him. With his free hand, his lover stroked his head and face, and then he felt wet. Sel was crying. He wiped the flowing tears with that hand, guarding both of them while the world around him plunged into chaos.

"Oliver," he said, his voice shaky with muffled sobs.

Ross felt everything more intensely with each passing moment. He could see quite clearly now what was happening around him. They were still on board. Sel held him in his arms as he sat on the planks. Sai was kneeling next to him, supporting Oliver, who was slowly recovering. She was calm about his fate, though her eyes expressed sadness. She looked at Ross, glad he was also alright. There were already others on board. Cora and the girl were standing nearby. Ross waved the little girl over to him, unable to speak yet. She clung to him, scared like a little bird, and he suddenly feared whether her little heart would endure so much fear and whether he had done the right thing to take her under his care.

He saw Lena over the shoulder of the child.

In the blink of an eye, fear seized him.

Lena stood, hiding her face in Victor's arm, who had aged strangely.

Oliver stood up as soon as he felt completely healed. He embraced Sai without saying a word.

He didn't notice - Ross was sure of it.

He saw no movement in the people's faces. A sailor who swore that what he saw was true, surrounded by a wreath of listeners. Tenan, who had looked overboard first, with a sincere look of regret on his face. Women whispering to each other in fear.

He did not know that the one and only person was missing among them.

"It happened so suddenly…" Sel said softly.

As if at a signal given to them, everyone fell silent. There was a tense silence.

"I had to choose: him or you," he almost whispered, looking at Ross. "I ran over to you. I left him…"

First, they grabbed him with a tangle of hands and bodies. Then they dragged them under the water. It crossed his mind that this time it was over. He will die right next to Ross's ship. Fear poured into his heart. The dark beings held him for a long time until he began to choke. Then they as if they remembered that he was a human, so they kindly pulled him out of the depths to dive him back into cruel joke in a moment. They tugged at him, tearing his clothes. They prodded painfully. If he survived this, he knew he would be battered. Apparently, that was the plan. Everything that happened on the way to the Bay was to distract him, weaken him. He had no chance of taking any action. It was too much like the events of the marketplace. He was torn by a wild fear that they eagerly fueled.

Lots of hands that touched him everywhere on the body tried to shut his mouth. They sucked him into the darkness where he couldn't even breathe.

He was thinking of nothing but survival, though it became more and more difficult with each passing moment. He was out of breath. He was dizzy. Plus, those pushy hands, touching the most intimate parts of his body. Even wearing clothes did not protect him.

They dragged him ashore, where he saw out of the corner of his eye that they were almost in the Bay. There, the beings dragged him into the darkness. Through the canals in which he could barely fit with them, dark alleys, empty spaces... Where they happened to meet people, they aroused fear and the desire to run away. He couldn't ask for help. Whores, sailors, thieves, fishermen... They all ran away from them in panic, not looking back.

The beings held him in an embrace. They entwined with bodies. They neither crawled nor flowed, at the behest of their master, destroying everything that stood in their way.

He couldn't imagine a bigger nightmare than this trip.

Suddenly, out of the darkness, they threw him to some place where the moonlight barely diffused the darkness.

Then they disappeared.

He was alone in the shadows. Abandoned, upset. Sore.

Above all, however, he was terribly lonely in his suffering.

Then he heard crying.

Baby cry...

A desperate cry of fear reached his ears shortly after the beings abandoned him.

The children had to be very young. Several years.

He couldn't even see them well, but he could feel them. Eight poor, unhappy little souls.

In the blink of an eye, he forgot about himself. He removed to the recesses of the soul the memory of ruthless groping, tearing at his intimacy. Ready to help, he made an effort. He sat up with difficulty, his eyes penetrating the darkness. He saw several pairs of fear-filled eyes.

His heart tightened with regret.

Suddenly he was enveloped in a glow and a screeching noise as the door of the dirty cell was opened. Because it was a cell, he only managed to see for a moment. The children screamed in agony, horrified at the sight of the light and the guards. It meant something monstrous for them that he couldn't even imagine. The guards, to the accompaniment of a great, soul-striking lament, fastened something around his neck and pulled him outside by a chain that flashed in the light.

Collar.

"Let the kids out, you bastards!" He shouted at them. "Let the children out of this hole!"

"Shut up!" One of them shouted, hitting him in the face.

Then he grimaced in disgust as he looked down at his hand.

"Fuck!" He called to his companions, "He's all in the gutter slime!"

"I know," replied one of them. "I got dirty when I was buttoning his collar, dam it!"

"We will not lead him through the chambers to the Dark One in this condition!" remarked another. "He's going to kill us for it!"

"We'll wrap some water on him, he won't smell like that! After that, they'll wash him better there!" ordered another.

"Going to be fun!" Said the one who spoke first. "Hurry up! I want to get this out of my head!"

They poured some cold water on him. The dirt had not completely left him, but the healer smelled less. Nevertheless, he trembled with fatigue and cold.

"To the Dark One with him!" The first guard ordered.

The one who struck him had clearly made a personal effort to make the prisoner feel enslaved. With evident satisfaction, he tugged on the chain, forcing Vivan to walk faster. The short distance caused the captured man's neck to ache soon. The three others were still with them, and on the way, they chose their deputies to guard the dungeons.

It was as if these little, poor, frightened creatures could try to escape...

The dungeons have turned into depots and warehouses. Then to the servants' quarters, laundries. A kitchen with a range of unusual fragrances and a separate exit. At the sight of the prisoner and the guards, they retreated in panic, but rarely with a scowl of disgust. He saw fear in the eyes of servants and cooks, and even looks full of genuine sympathy.

These people felt sorry for everyone the guard took to their dark lord.

They knew that the unfortunate victim would probably not come back alive.

Maybe they won't even see the body.

He felt these emotions. Full of fear of a similar fate. They were hastily resumed their activities. Nervous glances followed the guards stealthily as their interest and anger were feared. Nobody wanted to expose themselves to them.

Vivan could sense the moods. His instincts told him that fear had its source. The heavy atmosphere full of tension suggested that he must be prepared to fight for his life.

However, he lacked the motivation to do so.

But when he appeared in the kitchen, dragged down the corridor by the guards and the morning sunlight, fell on his tired face and he heard a voice.

He thought he would never hear him again.

"They have a separate exit," Ross pointed out matter-of-factly, as if a few hours ago, when Vivan last saw him, he wasn't close to death. "See that?"

He did not dare to believe this miracle. Ross sensed it.

"We're alive, Vivan. Me and Oliver. Good thing you came up with this gruesome idea with vials of blood. Sel had it."

"Whatever happens, remember: we won't leave you! You have to survive, Vivan!" Ross was clearly emphasizing the words, "Do you hear? You must survive! So please look around! Look for escape routes! Weak points! They can come in handy! They can save your life!"

Vivan staggered as the guards paused to catch their breath.

He didn't even have the strength to answer him.

Ross suspected that would be the case. Vivan wasn't talking to him. His thoughts were tangled, as if he were struggling to focus. Searching for escape routes was supposed to help him concentrate, but soon Ross abandoned the idea. It was clear to him that Vivan was about to become a victim, though he was certainly ready to fight for his life with the last of his strength. It is not enough. He didn't want an end for him.

That's why he already had an idea.

"We will give you what you have given us," he turned warmly to his friend.

Ross sat among the crowd of voices and weeping, focusing his will on his imprisoned friend.

It's been two hours since Vivan was kidnapped by dark creatures straight into the Bay of Slaves. His eyes followed his friend's arduous, even murderous journey into the city, and then deeper into the dark canals to the very dungeons of the castle. Mighty castle on top of the hill. Lots of narrow, unfriendly streets. People without a trace of joy. And most of all he... Vivan. Muffled by these bullies, barely alive from trying to catch his breath among the waves at first and then in the city itself. Ross could sense a paralyzing fear that had its origins in the past. The horror of this journey filled his heart with fear. It didn't stop with the guards. The fear clung to him, taking root with an almost human delight. He was there, in every nook and cranny of his soul. With such fear, Vivan had no chance of meeting the enemy. Plus, those poor, imprisoned babies... Ross's heart tightened when he saw them. He must get to them! Although getting them out of this nightmare will probably be just the beginning. But if they free Vivan, a return to normal life becomes possible. Not everyone has as much fortitude as he does. He knew it without a hint of pride. He saw children treated in a similar way, who only lived a few years or were devoured by the street... Vermod was not a very friendly place for the abandoned. Those who were not cared for by anyone died forgotten.

He stopped paying attention to his surroundings. Somewhere in the subconscious, he knew that they were standing there, not knowing what to do next. They thought Vivan was dead. He didn't have time to explain it to them now. He didn't want to lose that fragile bond with his friend, not right now. He was sure they wouldn't kill him. After all, this wasn't what they were trying to capture him for. They are definitely preparing something special for him. He was sure of that. His specific state, as his thoughts drifted away to Vivan, was quickly noticed by Sel and Oliver accompanying him, though they did not share this knowledge with anyone. Sel helped him back to the cabin. Oliver and Sai took the little girl and followed him. They waited patiently for him to speak. Ross barely nodded at them in thanks for their actions. Later. Everything after that.

With him, she had to reach the man the guards called the Dark One...

The castle mounted on the top.

The maze of corridors along which they headed for an undefined destination resembled the shell of an enormous snail. Vivan, free from the presence of ghostly beings, recovered enough to begin to carefully observe his surroundings. He was sure he had never seen a structure like this before. Not so much service. They squeezed through the crowd of people hurrying to their duties. Many looked with surprise combined with a hint of distaste at the guards and their prisoner. Fear dominated. The guards were feared as if they were the worst plague. They were fleeing from them in fearful movements, lest their attention accidentally fall on them for longer. The guards pushed themselves brutally, hitting the heads of the unfortunates who stood in their way. They wandered both corridors and rooms, and even sleeping quarters on the lower floors. It made it seem unimaginably long and incredibly complex, with a network of rooms, corridors, halls and doors visible all around. In addition, the stairs that led to the upper floors were sometimes like a snake's tail entangling the keep, and then they changed their position. The nightmare road up, tiring both for the captive and his guards, was intended to create a feeling of entrapment and confusion in the prisoner. That was probably the order.

"Stop!" ordered at one point the one who hit Vivan. "Damn it, we'll wear ourselves to a shadow before we get there!"

Each of them was panting heavily and pouring sweat. Vivan staggered, fatigued to the limit. A moment later he fell to his knees, barely catching his breath. They didn't have the strength or willingness to punish him for it.

"What the fuck is going on?" the commander asked him, pulling the chain. "Who the hell are you?! Why is there so much trouble with you?!"

Vivan looked at him grimly, still silent.

"Talk!" the guard angrily pulled him towards him. "Why are we playing with you like that?!"

Their eyes met for the first time since he had been captured.

Suddenly Vivan understood.

He knew this man. He knew him very well.

The other recognized him too. The shock on his face was too telling.

"Why did you let them catch you, you stupid bastard?!" He asked with painful astonishment. "I thought you would get away after all!"

Vivan managed only a hint of a smile.

"Hello, Garen," he raised his head.

Garen. Companion from childhood years. Son of the alewife Seme and her husband. He and Peran, his brother, were Vivan and Paphian's best friends. Always inseparable. A trustworthy team of colleagues though a bit too serious, the little healer was a bit out of place. But they knew he was like that. The buddy who saved their broken noses, healed the bruises from fights with other boys in the village so that their mothers wouldn't see (he didn't take part in them, no one picked at him), but he certainly wasn't queening over anybody.

It was never in doubt. Garen and Peran, like Paphian, his brother, saw him in different situations on a daily basis, they knew each other and had fun. They laughed together and got into trouble together. Vivan has had difficult times, it is impossible to hide. He cried sometimes when they were told that a man must be tough. For example, when he claimed he was fed up with it all. That he does not want to be a healer at all, because he cannot help everyone, he cannot. They understood. They were comforting. They advised as friends.

Friends.

Seme sent them back at the time of the plague when Vivan was kidnapped. She was afraid that they might get infected while he is gone. She was afraid that she would lose them, so she sent them out into the wide world.

And they didn't come back anymore.

When the plague passed, when they finally defeated the evil witch, and Vivan recovered - he missed them. At times when everything seemed less complicated. For the carefree waiting for the next day with the curiosity of the child. For their presence and friendship. He wondered if they would get along with his new friends. He imagined these meetings before he fell asleep, exhausted by another tryst with Vashaba, during which she again deprived him of the right to meet his relatives, and he, loving her, allowed it, because in his naive, first love, he thought it was right.

He thought that the witch Mayene had destroyed everything in his room that mattered to him, and that fate had taken his childhood friends from him. He did not make friends easily. People did not know whether their children should play with the count's son.

But Seme helped his mother when he was born. Then at Paphian. Therefore, her sons, who were only a year and two older, became friends, as did the women. And even more...

Now Vivan was kneeling in front of the man who had hit him brutally.

He already knew there was nothing left of the old Garen he was friends with. This man was responsible for the fate of the little children trapped in the dungeons deep beneath them. He was brutal. Behind his attitude was a history of violence and bloodshed.

This man is not going to help him. He will torment him without hesitation if he is ordered to do so. Coldly explaining that this was his duty.

At first, it seemed he was right to judge him that way.

Garen punched him in the face.

This time, however, he didn't do it with his fist, but hit the mold. Vivan didn't know if he should be thankful for that.

"Shut your mouth and get up!" His old friend bellowed in his ear in a completely strange tone, "Garen is dead! You better remember that!"

Walking between the guards again, Vivan was certain that his worst nightmare had indeed come true...

Ross, overwhelmed by his feelings, felt tears slowly running down his face.

"I want to be here!" Lena shouted, opening the door to the captain's cabin. "You can't forbid me to do that!"

She burst in, staring at Ross with a mixture of hopes and fears. Hungry for the answers he had to give her. He saw it before breaking the bond with her son for a moment, looking for a break.

"He lives?!" The question was almost the answer. An ardent desire.

He nodded silently to her.

Her joy lit up her face for just a moment, giving way to fears at the sight of his gaze.

"It's very bad?"

His silence became more meaningful than words.

"Who..." he asked quietly after a moment, "is Garen?"

She looked at him in surprise.

"Garen?"

"Vivan's former childhood friend," explained Victor, who followed her into the cabin, "He knew such a Garen."

"He obeys the advisor to the king he calls the Dark One," Ross explained. "He won't help him. He carries out orders."

"Ross," Lena moved towards him. "You know how to make him change his mind."

She waited a moment. Seeing that he was a bit confused, she added one important word:

"Ramsey."

Ross's gaze turned cold quickly.

Yes. He knew.

Only this man was measuring him. He felt disgust at the thought of even touching him with a finger, let alone with his mind and heart.

"Help me," he asked firmly.

"Tell me what you need?" Victor asked as he approached him.

Ross looked at him thoughtfully.

Vivan needs to feel we all care about him.

Victor sat down next to him on the floor. He thought for a moment, falling into deep reverie. He kind of knew everything. He knew he had an unusual grandson. This grandson of an extraordinary friend, which is Ross. It all had its own laws, which he didn't even try to interfere with. So, it was like that and that's it. Now this. How to understand it all?

He smiled at his daughter, and then at Ross, who was worried, waiting for his help.

"It's far from here to the Vermoda market, isn't it, son?" he asked. "Fate has taken you there. It tied you with one rope," he pointed to the Jewel on his neck. "Both hearts are large, although different..." he put his hand on his shoulder. "I love you, just like Vivan and Paphian," he confessed in a calm, warm tone. "I'm glad and I'm proud that I have three wonderful grandchildren." He paused for greater effect. "Who bust their butt to help others. And you," he looked into Ross's tearful eyes, "loved the old man he didn't want to know you. You're amazing. I'm going to kill anyone who tries to humiliate you. Tell Vivan that his grandfather is going to help him. Share it with all your heart. Let him know."

Ross nodded, touched by his words.

Vivan felt a wave of warmth from the depths of his heart. The mind grew brighter, as if someone had turned on a light. The bruised body stopped hurting. He lowered his head to keep the guards from noticing the changes in him. Garen, the present one, was too preoccupied with getting to his destination. He did not look at him, for which Vivan was grateful. They knew each other too well to be deceived. The fatigue he felt was certainly not helping him.

It was much better, though Vivan certainly needed a rest. The thirst was tiring him too.

They stood a few floors above again. It was close now, as Vivan had learned from Garen's companions, who clearly enjoyed sharing the news with him.

"Are you pleased with yourself?" Garen asked teasingly, panting between the words, "If you weren't such a cunt who finally let him catch you, we wouldn't have tugged you so much of the way!"

"Straight out of the dungeons," Vivan remarked, not indebted to him. "Apparently, you're only suitable for keeping an eye on small, vulnerable children. You fit this place. At the very bottom, close to the sewage..."

Garen grabbed him by the laps of his shirt, from which there was not much left after his adventures with strange sea creatures.

"Shut up!" He roared in his face.

Vivan suddenly realized that Garen was really furious with him. Because he got caught, as he said himself.

So, he hoped it would be otherwise...

It was important to him.

"Where's Peran?" He asked, ignoring the threat in his voice. "What did you do with your brother?!"

Garen cast a quick glance at his companions, who were surprised at Vivan's words.

"Hey, Gar!" One of them asked curiously. "Who is this one? How does he know you had a brother?"

Vivan paled. His suspicions have just been confirmed. He felt a chill in his heart.

"You killed him..." the words barely crossed his throat.

Garen released him angrily. For a moment Vivan thought he saw a flash of tears in his eyes. This death cost him dearly.

"You murdered..." he added softly.

Garen hit him hard on the jaw. Vivan fell on his back, surprised by the sudden attack, and then Garen straddled him, aiming to strike.

"Gar!" One of the guards shouted warningly.

Vivan already knew that his old friend was afraid. He hid his fear under a mask of roughness, as did the rest of them. Each of them displayed it in their own way.

"Who is this?" Asked the same guard, as did the others, measuring them both with his eyes.

Beneath his dark hair, his wide-open eyes expressed both fear and a need to satisfy the curiosity.

"Let's go!" He ordered glumly when asked.

"We're not going anywhere until you answer!" His companion grabbed his sleeve. The others surrounded them, refusing to let them go any further until they knew the answer. Garen realized he had no choice. He gasped angrily.

"He's a healer," he said shortly.

Taking advantage of their surprise, he tugged on the chain, forcing Vivan to walk.

Therefore, he did not see their expressions change. Tough men, who had not cared about their master's victims before, suddenly found that the presence of a healer was out of their way. He shouldn't be here. This is a living legend, a way to save when things get really bad. A man who never refused to help anyone. The dark-haired man felt something akin to pride, as he had saved Vivan from being beaten. Immediately afterwards, however, came a bitter reflection.

They won't be able to protect him.

The Dark One will tear their souls away for it.

Ross mused. Before Vivan reached the chambers of the king's advisor, he thought about what he could sense. The guards did not like that the healer had fallen into the hands of their master. Behind his brutality, Garen still hid the remnants of his humanity. It gave hope that these people, if they were close to Vivan, could become puppets in his hands.

Troublemaker of Thoughts.

That was also what he was called.

CHAPTER 39

They finally reached the right floor.

"It's here," Garen said shortly, "You're about to regret your stupidity!"

Vivan was silent.

"You won't say anything now?!" Garen tugged on the chain, barely suppressing his anger. "You're right! Don't waste your words!"

"You care..." Vivan looked up defiantly.

Garen hesitated as if he were going to hit him again, but then gave up.

"Fuck, I was counting on it! It's true! I thought neither of you can be captured! Happy?" He looked into his eyes. "There are rumors that he sent demons after you! After you and your new wizard buddy. And they didn't come back! It has never happened before! However, you are here! And now the whole world is going to hell!"

"What are you talking about?"

Garen looked at his companions, sharing with him a similar ironic smile on the verge of the madness they were headed for.

"They will eat you alive here, Vivan!" He explained ruthlessly. "And this time no one will stand in their way!"

The jewel around Vivan's neck glowed red unexpectedly and faded out.

Vivan smirked, feeling his friend's presence in his mind.

"I wouldn't be so sure," he replied coldly.

The first floor's chambers and corridors differed significantly from the interior of the king's palace, in which Vivan had once been forced to stay. They were permeated with the symbolism of these lands, full of paintings, elaborate mosaics filling the corridors. Each room passed by seemed to be a separate piece of architectural art, and the elaborately arched windows presented a view of the sea at the foot of the fortress, then unusual, sand and green views of the hills to the far horizon. Depending on which side Vivan might have looked at. It was very high up here. Higher than he had ever been in his life. The spacious corridors were airy due to the warm climate. In some rooms you could see panes in the windows or decorated stained glass. Judging by the time-consuming trip up the mountain, the castle must have been huge and had solid walls. But not only this aroused some respect in the healer. He sensed something else here that the others hardly knew. The enormity of the tragedy that took place in this place was crushing like a heavy boulder. There are memories of the builders who breathed their last breath here, often in pain and suffering. They were dying of exhaustion and hunger. They died bloody to take with them the secret of buildings, hidden chambers, covered corridors.

Their cries, sweat and blood are preserved within these walls.

Finally, they reached the proper chamber, which was guarded by only one guard. Knowing so much about his enemy's abilities already, Vivan didn't feel surprised.

This man needed no humans for protection.

He was powerful.

Besheram sat at the table, absorbed in the meal, the aroma of which pleasantly irritated the healer's nostrils. Perfect white crockery, next to a glass of red wine. Surprisingly modest, but that was clearly the style he liked. The plain simplicity and splendor of an exquisite dish that Vivan remembered he had eaten last night were probably meant to irritate the already scared prisoner.

The guards positioned Vivan in front of the table awaiting further orders.

Besheram winced in disgust, finally letting everyone know he had noticed their arrival.

"You smell," noticed in the tone of an aristocrat who cares about the aesthetics. "Cold water is not enough."

He stood up slowly, celebrating the act. Then he looked slowly at Vivan, as if he felt compelled to do so, and he did not feel like it. His eyes concealed the chill of the icy lands: almost entirely white, with a slight tinge of blue. Dark hair interspersed with white streaks and a handsome face without a trace of warm feelings completed the picture. Tall and slim, dressed in black, with numerous silver accents in the form of a buckle, buttons or ornamental motifs related to the culture of this kingdom in the form of mosaics, they gave him a majestic appearance, and at the same time a sense of distance from others, inferior to him.

Everything devoid of any emotions.

Suddenly, without a shadow of a warning, the image shattered as Besheram's face turned inhuman, demonically contorted, and his voice changed to dark and cold.

In the blink of an eye, he was by the prisoner, staring his ghastly gaze straight into his eyes.

"You thought you would outsmart me?!" He roared furiously, revealing his full, dark face. "Healer..." the word hissed contemptuously, referring to their meeting on the ship.

Vivan took hold of the fear, though it turned out to be quite a challenge. Besheram's face returned to its former appearance. It was puzzling that after the initial nervous shudder, the guards quickly regained their composure. Vivan understood that they were not surprised by this change.

It was well known to them. All too well.

Besheram was severely disappointed. He thought Vivan would be scared to see it. He was vain to the point of absurdity. But he hid his disappointment, resuming a somewhat exalted pose. Vivan looked at his friend. It seemed to him that the latter was playing this play for him on purpose. As if he was testing which his behavior would make a better impression on the prisoner. He expected to see other poses until his opponent chose the right one for his circumstances. Such instability, however, was very disturbing, which perhaps he did not know yet. Or he was just hiding it.

It made him unpredictable, and therefore extremely dangerous.

"Azram has been waiting for you for a long time," Besheram began. "Let's not let him wait any longer!"

He ordered the guards to escort the prisoner until he sent them back. They walked together to the audience hall. Vivan knew beforehand that this was where they were headed, thanks to the large group waiting for an audience. There were merchants, craftsmen, and representatives of the aristocracy. Azram did not care for the titles for ruling his kingdom with the help of demons.

The waiting people watched him closely. The sight of a ragged, half-naked prisoner, chained like an animal, was nothing special to them. They were accompanied by their slaves, whom they had acquired at the market, often in the same way that he himself was to be treated today. The more sensational was the fact that the prisoner was chained by the king's dark adviser himself, about whom there were disturbing stories in the surrounding lands.

The gates to the hall were swung open.

A huge, high-vaulted room loomed in front of them, rich in paintings that Vivan now had no time or desire to study. A long carpet led to the throne, on both sides of which other guests awaited the meeting.

The throne was placed on a platform. Before him, a group of merchants was presenting their gifts - shiny bales of deliciously colored silk fabrics. To the side, a group of musicians played their instruments subtly so as not to disturb the meeting. There was a soft buzz of conversation in the hall through which the words of one of the merchants assuring the king of his loyalty could be heard.

Everything went quiet suddenly as Besheram entered with his prisoner accompanied by a guard.

There was a silence, broken only by the sound of footsteps.

"My lord!" Besheram was only a little humble with the king.

Vivan recognized a certain amusement in his feelings, topped with a measure of respect. The adviser treated the presence of the king as a necessity in fulfilling his plans. Azram still respected his position, but there was recognition too. The healer shuddered at the mere thought of what the king deserved such feelings. There were legends about it...

At the moment, however, he was consumed by other feelings. Here he appeared before the king in a pitiful condition. Barefoot, near the end of endurance from fatigue. He was cold, hungry, weary and, most of all, helpless. Ross didn't say a word, though Vivan could sense his presence. It wouldn't really help him much now.

The crowd of people looked at him curiously. Their gazes traveled over his body without a trace of shame.

"Behold, my king," Besheram began in a loud voice, "I'm giving you a great gift! A cure for all your ailments!" He paused for greater effect, this time behaving without a trace of his previous exaltation. "King Azram, the most powerful lord! This is Vivan Beckert, his mother's bastard. THE HEALER!"

The king got up.

He was no longer young, but still far from old age. He had an angular jaw that looked like a wild dog's mouth ready to devour its victim. Hair, neatly styled, dyed dark to hide the first signs of gray.

It was not exquisite robes, worth a lot of money, nor a crown that seemed merely a symbol of power in its modesty, not even a face, that attracted the greatest attention of the viewer.

Big eyes, dark as darkness, marked by strength and ruthlessness, followed Vivan like the eyes of a predator waiting for a victim to move.

He walked slowly down the stairs, never taking his eyes off him.

"Are you sure?" He asked his adviser, his voice deep, cold, "I can't see the jewel on his neck..."

Besheram grimaced in disgust, then without a word walked over and tore the remnants of shirt off his prisoner, revealing to the king the healer's body, torn by teeth, blunt tools and flogging.

The crowd buzzed and rippled, moved by this discovery.

Vivan shivered involuntarily, feeling the eyes on him. Humiliated in front of strangers. Exposed like an animal, the collar around its neck, the chain still held by Besheram. He kept his eyes on the king, defending the remnants of his dignity. Among the crowd, he picked up comments about his own appearance. Some assessed its value on the market, strongly underestimated for this reason, some were of a different opinion. He was only a valuable asset for them. Attempts were made to convert its value into gold or the benefits it could provide. Even parts of his body were even valued, wondering how much he would be worth on the black market. Worth more than a slave. His humanity was relegated to the background. The quiet, enslaved unfortunates were perhaps the only ones who felt sorry for him. He could feel their silent support.

"Hmm..." Azram stretched the moment with the greatest delight, pleased with the gift.

Unexpectedly, he slipped Vivan's hand into his tattered pants, examining his penis and testicles with curiosity. Vivan felt the blood rush to his head. This study was not delicate. Abruptness and circumstances, and above all the good fun of Azram and his adviser, kept his will in check only from his old experience with the witch. Otherwise, he would have shown more weakness than a groan.

"Good stallion," the king muttered, reaching out his hand to nudge it on his pants. "They say a few drops of blood is enough to cure any disease, right?"

"Yes," replied Besheram, looking at Vivan with a hint of amusement. "That's for sure."

"He doesn't have to agree with it?" The lord of the Bay of Slaves asked.

"No," the adviser replied, ignoring the healer's hateful gaze.

The king held out his other hand. The glove on it had long, glistening silver claws.

The quick movement cut through the skin on Vivan's cheek. Two guards immediately restrained him, probably on the orders of the adviser. Garen held his head.

Azram waited until blood began to flow from the cut. Then, with his long claw, he scooped it up a little from the side, avoiding the sharp end, licking it carefully with his tongue.

He closed his eyes, waiting for the effect.

After a moment he opened them, illuminated by her benevolent effects that he did not deserve.

"Finally..." he whispered in delight.

The terror of this situation spread even to those waiting for an audience. Here was King Azram, who had so far been defeated only by disease (Vivan had already known from humiliating contact that the king had had a venereal disease), now he was in full strength. More powerful than before.

Vivan froze. It couldn't be something so banal. All this mysterious disease could not just be the result of a dissolute life. But Azram was recovering.

Suddenly, the solution to this riddle came to him when the king began to speak:

"So, it might actually help," muttered Azram. But seeing the healer looking at him strangely, he hastily changed his tone. "Take him to the chambers, wash him, dress him, and all the rest!" He waved his hand carelessly. "The collar and chain remain. I will decide when to take it off." He leaned slightly towards Vivan, beaming with the hope he only glimpsed. "Welcome to the Bay of Slaves, healer. You didn't want to be a guest, so you'll be a prisoner. By the time," he ended mysteriously, sending them away.

Besheram grabbed Vivan by the hair, pulling his head towards his shoulder.

"You think you can get a break from us now?" He asked coolly, as they stood in the room designated for Vivan. "You remember how you got here, don't you? Did you like the company? The Dark Folk can be very absorbing. Look everywhere. Apparently one of them put a fist in someone's anus. Interesting, isn't it? You'll have a chance to meet him again," he hissed in his ear. "They crawl out from every dark corner, and it's very dark at night. Have a nice dreams!"

He released him abruptly to leave the room quickly.

"Well, happy?" Garen asked him. "You wanted it yourself..."

He nodded to his own, showing him nothing but contempt. He left him to be guarded by the palace guard.

Vivan saw at last two young women waiting silently. Slaves. The door closed behind the guards. He glanced out the window, watching the sun go down.

A few hours left until dark...

"Let us take care of you, my lord," the first girl said, "We have prepared a bath. You are surely tired..."

"I can do it myself..." The words barely escaped his mouth, he was so tired.

"Lord," the other said gently, "We'll take care of everything..."

The last thing he wanted was to re-enter his intimacy, even as innocent as ordinary ministry. They must have noticed his mood as one spoke softly:

"If we fail to take care of you, my lord, we will face severe punishment."

"Perhaps even death..." added the second.

He looked at them warmer, sensing their fear and sincere kindness.

"You'll be punished, too," the other whispered, glancing at the door.

They shared a similar fate.

They discreetly helped him undress and get into the bath. He was forced to agree to it. He was barely on his feet. The hot bath helped more than he expected. It warmed up the frozen limbs. The girls dressed him for sleep, treated the cuts and chafing on the neck from the collar. Then they cleaned up.

Finally, although he was grateful for the help, they left.

He was left alone.

He crawled to the enormous bed. In the middle of it, he curled up in a fetal position, dreaming only of not feeling, hearing or seeing anything anymore. He knew he had about two hours until the dark beings would come.

He felt a numbness enveloping him, as if everything had suddenly started to flow around him. It was a good feeling. Without a hint of deeper emotions. Only standing.

As if he was drifting in a great ocean in endless solitude.

Suddenly he felt something that at first, he preferred to immediately dismiss. Warmth around the heart. Then a clarity enveloping his thoughts until he began to feel again. He felt the sheets feel pleasantly cool in the heat of the inevitable coming evening.

It was nice.

Only he didn't feel like feeling anything at all. He was falling asleep, as deep as death. His breathing slowed dangerously. The heartbeat was getting slower. He fell into a darkness he was not even afraid of. It just collapsed into him, as if slowly being drawn into a soft, cozy depth.

His heart almost stopped beating...

"Please..." He heard a warm, familiar voice in his head. "Don't go."

Let him ask. He is tired of it...

But that voice kept calling him. It wouldn't budge.

"Go away!" He ordered him sharply.

Ross wasn't going to listen to him. He did not yield. It was already starting to irritate.

"We're going to get you," he explained gently, "don't give up."

"Let me sleep..."

Ross paused for a moment, feeling the bond fading away. What could he do?

Just one.

Reveal a secret.

These words were supposed to be a mystery to others, but he did so.

Surprised, Vivan widened his eyes, feeling the knocks against his temples.

When he looked back at the setting sun, he felt a surge of power inside that he had never felt before. The gift lit a fire in his veins, completely regenerating his body. The weakness was gone.

He was ready to face the coming night.

They crawled out of the walls, as Besheram had said.

Black, faceless. Inhumanly skinny.

They encircled the bed, crawling along the walls, gliding across the floor. He did not try to run away from them. He knew it couldn't have worked.

As he sat, he supported his hands in his lap, trying to stay calm while his heart pounded in his chest like mad. His instincts told him that the crazy thought that came to his mind before the sun started to set was a good idea. It required discipline from him. But it was his only hope in this place.

From the Dark Folk, as Besheram called them, there was no escape...

Just before dark, he began to sing.

It was the lullaby his mother used to sing for him. She had learned it in this world from her first friend with whom she had strong ties - the alewife Semeralda, known by others as Seme, the mother of two sons, only a year and two older than her extraordinary son.

The once innocent child who was his old friend listened to the same words. He fell asleep to the rhythm of a lullaby, cuddled in his mother's arms. He thought of it, softly singing his beloved melody. Regret broke his heart as he recalled their meeting here. The man he had known half his life... He was gone. Fate took him away from him, as did many others. As if he was already dead. They will never talk like they used to.

The emotions that accompanied those thoughts colored the tone of his voice.

He hummed softly, keeping cool even as the beings began to touch him shyly, unlike before. He thought they were examining him this time.

Their movements were clumsy but inquisitive. Some touched his face. The many black hands and faces facing him suggested they were taken by surprise.

He did not expect what he saw in a moment.

One of the creatures was so close to his face that she allowed herself to reach out her hands again. This time, however, the blackness suddenly faded to reveal the hands of a child, and a featureless face appeared as a child's face. It could be no more than two years old. The rest of the body broke free of the blackness, revealing first an emaciated body, then, after touching his face, the body of a healthy child.

The child, staring at him in disbelief, tried to catch the melody from his lips. Apparently, it seemed familiar to him. He picked it up uncertainly, and then it stared at him intently as it listened to the lullaby. Then it smiled happily. He realized that it trusted him. The little boy cuddled up to him as if to hide. Vivan stroked his hair. He touched his face in a tender gesture, feeling his heart beating hard, filled with love. He covered the boy with a piece of bedspread. The other beings watched them closely, as if wondering where this was going.

The toddler closed his eyes.

"Sleep," he whispered in agitation. "Sleep in peace..."

The touch revealed to him the short, dramatic story of the child. His parents were murdered, and he was kidnapped to the dungeons. There, those disgusting creatures that tried to kidnap him rushed inside and devoured him alive.

Besheram, on the other hand, seized his terrified little soul and forced him into the darkness, where he was to obey his orders as a strange creature. The frightened child was so afraid...

The boy became transparent. His soul was at peace.

"You'll wake up in mom's arms, I promise," Vivan whispered, kissing his forehead goodbye.

The boy's ghost vanished with a soft sigh filled with happiness.

Vivan closed his eyes, and when he opened them, a baby was resting in his arms.

He smiled at the baby, knowing that other children were also waiting for his arms.

He lifted the baby staring at him, unsure whether to be happy, until he noticed a smile on its face.

"Hey baby," he said fondly, hugging them, "You want to be with your mom?"

This child had a similar story.

Before dawn, there was no dark creature left in his chamber.

CHAPTER 40

Besheram mused as he watched the dawn.

The healer fascinated him. He had not yet met such a strange specimen among the people he regretted he still belonged to. He hoped it would change soon, that he would gain immortality thanks to this young man. This was what was of general interest to him. How did this man endure such a horrible experience? What or who gave him strength? Woman? Friend - wizard? Family? The harm of which of them would hurt him the most? He had already killed the wizard… Overall, the healer had been too shattered the day before to scientifically conclude that he was impressed by this death. Too many emotions at once. He was barely on his feet. Well, tonight he'll give him some hours of sleep until lunchtime. After all, something like rape, as he expected from his Folk, must at least sleep off, otherwise the fun will end soon.

Three days left. He must make up for the long wait for one of them.

He threw a silk robe over his slim figure. It was exciting to know that it was the only thing he was wearing and that the fabric was sometimes showing through in the sunlight. He loved to embarrass the guards and the few servants on this floor. Sometimes he wondered if he would abandon his bathrobe and go naked. Even with an erection, he felt no discomfort. The king himself did not have the courage to comment on this. The growing numbers of the Dark Folk and the demons at their command effectively kept him from doing so.

So now Besheram, aware of his impunity, went back in that outfit, adding only high boots. It was possible that the healer was attracted to men, judging by his alleged friendship with a sorcerer who even had a lover on board. The thought of Vivan looking down made him feel like it. Maybe not with him, not at least now, but he would fuck someone furiously.

He walked down the corridor, mentally enjoying the furtive glances. Pleased with himself, he entered the healer's chamber.

Of course, this one was asleep. This is understandable, as are the floating candles burning in a rose water jar. He shone them in the dark. He probably thought it would help him. Naive! He found out how wrong he was...

He leaned over him.

Vivan slept so soundly... The dream was so deep that even the arrival of the intruder did not wake him up.

But that wasn't what surprised the Dark One.

A glow shone around the sleeping man.

The green shone with a soothing glow, choking the delicate shades of blue. In front of the adviser, the glow turned white as fluff, then faded out.

Suddenly Besheram realized that the night was just about to end. Dawn barely colored the sky. So why doesn't he see a swarm of bodies? Where has his dependable army gone?

He summoned her in his mind, promising himself to punish his Folk properly.

Silence answered him.

He felt a tingle along his spine. The people were silent!

Realization of the cause of this silence came a moment later.

Exhausted Vivan did not fall asleep because of the cruelty inflicted upon him...

Besheram felt the blood rush to his head. The damned freak! Cursed healer and his gift! He took them away from him! These souls would belong to him forever!

He wanted so much to throw himself on the sleeper! To beat, enslave with the utmost brutality. He should pay for it! But as soon as he made a move, he saw the necklace around his neck, previously hidden from his sight. The jewel glowed red, and the voice in his head rang like a bell. Many bells ordering him to withdraw from the healer immediately. He gripped his head in pain. Suffering vanquished all his thoughts. Only that voice mattered, a chorus of voices carrying the command echoing. One of these voices was dominant, but that was all he could say. He had to go! He had to get out! Get away from those voices before they crack his skull open! Tough, painful a thousand times! He fought them but couldn't win! Their strength grew as soon as he approached the sleeping man, unaware of his struggle. He relented in anger as he walked away. The voice haunted him even outside the room. The slightest thought that he might send a guard, any idea to harm a healer, would cause more suffering. He had to yield. Only then could he carefully consider who was stalking him. Not very long. The man was still in it. He followed his thoughts. It settled in his mind like a parasite. All that could be done was to quiet down until the other retired.

But... is it possible that he...? He should be dead! After all, he killed his twin by accident!

Who could have such tremendous power?

Lena held Ross tightly by both hands.

"Say it helped," she said softly, pouring all her motherly concern into the words.

They were surrounded by many people whom Sel hastily summoned. Before dawn, Ross woke him, urging him to bring some of them back to his cabin immediately. He didn't tell him what exactly was going on. All they knew was that Besheram was approaching. Sel ran out in a hurry, forgetting even to button his shirt. The girl sleeping between them immediately woke up, alert like a frightened animal. Ross smiled sadly at her as he hugged her. The memories of the children woven into his dreams were still floating in his head. Vivan saved them all! But he might pay a hefty price for it, and he wasn't going to let that happen.

They showed up quickly. Lena, Victor, Silas, Cora, volunteers from Leviron, Daryenne… They barely fit into this cabin, but no one complained. Lena sat down on the edge of the bed, the others, in silent agreement, placed their hands on both of them.

How was it possible that they could figure out what was expected of them? Ross looked at Silas.

"What's next?" The other smiled, hinting that he no longer wondered about anything about Ross and the Healer.

"Make Besheram get off Vivan," he said firmly.

"I even tell him to fuck off..." Marlene began, quickly silenced by the other girls, showing her the baby at the captain's side.

Yes. He had everything he needed.

"Ross?" Lena snapped him out of his memories. "Say something, please... Did you, do it?"

He smiled, making her tears of relief and a sigh of those present.

He nodded his head in agreement, which made them happy. He waited for a moment to enjoy her before he finally spoke up.

"It helped, but just this one time," he explained. "He begins to suspect that I'm alive. But there was nothing else I could do. I had to take a risk."

They had talked about it before. They discussed various strategies. But none seemed appropriate or as desperately insane as his idea. They knew that they had no chance against the demons. Therefore, they were left with a trick.

And this one seemed particularly idiotic.

However, they had no other.

"What about the costumes?" He asked Marlene, who had formally taken command of the members of the plot.

"Almost ready," she replied.

"And the dance?"

The women looked at each other uncertainly. Oliver stepped forward a little.

"We will try," he explained.

Ross looked him in the eye anxiously, but his brother replied with a calm smile.

"We can do it," he assured.

Ross looked at Daryenne. She nodded gravely.

"I'm ready. If you want, I can go right now!"

"On the water?" Silas asked jokingly, causing a wave of smiles.

Daryenne glared at him.

Ross looked at everything with emotion. He thought of how fate had led him down the path that had led him now to command these people. He, a bastard, a street kid.

Once upon a time he had almost nothing...

When they left, he put the little girl to sleep. Then he looked out the window, at the dawn, which in a moment would illuminate the bed of Vivan, temporarily sleeping safely in his chamber.

"Ross…" Sel started softly, but Sel immediately cut him off.

"Please..." he said fondly.

But Sel refused to give up without a fight.

"Don't send me away!" he asked. "I can be useful to you!"

"On the ship, you and the baby will be protected by shields," he reminded him.

"The little one does not trust me..."

"Sel," Ross cut in on his word with affection. "Look, to the Dark One, you are my weakness. He knows I love you! He'll kill you or do something horrible enough to hurt me! And I don't want, I CANNOT lose you!" He finished in a dramatic whisper. "You are my strength!"

Sel looked at him warmly.

"I would like to protect you..."

"At least protect my heart," he pleaded.

Sel surrendered, lightly touching his cheek. He realized he had to relinquish.

When he went to sleep, Ross was still pondering. He thought about things past and present. About good and bad deeds. Consequences of the choices...

He lay down, thinking about the future. He looked at the dormant face of his beloved. Then he looked for the girl's hand. He closed his eyes. Then he heard a shy whisper.

"Ross," the child whispered, filling his heart with joy. "My name is Christine."

He looked at her, feeling tears welling up.

"Hi, Christine," he replied, his voice trembling.

"Hi, Ross," the girl replied softly, squeezing his hand.

CHAPTER 41

Vivan awoke, unaware of the fight that was taking place over his head. It was getting dark. He recognized the position of the sun outside the window. It puzzled him. After all, he did an almost incredible thing. He released the hapless souls enslaved by Besheram. Surely the other found out about it already.

Meanwhile, silence surrounded him, barely broken by sounds from the palace. A quick look into Ross's mind showed him that his friend was asleep, as were most of his crew. It was also puzzling. Why was he sleeping right now? Shouldn't he appear here?

Maybe... he didn't want to save him?

No. It wasn't like that.

Even the two nice slaves who helped him yesterday did not come.

He was completely alone. Except for the guards at the door, outside.

For some reason it made him even more anxious. He had heard about the practices carried out in this place. He saw imprisoned children somewhere deep in the dungeons, under the palace.

These people were not famous for their hospitality and concern for the welfare of others. They murdered innocents.

He had a feeling he knew what might be causing it, and that didn't quite calm him down at all. They wanted to prepare him. Like the poor babies in the dungeons, his death was planned for a special occasion. Now they wanted him to rest and be ready.

His hair bristled on the back of his neck. Yes! This was it!

This apparent well-being was to reassure him. Lull his vigilance.

He knew what was at stake. Power over the world. And he was the victim to bribe the demons.

The imprisoned children were only an appetizer for them. Karma that will create the Folk...

He wrapped his hands around his knees, feeling the blue flame struggle to rise to the surface.

Then he saw it.

The loose shirt was rolled almost to the elbows, revealing smooth skin except for hair.

Without any bites or scars.

He took off the dragonskin gloves that he would not allow himself to take off while bathing.

The sight of the smooth skin of his hand, which was gripped desperately by the cross as the desperate inhabitants of Vermod attacked, made him hold his breath for a moment.

The royal medic was eager and determined to do everything in his power to save his hand. The muscles were damaged, the skin torn in many places, and the cross pierced the palm of his hand. Of course, Vivan could help him, but in those moments, he was fighting for his life, unaware of what was happening to him. He also didn't know how to direct his gift. Sedon has soared to the heights of his medical skill, saving the hand and restoring it to fitness. Vivan didn't change anything, as if he didn't want to.

Now the hand looked as if the brutal nail attack had never happened. It was smooth, with no prints from the hard work in a mine she had never known before. It was similar with the other hand, less injured in the attack.

He parted the fabric of his shirt, distrusting his eyes. He found no scars that all those gathered in King Azram's audience hall had seen the day before.

Finally, he got up, heading for the mirror in the room.

The claw cut vanished from his face.

Bitten by a witch, thirsty for his blood, too.

Everywhere he could look at his body, the scars just disappeared...
He remembered last night.

The smile of the children he restored to their peace of mind. Eyes looking at him confidently as he sang lullabies to them...

Their silent gratitude healed his body. Even a soul. He felt calmer, stronger and ready to face challenges. They helped him. Just like he helped them.

He smiled through his tears. In silence, he thanked the innocent little souls, promising that he would always remember them.

Then he went out the window, trying to escape for the first time... He had a job to do.

Ross opened his eyes.

Sel was asleep against his back. Christine clung to him, clutching his hand tightly. Her hair tickled his nose. They were both so close to him, as if they were afraid that someone would steal him from them. He could barely breathe freely. He felt terribly hot. In this situation it didn't help to know that Vivan was playing cat and mouse with the guards, as if he had been given some incredible superpower. He was fast. Agile. And cunning. He was captured once, but managed to slip away before reaching the second floor of the king's gloomy adviser. He was neither sore nor injured like he had last night. A mysterious force and a clearly defined goal pushed him to act.

The second time around, more forces were involved. Still, he almost managed to escape the palace. Almost because the panicked fear of the servants and the inhabitants revealed at the last moment his escape route through the kitchen, which he managed to see when he was led upstairs. Vivan seemed completely undaunted by the fact that he had been caught a second time. As if he expected it. Ross assumed that the friend was probably hoping for a stroke of luck, which, unfortunately, was not enough. But this happiness did not disappoint him at all. Moments later, he brazenly escaped from Besheram's own chamber, giving him a white fever. But this time it has disappeared for good. With a mixture of desperation and fear of being detected prematurely, he vanished from his pursuers so effectively that the angry Besheram wondered if he had succeeded this time. He threatened, thundering all over the palace, that he would tear everyone's heads off if they didn't find him. Perhaps it would have been funny were it not for the fact that Ross sensed in the guards passing by the unknowingly by Vivan's hideout that he was speaking quite seriously.

His anxiety had spread to Ross, who was unable to sleep anymore. He felt he was going to suffocate in a moment, so he needed a breath. He cautiously freed himself from the embrace of his beloved beings and left the room.

The cool air helped him dissociate himself from Vivan's emotions. He was in no danger or Besheram would have killed him long ago. They both knew the man was waiting for the right time. The words of Azram himself led them to this.

He glanced at the moon, which was a little short of full moon. It's the day after tomorrow. Could it be that?

Suddenly he longed for Alesei. It was the perfect time for the two to talk to each other freely. But he was gone...

Ross was under no illusions. The happiness that has been with him so far may finally fail him.

"I thought you were asleep," he had not heard that voice for a long time. "And you are walking on the deck in the darkness of the night..."

"Dinn?!" He was surprised to see the silhouette of the elf emerging in the light of a small lantern.

"I wanted to see you this morning," Dinn explained. "See, Alesei made me promise something before he died. But the two of us were never too close... I had a hard time keeping that promise when people were around you. I'm good for nothing."

Ross smiled at the cryptic words.

"I didn't come earlier," added the confused elf, "because I didn't know how to start. I'm not good at making friends."

"Alesei told you to befriend me?" Ross understood, still smiling.

Indeed, Dinn's choice might have come as a bit of a surprise.

"He didn't have a lot of choice," Dinn muttered.

"Oh, I'll start to blush!" Ross's smile widened.

"I'm telling the truth!" Dinn remarked in a slightly offended tone. He thought Ross was starting to mock him. "I came to tell you you can count on me. I will not do anything by force, even if Alesei wanted so, but you can call me for help whenever you want. And I will come. I hope you understand me, though," he hung his head, "what I said... It sounds a little pointless. I mean, I won't insist that I understand if..."

He was silent.

Ross looked at him warmly, fully understanding what the elf was trying to express. He felt grateful to his deceased friend who cared for him until the last moments of his life.

"You're just in time," he told Dinn.

Word to word, they moved on to a casual conversation that was very much like Ross once had with Alesei. Ross confided his dilemmas to a new friend. He revealed how much responsibility he had for the fate of others. He mentioned the plan to free Vivan, for neither he nor the healer himself had any doubts that his escape attempts would be unsuccessful. The goal was to irritate Besheram, or so Vivan explained it. It didn't sound very sensible, but he seemed to insist on his action, so Ross relented. Though he already suspected what it was really about.

He also mentioned this to Dinn. The elf listened. He advised and suggested ideas. He was good at it. Ross felt that there was finally someone, besides Vivan, to whom he could tell his version of their shared story, sometimes depriving it of its embellishments.

"I'm afraid," he finally revealed to Dinn the innermost fear that no one except Vivan knew. "I've been doing well so far, I've got everyone out of many dangers, but now I'm afraid that in the last skirmish I will run out of ideas and everything will fall apart. I feel like a blanket with too many darning. I still give warmth, but every time something happens, I get the feeling that there are more and more stitches and fewer and fewer of me. And I know that I cannot be patched endlessly, because in the end I will only become scraps of fabric... There will be almost nothing left to save. Do you understand me?"

"I understand," Dinn replied seriously, "Ross, it could just be fatigue. You have done amazing things..."

He spoke calmly, suggesting to the young, gifted sorcerer how he might direct his gift in the future. He used the example of people he met in the past. He was far from jealous or judging his actions. Ross listened to his heart. An unusual gift, born with the help of a healer (which Dinn had no doubts about) had found its way into troubling times. This had consequences, such as the sudden change in hair color to white. The invisible ones, under the guise of controlling the situation, could have grown into horrible irresistible wounds. So Dinn explained, told, comforted. Ross was carrying a burden that wouldn't have been so bad if all the changes had gone smoothly. But was it really that tiring? Was he not glad to help his friends, and his power grows stronger to save them?

Slowly his words dissipated the gloomy thoughts in Ross's heart. He had begun to hope that perhaps the future would bring him something good after all? Dinn was right. It would be good to have that kind of power. Though vanity was not close to him, he was glad that he finally meant something in his life. The initial joy of the skills received was back.

For the first time, these two could finally communicate. And it went as Alesei had expected.

They talked for hours, sitting next to the steersman, who was Silas again, discreet and secretive. Ross wasn't worried about Vivan. He knew he had made an appointment for himself, and he would quell any Besheram's anger at him immediately. He was no longer afraid of being discovered. You couldn't hide it anyway. Dark One was not a fool. Sitting under the starry sky, he took advantage of his last quiet moments by talking to someone who understood him at times better than his deceased friend.

He thanked fate for his presence.

"So, you say the whole plan is in your head?" Dinn asked at the end when they saw Victor, his usual cup of cereal coffee in his hand. It was an unmistakable sign that it was dawning.

"Yes," he replied, hiding his fears.

Dinn patted him on the shoulder, his gaze showing respect for his caution.

"Well…?" He began with a smile, which was a real rarity with him.

"He's totally and undeniably insane," finished Ross with a similar smile.

Dinn nodded, a gleam of mirth in his eye.

"Good luck," he shook hands with him.

Ross gave in to the memories. He remembered Alesei's handshake at Sel's house. Long long time ago…

"Dinn," he began softly.

"Yes?"

"It's never too late for friendship," he smiled at him.

He was sure that the spirit of the good-natured bully was behind him at the moment, though certainly no one had seen him. He could feel his presence. He imagined himself standing there with that broad smile of his, glad that everything had gone as he had dreamed of it.

Suddenly something strange happened.

Walking towards the waiting boat for him, Dinn nodded farewell. Then he looked over his shoulder, and finally, to Ross' amazement, he made the move again...

"Sel," he whispered softly in his lover's ear, not wanting to wake the child, "We need to write a few letters. Help me do this. You know how bad I am in this..."

"Kitten," Sel replied in a similar tone, "I'll do whatever you ask me to do."

Ross touched his lips in a light kiss.

Sel wrote one of the letters all by himself. He had added a few words to the last one under Ross's handwriting. Leaning over his shoulder, Ross silently agreed with what they said. The jewel glowed in two colors, reflecting the deepest feelings.

"You know this could end badly for us?" He asked as their last moments passed together.

Sel looked at him seriously. He loved him more than he ever could express it right now. But he didn't have to say it. They didn't always need words.

"I know," he replied, just like that.

With that one word, Ross felt he was ready to act.

From dusk until early dawn, he brought the entire palace to his feet with his attempts to escape: this is what Vivan did. The first one allowed him to discover that the wall of the building had easily helped him descend to the small balcony below. Then one had to sneak between the guards and numerous servants. He quickly concluded that he needed to disguise himself as a guard. This time, however, he did not. He was lost due to the unfamiliarity with the layout of the rooms on the floor below, and he fell right into the hands of the sentries. The second escape, taking advantage of the moment of inattention of the people watching him, allowed him in a mad plan to return to the same places, the layout of which he remembered well, to discover that the layout of the corridors was the same on the next two floors, and in addition, equally richly decorated with mosaics. The same was true of the number of guards. There were two lifts for transporting meals between the rooms.

This is where the servants saw him.

He found that the people living and working here fear the wrath of the Dark One, to which he was led in a hurry. Nobody dared to help him in his time of need.

With the third escape, he mocked them all.

He was led into the chamber. Besheram looked at him pityingly, probably mentally ridiculing his stupidity. Vivan acted instinctively. It was enough for the guards to let him go, facing Besheram. He dodged and dashed to the window that led to the balcony, one floor below. He wasn't afraid to jump down, even though it was really high up here.

After a while, he neutralized the guard and dragged him into the dressing room. It took several minutes for him to put on his uniform. He left the chamber at a steady pace, rounding a bend, passing the sentinels summoned by the furious Besheram, who did not even glance at him, rushing to obey the order. Vivan walked through the next floors in this way, while nervous guards paced the corridors leading to the palace exit. Once he was even summoned to search. By the time the unconscious guard under the bed was found, Vivan found himself on the ground floor, amidst the crowd of servants, in the midst of relentless pressure and urgency. The exit was nearby, guarded by the king's men. Lots of people.

But he wasn't going to leave. He already knew from above that there were too many sentries around for him to slip away, and that the uniform was only a temporary rescue. So, he went where he had been going from the beginning.

To the dungeons to save the imprisoned children.

"Ross," he said under cover as Ross was still talking to Dinn, "ask Daryenne to come to the place I tell you. I will need her."

"Are you sure this is going to be Daryenne?" Ross asked, "maybe..."

However, Vivan confirmed. Ross had no choice but to agree to it. So, he found her in the women's cabin and called her to him on the side.

It was the first time Daryenne had seen Ross connecting with a healer up close. In a low voice, he gave her directions as he waited for Vivan's next words. It was unlike anything she had seen before.

"Will you remember?" He asked at the end.

She nodded at him, looking at him closely for the first time.

"I thought you were much older, Captain," she blurted out as she looked down at his young face in the streetlight, with no stubble (which he hated anyway). White, disheveled hair beneath a triangular, slightly shabby hat. Eyes of an unusual color of chocolate. The slender figure made him look even younger. Not even the earring in the ear, nor the serious attire of the captain of the ship helped.

"It depends on how I feel on a given day," he replied mysteriously, with a slight smile. "Take care of yourself, girl!" He ordered solemnly "These people don't know what pity is."

She nodded at him seriously. Suddenly she felt that she had to hug him goodbye, although probably others would scold her for it with their eyes. She didn't care about their opinion. She just felt compelled to say goodbye. This desire filled her heart with dread. She hugged him tightly and spontaneously, feeling her heart pounding against her chest, not at all because of the hug.

"Hey!" surprised, he replied with a much gentler hug. "It's very nice, thank you. Although I don't know why I deserved for it?"

"Take care of yourself, okay?" She whispered in his ear.

Ross could feel sincere concern and anxiety in her voice. It touched him.

"I'll try," he replied seriously.

She slipped hastily from his arms, burning on her face like his Jewel. Another moment or two and she was gone. The sailors took her in a boat, sailing towards the distant shore at night.

Vivan watched his former childhood friend and his companions.

Garen.

Completely changed. Vivan had no doubts that the man standing in front of him, chatting in the distance with one of the guards, would have done with him whatever the Dark One would have ordered him to do without hesitation. It was no longer a companion for children's games and stalks. He's his own brother's murderer.

He didn't even have to exchange a word with him. And he wasn't going to do that.

He began to hum softly...

There were only six guards in this part of the dungeon. They looked after small children, so they didn't have to be particularly vigilant. Vivan crept easily into their bored minds. He dulled their senses with sleepiness. It wasn't long before all the guards were asleep. The last one to fold Garen's head. Vivan made sure, keeping his will to sleep like a beast on a rope, he saw him casually pushing him off the forged door and opening it. They didn't even close them. He looked into the dim eyes of his old friend, contemptuously observing his reaction when he noticed who was standing in front of him.

"You rotten apple!" He hissed as Garen closed his eyes to sleep. "May your fate pay you back!"

This meeting caused him almost physical pain. He did not want to touch the man with even a finger, fearing what he would see. Was Peran defending himself? Vivan was sure of it. The other brother was brave and strong. He couldn't imagine now how he would look Seme in the eye and reveal what had happened to her sons, whom she missed so much and looked forward to hearing from them. It was more horrible than he had expected. Garen imprisoned innocent children. In the dark, dirty and cold.

Seme will take it hard. It will break her heart.

He went inside.

Small children. Some of them desperately tried to hide in the corners. Others burst into tears when they saw him. They became hysterical. They didn't understand anything. They didn't know why they were here. What have they done? Why isn't mom with them? At first, from the rush of their emotions, he felt his knees buckle under him. He went numb, shocked by the sight of them.

But he shook himself quickly. He came to help them. He cannot succumb to this despair!

"Do not be afraid... How many are you, my darlings?" He asked softly.

Eight. Fortunately, no one miss.

He looked at the bars that blocked the entrance to the sewers in the wall. It's here. After all, dark beings could not attract a living man except through the place through which he would slip. They pulled him this way. He grabbed the bars. A little child might not move them, but a dark being could move them easily. This way they returned when they set out on secret journeys commissioned by their master.

He spread his hands in a reassuring gesture towards the terrified toddlers.

"Dear little frogs," he said to them warmly, ignoring the cries and screams for a moment. "Now you will go to sleep. And I will get you out of here," he announced calmly.

The children began to quieten. Tired and scared, they lay down where they were at the moment when he began humming them a lullaby. They fell asleep almost immediately.

He opened the bars and peered through the opening. The canal led to a light not far away. He also checked its depth. Just to the knees. That's good, because it smelled terribly there.

Nobody even suspected that the healer would enter the dungeons. All entrances, every chamber was covered. The dirty dungeons from which he was retrieved from the clutches of the gloomy people did not occur to anyone.

He took the two children and headed for the exit.

The canal led to a system of successive branches and an exit. The extensive network of canals beneath the city, the pride of the king, cost the lives of many slaves. Through the sewers leading into the streets, the dark beings dragged Vivan into the palace. The outlet outside led down the hill into the forest. The water ran down towards the thicket. Above this mouth there was no passage along the walls for the guards, but the palace building. Nobody thought to look out the windows.

Making the dungeon a place beyond suspicion, like the sewer outside, was entirely Ross's work. With a smile on his face, he felt the palace turn upside down, seeking a healer anywhere but there. This is just a fraction of his new power. He made Besheram his main link, which he spread to others as to how he acted. The Dark One did not even guess that he had become an element of manipulation, like Ross's mother's lover. Once he developed a similar bond with someone, he never lost sight of him again.

So, he knew every Besheram decision about the search.

It slipped into his mind like a snake.

Vivan had no way of carrying eight children alone without arousing any attention. So, he waited with a trembling heart at the mouth of the canal, warming the children with his warmth. By watching over the sleep of Garen and his companions, he cured the sleeping babies of all diseases. He also softened their thoughts, giving them peace.

Protected by a friend he could rely on at all times, all he could do was hope for a good end.

Fortunately, he didn't have to wait long. Dodging and hiding while Daryenne made her way to the meeting place, he lost several hours to finally reach the dungeons. During this time, Ross spent time with Dinn. When Vivan put the guards to sleep, he was alone. He could calmly help in the escape, counting on the fact that he would not have to implement his plan.

Vivan, protected from the sight of all but his friends, was relieved to see the brave girl and the two sailors accompanying her as dawn marked its light in the sky.

The visitors stared at the unusual phenomenon. Surrounded by sleeping, dirty, ragged children, the healer radiated a soft white glow. He put the children close together. Some of them were covered with a coat stolen from a guard's uniform. He lay next to them, warming them with his touch.

Daryenne smiled at him in greeting, intimidated by the sight. He looked like a creature out of this world.

But when he smiled back at her, she realized there was no need to be embarrassed. It was the same Vivan she had met. With him, she didn't have to feel embarrassed.

"We have blankets and scarves to carry babies," she said. "You asked the captain..."

He nodded to thank her.

The seamen greeted him warmly. Daryenne thought about how happy everyone would be to see Vivan come back. Their crazy mission will no longer be needed. She was also happy herself. This time, however, she felt uncomfortable hugging Vivan. She felt guilty about whether it was appropriate to show her feelings in this way, but at the same moment she felt warm arms embracing her.

"Thank you for coming," he told her.

She held him for a moment, enjoying that unusual warmth. Since he hugged her, better take advantage of it. She loved the feeling, spreading deliciously in her heart. It was as if her dear deceased father embraced her.

The children were divided among them all.

Everything was perfect at first. Just before dawn, the sleepy city was almost empty. Somewhere in the streets, a drunk admirer of alcoholic drinks was returning, trying to be quiet. The rope squeaked as someone drew water from the well. Sleepy guards walked slowly through the dark alleys. Only the main streets had lanterns where candles were changed. The immense capital of the ruler of the Bay of Slaves sucked life out of many lives, developing better and faster than in Vermod, in Tenchryz, or any other kingdom in this world. Its development never stopped. The crowds standing in the audience hall were composed of architects, artists, builders, and all masters of invention who were ready to render their services to the king in exchange for illusory freedom. The rich and merchants gave their gold to the treasury to ensure their peace. These people feared Azram's growing power. Most of the townspeople were just like them. Many people had their fingers in the criminal, slave practice, thus earning money. The city was rich. But everyone here was afraid of the demons, the minions of the Dark One. The night was the servant of an evil adviser. Demons liked to lurk in the dark. It was even said that Besheram liked to send them hunting. It was just a rumor. Besheram did not resort to such measures. The inhabitants of the city were needed by the king. Though it happened, it was rare, that he punished those who had somehow gained his disfavor with a visit of demons.

Hidden in the gates and dark alleys, the caretakers of the children slipped in silence. They rejoiced at the thought of leaving Azram's palace. They didn't have to worry about the kids. They slept soundly, cuddled up in their saviors. Ross made sure the group became apparently invisible to the others. If anyone, human or demon, saw them in the street, they would be ignored by his will.

So, it could work, even though dawn was drawing brighter and brighter in the sky.

Vivan was beginning to hope. In his mind's eye he could see the joy of his family and friends at his return.

But when they were halfway there, the military showed up.

Ross has given up guarding the dungeons by taking care of his friends. Besheram remembered that he hadn't sent anyone there to investigate this possible escape route. He wondered why he had only thought about it now.

He was furious when he found out about the sleeping Garen and his people.

The sight of the empty dungeon made him even more angry. He hadn't felt like this for a long time. He wanted to tear the healer to shreds right now.

Why didn't he send a guard there earlier?! He could only blame himself and his own stupidity. He assumed, in a persistent manner with no other arguments, that Vivan would not step over the threshold of the place that had shocked him so much at first.

Ross had the right arguments. Working in a brothel in the center of the capital, he got to know more than one side of human nature. People were great at deceiving themselves by refusing to admit their mistakes.

Besheram hadn't even guessed that the Troublemaker was guiding his thoughts.

But not everything was as the young sorcerer wished.

Had he been with the Dark One all the time, he might have prevented other things from happening. But he didn't know that yet.

Besheram did not send demons. They might be too zealous and hurt the healer.

He had not made the previous mistake. Vivan had broken free of their clutches anyway, so he would probably do it again. He was sure, however, that he would not defeat the entire army. He preferred to send people. His demons were too precious. Azram will finally achieve his goal, and it won't be if they accidentally kill the healer ahead of time.

The royal army was brought to its feet, ordered to enter the city and search every home for a fugitive. He preferred to think about the complaints later. The stakes were too high.

Chaos reigned in the city before the eyes of the refugees. There were knocking on doors and gates, even politely, but the awakened inhabitants, full of anxiety and anger, loudly expressed their dissatisfaction at the sudden wake-up call. Babies awake cried, excited men shouted. The women complained about the soldiers, dissatisfied with their task. It was getting brighter and louder.

The world around the fugitives tightened its loop. The army was getting closer. They were almost hot on their heels. Once or twice, one of the inhabitants discovered their presence, so they escaped quickly. There were fewer places to hide.

Finally, Vivan detained Daryenne and the sailors.

"They search me," he said calmly, "Besheram don't care about children anymore. Split up and go back to the ship," he gently gave the men the two babies he was carrying.

"No!" Daryenne shouted softly, feeling the burning sensation under her eyelids, "You're coming with us!"

The bearded sailor nudged her lightly.

"He's right, girl..." He looked sadly at Vivan.

The other cursed softly.

"Let's try..." he began, but Vivan shook his head.

"They search me," he repeated. "When I go out to see them, they'll stop searching. This is your chance."

With her free hand, Daryenne grabbed him by the drape of his uniform.

"Everyone is waiting there... I promised! I'm not leaving you here!"

He hugged her gently, taking care of the children. He touched the shoulders of the agitated sailors.

"We will set you free, my lord!" assured the bearded man. "The captain has a plan, you will see!"

"I know, Morgan," Vivan replied, bringing a slight smile to his face, though it was not easy for him.

The sailor was even more touched. The healer knew his name...

"Go," Vivan ordered them gently, turning toward the noise from the street.

Daryenne released him in pain. The sailors hung their heads.

Vivan felt a weight in his chest as he walked towards the soldiers. In captivity again. He could almost hear the malicious chuckle of fate. He saw an abandoned stick in the corner. Well, it's better than nothing. He took it and walked over to the group standing in the middle of the paved street. He grabbed the stick in both hands.

He won't win against the soldiers. He knew about it. He was going to amuse them with his resistance.

They looked at him curiously, interrupting their conversation.

"You are looking for me," he said calmly, "I'm Vivan the Healer."

"Why would we believe you?" One of them sneered.

Vivan looked into his eyes. The man staggered to a sudden sleepiness. He would have collapsed to the ground in a moment had he not been held down.

"It's just a sign you're a sorcerer!" Another noticed.

Vivan pulled the Jewel out from under his shirt, on which hung a cross given to him by his grandparents.

"Does that tell you something?" He asked.

It's the Jewel and the Cross!" said the sleeping one's companion. "As in stories!"

"He doesn't have white hair!" Another noticed.

"Well, well," nodded the one who had accused him of being a sorcerer before, "So that's you? Are you sure you want to drive us away with this stick?" He asked mockingly.

His companions laughed at the joke.

Vivan smiled as well, mockingly about his happiness in life.

"I'll try," he said firmly, gripping the stick tighter.

One of the soldiers called the other troops around the corner. The arrivals were quickly notified that the healer had been found. People were gathering around now, waiting for the spectacular capture of the fugitive.

Vivan winced in a parody of a smile.

It was just as he had predicted.

He waited for the first attack.

Ross slid down the cabin wall to the deck planks. His head was buzzing. However, this was not the most important thing.

Vivan had to turn back.

CHAPTER 42

"So, you decided to show off your courage?" Asked the king as Vivan was brought to his presence.

Vivan was silent, surrounded by guards. There was a collar around his neck again, this time lighter and thinner, but with a thick gold chain by which Azram grabbed.

He sent the guard away, looking into the eyes of his runaway.

"You freed the children..." he muttered, clucking loudly in disgust.

"He freed the children and destroyed my dark army!" Besheram roared furiously beside him, "You bastard! I'm gonna tear you, you hear!?" He roared in front of his face, his jaw lengthening unnaturally.

"Calm down, because your display doesn't impress anyone," growled Azram. "You still have a lot of demons."

"You would have many more, my lord!" The adviser replied resentfully. "I don't understand how he did it! Why can't he be punished for it? Give him to me and I...!"

"Not today!" Azram said sharply. "That was the deal! Tomorrow you're gonna slice him alive or skin him or whatever! Then you will create a ghostly toy out of his soul than this dark army of yours! But today he belongs to me!"

Vivan stiffened at the announcement of his fate. At the moment, however, one thing mattered. Until tomorrow, Azram won't let anyone touch him.

"My king," Besheram bowed to his lord. "You must know that disturbing things are happening here! Yesterday morning, when I visited him in his chamber, I had a strange feeling, as if someone were there. And tonight, I didn't even remember that there were dungeons in the castle..."

"Besheram," the king smirked. "You are only a servant, sent to me by demons as a pledge of future power, once I have given them the soul, they so desire. Maybe you are losing your mind? You went to our ideal victim without my permission, and without any underwear. Are these not just signs of insanity? Because only a madman would go against the will of the king, who will soon take over the world..." he finished menacingly, clutching the chain.

"Thanks to me, my lord," Besheram pointed out, "I am to make the appropriate sacrifice..."

"Look there!" The king asked mockingly. "He's still discussing here!" He looked menacingly at his adviser. "You know very well that you are only a tool. Like him! I will be the lord of demons and the whole world!"

Vivan sensed Ross was listening to this conversation.

"Hey," the king said cheerfully, as if he had just talked about something completely irrelevant. This made Vivanie more fearful indifference to his fate. "What are you so quiet? Relax, we will implement all our plans tomorrow..."

It was rather hard to remain calm after that.

"Lord..." Besheram said warningly.

"Shut up, Dark!" Azram ordered him half-jokingly, though his eyes were cold.

Besheram mused, suddenly struck by a strange thought.

"Come on, darling," Azram pulled on his slave's chain. "You'll come with me now and do something for me. I have to be sure everything will be as it should be."

"He survived," said the Dark One suddenly.

Vivan felt a chill envelop him.

"What?" Azram paused impatiently.

"This wizard survived," said Besheram firmly, now confident, "That explains it all! This strange confusion and oblivion! The white sorcerer survived!"

"It only shows how much you have bothered to do your job lately," the king muttered dissatisfiedly.

Besheram looked at Vivan, grimacing in anger.

"That little shit will regret being born! I'll skin him alive! I'll tear him from the ass to the head!"

"Lots of words, few deeds," Vivan muttered dismissively.

In his mind, he heard his friend snort.

Besheram looked furious. His face was pale with anger, his eyes bulged with a barely suppressed outburst.

Azram dismissed his behavior without fear as if he were an annoying fly.

"Calm down, Besheram!" He ordered his adviser as if he were his dog.

He tugged on the chain as he left the room and into the corridor where the guards were waiting for them. Vivan saw the Dark One's murderous glare before the door was closed behind them.

"I advise you not to upset my precious adviser today," Azram rebuked him fatherly as the procession started down the corridor. "You'll find out tomorrow," he continued in the same casual tone, as if he were discussing the weather. "By the way, I have to thank you for a few things. Killing those children to remake their souls for Besheram's purposes… I found it a bit distasteful now. Eventually, tomorrow I will have my own army of demons," Vivan listened to, feeling his heart beating faster. "And you, my dear, have done me a great favor. By freeing souls from this dark army of beings of his, you earned their gratitude. You must have noticed that already, right? You look perfect. Without a single scar. In addition, and I am sure of it - after all, I took by force many a virgin who was brought to me here, male and female, it makes no difference to me - you are a virgin again. There is something about the behavior of virgins, the way they react to intimate touch..." He touched his cheek fleetingly, to which Vivan instinctively stepped back. "So, you made yourself a perfect victim, pure body and spirit. Besheram will be delighted tomorrow. You probably want to mention that there is a second power in you? I got word from a fugitive in the diamond mine where you rioted," he explained to him. "Well, I have to worry you. It seems that the souls of these children did too well when they bestowed on you with their unconditional love. I don't sense any evil powers in you. Only a pure gift of healing! This is just what I need now!" He dismissed the guard in front of the chamber they reached. "Let's go!"

They entered a bright room, seemingly modestly furnished. He immediately noticed that it was a child's room. It was indicated by the delicate decor and the cradle next to which a dark-haired young woman was sitting. But there was something else just behind her, and a quick glance to the left and right made him finally sure of it.

Bars were installed in all windows of this chamber.

A strange thing for a small child's room.

The woman looked at them. Vivan saw fear mixed with disgust in her eyes as her gaze fell on the king. Her resemblance to Azram was beyond doubt. She could be his little sister.

"This is my darling," the king began freely. "The reason you are here, as far as purely practical. Gossip, which has apparently grown into a story passed from mouth to mouth by sailors, carefully concealed the truth. I'm not the sick person. Yes, I already know that you cured me of the diseases that I contracted while tasting this and that. By the way, this confirmed my resolve that you must be here in person. I don't believe in your healing power in this case. Therefore, you are not lying on the altar today. It could wait," the ease with which he spoke about his future, as if it were a meaningless thing, made Vivan shiver on his spine. "Child..." he muttered, showing unprecedented concern. "I don't make children here and there. I care about the purity of the blood, I'm sure you understand that," he pulled the chain. "But something went wrong here. And I don't want to have other children who will one day fight for fortune! I want my son whom I love more than my life, but..." He brought him to the cradle. "He needs you like no one else in the world," he finished, showing the child to his eyes.

Vivan saw the baby. A tiny creature, barely seeing the world, helplessly lying in a cradle. His sweet little face bore the marks of what others called disease here, but Vivan had some knowledge of an alien world. He knew that being called a disease was a mistake.

"He's defective," Azram explained to him, in case Vivan hadn't figured it out yet, "the Medic said he would have a weak mind for the rest of his life, and it is unknown how long he will live."

"He has a syndrome of..." Vivan whispered softly, recognizing the features.

"What?" Azram asked, and the woman leaned closer, fear in her eyes.

Vivan shook his head.

"What does it mean?" The woman spoke for the first time.

Healing reflexes, Vivan reached out to touch the baby. Clenched fist rested in his hand. The wide-set eyes seemed to search for him.

"He is two months old," he said quietly. "The heartbeat has stopped once. The medic brought him back to life. The mind is..." He hesitated, trying to put it delicately, "broken. Feet distorted. In the tummy..."

"You didn't even expose him!" Azram whispered in admiration. "Yet you already know that much?"

"What's going on with the tummy?" The woman asked quickly.

Vivan looked into her eyes.

"He has a month left. Maybe."

She covered her mouth, muffling a scream.

"Are you treating him now?" Azram asked nervously.

Vivan slowly released the boy's tiny hand, though his whole body was ready to help him.

The tyrant's child was before him. Because of him, innocent children, destined for food for demons, died. Through him and his servant, the demons tore the hearts of people. His mighty kingdom was fed on the blood of the enslaved, who were deprived not only of their freedom, but also the right to intimacy, and finally their lives.

This man built a palace by ordering slaves to be slaughtered, whose suffering settled forever in a silent scream among the walls.

He wanted a successor who would continue his work in the future.

"I'm begging you..." the woman whispered, taking his hand.

The mother of the future heir of the Bay of Slaves was King Azram's sister.

With one touch of her, Vivan saw Azram forcing her to conceive a child in the name of the purity of blood he so desired.

"No," he replied calmly to both of them.

His heart was breaking down. But he saw the future if it would help him.

Azram grabbed his chin, suppressing his anger.

"Are you avenging your fate on an innocent child?!"

Vivan was trapped. His gift even called for help. The aura glowed with a soft, green glow. Regret was squeezing his heart. But he couldn't forget that he had the monster's child in front of him...

"What do you want?" Asked Azram frantically. "Freedom? I'm supposed to set you free, right? It could be done! After all, the last word is mine! Instead of you, a white sorcerer would rest on the altar! He's good too! The demons told me that his heart remained pure despite how life treated him! You want that?!"

"Vivan..." Ross said softly, "Agree. I will not be captured."

"No!" Vivan replied firmly.

"It's just a baby!" A dark-haired woman begged in a pleading tone. "Azram, let him go! You hurt him and he won't save us!"

Azram let go of his chin in disgust.

"Look, Melempe!" he said sharply. "This man sees himself as someone better than me, because the fate of our child is in his hands!"

Vivan watched them with surprise mixed with horror. These people loved their baby! The great lord, who had kept even the Dark One in check, now stood before him, trembling for his son's fate. It would be so human and disarming... if it weren't for the awareness of what kind of human Azram is.

"Should I beg you for this?" He asked with mockery mixed with despair.

He would probably torture him personally tomorrow, if Vivan asked for it. But it didn't matter much to the healer, since he was going to die tomorrow anyway. It would only add more suffering to him, which he preferred not to think about now.

He looked at the baby. The only innocent creature in this room, because he didn't even consider himself, despite the king's words, to be one. Azram blurted out the words, persuading and threatening. Melempe was crying softly, in mute despair. She touched the head of her sick child painfully, thinking that she would lose it soon.

Her pain was so sincere. So was Azram's suffering, which he hid behind harsh words.

The child wasn't guilty of anything.

He had always felt this way when faced with matters that would affect the lives of tiny beings.

Innocent.

All people are born innocent. Then they stop being them.

Suddenly a thought flashed through him.

If he had ended this child's life... now.

A cruel, insane thought seeped into his mind, infusing his conscience with a sense of duty. It makes sense. It will just make the little heart stop and the world will stop rushing towards catastrophe.

The very idea that he could do it terrified him and made him tears burned under his eyelids.

Would he kill this boy, believing he was preventing the continuation of the nightmare?

"But you can have a second child," he observed, his throat dry.

He didn't think so, but he wanted them to feel a little bit of fear. Their involvement, when one thought of the children of the dungeon, whose fate was indifferent to them, awakened in him a strange need to hurt.

It was a sick feeling. Contaminated by the evil he has experienced. He didn't like it.

"That's what a man who is not a father says," Azram replied. "The world won't regret losing you if you treat a sick child so indifferently."

"Besheram murdered many children to create his dark army!" Vivan couldn't stand it. "You killed innocent people!"

"It's the law of the king!"

"A shitty law that allows killing on a sick whim!" Vivan hissed in his face, "Here's what your reward for this!" He pointed at the child. "Nothing lasts forever, Azram! You have to pay for everything you did!"

"So, you think the baby paid for my actions?!"

"Is he fit for a sacrificial altar?" He replied with a question.

"How dare you?!" Melempe shouted, shocked.

Azram was speechless.

"My son..." he said after a moment, still unable to shake off his amazement.

"He's the same candidate as I am," Vivan finished ruthlessly for him. "No, Azram, babies don't pay for adults' mistakes. You will pay for it! And it will be soon!"

"Are you thinking of your wizard friend?" The king asked mockingly, ignoring the fact that Vivan was addressing him without due respect. He treated him as a business partner he was going to end soon. "Melempe, do you see the same as me?" There are still fools in the world who believe that good will prevail!"

"It's ridiculous!" The young woman gasped, venting her frustration.

"The world lives by violence, Vivan," Azram lowered his voice. Now his voice was more paternal, as if explaining something to a silly child. "Without it, there would be no development. People like you or that Sorcerer of the Heart of yours are a relic. You can't just be good, or you will die in this material world. You have to be smart. Ruthless. This is why you will say goodbye to life tomorrow and I will survive. Because I'm not an idiot who does everything for others, and meanwhile they happily kick your's ass. I'm the ruler. I decide who deserves my attention. And tomorrow I will show this world that by allowing you to die, they have surrendered to an authority that only cunning men value. I'm sure that Besheram will make the right tool of your soul to help me maintain this power. Everyone will kneel before us!"

Vivan looked at him in the sudden silence, broken only by the soft voice of the child.

He thought about his words.

Then he reflected on what Cora had once said.

He closed his eyes.

"The world," he replied softly, "made me for who I am. Apparently it needed me."

"Yes. To make you my victim," Azram replied sarcastically.

"No," Vivan said calmly, opening his eyes. "He wanted something else."

He reached for the small fist with his hand. He smiled at the little man who was able to summon love in the heart of his cruel father.

"He wanted," he added softly, passing his power to the child, "that I would give people a chance."

"Chance? For what?" The surprised king asked.

"For a new life," replied the Healer thoughtfully.

At first the king wanted to laugh. But the longer they stood by the child who fell asleep peacefully, the deeper Vivan's words penetrated him.

New life.

Each of the cured people started their lives anew. It wasn't a discovery. Usually, people then start to wonder what they were doing and what they were striving for. Balderdash! He didn't say anything new. These things happened.

But...

People who were helped by Vivan usually changed. Azram remembered the news he had ordered his spies to get. Sorcerer of the Heart. Ross Hope. Formerly a bastard who ended up in a brothel. He had completely changed after meeting Vivan. Plus, this whole Jewel!

It was a glaring example, but Azram had heard of many who had changed after contact with the healer. About people who gave up their bloody professions to take up a normal life.

His son was changing in his eyes as well. The eyelids improved; the eye sockets shifted a bit. A small leg clearly kicked under the blanket. Melempe, tearfully, exposed the baby. Seeing his healthy legs, she cried with happiness. Vivan improved the condition of the organs. He strengthened the heart. He dealt with the mind of a child the longest, because there was unimaginable chaos there.

He finally released his fist with a soft sigh.

He waited for words that would probably come. For lack of gratitude. For mock this situation. A reminder of the coming future.

The silence dragged on, broken only by the sound of breathing.

Finally, Melempe took his hand and kissed him reverently, full of happiness. Then she gently lifted the baby from the cradle and hugged it, shivering with her motherly joy.

She touched the delicate features of the baby with tenderness. In inspiration she admired the small, healthy feet. The hand around her finger. Her eyes sparkled with tears as she pointed to Azram the child he leaned over in a rush of fatherly love.

Vivan stood looking at the scene in silence.

Azram, still holding the chain, looked at him finally. Then on a chain in his hand. He took a step closer, reaching for Vivan's neck.

After a while the hoop fell to the floor, dragging the gold chain behind it.

"You'll be my special guest," he told him. "That's all I can give you."

He smiled one last time at the child, thus bestowing his mother. Vivan saw the surprise on the woman's face.

Azram took a brisk stride for the exit, as if the whole event had given him new strength.

"Come with me," he said to Vivan, "I have to welcome my new followers to the Audience Hall. Like everyday. I don't advise you to refuse."

Vivan joined him slowly.

CHAPTER 43

Ross started by getting the ship ready.

He directed his hand to one of the shields Sel had prepared. He slowly formed the right thought in his mind. The light flickered on the disk as it moved to the next, and the disk to the next, until they were all illuminated by the same glow.

Then the ship began to disappear.

The stunned crew saw a shield around them that completely obscured the ship. Just like Ross has shielded the people in the village from the demons.

"Nobody will see you!" he assured people. "Nobody will hear you! And won't even feel! You are safe on the ship! And only here! Remember!"

Then he exchanged a few words with Silas, concerned about his fate. After what he saw in Azram's baby's chamber, he knew time was running out. He seemed completely calm, focused on his task. In fact, his inner anxiety, invisible to others, did not leave him. He was scared.

However, fate left him no choice, and he had to save face.

Daryenne returned with the sailors with young children from her trip. He personally went down to her boat to announce that she would go to the Judith. He hid the pirate ship and the Judith in the bay where the Judith had been stationed earlier. Breaking up with Vivan took a toll on Daryenne. She thought she had failed, so Ross used his influence to calm her down.

What happened was not her fault.

At last, the time has come for him and his assigned group of companions to leave the safe deck of the Valeria. He calculated that they would be at the palace before evening, just before the end of audience time. The king was fond of gifts and evidence of loyalty, so he eagerly welcomed his new followers for a long time. Then there was a party that sometimes lasted all night.

He still had to say goodbye to Sel.

He hugged him tightly, without saying a word. He held his warmth and scent in his arms, trying to keep it within him. It would only be enough for him. For all eternity.

Sel didn't say anything either. They didn't need words.

Before Ross released him, however, he gave him one last kiss. Like a blessing before a fight.

Because it would come to it, he knew for sure.

Ross changed his appearance, taking the form of Tenan, who hid his face under a black mask and his figure under a black cloak. Ross' perfect illusion revealed the companion's attire in every detail. Before that, he had taken a close look at him. He didn't need the camouflage for long. It was enough to enter the audience hall. That was no problem at all. He persuaded all the guards not to be suspicious and let them all inside. By the way, he was sure it was as expected.

Besheram was waiting for him.

He could feel this information in the mind of the guards, servants and palace guards. Everyone they met waited for a sign that a healer had arrived at the palace to report it to the Dark One immediately.

The king's advisor had prepared himself well. If it weren't for the gift of persuasion, Ross would certainly have been discovered by now.

So, they were all in the audience hall as he wanted. It remains to start action.

There was a large crowd. Both the powerful and merchants with various gifts waited in front of him. King Azram sat on the throne, delighted. Besheram sat at his right hand, glaring at the room.

On the left, Ross finally saw his friend.

The healer, seated on a decorative chair, looked at the room with his eyes devoid of any joy. The crowd watched him curiously.

However, no one asked the ruler out of concern for the title or privilege.

Anyone who came to plead for grace from the king was given a similar, subdued look. Even without a special bond, the young sorcerer knew what worried him.

He did not condemn him for the choice he made.

He understood his motivation perfectly. For his part, he would also add his own to them by making a similar choice in his place. After all, he himself was an example that having bad parents is not always the key to their child's character.

Here, according to the words of the queen, the king's soldiers proved not only numerous, but also effective. They exterminated the entire herd, proving that they can cope with even an extremely fast opponent. The young prince leading his army was proud of himself. He showed remarkable courage on the battlefield. For sure the fiancée will be proud of him. After all, he freed so many people. Many of them joined the fight. Some of the inhabitants of the city - fortress, already engulfed by fires, have already started their escape. Mostly women and children who were allowed to do so, although when some refugees found pirates, it could not be ruled out that their disappearance occurred under rather dramatic circumstances.

But all this was irrelevant to the king now, as Vivan had finally been led up the hill, where the sacrificial altar had already been prepared.

It remained to murder him to fulfill the prophecy and gain absolute power.

"Are you ready?" Besheram asked, dragging the leaning Vivan towards the altar.

The troop of soldiers was just waiting for it. Vivan also noticed horses near the altar. He felt a bad feeling come over him.

"We're waiting all the time, my lord," Garen bowed slightly, appearing with a torch. "Unfortunately, I had to change a few of my men. They didn't want to do this. Their hearts melted."

"I hope these sensitive souls are already under the altar," muttered Besheram, handing Vivan over to Garen's men whom he had brought. He breathed a sigh of relief to be able to walk as dignified as Azram among the others.

"Not otherwise," Garen replied coldly, pointing to the bloody mass of human organs lying in front of the altar, as requested by the Dark One.

Vivan went numb with fear. There was no doubt someone was fighting for his life here.

The worst nightmares have come true. In addition, at the side of an old childhood friend who lost that self a long time ago.

"Can we start?" Garen asked.

Besheram waved a dismissive hand at Azram's approval.

Garen grabbed Vivan by the skirts of his clothes.

"I'm a rotten apple, right?" He asked maliciously. "But you are a fool! You will be dying for a long time!"

He hit him with a hard blow to the face and pushed him to the ground. His companions - torturers joined immediately, without sparing their kicks.

"Not in the nose," Besheram said indifferently, looking at the whole scene, "I don't want him to choke on blood and die. He would thwart my plans."

"What are you doing this for?" Azram asked, feeling a bit uncomfortable. Somewhere deep inside, he felt his conscience quiver. After all, this man saved his son.

"I'm preventing the attack of his fury," the advisor explained to him. "And I don't want him to throw himself too much. Do you care? I can assure you that it will be much worse. Enough!" He ordered. "Spread his arms and legs!"

Vivan preferred to stay in that crouched position. He must have broken ribs as the pain in the chest was excruciating.

The soldiers obeyed the order. Besheram reached behind the altar, pulling out a large wooden hammer.

Vivan splashed in a cold sweat, knowing what this was up to. He desperately tried to get away. It only amused Garen and his people.

"I told you," he said without any warmer feelings.

"No!" Vivan could only think before the first strike came.

He screamed while he had enough strength. Besheram struck hard with savage delight. Each time he chanted words in an unknown language followed by the sound of distant thunder. The sky began to cloud over.

The next moments were drowned out by the roar of pulsating blood in his temples. He couldn't breathe freely. The blasting fear was worse than the pain. Besheram ordered to place him on the altar. Another wave of pain and terrifying loneliness among the torturers increased his desire to escape. The fingers touched the grooves of the previous victims, and then the hope faded abruptly, taking away all his strength. These victims did not run away, although they defended themselves very much. He will die a horrible death.

"Get the horses ready!" Besheram exclaimed, watching his victim with satisfaction.

Horses? What do he need horses for? Vivan looked around, fighting the last of his strength against the mounting panic. The tears made it difficult for him to see. The trembling of the body increased the suffering. His fingers were almost still. He could barely bend them, and not too hard.

To his right, he saw Azram watching him. As predicted, this man did not help him in any way. He looked like someone who would like to get it over with. His conscience tried to reach out to him, but he was already too hard after the previous murders committed in this place to succumb to him now. Therefore, his gaze was unbearable to Vivan.

"Hold him!" The Dark One ordered.

Garen and his companions proceeded to obey the order while the other soldiers harnessed the horses.

He looked at his former playmate. The man he had missed for several years. Formerly a friend and confidant of secrets.

"Why?" He asked with difficulty. "Why are you doing this?"

Garen looked at him. The desperation and madness in his eyes only made one thing clear to Vivan. This man sacrificed everything for one purpose. He hurt, murdered and tortured to achieve this. What was desire that took away his reason and humanity?

"For immortality," he replied in a fit of sudden honesty, "He promised me that I would live forever, Vivan. He's been whispering and whispering about it every day since they caught both of us. He enticed. Tempted. He said I had to kill my brother to be free from his voice. So, I finally freed myself. I freed myself from the voice in my head!" He laughed like a madman. "I'll start a new life! Eternal life! And it all doesn't matter anymore," the gleam in his eyes was a sign of madness that had been concealed so far.

Besheram confused him. Now he was standing here watching their conversation. Vivan realized he was amused by his emotions as he listened to his old friend's confession. Therefore, he did not disturb them.

"Playing with someone else's mind is my favorite pastime," added the king's immodestly gloomy advisor. "I will derive real pleasure from the successive victims who dare to oppose my master. And you will help me with this."

"Done, my lord!" One of the soldiers near the horses announced.

"Let me introduce you to the situation, Vivan," Besheram was excited. "We are running out of time. You see, I had a stake ready. I gave you a taste of fear by having you put you on our altar. Did you like it? It must have gotten comfortable after so many victims. It simply exudes all the power of the life that escaped from the victims. At first, I thought I had to cut you up there, but then I had a vision. You can't just die. Your death is going to mean something. It is supposed to be the beginning. That's why we'll put you down on the ground now, tie your legs to the horses, and you'll impale yourself on a stake. You'll hang on it for a day or two until you die. Then the sacrifice will be accepted and your soul will be mine. So maybe let's not prolong your waiting and just start."

"Do it at last," muttered Azram impatiently.

An irrational desire grew within Vivan. His strength was so overwhelming that he even ignored his awkward position. At least partially. But when he was abandoned, the feeling became excruciating, and he finally gave in, though the threat of madness has never been closer than it is now.

He started to laugh.

At first he was choking, unable to breathe freely. After a while, however, the laughter intensified, bearing the hallmarks of madness. He has reached the limit of his endurance.

But these fools saw nothing.

"A complete lack of manners," Besheram said, "You could at least keep this dignity to the end. I was starting to like it."

"I'm going to die..." Vivan croaked in a haunted voice, "...without your help?"

"Ridiculous question," Azram said, "Besheram..."

"I won't die," Vivan said, a hint of mad laughter in his voice, "You have to finish me off!"

"What are you talking about?" Besheram asked.

A jewel, a cross and a ring gave by Vashaba suddenly appeared on the neck of his victim, connected by an apparently thin chain.

"What is this?" Azram asked at the sight.

Vivan would have given them a mocking smile if he had only had the strength.

"A jewel from his mother," Garen explained. "The cross, a symbol of another world religion. And this ring..."

"Adamantis." Besheram paled with rage.

"It gives eternal life to the one who received it out of love," explained Garen's companion. "The gift of the elves."

Besheram was furious. The victim should die alone, as the healer asked, in pain and suffering. It was impossible to end his torment. It wouldn't be valid.

"We chose the wrong one," Azram whispered in shock.

His dream was never to come true.

"I'll have him impaled anyway! For pure satisfaction!" Besheram snapped.

The king abruptly stopped his aspirations, completely surprising him with his decision.

"If this death is not needed," he said seriously, "Why to do it?"

He waved his hand at the soldiers, ordering to untie the bonds.

He looked like a man who had experienced unimaginable relief.

"What are you doing?!" His adviser was surprised.

"The same as I would do!" Suddenly they heard a new voice.

Ross appeared on the hill.

As he stood on the hill, Ross realized a few things.

Most of all, he saw Vivan in a terrifying state. The sharpened stake still ominously lay between his legs.

There was only a small squad of soldiers on the hill, apart from Besheram and the king.

The others fought the soldiers of the future king of Tenchryz, amid the burning houses of the falling Bay of the Slaves. The sounds of fighting were quite close now. The prince is about to take the palace.

Lightning flashed in the sky. The ground trembled, not because of the battle that was taking place.

Something was coming this way.

"What a wonderful sight!" Besheram crowed in delight, "This is the right man in the right place!"

"Runaway!" Vivan ordered his friend silently.

Ross just looked at him warmly.

Besheram started toward him, intending to leap at close range. Suddenly, as he passed nearby bushes, a figure jumped out at him. The flash of steel with a unicorn hilt in the torchlight followed a moment later. Besheram fell to the ground with a crash, one limb missing, just below the knee.

Arrows sent from a bow by a woman with two long braids knocked Garen's three companions down. The fourth hit the king on the shoulder.

Besheram roared furiously, ready to turn to smoke. Ross didn't wait this time. He swirled the transforming figure in a vortex, stopping the process of that transformation. He drew fire from the torch at the altar and set fire to Besheram's clothes.

"I'm born of fire, fool!" Besheram roared, freeing himself from the trap.

Marlene killed another soldier. Garen sent people after her and her secret helper. He himself remained with the king.

Ross slashed a bush where Paphian had previously been hidden and sent a cloud of branches into the shaping silhouette. In response, Besheram sent them back to him. Prepared for this, the young sorcerer formed an air shield that crushed them to dust. Besheram summoned his demons in their language.

None, however, arrived. They were all knocked out.

Furious that he had only realized it now, he found a new way.

He started attacking in the form of smoke. He did it so fast you could hardly follow him with your eyesight. Ross created an air cocoon to resist sneaky attacks. Then Besheram reappeared as a human. His leg just grew back.

Busy in a sword fight with soldiers, Paphian no longer had the opportunity to help his friend.

Besheram was breaking into the cocoon, shedding the layers inside which the wizard was hiding. It was clear that Ross couldn't create them forever.

Vivan closed his eyes.

Blood pulsed in his veins. The body was on fire.

Nevertheless, he made his last effort.

He clenched his hardly shattered arm.

Besheram's heart, beating in human form, suddenly stopped.

At first Besheram did not understand what had happened. He tried to gasp, but nothing happened. Ross quickly understood why. He broke free from the cocoon and drew his sword.

The blade beheaded Besheram.

The body fell to the ground with a thud. He set them on fire again.

"You are dead this time, prick!" He spat into the fire.

Paphian defeated the last two soldiers with the help of brave Marlene.

Desperately, Garen aimed his sword at his opponents.

"Lower your sword, fool!" The wounded king admonished him. "We have lost!"

He turned towards the palace, looking at it sadly. He thought of his son, out there in the midst of the fighting. He quietly hoped they wouldn't kill the baby.

After all, they are not barbarians. As he was.

"We lost everything," he said once more, bidding farewell to his dreams.

A powerful fist unexpectedly crushed his body, crushing Garen as well.

It was close to crushing the healer as well. Frightened horses started to run away.

Facing the young sorcerer, a mighty giant was climbing the hill, his eyes ablaze with the fires of hell, enraged by the unfulfilled promise and the lack of the required sacrifice.

Ross stood slightly astride. With growing dread, he watched the enormous figure grow before his eyes, revealing its full enormity. He felt so tiny with him. He was obscured by the sky and the whole world.

"What now?" He asked himself.

"Captain?" Marlene asked fearfully.

"Get the healer out of here!" He ordered them quickly.

They obeyed this command with some caution. Ross noticed Vivan was unconscious.

"Come!" Paphian said to him. "We will seek help! You can't handle him yourself!"

"He's going to kill everyone..." Ross whispered, thinking of the battle that was taking place next to him, and it suddenly fell silent.

He also thought of his friends on the Valeria. A dedicated crew.

Past good and bad.

About Sel... About him for the longest time.

Then about brave little Christine.

He realized that he would not see them anymore.

"Sorry, Oliver," he conveyed the thought to his brother by chance.

"Sai will be desperate," he replied with a thought, lying by his wife's side in his cabin, "But I don't think she has any use for me after what happened."

"She would," Ross replied, feeling the earth rumble beneath the giant's footsteps, "You're going to be a father. You would certainly take care of her and the baby."

Oliver held his breath.

He turned to the sleeping woman. He studied her beautiful face. The mother of their child.

He will leave her. It broke his heart.

He hugged her to him. She sighed, enjoying his touch. Though she did not know about the conversation with Ross, she suddenly felt that she had to finally reveal her secret to her husband. She hoped it would help him get on with his life.

She put his hand on her belly.

He smiled through his tears.

"Ross..." Vivan whispered, waking up. "Don't take me..."

"Relax," whispered Paphian, mentally despairing over his condition. "We just moved away. If he loses, we won't be able to hide anywhere. And if he wins... He might need you."

Vivan fell silent.

Paphian glanced at Marlene. She was close to crying, and so was he.

Vivan was dying.

Witnesses said the clash was shocking. Ross drew lightning bolts from the clouds that the giant was trapping. Sea water. He smashed Azram's wooden altar to pieces and used them as a spear. He used whatever means he could think of. All abandoned the fight to await the outcome of this battle with fear. The enemies stood side by side in the streets and alleys of the city. The Valeria's sailors watched the giant from their hidden harbor.

Paphian swore that the petite Ross had raised his hands at one point and by the strength of his mind demanded that the giant go back to where it came from and never come back again. He had to repeat it several times. And when the mighty, immortal giant returned to the depths of the sea, from where it had come from, a roar of thousands of throats arose from beneath the earth. The gate has not been opened. Ross sealed it. The circle of hell did not break into the human world.

The sorcerer fell and didn't get up anymore...

Ross felt he was dying. The blood was flowing from his nose in a steady stream, and he was unable to stop it. He didn't even have the strength to raise his hand. It was also flowing from his ears.

He was tired. Terribly tired.

He felt he had had enough.

His blanket had too many stitches.

"Ross..." Vivan croaked. "Take me!"

"No, Vivan," he told him silently, "that's enough."

He closed his eyes.

He felt a stroking on his head.

Nanny.

Peace overwhelmed him. He was back in her warm arms. Words were not needed. The other hands that hugged him were Valeria's.

Happiness drove all his fears away.

He's gone.

Vivan howled in despair like a wounded animal.

Sel felt it in his heart. Ross was leaving and not taking him with him. He predicted it. He looked at the baby sleeping beside him.

"You promised me, Jewel," he recalled his plea, made as they both said goodbye in silence.

"YES," said the Jewel.

Ross didn't want to take his life. Except Sel couldn't live without him. He had known about it a long time ago.

He asked for Tenan to be brought in.

"Give those letters back," he asked softly when he appeared. "One of them is for you."

Tenan looked at him in surprise. He was asleep after crossing his cabin when summoned. He did not even know about the confrontation with the giant.

"Ask Vivan and his family to take care of the girl," Sel began softly. "She will need them very much."

"Okay. Sel…"

"I offer you my workshop," Sel interrupted, sitting down against the wall. He thought it was probably better than a cold corpse in bed. For a small child, for sure.

"I don't know what…"

"At first, you won't know for sure. But then you think it gives meaning to your life. There are designs for several inventions there. Properly sold will set you up for a long time. It will be a good start for you and Maya. House, ground, maybe you will create something too?" He smiled knowingly at him.

Tenan sat down next to him, unable to find the right words.

Time was running out.

"I know it wasn't you…" he said goodbye, feeling powerless overwhelming him.

Tenan knew what they were talking about now.

They looked at each other for the last time.

"Stay with you?" He asked softly, not wanting to disturb the moment.

Sel looked at him with sympathy and gratitude.

"You know… Actually, I want you to stay. For the little one."

Tenan nodded silently.

He waited.

Sel rested her head on his shoulder as if he was falling asleep.

His breathing stopped suddenly.

Tenan buried his face in his hands, clutching the letters that had been handed to him.

CHAPTER 44

The fortress city of the Bay of Slaves was deserted. Residents abandoned them for good. Only the decaying ruins of houses and the former, magnificent palace remain.

Prince Meron took care of the baby he found in the empty chamber. His mother stabbed herself with a dagger. The boy was certainly the son of King Azram, whose death he had also learned of. The young prince had no intention of killing the child. He decided to take care of him and raise him like a son.

With the help of his army, he smashed all the other cities that dealt with the grim slave trade. There was not even a trace of Azram's power left.

The pirates paid tribute to the fallen sorcerer and asked Violet to release the word. Apparently, she agreed to it willingly.

The Beckert family said goodbye to the elder of the family with great regret. The funeral was given to him with military honors. A commemorative monument was erected for him in the square. Anna, Victor's wife, never remarried.

Ross's funeral was an above-average event. King of Tenchryz himself and his family appeared at the ceremony. Ross's body in his new captain's clothes, along with his inherent hat, was placed in a glass coffin. For months, those who owed him life and freedom visited his tomb. Many white flowers and thanks were left. An amazing thing was happening. It is unknown if the coffin was this tight or if a healer interfered with it in some way, but Ross's body never decomposed.

He looked as if he had fallen asleep.

His monument stood on the seashore. He was depicted in a dignified manner, staring down at his subjects from the rocks, raising his hands in a brave gesture. It protects the inhabitants of the growing Leviron from danger.

Sel was buried in an oak coffin, as requested in his last letter. There was a glass coffin on his tomb so they could be as close to each other as they could be.

Tenan took over Sel's workshop. After a time of mourning, he dared to go inside, where he was amazed at the enormity of sketches and tools.

He followed Sel's words. He made his own inventions, in partnership with Alvar. He married Maya.

Oliver died at the same time Ross's heart stopped beating.

His life was inextricably linked with him.

Sai never recovered from this loss. She devoted her life to raising her son, who was born a few months later. She was social and was always close if Vivan needed her, though she was left alone.

She never played the lyre again.

Lena took care of little Christine. When Vivan recovered, he often visited the little girl. Thanks to him, she started talking to people again.

Sara Beckert visited her grandson during his convalescence. The conversation took place without witnesses, so its content was never known. Vivan hadn't even told her a word. He did not agree to her exile and confiscation of her property, although the king insisted on it. She lived for many years, forgotten by all, in her declining fortune. She never complained about her fate.

One day, on the anniversary of Ross's victory over the giant, Vivan asked Cora to dance.

Dinn, feeling guilty of Ross' death, drifted off to his land. He always wished he had obeyed him when the sorcerer asked him to stay on the ship.

The Valeria ship formally belonged to a healer. Like the house on the hill where Vivan often looked for solitude. It had to undergo a major overhaul, because without the help of a sorcerer it turned out to be too heavy. Alvar took care of it, sticking to Ross' directions whenever possible. Vivan didn't want to change anything. Silas was captained, unanimously elected by the crew.

Vivan could not recover for a long time. At first it was very bad with him. Eric and Cora took care of him, feeling the burden of responsibility. The king even sent his medic, Sedon, to them, still under guard, of course. Everyone wanted the healer to get better.

Vivan had three broken ribs, and numerous internal injuries. Cracked pelvis. Shattered hands and wrists. Both legs broken with displacement. Head damage.

Eric could not tell how serious the internal injuries were. But a hard belly did not bode well for him. The risk that shattered hands and wrists would remain inoperable, even if folded well, was very high. It was the same with the legs. If the healer doesn't help himself to heal himself, he can be crippled forever.

It was quickly realized that there was only one way to heal him.

Paphian and Lena stayed with him for the first nights, at the request of Vivan himself. Then Elron and Anna changed them. Sai also came, despite the despair emanating from her. Tenan appeared. Residents came in groups. Everyone supported Vivan as much as they could.

Cora, moved by their affection, watched these incessant processions.

The hands finally started to heal. Within a month of returning to Leviron, the condition of his left hand had improved considerably. Inside the body, healing happened almost immediately. The next limbs sat at a few days' intervals.

The pain in healing was almost equal to that in a fracture, which is why Vivan most often sought help from his brother.

"Please," he whispered to him, "Paphian, help me and stop worrying. I'm scared..."

Paphian tried his best to show him the support he so needed.

One night, when he was almost healed, Vivan awoke again, shivering with cold.

However, it was not only the cold that woke him from sleep. He was paralyzed by fear. He woke up seeing Besheram's hammer in a dream. Hearing his crazy laugh.

Cora hesitated. This time there was no one with him, and Vivan was freezing. Literally!

So, she stepped under the covers without thinking and hugged him to warm him. Her pregnancy belly was quite clear now. The baby moved in her womb.

Vivan accepted her help gratefully, knowing how much the struggle with herself had cost her to go to bed with a man, even if he was sick. Finally, he felt a warmth envelop him.

Then he felt something else: unusual peace. He felt the familiar sensation of sudden relaxation in only one case. When Ross was interfering with his emotions, trying to calm him down.

Now suddenly that feeling has come back.

After a moment, the heat from Cora's stomach penetrated him right through. He felt that he was beginning to cry with emotion. He couldn't hold back his tears.

He couldn't be wrong either.

"Hey," she said, "Has something happened?"

Quietly he replied:

"No. But I know that feeling. It's warm."

"I probably remind you of Lena," she smiled, not feeling fear in front of him.

"No," he replied, excitedly, "Ross. And not you..."

She looked at him, understanding nothing at first. Then she touched her belly.

"I was wondering if I would be able to love this child," she said slowly. "Now I don't have to ask myself such questions anymore. I felt the warmth you are talking about. I just didn't know why. Now I know," she looked at him warmly, moved by the news. "This is a new beginning for both of us. A chance for a new life. Mine and his. Ross. This is a chance for me to be a mother to a child that I have finally started to love. And for him, to live life with his mother in a better life. This is his reward for saving the world."

Vivan smiled through his tears. Yes, it made sense.

Their hands were found by accident. They stayed together, entwined.

Adamantis rested at the bottom of the sea.

Vivan revealed to Seme the story of her sons. When he was talking about Garen, he blamed Besheram. He explained to her that the Dark One's insidious actions confused her older son's mind, leading to a tragedy.

He wished she would never know the truth.

He wished he could forget. His brother did not recognize the changed playmate. Only he knew what it really was.

Weeks passed. Cora and Vivan closed up to each other carefully. Each of them had their own fears.

But when he whispered that she shouldn't hurt him, she felt the wall crumble within her. Vivan was seriously hurt by Vashaba. She treated his love badly. This was what united them, because she herself was afraid to trust anyone.

They gave themselves all the time they needed.

Finally, their hearts joined in the cabin on the hill. With a little heart that they passed into each other's arms. Nobody knew how the Jewel of Hope got into that little hand.

THE END

Printed in Great Britain
by Amazon

75287371R00364